William Howard Van Doren

A Suggestive Commentary on the New Testament; on an Original Plan

St. Luke-Vol. I.

SALZWASSER
VERLAG

William Howard Van Doren

A Suggestive Commentary on the New Testament; on an Original Plan

St. Luke-Vol. I.

1st Edition | ISBN: 978-3-75252-037-8

Place of Publication: Frankfurt am Main, Germany

Year of Publication: 2021

Salzwasser Verlag GmbH, Germany.

Reprint of the original, first published in 1867.

A SUGGESTIVE COMMENTARY

ON THE

NEW TESTAMENT;

ON AN ORIGINAL PLAN.

ST. LUKE—VOL. I.

BY

REV. W. H. VAN DOREN,

CHICAGO, ILLINOIS, U.S.

ὁ λύχνος αὐτῆς τὸ 'Αρνίον. Rev. xxi. 23.

LONDON:
R. D. DICKINSON, 92, FARRINGDON STREET;
REEVES & TURNER, 238, STRAND.

1867.

A

SUGGESTIVE COMMENTARY

ON

ST. LUKE:

WITH

CRITICAL AND HOMILETICAL NOTES,

ON AN ORIGINAL PLAN.

BY

REV. W. H. VAN DOREN.

ὁ λύχνος αὐτῆς τὸ 'Αρνίον. Rev. xxi. 23.

VOL I.

LONDON:

R. D. DICKINSON, 92, FARRINGDON STREET;

REEVES & TURNER, 238, STRAND.

—

1867.

PREFACE.

Our aim in this Work has been to simplify Divine truth, and to condense in some degree the results of Biblical Criticism. Many Ministers in our busy age, with little leisure for study amid pressing duties, and Bible Class Teachers with still less time, will welcome any aid, however humble. For such we have ventured to print this Synopsis in the form of Notes, usually prepared for the Lecture Room or Bible Class.

The Critical Notes, rays of the many-sided divine gems, may remind the Student of previous exegetical researches. These hints are intended to suggest parallel trains of thought during weekly preparation. We regret, the severe brevity of our plan rendered the dogmatic form necessary, for mere *suggestions*. As the English Notes only occasionally indicate the authorities, we freely acknowledge in every page, our obligations to the labors of the living and the dead. The work possesses the results of the Author's travels in Egypt, Syria, Palestine, &c. where they illustrate the Text. His weak vision rendering amanuenses necessary, will account for some errors throughout the volumes which may have escaped his notice. The Historical portions of the New Testament will follow as fast as the various scholars engaged, can complete the series. The Author records with pleasure the kind attentions of the Rev. Dr. James Hamilton, and Rev. William Ballantyne, to one who has felt a stranger in the land of his fathers. We commit the labors of eight years to the Adorable Lamb, whose Divine Light and Love invest these pages with whatever interest they may possess; trusting His blessing will follow, even after the Author's pilgrimage is closed.

London, August, 1866.

INTRODUCTION.

—o—

Luke. This name an abbreviated form of Lucanus or Lucilius.

Not to be confounded with Lucius, mentioned Acts xiii. 1.

Name Luke occurs three times in N.T., Col. iv. 14; 2. Tim. iv. 11; Phil. verse 24.

Probably in all three the third Evangelist is the person spoken of.

Born at Antioch, in Syria, according to *Eusebius* and *Jerome*.

Not born a Jew, not reckoned by Paul among those "of the circumcision."

Uncertain whether he became a Jewish proselyte before his conversion.

The date of his conversion to Christianity unknown.

His profession, a *physician;* called by Paul "the beloved physician." Col. iv. 14.

A late tradition makes him a painter, of no mean skill. *Nicephorus.*

Supposed by *Epiphanius* and others to have been one of the seventy disciples.

Probably because he only, of the Evangelists records the mission of the Seventy.

Thought to have been one of the two who journeyed to Emmaus with the risen Lord. *Theophylact.*

He alone relates the account of this journey, and in so graphic a manner as to warrant the presumption that he was an eye-witness.

Especially striking that he should leave the name of one of the disciples unmentioned.

A fellow-laborer of Paul; joined him at Troas, and accompanied him to Macedonia.

Journeyed as far as Philippi, where we lose him from the society of Paul and Silas.

When they were afterwards liberated, and departed thence, Luke remained at Philippi.

Passed through Miletus, Tyre, and Cæsarea, to Jerusalem.

Probable allusion to Luke as "the brother whose praise is in all the churches." 2. Cor. viii. 18.

Appears in company with Paul, in the memorable journey to Rome. Acts xxvii. 1.

Remained at his side during his first imprisonment.

Continued faithful to the Apostle till he received the crown of martyrdom.

Doubtless others were near him; but Luke was the last of his habitual companions who had clung to him.

Tradition says that after Paul's death he preached in Dalmatia and Gallia.

Much uncertainty as to his age and the manner of his death.

Probably suffered martyrdom between A.D. 75, and A.D. 100.

Luke and Mark, Evangelists, not Apostles; Matthew and John were both.

Luke's gospel written before the *Acts of the Apostles*. Acts i. 1.

Date of authorship probably about A.D. 56 or 58.

Place where it was written, uncertain.—Achaia and Bœotia *(Jerome)*; Alexandria *(Syriac Version)*; Rome *(Ewald)*; Macedonia *(Hilgenfeld)*; Asia Minor *(Köstlin)*; Cæsarea *(Conybeare* and *Howson)*.

Never any doubt Luke wrote his gospel in the Greek language.

There are peculiarities such as we should expect in the writings of an author like Luke.

Traces of his profession apparent. Note description of fever (chap. iv. 38); mention of the healing of the servant's ear (chap. xxii. 51); and falling of "the great drops, as of blood" (chap. xxii. 44).

We are plainly not listening to the Galilean fishermen, but to the educated citizen of Antioch, well versed in the literary language of the empire.

Composition of his sentences much more studied and elaborate than in Matt. and Mark.

The periods more rounded, the words far more numerous, and the idioms more classical.

Yet has many Hebraisms, mainly apparent in the hymns and speeches, embodied in the narrative.

Indicative of the Hebrew sources, whether oral or written, from which he has been careful to derive his information.

Citations from the O.T. show he frequently used the Sept. version.

Gospel we now possess unanimously acknowledged as that written by Luke.

About A.D. 120 it was in general use and familiarly known.

Quoted by Justin Martyr, and the author of the Clementine Homilies.

Christian antiquity testifies Luke wrote under the eye of Paul.

Irenæus says "Luke set down in a book the Gospel preached by Paul."

Remarkable agreement between Luke's account of the institution of the Lord's Supper (chap. xxii. 19), and that by Paul (1. Cor. xi. 23).

Origen, Eusebius, and Jerome understand the expression "my gospel," used in Rom. ii. 16, of *the Gospel of Luke.*

But the language of Luke's preface forbids the notion of any exclusive influence of Paul.

Paul, the Apostle, and Luke, the Evangelist, of the Gentiles.

Universality, the predominant character of Luke's gospel.

Jesus not mainly presented as the Messiah of Israel, or as the Incarnate Son of God, but as the Divine Son of Man.

His genealogy traced through the great Jewish ancestor up to the parent of mankind.

Luke principally records those sayings and acts of our Lord by which God's mercy to the Gentiles is set forth.

First sermon recorded is that of Nazareth, where the wide spread of the Gospel beyond the people of Israel is distinctly declared, chap. iv. 18-27.

His epitome of the Sermon on the Mount, unlike Matthew's, unmarked by frequent interpretations of Jewish law, and breathes only of universal love.

No restriction to race or nation shown by the mission of the Seventy, whose number was typical of the Gentile world.

Same principle indicated in the peculiar selection of miracles and parables.

Luke alone relates the pardon of "the woman which was a sinner."

Luke alone relates the conversion of the chief publican, *Zacchæus.*

Luke alone discloses the fact of the penitence of the dying thief.

Luke alone has given the parables of the Lost Sheep and the Lost Piece of Money.

Luke alone has given the most glorious of all parables, the Prodigal Son.

Luke dwells much on the priestly lineage and person of our Lord.

He alone mentions the relationship of Mary to the wife of Zacharias the *priest.*

He alone relates the angelic vision to Zacharias, ministering in t priest's office.

He alone describes the sacrificial offerings made for Christ, an infant, the temple.

Oftener than the rest he reveals Christ in prayer, and intimates His *mediatorial* office, as ever living *to make intercession for us.*

Hence the early Fathers represented Luke under the symbol of the sacrificial victim—the *calf. Augustine.*

More fully than the other Evangelists he sets forth the Lord's death as an atonement for the sins of the whole world.

Observe also how he notes His tender *human* sympathy; for instance, in the *first* parable recorded—The Two Debtors (chap. vii. 41-43), and in that of the Good Samaritan (chap. x. 30-37), and in all the miracles, especially the Raising of the Widow's Son (chap. vii. 11-17).

Moreover, he alone records that, when dying, He prayed for His murderers.

He alone describes the loving attitude of blessing, in which He parted from His disciples at the time of His Ascension, chap. xxiv. 50-51.

Of all the Gospels, that of Luke has the best claims to be considered a history.

With peculiar power he exhibits the Lord's conversations, with all the incidents that gave rise to them, the remarks of those who heard them, and the final results.

His acute spirit of enquiry collected many notices which either complete or explain the narratives of the other Evangelists.

He alone gives the reasons for the birth of Jesus at Bethlehem, the history of John the Baptist, the appearance of Moses and Elias on the Mount of Transfiguration, and many other circumstances in the Gospel narrative.

The numerous striking reflections with which his gospel is interspersed display the high culture of its composer.

Occasionally he manifests profound acquaintance with the constitution of the human mind, for instance—"*They believed not for joy*," chap. xxiv. 41.

The preservation of the glorious account of how the Lord *turned and looked on Peter*, displays the same philosophic insight.

He treats the subject of spiritual agencies, and their operation, with much more distinctness than the other Evangelists.

His notices of the future state are remarkable for vivid power,—witness the parable of the Rich Man and Lazarus.

Viewed in its general character, his gospel is the most complete and systematic account of the earthly life of the Lord Jesus.

As the four Gospel-trees stand in the midst of the true "Garden of the Soul," this is the most perfect in form.

It is emphatically the Gospel of the Redeemer, as the Personification of Divine Love.

It provides a rich storehouse of comfort and hope for all who *sit in darkness, and in the shadow of death.*

It is the Gospel which seems to bring heaven nearest to earth.

As Luke was a physician, so all his words are medicine for a languishing soul. *Jerome.*

See *Lange*, *Olshausen*, *Alford*, *Wordsworth*, *Prescott*, *Smith's Dictionary*.

LUKE.

CHAPTER I.

1. *Forasmuch as many have taken in hand to set forth in order a declaration of those things which are most surely believed among us.*

Luke and Mark evangelists, not apostles; Matthew and John were both.

Luke's Birthplace, Antioch. *Eusebius. Jerome.*

Tradition describes him as a painter of no mean skill. *Nicephorus.*

Supposed to have been one of the seventy disciples. *Epiphanius.*

Thought to have been one of the two who journeyed to Emmaus with the risen Redeemer. *Theophylact.*

A Gentile and Physician. Col. iv. 14. Fellow laborer of Paul. Ph. 24 ver.

At Troas, Philippi. Acts xvi. 10. Jerusalem. Rome. Acts xxi. 17, and xxviii. 16.

Imprisoned with Paul. 2 Tim. iv. 11. "The brother" probably. 2 Cor. viii. 18.

His style purest Greek of the Evangelists.

Many Annalists. Honest but uninspired believers.

Taken &c. Luke inspired, made no such *vain attempt.*

In order. God of *order* shown in Nature and Revelation. 1 Cor. xiv. 23.

Declaration. Historical Narration, but not in order of time.

Surely, &c. Christianity is built upon facts. 1 Cor. xv. 1-8.

Had others' labors been complete, Luke had not written.

Believed. Assured faith, begets confidence in others.

Neither Mark nor Luke, apostles. St. James and Jude, authors of epistles. Doubtful. *Tholuck.*

"*Many*" Luke includes Mark, *Grotius*, Including Luke himself, *Alford.* Apocryphal gospels innumerable. *Irenæus.* Egyptian gospel, *Mill.* "*Taken, &c.*" not a failure, *Major.* Attempted but failed, *Theophylact.* A rebuke for writing without divine commission, *Origen. Michaelis.* Happily pursued *Lightfoot.* "Declarations," family Traditions. "*Believed,*" a thing certain. *Wetstein.* Completae sunt, *Vulg Lightfoot.* Fully persuaded, Rom. iv. 21. Fully known, 2 Tim. iv. 17. Proved by arguments, *Theop.* Accomplished, *Campbell.* Performed, *Hammond.*

---

2. *Even as they delivered them unto us, which from the beginning were eyewitnesses, and ministers of the word.*

They. Apostles were eyewitnesses, evangelists partially.

Delivered. They taught orally. *Traditions* are not endorsed.

All that the evangelists wrote was *inspired* afresh.

The Scriptures are fully and *completely* the work of the Spirit.

The styles vary, but the shades of thought are preserved

Unto us, i. e. Christians.

Word. Gospel written amid fierce perescutions.

Composed without one single word of bitterness.

Gospel is received by the wisest, purest, and holiest of men.

Eyewitnesses. Apostles, 70 disciples, and 500 brethren, 1 Cor. xv. 6.

He gives Apostles no flattering titles, Job xxxii. 22.

Alludes to human, but not to divine sources of knowledge.

One must be more than an eyewitness, to be an Evangelist.

Ministers. Lat. servants, the form of the master, Phil. 2. 7.

"*Delivered,*" not the basis of the gospel, *Major*. Luke a compiler, *Schleiermacher*. Oral tradition, *Oosterzee*. Plenary inspiration, clearly taught, 2 Tim. iii. 16. *Variation* in styles caused by the *medium*. Gold cast by one artist, assumes the *varieties of moulds*, but the *materials* and *forms* are precisely as they were intended. "The truths inspired take the form of the varied minds and styles of each writer. Syllable by syllable as a harp doth give a sound according to the skill of the hand striking it." *Hooker*. ἀπ' ἀρχῆς official beginning, *Oosterzee*. Of Christ's ministry, *Doddridge*. Christian dispensation long time since, Acts xv. 7, *Lightfoot*. ὑπηρέται actors in the Gospel, *Elsley*. *Greek*. Under-rowers in the ancient war galleys, generally slaves. They sat one row above another. Their oars were of different lengths. Λόγου Christ, *Elsley*. Λόγου denotes here πράγμα v. 1. *Erasmus*. *Kuinoel*. Ministry of the Word, *Le Clerc*.

---

3. *It seemed good to me also, having had perfect understanding of all things from the very first, to write unto thee in order, most excellent Theophilus.*

Seemed. He neither claims nor denies inspiration.

Perfect, &c. This can be said of no *human* aids.

Uncertainty hangs round all, but God's promises.

His book is not "the word of man," but of God. 1 Thess. ii. 13

All things. The leading facts and doctrines of Christianity.

Very First. Dawnings of the gospel era.

To Write Antiquity, mode, and materials, Luke i. 63.

Christ's setting so many pens in motion, proves His history *divine*, and His enemies *insane*.

To Thee. Luke's gospel written, to build up *one* Gentile heart.

The Spirit aims to build up the entire Church in future.

Order. Not of time, but of *classifying* the events.

We find fidelity, accuracy, research, and order.

Excellent, applied to Felix, Festus in *official* station, Acts xxiv. 3.
Fawning servility, a common form of hypocrisy.
Yet "Honor to whom, &c." Rom. xiii. 7. "Be courteous." 1, Peter iii. 8.
Highest civil honors, *enobled* by citizenship in the Kingdom.
Titles of honor, *where* most merited are least coveted.
Theophilus. Some illustrious, but unknown Christian.
Gr. *Friend of God.* Most prefer the world's favors.
"Not many wise, not many noble are called." 1. Cor. i. 26.

Κἀμοὶ et Spiritui Sancto. An old translator adds, *Oosterzee.* Παρηκολ. Having investigated, *Major.* Followed closely. *Brown.*

ἄνωθεν Christ's *entire* life, *Alford.* Above or heaven, *Lightfoot,* very beginning, *Ellicott.* ακριβῶς extreme accuracy, *Major. Olshausen.*

Καθεξῆς as to time, *Grotius.* Distinctly, *Campbell.* Chronology, *Lange. Ellicott. Olshausen.* Consecutively, *Alford. Brown.* Classification of facts, *Elsley.* Κρατ. most noble, *Geneva* Christians in general, *Epiphanius. Hammond,* official. *Oosterzee.* As *optimus* of Senators, *Horace. Major.* Term omitted in Acts i. 1. Θεόφιλε dwelt in *Jerusalem, Josephus.* Alexandria, *Bengel* Rome, *Oosterzee.* A pupil of Luke, *W. and W.* Christian, *Athanasius. Michaelis.* Fictitious person, *Salvian.* A magistrate in Asia Minor, *Major.* A freedman of Nero, *Greswell.* Phil. i. 13.

---

4. *That thou mightest know the certainty of those things, wherein thou hast been instructed.*

Know. Gr. intensive—know perfectly.
Knowledge embraces *truths* revealed for our well-being.
Wisdom alone, puts that knowledge in *practice.*
Certainty of revelation, testified to by every *conscience.*
Equal evidence of the *divinity* of the *Sun* and of the *Bible.*
Bible divinity as self-evidencing as the light of the Sun.
God and human law hold us *responsible* for our belief.
Things. Gr. *words,* truths, doctrines, revealed by the Spirit
Instructed. Gr. *catechized,* instruction by word of mouth.
Refusing light to men, proves one an enemy of Christ. Matt. v. 15.
Ignorance is ever the enemy of devotion. Luke i. 77. Notes.

κατηχ. orally, *Major. Brown.* ἀσφά. Luke hints at the brevity, want of order, and even inaccuracy of the many. *Kuinoel.* Sceptics deny man's responsibility, if he errs honestly. *Brougham's Life of Voltaire.*

5. There was in the days of Herod, the king of Judea, a certain priest named Zacharias, of the course of Abia: and his wife was of the daughters of Aaron, and her name was Elisabeth.

It came. Prophetic harp had been silent for 526 years. Dan. vii. 12.
From the building of the second temple, no revelation was given.
A departed sceptre, proved the time of the Shiloh had come. Gen. xlix. 10.
Israel's bondage, shewed a Redeemer needed.
In the days. Christ born four years before our common era.
Herod the Great, son of Antipater, an Idumean.
Aided Rome by bribery, after robbing his countrymen.
At Antony's request, senate voted him a crown.
The first *foreigner* who reigned over Judea.
He slew Bethlehem babes, and 70 members of the Sanhedrin.
Also his wife, and sons Alexander and Aristobulus, through *envy*.
He rebuilt the Temple, adorning it with splendor.
Built several theatres in Judea, in honor of Cæsar.
Reigned 37 years a monster of cruelty.
King. Judea had been ruled by *Asmoneans* 100 years.
Judea. 1. named Canaan; 2 Land of Promise. Heb. xi. 9.
3 Land of the Hebrews; 4 of Israel; 5 of Judah; 6 Holy Land.
7 Palestine from Philistines on the north coast.
Length 170; breadth 65 miles. Division 12 tribes.
1 Galilee; 2 Samaria; 3 Judea; 4 Perea; 5 Idumea.
Plains. 1 Sharon. 2 Esdraelon. 3 Jericho or Jordan.
Rivers. Jordan. Arnon. Lakes. Dead Sea and Galilee.
Mountains. Lebanon. Hermon. Tabor. Olivet of Judea.
Harvest from April to June. The Vintage July, to October.
Products, Millet or wheat, barley, grapes, oranges, dates, figs.
Jerusalem 2400 feet, Hebron 2600 feet above the sea.
Barrenness supposed miraculous. Jer. iv. 27. xviii. 16. Ezek. xiv. 16. Mic. vii. 13.
Priest. First born was priest until the law of Sinai.
In their stead the tribe of Levi was chosen. Num. iii. 41.
Noah, Abraham, Job, Laban, Isaac and Jacob, sacrificed.
Exceptions. Melchisedec, Samuel, Saul, David, Solomon, Elijah.
They offered gifts, kept sacred fire, and made shew bread.
Nadab and Abihu slain for offering strange fire. Lev. x. 2.
Uzziah unauthorized, smitten with leprosy. 2 Ch. xxvi. 19.
They must always wash before sacrificing. Ex. xxx. 17. 21.
Touched not the dead, entered office at 30 years of age, left at 50.

No land given them, they inhabited 13 cities.
Skin, wool, select portions of victims, first fruits and tithes of the land, theirs. Lev. vii. 6.
First born of clean animals sacrificed; unclean, redeemed.
Judges and instructors in peace, bore the ark in war. Deu. xx. 2.
Course, not lineage, but order of service set by David. 1 Ch. xxiv.
24 Courses, one class ministering a week at the Temple.
Only four courses returned from Babylonish captivity. Ezra ii. 36.
These four were again divided into 24.
There may be a *succession* in a *forsaken* church.
It remained, when Christ was crucified, and Spirit quenched.
Wife. Marriage instituted in Paradise, for well being of society.
Finding a good one is of God's favor. Pro. xviii. 22.
Christ's first miracle, sanctioned a wedding at Cana. John ii. 1.
Abia, descendant of Eleazar, the eighth course took his name.
Daughter of a Levite, *lawful*; of the priests, a more *desirable* wife.
Pious parents among God's richest gifts. 2. Tim. i. 5.
Aaron. Son of Amram and Jochebed, three years older than Moses
Wife, Elisheba; sons, Nadab, Abihu, Eleazar and Ithamar.
Aged 83 at the Exodus, ascended Sinai. Ex. xxiv. 9.
First High Priest, because his rod budded. Num. xvii. 8.
He made the golden calf. Ex. xxxii. 4. Seditions. Num. xii. 11.
Died on Mount Hor in Edom, aged 123.
Elizabeth. Heb. "My God hath sworn."

ἡμέρασ λειτουργίαν *Hesychius.* The days of atonement. Greek and Roman Calendar rests on this hypothesis, *Doddridge.* ἱερεύσ priest, hence *presbyter*. Heb. *Cohen* a *Prince*. Zacha, an assistant of the High Priest, *Lightfoot*. "*His wife.*" He had a wife. *Lachman. Tischendorf.*

---

6. *And they were both righteous before God, walking in all the commandments and ordinances of the Lord blameless.*

Both. One in affection, one in interest, one in Christ.
Righteous. Either justification or sanctification.
They always go together in the believers spiritual life.
Christ our righteousness. 1 Cor. i. 30. Phil. iii. 9.
No one perfect. Eccles. vii. 20. 1. John i. 8.
"Who can say I am pure from my sin?" Prov. xx. 9.
Believers desire *to be* all that God demands. Ps. cxix. 47.
Far from being sinless, they are blameless. Phil. ii. 5.
Approved by God, and esteemed by men. Rom. xiv. 18.

Ancestral piety, not princely blood, was John's nobility.

Before God. In the sight of an all seeing Creator.

God. A Spirit, infinite in every divine perfection.

Walking. Orientalism for progress.

Habitual tenor of one's life. Psa. i. 1.

In darkest hours, houses still become temples of God.

Commandments and Ordinances. Moral and ceremonial laws.

Lord. Sax. *Bread Giver*, in capitals, *Jehovah*. Luke i. 11.

Blameless. Irreproachable in their integrity.

Righteous. Jewish laws, *Major.* ἐντ. & δικα. moral and ceremonial, *Besa Lightfoot.* Synonymous, *Kuinoel.* Justificationibus, *Vulg.* Good works here endorsed, *Rhemish Notes.* ἀμεμ, "Innocuos ambos cultores numinis ambos," *Ovid.* O. T. placed piety in *fear*, N. T. in *love*, *Stier.* Θεοῦ from τίθημι. Primitive with, Διοσ, &c., *Gesenius.* Jehovah, Existing One, Elohim, lost Hebrew root, *coluit.* *Havernich.* Jehovah not same as Jove, but Hebrew origin, Elohim *Deity*, Creator. Jehovah the Redeemer. Affix "Living," as opposed to idols, *Nicholson.* Jehovah the Redeemer, pain and joy, *Rosenmuller.* Arabic word Height, *Ewald.* Three words, Ex. xiii. 14. Contain proofs of Eternity, *Grotius*, *Crusius.* Isa, Egyptian God, *Von Bholen.* Essence and truth, *Buxtorf.* Essential personal being, *Olshausen.* Matt. xviii. 20. God, from Goda, Persian, same as *dominus*, not from Saxon goodness, *Smith.*

---

7. *And they had no child, because that Elizabeth was barren: and they both were now well stricken in years.*

No child. In the East, mourned as a reproach, 1 Sam. i. 10.

"Children are the heritage of the Lord," Ps. cxxvii. 3.

Here was desolation without murmuring.

Isaac, Joseph, Samuel, John, were special *gifts*.

Blessings long withheld, are more intensely prized.

Well stricken. Far advanced in age.

8. *And it came to pass, that, while he executed the priest's office before God, in the order of his course.*

9. *According to the custom of the priest's office, his lot was to burn incense when he went into the temple of the Lord.*

His course. The eighth in order. 1 Chron. 24.

They began in September, and ended at the Passover.

Custom. In sanctuary service nothing is left to accident.

His lot. Three priests each week entered the temple service.

1 removed ashes; 2 brought coals; 3 burned incense.

Incense. Gums from Arabia and India called *frankincense*, from the *freedom* with which it gives forth its odors.

Symbol of prayer accepted, Rev, v. 8; Ps. cxli, 2.
Temple. Gr. *shrine*. Our Lord never entered this Holy Place.
Priest taught, and Israel worshipped, in the *sacred enclosure*.
The money changers and merchandise were here, John ii. 15.
Built by Solomon, on Mount Moriah, B. C. 1011.
On the verge of the Mount, 500 feet above the valley of Jehoshaphat.
Threshing floor of Ornan, purchased by David, its site. 2 Ch. iii. 1.
Length 50 feet, Porch 15 feet, width 30 feet, height 40 feet.
Materials marble, gold, cedar, brass—Hiram builder.
Without window, *Shechinah* its only light, 1 Kings viii. 12.
Holy of Holies, veiled by a screen, looped at each end.
1 Court of *Priests*, 165 by 119 cubits, Court of Israel, 187 by 135.
Here Israel prayed in silence during sacrifice. Luke i. 22.
2 Court of the *women*, parted from Gentile by Beautiful Gate,
The Treasury, here Publican and Pharisee prayed. Luke xviii. 10.
Our Lord preached in these courts. John viii. 20.
3 Court of the *Gentiles* covered 14 acres, all walled in.
Ark in the first temple, two tables of stone, budding rod, manna.
Plundered by Shishak for 33 years. Ruined by Nebuchadnezzar.
It stood 424 years. Tabernacle *before this*. 480 years from Exodus.
In ruins 52 years. Under Cyrus Zerubbabel rebuilt it.
Twenty-one years in building.
This was larger than Solomon's, and Herod's larger than Zerubbabel's.
1, Ark and Mercy Seat; 2, Shechinah; 3, Holy Fire;
4, Urim and Thummim; 5, Spirit of Prophecy, wanting in the second temple.
It was profaned by Epiph'anes B.C., 163.
12 B.C., enlarged and beautified by Herod, and used after nine years.
Workmen engaged on it during all the Saviour's life.
Soldiers of Rome under Titus destroyed it, A,D. 70.
Mosque of Omar, built A.D. 637, now stands on the spot.
Lord. Luke i. 11. *See note on* **Lord,** *verse* 6.

θυμιᾶσαι This office only held once by each priest. *Wetstein*. *Flamen* (flame), Roman priest was robed in white (purity), remained out of Rome, but one night (ever ready to supplicate the gods), inaugurated and anointed, to offer sacrifice. Slave entering his house was *free*. He was ever for peace—touched no *leavened* bread. *Lewis Ant.* Zachariah was high priest. *Augustine*. ναὸν only used in N.T. for the *shrine*. Ἱερὸν the entire courts around t. Christ never entered the ναὸς *Trench*.

10. *And the whole multitude of the people were praying without at the time of the incense.*

Multitude. Hints that the season was the Sabbath.

Praying. A dictate of nature. Heathen all pray,

Our duty: Pray without ceasing. 1 Thess. v. 17.

Dependence on God for all things. Acts xvii. 28.

Christ's example. Luke vi. 12. Flock prayed *silently*, Rev. viii. 1.

Without. Daily sacrifice burned on the *great altar*, while the priest went *within* and offered incense on the altar.

No one could follow him within, under penalty of death,

A bell announced the burning of incense to the waiting people.

Levites sang, and the priests sounded the trumpets.

Time. Gr. Hour. Third and ninth hour, 7a.m. and 3 p.m.

Faithful frequented the temple for prayer. Acts iii. 1.

Day and night, each divided into twelve equal parts.

Nine o'clock was the third hour; twelve o'clock, the sixth hour;

Three o'clock, the ninth hour. The darkness of Crucifixion. Mark xv. 33.

Night was divided into four equal watches.

11. *And there appeared unto him an angel of the Lord standing on the right side of the altar of incense.*

Appeared. No angel seen since the building of second temple.

Angel. Called Messenger, Thrones, Dominions, Principalities.

Living Ones, Cherub, Seraph, Powers. Rev. xviii. 1.

Power. 185,000 Assyrians slain in one night. 2 Kings xix. 35.

Activity. "A flaming fire." Heb. i. 7. Immortal in *youth*. Mark xvi. 5.

Jehovah's agents. Ps. lxviii. 17., Ps. 24, Eph. iv. 8, Rev xxii. 9.

Celebrated Creation. Job xxxviii. 7. Present at Sinai. Ps. lxviii. 17.

Life-guard of our Lord. Ps. xxiv. 7, Matt. xxvi. 53.

Students of God's works. 1 Peter i. 12, Perfectly holy.

Halo round them, painters borrowed from *heathen.*

Lord. Luke i. 6. Jehovah, the first Person in the Trinity.

Jesus, Lord of angels, birth announced by angels.

Right side. Esteemed a favorable omen by Greeks and Romans

Two angels stood on the *right* side of the sepulchre. Mark xvi. 5.

Jesus told Peter to cast a net on the *right side.* John xxi. 6.

Christ, enthroned, sat at the *right* hand, &c. Ps. cx. 1.

Solomon's mother sat on his *right* hand. 1 Kings ii. 19.
Altar of incense, of acacia, 22 inches square, 44 inches high.
Four horns on the corners, and cornice, covered with gold.
Stood in the Holy Place, between candlestick and shew bread.
Germ of the first Patriarchal Church—its use *now*, a *perversion*.
Others built of stone, not soiled by a tool. Ex. xx. 25.
Altars are unauthorised since Christ came. Heb. x. 14.
Places of refuge. God of the altar chosen as protector. Ex. xxi. 14.
Covenants and marriages solemnized there in after ages.
Built of *sod*, of *stone*, of *marble*, and hung with wreaths.
Greeks and Romans, built them on hills and mounts.
Greeks laid their hand on the altar, and Levites on victim, and prayed. Lev. i. 4.

ϑυσία root to *slay*. Lat. *altar* altus high. Greeks and Romans *stole* from Hebrews the idea of making altars places of *refuge* for the guilty, as they did nearly all their *higher* class of ceremonies. Hom. Od. 22. To Jove's *inviolable* altar nigh. Virgil ii. 528. Euripides.

Altar never called merely a refuge. *Alford*. Horns at first intended for binding victims. *Kuinoel*.

Κύριοσ & δοῦλος correllative terms. Heb. *Adonai*, *Dominus*, Lord or master, implies inferiority. 1 Peter iii. 5-6. David called none but Jehovah κύριοσ Matt. xxii. 44. Jesus humbly attired, called κύριοσ by the leper. Matt. viii. 2. *Campbell*. δεσπότησ on account of the cruelty of masters, stood afterward for tyrant. In classics, applied to the gods. In N. T. absolute author of life. Synonym with βασιλεύσ *Paulus*, used nine times in N. T., once of Christ. 2 Peter ii. 1. *Trench*. Denied by *Erasmus*, of Arian tendency.

---

12. *And when Zacharias saw him, he was troubled, and fear fell upon him.*

Troubled. He who served in the *Master's* presence, was astonished at the presence of one of His *servants*.
Fear, caused only by sin. Perfect love casteth out fear. 1. John iv. 18.
Moses at the bush. Daniel at the Hiddikel.
Peter at the lake, women at the tomb, and John in Patmos, *feared*.

13. *But the angel said unto him, Fear not, Zacharias: for thy prayer is heard; and thy wife Elisabeth shall bear thee a son, and thou shalt call his name John.*

Fear not. Dread of evil tidings, terrifies sinners. Ps. cxii. 7.
Good men are well known to angels and fiends. 1. Ch. xxi. 1.
Prayer. For the coming of the Shiloh. "A few names in Sardis." Rev. iii. 4.

Prayer. The offering of our *sincere desires* to God.
Prayers offered to any other being, or name, is idolatry.
It involves a sense of our *unworthiness* and *necessities*. Gen. xviii. 27.
Penitence. Ps. li. 17. *Faith*. Heb. xi. 6. *Sincerity*. Jer. xxix. 13. *Fervency*. James v. 16. *Love*. 1. Tim. ii. 8. *Delight* in God. Isa. xxv. 9. *Perseverance*. Eph. vi. 18. Humble *submission to* His will. Mich. vii. 7. In the *name* of Christ. Eph. iii. 12. And a *confession* of our sins. 1 John i. 9.
Jewish prayers were chiefly praise and benedictions.
Always answered, but in God's sovereign way.
Our Redeemer prays, but an angel is sent. Luke xxii. 43.
Paul prays, but the promise comes, a thorn remains. 2. Cor. xii. 9.
Prayer of faith, never comes weeping home. *Henry*.
Prayers are filed, not forgotten in heaven. Acts. x. 4.
If unanswered, our sins are the cause. Ps. lxvi. 18.
Prayers oft granted, long before we know their success.
This doubly answered—Messiah comes in his day.
His son is to be the Lord's forerunner. Luke i. 17.
Heard. God creates a longing for an *intended* blessing.
Elizabeth. Females long in the back ground in O. T., advanced in the Gospel age.
Living faith made her a fellow heir of grace. I. Peter iii. 7.
Son. A small favor, unless a child of grace.
God's gifts, at times memorials of wrath, at others pledges of love.
Son in old age. John ranks with Isaac and Samuel.
John. Heb. bestowed of God, or God is gracious. Luke vii. 19.
Thought to be born at Juttah, 6 miles south of Hebron.
Coming foretold. Isaiah xl. 3. Mal. iii. 1—4—5. Resembled Elijah.
Sanctified from the womb. Trained a Nazarite.
30 years spent in deserts. Baptised many, Jesus also.
Preached repentance and announced the coming Kingdom.
Sanhedrim questioned him as to his official rank. John i. 19. 28.
Herod heard, and imprisoned him in Machaerus, Moab.
Thence, John sent two disciples to our Lord. Luke vii. 19.
Beheaded because of Herodias dancing, and mother's revenge. Matt. xii. 10.

δέη. desire for posterity, *Olshausen*. *Maldonatus W. and W. Brown*. Burden of former prayers. *Koecker*. Messiah. *Grotius*, *Major*. *Lange*. Neither. *Lightfoot*. For the world. Deliverance of Israel. *Doddridge*. The nation. *Elsley*.

14. *And thou shalt have joy and gladness; and many shall rejoice at his birth.*

15. *For he shall be great in the sight of the Lord, and shall drink neither wine nor strong drink; and he shall be filled with the Holy Ghost, even from his mother's womb.*

Joy. A double gift, to the parents and the church.
Many would *grieve* to know the future of their children.
Gladness. Gr. exultation. He may have seen in vision John's success.
Rejoice. A joy, not in Christ, often a source of tears.
He was "a burning and shining light." John v. 35.
Note the interest of angels in the affairs of earth.
Great, without title, wealth, office or power.
In wisdom, piety, eloquence, heroic fidelity, and usefulness.
Sight of, &c. What men esteem, God oft abhors. Luke xvi. 15.
Jehovah looketh not on the outward appearance. 1 Sam xvi. 7.
It here excludes all idea of worldly greatness.
Officially, as the herald of Christ, above all prophets.
Drink. i. e. a *Nazarite.* Heb. separate. Num. vi. 13. Law.
A Nazarite, symbol of holiness, as a leper of sin.
He ate not grapes, nor drank unfermented wine.
His hair was unshorn, and he avoided funerals.
The vow lasted a week, month, year, or for life.
Monkish asceticism opposed utterly to a Nazarite's vow.
Young men trained Nazarites, public blessings. Amos ii. 11.
Wine. 1, *new wine,* juice of the grape, unfermented. Gen. xl. 11.
2, *Fermented,* but free from all drugs. Luke v. 39.
3, *Boiled wine* of *honey.* Num. xviii. 12. Prov. ix. 2-5.
4, *Spiced wine,* Sol. Song viii. 2. 5. *Strong Drink.* Isa. v. 22.
Made of grapes, apples, pears, dates, aniseed, honey, barley.
First named in connection with sin. Gen. ix. 21. 2 Sam. xiii. 28.
A *mocker.* Prov. xx. 1. Source of *evil.* Prov. xxiii. 29.
Source of *woe.* Isa. v. 22. Of *error.* Isa. xxviii. 1, 7.
Impiety. Isa. v. 11. Hos. iv. 11. Forbidden. Num. vi. 3.
Common drink in Palestine, employed in Passover.
Named with corn and oil. Ex. xxii. 29. Luke v. 37, 38.
In Temple service. Ex. xxix. 40. Lord's Supper. Matt. xxvi. 27.
Alcoholic drinks discovered by Arabs, 10th century.
Holy Ghost. Third person in the Holy Trinity—Omnipresence, Psa. cxxxix. 7.
Divinity. Formula of baptism. Matt. xxviii. 19. Benediction. 2. Cor. xiii. 13.

Name, God. Acts v. 3, 4. Heb. iii. 7, 9. Jehovah. Num. xii. 6. Eternity. Gen. i. 2. Omniscience. 1 Cor. ii. 10. Almighty. Acts vi. 10. Works. Psa. xxxiii. 8. Worship. Acts. iv. 24. John xvi. 8. Eph. iv. 30.

Mother. I will pour my blessing upon their offspring. Isa. xliv. 3. This hints, that very young children are converted.

John and Jeremiah shared similar grace. Jer. i. 5.

οἶν. σικε. Sicera Lat., sidre Ital., Eng. cider. "He shal not drinke wyn nor sydyr." *Wickliffe*, *Wine*, translates ten different Hebrew and two Greek words. Mixed Wine. Prov. xxiii. 30. Cup of trembling. Isa. li. 17. Anything that inebriates. *Elsley*. Old wine. *Lightfoot*. Grapes, the forbidden tree in Eden. *Rabbis*. *πνεύμ.* 1 wind, 2 breath, 3 vital principle, 4 apparition, 5 soul, 6 angels, 7 Deity. *Major*. Κοιλίασ. children may be renewed from infancy. *President Edwards*. Sanctified before born. *Olshausen*. *Meyer*. Inde a puero. *Kuinoel*.

---

16. *And many of the Children of Israel shall he turn to the Lord their God.*

Many. Not all. "Thy people *made* willing, &c." Ps. cx. 3.

Children. Jews trusted generally to being *Abraham's seed.*

Israel. Heb. *who prevails with God.* Surname of Jacob. Luke i. 54.

Turn. His ministry of repentance confined to Jews.

John was the last of the Old Testament messengers from God.

Lord, as Jehovah, belongs to Adam's entire race.

Their God, does not confine mercy to Abraham's seed.

17. *And he shall go before him in the spirit and power of Elias, to turn the hearts of the fathers to the children, and the disobedient to the wisdom of the just; to make ready a people prepared for the Lord.*

Before. As the heralds in the East precede Kings. Luke iii. 4. Isaiah lvii. 14.

Him, refers to God, v. 16. Clearly asserts the coming of the Messiah.

Spirit. "I have been very zealous for the Lord of Hosts." 1 Kings xix. 10.

Of self sacrifice. "Girt with leather and eating locusts." 2 Kings i. 8.

A Reformer bold and faithful in a very corrupt age.

Single handed, both grappled with sin in high places.

Ahab and Jezebel persecuted Elijah; Herod and Herodias, John.

Power. Not of miracles, for John wrought none. John x. 41.

We say a Samson for strength, or Solomon for wisdom.
John turned hearts. Mal. iv. 6, 1 Kings 18, John i. 7, Luke iii. 14.
Searching, awakening ministry, under the same Spirit.
Elias, born at Tishbeh in Gilead. 1 Kings xvii. 1. Parents unknown.
Foretold famine, and enraged Ahab and Jezebel. 908 B.C.
Fed 40 days at brook Cherith, near Jericho, by *ravens*.
Cruse of oil increased, child raised at Zarephath.
God answered by fire, and 400 prophets slain at Carmel.
He anointed Hazael, King of Syria, and Jehu, King of Israel.
Ahab's wife charged with Naboth's murder; Ahaziah's death foretold.
He called fire from heaven which destroyed 100 men.
Crossing the Jordan, he ascended to heaven in a chariot of fire.
His mantle and office were left to Elisha.
He and Moses appeared with Christ in glory on Mount of Transfiguration.
Fathers's hearts would now faithfully train their seed.
And fervently pray, pointing to heaven and leading the way.
Children. Sin, cause of all discord, finds its cure in Christ.
Gospel alone reconciles all the jarring interests of earth. John xiv. 27
Wisdom, i.e., piety. God the Giver of the only true wisdom. Prov. ii. 6.
All the boasted treasures of *earthly wisdom* shall perish. Is. xxix. 14.
The church of God ever the only light of the world. Matt. v. 14.
Prepared, as a ship provisioned for a voyage.

Elias.—As John was the forerunner of Christ's first advent, so Elias will be of His second. *Theophylact.* "Fathers and children." Patriarchs to their descendants. *Elsley.* To the child Christ. *Pearce.* Believers of every age. *Bengel.* Discordant sects. *Hammond.* Parental piety restored. *Major.* General gospel benevolence. *Gilpin.* Jews and Gentiles. *Lightfoot.* Strengthening family ties. *Oosterzee.* Spirit of the ancient Church restored. *Calvin.*

---

18. *And Zacharias said unto the angel, Whereby shall I know this? for I am an old man, and my wife well stricken in years.*

Whereby. He doubts the character and message of the angel.

Abraham, Gideon, *with* faith, and Zacharias *doubting*. Gen. xv. 17, Judges vi. 17.

The request was proper, but this motive (unbelief) wrong.

Desire for miraculous signs, 1 explicable, 2 reprehensible, 3 superfluous.

Morbid desire of Jews for signs rebuked by our Lord and Paul. 1 Cor. i. 22.

I know. The sign given very different from any expected.

God's word trustworthy, without proof or pledge. Rom. iv. 20.

Men trust their own deceitful hearts *against* all evidence.

He permits defects in the exalted, to cheer the humble.

Mary's faith, seeking explanation, had doubt solved.

Zachariah's unbelief, requiring a sign, punished.

Old. His sin was in resting on earth, not on *Heaven*.

The very *messenger*, as well as message, were signs.

Angel. Luke i. 11. Mistaken for an *evil* spirit. *Lightfoot.*

---

19. *And the angel answering said unto him, I am Gabriel, that stand in the presence of God; and am sent to speak unto thee, and to shew thee these glad tidings.*

I am. Answer full of dignity, and plain to a priest.

Gabriel. Heb. God is my strength. Only two angels named in Scripture.

Michael. Heb. Who is like to God? An Archangel. Rev. xii. 7.

Gabriel's services seem *Messianic*, Michael's *Judicial*.

Zacharias, most probably knew that he had visited Daniel before. Dan. ix. 21.

Stand. Gr. *wont* to stand. The posture of an oriental servant.

Implies constant access to the royal presence.

He explained the vision, and foretold the 70 weeks. Dan. ix. 24.

He announced the birth of Jesus to Mary. Luke i. 26.

Presence. High in the confidence of Jehovah. Orientalism for favorite minister.

Glad Tidings. A Gospel. 1 The doctrines of Christ.

2 Blessings promised in the N. T. 3 New doctrine. Gal. i. 6, 8.

Am sent. Angels are ministering Spirits, sent, &c. Heb. i. 7.

'Gabriel,' names of angels learned in Chaldea, *Rosenmuller*. Holds the scales at judgment, *Mohammed*. Superstition now shows at Rome a *pink* feather, which then dropped from his wing. ἀπεσ. I *was* sent. *Tischendorf*. εὐαγγ. Eng. Gospel. *God spel*. Sax. good news. Luke iv. 15.

---

20. *And, behold, thou shalt be dumb, and not able to speak, until the day that these things shall be performed, because thou believest not my words, which shall be fulfilled in their season.*

Behold. Denoting surprise, and calling special attention.
Dumb. He became deaf, as well as dumb. Luke i. 62.
All who cavil, sooner or later will be silenced.
Wounds inflicted by divine love, become healing medicines.
The more tender the love, the surer the chastisement.
Speak. Denial joined to affirmation. Strongest possible assertion.
Fulfilled. Foretelling events has as ever belonged *alone* to God.
Josiah named 326, and Cyrus 120 years before born.
David's prophecies took 1000 years, Daniel's, 800 to fulfil them.
God knows and controls the heart's secrets. Psa. cxxxix. 2. Prov. xxi. 1.
Believest. *Believed* not, unbelief leads to guilt and punishment.
Holiest of men are not free from defects. Noah, Abraham, Jacob, &c.
Seasons of mercy and judgments mingle in saints' experience.
Jacob's importunity at once answered and punished.

σιωπ. deaf, *Euthymius*. Hebraistic word, *Kuinoel*. Moral and physical dumbness, *Rosenmuller*. Climax, *Bloomfield*. Deaf and dumb, *Lightfoot*. An apoplectic stroke, *Hase*. Speechless three days, *Theophylact*.

---

21. *And the people waited for Zacharias, and marvelled that he tarried so long in the temple.*

22. *And when he came out, he could not speak unto them: and they perceived that he had seen a vision in the temple; for he beckoned unto them, and remained speechless.*

People assembled to worship. Indicates the Sabbath.
Marvelled. His solemn errand deepened their interest.
Speak. The benediction belonged to another priest's office.
Vision. Divine revelation to one in waking hours. Job. iv. 12.

Beckoned. Gr. assenting by nods, to questions of surprise.
His unusual excitement prompted the crowd's curiosity.
Speechless. Gr. deaf and dumb, one follows the other in time.
The ear regulates the voice. Laura Bridgeman lost her hearing, and in a few months lost the power of speech.
The last word distinctly pronounced was "*Mother.*"
Silence of *anger.* 1 Kings xxi. 4. Of *philosophy.* The Stoics.
Of *policy.* 1 Sam. x. 26. A *forced* silence. Phil. ii. 30.
Of *despair.* A dying Pope seeing the *crucifix.* "It's too late."
A Roman crowd silenced by "*Cæsar's your friend.*"
Silence of *faith.* "I was dumb and opened, &c." Psa. xxxix. 9
A nine months' silence for one distrustful word.
God's jealousy burneth nearest the altar. Lev. x. 2. 1 King's xiii. 4.

κωφόσ, mechanical provisions in the ear for *music*, still leave to the *mind* the source of taste and skill. Loss of sight improves the ear, hence blind love music, *Sir Chas. Bell.*

---

23. *And it came to pass, that, as soon as the days of his ministration were accomplished, he departed to his own house.*

24. *And after those days his wife Elisabeth conceived, and hid herself five months, saying.*

Ministration. Great bodily defect excluded Levites from office. Lev. xxi. 17.
Accomplished. No haste of bearing good tidings, nor loss of speech,
Could persuade him to neglect the Lord's service.
Own house. Luke i. 40. Mode and materials of Eastern houses.
An *Orientalism.* The city where one dwells. Matt. xiii. 57.
Elizabeth, Sarah, Rebekah, Rachel, Manoah's wife,
Hannah: illustrate the *miraculous* workings of God.
Hid herself. Modesty ever the fruit of piety.

λειτ. civil or military service of religion, *Hammond.* Sacrifice of God's people, *Trench.* Accomplished. The week from Sept. 30th to Oct. 6th. Six years before Christian era, *Greswell. Hid* to avoid defilement, *Lightfoot.* Keep her state secret, *Grotius.* Peculiar devotion, *Kuinoel.* It excluded him from office, as a prelude to

25. *Thus hath the Lord dealt with me in the days wherein he looked on me, to take away my reproach among men.*

26. *And in the sixth month the angel Gabriel was sent from God unto a city of Galilee, named Nazareth.*

Looked on. Hebrew mode of speech implying favor. Psa. xxv. 18, 119, 132.
Only the chosen few ever behold the *king* in the East.
"Many seek the Ruler's favor. Heb. *face*," but few succeed. Prov. xxix. 26.
Reproach. Earth's judgments rest on ignorance of God's ways.
Jews held barrenness to be the result of great sin.
Offspring unrestrained, oft prove a bitter curse to parents.
Abraham murmured—"I go childless." Gen. xv. 2.
Spirituality of the N. T. *subordinates* temporal blessings.
Angel. Their character and history. Luke i. 11.
Was sent. Angels informed of what occurs on earth. Luke ii. 13.
From God. Angels and apostles do His pleasure. John i. 6.
Galilee included Palestine west of Jordan, and north of Samaria.
Scene of our Lord's youth, and most of his labors.
Apostles all Galileans, pronunciation peculiar. Mark xiv. 70.
People generally esteemed rude, stupid, and seditious.
Creed despised; hence "Galilee of the Gentiles." Matt. iv. 15.
The Emperor Julian dying, defiantly called Jesus "*Galilean*."
Nazareth. Heb. separated, not named in the O. T.. Population 3000.
Six miles N.W. of Tabor, 70 miles N. of Jerusalem.
Mounts of Hermon, Bashan; Valley of Jordan, of Esdraelon.
Tabor, Gilboa, Samaria, Carmel, and Mediterranean sea visible from it.
It had an evil name. John i. 46. Jesus dwelt there 30 years.
Rome, Jerusalem, Athens passed by in God's sovereignty.
While Nazareth, unknown or despised, was selected.

"*Reproach*," Keys of clouds, heart, womb, and the grave, in God's hands. *Rabbis.* "Da tantum nomen mane Conubii, liceat tumulo scripsisse Catonis, Marcia," *Lucan.* "Galilee," 204 villages, and 3 millions pop., *Josephus.* Under Hadrian 985 towns laid waste in Judea, *Dion Cassius.* Hence the multitudes following Christ, *Greswell, Andrews.* (Ναζαρέθ) Heb. separate, *Gesenius.* Crown, *Bengel.* Branch, Matt. ii. 23 Why Christ called a Nazarene;—an unsolved difficulty, *Alford.* Mary had property there, *Olshausen.* Ναζωραῖοσ in rude Greek, indicating a dweller in Nazareth, not referring to Num. vi. 13, *Michaelis.*

27. *To a virgin espoused to a man whose name was Joseph, of the house of David; and the virgin's name was Mary.*

Virgin. Foretold by Isaiah vii. 14. Jews did not expect this.
When scoffers cannot refute, they bitterly revile.
Council of Trent teaches her immaculate conception. viii, 5, 5.
A descendant of David, verse 32, a link in Christ's incarnation.
After her return from Egypt to Nazareth, she is named five times.
Three times reproved. Matt. xii. 46, 50. Luke ii. 49, 50. John ii. 4.
John enjoined by the Saviour to protect her. John xix. 26.
She is named among disciples after the Ascension.
She confesses her need of a Redeemer. Luke i. 47.
For nearly thirty years, known as Joseph's wife. John vi. 42.
Her sons and daughters doubtlessly but one family. Matt. xiii. 55. 6.
Espoused. God the author of marriage institutions. Psa. 68. 6.
Her reputation screened, and a protector provided.
No Jewess was married without being first espoused.
Joseph, a just man espoused a daughter of Israel.
Received angelic message. Matt. i. 20. Went to Bethlehem.
Presented the babe, and heard the prophecy of Simeon.
Went to Egypt, and returned to Nazareth as a carpenter. Matt. xiii. 55.
Took Jesus at 12 years of age to the temple, and the passover.
Here our knowledge of Joseph ends.
At the crucifixion, he is thought to have been dead. John xix. 27.
David, his character. Luke i. 32 hints at the promises.
Shiloh must descend directly from David. Psa. cxxxii. 11.
Mary. Heb. *Exalted.* Same as Miriam. Ex. xv. 20.

Virgin, Joseph, prominent in Matt., Mary in Luke. Our Lord never alludes to this miracle. Paul in Rom. i. 4, Gal. iv. 4. John is silent, *Oosterzee.* Romanists hold to her perpetual virginity, which the Scriptures contradict, Matt. xiii. 55., Carpenter, Matt. xiii. 55, a Smith, *Bede.* Goldsmith and Carpenter, *Jerome.*

---

28. *And the angel came in unto her, and said, Hail, thou that art highly favoured, the Lord is with thee: blessed art thou among women.*

Angel. Note the *simplicity* and *tenderness* of this record.
Came in within her dwelling, Sarah within the tent. Gen. xviii. 9.
He passes by palaces, and visits the carpenter's home.

God chooses the obscurest town for the greatest honor.
The greatest city seat of the most degrading crime. Luke xxiii. 33.
Mary must have recognised His heavenly character. Matt. xxviii. 3.
Hail. G. *joy to thee*, a usual oriental salutation.
Angels spake *Hebrew* to Daniel, *Greek* to Mary.
As executors of infinite wisdom, their knowledge is great.
Wondrous news destined to make the earth rejoice.
Because selected to be the mother of the infant Jesus.
The message of a son to sinning Eve, was one of sorrow.
This message of peace, revokes the former sentence. Gen. iii. 16.
Idolatrous Rome changes a salutation into idolatry.
Favored. A poor virgin of a humble town, Christ's mother.
Abraham and David esteemed being His ancestor an honour.
Gabriel saluted Daniel with the same title. Dan. ix. 23.
Noah, Joseph, and Daniel found *favor* with God.
Very many prefer beauty, wealth, pleasure, and honor.
Lord is, &c. Said to Gideon, Jeremiah, and Paul. Acts xviii. 10.
Referred originally to God, and then to men *sharing* it.
Often in N. T. refers to this life, as depending on God's favor.
Blessed. Said to the wife of Heber the Kenite. Judges v. 24.
Most happy as the destined mother of the *Incarnate One*.
Angel calls her "blessed *among* women."
Papists call her "Dispenser of divine favors."
"Immaculate Queen of Heaven." "Command thy Son," &c.

"Hail gracious person," *Hammond*. Ave gratiæ plena, *Vulg*. Not classical, an intensive form of speech, *Major*. Conferring of grace upon, *Alford*. *Favored* implies mercy, *Lightfoot*. Beneficent, *Grotius*. Distinguished favorite of heaven, *Doddridge*. One much graced, *Ryle*. Most celebrated, *Wakefield*. εὐλογ, cancelled by *Tischendorf*, *Alford*, *Meyer*. Bracketed, *Tregelles*. Retained by *Lachmann*, *Major*, *Brown*. Micat inter omnes Julium sidus velut inter ignes luna minores. *Horace*.

---

29. *And when she saw him, she was troubled at his saying, and cast in her mind what manner of salutation this should be.*

Troubled. Uncertain, whether about the angel or his message.
Guilty, dread holy angel's visits. Dan. v. 6. Gen. xli. 8.
Salutation. Luke x. 4. Customary modes in the East.
It has never been customary in the East to salute *females*.

As mere toys of husbands, they are kept in perpetual childhood.
Their intellects are debased, their passions receive incense.
Cast. Proof of her serenity, while Zacharias feared

Troubled. She might have thought him an evil Spirit, *Doddridge*. δια. intensive form, *Mayor*

---

30. *And the angel said unto her, Fear not, Mary: for thou hast found favour with God.*

Said. Direct converse to Mary, and to Joseph by a dream.
Fear not. Fifty-three times, God thus re-assures His Saints.
Fear hath torment. 1 John iv. 18. Perfect love, &c. Psa. xlvi. 5.
'Good cheer.' Matt. xiv. 27., carries with it God's *heart* and *arm*.
Mary. Her name familiarly called, quiets her apprehensions.
Good and evil, hear with diverse emotions. John xx. 16. Gen. iii. 9.
Favor. Gr. grace. All his favors to us are of grace. Eph. i. 7.
Sovereign grace is independent of *merit* in the recipient.
With God. Angel's receipt, an invaluable remedy to the timid.
Faith rests sweetly pillowed on His Omnipotence.

χάριν, charitas, gratiam, *Vulg*. χάρισ shewn to *sinners*, ἔλεοσ to *miserable*. Latter shewn to brutes, not the former. God's love to men is ἔλεοσ, giving his Son χάρισ. His kindness to the fallen race ἔλεοσ, *Trench*. Had God been bound to provide an atonement, there would have been no ἔλεοσ, in Redemption.

---

31. *And, behold, thou shalt conceive in thy womb, and bring forth a son, and shalt call his name JESUS.*

Behold. Expressing surprise, and calling attention.
Thou shalt, &c. An explicit prediction of the miraculous birth of Christ.
A Son. Incarnation. 1 *a fact*, revealed in life, words, works.
2 an *unfathomable miracle*, unprecedented, intimate, voluntary union of Divinity with humanity.
3 *Glorious benefit*; it is the glory, the light, the life of men.
Shalt call. As to His official work and character.

Jesus. Heb. *Saviour*, Salvation the beginning and end of Revelation.
Substance of Gospel truth. 1 light, 2 life, 3 liberty, 4 pardon.
5 sanctification, 6 comfort, 7 peace, 8 hope, 9 triumph.
Isaac, Ishmael, Josiah, Cyrus, John, named before born.
Saviour such as the world *needs*, not as Jews *expect*.
Patriots are called saviours of their country.
Human bondage never to be named with Satan's *slavery*.

"Conceive." No ground, grammatical, historical, or logical, for doubting that the Church in all ages has rightly regarded this passage, as an explicit foretelling, of the *miraculous conception*, and nativity of Jesus Christ, *Alexander*. 'Ιησοῦν, Heb. *to save*. Hiph. modified, add two letters. The salvation of the Lord, Is. vii, 14. Immanue same as Jesus. God with us, and God is on our side, are then equivalent. Ιασισ, healing, *Eusebius, Cyril*.

---

32. *He shall be great, and shall be called the Son of the Highest; and the Lord God shall give unto him the throne of his father David.*

Great. Adorned with the attributes. He wrought the *works* of God.
Promised to Moses as a Prophet, to Daniel as a King.
Son. Thou art Christ, the Son of the living God. Matt. xvi. 16. Heb. i. 8.
Called, God. Rom. ix. 5. True God. 1 John v. 20. Great God. Titus ii. 13.
Everlasting Father. Isa. ix. 6. Mighty God. Isa. ix. 6. Adonai. Mal. iii. 1. Eternal. Mic. v. 2.
Omniscient. John xxi. 17. Omnipotent. Rev. i. 8. Supremacy. Rom. ix. 5.
Unchangeable. Heb. xiii. 8. God a Triune Being, a Mystery.
Many things are *above*, not *contrary to* reason.
Highest. Gr. superlative 'The most High God.' *Doddridge*.
Anointed King. 1 Sam. xvi. 13. Psa. ii. 7. Psa. lxxxix. 28.
His proper Divinity not revealed to His parents.
Throne. Hopes and line of David had long been buried.
Human improbabilities, no barriers to God's plans.
1 raised after deep abasement, 2 among Israel.
3 among us, 4 raised, to fall no more for ever.
Father. "Jesus Christ our Lord, made of the seed of David." Rom. i. 3.
Proves Mary to be a lineal descendant of David.
David. Son of Jesse, tribe of Judah, born at Bethlehem 1085. B.C.
Anointed by Samuel at Bethlehem, short stature, ruddy cheeks. 1 Sam. xvi. 12.

Great strength. Psa. xviii. 34. Swift. Psa. xviii. 33. Bore staff and scrip. 1 Sam xvii. 40.
Genius for music brought him to the court of Saul.
Victory over Goliath roused Saul's jealousy. Fled with 600 men.
Took refuge with Philistines. Beloved of Jonathan.
Saul and Jonathan's death, opened the way to the throne.
Reigned in Hebron 7 years, then at Jerusalem 33 years.
Grievously fell into sin, as to Bathsheba and Uriah.
His parental duties sadly neglected with Absalom and Adonijah.
His generosity, humility, and piety, shine in the close of life.
He prepared the materials for the temple of the Lord.
He was a statesman, warrior, poet, and saint, in one.
Type of the Messiah in his kingly office. His Psalms abound with allusions.
Genius, integrity, fortitude, activity, perseverance, his characteristics.
Died, aged 71. Buried on Mount Zion. Heirs reigned 60 years. Writings. Luke xx. 42.

υἱὸν. Mistranslated by Wakefield, not *a* son, *Middleton*. Conception of Christ's character never could have sprung from the mind of sinful humanity. It does not exhibit the spirit of His own age. His Godhead was not humanized, his humanity was not deified, *Neander*. ὑψίστου applied to Jupiter, *Pindar*, *Diog. Laertius*. Plurality of persons in the Godhead, cardinal truth, Gen. i. 26, Gen. xix. 24. Taught in the O. T., Psa. ii. 7, Psa. lxxii. 1, Psa. lxxxix. 27. Holy Spirit. Is. xlviii. 16. Three Persons, Psa. xxxiii. 6, Num. vi. 24. Traditions floated from the Church to heathen, *Plato's Timaeus*. Brahma, Vishnu, Schiva of *Hindoos*. Equality of Trinity denied by Arius of Alexandria, 320 A.D., Servetus of Geneva, 1531 A. D., *Whitby*. Priestley, taught, the Holy Ghost a mere attribute of God, *Stier*. Joseph and Mary both of the family of David, *Alford*.

---

33. *And he shall reign over the house of Jacob for ever; and of his kingdom there shall be no end.*

Reign. Promising the crown to the Messiah. 2 Sam. vii. 12.
He had reigned from eternity,—now his sceptre is *owned*.
Mediatorial kingdom from the Father, to be delivered up. 1 Cor. xv. 24.
Sovereign Head over all things, for the Church. Eph. i. 22.
House. Kingdom of Israel, in mercy, embraces Gentiles as well as Jews.
Kingdom of the Saints, called "House of Jacob." Isaiah lviii. 14.
Jacob. Heb. *supplanter*, son of Isaac and Rebekah.
Twin brother to Esau, the elder born. Gen. xxv. 31.

Jacob by fraud obtains Isaac's blessing, and primogeniture.
Flies to Mesopotamia, 600 miles,—vision of the ladder. Gen. xxviii. 12.
Serves Laban 20 years, marries Leah and Rachel.
Returns to Canaan—wrestles with the Lord of angels.
Surnamed Israel, "*Prince with God,*" token of success.
Buries his beloved Rachel,—Joseph sold to Egypt.
Mourns his loss 13 years—goes to Egypt—lives 17 years—dies, aged 147.
Blessed prophetically his sons—buried near Hebron, 1695 B.C.
Mary did not understand *all*—implied *universal* empire.
Kingdom, universal, eternal, spiritual. Daniel vii. 14.

34. *Then said Mary unto the angel, How shall this be, seeing I know not a man?*

35. *And the angel answered and said unto her, the Holy Ghost shall come upon thee, and the power of the Highest shall overshadow thee: therefore also that holy thing which shall be born of thee shall be called the Son of God.*

How. Zacharias' question one of doubt—Mary's one of wonder.
All doubts concerning the Divine will, arise from unbelief.
Proves she knew Joseph *not* to be the father of the child.
Angel. Character and history, Luke i. 11.
Holy Ghost. Luke i. 15.
Highest. The energy of the Godhead conveyed by the Holy Ghost.
A human conception would give Him a depraved nature.
He must be born of a woman, that he might *die*. 2 Cor. xiii. 4.
That he might be tempted. Heb. iv. 15.
At once honors marriage, and avoids the taint of illegitimacy.
Adam and Jesus created sinless, called "Sons of God." Luke iii. 38.
Overshadow. "A virgin shall conceive and bear a son." Isa. vii. 14.
Fulfilled 700 years after in the Incarnation.
The only key to the sinless life of the son of the virgin.
Son of God. A contrast with his seeming *known* humanity. John i. 34.
"*Son of man,*" A contrast with his unseen, *unknown* Divinity. Matt. ix. 6. Mark ii. 28.
A name *never used by any one*, but the *Lord Himself.*
Declared to be the Son of God with power. Rom. i. 4.
His ordinary name at that time was *Son of David.*
Believers named "Sons of God." 1 John iii. 1. Rom. viii. 17.

πῶσ. She had vowed perpetual virginity, *Rheimish Test.*, answered by *Foulke*
Πνεῦμα. His humanity the work of the Spirit, called "Son of the *Father.*' Ἐπισκια.

Special divine protection, *Kuinoel.* 1 overshadow, 2 surround, 3 defend, 4 influence, *Bloomfield.* Figure of a bird, *Grotius.* Of a cloud, *Owen, Alford.* Nuptial canopy, *Gill.* A mystery concealed by a divine cloud, *Calvin.* Veiled as a bride, *Bengel.* A crying mystery, wrought in the silence of God, *Ignatius.* Not creation, humanity prepared, *Olshausen.* Πνευ. the act of Holy Ghost, creating his humanity, δύν. ὑψίσ. the act of the Father, uniting the humanity to the Divinity, *Rd. Watson.* This declaration of the angel, all we know on the subject, has been scrutinized by friends and foes for ages, and not a syllable found inconsistent with the surpassing sacredness and delicacy of the subject, *Brown.* εκ σου cancelled, *Stephen, Elzevir, Oosterzee.* Attributed to the *Eutychians.* ἅγιον notes singularity and sanctity of His birth. *Celsus* began, and the Jews followed by *Voltaire, Barhalt,* and *Paulus* the blasphemy which deprives the holy, lowly bride of her chastity, *J. Pye Smith.* Test. Mes. Sceptics dreading to face the miraculous conception, deny the authenticity of 1 chap. Matt., and 1 and 2 Luke, *A. Norton,* Notes, vol. 2, p. 482.

---

36. *And, behold, thy cousin Elizabeth, she hath also conceived a son in her old age; and this is the sixth month with her, who was called barren.*

Behold. Tidings of greater *curiosity*, but not of greater *interest* to our race, could be brought even by angels.

Cousin. Gr. Relative. Mary, of the tribe of Judah; Elizabeth, of Levi.
John and Jesus (humanly speaking) were relatives.

Elizabeth. Luke i. 5. The angel graciously aids Mary's faith.
Working of one miracle, paves the way for faith in others.
Christ's eating fish, aided disciples' faith in His Resurrection. Luke xxiv. 42.

A Son. The sex of the unborn child is foretold.
This sign was unsought by Mary.

Barren. Implied censure on the popular reproach of her sterility.
Sarah, and Hannah prepared the way for faith in a *virgin* conception.

"Cousin," Gr., any kind of relative. The relationship arose from marriage, *Ellicott.* γῆρα γῆρει, *Tischendorf, Alford.*

---

37. *For with God nothing shall be impossible.*

Nothing. Gr., every word is possible.

Impossible. God does not bind himself with laws of nature, as chains,
But cords in his hands are lengthened or shortened at will.
Miraculous conception did not interfere with Christ's humanity.
Adam's creation did not make him *literally*, the Son of God.
1 Unbelief put to shame. 2 Faith is strengthened.

3 Adoration and obedience exacted. 4 Loyalty crowned.
God's power shines in *Redemption triumphant.*
1. Over Philosophy. 2. It subordinates all interests and enmities.
3. Overcomes human depravity. 4. All other religions.
5. By its humble instrumentalities, fishermen and tax gatherers.

ῥῆμα, co-extensive with *thing*, *Wordsworth:* questioned by *Euthymius*, *Meyer*. Gibbon assigns five causes for the success of Christianity.—1, intolerant zeal; 2, doctrine of immortality of the soul; 3, claim of miraculous powers; 4, pure morals; 5, union and discipline, *Milman*, Notes, chap. 15. ἀδυν. Future. "It shall be," an enduring principle, *Brown.*

---

38. *And Mary said, Behold the handmaid of the Lord; be it unto me according to thy word. And the angel departed from her.*

Mary's faith repairs Eve's unbelief.
Feelings inspired were painful and embarrassing.
Handmaid. Gr. Servant: by *Rome* made Queen of Heaven!
1 Genuine humility, with joyful faith. 2 Quiet resignation, with active zeal.
3 Faithful love, with unwavering heroism.
Be it, &c. Contrast the silence of faith, with the silence of unbelief.
Mary's splendid future, weakens not her faith.
Departed. Walls no obstacles to the coming of angels. John xx. 19.
Heavenly visions, bright, brief, and parting blessings.
His work finished, he *hastens* to return to his God. Dan. ix. 21.
His stay in a world of dark rebellion, gladly ends.
Society of kindred spirits, invites his return to heaven.
Paul desired to *depart*, to be with Christ. Phil. i. 23.

δούλη, Luke vii. 3. γένοιτό, Virgin conscious of her begun maternity, *Euthymius*, *Mald. Grotius;* denied by *Lightfoot.* Beyond the written word, all is *bold hypothesis.* God's sovereignty in harmony with man's free will, *Quesnel.* Condemned by *Clement*, in Bull *Unigenitus*, 1713. Here the Pope is right in principle. Quesnel himself denies man's *freedom of will, except to sin*, but teaches *his responsibility*, zealous of the divine honors of Jesus, *vainly. Luther.*

39. *And Mary arose in those days, and went into the hill country with haste, into a city of Juda.*

Arose. Refers to oriental *sedentary* life.
Went. Distance from Nazareth to Hebron, 40 miles.
To confirm her faith, and share her wonder and joy.
They are led by one Spirit, to a sacred friendship. Mal. iii. 16.
Happiness shared is doubled, grief revealed is lessened.
Hill country. Five-sixths of Judea are hilly and barren.
38 Cities of Judah's mountains named. Josh. xv. 48. 60.
Haste. Not of fear, but of holy transport.
She leaves it to God to enlighten Joseph, as He had her.
City believed to be Hebron, 'an ancient city.' Num. xiii. 22
Kirjath Arba, or Hebron, Mamre, home and grave of Abraham, Isaac, Sarah, and Jacob. Gen. xxiii. 2.
There God met Abraham, promised a son, and gave circumcision. Gen. xvii. and xviii.
David crowned, and Absalom rebelled, there. It was 22 miles south of Jerusalem.
A City of refuge, noted for its pool. 2 Sam. iv. 12. Still there.
The tomb of Abraham, with massive walls, without windows, described by Josephus as ancient in Christ's time, is there.
Grapes of Eschol grew there. City now called *El Khulil*, "*The Friend.*" *i. e.* of God, Mohammedan name of Abraham.

σπουδῆς. Jesus to be henceforth the principle of action, *Quesnel.* She had married Joseph before this journey, *Hug*, *Ebrard.* Had informed Joseph of her pregnancy, *pronubæ*, about a month before, *Alford.* Journey, inconsistent with O. T. decorum, but not with realities, and freedom of the Cross, *Stier.* 'Ioύδα, south of Hebron, *Oosterzee*, *Roland.* Josh. xv. 54. Hebron, *Bengel*, *Beza*, *Brown.* Here our Lord's conception took place, *Bengel.*

---

40. *And entered into the house of Zacharias, and saluted Elizabeth.*

Entered. Mary felt she would be welcomed, where God was honored.
House. No word for *home*, in Greek or any other language, unbaptized by the Bible spirit.
Honored roof, to protect mothers of Jesus and John for 3 months.
Material of reeds, brick, stone, mud, wood: last, very scarce.
Anciently of marble, porphyry, granite, chalk, mortar, asphaltum, ivory, 1 Kings xxii. 39.

They form a hollow square, with a court in the centre.
This court paved, or planted with shrubbery. Psa. lxxxiv. 3.
Sometimes a fountain. 2 Sam. xvii. 18. Covered with an awning. Psa. civ. 2.
Windows all open on the court, solid walls front the street.
Rarely a latticed window is on the street. Entrance is *indirect.*
Roof of stone, or earth, oft cracked by rain and sun. Prov. xxvii. 15.
Always flat, and guarded by parapets. Deut. xxii. 8. 2 Kings i. 2.
Breezes enjoyed. I Sam. ix. 25. Devotions offered. Jer. xix. 13. Acts. x. 9.
Booths pitched there. Neh. viii. 16. Grass grew. Isa. xxxvii. 27.
Walls of unburnt clay often dug through. Matt. xxiv. 13. Job xxiv. 16.
The writer saw a whole village swept away by the Nile. Matt. vii. 24. 27.
Zacharias. Luke i. 5. Character and office.
Saluted. Forms of oriental civilities. Luke x. 4.
Christianity tends to refine and elevate social life. 1 Peter iii. 8.

"House," Domum, *Home.* The name as well as the *thing* signified, *alone* found in Christian lands or *tongues*, Heathen do not understand the word.

---

41. *And it came to pass that, when Elizabeth heard the salutation of Mary, the babe leaped in her womb; and Elizabeth was filled with the Holy Ghost.*

42. *And she spake out with a loud voice, and said, Blessed art thou among women, and blessed is the fruit of thy womb.*

Elizabeth. Inspired to give Mary a proper reception.
Heard. Mary's tongue was filled with blessings.
Babe. Mother, and unborn offspring, rejoiced together.
Unborn, John offers involuntary homage to his Lord.
Filled. Loving the Redeemer, we are not forgotten by the Spirit.
Holy Ghost. Luke i. 15. Third person of the Holy Trinity.
Spake. She forgets her own, in the superior honors of Mary.
Loud voice. Not ashamed, or in a whisper, to praise God.
Orientals generally speak in a low sad key.
She rejoiced to proclaim her immediate inspirations.
Blessed. Repeats the very words of the angel, revealed to her also.
Blessed from heaven, and praised among men.
The new covenant, greeted at its entrance with hymns of praise.

1921 years before, all nations blessed in *promise* to Abram. Gen. xii. 3.
A greater blessing was hers, to be a *believer* in Christ. Luke xi. 22.

ἀνεφώνησε, classic use, "one breaking into a poetic exclamation," *Brown.* βρέφος, Pappoos, Indian; Bube, Ger.; Baban, Ir.; Babe, Eng.; probably all dialects were one.

---

43. *And whence is this to me, that the mother of my Lord should come to me.*

Whence. Elizabeth's *outward state*, doubtless superior to Mary's.
True piety divests the mind of all envy.
Saints delight to honor those whom God honors.
To me. Elizabeth confesses her inferiority to Mary.
With similar humility afterwards, her son, "Comest thou?" Matt. iii. 14.
Mother. Never afterwards called, Virgin.
Superstition changes terms, and then *worships* the *creature.*
Henceforth, she is called *Mary.*
My Lord. Luke i. 11. She acknowledges both His Divinity and humanity.
Before born, she openly rejoices to submit to his sceptre.
It compares with Peter's noble confession. Mark xiv. 61.
As Lord, he has the *right* to rule, and the *power* to save.

"Mother." In the very face of this, Rome calls her, the "*Blessed Virgin.*" κυρίου. How can an unborn child be called *Lord,* if not *divine? Olshausen.*

---

44. *For lo, as soon as the voice of thy salutation sounded in mine ears, the babe leaped in my womb for joy.*

45. *And blessed is she that believed: for there shall be a performance of those things which were told her from the Lord.*

As soon. This fact cheered its mother, and confirmed Mary's faith.
Blessed. Man's blessings are mere *breath,* God's carry *heaven* with them.
Believed. Zacharias' unbelief tenderly referred to.
He at that time continued both deaf and dumb.
He was unable to speak to Mary, a guest three months under his roof.
Faith, a source of joy, a mystery to the world.
The only ground of the Church's hope, is God's faithfulness.

All the moral wonders of heroism, are the fruits of faith.
Eve, through pride, believed the tempter.
Mary, through humility, believed Gabriel.
Eve hoped, that man would become like God.
Mary, that God would become like man.
Eve presuming, admitted falsehood and death.
Mary believing, becomes the mother of *truth* and *life*.
Performance. The Bible teems with divine promises to believers.
Not one, has ever, will ever, can ever, fail. Josh. xxi. 45. 1 Kings viii. 56.
God's promises during 6000 years have not failed in one *letter*.
All His covenants have been fulfilled with *exactness*. Josh. xxiii. 14.
Faithfully, He rewards His friends and punishes His foes.

αγαλλιάσει, to exult, to rejoice exceedingly, to leap for joy. Lat. salire, to bound as young cattle, Mal. iv. 2, *Major*. Rabbis assert, that the joy of mothers at the escape at the Red Sea, caused their unborn offspring to leap for joy. *Lightfoot*. Mysterious effects of sympathy, *Alford*.

---

46. *And Mary said, My soul doth magnify the Lord.*

Said. *Visit* of the angel to Mary later, her *song* earlier, than Zacharias'.
Faith is singing for joy, while unbelief is silent.
This ode immeasurably more sublime, than any of Greece or Rome.
My soul. True praise. 1 Clear eye to estimate God's works.
2 A glad heart to rejoice in them. 3 A loosened tongue.
Magnify. Extol. Creatures cannot add to His greatness.
Songs from humble, grateful hearts, magnify God. Psa. lxix. 30.
Lord. Luke i. 11. "Praise God" is the name of the unborn babe.
All the glories of the Messiah's reign, seem to rise before her.
The grace of God, verse 30. Omnipotence, 49, 51.
His Holiness, 49. His justice, 52, 53. His faithfulness, 54, 55.
We have here the inspired echo of Miriam's and Deborah's harps.

"Said," Song, Hebrew-like is in parallels, *Rosenmuller*. Mary did not comprehend it, *Bloomfield*. But one must be inspired to *know* this fact. ψυχή, lower regions of the spiritual man. πνεῦμα embraces νουσ, the conscience, latter *spiritual*, former *carnal*, *Olshausen*. The whole inner being, *Alford*. "*Magnify*." In Romish and other litanies, song is styled *Magnificat*, the first word in the *Vulgate*.

47. *And my spirit hath rejoiced in God my Saviour.*

Spirit. The living soul, all that is immortal. Gen. ii. 7.
Rejoiced. Christ the gift—God the giver is thanked.
None but believers have a right to rejoice. Ecc. ii. 2.
1 A thankful joy. 2 Humble joy. 3 Hopeful joy. 4 God-glorifying joy.
As a Saviour, He is only a cause of joy to sinners.
As a Judge, (unreconciled) an object of infinite *dread.*
My Saviour. A helpless guilty one, she claims Him *her Redeemer.*
She esteems her relations to the Redeemer, *above* those of a *mother.*
"Queen of Heaven," "Mother of God," were *blasphemy* to *her*, a *sinner.*

σωτῆρί, one recovering that which is lost, *Valkner.* Rome, 1854, decreed Mary's conception immaculate. The author, with about 75,000 spectators, witnessed the scene in that wonder of architecture, St. Peter's. It covers nearly 5 acres. Henceforth to name a child *Mary* is pronounced *blasphemy.*

---

48. *For he hath regarded the low estate of his handmaiden; for, behold, from henceforth all generations shall call me blessed.*

Low estate. Not her *humility*, but God's *mercy*, is celebrated.
God often makes something out of nothing. Illustrations—
Leah. Hannah. Jepthah. David.
The greater His favors, the deeper should be our humility.
Generations. Embracing Gentiles, as sharing with Jews.
Blessed. This word has long been *prostituted* by *superstition.*
All believers *admire* and *adore* the grace that gave us
The *Incarnate Word;* but abhor all *Mariolatry.*

"Low estate," abjectness, *Elsley, Alford.* Under disgrace socially, in poverty, *Olshausen*, Childlessness, *Oxford.* Strange exegesis. μακαρ. Happy, *Doddridge.* James v. 11 refers to mercy, not humility, *Lightfoot.* Afflictions, *Grotius.* Rome blasphemes with such terms, "*Ladder of Heaven,*" "*Gate of Paradise,*" "*Throne of God,*" "*Jube Natum,*" and "*Coge Deum,*" *Fulkes,* Notes on *Rheimish* Test.

---

49. *For he that is mighty hath done to me great things; and holy is his name.*

50. *And his mercy is on them that fear him from generation to generation.*

Mighty. God the source of all Power.
Great things. The angel's visit. The glorious promise of a Son, Jesus.

When Infinite power, and boundless Mercy unite,
Results, worthy of Jehovah may be expected.
Holy. God's holiness renders Him terrible to sinners.
By the Cross, it fills saints with adoring wonder and love.
His name. All by which Jehovah *reveals* Himself to men.
Mercy. All blessings from God are fruits of *sovereign grace.*
Not seeming, but real believers, objects of His care.
On them. *Celsus*, A.D. 120, the first writer against Christianity.
Denied, God cared any more for believers, than for lions, or eagles.
Fear. *Filial* dread of offending one loved, not *slavish.*
Generation. The reign of Grace extends back to Abel.
Embraces ALL who will believe, to the end of time.

ἔλεοσ, mercy of God to men as *miserable*; χαρισ, to men as *sinful.* Wicked ever envy saints the divine regard, *Neander*, vol. 1, p. 229. Providence answering prayer to scatter an enemy's fleet, ridiculed, *Macaulay.* Hist., vol. iii. page 399. American Ed.

---

51. *He hath shewed strength with his arm; he hath scattered the proud in the imagination of their hearts.*

Strength. Power of God. 1 Creation. 2 Providence. 3 Redemption.
Arm, shews His greatest power, *hand*, less, *finger*, least.
Scattered. Gr. Utterly discomfited—figure of a defeated foe.
He defeats the counsel of many an Ahithophel.
Pharaoh, Sennacherib, Haman, Julian, illustrate this.
Babel meant a bond of union, but really a source of scattering.
Proud. Pride the parent sin of our race, and devils. 1 Tim. iii. 6.
It creates the widest gulf, between Creator and creature. Dan. iv. 37.

'Εποίησ. A principle in God's kingdom is here expressed by the words down to ἐξαπέσ, *Brown:* Arm, Isa. lii. 10; hand, Ex. iii. 20; finger, Ex. viii. 19. ὑπερηφ. Appearing above others; haughty in thoughts; primarily to Herod, the Idumean. διαν. Inmost thoughts, *Olshausen.*

52. He hath put down the mighty from their seats, and exalted them of low degree.

Put down. Dethroning and casting down Satan. Luke x. 18.
Mighty. Nebuchadnezzar, from a throne, goes among beasts.
Belshazzar, in the very act of insulting God, perishes.
Seats. Gr. Thrones. Earth's heights are slippery. Deut. xxxii. 35.
Exalted. "Promotion cometh neither from the east," &c. Psa. lxxv. 6.
Believers ought to trace the footsteps of the flock. Sol. S. i. 8.
Joseph, Moses, Samuel, David. Esther, Daniel.
Low degree. Affected humility, a subtle, dangerous pride.
Humility no *stage-virtue*, the *chosen* state of the heart.
One has just as much Christianity, as he has humility.
Characteristic of the King of Kings. Matt. xi. 29. Rom. viii. 9.
True believers attain the possession of all God's rich gifts.
Humility within the reach of *all*.
Pride overcame man *first*; he overcomes at *last*.
Other sins need temptations, this feeds like the moth, on our graces.
Graces with pride, are powders uncovered carried in the wind.

Δυν. Invested with political power. Valerian, a persecuting emperor, A.D. 246, dethroned, was used as a stepping block by Sapor, the Persian monarch, mounting his horse, *Jortin*. Hist. of Saul, Herod, &c., *Bengel*.

---

53. He hath filled the hungry with good things; and the rich he hath sent empty away.

Filled. God and Christ alone able to fill the soul. Col. i. 19.
Hourly wants, need hourly supplies. Matt. vi. 11.
Hungry. Poor in the East, find life a long battle for bread.
Promises are rich to those hungering only after righteousness. Luke vi. 21.
Keenly sensible of want, they seek favor of their God.
Worldlings boast of fulness, a proof of madness. Ecc. ix. 3.
Good things. Oriental simplicity of speech., i.e., necessities of life.
Grace, Ep. ii. 7; Goodness, Rom. ii. 4; Wisdom, Rom. xi. 33.
Rich, in honors and treasures, of earth: poor, in God's eye. Luke xvi. 24.
Pharisees, Laodiceans, and all self-righteous ones. Rev. iii. 17.
Empty. Unbelieving soul, an "aching void," earth's honors hollow. Ecc. i. 2.
Deepest curse, when God sends men to the gods they serve.
Sent away with their hypocritical petitions disregarded.

54. *He hath holpen his servant Israel, in remembrance of* his *mercy.*

55. *As he spake to our fathers, to Abraham, and to his seed forever.*

Holpen. Gr., upholden. *Sending the Messiah, Bengel.*
Sinners under crushing weight of broken law, need help. Psa. lxxxix. 19.
Redeemer "travels in the greatness of his strength." Isa. lxiii. 1.
Servant. Gr., a *child*, or *boy*. Term of endearment. Jer. xxxi. 20. Matt. viii. 6.
Israel. Jacob's surname. Prince with God. Here, *all Jews*. Luke i. 33.
Name given after wrestling at Peniel with the *Angel*. Gen. xxxii. 28.
Remembrance. Reference to promises made 2093 years before. Gen. xii. 3.
Spake. Words recorded many ages before, now fulfilled.
The Incarnation, the accomplishment of many prophecies.
The source of all true blessings to the redeemed.
A bud enclosing the hopes of patriarcks and prophets.
Election. Conversion. Sanctification. Salvation.
Fathers. Patriarchs, a nobler ancestry than kings.
Abraham. Heb. Father of a multitude. Son of Terah.
Born in Chaldea, B.C. 2153. City of Ur, site unknown.
At 70 God called him in Mesopotamia, to Charran, or Haran. Acts vii. 2, 4.
At God's call he went to Shechem, in the Land of Promise.
Driven by famine, he went to Egypt—returned to Canaan.
Dwelt in Mamre, close to Hebron. Met Melchisedec at Salem.
Visited by 3 angels, he intercedes for Sodom to be spared.
Ishmael by Hagar, born, Isaac by Sarah, son of promise.
His offering of Isaac upon Mount Moriah, 25 years after.
12 years after, Sarah died, aged 127, buried in Machpelah.
Abraham marries Keturah, by whom he had six sons.
Died aged 175, called "father of the faithful." Rom. iv. 11.
As ancestor of Christ, all nations to be blest through him.
Integrity, hospitality, generosity and devotion, traits of character.
Styled friend of God. Isa. xli. 8. James ii. 23.
Seed. God's elect. Psa. xviii. 50. Gen. xvii. 19. Gal. iii. 16.
For ever. Duration of the blessings of the Messiah's reign.
God never forgets promises of mercy, or threats of punishment. Hos. i. 4.

"Israel." Heb., Man of God, *Jerome*. Thou hast contended, *Rosenmuller*. Soldier of God, *Gesenius*. Wrestled with God, *Robinson*. "*Seed.*" Our Lord honored not

Mary alone, but allied Himself to redeemed humanity, *Oxford*, *Olshausen*. "*For ever*" refers not to remembrance, but to *the seed*. παῖς. Gr., Child, Luke ii. 43. Maiden, Luke viii. 51. Son, Jo. iv. 51. Young man, Acts, xx. 12.

---

56. *And Mary abode with her about three months, and returned to her own house.*

Returned. With confirmed faith, returns to abide the will of God.
Own house. God is glorified by domestic, as well as Church duties.
A privileged spot where Jesus comes to abide.
Joseph desiring a divorce, is warned of God. Matt. i. 19.

57. *Now Elisabeth's full time came that she should be delivered; and she brought forth a son.*

Elizabeth. Luke i. 5. Nature's laws suspended at will by the Lord.
Full time. Promises of love, or threatening of vengeance, tarry not.
Pious mothers, blessings to the entire Church of God.

"*Son.*" Church of Alexandria, at first celebrated John's birthday April 23; this settled, Christ was born in *November*, six months after. Christmas was an after thought of Julius, prelate of Rome, A. D. 352, to correspond with the Saturnalia.

---

58. *And her neighbours and her cousins heard how the Lord had shewed great mercy upon her; and they rejoiced with her.*

Cousins. Gr. Any kindred near or remote.
Mercy. Zacharias' priestly family built up a child's greatness.
Rejoiced. Sympathy costs little, but is like oil to wheels.
A pin in the tabernacle, not to be left in the wilderness.
Jews in sympathy, witness a stupendous miracle by Jesus. John xi. 45.
Naomi's friends blessed the Lord at Obed's birth. Ruth iv. 14.

59. *And it came to pass, that on the eighth day they came to circumcise the child; and they called him Zacharias, after the name of his father.*

Eighth. The day enjoined, even if it was Sabbath. Ex. xii. 44. Jo. vii. 22.
Circumcise. Neither the place, nor the performer appointed.

This seems to have been done at Zacharias' house.
Sanctified from birth, yet must the law be honored. Matt. iii. 15.
A seal of Abraham's faith, before circumcised. Rom. iv. 11.
John, the first preacher of a righteousness without circumcision.
A rite, not sacrament—*Tree* in Paradise.
The *Rainbow*, *Baptism*, *Seals* of various covenants.
Visible symbols, of invisible blessings, as water, a symbol of purity.
Rite performed at home, sometimes in synagogue.
The uncircumcised Hebrew, was to be *cut off*. Gen. xvii. 14.
God's ordinances are neglected at a fearful peril. Ex. iv. 24.
This and Sacrifice traceable to a divine origin.
"Uncircumcised," a term of reproach and infamy. Jer. ix. 26.
Sign of social degradation, and treason towards Jehovah. Acts vii. 51.
Jews thought it infidelity to Moses, and reprobation, to eternity.
Egyptians and other heathen, borrowed it from the Jews.
Baptism taking place of circumcision, enlarged to both sexes.
Called. Abraham and Sarah's names changed at this rite. Gen. xvii. 5. 10.
Athenians named their children on the 10th day.
Girls named by Jews when weaned. Roman girls 8th, boys 9th day.
Jews seldom named them after parents, as Christians do.
Greeks and Romans named theirs after *ancestors*.
Heathen converts baptized, had their names changed.
'Christening' at baptism, a relict of Rome's superstitions.
Indenturing our children to God in baptism, a Christian's privilege.
The church always enjoyed *Seals* of the Divine Covenants.
Not the *want* of, but the *contempt* of ordinances, destroys souls.
John. His history and character. Luke i. 13. See Notes.
No son in the O. T. is called after his father.
This is the first instance proposed in the N. T. **Zacharias.** Luke i. 5.

περιτε. Gr. and Lat., Circumcise, *cut around.* Its divine origin contested by infidels. Herodotus no authority when opposed to Revelation. Herodotus makes Egyptians or Phrygians the first inhabitants of the earth. Ishmaelites took this rite with them, and from them it spread to other peoples. The scriptures ever called all heathen, the *uncircumcised.* Sacrifice and circumcision, from their very *nature*, could have *no human origin*, *Lewes*, *Heb. Ant.*, vol. ii. p. 448. *Cut off*, implied put to death by the magistrate, Ex. xiii. 14, *Poole;* childless, *Jarchi;* excommunicated, *Maimonides;* an untimely death, as Sabbath breakers were put to death, Ex. xxxi. 14, called *cutting off*, so here also. Its neglect nearly cost Moses his life, Ex. iv. 24. Enoch also preached, (Jude 14,) a righteousness *without* circumcision, *L. H. Van Doren.* "*Called*," Gr., were calling. Mother refused the name, *Trench.*

καὶ γάρ preferred, *Lachmann, Tischendorf, Oosterzee.* ἄρα refers back to the circumstances which have happened. "What then shall," &c., see chap. viii. 25. καὶ γάρ χεὶρ, &c., a remark inserted by the Evang. himself, *Alford.*

---

67. *And his father Zacharias was filled with the Holy Ghost, and prophesied, saying,*

Filled. God forgave his sin, and *inspired* his heart.

Holy Ghost. Luke i. 15. We are spiritually dumb, until God opens our mouth.

Prophesied. 1, foretell future events, 2, preach the gospel.

He forgets *family* splendors, in the *Redeemer's* glories.

προεφήτ. 1, foretelling; 2, χαρισ, imparted to primitive Christians; 3, acting as God's ambassadors. Ordinary Heb. word for prophet is *nâbi*, from verb *nâbâ* "to bubble forth." Two other Heb. words, *Rôeh, Chôzeh,* meaning *one who sees.* Sept. translates *nâbi* by προφήτησ. In Classical Greek this word means *one who speaks for another*, specially *one who speaks for a god*, and interprets his will to man. *Smith's* Dict. Prophet. μαντει. predictions of heathen oracles, *Olshausen.* Celebrating God's praise, *Rosenmuller.* Committed to writing later, *Kuinoel.*

---

68. *Blessed* be *the Lord God of Israel; for he hath visited and redeemed his people.*

Blessed. Luke i. 28. God must of necessity be eternally blessed.

What an everlasting mystery and wonder of love!

God's entering and shrouding Himself in a house of clay.

God. Luke i. 6. See Notes.

Israel. Chosen type of all the elect. Romans viii. 33.

Visited. God had apparently forgotten a rebellious people.

One visit recorded Ex. iii. 2, another Jud. vi. 11, Ruth i. 6.

Church often waits long for a merciful visitation.

At His coming, Judaism had lost all its glories.

Redeemed. Gr., pay the price of the freedom of a slave. Lev. xxv. 51.

Men were enslaved. Christ gives his blood to redeem.

By a *price*, from God's justice; by His *power*, from Satan's bondage.

"Redemption of the soul is precious, it ceaseth for ever." Psa. xlix. 8.
It contains the germ of the idea of *preciousness*. 1 Peter i. 18, 19.
Vicarious sacrifice, the key note of all the Apostles' teachings.
Man's salvation, counted *finished*, because fact is announced.
Zacharias says nothing of his relationship to the child.
He lost sight of self, in the glory of the unborn Christ.

λύτρωσιν. 1, equivalent for life taken; 2, price of a slave; 3, propitiation for life, Prov. xiii. 8; 4, vicarious sacrifice, Matt. xx. 28, endorsed by our Lord, *Olshausen*. Bishop of *Nola* sold himself in Algerine slavery, to redeem some of his flock taken captive, *Alexander*.

---

69. *And hath raised up a horn of salvation for us in the house of his servant David.*

A Horn. Emblem 1, of *Victory*, Ps. xviii. 2; 2, of *Power*, Ps. cxxxii. 17; 3, of *Glory*, 1 Sam. ii. 1; 4, of *Strength*, Mic. iv. 13; 5. *Safety*, 1 Kings ii. 28; 6. *Plenty*, Isa. v. 1; 7. *Honor*, Job xvi. 15; 8. *Kingdom*, Dan. vii. 8. Wicked slain, Jer. xlviii. 25.
Druse females, wear silver horns as tokens of victories.
Horns on the altars, grasped by criminals escaping.
Ancient conquerors fastened steel horns to their shields, returning in triumph.
"Lift not up your horn on high," &c. Ps. lxxv. 5.
David. Proving Mary to be of his royal line.
Luke i. 32. David's triumphs foreshadow Christ's.
Christ's glories, unearthly; kings covet them not.

"*Horn.*" Alexander's coins have horns, *Becker's Char.* Bacchus cornutus, *Euripides*. Royalty, *Euthymius*. Emblem of strength, *Ewald*. Of victory, *Rosenmuller*. Abundance and kingly vigor, *Bengel*. Metaphor from horned beasts, *Alford*.

---

70. *As he spake by the mouth of his holy prophets, which have been since the world began.*

Spake. Probable reference to the promise, Gen. iii. 15.
Mouth. One key note. Divine *harmony* among many witnesses.

Holy. God being holy, can inspire even unholy men. Num. xxiii. 5.
Prophets. Inspired of God to reveal secrets of heaven to man. Lk. i. 3.
O.T. prophets expounded scriptures. Called to repentance.
Aided priests, Levites, and kings in teaching religion.
Humble, faithful, fearless, self-denying, holy men.
Slain as witnesses for the truth, taken from the herd and the plough.
Schools of the prophets at Gibeah, Naioth, Bethel, Gilgal, Jericho.

ἐλάλ. Zach. begins where Mary left off, *Bengel.* ἀπ' αἰῶνος, time before Christ, *Lange.* During the Messiah, *Hammond.* Future, *Le Clerc.* From the earliest period, *Mayor.* Prophets from the beginning, *Bengel.*

---

71. *That we should be saved from our enemies, and from the hands of all that hate us.*

Saved. He laid help on One mighty to save. Ps. lxxxix. 19.
First type from Egypt. Ps. cvi. 10; second from Saul, Ps. xviii. 18.
Enemies. Romans the *most* dreaded, but to be *least* feared.
Evil spirits—sin and death—wicked men. Matt. x. 17.
Our most dangerous foes are within our breasts. Jer. xvii. 9.
Principles, maxims, customs, fashions of earth.
Christians were hated and persecuted simply for the *name.*

"Saved," the means of salvation, *Campbell.* μισούν. Proofs of Christians being hated for their *name*, Luke vi. 22—see Notes. Old Test. language in describing spiritual blessings, *Bengel.*

---

72. *To perform the mercy* promised *to our fathers, and to remember his holy covenant.*
73. *The oath which he sware to our father Abraham.*

Mercy. Luke i. 50. Restoration to God's favor.
Mercy here refers to the gift of the Messiah.
Promised. 1. Purpose of redemption. 2. Nature of the service.
3. Its freedom. 4. Fearlessness. 5. Its duration.
"There hath not failed one word of all his good," &c. 1 Kings viii. 56.
Remember. God's faithfulness. 1. In His Holy Providence.

2. In His Word, promises and threatenings. Num. xxiii. 19. Jer. iv. 28.
3. In the last Judgment, all proofs will be centred there.
Covenant. "I will be a God to thee," all that he needed. Gen. xvii. 1.
"Then will I remember my covenant." Lev. xxvi. 42.
God only *seems* to forget. Isa. xl. 27-31., Isa. xlix. 15.
As God's Covenant with day and night cannot be broken, neither can His Covenant with His people. Jer. xxxiii. 20-5.
Covenant of mercy, only hope of children of wrath. Eph. ii. 3.
Oath. He could swear by no greater, He swore by Himself. Heb. vi. 13.
Embracing all revealed to the O. T. saints and prophets.
Something inviolable, now first fulfilled.
Bonds loosed by grace, only bind saints more firmly to God.
Chains fell from the slave entering the house of a pagan priest.
How much more entering the service of Heaven's High Priest.
Abraham. Life and history. Luke i. 55. See Notes.
This Patriarch living, dying and glorified, ever in God's eye.
Promises to Abraham, extend to saints to the end of time.

διαϑήκησ, a will; a covenant; the new covenant sealed with Christ's blood. Gospel dispensation, Gal. iv. 24, *Campbell.* Used also for *the Writings* of the Old Covenant. 2 Cor. iii. 14. *Ed.*

---

74. *That he would grant unto us, that we, being delivered out of the hand of our enemies, might serve him without fear.*

Grant. Patriarchs fed on promises, and walked by faith.
Christ's Life, Death and Resurrection, were mysteries to them.
His name a *seal* on every promise, although they never saw it. Heb. xi. 13.
Delivered. Prophets thus painted the Messiah's golden reign.
"Oh Lord! thou hast loosed my bonds." Ps. cxvi. 18.
Enemies. All destroyed, peace and piety would be restored.
Fear. Luke i. 12. Christ's yoke remains, but His obedience makes it easy.
Slavish fear ceases, cords, are bands of love, now. Hos. xi. 4.
Spirit by adoption, is not that of law, or bondage. Rom. viii. 15.
Legal restraints and rites have vanished, holiness remains.
Fear arises in all, conscious of guilt unpardoned.
Such was Felix; but he held fast to his iniquity. Acts xxiv. 25.

Day Spring. Jesus, "Sun of righteousness," Mal. iv. 2. "Day star" 2 Peter i. 19.
"Morning star" Rev. xxii. 16. "Light of the world." Jo. viii. 12.
Mankind had groped long in darkness. 1 Cor. i. 20, 21.
John, the morning star, about to fade before the rising Sun. Jo. iii. 30.
Levitical economy had partially relieved the gloom.
Human *wisdom* had exhausted all plans for restoring man.
The Scriptures reveal our *chains*, and ourselves "*prisoners* of *hope*." Zec. ix. 12.
On High. Sun light lingers longest on the mountain tops.
The Gospel, a supernatural descent of God *from* heaven *to* earth.

σπλαγχνα, vitals, heart, bowels: hence *heartless*, *unmerciful*. We feel an oppressive pain, unable to relieve misery, Col. iii. 12; and gratify, ἐλέουσ, *Bloomfield*. ἀνατολή, used, 1, four times for a "branch," in O. T.; 2, east; 3, sun rising, *Lightfoot*, *Wetstein*. Day Spring, *Grotius*, *Campbell*, *Kuinoel*. Sun of righteousness, Christ, *Calvin*, *De Wette*, *Olshausen*, *Brown*. Light, *Alford*. Refers to John, *Mayor*. *Horne*. Ut valesceret oriens. *Tacitus*, quoting the Sybilline Leaves: similar prodigies are noted, *Virgil*, *Eclogues*.

---

79. *To give light to them that sit in darkness and in the shadow of death, to guide our feet into the way of peace.*

Light. God is Light. 1. Jo. i. 5. Light reveals all things. Ps. xxxvi. 9.
Its own evidence. Ps. cxix. 105. It uncovers wiles of Satan. Eph. v. 13.
"Thy *word* a lamp." Ps. cxix. 130. A guide, 2 Tim. iii. 16.
A quickening light. Jo. viii. 12. Cheering light, Ps. iv. 6. Satisfies, John xi. 9.
Darkness. "The world by wisdom knew not God," (nor cared to know.) [1 Cor. i. 21.
Darkness covered the world at Christ's coming.
No command to the Jews for 4000 years, to evangelize the nations.
The slow movements of Providence in regenerating the world.
"Cease Philip, in trying to govern the world." *Luther to Melancthon.*
Shadow of death. Mountains of sin obscuring the light of Truth.
Heathens helplessly *resting*, amid this terrible gloom.
The heart of darkness, the chosen *home* of the sinner.
Heathenism, like a damp cavern, chills the soul.
Pagans are the saddest of all men, seldom smiling.
Peace. All rest out of Christ, a *mockery* of repose.
"There is *no peace*, saith my God, to the wicked." Isa. xlviii. 22.

"I will have peace, adding drunkenness, &c." Deut. xxix. 19.
Guide. Christ, the Shepherd and Bishop of souls. 1 Peter ii. 25.

80. *And the child grew, and waxed strong in spirit, and was in the deserts till the day of his shewing unto Israel.*

Grew. Evidence of our Lord's proper humanity. Compare Luke ii. 40.
Spirit. Wiser and stronger in spiritual life.
Deserts. 2 kinds. 1. Vast labyrinths of rocky hillocks, 30 feet high.
Intervals covered with flinty pebbles of granite.
Not a blade of grass, or shrub, or any sign of life.
Camels passing over them 1000 years, leave no vestige.
Hapless pilgrims wandering from the caravan, or sound of voices, without the magnet in great danger of being lost.
500 Pilgrims from Persia to Damascus, lately perished
Water is found everywhere, a few feet beneath the surface.
But is far more *briny*, than the ocean.
2. Waves of shifting sand, of exceedingly minute particles.
Retirement often useful for public service.
Moses in Midian. Elijah in the Desert. John the Bap.
Our Lord at Nazareth. Paul in Arabia. John in Patmos.
Luther, Zuinglius, &c. Bunyan in Bedford Prison.
Day of his shewing. At 30 years of age he began to preach, Luke iii. 23.

"*In spirit*," strength of mind, *Campbell, Wakefield.* "*Deserts*," hill country, *Lightfoot.* Engedi, *Lange.* "*Till.*" At 30, *Mayor.* To avoid Rabbinical perversions, *Gillmore.* To avoid suspicion of collusion with Christ, *Basnage.* No connection with *Essenes, Alford.* From infancy, *Chrysostom.* After educated in the law, *Paulinus, Grotius.* αναδείξεως, of Christ as divine, *Wetstein.* A deus presens, *Bloomfield.* Appointment as preacher, *Wakefield.* In full office, *Bengel.* Opening of his official life, *Alford.*

CHAPTER II.

1. *And it came to pass in those days, that there went out a decree from Cæsar Augustus, that all the world should be taxed.*

Those days. General reference to the birth of John.
"The fulness of time," the centre of the world's history. Gal. iv. 4.
The most brilliant period of all Revelation.
1. *Divine Power* in the Incarnation. 2. Wisdom in the time, place and circumstances. 3. Faithfulness. 4. Holiness, hiding His wonders from unbelievers. 5. Love. Jo. iii. 16.
Decree, of a heathen emperor, unconsciously fulfils prophecy. Gen. xlix. 10.
Cæsar. Second of the *twelve* Cæsars, nephew to Julius.
Republic lasted 478 years, till Augustus, 31 B.C.
Augustus. Son of Octavius and Atia; licentious and treacherous.
Superstitious, oft borne to the temples before day, for prayer.
Generous, vain, ambitious, warlike, another Louis 14.
Cruel, 300 senators, 200 knights, murdered with his consent.
Defeated at sea, he *dragged* Neptune's statue into the sea.
Daughter Julia by her infamy, embittered his last days.
His dying words were "Have I not acted well my part?"
Reigned 44 years, died aged 76. A long and splendid reign.
In Augustus, see man's nothingness, amid earthly splendor.
In Mary, see highest destiny, amid earthly meanness.
Augustus intends simply to promote the glory of his reign.
But he only advances prophecies, and the birth of a King, unknown.
By the web of Providence, a monarchy begins, which will absorb Rome and all others. Dan. ii. 44.
Cæsar, unintentionally, a mere *official* in God's kingdom.
World. Name assumed by ambition and given by flattery to Rome.
The civilised world was then all subject to Rome.
All the world are now summoned to be enrolled, subjects, of a *higher King*.
Taxed. Gr. *Registered* census, basis of taxes and enlisting.
Every five years as in the U.S. Rome took a census.

Καίσαρος, *adorned with hair.* Augustus. *Magnificent.* "*World.*" Gr., inhabited world Crete called "my world," *Ovid.* Inhabited by Greeks, *Aelian,* Judea, *Greswell.* ἀπογρά. *Julian* cavilled at Christ's claims, because born Cæsar's *subject*, but he only confirms Jacob's prophecy. World, all subject to Rome, *Hammond.* All claimed, *Meda.* Judea, *Macknight.*

2. *And this taxing was first made when Cyrenius was governor of Syria.*

Taxing. First named, 2 Kings xv. 20. Renewed by Romans at Archelaus's fall.
Males from 14, and females 12 years of age to 65, paid 2 drachmas.
Continued by Vespasian and Domitian, and abolished by Nerva.
Rulers and Jews swore allegiance to Herod and Cæsar.
All seems chance, but God thus sets His seal on Christ's *descent*.
First made. Begun now, but finished eight years after.
Three years ordinarily taken by Rome to furnish census.
Doomsday book of Wm. the Conqueror took 6 years.
Joab was nearly a year taking that of Israel.
Cyrenius, or Quirinus was Proconsul about 8 or 10 years after Christ's birth.
Sulpicius Quirinus, ancient patrician family of Rome.
Was honored with a public funeral by the Senate.
Syria. Heb. Aram. Syria or Tsur (Tyre). Probably the origin of the name. Tyre being the first town of Syria known to the Greeks. *Smith.* Dict.
Subdued by Cyrus 528, B.C. Alexander 352, B.C. Pompey 65 B.C.
Druses, Maronites, Nestorians: Damascus is the capital.
Population one million. Ruins of Baal-bec and Palmyra.
Theatre of Greek, Jewish, Parthian, Roman, Saracen, Crusade wars.

Κυρηνίου. The 2nd verse a gloss, *Volkner*, *Kuinoel*, *Olshausen*. Article omitted, *Marsh*, *Lachmann*. Five taxings under Cyrenius, *Zumpt*, *Wordsworth*. Census made before C. was ruler, *Tholuck*, *Wieseler*. Assessment and census, *Ebrard*. Priestly census confounded with Roman, *Schleirmacher*. αὐτὴ for αὔτη, discriminating between the *decree* and the *enrolment*, *Lange*, *Oosterzee*. προτησ for πρώτη, *i. e.* previous, *Casaubon*, *Greswell*. Saturnius joined with Cyrenius, *Grotius*, *Elsley*. Luke alludes to one of two taxings, *Prideaux*. Enrolment confined at first to Judea, *Rosenmuller*, *Kuinoel*. Registry in Herod's time, and the taxing some ten years after, *Campbell*. Begun now, and completed under Cyrenius, 8 or 10 years after, *Hales* *Doddridge*. Highly probable that Quirinus or Cyrenius was *twice* governor of Syria, *Zumpt.*, *Alford*, in *loco*. The Geeek text is not the usual elegant style of Luke, *Marsh*.

---

3. *And all went to be taxed, every one into his own city.*

Taxed. Angelic announcement of greatness, not *earthly*.
Enrolment, subjects her to *trouble*, *want* and *danger*.
Cæsar's pride prompted, God's purpose directed the census.
To locate an infant's birth, 60 millons of persons are enrolled.

Church and State records prove Him to be David's Son.
Augustus thinks not of laying the foundations of a lasting empire.
Thus Darius, Cyrus, Sennacherib, fulfil God's designs.
Every one. Rome included men, women, and children *at home.*
But then this census was made at their *dwelling place*, not at that of their *extraction.*
Own city. Pagan laws executed by Jews after their customs.
Jews clung to the shadow, long after the substance was gone.
Judea under Roman rule, *civil*, but under Jewish, *ecclesiastical.*
Each family had to be enrolled with its own tribe.
Ancestral city, that was legally Mary's and Joseph's home.
If the law were enforced, their *inheritance* was there also.

4. And Joseph also went up from Galilee, out of the city of Nazareth, into Judea, unto the city of David, which is called Bethlehem, (because he was of the house and lineage of David.)

Went up. Travellers from all points *ascend*, going to Jerusalem.
Journey a type of our pilgrimage. 1. Dark in the beginning.
2. Difficult in progress. 3. Glorious in the end.
A badge of their lost independence.
A humble carpenter represents the royal house of David.
Galilee. Luke i. 26. **Nazareth.** Luke i. 26. **Judea.** Luke i. 5.
David. Luke i. 27. **Bethlehem.** Heb. *House of bread.*
David a Shepherd, **Shepherd of Israel** was born there.
Bethlehem Ephratah, foretold as Christ's birthplace. Micah v. 2.
Six miles south of Jerusalem, built of white stone.
Here David was anointed King by Samuel. 1 Sam. xvi. 13.
Water coveted by David, was poured out to the Lord.
Rachael buried; Naomi, Ruth and Mary dwelt here.
Empress Helena built a church over the grotto, 330 A.D.
Population 1500—ferocious, indolent, rapacious beggars.
House. Materials and form. Luke i. 40. See Notes.

At this time the *house* of David had probably become reduced to one *family*, *Bengel.* "*Lineage.*" Mary had property in Bethlehem, *Olshausen.* A mere conjecture, *Oosterzee.* Joseph unwilling to leave her in Nazareth. "Socii Latini nominee," ordered to their own City, *Livy*, Book 23. "Bethlehem." The actual spot of the Nativity is entirely lost. The cave now shewn, may, or may not be the place. Its present tinselled ornaments, banish all idea of the stall, where the Infant Redeemer was laid.

5. *To be taxed with Mary his espoused wife, being great with child.*

Taxed. Fulfilling the mark of Nativity, set up *seven centuries* before.
Pharaoh must dream, that Joseph may be governor.
Ahasuerus is wakeful, that Mordecai may save the Jews.
Belshazzar must dream, that Daniel may prophesy.
Nazareth was Mary's home, but not Christ's birthplace.
Rulers decree, but "There be higher than they." Eccl. v. 8.
Espoused. Betrothed—honour put on the marriage state.
Child. "Unto us a child is born." Isa. ix. 6
"The stem of Jesse" hewn down, but shooting anew. Zech. vi. 12.

γυναικί, cancelled, *Lachman, Tischendorf, Oosterzee.* Rome oppressed royal lines intentionally, *Calvin.* With Mary, Jesus was also enrolled, *Justin, Tertullian, Chrysostom.*

---

6. *And so it was, that, while they were there, the days were accomplished that she should be delivered.*

7. *And she brought forth her firstborn son, and wrapped him in swaddling clothes, and laid him in a manger; because there was no room for them in the inn.*

There. Called by angels, "City of David," seat of his royalty.
Accomplished. God's time up; a deluge flows; a sceptre departs, or Shiloh comes.
Brought forth. Ambition, curiosity, or avarice had devised the taxing.
But Augustus unconsciously ministers to the *Divine* decree.
Yet follows the unfettered dictates of his own heart.
Christ's birth, a hiding of His glory, teaches us humility.
On a journey, teaches we are all pilgrims on earth.
Stable, teaches self-denial, and puts a stain on earthly pride.
The day or month of the nativity utterly unknown.
The precise year is believed to be 4 years *before* A.D. 1.
Firstborn. Privileges of birthright. 1. Special consecration to God. 2. Authority over the others. 3. Priesthood. 4. Double inheritance. 5. Father's dying blessing. "Christ, firstborn among many brethren."
Mary and Joseph's *other sons* are named. Matt. xiii. 55. Luke viii. 20.
Son. Jesus born in the fullness of time. Gal. iv. 4.
"The Sceptre shall not depart," &c. Gen. xlix. 10. "Desire of all." Hag. ii. 7.

"Messenger shall suddenly come." Mal. iii. 1. "Seventy weeks."
The temple of Janus was shut 12 years for the fifth time. [Dan. ix. 24.
Monarch, universally expected, *Suetonius*, *Tacitus*, *Josephus*.
Swaddling bands. With which Hebrews closely bound infants.
Used to prevent distortion of limbs by weakness.
Foundation stone of a new heaven and a new earth. 1. School of deep humility. 2, of steadfast faith. 3, of ministering love. 4, of joyful hope.
Jesus has *consecrated* all the hard places where His people must lie.
Manger. Heb. trough. Having no *hay*, mangers not found in the East.
God and Man, Heaven and Earth, Old and New Covenants meet.
Manger. 1. Scene of God's glory. 2. Sanctuary of Christ's honor.
The precise spot of the Nativity is now unknown.
Stupendous contrasts oft occur in the life of the Redeemer.
No room. Not a sign of poverty, but of necessity.
Oriental pilgrims still place infants in as rude quarters.
The world never has room for Christ or His followers.
We should sigh, if the same world *rejecting* Jesus, should *receive* us.
Yet *He* rejects none. In His **heart there is room** for all! Luke xiv. 22.
Inn. Gr., *unloosing*. A place where travellers lay aside their burdens.
Blessings of ransomed millions through eternity rest on that child's [head.
The tinsel of Earth's greatness, fades before the Son of God.
Simple record of the wonders of God's empire, without one comment.

ἔτεκε, painless birth, (a superstition of Rome,) *Bossuet*. πρωτότ. ordinarily implies, parents had other children; thus Matt. xiii. 55 distinctly teaches. A Papal dogma teaches her perpetual virginity. Even *Augustine* was deceived. Luke viii. 19, "swaddling," used to prevent distortion of limbs through weakness, *Euripides*. φατνη. Mardonius the Persian carried a manger of *brass* with him, *Herodotus*. Lodging place, *Wetstein*, *Kuinoel*. Roof with open sides, *Bloomfield*. Modern kahns have walls, but no roof. Heli resided here, *Lightfoot*. A manger, *Campbell*, *Mayor*. A cave,—*Justin Martyr*, born 100 years after, within 40 miles of the spot, *Ellicott*, *Olshausen*. Feeding trough, *Owen*. Was Christ born on 25th December? Rome answers, Yes. March, *Bochart*. October, *Scaliger*. 15th September, *Lightfoot*. April 5th, *Greswell*. *Alford*. Autumn, *Robinson*. 15th August, *Lardner*. September, *Newcombe*. May 20, *W. & W. Clem. Alex.* 200 A. D., writes, that the time was unknown then. *Maximus of Turin*, 500 A. D., uncertain. Bishop of Eglesia, 600 A. D., first observed in time of *Chrysostom*, 386 A. D. Lately established, *Gregory of Nyssa*, 388 A. D. First fixed in the west, December 5th—352 A. D., by *Julius I*, Bishop of Rome. The period of the *Saturnalia*, *Bruma*. Solstitial Festival charmed Christians from the Church, *Faustus*. Mingling Pagan and Christian festivals would purify the former, *Peter Chrysologus*, *Neander*, vol iii., page 416-421. 400 A. D., Christmas *not* celebrated by the *Christian Church, Augustine.* As the *day*, so is the exact *year* of Christ's birth unknown; 41 of Augustus, *Ireneus;* 42, Tertullian; 22, Epiphanius; year of Rome 747, *Hardium;* 748, *Capellus, Kepler;* 749, *Petairus, Usher, Bengel;* 750, *Oosterzee, Wieseler;* 751, *Baronius, Scaliger;* 785, *Dionisius Exigius.* Some add 3, others 4, others more, *Kuinoel.* καταλ. Guest chamber, *Wakefield.* House allotted to strangers, *Campbell.* Reception room, *Lange.* Lodging house, *Oosterzee.* Hostelry, *Tyndale.* In diversorio, *Vulgate.*

---

8. *And there were in the same country shepherds abiding in the field, keeping watch over their flock by night.*

Country. Regions of Bethlehem.
Shepherds. Patriarchs by digging a well, claimed pasture right.
In Bible history God has singularly honored toil.
While Moses watched the flock, Angel of the covenant came.
David was anointed, and Jacob blest, tending flock.
Jesus Himself the "Good Shepherd." Jo. x. 14, Psa. xxiii, Isa. xl. 11.
God sanctions honest toil, by giving the shepherds the first tidings.
Abiding. In tents or towers. Gen. xxv. 21.
They were responsible for lost sheep,—exposed to wild beasts.
Watch. Luke. xii. 38. This humble unknown circle, known to God's
Under shepherds vigilant, receive divine visits of mercy. [angels.
Lord begins to shew where Sovereign mercy selects.
Proud sensual dwellers at Jerusalem, passed by.
Flock. The *wealth* and *comfort* of Orientals, greatly in flocks.
Night. God visited Abraham, Gen. 15. Jacob, Gen. xvi. 2, by night.
Like Simeon and Nathaniel, they may have looked for the Messiah.

"*Shepherds.*" Tradition gives the names of four. *Philo, Andrews.*

---

9. *And, lo, the angel of the Lord came upon them, and the glory of the Lord shone round about them; and they were sore afraid.*

Angel. Luke i. 11. Christ's humiliation ever joined with *Divine* honor.
His birth announced, His birthsong sung by angel choir.
In His presentation, Simeon prophesies—Baptism, heaven opens.
In the garden, an angel aids Him—ascending, angels honor Him.
For 4000 years the Church had been looking for the Shiloh.
Now, the august proclamation has a worthy herald.

Upon them. Gr. *poised above;* idea of unexpected appearance.
Angel, visits not the manger, but the field.
Shews the *hidden greatness* of the Lord's coming.
The three embassies of God. 1. His Son to redeem. 2. The Angels to announce. 3. Men to adore Him.
Glory. "On wheels of light, on wings of flame,
The glorious host of Zion came."
Half the world seemed illumined by one angel. Rev. xviii. 1.
Moses' face by communion with God, caught the lustre. Ex. xxxiv. 29.
1. Majesty. 2. Wisdom. 3. Love. 4. Holiness.
1. Hearers. 2. Preachers. 3. Key note. 4. Summoning. 5. The Sign.
Shone. Light, that by which God, reveals Himself. Luke. xii. 49.
Light in the darkness. 1, of Sin. 2, of Ignorance. 3, of affliction. 4, of Death.
Mid-day darkened at the Redeemer's *death.*
Midnight illumined into day, at His *birth.*
Afraid. Gr., *exceedingly terrified.* Supernatural objects. Luke v. 8.
Adam. Gen. iii. 8. Israel. Ex. xx. 19, dreaded the Divine Being.
Ancients thought death followed these visions. Judges. xiii. 22. Exodus xxxiii. 20.

"*Angel of the Lord.*" Hebraism for splendid angel. Cedar of the Lord—Noble Cedar. δόξα, Shechinah, *Townsend.* Miracle of light, *Campbell.* "Afraid." *Semele* struck dead by the effulgence of Jove, *Ovid* 8. Saturn's laws punished one for seeing immortal gods, *Callimachus.*

---

10. *And the angel said unto them, Fear not: for, behold, I bring you good tidings of great joy, which shall be to all people.*

Fear not. Saints need not fear *friends,* much less *foes.*
Conscious guilt fills the wicked with constant dread. Ezk. xxi. 7.
Behold. If *angels* wonder, *man* surely should regard.
Bring you. Each fallen creature feels the loss of peace.
Good tidings. Gr. gospel, first proclaimed by angels.
Final coming will be announced by an archangel.
Great joy, is often, 1. Secret; 2. Silent; 3. Childlike; 4. Modest; 5. Elevated.
Christ the only source of rational joy, among fallen men.
All, whose hearts were open to receive the Saviour.

No joy to Herod, envious and cruel—to Pharisees, proud and covetous.
To earth's down-trodden millions, the news was welcome. Mark xii. 37.

11. *For unto you is born this day in the city of David a Saviour, which is Christ the Lord.*

Unto you. 1. A Saviour is *born*; 2. A *Saviour* is born; 3. A Saviour is born unto *you;* 4. *To-day.*
The Shepherds were Jews. "He came unto His own." John i. 11.
This day. God's set time was come, though *hope was weary.* Isa. ix. 6.
City of David. For long ages, God eyed this chosen spot. Jer. xxiii. 5.
1. Son of **David,** regal birth; 2. **Saviour,** sovereign goodness;
3. **Christ,** fulness of the Spirit; 4. **Lord,** Divine and Prophetic.
Christ. Gr. anointed. Messiah. Heb. The O. T. foretold,
Him, as God and man; Exalted and debased; Master and servant;
Priest and victim; Prince and subject; Victor though dying.
Rich and poor; King—yet a man of sorrows and infirmities.
He allowed not demons to proclaim His office. Luke iv. 41.
Name "Christ," occurs 514 times in the N. T.

ὑμῖν—ἡμῖν, *Bodleian.* The angels, their spirits; and redeemed ones, *Kuinoel.* "*Christ the Lord.*" Magnificent appellation, *Bengel.* These words meet only here, *Alford.* κυρίοσ only applicable to Jehovah, *Bengel, Alford, Brown.* δεὸσ, σωτὴρ, august terms given the Sin-destroyer, but no created being, *Olshausen.* Χριστὸσ, official title, *Messiah,* xxii. 42. David, Isaiah, Daniel call Him *Messiah. Christ, anointed, i. e.* the anointed Prophet, Priest, and King, divinely chosen and qualified, *J. P. Smith.* He had no external official unction. *Ed.*

---

12. *And this* shall be *a sign unto you; Ye shall find the babe wrapped in swaddling clothes, lying in a manger.*

Sign. Divine, certainly, but not necessarily miraculous.
Babe. Hopes of millions, will yet cluster round that babe. Zec. ix. 9.
Manger. In His nativity: in His temptation, among *beasts.* Mark i. 13.
Believers, ambitious of *high place,* forget their Master's *cradle.*
A manger honored above a thousand glittering thrones.
An ornament of His royalty; a throne of His glory.
He *comes* in humility, He *reigns* in humility.
He *leads* by humility,—manger and cross, a stumbling block to many.
His infancy and death, are still rocks, wrecking human pride.

σημεῖον, τερασ, both ordinarily miracles, but the former a miracle wrought as a sign. σημεῖα, were not supernatural. In N. T., tokens of a higher power, *Olshausen.* βρέφοσ, *a*, not *the* babe, *Brown.* The lowliness of his condition was a sign for believers, *Bengel.*

---

13. *And suddenly there was with the angel a multitude of the heavenly host praising God, and saying,*

Suddenly. The instantaneous *flashings* of the heavenly throng.

Angel. Supposed to have been *Gabriel.*

Multitude. Myriads of angels. 1 Kings xxii. 19.; Psalm lxviii. 17. Rev. v. 11.

Heavenly host. Gr., *Army.* Celebrating peace; *starry host.* Acts vii. 42.

Thousands of angels. Psa. ciii. 20. "Praise Him ye His *hosts.*" Psa. cxlviii. 2.

Praising. Heavenly courtiers; models of those rejocing in royal favor.

Happy beings, free from envy; the *life-guard* of the royal child.

The first hymn to the Incarnate, sung by angels.

They know the misery sin has caused: the door of mercy now open.

Their deep compassion to man revealed by their deep interest.

1. The choir singers from the new Jerusalem.

2. Salvation the theme, 3. Dwellers in heaven and earth the listeners.

Saying, or "singing,"—usual among the classics.

στρατ. Acts vii. 42. "Knighthood of Heaven," *Wickliffe.* Stars of the sky, *Tyndale.* Host of the sky, *Crammer.* "Saying,"—dicere for cantare, *Hor.*, Car. 1, *Mayor.*

---

14. *Glory to God in the highest, and on earth, peace, good will toward men.*

Glory. Light, chosen emblem of the Deity. 1 John i. 5.

1, of Sovereignty. 2, of Wisdom. 3. Power. 4. Purpose. 5, of His Justice. 6. Holiness.

In the plan and execution of Redemption.

Redemption far more than *Creation* illustrates His Glory.

Highest. Heavens, where even angels tremblingly venture. Heb. i. 3.

Peace. Prophecy cheered the church with hope: Prince of Peace. Isa. 9. 6 and 7.

1. Among nations. 2. Neighbours. 3. Families. 4. One's self.

By sin, man is *at war* with himself, his neighbours, and his God.

Thirty-five times the present population of the globe has perished in war, *Burke*.

German war of 30 yrs. 1,000,000 perished. In Napoleon's wars, 6,000,000.

1,000,000 perished during the late *American* Rebellion.

50 times the amount of *property* of the earth, has been destroyed in war.

Peace, fruit of faith, repentance, reconciliation with God. Phil. iv. 2. Prov. xvi. 7.

Goodwill. 1. Power in Creation. 2. Goodness in Providence. 3. Mercy in Redemption.

Elements of Heaven, transferred to earth, by Christ. Eph. ii. 14.

εἰρήνη. Peace of God's good-will, *Wakefield*. Way of Peace, *Collyer*, *Lange*. By three angelic bands, in three strains of 1, Glory; 2, Power; 3, Goodwill, *Brown*. εὐδοκ. reconciliation, *Chrysostom*: armistice, *Theophylact*. Not so much a proclamation, as doxology, *W. & W.* ὑψίστοισ. *Heavens*. God's peculiar dwelling, *Bengel*. For εὐδοκία, read εὐδοκίασ in genitive, *Tisch.*, *Lachmann*, *Olshausen*, *Meyor*. The sentence must then be translated, *peace on earth to men of (God's) good pleasure*, i. e. *his chosen people*, *Alford*. The *Vulgate* reads "bonæ voluntatis." Rom. Cath. interpreters adopt this reading, and translate "peace on earth for those who like it." Received text preferred by *Alford*, *Oosterzee*, *Brown*. *Ed.*

---

15. *And it came to pass, as the angels were gone away from them into heaven, the shepherds said one to another, Let us now go even unto Bethlehem, and see this thing which is come to pass, which the Lord hath made known unto us.*

Gone away. Angel visits *bright*, but *brief* visions on earth.

Their errand ended, they return home to their blest seats.

Heaven. Had they guaged our woes, *sad tidings* they might take back

Let us go. Love to Christ, lessens our *interest*, loosens our grasp, on earth.

Faith, rather than curiosity, led them to Bethlehem.

This thing. The *babe* fills their whole soul, as they forsake their flocks.

Unto us. "If any man will do His will, &c." "Secret of the Lord, &c." Jo. vii. 17. Psa. xxv. 14.

ἄνθρ. retained. These shepherds I mean of whom I spoke, *Volkner*, *Owen*. Cancelled, *Tischendorf*. Διέλθωμεν. Let us cross the country, *Wakefield*. ῥῆμα a thing that is *true*, untruth is *no* thing; referred to Jesus, *Ambrose*.

16. *And they came with haste, and found Mary and Joseph, and the babe lying in a manger.*

Came. They were "not disobedient to the heavenly vision." Acts xxvi. 19.
In haste. "What thy hand findeth, &c., do it with thy might." Eco. 9-10.
"My soul made me like the chariots of Amminadib." Song vi. 12.
Mary. Wife, named first. Creature before Creator.
It shews the inversion introduced by the Incarnation.
Babe. "As much when in the manger laid, Almighty ruler of the sky."
"As when the six day's work He made, and filled the morning stars with joy." *Cowper.*
Manger. The deep poverty of the virgin, no shock to their faith.
They mutually told all the wonders, each had heard, and seen.

"*Came.*" Mysteriously guided in the dark. *Olshausen* hazards a conjecture that the stable or cave may have *belonged* to these shepherds. Seems clear the spot was somehow known to them by the angel's description. "*with haste,*" martyr prisoners, taken for praying in Bow church-yard, cheered by the cheerful obedience of the shepherds, *G. Hooper* 1554. Parker, vol. 2., p. 617. "*Manger,*" home stall, *Campbell.*

---

17. *And when they had seen* it, *they made known abroad the saying which was told them concerning this child.*

Seen it. These worshippers not offended at the poverty of the manger.
Halo of pictures round the head, borrowed from Heathen.
Made known. Good news would not let the lepers be silent. 2 Kg. vii. 9.
"My cup runneth over," said David, rejoicing. Psa. xxiii. 5.
Shepherds, the first *earthly*, angels, the first *heavenly* preachers.
Unselfish "love of Christ, constraineth" the believer. 2 Cor. v. 14.
"We cannot but speak the things which, &c." Acts. iv. 20. 1 John. i. 12.

18. *And all they that heard* it, *wondered at those things which were told them by the shepherds.*

Wondered, that angels should tell *shepherds*, and not the *priests*.
Myriads since have heard, wondered, despised, and perished. Acts xiii. 41.
Infinite Mind notes the secret *yearnings* of the humble. Psa. lxxix. 11.
Many admired His words, but stumbled at His birth. Rom. ix. 32.
Crowds wondered at His miracles, but rejected His gospel. Jo. vi. 66.

19. *But Mary kept all these things, and pondered them in her heart.*

Mary. Leaves to Providence to clear up her good name.
Pondered. Gr. kept in active remembrance; "revolving them."
She was doubtless ignorant of many things concerning her mysterious babe.
Her heart. She had "the ornament of a meek and quiet spirit." 1 Peter iii. 4.
Heart in *Scripture* is used for the seat of understanding, will, affections, &c.
Her faith in the "angel tidings," had full exercise.

συνετ. carefully preserved, *Mayor.* συμβ. weighing, *Campbell.* Carefully observing, *Wakefield.* Especially of oracles or dreams, *Mayor.* Reflecting with pleasure, *Olshausen.* Entered into their meaning, *Doddridge.* Thought over them, point by point, *Bengel.*

---

20. *And the shepherds returned, glorifying and praising God for all the things that they had heard and seen, as it was told unto them.*

Shepherds. The first fruits of the Gospel Dispensation.
Returned. Earth as well as the church, has its cares and joys.
Glorifying. They seemed to join in the chorus of the angels' song.
Praising. Implicit faith, and prompt obedience, ever rewarded.
Their simple faith, and sublime songs linger round Christ.
The Manger and Cross, foolishness to Greeks and Jews. 1 Cor. i. 23.
But saints ever draw thence, their inspiration and life of love.

21. *And when eight days were accomplished for the circumcising of the child, his name was called JESUS, which was so named of the angel before he was conceived in the womb.*

Eight. Law was exacting as to the time, even Sabbath. Gen. xvii. 12.
Circumcising. Luke i. 59. History of this ancient right. See Notes.
Bloody symbol of the removal of sin. Col. ii. 11-13. Jer. iv. 4.
"Was in all points made like unto his brethren." Heb. ii. 17.
In Him, a virtual pledge to die. Phil. ii. 8. *sinless.* 1. Jo. 3-5.
The law was honored,—scandal of uncircumcision failed. Gal. v. 11.
He could thus alone be heard as a teacher in Israel.
Jews would have held him an uncircumcised apostate.

Above the law, He obeyed it, to free us from the law.
Under the law, Rom. viii. 3. He became a debtor, &c. Gal. v. 3.
This rite counted Him a stranger, now a "Beloved Son." Mat. iii. 17.
Innocent, He still takes the mark and shame of sin.
This Divine Infant dignifies the rite, and silences the ignorant.
What good is there in circumcising, or baptising a child?
Answer—Jehovah ordained it, and submitted to it.
He now honors the *indenturing* of children to Himself, by baptism.
Jesus. Luke i. 31. A Prince, Law-giver, Prophet, Priest and King,
He passed by all these, for a name full of *mercy*, **Jesus.**

"*Circumcising.*" This disproved His body being a *phantom*, as *Docetae* and *Manicheans* held. Not actually necessary, but in the divine plan, *Olshausen.* Jesus, Greek form of the name Joshua or Jeshua, a contraction of Jehoshua, that is "Help of Jehovah," or "Saviour," *Ellicott.*

---

22. *And when the days of her purification according to the law of Moses were accomplished, they brought him to Jerusalem, to present him to the Lord.*

Purification. Male required 40, a female 80 days.
The rite demanded for the sake of his *mother*, not the child.
Sprinkling of hyssop and of blood, refers to the *pollution* of sin.
Law. Levitical system of types and shadows.
Moses. *Heb. drawn out of the water.* Was exposed on the Nile.
Adopted and educated as a prince, by Pharaoh's daughter. Acts vii. 21.
Returning to his kindred, he slew an oppressing Egyptian.
Fled to Midian in Arabia, married Jethro's daughter.
At Horeb, God appeared in a burning bush.
Divinely authorized with his elder brother Aaron, returns to Egypt.
1. Miracle of rod turned into serpent. 2. Nile changed to blood.
3. Frogs, 4. Lice, 5. Flies, 6. Murrain, 7. Boils, 8. Hail, 9. Locusts.
10. Darkness, 11. First born slain. Passover instituted.
Leads out Israel to the Red Sea, divides it, crosses it.
Quails, Manna in the desert, Law given at Sinai.
Rock gives water, Aaron's rod blossoms, Corah, &c. destroyed.
Amorites overcome, Balaam's curses changed to blessings.
In full strength at 120 years of age, dies, and God hid his body.
He wrote the Pentateuch. 90th Psalm, and possibly Job.
Jerusalem. Heb. Vision of peace. *Surname* of *Heaven.* Rev. xxi. 2.

Salem. Gen. xiv. 18. Jebus, Judges xix, 10. Holy City. City of David.
Now *El Khuds* The Holy. 37 miles east of Joppa.
Taken by David 2 Sam. v. 6. Made it capital. *Temple.* Luke i. 9.
Captured 588, B.C. by Nebuchadnezzar. Jews led to Babylon.
Rebuilt by Zerubbabel, 526. Taken by Alexander 352 B.C.
By Ptolemy, 324. Antiochus, 170. Retaken, Maccabees, 163. B.C.
Pompey 63 B.C. Destroyed by Titus 70 A.D.
Jews banished by Hadrian 135 A.D., named the new city *Aelia Capitolina,* A.D. 136.
Helena, mother of Constantine built church of the Holy Sepulchre 326.
Julian miraculously baffled in attempts to refute Christ A.D. 363.
Taken by Chosroes. 613. A.D. by Greeks 625. A.D. Omar 637.
By Ahmed Turk 868. Saracens 969. Jews suffered much till 1048.
By Crusaders 1099. Saladin 1187. By Raymond's treachery restored 1242. to the Latins. Sultans of Egypt 1291. Selim 1517. Turks hold it 1865.
It stands on Mountains of Judea 2400 ft. above the sea.
The promontory with steep descent 500 feet above Kidron Hinnom.
The city stands on three Mounts, Moriah, Zion, Acra.
Is 32 miles distant from the sea, 18 from the Jordan, 20 from Hebron, 36 from Samaria.
Wall 2½ miles around, 60 feet high, 8 feet thick, built 1534.
4 Gates, 2000 houses, 5000 Jews, Orientals 25,000.
One Christian Mission sustained by Prussia and England.
Jerusalem in ruins, fulfilment of our Lord's prophecies. Luke xxi. 5, to 20, [verses.
Present. i. e. *publicly* Joseph, could do it.
Believing parents desire to consecrate their children to God.

"*Purificat.*" For seven days she could not enter the sanctuary, nor eat with her husband, *Lewes* Antiq. Mothers stood at Nicanor's gate, *Lightfoot.* "*Jerusalem.*" Name given by Shem, *Rabbis.* Vision of peace, *Reland.* Possession of peace, *Ewald.* People or house of peace, *Gesenius.* Given by Shem, *Lightfoot.* Called, *Ariel.* The Lion of God. Isa. xxix. *Beit el makdis,* holy house. A foundation, *Rabbis.* αὐτὸν, *Tischendorf.* αὐτῶν, *Origen, Jerome, Brown.* Neither needed it, *Bengel.* Jesus mortal, though sinless, *Alford.* αὐτῆς adopted by the Eng. version is almost without authority, a manifest correction, *Alford.*

---

23. *(As it is written in the law of the Lord, Every male that openeth the womb shall be called holy to the Lord.)*

Written. Every step of our Lord's life fulfills some prophecy.
Lk. i. 63. First born, holy since the 1st Passover. Ex. xiii. 2.

First born offered, and redeemed for 5 shekels. Num. xviii. 15 16.
Redeemed from the earthly, He founded a spiritual temple. Heb. ix. 11.

"*Law.*" Redemption from being sacrificed. διαν. First-born of his mother, *Campbell.*

---

24. *And to offer a sacrifice according to that which is said in the law of the Lord, A pair of turtle doves, or two young pigeons.*

Sacrifice. Its origin was *divine* like circumcision.
Established immediately after the fall. Gen. iv. 4.
If not divinely sanctioned, would have been superstition.
Pair. One a burnt offering, the other a sin offering.
Mary had no idea of her *immaculate* conception.
Had she been able, a *lamb* was required.
The Magi had not yet brought their princely present.
She in the Temple publicly declared her poverty. Lev. xii. 8.
Jesus nursed and tended by a poor woman. 2 Cor. viii. 9.
He ate poor man's food, wore a poor man's apparel.
He wrought at a poor man's work, shared his troubles.
This should silence the murmuring of the poor.
Turtle doves, noted for rapid flight. Ps. lv. 6. Plumage. Ps. lxviii. 13.
Dwelling in the rocks. Jer. xlviii. 28., mournful voice. Is. xxxviii. 14.
Harmlessness, Matt. x. 16. Simplicity, Hos. vii. 11. Modesty, Cant. ii. 14.
Beauty of eyes. Cant. i. 15. Emblem of Peace, Gen. viii. 8.
Semiramis placed them on Assyrian standard.
They were the only birds offered in sacrifice. Lev. v. 7. xii. 6.
Pigeons, larger and more easily *domesticated* than doves.
Redemption price paid for Jesus, very *small.*
The price He paid for our Redemption *infinite.* 1 Pet. i. 18-9.
The holiest are not the richest, therefore despise not the poor
Mary cannot bring a lamb, but brings the "Lamb of God."

ζευγος. Index of poverty unnoticed by the fathers, *Ellicott.* τρυγόνων. from τρυζω to murmur or mourn, *Mayer.*

25. *And, behold, there was a man in Jerusalem, whose name was Simeon; and the same man was just and devout, waiting for the consolation of Israel: and the Holy Ghost was upon him.*

Behold. Calling special attention. **Jerusalem.** Luke ii. 25.
Simeon. Heb. *One who obeys.* First prophet to proclaim the Advent.
Devout. God has His elect in the darkest times.
Lot in Sodom. Obadiah in Ahab's train.
Daniel in Babylon. Jeremiah in Zedekiah's court.
Waiting, expecting life in Heaven, the way to live on earth.
Consolation. The Church had been waiting for many ages. Gen.
The sufferings of the Jews had been, and were then, great. [xlix. 18.
For ages the Messiah had been styled the *Consoler.*
A common oath "*May I never see the Consolation of Israel*".
A long sad silent preparation for earth's noblest scene.
Not like the sensual crowd, for an earthly deliverer.
"I waited for the Lord, more than they who watch for the morning". Ps. cxxx. 6.

"*Simeon,*" hearing with acceptance, *Gesenius.* Supposed to have been son of Hillel, and father of Gamaliel, *Lightfoot, Alford.* ανθρ. merely hints a lower rank, *Olshausen.* "*Just*" in performance of duties. "*Devout*" in disposition towards God, *Bengel.* "*Tradition*" says he received sight on Jesus' approach, *Oosterzee.* "*Waiting.*" God fulfils His word in silence, without leaving the threads of the web in mortal hands, *Alford.* Expectations of all nations of a Deliverer, *Trench.* "*Consolation.*" Paraclete refers to suffering state, Messiah would remove, *Olshausen.* "If I speak not truth, may I never see the Consolation of Israel," *Lightfoot.*

---

26. *And it was revealed unto him by the Holy Ghost, that he should not see death, before he had seen the Lord's Christ.*

Revealed. Here, we cannot know, to *doubt* is presumption. Luke i. 8.
Return of prophecy, a token of the Messiah being come.
It was the earliest dawn of the Gospel Day.
See Death, feel the pains of dying. An Orientalism.
Saints *before* Christ were taught as really by Him as *after.*
Before the angel Gabriel had fixed the date. Dan. ix. 25.
The Eastern World expected some great personage.
Lord's. Seeing the Messiah, gilded the gloom of the grave.
Christ. Gr. *Anointed.* Luke ii. 11. Alone anointed by Jehovah.

κεχρη., to transact business, or guide public affairs, also to consult an oracle. In N.T. sense—to be Divinely warned or instructed, *Ed.*

---

27. *And he came by the Spirit into the temple: and when the parents brought in the child Jesus, to do for him after the custom of the law.*

Spirit. An irrestible impulse from the Lord.
Temple. Outer Court, none but priests entered within. Luke i. 9.
Like Anna, his heart draws him to the house of prayer.
1. The Holy Ghost his Leader. 2. Faith his *consolation.* 3. Piety his life. 4. Saviour his joy. 5. To depart for heaven, his *desire.*
Parents, came to register Him among the firstborn.
Child. They who seek Him, will find Him in the sanctuary. Heb. x. 25.
He never fails to reveal His mercy to those who seek. Ps. lxiii. 2.
Prophet enters Jerusalem and sees God's glory. Ezek. viii. 3.
Custom. Verse 24. See Notes.

28. *Then took he him up in his arms, and blessed God, and said.*

His arms. Promises of God, are often more than fulfilled.
He was to *see*, but he *embraces* the Consolation of Israel.
Thus the priest presented the child to God by consecration.
No classic scene recorded, approaches this in *tender sublimity.*
Ministers taking infants up in baptism here sanctioned, Mark x, 16.

αὐτὸς of his own accord, *Bengel.* Simeon thought to be a priest, *Winer.* The child held during the blessing, *Meyer, Ellicott.*

---

29. *Lord, now lettest thou thy servant depart in peace, according to thy word.*

Lord. Luke i. 11. **Servant.** Luke vii. 2. See Notes.
The sight kindles his heart to a farewell song.
His song the last note of O.T. Psalmody. *Christian's death.*
1. God for his glory. 2. Has a song on his lips. 3. Christ in his arms.
4. Heaven in his eye. "Let me die the death of the righteous." Num. xxiii. 10.
Depart. Gr. dismiss, slaves were thus sent from masters.
The spiritual office of the aged servant was closing.
Peace. 1. Christ the King. 2. His gospel of peace. 3. His Kingdom of peace. 4. Heaven's reward of peace.

Peace, promised ages before to distracted Israel. Is. lxvi. 12.
Christian dies in peace with 1. The world 2. Conscience. 3. God.
Martyrs *sleep*. Acts vii. 60. "They rest from labors." Rev. xiv. 13.
Thy word. Promise fulfilled, he is willing to die.

ἀπολ. Thou art now releasing, *Brown*. Dimittis, *Vulg*. Servant dismissed, future hope at death, *M. Antoninus*, *Plutarch*. Prisoner released from captivity. εἰρήνη, Thousands of Christian martyrs sleep in the catacombs of Rome. Many epitaphs are seen in the Vatican.—"*Pax! Pax! Pax!*" Another,—"*Saturna dormit in pace.*" "*Lucius dormit* et vivet in pace in Christo," *Macfarlane*, p. 145. Sim. thinks of his death as the termination of, and dismissal from *his servitude*, *Meyer*. By the Divine promise Sim. receives at once a twofold blessing: the sight of his Saviour, and departure in peace, *Bengel*.

---

30. *For mine eyes have seen thy salvation.*

Seen. No eye is satisfied with seeing, until it sees Christ. Ecc. i. 8.
The eye of faith with Divine power, rests not there.
It receives rays of light, streaming from His entire Life.
It embraces His manger, His cross, His triumphs, as the Redeemer of men, the Conqueror of sin, death, and hell.
God's elect never die, until they have seen Jesus. 1 John iii. 6.
"The King in *all* his beauty" cannot be seen on earth. 1 Peter i. 8.
Salvation, everlasting, from the guilt and curse of sin. Luke xix. 9.
He beholds the world's Saviour in that helpless babe.
His mind fastens on the thing, not the person.
Some saints before the time of Christ had clear views of the gospel.
Abraham saw my day and was glad. John viii. 56.

31. *Which thou hast prepared before the face of all people;*
32. *A light to lighten the Gentiles, and the glory of thy people Israel.*

Prepared, by types, shadows, and prophecies, for 4000 years.
All people. Christ the forming centre of His saints. Isaiah xi. 10.
God's blessings no secret charm, kept only for the few.
Full and free as sunlight, without money or price. Isaiah lv. 1.
A *Jew* publishes the Saviour to the world, at His birth.
Light. Luke iii. 16, and xii. 49: is essentially active and spreading.
Christ, like light, renders visible the beauty of all things.
His absence also leaves all in gloom and woe.

Gentiles. Learned and polished, yet childish idolators, or secret sceptics

Selfish men are willing to enter heaven alone.

Fanaticism would exterminate, rather than convert, heathen.

Gentiles, placed before Jews (verse 32), hints at a future *preference.*

Glory. Christ in Simeon's prophecy. 1. Glory of Israel.

2. Glory of the Gentiles. 3. Highest gift to both.

Christianity the true glory. 1. Of every being. 2. Of every home.

3. Of every government. It alone elevates the *masses.*

With this swan-like song, he bids farewell to earth.

His prophetic views, much clearer than the disciples'.

φῶσ, to make the Gentiles known, *Wakefield.* That God, Christ, and their own condition may be revealed in the *light* of Christ, *Bengel.* αποκάλυψιν, 1. Uncovering. 2. Disclosing divine mysteries. 3. Appearance. ἔθνοσ and λᾶόσ used for the Jews; plural ἔθνη always refers to Gentiles. In the face of these prophecies, the Jews ignored the Gentiles, *Elsley.* "*Gentiles*" first named, as their conversion precedes the Jews', *Ford.*

---

33. *And Joseph and his mother marvelled at those things which were spoken of him.*

Joseph. Luke i. 27. **Mother.** Joseph not called father of Jesus.

Marvelled. At the divine evidence of their previous views.

Fresh wonder at each new sign, filled their minds.

No outward facts prepared them for the mysterious welcome of their Son, in His Father's house. *i. e. the temple.*

ἦν remnant of early simplicity for ησαν, *Beza.* 'Ιωσὴφ, *Oosterzee, Bengel, W. & W.* πἄτὴρ retained, *Mayor, Tischendorf. Brown, Olshausen, Alford.* Cancelled by *Lachmann.*

---

34. *And Simeon blessed them, and said unto Mary his mother, Behold, this child is set for the fall and rising again of many in Israel; and for a sign which shall be spoken against;*

Blessed. Inspired, a pledge of Jehovah to fulfil his words.

Mary. Simeon hints the Divine paternity of the child.

Behold. Solemnly directs attention of the hearer.

Set. Gr. *lieth.* "Behold I lay in Zion" (appoint). Isaiah xxviii. 16.

A figure taken from a stone in path of travellers.

Divinely set, but ever caused by man's own unbelief. 1 Peter ii. 8.
Many eyes fixed upon Him, many tongues against Him.
Fall. Proud *stumble* at our *foundation* stone.
Unbelief alone ruins. "Savor of life," &c. 2 Cor. ii. 16.
"Rock of Salvation." Psa. lxxxix. 26, is the place of shipwreck.
Jews and Greeks stumbled at His birth and death. 1 Cor. i. 23.
His self-denying doctrines, His holy life, His trade.
The first hint of unbelief, *opposing* Messiah's throne.
Angels had only announced great joy.
Fall. 1. It is not otherwise. 2. It cannot. 3. It ought not. 4. It will not be otherwise.
The Gospel, the great *Touchstone* of moral character.
Men perish without God's urging. "Love death." Pro. viii. 36.
Spirit quenched, is withdrawn. Mercies despised tend to ruin.
Privileges high; condemnation deep. Jo. xv. 22. Mat. xi. 23.
Rising. Not "again," but for the fall and rising of many.
Spoken. Satan's malice, man's contempt. Isaiah liii. 3.
Men, however diverse in customs, agree in maligning Jesus.
Sign. Set for a mark. Job xvi. 13. For signs. Isaiah viii. 18.
Implies pointed hatred, and deliberate malice.
Against, called Glutton. Matt. xi. 19. Insane. Mark iii. 21.
Had a devil. John viii. 52. Blasphemed. Mark xiv. 64.
At Antioch. Acts xiii. 45. At Ephesus. Acts xix. 9. Rome. Acts xxviii. 22.

Κεῖται shall be, *Tyndale.* Lies in my arms, *Meyer.* Appointed for, *Mayer.* Mistranslate to vindicate God from being the Author of Sin, *Michaelis.* "*Fall.*" Penitence preceding conversion, *Alford, Bengel, Brown.* Wilfully and finally impenitent, *Oosterzee, Grotius.* Disappointed as to a temporal Messiah, *Le Clerc.* "*Rising.*" Resurrection, *Tyndale.* αὐτοὺσ Jesus and parents, *Poole.* Parents, *Bengel.* σημεῖον, figure from a target, *Macknight.*

---

35. *(Yea, a sword shall pierce through thy own soul also;) that the thoughts of many hearts may be revealed.*

A Sword. A javelin used in Thrace.
The infamous treatment of Jesus, a dart in a mother's heart.
This casts a shade over the joyful tone of the prophecy.
Mercies and trials go hand in hand with saints.
Thoughts. Gr. reasonings. Disputations, indices of the heart. N.T.

Ambitious thoughts of a Messiah were sadly disappointed.
Hearts. Bible regards the heart, the central point of personal life.
Errors of the head less dangerous, than those of the heart.
Believers with a right heart, may hold erroneous creeds.
We need the head for *life*, but the heart for *death* also.
Revealed. Wherever Christ goes, His claims *compel* a decision.
Jesus ever appears a judge, during the progress of the race.
Continued *neutrality* towards Him, is impossible.
No mask can long keep the chief desires of man *secret*.
Self-love may work secretly, but unfolds powerfully.
Life a scene of constant *unfolding* of character. Mat. xiii. 30.

"*Sword.*" Mary's martyrdom, *Epiph*, *Lightfoot*. Her woe at the cross, *Euthymius*. Sorrows of repentance, including Mary herself before receiving Jesus as Lord, *Alford*, *Olshausen*. Alternations of hope and fear concerning Him, *Brown*. "*Soul.*" The very heart, *Tyndale*.

---

36. *And there was one Anna, a prophetess, the daughter of Phanuel, of the tribe of Aser: she was of a great age, and had lived with a husband seven years from her virginity.*

Anna. Heb. *gracious*. Another of the pious circle of Jerusalem.
Prophetess. The spirit of Deborah and Huldah rested on her.
Phanuel or Peniel "vision of God." Gen. xxxii. 30.
Aser. This tribe returned not after the captivity. 2 Kings xvii. 6
Tribe dwelt near Carmel in the rich plains of Esdraelon.
"Dipped his foot in oil, had iron and brass shoes." Deut. xxxiii. 24, 25.
Others fought Sisera, but "Aser remained in the creek." Judges v. 17.
Husband, not named, but her father is.
Seven years married, the rest is honored widowhood.
Her tender fidelity in treasuring her husband's memory.
Jews anciently highly praised characters of this class.
Prophetess as one celebrating God's praises, a female teacher. 1 Cor. xiv. 3. *Stier*.
She brought up Mary. *Sepp*.

37. *And she was a widow of about fourscore and four years, which departed not from the temple, but served God with fastings and prayers night and day.*

Widow. Gr. *bereaved*. "The widow's God." Psa lxviii. 5. No false God ever bore this name.

A term of loneliness, helplessness, and woe, in all languages.

Eighty-four. Extreme old age, and infant Jesus, in contrast.

Departed. Loved God's house. Psa. lxxxiv. 2. Model Christian female.

Forsaken and forgotten by the world, but not by God.

" In Christ neither male nor female, but faith." Gal. v. 6.

Departed not, till her patience was crowned at last.

Aged saints feel the need of prayer. " Grey hairs a crown." Pro. xvi. 31.

Temple. Luke i. 9. **Served.** Females had no public service. Ex. xxxviii. 8.

The extreme retiredness of Oriental females, explains this.

A screen now separates them in Eastern synagogues.

Fastings. Nature and seasons of fasting. Luke v. 35. See Notes.

Prayer. Luke i. 10. Never weary while communing with God.

Regular hours of temple worship nine A.M. and three P.M.

Night. Songs, sung in night watches. Psa. cxxxiv. 1. Job xxxv. 10.

The first breakings of the silence of the grave by songs. Isaiah xxvi. 19.

Music at night, sweet ; discordant sounds are hushed.

Day. Prayer and praise must be unceasing. 1 Thess. v. 17. Lev. x. 7.

Next to angels, the aged celebrate the coming of Christ, hope of future life. 2 Tim. i. 10.

ὡσ—ἕωσ, *Meyer*, *Oosterzee*, *Tischendorf*. Aged 103, *W. & W.* "*Temple.*" Females had no office there, *Lightfoot*. Deaconesses in primitive Church. Rom. xvi. 1. *Servant*, Gr., deaconess, *Chrysostom*, *Epiph.* Office abolished, Council of Laodicea. Council of Nice' forbade laying hands on them. Found in Constantinople in 12 century, *Herzog's Cyclo.* "*Night*" service more solemn, *Alford.* Copts near Thebes spend a night monthly, in tents around their roofless church.

---

38. *And she coming in that instant gave thanks likewise unto the Lord, and spake of him to all them that looked for redemption in Jerusalem.*

Coming. Gr. Suddenly entering, joining in the praise.

That instant. Gr. hour, of Simeon's blessing.

Many expected the Messiah, but were not looking for *Jesus.*

Thanks. *First female testimony to Christ.* 1. Excited by long expectations. 2. Based on personal sight. 3. Given with full candor. 4. Sealed by holy walk. 5. Crowned by a happy old age.

All. "A little flock." Luke xii. 32. Among the thousands of Judah.

Looked. Joint expectants of mercy, will be sharers of His praise.

Redemption. The yoke lay heavily on the Jewish nation.
Freedom from temporal bondage, and spiritual tyranny.
The daughter of Phanuel, the first preacher of Christ in Jerusalem.
Anna richly rewarded, for her pious assiduity in watching.

ἐπισ. coming suddenly, *Olshausen.* Standing by, *Brown.* ἀνθωμο. Praised in turn, *Oosterzee.* Publicly acknowledged, *Bengel.* Responsively, *Brown.* κυριω. To Jesus, as Simeon called Him *Messiah, Doddridge.* θεῳ refers to the *Father, Tischendorf, Lange, Oosterzee.* *To all,* implies an *audience,* perhaps the hour of prayer. *Alford.*

---

39. *And when they had performed all things according to the law of the Lord, they returned into Galilee, to their own city Nazareth.*

Harmonists here insert the records of *the visit of the Magi.* Matt. ii. 1.
The flight of Mary and Joseph into Egypt. Matt. ii. 14.
And the massacre of the babes of Bethlehem by Herod. Matt. ii. 16. All omitted by Luke.
Returned, from Egypt to Nazareth, as bid by the angel. Matt. ii. 20.
The gold of the "wise men" help to bear their expenses.
When God has a work, *means* will never be wanting.
When the Tabernacle needs gold, Pharaoh's treasures supply it. Ex. xii. 36.
When the Temple is to be rebuilt, Babylon has to pay its share. Ez. vii. 15.
Galilee. Luke i. 26. **Nazareth.** Luke i. 26. Their home.
Our Lord reveals Himself only to an elect few.
He then retires for 30 years, to an obscure place. Phil. ii. 7.
The *silence* of the Bible, not the least sign of its *divinity.*
He waits His Father's command to reveal Himself.
At a set time, He will preach, work wonders, and die.

ἐτέλεσαν. At the Presentation an old man and woman are attendants. Poor mother, equally poor husband, with the Lord, an infant, in his arms. Verily God's ways are not our ways. Matthew's account of Magi, &c., Luke had not *heard, Alford.*—If not untrue, unquestionably an irreverent note, *Author.* Events before the Presentation, *Lange.* After, *Oosterzee.* Different traditions, *Olshausen.* "*Returned.*" About to settle in Bethlehem to educate Jesus, *Foote.*

40. And the child grew, and waxed strong in spirit, filled with wisdom; and the grace of God was upon him.

Child. Sinless in infancy, and innocent in childhood.
His manhood mysterious, union of humanity and Divinity.
To Him the *Source* of life, *old age*, alone, was unsuitable.
Strong, in spirit; evident tokens of innate Divinity.
Other children unfold inherent depravity of nature.
To others, He must have seemed an "incarnate angel," born on earth instead of heaven.
Filled with the fulness of the Godhead, from His Incarnation. Col. ii. 9.
Wisdom. His Divine wisdom at 12 illustrates this point.
Grace. Divine regard manifested increasingly toward *Him*.
By nature, all others "are children of wrath." Eph. ii. 3.

ηὔξ. body. ἐκρ. the soul, *Alford.* εν πνεύματι cancelled, *Tischendorf Tregelles, Lachmann.* Retained, *Oosterzee.* χάρισ, greatness, *Wetstein.* Graceful dignity, blended with superhuman authority and sweetness, *Campbell, Mayor.* Divine comeliness, used by *Homer* and *Virgil, Wakefield.* God's love in active exercise, *Olshausen, Brown.* Now first conscious of His Divinity. *Olshausen.* Proves His human soul against Arians, 325 A. D., *Council of Nice.* Unhistorical. He learned wisdom of Egyptians, *Paulus.* (Rationalistic and sceptical.) Divinity then became incarnate, *Quesnel.* No foundation for this statement, *Ed.*

---

41. Now his parents went to Jerusalem every year at the feast of the passover.

Christ at 12 years old in the Temple.

Went. Gr. *accustomed.* Public and family worship go hand in hand.
But one incident recorded of a life of 30 years.
Such historical *reticence*, indicates a *Divine origin.*
The journey fatiguing, troublesome, and expensive.
No danger, Archelaus had been banished by Augustus.
Jerusalem. Every year. They may have gone oftener.
Parents are enjoined to observe God's appointed ordinances.
Marriage leads them nearer to heaven or hell.
Elkanah to Hannah "Do what seemeth thee good." 1 Sam. 1. 23.
Rachel to Jacob "What God hath said unto thee, do." Gen. xxxi. 16.
Their Son was better able to teach them, than Rabbis.
"My soul fainteth for the courts &c." Ps. lxxxiv. 2. "God loveth gates of Zion. Ps. lxxxvii. 2.
Passover. A lamb. "Christ a Lamb without blemish." 1 Peter i. 19.

Set apart 4 days. Christ prepared for the Sacrifice.
Bitter herbs, Christ received with bitter repentings.
No bone broken. Fulfilled in Jesus. Jo. xix, 36.
Blood sprinkled on the doors. Christ's on the heart.
No leavened bread eaten, no leaven of pride or malice. 1 Cor. v. 8.
A herald announced through all Judea the coming feast, Nisan.
The angel *passed over* the Hebrew dwellings. Ex. xii.

42. ***And when he was twelve years old, they went up to Jerusalem after the custom of the feast.***

Twelve. The established Jewish age of first sharing the Passover.
Went up, to Jerusalem, both as a metropolis, and high position.
The city stands among the highest mountains of Judea.
Custom, when holy, deserves attentive obedience.
Feast. 1 *Passover*—Deliverance of the first-born. Ex. xii. 43.
2. *Pentecost* or Harvest home, fifty days after Passover. Lev. xxiii. 16.
3. *Tabernacles*, or their tenting 40 years in the wilderness. Lev. xxiii. 34.
4. *Purim*—Deliverance from Haman, the Persian. Jo. v. 1. Esth. ix. 28.
Three times a year, all the males went up to Jerusalem. Ex. xxxiv. 23.
Women, according to the maxims of Hillel, bound to go up once a year, to Passover.

At 12, called "Children of the Commandment," *Rabbis, Lightfoot.* Son of the law, *Grotius.* "*Feast*," *Nisan*, the first month of the Jewish year after the Exodus, corresponds nearly to our *April*, depended on the full moon. *Purim*, celebrated in March. *Tabernacle*, 15 days after new moon, *October*. Feast of trumpets, *origin* unknown. Lev. xxiii. 24. Dedication of the Temple after pollution by Antiochus. Jo. x. 22. The 7th year Jubilee. All slaves of Jewish origin freed. Aliens left in servitude, *Lewes Antiq.* "*Custom*," to go with his parents, *Cyril Alex.* To worship, *Greswell, Ellicott.*

---

43. ***And when they had fulfilled the days, as they returned, the child Jesus tarried behind in Jerusalem.***

Fulfilled. Observed all the solemn rites of the seven days.
Days. Seven for unleavened bread, one for Passover.
Returned. Jerusalem is good, so also is Nazareth.
Work and worship, serve to relieve each other.
Child. Youth always welcome at God's house. Matt. xix. 14.
Redeemer enthroned, listens to their infant praise. Matt. xxi. 15.

David, on his throne, loved to lead the youthful band. Psa. viii. 2.
Behind. Jesus sometimes hides Himself from the best of saints.
Mother. Joseph, by the Evangelists, never called *Father.*
Mary, unwilling to acknowledge His Divinity, calls Joseph "Father."

"*Fulfilled,*" Jews must remain 7 days. Deut. xvi. 8. Peter and Cleophas left the *third.* Luke xxiv. 18. *Lightfoot.* "*knew not,*" accustomed to his thoughtfulness and obedience, they were free from anxiety, till they discovered he really was not in the company. *Olshausen,* μητηρ, *Mayer.* οἱ γονεῖς, *Griesbach, Lachmann, Tischendorf.*

---

44. But they, supposing him to have been in the company, went a day's journey; and they sought him among their *kinsfolk and acquaintance.*

Company. Orientals dare not travel, nor dwell alone.
Villages stand like islands in the ocean—nothing between.
A festal caravan is secure from robbers, and source of pleasure.
Days, &c. Ordinarily now 20 miles—then, likely a few miles.
Sought. Gr. extreme solicitude, the child being the subject of many *miracles.*
His deep reverence, and uniform obedience, afforded great comfort.
Devotion in Him, was nowise disrespect to *them.*
Too many try to seek Jesus *now* among worldly friends.
Oftener is He lost in prosperity, than in adversity.

45. And when they found him not, they turned back again to Jerusalem, seeking him.

Found not. The Son of man, once a lost Son.
Jesus lost amid the world's bustle, and found in the temple.
Losing comfort in Christ, we must look for the *cause.*
Turned back, not to be discouraged, when failing once.

46. And it came to pass, that after three days they found him in the temple, sitting in the midst of the doctors, both hearing them, and asking them questions.

Three days. He teaches his parents, He could live without them.
A type of His disciples losing Him for *three days.*
Found. They had come to pray for guidance and success.
Assured if they could find *God,* they soon would find Jesus.
Temple. Luke i. 9. No time wasted, nor idle company sought.

As a child, He desired ever to be God's servant.
Christ in the Temple, "*The* glory of the latter house." Hag. ii. 9.
Sitting. Pupils sat at the feet of their teachers. Luke x. 39.
In the seat of the scholar, He predicts the Throne of the Teacher.
He could have *taught*, but in humility, He *learns*.
Doctors. 71 members in the Sanhedrim sat on raised seats.
Hearing. "Let every man be swift to hear, slow to speak." Jas. i. 19.
Asking. "*Disputing*" with doctors, a wrong interpretation of his act.
Questions. The teachers carried on their instructions by questions.
Rightly to *question*, the highest wisdom of the learner.
His after teachings intimate the nature of these questions.
He will soon denounce heavy woes on these Rabbis.

"*Sitting.*" Scholars sat on the floor, *Vitringa*, *Kuinoel*, *Trench*. Stood, *Lightfoot*. "*Asking, &c.*" *Discussed*, *De Wette*. A child lecturing, an anomaly with a God of order, *Olshausen*. "*Doctors.*" Rab, lowest; Rabbi, my master, next higher; Rabboni, highest, my great master, *Lightfoot*. Hillel the *Looser*, Shammai the *Binder*, were there, *Ellicott*. Sat among the teachers, not pupils, *Lightfoot*. Questions meant as instructions, *Hall*. Disputing a vulgar error, *Doddridge*. Asking, not teaching, *Stier*.

---

47. *And all that heard him were astonished at his understanding and answers.*

Astonished. Gr. transport of admiration—A child excites astonishment, but shews none. Their surprise greatly increased by His modesty.
His great faith, the cause. David wiser than teachers. Psa. cxix. 100.
He gave men a taste of His Divine knowledge.
Understanding. "I have more understanding than my teachers." Psa. cxix. 99.
Answers. Rabbis must quickly have questioned Him in return.

48. *And when they saw him, they were amazed: and his mother said unto him, Son, why hast thou thus dealt with us? behold, thy father and I have sought thee sorrowing.*

Amazed. Such a scene had not been witnessed before on earth.
Mother. Had Joseph been His father, Mary would not have spoken.
Contrary to all custom the foster father is silent.
Said, *privately*. She could not *rebuke* after such a scene.
Thy father. Knowing the secret mystery, she says not, *parents*.
Father by *representation*, head of the family, *tutor*, *guardian*.
Dealt. The *first* and *last* reproof He ever received.

This word, proof of Mary's infirmity, fretting over her son.
Note Mary's over hasty zeal, and Jesus' heavenly tranquility.
Sought. Those who find Him, have ever sought Him *sorrowing.*
Sorrowing. Betrays the weakness of affection and humanity.
Self love comprehends not Christ's *holy rigor* to friends.
No grief like his, who has *lost* a Saviour *once loved.*
The miracles around His nativity, had already become *dim.*

ἰδοντεσ, Rabbis and spectators, *Campbell.* Parents, *Meyer.* Privately, *Hall, Ellicott, Brown.*

---

49. *And he said unto them, How is it that ye sought me? wist ye not that I must be about my Father's business.*

Said. The *first recorded words of the Redeemer on earth!*
Words of Consecration, Self-denial, Zeal, Sacrifice.
How is it, implies, He gave them *ground* to know him better.
The stupendous miracles of which He was the *subject.*
They should have known *more;* but the heart is *dull.*
With more *faith,* she herself would have led Him hither.
Twelve years of quiet life, found not Mary's faith always *awake.*
Sought. He acknowledges no error, expresses no anxiety.
Wist. Sax, think or know. A *rebuke,* not reproach.
I must. Sacred germ of the Divine *decree.* He bound himself. Heb. x. 7.
My father. Mary said "*Thy* Father," He replies "**My** *Father.*"
"Thy husband, you soon will learn, *is not My* Father."
"*My* Father sought me not, for I am always with *Him.*"
A seal is now set to the angel's mysterious words. Luke i. 32.
A ray now gilds the obscurity of the angel's visit at Nazareth.
The *key note* of the whole future life of the Lord.
His conscious Divinity begins to reveal itself.
The mother of *Our Lord,* must not interfere with His work.
Children if able, may modestly instruct even parents. 1 Sam. xix. 4.
They were not prepared for a direct appeal to *His Father.*
Business. My Father's pleasure, is His only apology.
Implying He would need no further guidance from them.
He clearly claims Jehovah as His Father.
Under that Divine Guide, He could not err, nor stray.
Hereby He claims to be the *Messiah,* the **Son of God.**

τοισ i. e. πράγμασιν, *Calvin, Buxtorf, Besa, Rosenmuller, De Wette, Stier, Alford, Oosterzee.* οικήμασιν, Father's, *Erasmus, Grotius, Bengel, Wetstein, Kuinoel, Olshausen, Meyer, Trench, W. & W., Ellicott, Brown.* Mary says, *thy father and I;* Jesus answers; he is not my father, or I would have been *in his house.* God is my father, therefore I am found *in His House, Theophyl.*, in *Meyer.* Till now Jesus and others had called Joseph his father, but never after this, *Stier.* An unintentional rebuke is given Mary. δεῖ, earing time of human progress, *Olshausen.* Appointed and undertaken course of Christ, *Alford.*

---

50. *And they understood not the saying which he spake unto them.*

Understood not. Until "mother" was changed into "woman." Jo. ii. 4.

And **My Father.** Publicly resounded in the temple.

The Holy mystery again folds up for 18 long years of trial.

We must not despise, what we do not comprehend.

Unto them. Henceforth Joseph disappears from the Gospels.

Mary perhaps dreamed of a Messiah, such as the Jews expected.

"*Understood not.*" Priests are to be *reticent* towards parents, *Quesnel.* Alas! for Rome and prejudice. What neither they, nor Rabbis had taught Him, *Oosterzee.* They considered not attentively, *Grotius.* Their ignorance was *strange, Meyer.* Because the unfolding was so gradual, *Stier.* O. T. veil yet upon these, *Olshausen.* His parents understood not even the *first* wonders of His birth, *Alford.*

---

51. *And he went down with them, and came to Nazareth, and was subject unto them: but his mother kept all these sayings in her heart.*

Down. Roads descend every way from Jerusalem.

Nazareth. Luke i. 26. His heart drew him to the temple, duty calls to Galilee.

Subject. Gr. habitually subject.

He could attend *Divine*, and not neglect *filial* duties.

The Ruler of the world, an obedient child. Isa. ix. 6. 1 Cor. xv. 25.

He left Heaven, now His Father's house, for an humble home.

The settled custom of Jews taught sons a trade.

"*Nazareth.*" Place, out of which men fancied no good thing could come, only truly good one had his dwelling, *Vers. Germania.* "*Subject.*" Mark vi. 3 proves He wrought at

His father's trade, *Oosterzee*, denied by *Alexander*. "Christ among men made yokes and ploughs as worker in wood, &c.," *Justin Martyr*, 100-150 A. D. ῥήματα passages, acts as well as words. A Hebraism, *Heyne*. Used thus by *Sophocles*. *Blackwall*. Things, *Rosenmuller*, *Wetstein*.

---

52. *And Jesus increased in wisdom and stature, and in favour with God and man.*

Jesus. Luke xxxi. **Increased,** disclosing the Incarnate Deity.
Moses endured, and prayed 40 years in Midian, till called.
A 1000 *years* with God, in His plans, as *one day*. 2 Peter. iii. 8.
Wisdom, only as a *man*. Samuel a child. 1 Sam. ii. 26.
No human learning furnished His mind. Jo. vii. 15.
Youth, increasing in years, and decreasing in knowledge, hopeless.
Stature. The Spirit minutely gives proofs of His *humanity*. Luke xxiv. 43.
Favor, i.e, this was *unfolded* to the eye of man.
His testimony against sin, soon wrought another feeling.
"*Me* the world hateth." Jo. vii. 7. Scene at Nazareth. Luke iv. 28.
God. His friendship essential to our well-being.
Man. Those securing God's, in the end, will have man's interest also.
Men have attempted to tell us, *how* these things were.
The Bible *silent*, the wisest know just *nothing at all*. 1 Tim. iii. 16.
The Incarnation is a truth for *humble faith*, and *adoring love*.
For thirty years our Lord dwelt in obscurity.
Nathaniel, only 9 miles distant, never heard of Him.

προέκοπτεν 1. Cut through thickets. 2. Make progress, *Wetstein*. Disclosed *Ellicott*. ἡλικία stature, *Beza*, *Bengel*, *Meyer*. Age, *Calvin*, *De Wette*, *Alford*, *Oosterzee*, *Brown*. Whole physical life, *Olshausen*. Wise beyond His age, *Wetstein*. σοφία, derived from Rabbis. Egyptian sages. Learned Essenes, *Paulus*, *Meyer*. Literally used, *Waterland*. Natural genius, *Hase*. Result of pious training, fine scenery, reading Scriptures, journey to Jerusalem, and heavenly communion, *Oosterzee*. χάριτι flashings forth of divinity, beauty, John xviii. 6, *Ellicott*. Divine Good-will, and approval, *Olshausen*. Grace of soul and body, *Bengel*. Luke shews historic fidelity in his silence concerning Christ's retirement, *Oosterzee*. His great work in fact was then being wrought, *the obedience of one* by which many were made righteous, *Alford*.

CHAPTER III.

1. *NOW in the fifteenth year of the reign of Tiberius Cesar, Pontius Pilate being governor of Judea, and Herod being tetrarch of Galilee, and his brother Philip tetrarch of Iturea and of the region of Trachonitis, and Lysanias the tetrarch of Abilene.*

Now. Eighteen years of the life of Jesus utterly veiled.

Divinity of the Bible noted in its *silence*, as in *speaking*: lesson of humility.

Fifteenth. Year of Rome 779, and autumn of A.D. 27.

Reign. The date when Tiberius was associated with Augustus.

Tib. Cæsar. Successor to Augustus, and second Emperor; born 42 B.C.

Won the esteem of the people, and love of his soldiers, by victories and kindness.

Honored by four triumphs, he ascended the throne with the brightest prospects.

But no sooner had obtained imperial power, than he displayed his odious character.

Talented, ambitious, cruel, licentious, infamous, inhuman.

Brutal towards his wife, and mother; poisoned his nephews.

Kept secret spies as royal pensioners in many noble families.

It is said, that there was not a noble family in Rome that escaped his vengeance.

At length, dreading the rage of his people, he entrusted the government to Sejanus.

Shutting himself up in the Island of Capreae, for 10 years, indulged in infamous crimes.

Falling into a swoon, his attendants thinking him dead, proclaimed Caligula.

Recovering, he would have punished them, but they smothered him, A.D. 37. Aged 79.

Pilate. Character and history. Luke xxiii. 1. See Notes.

Governor. *i.e.* Procurator, decided civil and criminal cases.

Judea. Geography and divisions. Luke i. 5. See Notes.

Herod, *Antipas*, son of Herod the Great, and Malthace a Samaritan.

Made by Augustus, Tetrarch, *i.e.* "Governor of a fourth."

Weak, cunning, sensual, capricious, superstitious, and yet a Sadducee.

He built *Tiberias* in honor of *his Patron.* Murdered John the Baptist.

Went to Rome for a *crown*, was defeated by a nephew.

Banished with Herodias, to Lugdunum (Lyons in Gaul,) died in Spain.

All *three names* linked with political and moral *misery.*

Earth in the hands of the wicked, mourned. Job. ix. 24.
Mankind, like a starving crowd, in a besieged city. *Seneca.*
But the "stone cut out of the mountain" will overthrow and destroy all evil powers, Dan. ii. 34.
Galilee. Geography and Divisions. Luke i. 26. See Notes.
Philip. Son of Herod the Great and Cleopatra of Jerusalem.
The only *virtuous* member of a proud and wicked family.
Married Salome, rebuilt Paneas, calling it *Cæsarea.* Matt. xvi. 13.
Rebuilt Bethsaida, calling it Julias, died there A.D. 34.
Iturea. From Jetur, son of Ishmael. 1 Chron. i. 31. It lay N.E. of Jordan.
Trachonitis. North-eastern part of Palestine; mountainous.
Lysanias. Unknown, probably a descendant of Lysanias son of Ptolemy, put to death by Antony.
Abilene. Abila, 18 miles from Damascus, near Baalbec.
These facts shew Luke's accurate historical knowledge.
Dates of Christ's birth, death, resurrection, and ascension, not so accurately noted as this.

"Fifteenth." Chronology omitted by Matt. and Mark, coincides with John's imprisonment, *Wieseler, Ellicott.* Common era, 4 years too late, *Usher.* Tiberius' statue is now in the Louvre. He and our Lord the only ones who received divine worship at that day, *Conybeare.* ἡγεμον. administration, *Horne.* Lieutenant, *Tyndale.*

---

2. *Annas and Caiaphas being the high priests, the word of God came unto John the son of Zacharias in the wilderness.*

Annas. Deposed, but secured office for his *five sons.*
Caiaphas. Son-in-law to Annas. In office from 27 A.D. to 36.
He was a Sadducee and counselled Christ's death. Jo. xi. 49, 50.
Examined Christ before the Sanhedrim, and condemned Him. Matt. xxvi. 65-66.
He persecuted the Church. Acts iv. 6. Was deposed by Vitellius.
High in privilege like Balaam, we fear, like him perished.
High Priest. There could be but *one* legal H. P. in office at one time. Luke i. 15.
Word of God. Special divine message to preach *repentance.*
Ministers should have an *inward* and an *outward* call.
John. History and character. Luke i. 13. See Notes.

Prophet. Luke i. 70. See Notes. **Voice.** His whole *life* a *burning sermon* on repentance.

Crying. An exclamation, as Hark! one is crying.

Original, *crying aloud*, indicates his vehement manner.

Wilderness. Luke iii. 2. See Notes.

Prepare. Reformation must begin *then* and *there*.

Clearing away of all obstacles to the Redeemer's approach.

His paths. A highway for the Lord to return with His elect. Isa. lvii. 14. lxii. 10-11.

Troops preceded Titus, preparing the way for the army.

Highways in Judea and the East scarcely passible, for a single camel.

No roads ever repaired except by careless reckless rulers.

"Isaiah," sawn asunder, Tradition of *Talmud. Fathers.* Heb. xi. 37. His histories of Uzziah. 2 Chr. xxvi. 22. And of Hezekiah are lost. The *authenticity* of Isaiah's prophecies settled by *Kleinert.* Questioned by *Spinoza, Eichhorn* Some modern critics suppose there were two Isaiahs, 1st wrote Book of, to chap. 40, 2nd wrote the remainder. Great difference in style the assigned reason. Contrary opinion founded on 1. Unanimous testimony of Jewish and Christian traditions. 2. Evidence of N. T. quotations. 3. Unity of design. *Smith's Dict.* Isaiah. "*paths.*" Semiramis, marching into Medea. had her way prepared, *Diodorus*, Caligula, his way, *Suetonius*. Xerxes, his way, *Justin*.

---

5. *Every valley shall be filled, and every mountain and hill shall be brought low; and the crooked shall be made straight, and the rough ways* shall *be made smooth.*

Valley. Typical: humble, exalted; despairing rebuked. Isaiah xl. 4.

Mountain. Implies; proud, humbled; difficulties levelled. Isa. liv. 10. Mic. i. 4.

Hills. Obstacles high as hills, brought down by the Gospel.

Low. Loftiness of men brought down, haughtiness made low. Isa. ii. 17.

Far easier to level hills, than subdue the proud will.

Crooked. Sinners converted. Truth repairs deformities of sin.

Rough ways. Asperities of temper, passion, plans, and habits.

Selfishness, pride, sensuality, bigotry, fanaticism.

Thorns and briers, spring, like sins, *spontaneously*.

Valleys and hills. Spiritual states, *Olshausen.* For forty years the pillar of fire smoothed the road for Israel, *Rabbis, Lightfoot.* Repentance as hard to the self-righteous as levelling mountains, *Stier.*

6. *And all flesh shall see the salvation of God.*

Flesh. All unsanctified humanity in the millenium. Psa. lxv. 2.
Had the church been faithful, all nations would have *heard* the Gospel.
The "middle wall" is now levelled by the Gospel, all men are equal before God.
See. All barriers removed, nothing will then hinder men from believing.
Salvation. The O. T. view of Christ's atonement, *completed.*
A prophetic glance at the millenial reign of grace. Isa. lxvi. 12.

"*Salvation of God.*" The Messiah "*shall see*" every object that could cast a shadow removed; every point exposed to light, *Bengel.*

---

7. *Then said he to the multitude that came forth to be baptised of him, O generation of vipers, who hath warned you to flee from the wrath to come?*

Multitude. Gr. *crowd.* Reckless curiosity urges Oriental mobs.
Pharisees, envious and jealous of their vain *traditions.*
Sadducees though sneering at futurity as a dream, are anxious. Scepticism hollow.
Baptised. Luke iii. 3. See Notes.
Generation. Gr. Ye *brood of vipers.* Sin's intense malignity.
Vipers. Serpent from 2 to 5 feet long, an inch thick, flat headed.
Ash color, brown spots, 16 small teeth in each jaw.
One tooth hollow, through which poison distils.
They were thought to possess mysterious knowledge and power.
Traditions of *all nations* filled with references to them. Luke x. 19.
Points to Satan. Rev. xii. 9. Diabolical nature of hypocrisy.
Crafty, malignant, poisoners: cunning enemies.
Ungrateful to benefactors, *descendants* of the same.
Seed of the woman always at war with the seed of the serpent.
With various results, a contest of 6000 years has been going on.
It approaches a crisis, yet men love to hear "smooth things." Is. xxx. 10.
Nature of *love* is, plainly to call evil, evil.
The world intends to *please*, at any sacrifice of truth or of heaven.
Morbid fears dread giving offence. Silence is treachery to the soul.
It is no charity to flatter the wicked. Gal. i. 20.
A religion without threatening, is not of Christ.
N. T. unfolds a revelation of wrath, not less terrible than the Old.

Solemn tones of truth *attract*, rather than *repel* the multitude.
No pulpits attract more than those, proclaiming the *law* in *love*.
Teachers of a God of mercy, without justice, find *thin* churches.
John's severity to sinners, marked with humility towards Christ.

Warned. *Forewarned.* None perish innocent. Rom. ii. 15.

You. Emphatic. Denotes *surprise* at *such* a class coming.

Wrath. No motives as strong as those of the Bible.

To come. "The mills of God grind slowly, yet they grind exceedingly small."

---

* ὄχλος, confused crowd. δῆμος, regular assembly, *Gesenius*. ὑπέδ. secretly give a glimpse at anything, *Alexander*.

---

8. *Bring forth therefore fruits worthy of repentance, and begin not to say within yourselves, We have Abraham to our Father: for I say unto you, That God is able of these stones to raise up children unto Abraham.*

Bring forth. Gr. a continual habit, not a single act.

Fruits. Humility, patience, faith, love, equity, mercy.
Profession without fruit only sears the conscience. 2 Cor. iv. 2.
"The talk of the lips only tendeth to penury." Pro. xiv. 23.
"Herein is My Father glorified that ye bear *much fruit*." Jo. xv. 8.

Repentance, always accompanied by faith, if *genuine*. See Notes. Luke iii. 3.
The theme of all true ministers in every age. Mark i. 15.
"Godly sorrow," leading to reformation, forsaking forms. Acts xx. 21.
Sincerity, "a broken heart and contrite spirit." Psa. li. 17.
Motives to repentance found in, 1. Divine precepts. 2. Penalty. 3. Promises.
Delays, dangerous, Time may fail, or Spirit's aid be refused. Jo. iii. 27.
Habits are formed. Jer. xiii. 23. The *will* inefficient. Jo. vi. 44.
The flower of existence spent in sin; blind and lame, a mere wreck, brought at last to God. Gal. vi. 10.

Begin. John anticipates their stereotyped objections. Matt. xii. 25.

To say. Secret thoughts are heard on earth, and in heaven. Prov. xxi. 2. Luke ii. 35.

Within. Conscience stung is *ashamed* to speak out. Ps. xiv. 1.

Abraham. Life and character. Luke i. 55. See Notes.

Father. Pharisees taught that no child of Abraham could perish.

His name used as a *shield* to turn aside the arrows of truth.
Ties of blood, ancestral piety, or rites of Church, cannot save.
Abraham's *blood*, without his *faith*, will avail only to condemn.
Church of Luther, Calvin, Knox, Cranmer, Whitfield,
Can give the unrenewed *no* passport to heaven.
Paul in the pulpit would perish, if Paul were not *in Christ*.

God able. No one can limit His sovereignty, and be innocent. Ps. lxxviii. 41.

Stones. Jews always angry at any allusion to the *calling* of the *Gentiles*. Luke iv. 28.
God is not tied to *succession* in the Church.
There is a Successor without a church, and a church without Succession.
They forgot that the calling of the Jews was an act of Sovereign *grace*.

Πατέρα As Members of the Theocracy by birth and circumcision, *Lange*. λίθων Doubtful, if allusion to Gentiles, *Olshausen*. To original creation out of dust. *Oosterzee*. Gentiles worshipped stones, *Clemens*. Hearts hard as stone, *Jerome*, Ironical, *Lightfoot*.

---

9. *And now also the axe is laid unto the root of the trees: every tree therefore which bringeth not forth good fruit is hewn down and cast into the fire.*

Axe. Anciently of *Hatchet*-shape, and tied with thongs to the handle.
Emblem of Divine justice, ever suspended over barren souls.
Ye long for national *deliverance*, beware of national *judgments*.
Jewish nation, the tree; the Romans, the axe.

Is laid. Hebraism; the present for future, intensifies the sense. Jo. iii. 18.
He passes from *possibility* to *certainty* of coming wrath.
In salvation's business, an hour lost, may peril *all*, for eternity.
God's patience, though infinite, to *sinners*, has its *limits*.
What *Justice* lays at the root, *Mercy* leaves *still lying* there.

At the root. Not the useless branches lopped, such warning is ended.
Points to a judgment of extermination in the case of the incorrigible.
Annihilation of the wicked, a *dream*, not found in Scriptures.

Every tree. No class of high, or low, impenitent individuals, excepted.

Bringeth not. Sentence against the barren tree. Pro. i. 24.
1. Surely expected. 2. Perfectly justified. 3. Still to be avoided.

Good fruit. God and men expect fruit from toil. 1 Cor. ix. 7.

Hewn. No height, nor value can save. "God no respecter of persons."
Cast. The fierceness and strength of Almighty justice.
Fire. The type of earth's most exquisite conception of agony.
Brambles in valleys, cedars of Lebanon on "the mount of God."
No fruitless soul, however exalted in mercies, will be spared.

10. *And the people asked him, saying, What shall we do then?*

People. Promiscuous crowds of the dwellers drawn by curiosity.
What. Roused *consciences*, proves John's *power* as a preacher.
Honest hearted ones among them, gave up their hope in Abraham.
Do. The greatest of all questions. "How shall man be just? &c." Job ix. 2.
The soul convinced of sin always first thinks of an *atonement*. Mic. vi. 7.
The young ruler. Mark x. 17. The jailor. Acts xvi. 30. Naaman, 2 Kings, v. 13.
Heathen pour out their *treasures* and *blood* to atone for sin.
With painful earnestness they ask, "Who will show us any good?" Psa. iv. 6.

ὄχλοι, Cretans, *Folk.* Embracing Pharisees and Sadducees, *Stier.* Luke obtained particulars of John's preaching from unknown sources, *Oosterzee.* "*What shall we do?*" A question characteristic of a soul seeking salvation, Acts ii. 37, *Bengel.*

---

11. *He answereth and saith unto them, He that hath two coats, let him impart to him that hath none; and he that hath meat, let him do likewise.*

Two. *Ascetics* deemed it *religion* to have but *one* coat.
Coats. Luke vi. 29. Gr. *tunic.* At first, was worn next the skin. See Notes.
Impart. Jews then sadly failed in the grace of *charity*.
Fanaticism burns out all kindness from the soul.
Sin ever supremely selfish, repelling all claims of mercy. Isa. v. 8.
Covetousness, the thirst of *devouring fire*, self-love, thirsty as earth for rain.
Avarice, selfishness *hoarding*,—prodigality, the same, *indulging*.
A religion without charity, is not from above. Matt. xvi. 24.
Meat. Gr. Any *solid food*, as flesh or vegetables.
John's morality *external*. Jesus bound the *inner* life.

12. *Then came also publicans to be baptized, and said unto him, Master, what shall we do?*

Publicans. Gr. *Tax-gatherers*, infamous with Jews and Greeks.
Taxes were farmed out to Roman nobility, and they underlet to others.
Hated by the Jewish nation as the tools of a *foreign heathen* power.
Despised as far meaner than pagans.
Paid a fixed sum to Rome, and *extorted* for themselves.
Their cupidity made lawful taxes extremely oppressive.
Exceedingly rapacious, the burden was an intolerable grievance.
As officers of Rome, called *traitors* to their country, and to their God.
Rigidly excluded from temple, synagogue, and court.
Nevertheless, the most forlorn and despised of humanity desire to reach heaven.
Our Saviour himself classed them with *harlots*. Matt. xxi. 31.
In parable of the publican, He selects the *veriest outcasts* of men.
In selecting this abhorred caste for *apostles*, He enraged the Jews.
None but the most reckless Jews dare assume the office.
Vespasian wrote on Sabinus' monument, "HONEST PUBLICAN."
Under lawful business direst evils have been inflicted.
Baptized. The history, object and mode. Luke iii. 16. See Notes.
Master. G. *Teacher.* Instruction *the* work of the ministry.
Publicans shew more respect than any other class, *Bengel.*

τι "*what.*" How shall we show the genuineness of our repentance, *Stier.*

---

13. *And he said unto them, Exact no more than that which is appointed you.*

Exact. The nation *condemning* the office, John *sanctions* it.
He requires *none* of them to *leave* their lawful calling.
But to honor the king, and serve their God. 1 Peter, ii. 17.
Obedience to Cæsar; but to avoid oppressing the people.
Defrauding government, is thought quite a *venial* offence.
Corporate members at times perform actions, which no one *singly* could satisfy his *conscience* in doing.

διατετ. arranging for a levy. *πράσ.* to *extort*, as by the bastinado. In Turkey all classes now try to conceal their means. The rich live like beggars to avoid extortion, *Chardin.*

14. *And the soldier likewise demanded of him, saying, And what shall we do? And he said unto them, Do violence to no man, neither accuse any falsely; and be content with your wages.*

Soldiers. Jews enlisted as auxiliaries under *Xerxes*, *Alexander*. *Pompey*, *Antiochus*, *Demetrius*, and the *Ptolemies*.
If soldiers Gentile, John would have forbidden *idolatry*.
War presents great obstacles to soldiers' religious interests.
The state *must* be defended, but not with the price of *souls*.
But for the *lawless*, civil rulers were a useless burden.
Violence. Ancient soldiers were *defiant* to friends and foes.
Quartered on families, insolent and licentious spies.
Many in the British and American armies have been burning and shining lights.
Christianity will remove the cause of all war on earth.
Accuse. Gr. *act the sycophant;* a flatterer, or busy informer.
Wages. Gr. *Fish* eaten with bread; *rations*, then, soldiers pay.
Roman soldiers, first paid in barley and salt fish.
Three oboli (cents) per day, at times they slew their leaders, for wages.
A warning against mutiny, which is a sin against God.

στρατευ. Men going to battle. Herod's army passing at that time, *Stier*. διασει. Intimidate, *Brown*. Put in fear, shake by violence, *Major*. Bullying character of all half civilized troops. Soldiers noted for rapine, *Tacitus*, *Juvenal*. ςυκοφ. An informer against those who exported figs in Athens contrary to law. *Potter*, *Ant*. Calumniate under pretence of law, Gen. xliii. 18, Sept., *Bengel*. Lay vexatious charges of disaffection, *Alford*. ὀψων. First eaten with bread, used for that which buys bread, *Major*.

---

15. *And as the people were in expectation, and all men mused in their hearts of John, whether he were the Christ, or not.*

Expectation. The *wonders* of John's birth, and Christ's, the cause.
Daniel's seventy weeks were expiring. The sceptre seemed departing.
All the great lines of prophecy converging.
A corrupt nation needed, and cried loudly for a Reformer.
Society thoroughly sick of life, and wearied with hope. Anything that *hinted* of a change was welcomed by all.
All men. General terms, but confined to Palestine.
Mused. Gr. *pondered.* Faithful ministers arouse the mind.
Unrenewed world strives to remain *thoughtless*. Isa. i. 3.

John. Luke i. 13. **Christ.** Luke ii. 11. Heb. and Gr. *Anointed.* Luke ix. 20. See Notes.
Had John come in *grandeur*, all would have welcomed him.
His moral strictness, deeply impressed the multitude.
His retiring modesty, proves his moral greatness. Acts xiv. 15.
By John; Christ was now standing and knocking at the door.

Whether *he himself might be, &c.* Implies they could hardly believe it, yet could not help asking, Whether, &c.? *Brown.* Pharisees generally rejected John's baptism, *Andrews.* The fact of their thinking thus of John, shows, that the coarse idea of Messiah's temporal glory had not yet taken root, *Bengel.*

---

16. *John answered, saying unto* them all, *I indeed baptize you with water; but one mightier than I cometh, the latchet of whose shoes I am not worthy to unloose: he shall baptize you with the Holy Ghost and with fire.*

Answered. A deputation from the Sanhedrim had inquired. Jo. i. 19.
Baptize. Luke iii. 3. **Water** can only cleanse the flesh. See Notes.
It marks the intimate connection between *Atonement* and *Sanctification.*
Mightier, in name, nature, wisdom, power and aims.
Superior to John. 1. Sinless. 2. Office. 3. Miracles. 4. Baptism.
Note an infinite chasm between Christ and His holiest minister.
Latchet, to *unloose*, office of a servant, the guest entering the house.
Shoes. Gr. *Underbound.* Sandals, then universally worn.
Made of leather or wood, bound to the feet by a thong, or *latchet.*
Of interlaced palm leaves, or papyrus stalks.
Sandals in Egyptian tombs, and in Turkey, highly ornamental. Sol. Song. 7. 1.
"To loose a sandal," was to enter a house or temple. Jos. v. 15.
"To bind them," was to prepare for a journey. Acts xii. 8.
Unloosed by the seller, and given to the *buyer*, of real estate. Ruth iv. 7.
Slaves went barefoot. Prodigal thus had *sunk.* Luke xv. 22.
The rich, when mourning, also went barefoot. Is. xx. 2-4.
Roman soldiers had shoes, soles covered with *nails.* Deut. xxxiii. 25.
John's humility, contrasts with the lofty views of the people.
One word, could have enlisted thousands with him.
Worthy. He retires into the back ground, and rejoices in his abasement.
Unloosed, especially at baths, and borne by newly bought slaves,

Baptize. Luke iii. 3. See Notes. Jesus baptized no one, but with His Spirit. Jo. iv. 2.

Holy Ghost. Luke i. 15. Third Person in the Adorable Trinity.

Fire. Baptism foretold. Is. iv. 4. Jer. v. 14. Pentecost. Acts ii. 3.

Transforms a cold *iron* mass, into its own *glowing nature.*

The Spirit transforms the soul, into image of *Love* and *Light.*

Fire, chosen emblem of Jehovah in His manifestations.

Examples. Flaming Cherubim, Gen. iii. 24. Burning lamp, Gen. xv. 17.

Burning bush, Ex. iii. 2. Divine Majesty, Ex. xix. 18. Wrath, Num. xi. 2.

Angel, Jud. xiii. 20. Mount Carmel, 1 Kings xviii. 38. Sacrifice, Ex. xxx. 9.

Consuming, 2 Kings i. 10. Chariots, 2 Kings ii. 11; vi. 17.

Cloven tongues, Acts ii. 3. Mal. iii. 2. God's *Word*, Jer. xxiii. 29.

Baptism of the Spirit, 1, of *Truth* to enlighten us. 2, of *Power* to renew. 3, of *Grace* to comfort. 4, of *Love* to unite.

Mightier, differed from Christ in *accidentals*, not *essentials*, *Spanheim*. Differed as water and fire, *Quesnel*. "*Fire.*" The Holy Ghost, *Erasmus*, *Brown*, *Alexander*. Judgment, *Oosterzee*. Punishment, *De Wette*. Perdition, *Neander*, *Lange*, *Meyer*, *Origen*. Triumph of the new life. *Olshausen*. Tongues of fire, *Ebrard*. Discriminating work of John, *Kendrick*. As regards believers, the fiery power of the Spirit. As regards the unrepenting, fire of wrath, verse 17, *Bengel*. "*Cometh.*" His personal acquaintance with Jesus was by no means certain, *Ewald*, *Ellicott*. Contrary opinion, *Alford*.

---

17. *Whose fan is in his hand, and he will thoroughly purge his floor, and will gather the wheat into his garner; but the chaff he will burn with fire unquenchable.*

Fan. A fork or shovel, for flinging the grain in the wind, means a *judicial fan.*

1. The thresher and the fan. 2. Wheat and the barn. 3. Chaff and the fire.

Hand. Implies a readiness, a warning to His foes.

Purge. Gr. *through* and *through i.e.* from end to end.

Either separate chaff from the grain, or gather the grain.

Floor. Gr. a *circle*, a spot, where grain is trodden by oxen.

Visible church will be thoroughly purified, sooner or later.

In life we are in the *field*, in judgment on the *floor.*

Temple, type of the church, built on *Araunah's* floor. 2 Chron. iii, 1.

The holy, and unholy, cannot be separated by discipline. Matt. xiiii. 30.

Gather. First the scattered sheaves, then the threshed grain.

Wheat. Matt. *His wheat*: *i.e.*, worthless chaff belongs to no one.
Oriental wheat has six or seven ears to every head.
Garner. *Barne*, *Tyndale*, any repository for safe keeping.
In Palestine, generally a place under ground, covered with straw.
God, the heavenly Husbandman, Jo. xv. 1. He has *Vineyards*.
Cornfields, *Shepherds*, *Flocks*, *Herds*, *Wine-Press*.
Threshing-floors, *Laborers*, *Garner-houses*, and Place for burning chaff.
Chaff. Anciently burned, now food for beasts.
In the East there is no hay found for brutes.
"Ungodly like the chaff which the wind driveth." Ps. i. 4.
Israel, sifted. Amos ix. 9 Incorrigible, cast off.
Fire. Souls sustained by God, immortal in woe.
No church without chaff. Matt. xiii. 30. No garnering the stubble.

Fan. Sheets are now used. American fan, or mill, unknown in the east. "*Floor.*" Theocracy, *Lange*. Messiah's sphere of action, *Ewald*. Judea in ideal sense, *Meyer*. Mankind, *B. Crusius*. Jews, *De Wette*. ἄσβεσ. Homer's favorite, unceasing, *ever burning*. With us, *cannot burn*. Applied to fame, laughter, strength, flowing ocean, *Aeschylus*. Utter destruction, joined with continued conscious existence, *Brown*.

---

18. *And many other things in his exhortation preached he unto the people.*

Preached. Gr. *Glad tidings*, given as by a *teacher*. Luke i. 19. See Notes.
As a preacher John was 1. Affectionate. 2. Practical. 3. Popular.
4. Evangelical. 5. Faithful. 6. Bold. 7. Zealous. 8. A martyr.
He preached Christ's Kingdom 1, not of this world, but world wide.
2, not ostentation, but truth. 3, not false peace, but true help.
4, not of law, but salvation. 5, not demands, but grace.
Many. Gr. *Other exhortations*. Variety of subjects, as hearers needed.

19. *But Herod the tetrarch, being reproved by him for Herodias his brother Philip's wife, and for all the evils which Herod had done.*

Herod, Antipas. Luke iii. 1. A frivolous worldling, yet desired to see Jesus.
Our Lord did many things, and Herod heard Him gladly. Mark vi. 20.
Reproved. John spared no sins, was not afraid of the king's wrath.
No time server, neglecting duty, for the favors of the throne.
He might excuse himself with, "I am not responsible for the king."

"I might lose the king's support and frustrate my labors."
"I may expose myself and my disciples to danger." &c.
John before Herod. 1. A faithful preacher. 2. An innocent victim. 3. An avenging accuser.
The evils. Rulers amenable to the gospel pulpit. Luke xx. 25.
Ministers unfaithful, unless, they rebuke those in high places as well as the poor. Lev. xix. 17.
Herodias. Herod's niece and sister-in-law, grand daughter of Herod the Great.
He forsook his beautiful wife, daughter of Aretas, king of Arabia, and wickedly married Herodias. Salome, *her* daughter by Philip, trained to follow in a similar course. See Matt. xiv. 6.
Incest, murder, and adultery characterize the Herods.

Φιλίππου, "*Philip's*," omitted by *Tisch.* and *Alford.* Read "*his brother's wife*," Cod. Sina.

---

20. *Added yet this above all, that he shut up John in prison.*

Above all. Herod's sins had already reached a fearful height.
Against light revealed, and conscience condemning.
Licentiousness pre-eminently begets *shamelessness* in the guilty.
The soul hardens rapidly, under the fires of lust.
In prison. Imprisoned two years before Christ began to preach.
It is only *mentioned before* our Lord was baptised.
God doth not reward His servants in *this* world. 1 Jo. iii. 13.
Let us take heed, if the wicked *applaud* us. Luke vi. 26.
Ancient prisons, were dark cells, under palaces and castles.
Bound to wood-blocks, sleep was difficult, ease impossible.
"Iron entering the soul." Ps. cv. 18. Illustrated in the history,
Of the *Bridge of Sighs*, and *Bastiles*, victims lost their sight.
Some desperate ones begged visitors to put them to death.
Le Motte was in prison 54 years, another in *Venice* 30 years.
The world might say "See what John hath brought upon himself."
Christ, "See my faithful witness, great will be his reward!" Luke xviii. 30.

Prison. Thus treated by Herod through *envy*, *Josephus.* Προσέθ. added guilt to guilt, in classic use, *Foote.* To persecute, adds to one's sin, *Bengel.*

21. *Now when all the people were baptized, it came to pass, that Jesus also being baptized, and praying, the heaven was opened.*

The people. With *Divine* meekness, He waited till all was done.
Jesus also. Circumcised, purified, baptized, fulfills all righteousness. Matt. iii. 15.
Baptized. Proved it a rite of no small import.
Some exalt it above, others degrade it below its value.
Others invest it with magic charms against sin.
Divine grace is *tied* to no sacrament. Luke xxiii. 43.
Praying. *Thrice* the Spirit descended while He prayed.
Original Gr. hints at a *specially fervent* manner of prayer.
Prayer hallowed His baptism, and choice of Apostles. Matt. iii. 15. Luke vi. 13.
Renunciation of a crown. Jo. vi. 15, and His transfiguration. Luke ix. 29.
His journey to Calvary, scene of Gethsemane, and the Cross itself.
The hour of baptism should ever be a season of prayer.
John reverently declined. Matt. iii. 14. With O. T. saints, he trusted the Messiah as his Saviour.
His baptism, His solemn *inauguration* as the Messiah.
As Levites were consecrated in office, *by sprinkling*; this, the only end attained, as He had no *sins* to wash away. "*All righteousness*" was thus carefully "*fulfilled.*"
Our Lord solemnly engages *thus* to fulfil the entire law.
Though *sinless*, He identified himself with penitents.
Not *ashamed* to come among a crowd of sinners. Heb. ii. 11.
Heaven. A stupendous miracle witnessed by *all*.
Our Lord first *officially* made known to John. Jo. i. 31-34.
Opened. Figure of a door. Mark, i. 10. Gr. *rending*.
Prayer, a key, unlocks the treasures and doors of Heaven.

Chronology. In September, *Lightfoot*. Tradition reports a fire kindled on the Jordan, *Justin M.* Jesus incapable of regeneration. Infants being the same, are to be baptized, *Foote*. His object.—His mere *contact* with humanity, He would *cleanse*, *Stier*, *Lange*. Subject to death, *Ebrard;* to elicit the declaration of His Messiahship, *Paulus*. Feeling of sinfulness, *Baur;* incompatibility of weakness of the flesh with life of the Spirit, *Hoffman;* confirm his followers, *Ammon;* sanction John's baptism, *Kuinoel;* obligation to the law, *Osiander*, *Brown*. Before Spirit's descent, He acted like an ordinary Israelite, *Olshausen*. "*Opened.*" A violation of decorum, if in presence of the people, *Oosterzee*. Only witnessed by John, *Meyer*.

22. *And the Holy Ghost descended in a bodily shape like a Dove upon him, and a voice came from Heaven, which said, Thou art my beloved Son; in thee I am well pleased.*

Holy Ghost. Luke i. 15. Third Person in the adorable Trinity. See Notes.

Descended. Heaven *above*, as opposed to *earth* and its *impurities*.

Bodily, &c. No vision, actual form of a dove was seen.

Dove. Its character. Luke ii. 24. See Notes.

It rendered visible, *spiritual union* of the Son and Spirit.

Symbolized *purity*, *peacefulness*, and *meekness*.

Upon. Hence the Church lays on its hands in consecrating acts.

A voice. Audible, pointing out *The Son.*

Beloved. *God Himself* gives this title. Eternal Sonship.

The nearness of relation, and infinite love, are noted.

Pleased. Gr. *Delight.* The ineffable complacency of the Father.

"Mine Elect IN WHOM MY SOUL DELIGHTETH." Isa. xlii. 1.

The ETERNAL GODHEAD of Christ, *alone explains such words*

Son. 1. By eternal generation. 2. Miraculous conception.

3. By special consecration. 4. By resurrection and enthronement.

Doctrine of the Triune God here exemplified.

The Father speaks. The Son acknowledged. The Spirit descends.

"*Bodily, dove.*" Flame, like Shechinah, *Major*. Ray of light, gently, swiftly, evenly. Jews did not regard dove, emblem of the Spirit, *Oosterzee*. Undulating light, *Milman*. Its rapidity, *Fritzsche*. Purity, *Olshausen*, Creative power, *B. Crusius*. Fulness of life, *Lange*. A chance dove, *Paulus*. A meteor, *Meyer*. Lightning, *Kuinoel*. Swift flight, *Neander*. Straight course, *Winer*. A vision, *Origen*, *De Wette*. A real dove, *Augustine*. Go to the Jordan and see the *Trinity*, *Augustine* agt. *Marcion*. Trinity first distinctly revealed, *Lange*. Sacrificial use of the dove, *Cocceius*. Actual fact as recorded in the form of a dove, *Alexander*, *Brown*. Luke's account concise, wholly independent of the others, records three additional particulars, 1. All the people *had been baptized before the Lord's baptism*. 2. He was *praying* at the time of the descent of the Spirit. 3. The Spirit appeared in a bodily form, *Alford*. (*Ed.*) λεγουσ., cancelled, *Tischendorf*, *Oosterzee*. Omitted, *Cod. Sina*. το πνευ. article, definite with *emphasis*. *Middleton*. αγαπητὸς, more expressive than only-begotten of *Homer*. ηὐδόκη, the *time* of assuming the Messiahship,—aorist. *Viger*.

---

23. *And Jesus himself began to be about thirty years of age, being (as was supposed) the son of Joseph, which was* the son *of Heli.*

Jesus, His *spiritual* name. Christ, His *official* name. Had other names, Second Adam, 1. Cor. xv. 45. Advocate, 1. Jo. ii. 1. Amen,

Rev. iii. 14. High Priest, Heb. iii. 1. Author of our faith, Heb. xii. 2. Bishop, 1. Peter, ii. 25. Bread, Jo. vi. 33. Brightness, Heb. i. 3. Captain, Heb. ii. 10. Door, Jo. x. 7. Firstborn, Col. i. 18. Forerunner, Heb. vi. 20. Foundation, 1. Cor. iii. 11. Heir, Heb. i. 2. Hope, 1. Tim. i. 1. Judge, Acts x. 42. King, Luke xix. 38. Lamb, Jo. i. 29. Light, Jo. viii. 12. Lord, Acts x. 36. Master, Matt. xxiii. 10. Mediator, 1. Tim. ii. 5. Nazarene, Matt. ii. 23. Passover, 1. Cor. v. 7. Resurrection, Jo. xi. 25. Shepherd, Jo. x. 11. Beloved, Matt. xvii. 5. Teacher, Jo. iii. 2. Way, Truth, Life, Jo. xiv. 6. Vine, Jo. xv. 1. Bright and Morning Star, Rev. xxii. 16. &c.

Began. Refers to the commencement of His ministry.

Thirty. The time priests entered on official service. Num. iv. 35.

Joseph stood before Pharaoh, and David began to reign, at thirty.

He patiently conceals himself about thirty years.

No ministry could have been more useful or necessary.

The silence and humility of His quiet labor, instructive.

Seventy-five generations extend through 4000 years.

No living monarch's line extends over a *thousand* years.

Isin, B. C. burned Chinese Records, and 460 *scholars*, that his dynasty should seem *one*, from the *beginning*, to the *end* of time.

Mary's genealogy in Luke, *Joseph's* given in Matt.

Writing for Jews, Matt. traced Christ to *Abraham*.

Luke for Jew and Gentile, traced Him to Adam.

Luke's record *ascending*, Matt.'s, *descending* ancestral line.

From David to Babylonian Cap. Luke gives 21; Matt. 14 names.

The hope of ancestral *relation* to the promised Messiah, preserved jealously these family records of the Jews. Luke i. 55.

Joseph. Luke i. 27. Biblical notices. **Heli.** The legal father of Joseph.

ἀρχμενοσ. of His ministry, *Justin*, *Euthym.*, *Bengel*, *De Wette*, *Meyer*, *Olshausen*, *Alford*, *Tischendorf*, *Oostersee*, *Brown*. His thirtieth year, *Calvin*, *Grotius*, *Beza*, *W. & W.* E. V, was about thirty, *Origen*, *Rosenmuller*, *Doddridge*. About 31, *Vogel*; 32, *Allin*, *Lardner*; 33, *Paulus*, *Macknight*. "*Supposed*," believed, *Bengel*. "*Heli*." The genealogies of Luke and Matt. are harmonized; 1. By each one from David to Joseph having *two names*. 2. Joseph's mother marrying twice, son of one by birth, son of the other by adoption. The two records, those of these two fathers. Luke traces the line through Heli, and not through Jacob, *Julius Africanus*, A. D. 220. This makes Christ's descent from David not through *Joseph*, but *Mary*. 3. Mary, an heiress, married in her own tribe, her husband assuming her father's name. Neh. vii. 63. 4. Mary the daughter of Heli. An unsolved difficulty, *Alford*, *Meyer*. Luke's record of

Mary, and Matt.'s of Joseph, *Bengel, Lightfoot, Hale, Major, Lange, Oosterzee, Olshausen, Ebrard.* Anciently both were thought Joseph's. Others make Matt.'s the *regal* descent from Solomon. Others, natural descent through Nathan from David, *Mill, Ellicott.* Jewish records burned by Herod, *Eusebius* quoting Apocryphal Gospel of *James.* Questioned by *Oosterzee. Heli.* It is maintained by Lord A. Hervey, the latest investigator of the genealogy of Christ, that Heli was the real brother of Jacob the father of the Virgin herself. *Ed.*

---

24. *Which was* the son *of Matthat, which was* the son *of Levi, which was* the son *of Melchi, which was* the son *of Janna, which was* the son *of Joseph.*

25. *Which was* the son *of Mattathias, which was* the son *of Amos, which was* the son *of Naum, which was* the son *of Esli, which was* the son *of Nagge.*

26. *Which was* the son *of Maath, which was* the son *of Mattathias, which was* the son *of Semei, which was* the son *of Joseph, which was* the son *of Juda.*

27. *Which was* the son *of Joanna, which was* the son *of Rhesa, which was* the son *of Zorobabel, which was* the son *of Salathiel, which was* the son *of Neri.*

28. *Which was* the son *of Melchi, which was* the son *of Addi, which was* the son *of Cosam, which was* the son *of Elmodam, which was* the son *of Er.*

μαδάμ for μωδαμ. *Lachmann, Tischendorf.*

---

29. *Which was* the son *of Jose, which was* the son *of Eliezer, which was* the son *of Jorim, which was* the son *of Matthat, which was* the son *of Levi.*

30. *Which was* the son *of Simeon, which was* the son *of Juda, which was* the son *of Joseph, which was* the son *of Jonan, which was* the son *of Eliakim.*

31. *Which was* the son *of Melea, which was* the son *of Menan, which was* the son *of Mattatha, which was* the son *of Nathan, which was* the son *of David.*

David. Life and history. Luke i. 27. No caviller ever denied Jesus being of David's line.

Had both these genealogical records perished, we have the positive declaration of the Holy Ghost. Luke i. 32. 35.

Naturally and legally his son and heir. Acts ii. 30; xiii. 23. Rom. i. 3; 2. Tim. ii. 8.

A royal bearing given to His *words*, *deeds*, and even *silence*.

Bright and morning star, yet root and offspring of David. Rev. xxii. 16.

Μεννᾶ for Μαϊναν, *Lachmann.*

32. *Which was* the son *of Jesse, which was* the son *of Obed, which was* the son *of Booz, which was* the son *of Salmon, which was* the son *of Naasson.*

33. *Which was* the son *of Aminadab, which was* the son *of Aram, which was* the son *of Esrom, which was* the son *of Phares, which was* the son *of Juda.*

τοῦ 'Ἀρὰμ—Ἀδμεὶν, *Tischendorf.*

---

34. *Which was* the son *of Jacob, which was* the son *of Isaac, which was* the son *of Abraham, which was* the son *of Thara, which was* the son *of Nachor.*

Abraham. Luke i. 55. Life and character. See Notes.

35. *Which was* the son *of Saruch, which was* the son *of Ragau, which was* the son *of Phalec, which was* the son *of Heber, which was the son of Sala.*

36. *Which was* the son *of Cainan, which was* the son *of Arphaxad, which was* the son *of Sem, which was* the son *of Noe, which was* the son *of Lamech.*

"*Cainan.*" Not in original Heb. but in Septuagint, translated B.C. 300. Several theories: 1. Luke copies, but does not endorse the record. 2. Name omitted in the Heb. text by the translators' error, *Alford.* 3. It crept into the Greek of Luke by transcribers' error, *Lightfoot.* Neither Moses nor Luke wrote it, *Spanheim.* By mistake copied from ver. 37, *Bochart.* By the seventy, *Grotius.* Before Luke's time, *Usher.* Septuagint more reliable than Heb., *Mill.* Luke had access to unrevealed O. T. Hist., *Oxford.* Cancelled, *Beza.* Retained, *Bengel.* Retained, *Cod. Alex.* Omitted, *Cod. Cant.* Καϊναμ *Cod. Vat.* and *Cod. Sina. Tischendorf.* *Noe.* Luke xvii. 26. See Notes.

---

37. *Which was* the son *of Mathusala, which was* the son *of Enoch, which was* the son *of Jared, which was* the son *of Maleleel, which was* the son *of Cainan.*

Methuselah, died the year of the deluge, 969 years of age, oldest of men Gen. v. 27

38. *Which was* the son *of Enos, which was* the son *of Seth, which was* the son *of Adam, which was* the son *of God.*

Of **Adam,** by creation, of God, by eternal generation.
He disdains not to be numbered among *mortals.*
His low appearance, and exalted dignity. 1. His Person.
2. His work. 3. His Kingdom. 4. His Future.

Son of God. First Adam, and Jesus the Second Adam, both sons of God.

Genealogy with respect to redemption.

1. Adam, head and representative of humanity, needs redemption.
2. Christ, His greatness, who undertakes redemption.
3. The glory of God, who ordains redemption.

What shortlived being is man, 75 *generations* have come and gone.

How little we know of their glory or shame.

Their joys, sorrows, hopes, fears, cares and plans!

This dying state, made a living one, throught Christ. Jo. xiv. 19.

All things are of God through Christ, by Christ all things are restored to God.—*Bengel.*

CHAPTER IV.

1. *AND Jesus being full of the Holy Ghost returned from Jordan, and was led by the Spirit into the wilderness.*

Jesus. Luke i. 31. See critical Notes.
Full of the *Spirit.* The Lord and Giver of Life.
Holy Ghost. The Third Person in the Adorable Trinity. Luke i. 35. See Notes.
Returned. Having been baptized by John. Luke iii. 21.
Jordan. Luke iii. 3. See Notes.
Led. By an extraordinary, but not miraculous impulse.
Those led *into* temptation by the Spirit, will also be led *out.* 1 Cor. x. 13.
He did not seek the conflict, nor shun its violence.
Led not into unknown results, but for special purposes.
Spirit. Not His own, but the Spirit of God. John iii. 34.
Wilderness. The exact spot unknown; it was far from human aid. Luke i. 80.
The Divine Victim was prefigured by the scape-goat. Lev. xvi. 22.
Adam's fall changed Paradise into a wilderness.
Jesus' victory changes a wilderness into a Paradise.
A monkish *delusion* that *cities* alone expose to temptation.

"*Was led by the Spirit,*" ηγετο, was carried, *Lightfoot*; irresistibly led, *Oosterzee.* Matt. ανηχθη, *was brought up.* Mark, εκβαλλει, *putteth him forth, i.e.*, the Spirit *hurrieth*, or *driveth* him; In each case the Evangelist attributes the impelling agency to the *Holy Ghost*, not to *Satan. Dr. A. Clarke.* εν, into the very *midst*, *Major.* "*wilderness.*" Supposed scene called Quarantaria in memory of the forty days, *Kitto.* A rock, perpendicular, and nearly as high as Gibraltar, *Thompson:* 1200 or 1500 feet high, *Robinson.* Scene, east of Jordan, *Stanley.* Lofty, naked peak, overlooking Jordan and Dead Sea, *Lightfoot, Lange, Oosterzee, Major.* Arabian deserts, *Greswell, Alford.* τῇ ἐρήμω, *Cod. Sina., Alford.* Milton's *Paradise Regained* founded on this Temptation Scene.

---

2. *Being forty days tempted of the devil. And in those days he did eat nothing: and when they were ended, he afterward hungered.*

Forty days. Time of the Deluge coming. Time Moses and Elijah fasted.

Goliath dared the armies of Israel forty days, and *fell* the *last*.

Ezekiel commanded to lie on his right side, forty days. Ezekiel iv. 6.

The time Jesus fasted, not the duration of the conflict.

Equalled by the forty days of victory in his life, after His resurrection.

Tempted. Gr. *Tested*, as metals by fire, and of standard purity. Luke xi. 4.

God thus *tries*. Gen. xxii. 1, but never *tempts*, *i. e.*, entices to sin. Jas. i. 13.

Satan's *means* are wiles, darts, snares, depths, deceivableness, &c.

He darkens the mind, perverts judgment, excites pride, envy, malice, &c.

Seasons of great mercies, are often followed by severe trials.

Pirates assault *freighted* vessels, letting *empty* ones pass.

Abraham, David, Peter, and Paul, illustrations.

Christ's *entire life* a conflict with the enemy.

First Adam overcome in a garden. Second Adam conquers in a desert. Heb. iv. 15.

The Divine *Awarder* of prizes, Himself among the *wrestlers*.

He who crowns His saints, Himself crowned Victor.

The most remarkable scene described in Scriptures.

The Almighty Son, meeting the foe, face to face, in trial.

He attacks human corruption at its *root*, by subduing Satan.

Idea of *redemption*, presupposes bondage to a foreign power.

First and second Adam, were tempted from *without*.

But Satan could not appear under a *mask* to Christ.

Satan's ordinary daily assaults on us, a *perfect mystery*.

How he tempted Jesus, must for the *present*, be one also.

Devil, the *slanderer*. Mark calls him Satan, the *adversary*. chapt. i. 13. Matt. emphatically designates him *the tempter*, chap. iv. 3.

Chief of *fallen* angels, he has raised himself "to this bad pre-eminence."

A gigantic *intellect* without *goodness*, *mind* without *love*.

Variously described in Holy Scripture; each name sets forth some phase of character or work; as—

"A murderer," John viii. 44., "god of this world," 2. Cor. iv. 4., "prince of the power of the air," Ephes. ii. 2., "wicked one," 1. John v. 15., "roaring lion," 1. Peter v. 8., "angel of light to deceive," 2. Cor. xi. 14., "liar," John viii. 44., Beelzebub," Matt. xii. 24., "Belial," 2. Cor. vi. 15., "tormentor," Matt. xviii. 34., "accuser of our brethren," Rev. xii. 10., "leviathan," Isa. xxvii. 1. "Apollyon," Rev. ix. 11. "dragon and old serpent," Rev. xii. 9. "lightning," Luke x. 18., "wolf," John x. 12., "fowler," Psalm xci. 30., "dog," Psalm xxii. 16., "adder." Psalm xci. 13. &c.

His attempts to *defeat* only *advance* God's designs in the end.

Eat. Jewish customs at their meals. Luke vii. 36. See Notes.
He doubtless knew that Christ had left heaven.
He had witnessed the Lord's baptism and miracle.
Success over the first Adam, assured Him of a victory over the *Second.*
He had robbed us of *Paradise*, why not rob Jesus of His *crown!*
Whom will the vanquisher of Job, David, Peter, spare now?
False teachers never warn men of Satan's power and malice.
The Scriptures abound with exhortations, to be on our guard.
Nothing. A miracle. No one has survived hunger *eighteen* days.
Hungered. Divine aid withdrawn, proves His humanity.
Beasts. Mark i. 13. Adds terror, and aggravates the horrors, of the scene.

ἡμ. τεσσαρ. Temptations began at their end. *Pearce, Major.* The words of the Evangelists rather imply that He was tempted at intervals during the *forty days*, and that at the close of them the Tempter assailed Him with greatest violence. *Wordsworth.* Tradition makes Adam's trial *forty* days. *Andrews.* πειραζόμενος, 1, *to make proof or trial.* 2, *to make an attempt.* 3, *to seek to seduce, to tempt to sin.* In the first sense only God is said to *tempt, i.e. to try.* Comp. Gen. xxii. 1, and Jas. i. 13. ὁ διάβολος, *the Devil.* The derivation of the word implies the effort to break the bonds between others, to "set at variance;" and common usage adds to this general sense the special idea of "setting at variance by slander." Both these should be kept in view. The general object of the devil is to prevent the union between God and man; and to break those bonds of truth and love which bind men to each other. His slander of God to man is seen in Gen. iii. 4-5. His slander of man to God, in Job i. 9-11; ii. 4-5. The Scriptures speak of the devil as a "spirit," Eph. ii. 2; as the prince of "demons," Matt. xii. 24-26; as having "angels" subject to him, Rev. xii. 7-9. We conclude he was an archangel, one of the "princes" of heaven, but of the *time, cause,* and *manner* of his fall, the Bible is almost silent. Comp. 2 Peter ii. 4, and Jude, verse 6, although it is hardly possible to consider Satan as one of the angels spoken of, seeing he is permitted to go about as the Tempter. From 1 Tim. iii. 6, it would appear that pride was the cause of the devil's condemnation. He is the leader of a host of evil spirits, described as "principalities," &c., Eph. vi. 12, opposed to man. In Rev. xii. 7-9, they are spoken of as fighting under the "dragon," &c., against "Michael," &c., and as cast out of heaven, with their chief. Matt. xii. 24-26 identifies them with the δαιμόνια, who had power to possess the souls of men.

If Christ, the Second Adam, was to be tempted, in order to be like us (Heb. ii. 18), it must be, as the first Adam was, by the devil; for he could not be tempted from *within. Gregory.* It is evident our Lord's temptations were literal transactions; to suppose them visionary does violence to the narrative, and robs His example and victory of all value. If Satan appeared in a *visible* form, it is the only instance on record of the *visible* appearance of an evil spirit on this earth, while appearances of holy angels are frequent. The presence of the Tempter was not less real if invisible, see John xiv. 30. ὕστερον, "*afterwards*," cancelled, *Tischendorf, Alford, Oosterzee;* omitted, *Cod. Sinai.* See *Alford, Lange, Ellicott, Wordsworth, Smith's Dictionary*, Article, Satan, &c.

---

3. *And the devil said unto him, If thou be the son of God, command this stone that it be made bread.*

If Thou. Either doubt your Sonship, or prove it by a miracle.

He tries hard to make believers doubt their adoption.

Son. Jesus, *common* name. Christ, *official*. Son. His *filial* name. Luke i. 35.

Father of lies unintentionally a *witness* for the *truth*.

Temptations in the O.T., and in the N.T., begin by doubts being insinuated.

Command. *Ironically ;* appealing to His hunger and confidence.

Stone. Wicked trying to convert stone to bread, oft change bread into stone.

Satan in temptations, often offers *stones* to the hungry.

Bread. Materials, baking, &c. Luke vii. 33. See Notes.

"If God be Thy Father, He hath forgotten Thy wants."

The sin not one of gluttony, but distrusting Providence.

The Hebrews' sin, questioning his willingness to relieve them. Exod. xvi. 3.

The Lord had meat the world knew not of. John. iv. 32.

The world prepares *magical* manna for its devotees, in the wilderness.

Its origin, wicked devices. Its character, selfish gratification.

Its guilt and poverty in the inner and outer man.

"*Command*," &c. As if to say, Thou art hungry, how unworthy the Son of God! *If he*, free thyself from this weakness and want. Else no man will believe thee, *De Wette*. The tempter acknowledges the Son of God to be omnipotent, *Bengel*. Distrust Divine Providence, and make use of unlawful means to supply thy wants, *A. Clarke*.

---

4. *And Jesus answered him, saying, It is written, That man shall not live by bread alone, but by every word of God.*

Answered. He often replied to the *secret thoughts* of men.

He might have hurled him back to the prison of despair.

But His every word and deed, for the *instruction* of the church.

Written. Materials, manner, antiquities. Luke i. 63. See Notes.

First quotation refutes false doctrines, second false interpretation.

Third false authority. *Faith* transforms bread into *manna*.

Eve rightly repelled the Tempter with "The Lord said."

From His birth to His death, He ever recurs to "The Word."

Live. "Life hid with Christ in God," alone *true life*. Col. iii. 3.

Alone. Gives great *breadth* to the fourth petition of the Lord's prayer.

If *He* needed such bread, how much more, *man*.

Desiring the bread of disobedience, one is already Satan's captive.

Having Christ, the Heaven-descended bread, we shall never hunger. John vi. 58.
Israel, hungering, saw bread rained down from heaven.
No strait, however pressing, should shake our faith in God.
Word. Preservation, a constant act of creation.
By His Word, all things at first were created. John i. 3.
The first *perfect* resistance, since Tempter ruined Adam. Luke xi. 4.
Heretofore a conqueror, Satan is now a vanquished foe. Ps. lxviii. 18.
Adam's yielding, stands at the *threshold* of the Old Testament.
Christ's *vanquishing*, stands at the *threshold* of the New.
A surprise, as well as consternation on Satan's part.
David chose three stones, Our Lord three texts to meet the foe.

ῥήματι. A thing, a truth, *reality*. *ῥήματα*. Words of Jesus, *Luther*. Creative cause of all nourishment, *Olshausen*. Deut. viii. 3, Moses refers to *manna*. Italics in English version have nothing in Hebrew, *Trench*, *Oosterzee*. λέγων, "*saying*," also the clause "*but by every word of God*," omitted by *Tischendorf* and *Alford*. "Wanting bread, I have made meals on God's promise." *Henry*. Order of the temptation, 1, a distrust of providence. 2, presumption. 3, ambition, *Brown*. Adam fell in the garden, surrounded by beauty and abundance. Christ triumphed in the desert, surrounded by desolation, and pinched with hunger, *Ed.*

---

5. *And the devil, taking him up into a high mountain, shewed unto him all the kingdoms of the world in a moment of time.*

High mountain. Tradition has selected *Quarantaria*, near Jericho.
Balak thus *changed* the ground for Balaam's ungodly work.
Tempter, defeated, returns as cunning as ever.
The mountain tops of spiritual life are dangerous.
Highest elevations, border on the deepest precipices.
Sheweth. *How* the Tempter works, is still a *profound mystery*.
Kingdoms. An overwhelming appeal to the ambition of a mere man.
Moment. Superhuman *power*, in this *violent* assault.
A general collects his forces, and hurls them against one point, often the weakest.
The imagination dazzled, and judgment surprised in this temptation.
But Earthly joys, and glory of *momentary* duration.

ο διαβολοσ, "*the devil*," cancelled, *Tisch.*, *Alford*. εισ οροσ ὑψηλον, "*into a high mountain*," cancelled, *Tisch.*, *Alford*. Omitted, *Cod. Sina.* Scene of this temptation, see Matt. iv. 8. Quarantaria, *Porteus.* Bethabara, *Lightfoot.* Nebo or Pisgah, *Ellicott.* Horeb, *Origen.* "*world,*" Palestine, *Kuinoel.* Heathendom, *Meyer.* World in widest sense, *Alford.* "*shewed.*" Actual exhibition, *Lange.* Palace splendors, *De Wette.* Scenes of pleasure and triumph, *Doddridge.* The temptation *inward,* since no literal mountain commands such a view, *Olshausen.* To his eyes as far as the horizon; the rest possibly by enumeration and indication, *Bengel.* "*moment of time.*" Pointing out the supernatural character of the vision, *Alford.* The display was sudden, hence the temptation was strong, *Bengel.*

---

6. *And the devil said unto him, All this power will I give thee, and the glory of them: for that is delivered unto me; and to whomsoever I will, I give it.*

Power. Sceptres, robes, thrones, armies, reins of empire, often Satan's gifts.

Give thee. They had for ages been pledged to Christ by Jehovah. Ps. ii. 8.

Never consent to receive from Satan, what God promises.

Temptations, striking at God's *throne,* are most perilous.

Glory. Crowns, palaces, gardens, equipages, armies, what men call glory.

Courts, life-guards, pomps, field-shows, country seats, &c. &c.

Man everywhere naturally loves and longs for "glory," indicative of immortality.

Satan conceals cares, dangers, calamities, treasons, sorrows.

Woes skilfully hid under false colors, and delusive splendors.

The temptation implies, that His Father had abandoned Him.

Delivered. Jesus names him "prince of this world." Jo. xii. 31.

He offers to abdicate his seat, in favor of Christ.

He confesses a *Greater One* in creation, than *himself.*

I will. He does not speak the truth, he is "father of lies."

To dispose of the world and its interests, belongs finally to God.

He never lies more boldly, than when he *promises.*

The realm of futurity, is held supremely and solely by God.

I give. Three lies, against, 1. God's justice. 2. His sovereignty. 3. His providence.

Boasting, while the chains of fire were checking his wrath. Jude 6 verse.

He does not say "*Resist,* and I will *arm* the world *against Thee!*"

He promised to *Eve,* to *Jesus,* and will to us.

δοξαν. "*glory.*" Satan appeals to the *same motive,* which cost him heaven. Isa. xiv. 12, 13. 1. Tim. iii. 6. "*is delivered;*" this was not entirely false, *Bengel.* The enemy reveals himself openly as "father of lies;" for though power is given him over this world and its sons, his assertion here is most untrue, *Alford.* His object to tempt our Lord to accept worldly pomp and pride, instead of a *spiritual kingdom.* This would gratify Jewish expectations, and save him from bitter persecutions, *Jacobus.*

---

7. *If thou therefore wilt worship me, all shall be thine.*

Worship. Kissing the hand, and prostrating one's self as Persians do.
An act of a subject to a sovereign, *worship* in the higher sense, due to God only.
Boldly dropping his mask, Satan stands out as God's rival.
Hebrews yielded (Deut. xxxii. 17), and were punished. Lev. xvii. 7.
Resist unto blood. Heb. xii. 4. *Death* better than *sin.*
Satan true to his ruling passion loves honor even in ruins.
Worship given to heathen gods, really given to Satan. 1 Cor. x. 20.
If once made *partner* with God in the heart, Satan will soon be *proprietor.*
Adopting a new religion for *honor*, one worships Satan.
All Thine. Herod hazarded but *half* his kingdom.
Many peril *all* for honor; sell heaven for a *bubble.*

προσκυνήσῃς, 1. To kiss one's hand extending toward one in homage. 2. To worship, prostrate on the ground, as a suppliant, *Soph.* Adore, *Aesch.*, Prom. 988, *Gesenius.* From κυων, crouch like a dog; Orientals fawn, *Major.* From κυνέω. "*to kiss,*" *Donnegan.* Prostrate thyself, *Elsley.* Satan proposes no act of immorality, but asks the Lord to take from him (Satan) the sovereignty of the world, until He accomplishes His designs, *W. & W.* The tempter does not demand the highest degree of adoration; but Jesus shows that no degree, however low, can be given to a creature, much less to Satan, *Bengel.*

---

8. *And Jesus answered and said unto him, Get thee behind me, Satan: for it is written, Thou shalt worship the Lord thy God, and him only shalt thou serve.*

Get thee, &c. Begone! An expression of the deepest abhorence.
These identical words were afterwards addressed to Peter. Matt. xvi. 23.
All kingdoms of earth, cannot balance one sin.
Written. Luke i. 63. Deut. vi. 13. Christ peculiarly honors the *Pentateuch.*
Our Lord is the very highest authority for its *inspiration.*
Assaulted, let *us* also draw our weapons from the Bible. 2 Tim. iii. 16.

Our Lord's reply was a renewed declaration of *war*. Gen. iii. 15.

He yields not a moment's advantage, or a hair's breadth.

Sword of the Spirit: 1. How dazzling its brightness. 2. How deep its wounds. 3. How decisive its triumphs.

Only. Not in the Hebrew. Deut. vi. 13. But Christ the AUTHOR of both, can *add* or *detract* as He pleases, in Infinite Wisdom.

What we supremely love, is our object of *worship*.

Serve. The Papacy discriminates the worship of *God* from worship of images.

All religious worship of every kind, *not* to GOD, is *idolatry*.

ὕπαγε, &c. "*Get thee behind me Satan.*" Cancelled, also γαρ, "*for*," *Alford*, *Tischendorf*, *Oosterzee*. Omitted, *Cod. Sina.* Retained, *Wetstein*, *Brown*. Supposed that later Greek copyists had translated thus from Matt., *Bengel*. Satan must obey, hence Matt.'s order preferred, *Brown*. Some led by *pride* to *ambition*, Matt.'s order, others *vice versa*. Luke's order preferred, *Mills*. λατρεύσεις. Classical meanings, 1, to work for hire or pay. 2, to subject to. 3, to serve the gods with prayers and sacrifices. In N. T. sense, to render religions homage, or worship. Confined to religious worship in the Sept. Sometimes used in the N. T. for external religious service. Heb. viii. 5. Used also in the sense of offering sacrifice. Heb ix. 9. *Ed.*

---

9. *And he brought him to Jerusalem, and set him on a pinnacle of the temple, and said unto him, If thou be the Son of God, cast thyself down from hence.*

Brought. Led. Nothing however which implies *compulsion*.

No more inconsistent with Divine *dignity*, than being *scourged*.

His humiliation, was not in being *led*, but in being *tempted*.

A depth of Divine *repose*, demons could not *disturb*.

Jerusalem. Luke i. 15. History and antiquities. Luke xxi. 24. Ruins. See Notes.

Pinnacle. Gr. *Wing*. The roof receded like a bird's wings.

The roof was flat, surrounded by a *balustrade*. Deut. xxii. 8.

High places of earth are slippery places.

Victims of ambition, raised by the tempter to *high honors*.

Temple. Luke i. 9. Mount Moriah was 500 feet high, very steep.

If Thou. Insinuates a groundless, vain confidence, on the part of Jesus.

Born in a stable, fleeing to Egypt, living under a carpenter's roof.

Thirty years in obscurity of a humble village, now hungry.

Unhonored, unattended, unpitied, among beasts. Mark i. 13.

Cast. Unbelief, worldliness, presumption, Satan's three great motives.

The sin. To *parade* a miraculous deed before the crowd.

If evil is done, Satan *persuades*, but cannot *compel*.

"*Pinnacle.*" The temple had no spires. The battlements were to prevent persons from walking off, *Doddridge, Major.* An outbuilding of the temple, *De Wette.* Perhaps the royal portico of Herod overlooking, at a fearful height, the Valley of Jehoshaphat, *Meyer, Alford.* Christ was tempted by *heights* and *depths, Bengel.* τοῦ "*the*" before *Son of God,* cancelled, *Campbell, Major.* Omitted by Satan through malignity, *Oosterzee.* This temptation scene a compromise of dignity, *Paulus:* if so, crucifixion was too, *Gregory.*

---

10. *For it is written, He shall give his angels charge over thee, to keep thee:*

Written. Satan with Bible in *hand*, and a text in his *mouth*.
A head full of Scripture, and a heart full of rebellion.
Devil turns theologian, opposes Jesus with his own weapons.
Abuses of Scripture: 1. Letter against the Spirit.
A poetical sentence, quoted against demands of Law.
The part that would have condemned the temptation, skilfully left out—
"*To keep thee in all thy ways.*" Psa. xci. 11.
2. *Dangerous.* Holy words finds an echo in the heart.
3. Only conquered by persistent searching of God's Word.
Angels. Luke i. 11. Not guardian angel, the plural is used.
Ministering spirits, instrumental agents of God. Heb. i. 14.
Charge. Providence, a ground of *confidence*, not *presumption*.
Satan intent on the *ruin*, angels on the *salvation*, of saints.
Angels, guides for *paths*, not precipices; *necessities*, not *passions*.
Teachers are to *enlighten* us, not to follow our *infatuation*.
Promises embraced, "munitions of rocks" to the soul. Isa. xxxiii. 16.
So often baffled by the Bible, Satan hates it intensely.
Men "*wrest* the Scriptures," and grace is changed to lust. Jude, ver. 4. 2 Peter, iii. 16.

"*It is written.*" *That* temptation is the most specious which appears to cite Scripture appropriately, *Bengel.* A vile abuse of Scripture to persuade thereby to sin, or plead for sin, *Trapp.* That God has promised to protect and support His servants is true, but only when they walk in the *path* of *duty*; out of that *path* there is no *safety*. *Dr. A. Clarke.*

---

11. *And in their hands they shall bear thee up, lest at any time thou dash thy foot against a stone.*

Bear. The tender care of nurses towards infants.
Lest. Peradventure. **Dash.** Strike or stumble. Ps. xci. 11.

Stone, in the path, "Thy foot shall not stumble &c." Prov. iii. 23.
A proverbial expression indicating *danger*.
God's entire attributes are pledged to protect us *in* duty.
"As thy day is so shall thy strength be." Deut. xxxiii. 25.
But promise not thyself, *more* than God has pledged.
Satan quotes a correct *principle*, but makes a wrong *application*.
The text is both misquoted, and misapplied.

"*And in their hands they shall bear thee up,*" literally, *on their hands;* a metaphor taken from a nurse's management of her child, *Dr. A. Clarke.* "*Lest at any time thou dash thy foot against a stone.*" Whereof the temple was built, *Bengel.* The words indicate the tender watchful care of our Heavenly Father, *Trapp.* Christ had repelled the first temptation by an act of faith, now the devil solicits him to make trial of his faith, to prove how far God would honor it. Learn, that the means we use to repel one temptation may be made through the subtlety of Satan the groundwork of another and a more dangerous temptation, *Dr. A. Clarke.* Most of the ancient saints failed in that point which constituted the strength of their character, Abraham, Moses, Elijah, &c. Even a virtue when in *excess* becomes of the nature of vice. *Ed.*

---

12. *And Jesus answering said unto him, It is said, Thou shalt not tempt the Lord thy God.*

Said. All three answers were from the *Pentateuch.* Deuteronomy.
Satan cried; "It is written," Jesus answered, "It is written."
Tempt. *i.e.*, try thoroughly by criminal presumption.
Applied to God, it demands proof by further evidence.
Christ will not be tempted by presumptuous solicitation.
Neither will he tempt God, by presuming on *His* Providence.
This temptation was, 1. *Unbelief* in God's Word.
2. *Presumption* on God's Word. 3. *Apostacy* from God's Word.
"Christ was tempted in all points like as we are, yet without sin." Heb. iv. 15.
"The prince of this world cometh, and findeth nothing in *me*." John xii. 31.
No one of a fallen race tempted, is without sin. Heb. iv. 15.
Our Lord's vanquishing the tempter by the Scriptures—
1. A *light* to our blindness. 2. A *spur* to our sloth.
3. A *staff* to our weakness. 4. A *crown* in our victory.
God's dealing with christians 1. Old way, yet always new.
2. Hard, yet kind. 3. Dark, yet full of light.
4. Solitary, yet ever a blessed way. Proverbs iv. 18.

"*Tempt.*" Wantonly testing a kind Providence, *Wakefield.* God is tempted when men are too much addicted to means as Thomas; or when they reject them as Ahaz, *Trapp.* To expose myself to any danger, with the vain presumption that God will protect and defend me from the consequences of my rashness and folly, is *to tempt God, Dr. A. Clarke.* Uncalled fanatics and reformers have sinned through presumption, in forgetting this word of the Lord, *Stier.* Notwithstanding Satan's retort of the words, "it is written," Jesus did not allow them to be wrested from Him, but applied them three times. Scripture must be interpreted by and reconciled with, Scripture, *Bengel.* The plan of building theological or moral opinions on isolated fragments and texts of Scripture may be used to support any heresy or any crime. The History of the Church affords mournful proof of this, *Ed.* Christ had *minimum* of *peccatum originale, Irving.* No sin in Eve, seeing attractions in forbidden fruit, but the *will* to eat, was sin, *Oosterzee.* No believer vigorously tempted, escapes a stain, *Brown.* Saints must offer this petition, "*Forgive us our trespasses,*" until they leave this world.

---

13. *And when the devil had ended all the temptations, he departed from him for a season.*

Ended. Our temptations limited, "Thus far, and no farther, &c."
Temptations. If Satan cannot *ruin* our *soul*, he *bruises* our *heel.* Gen. iii. 15.
In the wilderness, every allurement to ambition is often found.
In the garden, or on the cross, every avenue to pain is tried.
Thus the world tries *seductions*, then *threatenings* of wrath.
The greatest victories of Christ's Kingdom cause reaction.
Satan powerfully withstood Moses in freeing Israel.
Christ coming to atone, demons strenuously resisted Him.
In the coming "end," they will "come down in great wrath." Rev. xii. 12.
If they gain no *victory*, there is still *revenge.*
Departed. But ceased not continually to *torment* Him.
Satan's victims thrown off their guard, often are lulled to sleep.
Season. Renewed. Matt. xxvii. 40; John vii. 3-4; vi. 15.
He sees the back ground of Peter's request. Matt. xvi. 22.
If Satan returns to tempt, so God does to aid us.
Implying that we must be ready for *new onsets.*
He vanquishes the *first* Adam, but is vanquished by the *Second.*
With the sword of the Spirit, *He* comes off Victor.
Capability of temptation, proves His perfect *humanity.* Heb. ii. 17.
Angels came. Mark i. 13. As hostile powers fled, heavenly powers surround Him.
Receives Heaven's homage and Father's smile among beasts. Mark i. 13.

Heaven a sympathising witness of the conflicts of earth.
The greatest triumph over the dark king, celebrated *secretly*.
None need dread demons or deserts, since *angels* are *near*.

Beasts. Mark i. 13. Daniel from the den of beasts advances near the *throne*. Dan. v. 29.

Our Lord from similar perils, proceeds to take the *crown*.
Objects of temptation: 1. Gives the Lord experience of His work.
2. Makes trial of the glorious qualifications He had received.
3. Encourages Him in the great work of redemption.
4. He learns how to succour them that are tempted. Heb. ii. 18.
5. Pledge that He will destroy the works of the devil. 1. John iii. 8.

"*Ended.*" In the course of this trial our Lord was tempted 1stly. To DISTRUST. "*Command these stones,*" &c. 2ndly. To PRESUMPTION. "*Cast thyself down.*" 3rdly. To WORLDLY AMBITION. "*All these will I give thee.*" 4thly. To IDOLATRY. "*Fall down and worship me.*" There is probably not a temptation of Satan but is reducible to one or other of these four, *Dr. A. Clarke.* There is no temptation against which this example may not furnish us with weapons and teach us how to use them, *Bengel.* "*For a season,*" lit. *till a time.* It expresses the devil's intention to return, *Meyer.* From this time forth the devil knew Jesus, *Stier;* more especially on the approach of our Lord's passion, the prince of evil returned, *Vers. Ger.* Matt.'s order preferred, *Schleiermacher, Major, Brown, Alford.* Narrated by our Saviour to His disciples, *Olshausen, Norton.* Unnecessary if inspired, The *Author.* "*Temptations*" addressed to the threefold division of our nature, body, soul, and spirit, *Ellicott.*

---

14. *And Jesus returned in the power of the Spirit into Galilee: and there went out a fame of him through all the region round about.*

Returned. After John's imprisonment, a year after His baptism.
Events of the interval, briefly stated by John iv. 43.

Galilee. Luke i. 26. The records of Our Lord, confined mainly to His last year. See Notes.

Spirit. Luke iii. 22. He needed no *call* to preach the Gospel.

Fame, of miracles wrought by Him in Capernaum.
They brought crowds of hearers to His presence.

"*Spirit.*" His human soul, *Crosby.* Divine nature, *Owen.* Power of the full anointing of the Spirit *received at baptism, Alford.* "*Fame.*" Result of His preaching, *Oosterzee.* Men felt the power of the Spirit, *Bengel.*

15. *And he taught in their synagogues, being glorified of all.*

Taught. The *Great* Teacher. His hearers the most favored of men.
Saviour, thus glorified in a corrupt church.
Many reformers, so called, are only schismatics.
Synagogues. 1. Assembly. 2. Edifice. 3. Festal assembly of heaven. Heb. xii. 23.
First named 174 B.C. Small, without windows.
Men first worshipped in open air. Gen. xviii.
Then built a wall round the altar, but without roof.
In Greece, a mere *cord* marked the limits of a holy place.
Temples of Greece, without windows—lamps gave light.
Worshippers stood *without*, priests alone were *within*.
Synagogues built, when ten men of piety and means were found.
To erect one, was supposed a passport to heaven. Luke vii. 5. Hence multiplied.
In Jerusalem there were 460 in number. People sat facing the temple.
Rome has 360 churches, population 120,000, about 160 to a church.
The ark was in the western part, 19 prayers said, phylacteries read.
Law read. Twenty verses of Scripture expounded.
Antiochus forbade the reading of the Law under penalty of death.
Teachers *sat*. Matt. xxiii. 2. Service on sacred days, 2nd and 5th of the week.
Synagogue and mosque divide females from the audience by lattice.
Glorified. To be humble under honours—a rare virtue.

ἐδίδασκε, announcing good or evil tidings. *κηρυσσ.*, critical notes, Luke ix. 2. Same as *caduceator*, *caduceus*, wand of peace, borne by the herald in time of war. Proclamation made on *authority*. *ευαγγελ.*, *always* good news. Luke xx. 1 discriminates, *Trench*, *Campbell*. *συναγω.*—Assembly of Greek freemen, and *ἐκκλησ.*—Called *out of the people*, Church summoned *out of the world*. Christ, Matt. xvi. 18, engrafts a more august sense on it, *Campbell*. First, assemblies, then, buildings—similar to *Theseus*' temple now at Athens. One at Hebron described by *Josephus*. Pantheon at Rome, without window, massive and dark. Females invisible formerly, as in mosques now. "*Glorified*." Universal applause, *Campbell*. Exceedingly admired, *Hammond*. Having withstood *temptation*, gains glory, *Bengel*.

---

16. ¶ *And he came to Nazareth, where he had been brought up: and, as his custom was, he went into the synagogue on the sabbath day, and stood up for to read.*

Came. Properly *identical* with the record in Matt. xiii. 54.
Nazareth. Luke i. 26. His sisters dwelt there. Matt. xiii. 56.

Mary had retired to Cana, her permanent home.

Brought up, His entire life to 30 years of age, the priestly age.

This the turning point in our Saviour's life.

Hitherto He had met with a kind of toleration.

Henceforth the city of David is no safe dwelling-place for Him.

Custom. Creatures of habit, men's minds become set. Jer. xiii. 23.

An element of great power, in controlling mankind.

Our Lord thus bids us cultivate *regularity* in religious duties.

If the sinless Jesus, how much more ought *sinners!*

Went, &c. His Father's *day*, *word*, and *worship*, acknowledged.

Sabbath. Heb. *Rest.* Luke vi. 2-5. See Notes.

In Sabbath battles, the assailants are generally defeated.

Those firms desecrating it, generally become *bankrupts.*

Nations despising God's day, uniformly punished. 1. Sam. ii. 30.

Stood. Hitherto a hearer. Henceforth *the Great Teacher.*

It implied, He desired to read a Scripture Lesson.

Read. Bible ought ever to be heard in God's worship.

"*Nazareth.*" His enemies had little opportunity to arrest Him, *Ellicott.* They could only watch and annoy. *Andrews.* He took Capernaum on His way. Luke iv. 23. *Alford, Kraft.* Same as Matt. xiii. 53. Mark vi. 1. *Lange, Alford, Schleiermacher, Brown.* Different, *Meyer, Stier, Robinson, Tischendorf, Wieseler, Ewald, Andrews.* "*Custom,*" as having preached for some time, *Brown.* Time preceding His 30th year, *Oosterzee.* He returned after brief intervals to the Feasts, *Olshausen.*

---

17. *And there was delivered unto him the book of the prophet Esaias. And when he had opened the book, he found the place where it was written.*

Delivered, by the Minister, a roll, the day's lesson.

A solemn moment, after thirty years of silence.

Book. Materials and method of writing. Luke i. 63. See Notes.

Prophet. Luke i. 70. **Isaiah.** Luke iii. 4. Character and life. See Notes.

Opened. Gr. *unrolled.* Parchments rolled. Christ first opens the O.T's matchless treasures, Himself the Inspirer.

Found. Selects it, to correct *worldly* views of the Messiah. Isa. lxi. 1.

Written. He read from the Septuagint, not the *Heb. original.*

Antiochus 174 B.C., put to death those who read the Law.

"*Opened*," evolvere volumen, frequent phrase. By divine direction, *Meyer*: corresponding with the prophecy, verse 22, *De Wette*. By Providential guidance, *Alford*. "*The place*," a text, *Vitringa*, *Le Clerc*. A section, *Lightfoot*. A section read last of Aug., first of Sept., *Major*. An infallible date of chronology, *Bengel*, *Oosterzee*. Doubtful, *Greswell*. "*Written*." Luke quotes *memoriter* from Sept, *Oosterzee*. First received its accomplishment, in Christ, *Hoffman*.

---

18. *The Spirit of the Lord is upon me, because he hath anointed me to preach the gospel to the poor; he hath sent me to heal the brokenhearted, to preach deliverance to the captives, and recovering of sight to the blind, to set at liberty them that are bruised.*

Spirit. Luke i. 15. Passage seems inspired for *this hour*.
Upon me. On Prophets, at *seasons*, on Christ *always*.
Me, claiming *conscious* inspiration direct from God.
Lord. The *Three Persons* of the Trinity pass before us.
Anointed. Common practice, Jews, Greeks, Romans. Mic. 6. 15.
Its objects were health, strength, beauty and consecration.
Its absence a sign of mourning at Egyptian feasts.
Prophets. 1. Kings xix. 16; Priests. Ex. xl. 15; Kings. Judg. ix. 8.
Spiritual anointings. Ps. ii. 2. Oil of gladness. Ps. xlv. 7.
Christ anointed with the Holy Ghost. John i. 32; Acts iv. 27.
Here He was inaugurated for the work of the Atonement. Ex. xl. 15.
Preach. Luke viii. 1. & ix. 2. Glad tidings. His life, labors, miracles.
1. Inspired with wisdom to preach the Gospel to the poor.
2. Grace to heal the broken-hearted.
3. Righteousness and sanctification, deliverance to the captives.
4. Redemption, to preach the acceptable year of the Lord.
Each sermon like Christ's, should be: 1. Founded on Scripture. 2. Suited to the hearers. 3. Attractively set forth.
Gospel. *Glad news.* Afflicted are comforted when Christ appears.
Poor. Chasm between rich and poor, *wide* in the East. Jo. vii. 49.
Jews believed the Messiah would favor the *higher* classes.
In India, a Sudar reading the *Vedas*, hot oil is poured in his ears.
To *break* these iron walls of caste was Christ's great work.
A church which recognizes, and acts on the principle of social caste, see James ii. 1-9, is *Antichristian*.
Jubilee liberated slaves, and released debtors. Ezek. xlvi. 17.
Poor in spirit, not intellectual weakness, nor bodily want, *merely*.
The saints are sufferers, destitute of worldly felicity. Luke vi. 20.
Heal. Gr. as a physician. "Balm of Gilead." Jer. viii. 22.
Broken. Gr. *crushed*. Alludes to the gentle ministry of Christ.

"He will not break the bruised reed, nor quench the smoking flax."
Opposes the formalists, self-righteous, lovers of themselves.
Deliverance. Oriental prisoners in every age treated most cruelly.
Captives. Gr. taken by the point of the spear—generally sold, as slaves, if not put to death, regardless of color.
Blind. Prisoners' eyes put out. Zedekiah's, Samson's. Jer. xxxiv. 3. Jud. xvi. 21.
Bolts and bars typify the desperate *strength* of sinful habits.
Kings oft opened the doors to prisoners at their coronation.
Our Lord restores Satan's captives to *liberty* and *sight.*
Sinners blinded by Satan, are "*blind, who have eyes.*"
Liberty. Many hearts are bound by chains of care and remorse.
Bruised. Gr. the scars, from the fetters in stocks. Acts xvi. 24.
1. Poor. 2. Captives. 3. Blind—representatives of suffering humanity.
1. Light. 2. Health. 3. Liberty—images of Christ's *Salvation.*

οὗ ἕνεκεν. Inasmuch, *Wakefield.* Because, *Major.* πτωχοῖς, Heb. has "meek," *Lightfoot.* ἰάσασθ., omitted, *Cod. Sina. Vat.,* and *Cant.* Retained, *Alex.* Doubtful, *Lachmann.* Cancelled, *De Wette, Meyer.* Retained, *Bengel, Stier.* "*Deliverance.*" Jubilee, *Alexander.* Crept in from the margin, *Le Clerc.* "Sight," &c. Orig. Heb. has *bound in prison, Lightfoot.* Heb. opening of the prison, *Kimchi.* Complete opening, *Gesenius.* Deliverance from darkness, *Ewald.* Spiritual blindness, *Alexander.* Speaker, is Isaiah, *Umbreit.* Our Lord, *Vitringa, Alexander.*

---

19. *To preach the acceptable year of the Lord.*

Preach. Gr. Herald. Luke viii. 1; ix. 2.
Acceptable, *i.e.,* the Jubilee.
Jubilee. Heb. The prolonged sounding of the trumpet. Lev. xxv. 9.
Slaves, except strangers, freed: debts, mortgages, released.
Every fiftieth year, social state, founded by Moses, restored.
Every seventh and every fiftieth year, the land was not tilled.
Holy Ghost made Christ's advent a spiritual Jubilee.
No Israelite, by the *Jubilee trumpet,* gained *such* an inheritance.
"Blessed are the people who know the joyful sound." Psa. lxxxix. 15.
"Acceptable year," precedes "the day of vengeance." Isa. xxxiv. 8.
Year. All the ages from Calvary to the day of judgment.
How brief our *hour,* to do the work of eternity.
1. Moments of mercy. 2. Hours of trials. 3. Eternity of joy.

δεκτον, not classical, *Wetstein*. Accepted time, *Major*. Our Lord's ministry probably lasted two years and three months, The *Author*. One year. *Clement Alex.*, *Origen*, *Julius Africanus*. Three years. *Melito* of *Sardis*, *Irenaeus*, *Tertullian*; but the record is mainly confined to the last, *Ellicott*. Refers to the Jubilee, *Lightfoot*, *Grotius*. Passage interpolated from *Vulgate*, *Campbell*, *Tischendorf*. Retained, *Alford*. Chronological datum.—Passage read on Atonement season, *Bengel*, *Mc Knight*.

---

20. *And he closed the book, and he gave it again to the minister, and sat down. And the eyes of all them that were in the synagogue were fastened on him.*

Closed. Gr. rolled up the scroll. One *inspired*, may *close* the Bible.
Offers of mercy, and days of grace, alike have limits. Heb. iv. 7.
Sat down. Ancients sat, when they gave instructions.
A divine dignity characterizes all His movements.
Minister. Gr. *Under-rower.* Luke i. 2, humble servants.
Fastened. Gr. *Sharply fixed*, expecting great things.
Thirsty souls ever *drink in* the truth as it is in Jesus.
His Divinity seemed to flash through His earthly garments.

"*Minister*," angel of the church, *Lightfoot*. One of the deacons, *Prideaux*. It was the duty of the minister to keep the sacred books, *Alford*.

---

21. *And he began to say unto them, This day is this Scripture fulfilled in your ears.*

Began, with solemn, weighty truths, to preach the Gospel.
This day, of "merciful visitation," which they believed not.
Had they *power* as *malice*, it would have been His *last day*.

"*Fulfilled*." His course of ministry, *Alford*, *Brown*. ὠσὶν, by hearing *Me*, *De Wette*. Jesus is the fulfilment of all prophecies, types, and promises, *Quesnel*.

---

22. *And all bare him witness, and wondered at the gracious words which proceeded out of his mouth. And they said, Is not this Joseph's son?*

Witness. Prejudice and guilt must approve the truth. Num. xxiii. 10.
Wondered. Solemn sermons don't prevent men loving the world.
His *manner* must have made an irresistible impression. John vii. 46.
Preacher often *admired*, and yet his message *rejected*.

How many heard the Redeemer on earth cry "Come unto me." Who will hereafter hear Him cry "Depart ye cursed!"

Gracious. Sweetness of manner, and richness of matter.

Is not. His humble earthly relatives, the great stumbling-block.

His deep humility, a strong evidence of Divine condescension.

With incredulity and contempt, they recount His brethren. Matt. xiii. 55.

We know this Wonder-Worker and friends, as *common people.*

In the carpenter's son, they *resolve* not to find the Messiah.

Joseph's Son. They knew he had received no Rabbinical education.

A challenge for Him to work a miracle.

Proves how little they knew of His miraculous birth.

Prejudice *weakens* judgment, pride *blinds* the mind.

Infidels ever *deride*, but cannot *disprove* His claims.

As usual, their *wondering*, gives witness *against* themselves.

Their wretched pride cannot comprehend the *humility* of the Great One.

Such quench the Spirit. 1. Thess. v. 19, and believe a lie. 2. Thess. ii. 11.

A divine impression of truth, resisted, maddens the Nazarenes.

ἐθαύμ.—Dislike, not admiration, *Pearce.* At the matter, not manner, *Oosterzee.* Surprise, *Major.* Praise and admiration, but, unaccompanied by settled faith, give place to perversity, *Bengel.* Wonder with *envy*, *Alford.* Enemies astonished, *Oosterzee.* "*Witness.*" Favorable testimony, *Campbell.* Testimony of admiration, *Wakefield.* λογοίς. Eloquent expressions, *Wetstein.* Their divine power, *Grotius.* The subject matter, *Wolfius.* Joyful nature of subjects, *Kype.* "*Gracious.*" Sweetness, benevolence and grace, *Stier.* His matter and manner, *Brown.*

---

23. *And he said unto them, Ye will surely say unto me this proverb, Physician, heal thyself: whatsoever we have heard done in Capernaum, do also here in thy country.*

Surely say. Knowing, they in *heart* believed, the prophecy did not suit *Him.*

Infinitely wiser than human teachers, *He* could place His finger on the *secret keys* of the minds of His hearers.

He plainly tells them,—Why He would work no miracles there.

Proverb. Gr. parable. Spiritual truth illustrated by a representation in nature. Luke v. 36.

Physician. Luke v. 31. As their countryman, they held Him bound for a miracle.

Heal. Make yourself rich, honored, happy, great.

A physician *despised*, but healing all who came.

A prophet deserving highest honors, but receiving none.
Thyself. This reproach was repeated under the *cross.*
Others. One so ignorant, ought not to instruct others.
Heard. Choosing Capernaum as residence, known at Nazareth.
Done. Miracles recorded. Matt. viii. Mark, chap. i. ii. iii. iv.
Appetite for miracles easily excited. Never satisfied. Matt. xii. 39.
Severely rebuked, "Except ye see signs and wonders" &c. John iv. 48.
Long after His ascension, Jews *called for miracles.* 1. Cor. i. 22.
Miracles not to *compel* faith, but to leave unbelief inexcusable. Luke xvi. 31.
Miracles on earth, are only *nature* with the Creator.
Capernaum. Heb. *Town of pleasure*, or of Nahum.
Not named in O. T., once in Josephus; built after The *Exile.*
Stood north-west of sea of Galilee, chosen home of Jesus. Mark ii. 1.
The spots which lay claim to its site are, 1. *Khan Minyeh*, and 2. *Tell Hûm*, three miles north.
Honored by His miracles, His second birth-place.
Violence of Nazarenes, not the *cause* of the change.
Here paid tax. Matt. xvii. 24. Twelve months residence made a citizen.
Matt. here chosen apostle. Matt. ix, 9. Peter and Andrew dwelt here. Mark i. 29.
The centurion's servant, Simon's mother-in-law, and the paralytic, healed. See Matt. viii. and ix.
Here our Lord delivered the wonderful discourse recorded John vi.
Do also. "Why not begin Thy mighty works among *us?*"
"Thou hast passed Thy neighbours by, for strangers."
He knew them too well, to hope for any good result.

"*Heal,*" &c. Kinder to strangers than friends, *Grotius.* Help your own countrymen first, *Oosterzee.* Enrich yourself, *Olshausen.* Exalt your own connection, *Meyer.* This proverb seems to have been current among Greeks, Romans, and Jews, *Wetstein.* "*Capernaum.*" Khan-Minyeh, north of the Plain of Esdraelon, *Robinson.* Tell-Hum, *Thompson, Ellicott, Winer, Ewald.*

---

24. *And he said, Verily I say unto you, No prophet is accepted in his own country.*

He said. A formula of the O. & N. T.; implies a previous pause on [speaker's part.
Verily. No unmeaning term, solemn attention called.
Prophet. Luke i. 70. Divine Physician for soul diseases.
Accepted. A deep principle, in our *fallen* nature.
An unwillingness to esteem virtue, due to *envy.*

Unrenewed heart would pull down all *higher* than itself.
Envy, key-note, ending in the *death* of 50,000,000 Christian martyrs.
Familiarity takes away the charm of *novelty*.
It reveals the *tinsel* glittering in hollow, but showy virtues.
We seem unable to associate every day life, with a *loftiness* of spirit.
Thus the matchless powers and graces of Jesus, not esteemed.
Wicked Nazarenes, did not *want* to honor *such* a Messiah.
Had He *half* Caesar's pomp, all Judea would have been in His train.

"*Accepted.*" Nearer the vision, less the attraction. Christians should therefore labor among *Strangers*, *Brown*. Human heart is ever *jealous* of superior virtue, *Author*. Earthly mindedness, prejudice and pride, the real causes, *Oosterzee*. Your own fault, if the Physician care less for you, than for those more remote, *Bengel*.

---

25. *But I tell you of a truth, many widows were in Israel in the days of Elias, when the heaven was shut up three years and six months, when great famine was throughout all the land.*

I tell. He claims omniscience, for the Bible may not have recorded all the cases cured by Elijah and Elisha.
Truth. He knew all Jewish feelings, would rise against Him.
Their national vanity finally rose to absolute *infatuation*.
Widows. Gr. Bereaved. Luke xviii. 3. Sad term understood in every language.
Elias. Luke i. 17. Heavens shut in answer to Elijah's prayer. Jas. v. 17.
Early rains fall in April, *latter* in October, in Judea. Hosea vi. 3.
He pronounced that judgment inspired of God. 1. Kings xvii. 1.
Six months. Preceding the commencement of the three years.
Famine, Sword, and Pestilence, God's messengers. Ezek. v. 17.

"*Six months,*" added in advance, *Lightfoot*, *Major*. A Jewish mode of speech, *De Wette*. O. T. and N. T. Chronology vary, *Geisler*. Reckoned from Elijah's arrival at Sarepta, *Olshausen*. Luke's information derived from authority unknown to us, *Kuinoel*.

---

26. *But unto none of them was Elias sent, save unto Sarepta,* a city *of Sidon, unto a woman* that was *a widow.*

Sent. Gracious display of sovereign power. Eph. ii. 17.
Finger of the *Inspirer*, invests a line of the O.T. with deep interest.

Sarepta. Site lost, near Surafend, between Tyre and Sidon.
A sea-port, made a Latin bishopric by the Crusaders.
Sidon. Named for, and built by the oldest son of Canaan. Gen. x. 15.
Now Saida, a Phoenician city once celebrated for commerce.
Twenty miles south of Beyrout—very ancient. Gen. xlix. 13.
Belonged to Asher. Josh. xi. 8. Watered by streams of Lebanon.
Famous for making glass, and for their ships in the Trojan war.
The harbour choked with sand, old city now complete ruins.
Paul found friends there. Acts xxvii. 3. Present population, 7,000.
Widow. Foreigner and poverty, contemned by Jews. Matt. xv. 27.
Miraculous increase of oil and meal supplied her wants. 1. Kings, xvii. 16.
Jehovah, covenant God of the widow and fatherless. Deut. x. 18.
Heaven closed three years in vengeance, opened three years by Christ's preaching.

"*Sarepta.*" Heb. Zarephath. Theophilus, (Luke i. 3,) must have praised God's grace to the Gentiles, *Stier*. "*Sidon.*" Hebrew signifies "*Fishing.*" 400 stadia from Beyrout, *Strabo*. Its fleet named by *Homer*, employed by *Xerxes*, *Polybius*. Famous in ancient history. Fifty miles from Nazareth, the most northern city of our Lord's journeys, *Ed.*

---

27. *And many lepers were in Israel in the time of Eliseus the prophet; and none of them was cleansed, saving Naaman the Syrian.*

Lepers. Gr. scaly. A disease indigenous in Egypt and Asia. Compare 2. Kings, 5 chap.
Promoted by damp air, want of cleanliness, and eating greasy or oily food.
Skin is silvery, resembling and named *Elephantiasis*. 2. Kings, v. 27.
Bones and marrow infected, feet lost their power.
Supposed to have been Job's disease. The lepers dwelt *alone*. 2. Kings, [xv. 5.
A bright spot on the skin, Lev. xiii. 2, a proof of its presence.
Garment on his head, like mourners, his look that of a beast.
Hand on his lips, and cried, "unclean, unclean!"
Carried with him the emblems of death, "garments rent."
Head bare, all the springs of life poisoned.
Introduced in Europe by Crusaders, leper was clothed in a *shroud*.
Masses were said for his soul, as one *dead*, property given to heirs.
Bodily *anguish* rendered the victim miserable.
House infected, walls razed, and carried out of the city. Lev. xiv. 34.

Incurable. "Am I a God, to kill, or make alive?" 2. Kings, v. 7.
Instead of sacrifice cleansing, his touch *polluted* the *altar*.
That altar, useless, defiled, was torn down and scattered.
Symbolized the *incurable* malignant nature of *sin*.
Miriam, Gehazi and Uzziah struck by God. Num. xii. 10; 2. Chron. xxvi. 23. 2. Kings v. 27.
Author saw a family of *children lepers* in Judea from 2 to 10 years of age.
Eliseus or Elisha. Heb. Salvation of God; pupil and successor of Elijah 903 B.C.
1. Miracle.—Divided Jordan, with Elijah's mantle.
2. Sweetened waters of Jericho. 3. Punished 42 youths for cursing.
4. Relieved Jehoram. 5. Widow's cruse of oil. 6. Predicts a son.
7. Raises dead child. 8. Cures poisoned food. 9. Increases bread.
10. Cures Naaman. 11. Iron swims. 12. Syrians blinded.
13. Predicts plenty. 14. Foretells death of a prince. 15. Foretells king's death, and Hazael's reign. 16. Predicts Syrians' defeat. 17. His bones restore a corpse to life, let down into his grave.
Naaman. Heb. *Pleasantness.* General of Benhadad.
A Syrian, high in honor and wealth, but a *leper*. 2. Kings, v.
A Hebrew slave, "a little maid," informs him of cures having been made.
The king gives him a letter to Joram the king of Israel, an old enemy.
He felt insulted. Elisha advises they send him to him.
As a *leper*, he could not enter the prophet's house.
Elisha refuses to come out, merely sends a messenger.
Enraged, Naaman refused to wash 7 times in Jordan. Lev. xiv. 7.
Repents, goes, and is healed. Elisha refuses all reward.
Gehazi by fraud obtains treasures, and becomes a leper.
Naaman asks for two mules burden of earth, for an altar. Ex. xx. 24.
Knowing God's holiness, asks pardon for bowing in house of Rimmon.
Naaman's name, a reproach to the Jews for unbelief.
The Syrian, and a Shunammite, both Gentiles, grace truly *sovereign*.
Proved God loved believing *strangers*, more than unbelieving *Jews*.
He often passes by *formalists*, saves *profligates* and *Pagans*.
Syrian. Luke ii. 2. This implies an answer, *No!*
Ye are *unworthy* of miracles, as the Jews of old of prophets.
Hence they were sent among the Gentiles.

λεπροὶ. Levitical laws, mere Board of health, *Michaelis*. Persians and Polynesians exclude them also, *Wakefield*. Sum of all diseases; midway between demoniacal possessions and ordinary diseases, *Alexander*. Jews, not Pagans, feared the touch. Naaman talked with the king, *Major*. A living parable of moral death, *Trench*. Touch cleansed by hyssop, *Lightfoot*. Excluded from walled towns. Ancient, a more dreadful *type*, than modern, *Alexander*. The Author having seen a number of lepers, hardly thinks it possible. Hebrews expelled from Egypt, on account of this disease, *Tertullian*. *Eliseus* or *Elisha*; of such importance is the prophet esteemed by God that his name is given to an epoch, *Bengel*. Νεεμὰν, Ναιμὰν, *Lachmann*, *Tischendorf*.

---

28. *And all they in the synagogue, when they heard these things, were filled with wrath.*

All they, who admired His kind and winning eloquence. Verse 22.
Each fact kindled Jewish pride and fanaticism.
These things. He (the son of Joseph) compared Himself to the *greatest prophets*.
He had hinted, God had kind thoughts towards *Gentiles*.
Proud man scorns being told, "*God owes him nothing*." Matt. xi. 26.
The unrenewed heart angered now at "*few saved*." Matt. vii. 14.
Wrath. Fanaticism roused, the *fiercest* of all man's passions.
Their pride wounded, He left them spiritual *beggars*.

29. *And rose up, and thrust him out of the city, and led him unto the brow of the hill whereon their city was built, that they might cast him down headlong.*

Rose up. In a malignant, boisterous rage.
Thrust. Gr. *Hurried him along*. Service solemnity, broken.
In frenzy, they resolve to *murder* Him, for His good works.
"He came to His own, but His own received him Him not. John i. 11.
A good comment on Nathaniel's question. John i. 46.
Same reckless frenzy carried out, nails Him to the cross.
City. Nazareth. **Brow.** Several are now near it.
Hill, of Nazareth, contrasted with the Hill of Temptation.
Nazareth shows the fruits of faithful, *perfect* preaching.
1. Blossoms, no sure signs of fruit. 2. Fruit sadly blighted.
3. Harvest may be better than the promise.
Marvelled. Mark vi. 6. At Gentile faith, and Jewish unbelief.
To His Divinity, nothing was new; to His humanity, wonder was *natural*.
Headlong. Idumean captives, thus were slain.
At Rome, the capital bordered on the Tarpeian Rock.
Ever thus with a fickle populace, "*Truth begets hatred*."
His first open insult! From "His own household." Matt. x. 36.
The whole occurrence, a foreshadowing of subsequent treatment from the nation.

ἐξέβαλον. Hurried, *Bloomfield*. With violence, *Brown*. "*Brow*" taken like *dorsum* from the body. "*City*." Nazareth, *Major*. Capernaum, *Whitby*. "Brow" Tradition points to a cliff some 90 feet high behind the present Maronite Church, *Andrews*, *Robinson*. Crumbled away by earthquakes, &c., *Vander Velde*.

---

30. *But he, passing through the midst of them, went his way.*

Passing. He neither blinds them, nor becomes invisible.
He turns on them one look of Majesty, sign of His *Almightiness*.
Supernatural power, as in Gethsemane. John xviii. 6. Hour not yet come.
His ministers invulnerable and immortal, till their work is done.
His intrepid calmness, contrasted with their blind fury.
It depended on Himself to suffer, or not suffer. John x. 18.
He is Lord of *times*, as well as of *things*.

διελθὼν, overawed by *courage*, *Ammon*. Dignified tranquility. "Slave, wilt thou kill Marius?" disarmed an assassin, *Hase*, *Stier*, *Oosterzee*. Escaped through narrow streets, *Robinson*. Miracle, *Doddridge*, *Euthymius*, *Olshausen*, *Alford* Gleam of divinity flashed on the crowd, *Owen*. Special Providence, *Meyer*. Mob confounded, *Pfenninger*. By flight, *Tertullian*. Ministry of angels, Heb. i. 14, *Brown*.

---

31. *And came down to Capernaum, a city of Galilee, and taught them on the Sabbath days.*

32. *And they were astonished at his doctrine: for his word was with power.*

Capernaum. Luke iv. 23. His "own city." Matt. ix. 1. **Galilee.** Luke i. 26.
It was in a direct road from Jerusalem to Damascus.
Taught. Gr. *Continued teaching*, from the very first Sabbath, and on.
Discouragements will not check faithful laborers.
Sabbath. Luke vi. 2, 5. **Astonished.** Gr. *Strike with wonder*.
A blameless life, and faultless system, did not *convince*.
They knew his humble mode of living, and were offended.
Familiarity with sacred things, too oft begets contempt. 1. Sam. ii. 29.
Heaven-descending manna, is at length despised. Num. xxi. 5.
Doctrine. Not principles, but His unsurpassed *manner*.
Word. *Course* of teaching, by parable and miracle.
Power. He expounded the Law as Law-*Maker*, not *Interpreter*.

Rabbis enforced theirs, by appealing to eminent *teachers*.
Sermons *applauded*, no sign of hearers *improving*.
The inspiration of the Bible, and sunlight, both *self-evidencing* alike.

"*Capernaum.*" Joseph had possessions there, *Lightfoot*, *Ewald.* Resided in Peter's house, *Norton.* Peter opened a house for his master's convenience, *Alexander.* Whole family, except sisters, removed thither, *Alford.* Tribute money proves him a legal inhabitant (Matt. xvii. 24) *Greswell.* "*Power.*" Self-evidencing light and self-asserting force, accompany all God's teachings, *Alexander.* Conscience created for *truth*, as lungs for *air.* Scribes appealed to masters, *Grotius.* διδαχῇ, learning, *Tyndale.* Teaching, *Wycliffe.* 1. Art. 2. Manner of teaching. 3. Things taught.

---

33. ***And in the synagogue there was a man, which had a spirit of an unclean devil, and cried out with a loud voice.***

Synagogue. Luke iv. 15. **Man.** Demoniac, an object of *compassion*.
Persons were actually subject to the control of demons. Evidences—
1. Supernatural strength. Mark v. 4; 2. *Mind*, not source of blindness. Matt. xii. 22.
3. Insanity cannot *divine*. Acts xvi. 17; 4. Demoniacs confess it. Mark v. 9.
5. Demons knew Jesus. Mark i. 24; 6. Jesus addresses them. Matt. viii. 32.
7. Apostles assert it. Luke x. 17; 8. Jesus admitted it. Matt. xii. 28.
9. A female bound. Luke xiii. 11; 10. Peter assures us of it. Acts x. 38.

Unclean. Vileness, and moral loathsomeness of the demoniac.
Indicates the kind of sins Satan encourages in men.
Unclean heart, far more miserable, than *possessed* body.
Devil. Luke iv. 2. See critical Notes.
Cried. Denotes a more powerful agent, *mastering* a human being.

"*Spirit,*" of deceased wicked ones, *Josephus.* Disease, the substratum, *Trench.* Bodily disease, *Semler*, *Farmer*, *Paulus.* Superstitions, vulgar opinion, *Strauss.* Insanity, *Mede.* Magnetic clairvoyance, *Ebrard.* Demons acted on the nerves, *Oosterzee.* Lunacy.—Unlucky cast of dice, as Romans called the "*Cast of Venus.*" St. Vitus' dance, or St. Anthony's fire, *Wakefield.* Mainly among rude Gentiles, *Smith*, *Barry*, Possession admitted by Greek and Roman writers, *Plato*, *Lucian*, &c. Possessions found still,

Kerner, *Esquirol*, *Rhemius*, an Indian missionary, *Bacon*, *Sir M. Hale*, *Bp Hall*, *Baxter*, *Lavater*, *Dr. Thos. Brown*, *Ellis's Polynesian Researches*. "*Spirit of an unclean devil.*" *Spirit*, implies its operation, *devil*, its nature, *Bengel.*

---

34. *Saying, Let* us *alone; what have we to do with thee,* thou *Jesus of Nazareth? art thou come to destroy us? I know thee who thou art; the Holy One of God.*

Let us. Consciousness lost, he seems *identified* with the demon. Mark v. 7.

Demons unbound, unwillingly honor Christ.

The old hate and contest, ever breaking out. Gen. iii. 15.

The Anointed of the Spirit, and demoniac, both in the synagogue.

Heaven, *Earth*, and *Hell*, all meet in *one* place.

Alone. Gr. a *complaining interjection*, equivalent to "ah!" indicates [terror.

Jesus' blessed presence a *torture* to devils. Mark v. 7.

This insolent demand, a witness of Jesus' Godhead.

Satan dreads all such interference with his domain.

Do with, &c. They want nothing to do with *Him*.

But He has determined only the more to do with *them*.

Art thou come? Note, How Satan meets Jesus.

1. With hypocritical homage. 2. Irreconcilable hate.

3. Cowardly fear. How Jesus meets Satan.

1. Intrepid calmness. 2. Pitying love for his victim. 3. Triumphant power.

Destroy. Hints at destruction, as their sure doom.

Terrified demons recognize Him, as their future *Judge*.

I know. It is no longer, "*If* thou be the Son of God."

These demons had *met* their Creator *before* in unholy warfare.

In the dread conflict in heaven, they felt His wrath. 2. Peter ii. 4.

They knew they would surely meet Him again. Jude, verse 6.

They manifest supernatural knowledge of the *past*.

But can only successfully *surmise* concerning the future.

Devils have clear knowledge of religion. Jas. ii. 19.

Unsanctified wisdom, a dangerous inheritance.

Holy One. The term taken from the Messianic Psalm, xvi. 10.

Note their entire sense of impotence and subjection.

His presence wrings out from them, a confession of His Godhead.

They know full well, He and they, could not dwell together.

They wonder, if the judgment day is coming before its time.

It opens glimpses of the *oneness* in character, between the wicked and Satan.

λεγων omitted, *Cod. Sina.* Cancelled, *Tischendorf.* ἔα. Doubtful, *Lachmann, Oosterzee.* Verb, *Vulgate, Luther.* Interjection, *Brown.* ἅγιος. 1. Perfect. 2. Blameless. 3. Reverential; with the article, always refers to the Divine Being, *Campbell.* "*Know*," officially, not by the Divine nature, *Stier.* ἀπολ. utterly destroy, used by Annihilationists, *Jo. Taylor, of Norwich.*

---

35. *And Jesus rebuked him, saying Hold thy peace, and come out of him, And when the devil had thrown him in the midst, he came out of him, and hurt him not,*

Rebuked. Praises of the vile, no ground of credit to the virtuous.
Saviour's first miracle at Cana, John ii. 11. First in Luke is exorcism.
Hold. Gr. *muzzled.* Were dumb *Wycliffe.* Implies coercion.
He would not have people believe, on a *devil's testimony.* Matt. viii. 29.
If the tempted knew the source of assault, they would be oftener victors.
He knew the homage from *unclean* lips, and rejects it.
Come out. Breaking up of *two* distinct personalities.
On Jesus' arrival, demons cannot long stay.
Thrown. Shows what the demon would have done, if he *could.*
Torn. Mark i. 26. Denotes, how reluctant to lose his terrible grasp.
Jews and heathen *then* peculiarly under the power of fiends.
Jesus chose this awful hour of darkness, for His Advent.
Note the fearful peril, of resigning a soul, to the *full power* of evil.
Hurt not. The rage of devils under Christ, always *impotent.*

ῥιψαν. Demoniac deserves our *sympathy*, the demon, *punishment*, *Stier.* Demoniacs expressed desire of deliverance, *Olshausen.* "*Hurt not,*" the devil had wished to hurt the man, *Bengel.*

---

36. *And they were all amazed, and spake among themselves, saying, What a word is this! for with authority and power he commandeth the unclean spirits, and they come out.*

Amazed. Gr. *amazement was upon all.*
Strange teachings, were more *strangely confirmed.*
Spake. They had faith, but no living, *working faith.*
Word! Omnipotent arm of God was laid bare before men.
Sacred solemnity of the Sabbath, broken by miracles.
Where the *old Creation* ended, He begins a *new Creation.*
Authority. *Right* to act, and an effective *power* to do so.

With authority incontrovertible, and power irresistible.
Commandeth. Outward effects of the Redeemer's power.
Far surpassed by *His invisible works of mercy* on the soul.
His *hidden* strokes at sin, were infinitely mightier.
Come out. No guilt too desperate for infinite grace. Isa. i. 18.
Power and *weakness* of Satan's kingdom.
1. Has power to tyrannize over men. 2. To deride the Son of God.
3. Too weak to resist His word. 4. Or ruin one of His lambs.

τίς ὁ. What meaneth this? *Campbell.* Miracles over *licentious*, most wonderful, *Quesnel.* Such an inference could only arise in *monasteries* among *monks.* The *Author.* "*Authority*," indisputable, "*Power*," irresistible, *Bengel.*

---

37. *And the fame of him went out into every place of the country round about.*

38. ¶ *And he arose out of the synagogue, and entered into Simon's house. And Simon's wife's mother was taken with a great fever; and they besought him for her.*

Fame. A wonder-worker, rouses a nation's interest.
Synagogue. Luke iv. 15. **Simon.** Heb. *Heard.* Gr. Peter, a *stone*
His history. Luke vi. 14. **House.** Luke i. 40. Form and materials.
Simon's house. 1. Chosen of our Lord. 2. Visited by sickness.
3. Gladdened by Almighty power. By miracle changed into the house of the Lord.
One believer, often by *covenant*, a blessing to the whole house.
He scarcely enter's Christ's circle, before his family are blessed.
Wife's. Contradicting Rome's dogmas. St. Peter sanctions marriage.
A *slanderous* tradition makes him divorce her, on becoming an apostle.
All apostles, under God's authority, had this right. Gen. ii. 18; 1. Cor. ix. 5.
Fever. Christ's favored friends, not free from afflictions.
Suburbs of Capernaum always marshy and unhealthy.
Besought. He waited to be asked. He encourages prayer. Ezek. xxxvi. 37.
He never refused to heal the sick by miracle, if asked.

πενθερὰ, mother-in-law. Rome, to be consistent, teaches that Peter, when he said, "*We have left all,*" then forsook his wife and became a *celibate*, *Bossuet*, Rheimish Notes. Such exegesis is *wresting* Scripture, 2. Pet. iii. 16, *Horsley*.

39. *And he stood over her, and rebuked the fever; and it left her; and immediately she arose and ministered unto them.*

Stood. Attitude anciently symbolized a *conqueror*. Eph. vi. 13, 14.
War, famine, and pestilence, His servants. 2. Sam. xxiv. 13; Matt. viii. 9.
Rebuked. Figure taken from a boisterous sea. Mark iv. 39.
Diseases treated like demons, as hostile powers.
Dumb elements of nature can *hear* His voice. Jer. xxii. 29.
Left. Gr. *set her free.* Fevers bind with chains of *fire.*
Immediately. In nature, they subside very gradually.
Ministered. Gr. *act as deaconess*, supply with food.
Luke notes *female believers*, more than any other evangelist.
Happy are they who share the privileges of angels. Mark i. 13.
Lives spared by God's grace, consecrate to His service.
Highest medical science, *useless*, without His blessing.

πυρ. μεγάλῳ, an epithet used by Luke, *as a physician*, *Wetstein*, *Alford*. επαν. αυ. *over her.* His approaching so near, proved that the disease yielded to his power, and could cause him no danger by infection, *Bengel.*

---

40. *Now when the sun was setting, all they that had any sick with divers diseases brought them unto him; and he laid his hands on every one of them, and healed them.*

Sun setting. "Sabbath, from even to even." Lev. xxiii. 32.
Cool of the day, favorable for removing invalids.
He did not hesitate to cure on the Sabbath. John v. 17.
A *busy* Sabbath-day, of our Redeemer.
Refusing an act of mercy on the Sabbath, one becomes a *Sabbath-breaker.*
Sick. "All that a man hath, will he not give for his life?" Job ii. 4.
Divers diseases. 1. Many kinds, but one Great Physician.
2. Many cures, but one Healing Power. 3. Many voices, but one Key note, viz., *Grace.* "Unto him," &c. Rev. i. 5.
Brought. Favours not to be expected, if we are too *proud* to seek.
Malady of body and soul. 1. Same misery in both. 2. Same confession.
3. Requires same faith. 4. Uses same remedies.
5. Excites same opposition. 6. Deserves same homage.
Hands, convey no virtue, but *point out* the objects. Heb. vi. 2.
Every one. How deep His heart-felt sympathy for suffering.
Many grievously err, in thinking His miracles *few.*
While healing the body, could He forget the soul?
Many *vows*, made in sickness, forgotten in health.

δύνον. after sun-set, *Campbell.* At setting, *Wakefield.* Not *legally* until after setting, *Theophylact*, *Lightfoot.* Indicates *secular time* for secular *labors*, *Dwight.* ἐπι ἑκαστῳ; "*on each one.*" Thus Christ cares for every separate soul, *Vers. Ger.*

CHAPTER V.

1. *AND it came to pass, that, as the people pressed upon him to hear the word of God, he stood by the lake of Gennesaret.*

Pressed. Regarding in the rush to be healed, neither time, nor place.
Note the patient endurance and humility of the Saviour.
No church can contain the crowds, if a nation *will* to hear.
"Not many *mighty*," 1 Cor. i. 26, but "many *sons* to glory." Heb. ii. 10.
Gennesaret. Heb. a *garden*. Chinneroth, Num. xxxiv. 11. Jos. xii. 3.
Sea of Galilee, called also sea of Tiberias, thirteen miles long, six broad.
Water fresh, cool, clear, beach abounding with pebbles. Jordan flows through it.
700 feet below the Mediterranean sea; Fish plentiful.
Nine cities on its shores, Capernaum, Chorazin, Bethsaida, Magdala, &c.
Tiberias and Magdala alone of the nine remain.

"*Gennesaret.*" Land of Gen. identified with El-Batihah, *Robinson*. In harmony with Josephus, *Tregelles*. For τοῦ ακούειν, "*to hear*," read και ακούειν, "*and heard*," *Tischendorf*.

---

2. *And saw two ships standing by the lake: but the fishermen were gone out of them, and were washing* their *nets.*

Saw. The *third call*. First, John i. 35-42. Second, Matt. iv. 18-22.
Ships. Different kinds. Anciently frail, driven by oars—first made of a hollow tree.
Rafts tied with leather thongs. First built 700 B.C.
Wicker bulwarks, with stones for anchors, but one sail.
Guided by sun and stars, carrying from 7 to 4000 persons.
Ptolemy's had 4000 rowers, they sat in tiers, one above another.
230 fishing ships were on the Lake of Tiberias in the days of Josephus.
Jews an agricultural people, to preserve their *integrity*.
Fishermen. Servants attending the owners of vessels.

"*Saw.*" Same history as Matt. iv. 18, *Lightfoot, Oosterzee, Trench, Robinson, Wieseler, Tischendorf, Andrews.* Distinct, *Augustine, Stier, Alford, Greswell, Brown.* Second call, *Bengel, Alford, W. & W.* Third call, *Brown.* Apostles followed fishing whenever the Lord was at Capernaum, *Alford;* impossible amid the pressure of duties, *Andrews, Ebrard.* "*Standing,*" aground, *Campbell.* At anchor. Stant littore puppes, *Virg., Major.* "*Washing.*" After they had washed, *Hammond.*

---

3. *And he entered into one of the ships, which was Simon's, and prayed him that he would thrust out a little from the land. And he sat down, and taught the people out of the ship.*

Simon's. Peter's history. See Notes on Luke vi. 14. He soon would leave his humble bark.
Prayed. Note the courtesy of Jesus. Domineering spirit rebuked.
"Learn of me, for I am meek and lowly." Matt. xi. 29.
He might *command*, but for love's sake, He asked.
Sat. Ancient posture of instructors. Luke ii. 46. See Notes.
Taught. Peculiar work, next to His atonement.
His resurrection, God's seal, on all He taught and did.
Needing a pulpit, souls perishing, He waited for no *consecration*.
A mountain, a well, a ship, sea side, all were *pulpits* to Jesus.
Sinners might well lend a *pulpit* if He gives His *life*.
Fishermen, unconscious *prophets* of their future work. Jer. xvi. 16.
David, a shepherd, foretold his tending God's flock. Psa. xxiii.
People. He passes by courts, senates, schools, for the *poor*.
Sabbath was past, but earthly toil hinders not spiritual work.
After their devotion, disciples had prodigious success.
Being in the mount with God, brings a double blessing. Luke ix. 33.
Out of the ship. In order more advantageously to fish for men.
He had His eye on two noble brothers near, but then strangers. Ver. 10.

"*Which was Simon's.*" Even at this period precedence is given to Peter, *Bengel.*

---

4. *Now when he had left speaking, he said unto Simon, Launch out into the deep, and let down your nets for a draught.*

Launch out into the deep. This is God's command to each of us.
Lord at Thy word, should be our answer. He will bless our net.
Cheering to the care-worn sons of toil, is that word, "*Launch.*"

Let down. He would first test Peter's obedience; no success is promised.

Obedience is our *duty*, *results* are with the Lord.

His former Word had taken root in Peter's heart.

He moulds into His own image some like Paul, in an *instant*.

Others, like Peter, are laboriously *hewn* and *polished* by sore trials for years.

The beginning of Peter's apostleship; Christ "chooses weak things." 1. Cor. i. 27.

Amos, a herdsman, David, a shepherd, Matthew, a publican.

By humble *fishermen*, Christ will yet win *many nations*. Ezek. xlvii. 10.

"*Launch.*" Omitted by John. A discrepancy, *Baur*, *De Wette*. Out of many omissions, natural, *Ebrard*. John refers to an *interview*, *Oosterzee*. "*Into the deep.*" This was further than *a little*, verse 3. "*For a draught.*" This implied a promise of success; comp. John xxi. 3, 6, *Bengel*.

---

5. *And Simon answering said unto him, Master, we have toiled all the night, and have taken nothing: nevertheless at thy word I will let down the net.*

Master. Indicates an acquaintance already formed.

Filial faith soon enabled him to call Him, LORD.

Toiled. Fishing proves neither abject poverty, nor social degradation.

He selects humble, hardy laborers, over sages and kings.

All night. The proper time for fishing in that lake.

Even the Lord's apostles, have their *dark nights* of toil.

He thus tested the Satan-bound female, 18 years, Luke xiii. 16.

Another, 12 years, Mark v. 25. A man 38 years, John v. 5. Abraham 25 years.

At evening time, it shall be light. Zech. xiv. 7.

Sorrow may endure for a night, but joy cometh in the morning. Ps. xxx. 5.

Our calling not to be left abruptly, for want of success.

Nothing. Diligence not always rewarded. "The race is not to the swift nor the battle to the strong." Eccl. ix. 11.

Laborers in Christ's vineyard, not to be discouraged. Isa. xli. 10.

Crossed in *our* chosen plans, *Christ* welcomes us.

Nevertheless. Peter sacrifices practical knowledge to *faith* in Christ.

Thy word. This answer implies modest doubt of success.

To experienced fisherman, the effort, a *sure* failure.

After Christ's *sermon*, look for the outgoing of *power*.
I will. Peter sets aside a life-time of experience, for Christ's *word*.
Our *duty* often *clear*, when God's *reasons* are *hidden*. Jer. x. 23.
Obedience of faith: 1. Its foundation. 2. Its existence. 3. Its blessing.
Transitions in the life off aith: 1. From doubt, to wonder. 2. From want, to abundance. 3. From terror, to joy. 4. From fear, to hope. 5. From failures of earth, to triumph in God.

"*Toiled.*" Fishing, type of hardship, peril, destitution. Greek proverb, *Trench.* No evidence of either ignorance or rudeness, *Alexander.* "*I will,*" a vow to Christ's dignity, not faith, *Olshausen.* Obeys, to prove the command useless, *Trench.* Ἐπιστάτα, equivalent to Rabbi. Luke translates for Greek readers. Matt. uses Κύριε. Mark Διδάσκαλε, *Olshausen.* Peter thought our Lord more *skilful* in fishing than himself, *Bengel.*

---

6. *And when they had this done, they inclosed a great multitude of fishes: and their net brake.*

This done. Obedience, active, prompt, and unreserved, obtained the blessing.
Multitude. The secret, "He hath dominion over the sea."Ps. viii 8.
This part of man's inheritance *lost* by the apostacy.
Quite as easy for the Lord to *collect* fish, as to *create* them.
Mysterious instincts guide the annual flight of birds. Jer. viii. 7.
He creates the wealth of the sea, as well as commands its waves. Job. xxxviii. 11.
God's blessing secured by His promise, by faith, and by labor.
We should confess our unworthiness, and rightly use our blessings.
A miracle compensates at once, for past loss, and present obedience.
It foreshadowed apostolic success in the ministry.
"Lo! I am with you," guarantees success to faithful toilers. Matt. xxviii. 20.
Brake. Gr. *began to break.* A faithless net, *perils* all.
A munificent recompense, for the use of his boat for a pulpit.
Our prayers always answered, would perhaps ruin our interests.
Christ rewards all receiving Him, or His servants as their guests.
At Cana, He multiplied their scanty stores. John ii. 1-10.
Blest Obed-edom, Barzillai, Shunammite, widow of Sarepta. 2. Sam. vi. 11. 2. Sam. xix 39. 1. Kings, xvii. 9; 2. Kings, iv. 8.
Potiphar for Joseph's sake. 276 souls for Paul's sake. Acts xxvii. 24.
No one has lost, or ever will lose in the service of Jesus.

ἰχθύων. Primitive Christians mistook the allegory, verse 10. Resemblance is only as to the mode of taking fish by net, and converts by the gospel "*Brake.*" Heretics do this, by corrupting truth, and schismatics also, *Quesnel*, (Roman Catholic Divine.) At the point of breaking, *Trench*. Was bursting, *Alford*.

---

7. *And they beckoned unto their partners, which were in the other ship, that they should come and help them. And they came, and filled both the ships, so that they began to sink.*

Beckoned. They were too far off to hear their call.
Partners, of our toil, oft sharers of our triumphs.
Ship. John, the owner, a man of means in Capernaum. Ver. 10.
Help. "A friend loveth at all times, and a brother is born for adversity."
Filled. Gospel on board, or in a house, carries a blessing. Luke xix. 9.
Shutting a door, or kindling a fire in God's house, is not unrewarded, Mal. i. 10.
Godliness profitable for all things, for this life, and that to come. 1. Tim. iv. 8.
Sink. They were dragged down in the water by the weight of the fishes.
How often prosperity proves the ruin of body and soul!
A far harder test to human character than adversity. Deut. xxxii. 15.

"*Beckoned.*" Lest *speaking* frighten the fish, *Trench* Overcome by fear, *Euthymius*. The distance, *Alford*; reverence, *Bengel*. βυθίζεσθαι, exaggeration, *De Wette*. Cum grano salis, *Oosterzee*. Actually sinking, saved by partners, *Stier*. Ready to sink, *Doddridge*.

---

8. *When Simon Peter saw it, he fell down at Jesus' knees, saying, Depart from me; for I am a sinful man, O Lord.*

Saw it. The *impulsive* Simon, is all himself again.
Fell down. Had Jesus been *mere man*, He had *rebuked* him. Acts xiv. 15.
Jesus' knees. Ancients thought *mercy* dwelt in the *knees*.
Praying, the Greeks clasped the knees of their idol gods.
Depart. He forgets the fishes; and turns to the Saviour.
Hebrews, seeing spirits, feared death. Judges vi. 23. Dan. x. 17. Isa. vi. 5. Ex. xxiv. 10. Luke ii. 9. See Notes.
Greeks permitted no gods on board their ship.

Lest offended, their vengeance might raise a tempest.
A wide gulf separates sinful man, from the holy God.
Humility, not fear, fills his wondering, adoring soul.
God always *enters* the broken heart, dreading His presence. Isa. lvii. 15.
Woe! unto us, if the Lord indeed depart from us. Mark v. 17.
Nothing *humbles* a believing soul so deeply as *grace*.
Sinful. Sinner like me, not fit company for *Thee*.
"Art thou come to call my sin to remembrance?" 1. Kings, xvii. 18.
The nearer to God, the clearer becomes our vileness. Job xlii. 6.
Even divine blessings, should fill us with holy *fear*. Psa. cxviii. 4.
Peter while drawing in fish, is *taken* in the net of Christ.
David, tending a flock, follows the Divine *shepherd*.
Capernaumites following for food, get the *bread of life!*
Samaritan coming for water, obtains *water of life!*
Paul, going to Damascus, to *capture* saints, is *captured* himself.
Magi, following a star, are led to the *Star of Bethlehem!*

ἔξελθε, &c. Fear as of an arch-sorcerer, *Ammon*. Upbraided by conscience for returning to his nets, *Stier*. The effect of deep humility, *Lightfoot*. Had seen diseases cured, now fish of the sea obey, *Wetstein*. Superstitious dread, *Olshausen*. Horror, *Kuinoel*. Christ chose apostles from the *greatest* sinners, *Ignatius*, *Jerome*. We best recognize our sinfulness when we best recognize the glory of God, *Vers. Ger.* Christ here appears as the *ideal man*, the second Adam of the 8th Psalm.—"Thou hast put all things under His feet: the fowl of the air, and *the fish of the sea*," &c., *Trench*.

---

9. *For he was astonished, and all that were with him, at the draught of the fishes which they had taken.*

Astonished. Grace appears more glorious, the weaker the instrument.
Our Lord's Divine Power established in all those coasts.
Draught. The miracle concerned *his own* craft, in *his own* vessel, and with *his own* net, after *his own* fruitless efforts.
Far more wonderful, the draught of souls on the Pentecost. Acts ii. 41.

θάμβος. More at this, than, at the healing at Capernaum, *Le Clerc*. In his own occupation, *Stier*. Ecstatic awe—hic numinis ingens horror, *C. Val. Flaccus.*, *Schleusner*. Admiration, *Augustine*. Humility, *Lightfoot*, *Grotius*, *Alford*, *Trench*. περιέσ, took possession, *W. & W.* Each side astonished, *Wickliffe*. Utterly amazed, *Tyndale*. Even God's benefits should teach us to fear him, *Bengel*.

10. *And so was also James, and John, the sons of Zebedee, which were partners with Simon. And Jesus said unto Simon, Fear not; from henceforth thou shalt catch men.*

Our Lord had been teaching about six months.

James and John. Sons of Zebedee and Salome; had hired servants, Mark i. 20.

Owned two ships, acquainted with High priest. John xviii. 15.

James, John, and Peter, at His transfiguration, at raising of Jairus' daughter, and at Gethsemane.

Former, called Boanerges or "the sons of thunder," for their zeal. Mark iii. 17.

James became an apostle, one year after this miracle.

He was the first Christian *martyr* under Herod. Acts xii. 1-2.

John. Son of Zebedee of Bethsaida, time of calling uncertain.

A disciple of John the Baptist, and by him, directed to Christ. John i. 29.

Social position indicated by acquaintance with High priest. John xviii. 15.

Resided at Jerusalem, at the time of the crucifixion. John xix. 27.

Gave Mary, the mother of Christ, a *home*. John xix. 26.

Author of the Gospel, 3 Epistles, and the Apocalypse written in Patmos.

A chief "pillar" in the church. Gal ii. 9. At first vehement in zeal.

Wrote his three epistles in Ephesus, during the reign of Trajan.

Supposed to have died at Ephesus A.D. 100, aged 102, but mere conjectures.

Fear not. A word of kindness from the Friend of sinners.

Highest pledge of God's love. Isa. vii. 4; Hag. ii. 5; Zech. viii. 13, 15.

Sown in tears, His word cannot return void. Isa. lv. 11.

Peter's inauguration to the apostolic office.

Catch. Gr. *take alive.* From element of death, to life.

Fish taken for *death*, converts for eternal *life*.

Their anxiety hitherto for the *body*, henceforth for the *soul*.

By the Gospel net, all kinds taken, will be separated at the Day of Judgment.

Catching souls, like fishing, needs *skill*, not *violence*.

"I will send for many *fishers*, saith the Lord." Jer. xvi. 16.

Peter learns that winning souls is *above* material miracles.

Sea, the *world*, fishers, *preachers*, net, the *gospel*.

Ships, the *churches*, draught, the *success*, shore, *eternity*.

Fish, a symbol dear to the primitive saints, seen on *monuments*, *rings*, *cups*, &c.

JOHN, *the beloved disciple;* wrong to esteem him gentle by nature, only became so by reception of the Spirit of Jesus, Ed. A chair now at Jerusalem, said to be his relic, *Williams*. His brothers, Levites, *Ewald*, *Wieseler*. His disciples, Polycarp and Ignatius,

Jerome. When too aged to preach was carried into the church, and would say, "*Little children, love one another,*" *Jerome.* Tradition says that in the persecution under Domitian, he was taken to Rome, and thrown into a caldron of boiling oil, but taken out unhurt, *Ed.* ζωγρῶν, take them alive, *Robinson.* Used allegorically by Jesus. Success due to His power, not their skill, *Grotius.* Ethical mode of winning souls, *Meyer, Stier.* Catch, *Alford.* Unto salvation, *Wakefield.* Captivate, *Doddridge.* ΙΧΘΥΣ inscribed on tombs in Catacombs of Rome, indicating their memory of the Saviour's charge to Simon. Initials of Ἰησοῦσ Χριστὸσ Θεοῦ Υἱὸσ Σωτὴρ, *McFarlane.*

---

11. *And when they had brought their ships to land, they forsook all, and followed him.*

Forsook. Visible miracles useless, without *invisible* ones.
Calling of Christ vain, unless heard and obeyed by the *heart.* Matt. vi. 21.
All. Fish, nets, ships, home, habits, hopes, friends.
Their all, of little *value;* our Lord notes the *spirit.* Luke xxi. 2.
Many forsake their all, in *form,* but not in *heart.* 2. Tim. iii. 5.
Followed. One who was poor, persecuted, friendless, homeless. Matt. viii. 20.
Some put out the *covetous eye,* but retain the *covetous heart.* Ezek.
After crucifixion, they returned to their fishing. John xxi. 3. [xxxiii. 31.
After the Pentecost, they renounced their nets for ever.

12. ¶ *And it came to pass, when he was in a certain city, behold a man full of leprosy: who seeing Jesus fell on his face, and besought him, saying, Lord, if thou wilt, thou canst make me clean.*

Certain city. Supposed to be Capernaum. Mark ii. 1. Luke iv. 23.
Leprosy. Luke iv. 27. The leper still lingered in the outskirts.
He had heard of *the* Physician, and his heart throbs with *hope.*
Leprosy symbolized the incurable nature of sin's disease.
Over this sacrament of death, our Lord's power was supreme.
Fell, &c. In the East, profound respect, not necessarily adoration.
Face. *Prostrate.* In Oriental lands prostration to superiors is not unusual. But Copts, Greeks, and Moslems, are *daily* seen *prostrate* in worship.
Faith speaks little, *sighs* speak much in His ear. Mal. iii. 16. Psa.
The sinner full of confusion at the sight of the Holy One. lxxix. 11.
Besought. His importunity could neither be resisted, nor silenced.
Sinners must be intensely earnest, to be cleansed.
Mercy might do, what *skill* had never done.
Lepers the *last* that dared to hope, or apply for a cure.

Wilt. The leper doubted not His *power*, but His *willingness*.
He *could*, if He *would*. Would He deign to notice?
Leper *conceded* Him omnipotence, and Christ *seals it*, by healing him.
For man to attempt a cure, were downright folly.
Me clean. No man is too mean for Jesus to love. John iii. 16.
No misery too great for His power to reach. Heb. vii. 25.
Condition of Salvation, not beyond the reach of any one. Rev. xxii. 17.

"*Full of leprosy.*" A touch of medical accuracy from the beloved physician, (Luke) indicates the soreness of the disease, *Alford*. "*Fell.*" Some regarded Messiah *divine*, others *human*, *Gerlach*. *κύριε*. The leper probably used Adonai, *Elsley*. "*A man,*" supposed to be Simon the leper, *Brown*. No leper could approach Him, surrounded by multitudes, hence privately done, *Greswell*, *Andrews*. This cure made it impossible for Him henceforth to enter any city, *i. e.* Capernaum, *Norton*.

---

18. *And he put forth* his *hand, and touched him, saying, I will: be thou clean. And immediately the leprosy departed from him.*

Hand. Pointed out special object of grace. Heb. vi. 2. 1. Tim. iv. 14.
Our Lord never required belief in any well defined doctrine, or creed.
Only conditions, personal need and believing trust.
Touched. Law forbade the polluting touch. High priest might enter a leper's house.
Our High Priest is *touched* by our infirmities. Heb. iv. 15.
The *touch* of *this King* cures diseases of soul and body.
A mere *man's* touch would have contracted *impurity* only.
But God in Jesus, overcame death. "In Him was *life*." John i. 4.
No human will resists the power of saving grace. It is written—"Thy people shall be *willing* in the day of thy *power*." Psa. cx. 3.
The purity of Divine love removes the impurity of human misery.
A visible sign, imparted an invisible blessing.
His Divine touch, henceforth hallowed the sufferings of saints.
I will. *I can! I will!*—Echoes of mercy, to his fervent prayer!
Either the word of the true God, or fearful impiety.
Be clean. Human language hitherto, had no such words.
No prophet had *dared* to heal after this manner.
The majestic utterance of the Godhead, not transferable *tongue*.
No hand but that of Christ, can uproot the leprosy of sin.

Sin's deeply-seated curse, removed, a still greater miracle.
Our Saviour, true Jehovah. "The LORD healeth thee." Ex. xv. 26.
Departed. The Prince of Life, conquered "the king of terrors." Job xviii. 14.
Leprosy of body and soul, instantly left him.
Restored to health, society, friends, and sanctuary.

"*Touched,*" not unlawful, Elijah and Elisha did the same, 2. Kings iv. 34, *Elsley.* *καθαρ.* on seeing signs of convalescence, *Ammon.* Fullness of divine power, *Stier.* *θέλω* "*I will.*" An instantaneous result of his prayers, *Vers. Ger.* Divine grace is irresistible, *Quesnel.* This Gospel truth honored by the anger of the Pope. Clement II, A. D. 1713, *condemned* it in the Bull *Unigenitus.*

---

14. *And he charged him to tell no man: but go, and shew thyself to the priest, and offer for thy cleansing, according as Moses commanded, for a testimony unto them.*

Charged. Discouraged gossiping habits of men.
Tell no man. Popular excitement would only retard His holy work.
Popular applause unsought by Him in the depth of humility.
He turns the patient's mind from the world, to his own state.
Go shew. Christ's work ever invites *investigation.* Acts xxvi. 26.
Priest. Luke i. 5. He honors the Old, while building up the New Dispensation.
The priests pronouncing the leper healed, a *testimony in the temple for* CHRIST.
The Sun of righteousness shall arise with *healing* in His wings, &c. Mal. iv. 2.
Not a tittle of the law can fail, till all be fulfilled. Matt. v. 18.
Offer. Sacrifice required. Lev. xiv. 10. Altar, the *bud.* Gospel, the *flower.*
To revive the altar, &c., were to light a candle at noon-day.
Moses. Luke ii. 22. Life and miracles. See Notes.
Testimony. To the dignity and validity of His *Messiahship.*

παρ.—*εμβρ*, in Mark. Decided tone, *Oosterzee.* Denotes *anger* at leper, *Major.* Greek etymology implies discrimination, *i. e.* command fixed by no rule, but Christ's pleasure, *Alexander.* "*No man.*" Prevent tumults, *Major, Lange.* Lest He prejudice priests, *Grotius.* First duty to the priest, *B. Crusius.* Repress vanity, *Olshausen.*

Teach him caution, *Oosterzee.* Humility and charity, *Luther.* To keep Pharisees ignorant. Fulfil Isa. xlii. 1. Avoid all seeming *fore-plan.* His resurrection might seal His words. His mission revealed by *facts* not *words.* To avoid being made king, *Elsley.* Till shown to the priest, still separated, *Bengel.*

---

15. *But so much the more went there a fame abroad of him: and great multitudes came together to hear, and be healed by him of their infirmities.*

The more. Honor like a shadow pursues the deserving.
His whole course was sublimely *noiseless* and divinely humble.
A fame. Healed man forgets the Lord's injunction. 1. Sam. xv. 22.
Joy overflowing, makes silence a hard task.
Enthusiasm of his admirers drives Him into retirement. Verse 16.
Those breaking a like command were *not* rebuked.
Christ's miracles: 1. Witness of His Gospel. 2. Works of Love.
3. Seals of His Power. 4. Signs of New Testament Freedom.
5. Keys of Divine Glory. 6. Revelations of God to man.

ὑπ' αὐτοῦ. "*by him.*" Omitted by *Tischendorf* and *Alford.*

---

16. ¶ *And he withdrew himself into the wilderness, and prayed.*

Withdrew. Gr. *kept withdrawing.* Over zealous leper thwarts the Lord's designs.
He retires to prevent a premature *crisis.*
Those serving *men* best, have the most leisure for *God.*
Satan tempts saints to *ostentation*, or, by *distraction*, in devotions.
Retired communion with God, braces up the soul for conflict and duty.
To plead for men's souls *secretly*, is not *forsaking* them.
Wilderness. Luke i. 80. Excessive hearing, reading, talking, visiting, endanger *modern* piety, as to its *depth* and *strength.*
The secret of the believers' *strength* and *purity*, lies at the Mercy-Seat.
Too much, or too little *Church machinery*, is perilous.
Prayed. Luke above other Evangelists, notes Christ's *devotions.*
Some scream their prayers at God, He hears a "secret sigh." Ps. lxxix. 11.

"*Withdrew himself.*" Thus obtaining time for prayer and rest, *Bengel.* If Jesus needed seasons of retirement to recruit his energies, and obtain spiritual refreshment and help.—How much more His ministers! Do not ministers live too much in public in these days? *Ed.*

---

17. *And it came to pass on a certain day, as he was teaching, that there were Pharisees and doctors of the law sitting by, which were come out of every town of Galilee, and Judea, and Jerusalem: and the power of the Lord was* present *to heal them.*

Certain day. A short period before the Lord's second passover.
This incident probably took place in Capernaum. Mark ii. 1.
Teaching. This was His work, the miracle, a mere *incident.*
Pharisees. Heb. *separate.* (Luke vi. 2.) From their sanctimonious pride.
First noticed 144 B.C. Ecclesiastical *demagogues* of that age.
They and Scribes, the expounders of sacred and civil Law.
The most persistent and malignant enemies of Christ.
They esteemed the poor as so many beasts to bear their burdens.
Characteristics. 1. Excessive zeal in proselyting. 2. Careful to hide the key of knowledge from the people.
3. Intense regard for externals. 4. Affectation of superiority.
5. Supreme hypocrisy. 6. Sacrificed justice and mercy to *forms.*
7. Contempt of the humble. 8. Idolaters of tradition.
9. Contemned motives. 10. Scrupulous in their tithes.
11. Professing self-denial, but sensual. 12. Constant spies on Christ.
13. Wearing the broadest phylacteries. 14. Claimed to be Heaven's favourites.
Traitors to their God and Saviour, and betrayers of their country's hopes. Isa. viii. 12.
Their knowledge of prophecy, left them without excuse.
Doctors. Eminent Pharisees, exalted to teach the nation.
All were emissaries of the hostile Sanhedrim at Jerusalem.
His miracles attract attention, deceivers avoid all such as are intelligent.
Even the boldest deceivers avoid the intelligent, as judges.
Galilee, Luke i. 26. **Judea,** Luke i. 5. **Jerusalem,** Luke ii. 25.
Sitting by. Many do not *sit under,* but *sit by* the Gospel.
To such it is a thrice told tale, "What a weariness." Mal. i. 13.
Power. Miraculous, but invisible energy of the Almighty.
Jesus Himself the *Power,* and the Gospel—Both seen in His life.
Lord. Denoting the supreme Godhead of the Saviour.

Our Lord's miracles proved Him a messenger from *above*.

Heal. Not the scornful Pharisees, but the audience.

His mission, not to self-righteous doctors, but to broken hearts. Isa. lxi. 1, 2.

"*Pharisees.*" Pharash, Divider, *Beza.* No nick-name like *Cathari*, or *Huguenot*, &c. The Pharisees were fatalists, held that the soul enters another body, that works of supererogation are acceptable to God, that an oath is not binding, that mental reservation may be practised, that anger and lust are venial offences, that pleasure is the chief good, given to ornamenting tombs of prophets and martyrs, thought a sinner's touch polluting, addicted to washing hands, cups, &c., to fastings and tithings, &c., *Major.* "*Doctors,*" teachers of *oral*, Scribes, of *written* law, *Lightfoot.* Doctors, private students, *Macknight.* Teachers, *Lardner.* Village schoolmasters or inferior magistrates, *Greswell.* Possibly came on a friendly conference, *Trench.* *δύν. κυρ.* Does this mean *the power of God*, or *the power of the Lord, i. e.* Jesus? Meyer remarks that Luke uses *κύριοσ* frequently for Jesus; always with the article; but the same word without the article for *the Most High:* whence we conclude that the meaning is "*the power of God working in the Lord Jesus wrought so that He exercised the power of healing,*" *Alford.* Faith of the leper active, of the next passive, *Oosterzee.* *δύναμις*, outgoing of Almighty power. *τερας.* Miraculous portent. *θαυμασια.* All God's works, natural and supernatural, being alike to Him. Christ's *τέρατα* prove His message from *above.* Satan's *τέρατα*, from *beneath*, *Olshausen.* *σημεια*, natural signs.

---

18. ¶ *And, behold, men brought in a bed a man which was taken with a palsy: and they sought* means *to bring him in, and to lay* him *before him.*

Behold. A *three-fold* miracle, thoughts read, sins forgiven, palsy healed.

Brought. They are our truest friends who bring us near to Jesus.

Advancing us to honors of earth oft ruins the soul.

Bed. Ordinarily a pallet, or rug, sometimes both portable and ornamental.

Bedsteads in the East, quite unknown.

A raised platform of wood, stone, mud, or rugs, now used.

Ulysses tied timbers to trees for his bedstead. *Homer.*

The bed *pledged*, not to be *retained* after sunset. Ex. xxii. 27.

Poor, *wrap* themselves, the rich *cover* themselves. Isa. xxviii. 20.

They *sit* on beds in day time, and *sleep* on them at night.

Orientals in humble life, carry their beds to harvest field. Ruth iii. 4.

Palsy. A weakening of nervous energy and activity.

Muscles lose their *tone*, *i.e.*, power of contractility.

Generally affects the *left* side, and vital organs.
He who could heal the leper, might cure the palsy.
Sought. Crowd blocked up all avenues to the Saviour.
Before Him. *Proximity* necessary to healing.

"*Palsy.*" Cessation of nervous action, anciently called *apoplexy*, modern name *paralysis*, *Oosterzee*, *Hug*.

---

19. ***And when they could not find by what way they might bring him in because of the multitude, they went upon the housetop, and let him down through the tiling with*** his ***couch into the midst before Jesus.***

Could not. God often places *obstacles* before our faith.
There can be no blocking up the avenue to His heart. John iv. 23.
House-top. Luke i. 40. Interior stairs crowded by people.
Carried the patient up a neighbouring house, roofs being flat.
Tiling, being removed, the pallet was let down, in His presence.
Well pleased, to see His *teaching* disturbed by their *faith*.
What energy, men in real earnestness, display everywhere!
If we cannot reach Christ's *presence*, He can still heal our sick.
If baffled, the widow's importunity encourages us. Luke xviii. 1.
Centurion believed, that He could heal at a *distance*. Matt. viii. 8.

δῶμα, used in N. T. for *roof*; by classical authors.—*House*, *chamber*, *chief room*, *or hall*, *Liddell & Scott*. *κεράμων*, burnt clay, *Gesenius*. Court, or impluvium, generally in ancient and modern Oriental dwellings, *roofless*. Sometimes covered with *leather*, or canvass, *Jerome*, Thin stone slabs, *Ellicott*. Painted tiles on the sides of the house, *Doddridge*. Burnt tiles, *Alexander*.

---

20. ***And when he saw their faith, he said unto him, Man, thy sins are forgiven thee.***

Saw. Jesus attends oftener to our *wants*, than to our *desires*.
Faith. The passive sufferer rests on the faith of *friends*.
Their Faith, was of service in all, but the forgiveness of sin.
Man, Son, Matt. Hints at a new relation begun.
Cheer. Matt. ix. 2. "Have a good heart." Love casteth out fear.
Thy sins, sin the cause of all human disease and suffering.

God, best interpreter of our prayers, knows our necessities.
This patient puts up no prayer, his palsy pleads.
Forgiven, not a prayer, but DECLARATION of a FACT.
A delightful paradox, *surprising* both friends and foes.
Hints at his being cast down, under some spiritual *burden*.
A curse possibly pressed heavier on his *heart*, than on his *limbs*.
Pardoning, precedes healing, *One* present can *forgive*, as well as *heal*.
Bodily and spiritual healing, often *coincident*.
Christ rejoiced more over *his penitence*, than over their faith.
He ever kept back the sublime words, "*I am God*"!
God gives *before* we ask, *better* than we ask, and *after* we have asked.
He did not stop *giving*, till Abraham stopped *asking*. Gen. xviii. 32.

αφεωνται. A Doric form. A thing done, *Alexander*. Pangs of conscience hindered healing, *Oosterzee*. Near despairing, *Stier*. Needed comfort before healed, *Neander*. An answer to secret penitence. *Olshausen*. Some secret link between his sin and disease, *Hedinger*. Moderns err in denying any connection. *Oosterzee*.

---

21. *And the scribes and the Pharisees began to reason, saying, Who is this which speaketh blasphemies? Who can forgive sins, but God alone?*

Scribes. Generally Pharisees, at first, copiers of the Law.
Afterward, teachers, esteemed as oracles of wisdom.
Old Test. recorders of acts of kings, revenues, muster-rolls.
Belong to a state of society founded on *law*, not on *force*.
The pen, a symbol of power; *thought* rules the world.
Writing, a sacred art, scribes copied, and expounded the Law.
Ezra, first scribe, a *guardian* of the sacred text.
Sanhedrim, made up of Scribes and Pharisees,—The supreme Court.
Their vigilance constant. Had great influence with the people.
Pharisees. Luke v. 17; vi. 2, 4. Secretly sneering at the Lord's claim.
Who is this? Fish taken, tempest stilled, answer, *God!*
Demons obey, lepers cleansed, sick healed, answer, *God!*
Thousands fed, blind seeing, deaf hearing, answer, *God!*
Gospel has led *Philosophy herself*, a captive to Christianity.
Blasphemies. *A profane speech, slander*: see *Liddell & Scott*.
It denies honor and truth essentially belonging to Jehovah.
In their heart. Mark. He heard no voice, but heard *silent thoughts*.
Forgive. Earth has thousands of altars, but only one Mercy-Seat.

God alone. Evil hearts, change balm of Gilead, into poison.
Scribes and Pharisees had a *true idea* of the act of forgiving sin.
It presupposes a knowledge of the secrets of the heart.
No one can remit a debt, but He, to whom, it is due.
Who can. "*I can*, and I will prove it by miracles," saith Jesus.
Christians, like their Master, doing good, are reviled.
Jesus claims the highest prerogative of Jehovah.
They charged Him, with daring to assume the authority of God.
Instead of correcting a mistake, He *vindicates* His claims.
He received adoration, and challenged it as His *due*.

"*Scribes.*" First inquisitorial assembly, *Sepp.* "*Reason.*" Ironical, *Stier.* Philosophical vanity, *Gerlach.* οὗτος. Classic Greeks fill the ellipsis with "*fellow*," *Stier.*

---

22. *But when Jesus perceived their thoughts, he answering said unto them, What reason ye in your hearts?*

Thoughts. "All things are naked and opened unto the eyes of Him, with whom we have to do." Heb. iv. 13.
He tells them the *exact line*, their thoughts were taking. Ps. cxxxix. 2.
Peter exclaimed "Lord, Thou knowest all things." John xxi. 17.
Answering. Their secret reflections. No question being put.
In His judgment, their secret cavils needed an open reply.

23. *Whether is easier, to say, Thy sins be forgiven thee; or to say, Rise up and walk?*

Easier. Both demand omnipotence, both acts of Jehovah alone.
Enemies *unconsciously* and unwillingly ever advance His glory.
Forgiven. This *unexpected* act, the *key-note* of this narrative.
Rise up. He offers to cavilling Scribes and Pharisees a clear *test.*
He had performed an act of God, which was *invisible.*
He proposes to do an act of God, which will be *visible.*
If He fail, He is an *imposter*, if He succeed, He is Jehovah.
He thought it no robbery to be equal with God. Phil. ii. 6.

24. *But that ye may know that the Son of man hath power upon earth to forgive sins, (he said unto the sick of the palsy,) I say unto thee, Arise, and take up thy couch, and go into thine house.*

Son of man. Used *of* no other, and *by* no other, except Jesus.
Occurs about 60 times. Our Lord's chosen title.

Preached in Ethiopia, probably died without a martyr's crown. (tradition otherwise).

Receipt. Custom house. Government sanctioned by Jehovah. Rom. xiii. 1.

Saw. 1. Jesus looks on him in love. 2. Calls him by His word.
3. Faith springs instantly. 4. Love in its activity.

Follow me. A conversion, and an apostle's *call.*
Resistless efficacy seems to have accompanied His words.
1. Grace is glorified. 2. Faith opened. 3. Sacrifice demanded.
4. Compensation promised. 5. The blessing he would prove.
6. The throne, he would ascend. Rev. iii. 21.
Christ's first four apostles, *fishermen*, fifth, a *publican.*
Called to the very highest office and honors of God's church.
Yet Pharisees would not deign *to eat* with him.

"*Levi.*" Matt.'s family name, *Brown.* One of the ascetic Essenes, *Clement* of *Alexandria.* Different from Matthew, *Grotius.* Same as Lebbœus, *Schleusner.* Doubtful, *Alford.* Identical with Matthew, *Alexander*, *Brown*, and nearly all antiquity. Previously a follower of Christ, *Oosterzee*, *Lange.* Preached in Macedonia, *Isidore.* Remained in Jerusalem 15 years after the crucifixion, *Clement.* Wrote his Gospel in Hebrew and Greek, *Lange.* In Aramaic, *Olshausen.* Greek, *Alford.* In Hebrew, *Michaelis*, *Mill.* Ακολούθει. Instantaneous conversion, *Oosterzee.* Questioned, *Stier*, *Alexander.* "*Receipt.*" The place of toll at the entrance into the city, *Lietenstein.*

---

28. *And he left all, rose up, and followed him.*

29. *And Levi made him a great feast in his own house: and there was a great company of publicans and of others that sat down with them.*

All. Faith alone *mates* and *masters* Earth's attractions.
Matthew *enlisting*, immediately becomes an *enlister.*
Proves his *depth* of humility, (Matt. x. 3.) worthy to be "among princes." Ps. cxiii. 8.

Feast. Gr. *reception.* Feast an epoch in oriental life.
Conversion ever the best cause of festal joy.
Worldlings esteem the blessed change, a great *misfortune.*
Angels, heavenly students, knowing the soul's value, rejoice. Luke xv. 10.
Soul's birth-hour, adoption into the King's family. John viii. 36.
"It was meet that we should make merry." Luke xv. 32.

Matthew's feast a farewell to his companions in office.
In his *humility*, he omits to mention the *greatness* of the feast. Matt. ix.
Own. Emphatic, to the shiftless, homeless wanderers. [10, 13.
Wide *chasm* between the *favored* and *poor* class, only filled by the
House. Materials and form. Luke i. 40. See Notes. [Gospel.
Sat. Gr. *reclined.* Learned from Greeks, habit of *reposing* during meals.
In Old Test. times, Hebrews sat, women and children always *sat.*
Leaning on the left elbow while reclining, illustrated John xiii. 25.
Cups always used. Psa. xvi. 5. Knives invented in Parma, 1490 A.D.
With the right hand, they took the food, back resting against a cushion.
Couches were a little higher than the table. 3 feet high.
Orientals now carefully collect their food in their *fingers.*

"*Followed.*" Had taken previous steps for retiring, *Olshausen.* No authority for this inference, *Stier.* "*Feast.*" Different from Matt. ix. 9, *Greswell*, *Major.* Same, *Ellicott*, *Brown*, *Alexander.* "*House*" of Jesus, *Meyer.* Matthew's, *Lange*, *Oosterzee.* "*Feast.*" Immediately following the call, *Lichtenstein*, *Tischendorf.* Later, *Lightfoot*, *Townsend*, *Robinson.* The ancient mode of reclining at the feast according to the usage of society and grades of honor, *Author.* Quum primum istorum conduxit mensa choragum, *Suet.*

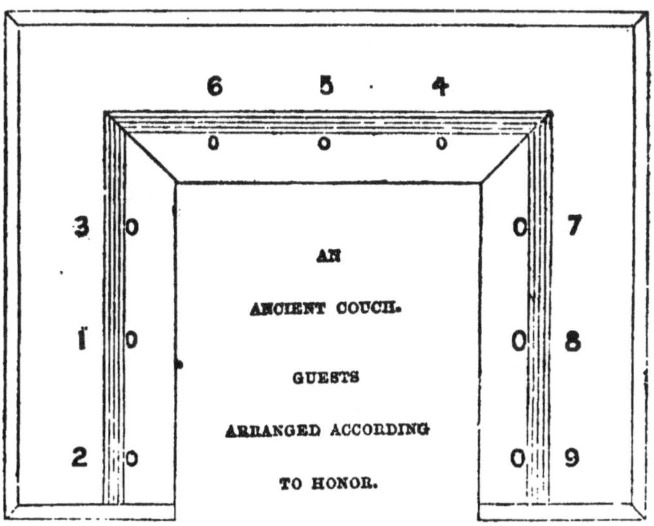

1. Host. 2. Hostess. 3 Guest. 4. Highest place. 5, 6, 7, 8, 9 for Guests.
Servants moved inside.

A Couch found in Pompeii. History of Ruins, vol. 2. p. 89.

80. *But their scribes and Pharisees murmured against his disciples, saying, Why do ye eat and drink with publicans and sinners?*

Scribes, Pharisees. Luke v. 17; vi. 2. Sanhedrim, 70 members.
Superior claims for *patriotism*, not *piety*, made them popular.
A temporary union, proves no real alliance.
Both, thus far, artful *spies*, but not open *enemies*.
Murmured. Gr. *muttered.* Luke xv. John vi. 41. 1. Cor. x. 10.
Dissatisfied with themselves, men keenly censure others.
Sign of a bad heart, to be ever *cavilling* at the virtuous.
He in humility, "endured contradiction of sinners." Heb. xii. 3.
Jesus came to take up the quarrel between man and the Creator.
Under pretended zeal for God, envy and murder are *hidden*.
Disciples. Their recent *defeat*, prevents their attacking Jesus.
Ye. They use the plural, but *aim* alone at the *Master*.
Sin made them *cowards*, afraid to assault Jesus.
Eat. Not Moses' law, but tradition was violated.
Greeks deemed it *impious* to eat with those denying honor to their gods.
Jews dreaded ceremonial uncleanness; indifferent to moral purity.
Our Lord never was invited to a priest's table.
Bigoted, are ever the most *desperate* subjects of hope and prayer.
Oriental usage permits strangers to enter and view the company.
Social retirement, a fruit of advanced civilization.
Eastern populace know no law, but life-guard's bayonet.
Publicans. Luke iii. 12. **Sinners,** despised as *dogs* in the East. Job. xxx. 1.
Pharisees dreaded touching *sinners*, but indifferent as to *sins*.
God condemns *chosen* intimacy with the wicked. Psa. cxix. 115.
Yet, pure religion leads believers to hovels of woe. James i. 27.
Despising the humble, the Pharisees *envied* the least favor conferred on them.

ἐγόγγ.—Gruochiden, *Wickliffe*. Sullen discontent, *grumbling*. "*Scribes.*" Galileans, scribes of that place, *Kuinoel*. John's disciples displeased with his imprisonment, unite in this censure, Mark ii. 18, *Oosterzee*, "*Pharisees.*" Matt. corrected by Luke, *De Wette*. Luke corrected by Matt., *Meyer*. Pharisees put it, in behalf of John's disciples, *Lange*. και ἁμαρτωλῶν, "*and sinners*," cancelled by *Tisch*. retained, *Alford*.

---

81. *And Jesus answering said unto them, They that are whole need not a physician; but they that are sick.*

Answering. To shame His foes and justify His cause.

He would always rescue His perplexed disciples.
Whole. Those only owning themselves sick, were healed.
Pride, *the* disease which flatters the sick as being in health.
A word of *consolation* to the humble, but of *woe* to the proud.
Physician. Jews thought diseases sent directly from God.
If curable, to be learned by *priests*, consulting the *Oracle*.
Heathen also by *charms* and brutal rites, consulted gods.
Jehoram sent to Baal of Ekron, a *bribe*, for their physicians.
First named in the embalming of Jacob in Egypt. Gen. l. 2.
"Daughter of Egypt use many medicines, not cured." Jer. xlvi. 11.
Anciently, law, medicine, and divinity, belonged to *one* person.
Sick. God's church on earth a blessed Asylum, or rather, a spiritual Hospital.
Our Lord alludes to no *sinless* class on earth,
Sin, unconsciously *deforms*, *weakens*, *wastes*, *destroys* the soul. Rev. iii. 17.
Nature will not, *reason* cannot, *science* attempts not, a cure.
Our Physician is skilful, faithful, compassionate, self-sacrificing.
His success, *infallible*, "Healing in His wings," Mal. iv. 2.
Selfish Pharisees thought the Messiah came for His own *glory and ease*.

ὑγιαί.—Righteous in the Jewish sense, *De Wette*. Ironical, *Calvin*, *Meyer*. Subjectively, *Alford*. Really holy, *Elsley*. Ἰατροῦ—not *a*, but *the* physician. Thus announcing Himself Physician of souls, *Oosterzee*.

---

32. *I came not to call the righteous, but sinners to repentance.*

I came. The Advent of One who belongs to the Highest order of Being.
His Coming heralded 4000 years;—announced and hailed by Angels.
Ought to have been *welcomed* by all our fallen race.
Call, pervades His eating, drinking, and entire life.
His graciously condescending fellowship, a *Divine call*.
He came not so much as a *Teacher*, as a *Saviour*.
Righteous. Absolutely free from sin, as *no man* is. Rom. iii. 23.
Sinners. "It is for sinners I am here," not for holy, but *fallen* men.
A great encouragement to *sinners*, but none to *sin*.
Expecting to retain *them*, and receive *Him*, a sad delusion.
1. A moral frenzy *denies* the soul is sick.
2. Tempted, they *despair*, as being past all remedy.

Truly renewed hearts, have changes of light and gloom. Isa. l. 10.
Bridegroom, denotes His tender love for all believers.
The intimate *vital* union between the Head and members. Eph. v. 23.
Participated privileges, 1. Home. 2. Wealth. 3. Home joys.
Christ's exaltation did not consign the church to *grief.*
Fast. Principle condemned, is that of *stated* fasting.
Hankering after artificial fasts, ever follows Rome's idolatries.

υἱοὶ like כן added, implies partaken of, *Wetstein.* *νυμφ.*—Greek root, a *veil*, associated with marriage in all nations, *Major.* Christ compares himself to one welcoming guests to a wedding banquet, *Rosenmuller.* *νεστ. to fast*, sacraments give grace by the work wrought, *ex opere operato*, and who denies it, *let him be accursed.* *Corpus Juris Gregorii* XIII. *Pont. Max.* Leyden, 1614. *Council of Trent*, 6. Can. *De Justificatione.* This Antichristian doctrine is here *prophetically* condemned, *Alexander.* Rome teaches, Christ left a *fasting Church*, *Bossuet.* Tradition pretends the disciples fasted 40 hours, our Lord's stay in the *grave*, *Wetstein.* Not His bodily presence, but spiritual absence, *Olshausen.* The period between His first and second coming, *Stier.*

---

35. *But the days will come, when the bridegroom shall be taken away from them, and then shall they fast in those days.*

Days. Censors defeated, in desiring John to be *condemned* by Jesus.
Times of the Spirit's absence, the Church in a cold, barren state.
Will come. The Lord called the church to weeping. Isa. xxii. 12.
In times of self-denial, the believer's *privilege* is to fast.
They will have *time* and *cause* enough to mourn. Acts xiv. 23.
Taken away. Sad words, contrasting with sun-light of Bridegroom's [presence.
The first allusion to the Redeemer's *violent* death.
Neither the Gospels, nor any apostolic Epistle, hath a *command* to fast.
Although oft practised. Acts x. 30. xiv. 23. 2. Cor. vi. 5. xi. 27. Dan. ix. 3.
Fast. At Christ's death, and consequent famine in the Kingdom.
"But when the candle of the Lord shines brightly on their head." Job. xxix. 3.
Christ's *presence* should be a continual feast. John xiv. 23.

ἡμέραι, v. 34. *ἀπαρθῇ*, not *απελθῃ*; used nowhere else, "*bear away*," violent death, *Oosterzee.*

36. ¶ *And he spake also a parable unto them; No man putteth a piece of a new garment upon an old; if otherwise, then both the new maketh a rent, and the piece that was* taken *out of the new agreeth not with the old.*

Parable. Natural similitude used to illustrate religious truths.
Used much by our Lord in Matthew, Mark, and Luke, but not elsewhere.
Sanctioning novels by this word of Jesus, mere folly.
Abstract doctrines are intelligibly and vividly brought out.
These analogies, often arguments and witnesses of truth.
The Lord's *train*, filled the temple above, His *skirts*, the temple below.
Soil full of weeds and thorns, a *parable* of the depraved heart.
Characters of nature, to eye of faith, the *hieroglyphics* of God.
To the stupified mind, the *key* of knowledge is lost.
Amid a worn-out world, Christ *renewed* old truths at His touch.
Common customs of life, under Him, are *sermons* to us.
Garment. Luke vi. 29. Wedding figures, such as "*robe*," "*preparation*," "*wine*," run through the N.T.
Unfulled cloth. Mark ii. 21. Has greater *strength* and *shrinkage*.
Worn-out texture of the old, could not stand the strain of the new.
Rent. *Schism.* Mark ii. 21. Happy if those were the only rendings of the church.
Messiah's work, was not to patch up old finished rites, such as old types, ceremonies, sacrifices, washings, fasts, &c.
Completed garment of salvation, rejects worn-out trimmings.
No empirical repairs, can detain the fleeting Levitical shadows.
The vital principles of the church, *unchangeably* the same.
Yet the Messiah, changed all its outward forms and robes.
"Behold, I make all things new," saith Christ. Rev. xxi. 15.
His concealed sarcasm, refers to the excrescences of tradition.
Agreeth not. Old garment by nature cannot be mended with a *new patch*.
Some duties more difficult than others. Matt. v. 19.
Hearts renewed in times of peace, may not have a martyr's faith.
The trees of the garden, are not *all* as cedars of Lebanon.
God did not lead unarmed Hebrews, by the way of *Philistia*.
The good Shepherd gently *carries* the lambs of His flock. Isa. xl. 11.
Gospel meat, may be too strong, for babes in Christ. Heb. v. 12.
Over-doing even in *well-doing*, is injurious—"Be not righteous overmuch." Ecc. vii. 16.
Kindness and gentleness will bear with weakness and ignorance.
"If the lambs and mothers be over-driven, they perish." Gen. xxxiii. 13.

"*Parable.*" External worship cannot improve sinful nature, *Neander*. Difference between O. and N. Test., *Oosterzee*. New necessities, require new means, *Alexander*. Mosaic economy, not only old, but antiquated, *Lange*. New spirit requires new forms, *Olshausen*. Churches of Galatia mixed Law and Gospel, and perished, *Oxford*. παλαιῷ, αγναφου. Mark, *unfulled*, apt to shrink when wet, *Brown*. *Imprudent* counsels to new converts, or enquiring souls, *Ryle*. Read σχισει, "*shall make a rent*," for σχιζει, "*maketh*." and οὐ συμφωνήσει, "*shall not agree*," for συμφωνεῖ, "*agreeth not*." ἐπίβλημα, "*the piece*," omitted, *Tischendorf*. *Alford*.

---

37. *And no man putteth new wine into old bottles; else the new wine will burst the bottles, and be spilled, and the bottles shall perish.*

Wine. Luke i. 15. An emblem of spiritual mercies. Isa. xxv. 6; lv. 1.
Bottles. Gr. *skin bottle.* Gen. xxi. 14; 1. Sam. x. 3; Job. xxxviii. 37; Jer. xiii 12.
Drawn entire from animals, tanned in Arabia, with acacia.
In Hebron, with pitch. Gibeonites deceived Joshua. Josh ix. 4.
Cairo, the population 250,000, bring all cooking water 2 miles from the Nile, in skins.
Bottles of clay. Judg. iv. 19; Jer. xix. 1; found in old tombs of Romans.
Glass bottles found in Babylon, by Layard, made 800 B.C.
"Put my tears in thy bottle,"—ancient custom at funerals. Ps. lvi. 8.
Placed with burning lamps, in sepulchre, to dissipate the gloom.
The Author found tear bottles, holding two spoonfuls, in Alexandrian tombs.
Burst. Religion oft misrepresented by ill-timed severity.
Spirit of the Gospel strong enough to break up old forms.
No compromise of principle, no *policy*, yet *allowance* made for customs.

παλαιούς. Pharisaic austerity,—*new wine*. Jews—*old bottles*, *Wetstein*. "*Old bottles*." Romish superstitions and the Gospel cannot coalesce, *Stier*. ἀπολοῦνται. Rigid austerities imposed on My disciples, fatal, *Harwood*.

---

38. *But new wine must be put into new bottles; and both are preserved.*

39. *No man also having drunk old* wine *straightway desireth new; for he saith, The old is better.*

New bottles. Fetters of the old form restrained Gospel liberty.
The life-giving power of the Gospel weakened by Mosaic rites.

Better. Old habits of the Jewish converts, hard to yield.
Purer spirituality of the N. T. dispensation disliked by those long accustomed to the forms of the Old.

συντηροῦνται doubtful reading, *Griesbach;* cancelled, *Alford, Tisch.;* omitted, *Cod. Sina.* εὐθεωσ, "*straightway;*" omitted, *Tisch., Alford.* ὁ παλαιὸς. A pure Iambic verse. He uses a Gentile proverb, *Wordsworth.* Uttered at another time, *Kuinoel.* Men reluctant to part with old customs, *Olshausen, Alford.* Disciples unwilling to adopt the austerities of Pharisees, *Doddridge.* Disciples accustomed to John's, not to Christ's teachings, *Ryle.* Our Lord *above* Moses, ready to break the law,—but meeker than Moses, will not quench the smoking flax, *Oosterzee.* Their own old doctrine more acceptable to Pharisees, than the teaching of Jesus, which, though they regarded new, far older than their own, *Bengel.* For χρηστότεροσ, "*better,*" read χρηστόσ, "*good,*" *Cod. Sina., Tischendorf, Alford.*

CHAPTER VI.

AND it came to pass on the second sabbath after the first, that he went through the corn fields; and his disciples plucked the ears of corn, and did eat, rubbing them *in* their *hands.*

Came to. This incident occurred near Capernaum.

Second, &c. Gr. *second-first.* First, after the second day of the Pass- [over.

The barley harvest—close of March and beginning of April.

Wheat harvest gathered in May and June.

Went. Gr. *went along.* He only crossed *through*, to reach another place.

Corn. Gr. *sown fields*, barley or wheat. Luke xvi. 7.

Began. Mark ii. 23.. Interrupted by the spies, while satisfying their hunger.

Plucked. Expressly allowed, but not the use of the reaping hook. Deut. xxiii. 25.

God shewed by this slight restriction, He was *proprietor* of the land.

The disciples were not curious about diet, but took what came first.

Sabbath, instituted at Creation, to commemorate God *resting*.

It was re-enacted at the Exodus, as Israel's rest from Egyptian bondage.

Its character binding to the end of time, as seen from its *place* in the Decalogue.

Jews, unable to sacrifice in captivity, distinguished from heathen by the *Sabbath.*

Prophets predicting the exile, laid peculiar stress on *its* obligations.

At the restoration, Rabbis burdened the duty, by gratuitous restrictions.

They lost sight of the *spiritual* purpose, in outward extreme acts.

Disciples knowing these traditions, must have been instructed by Christ.

σαββάτω—Heb. *rest*, total cessation from labor; a fire could not be kindled. δευτεροπρώτω. Reading doubted, *Alford;* retained, *Tischendorf;* cancelled, *Meyer;* marginal gloss, *Olshausen.* *Second first* sabbath after the festival of unleavened bread, *Gesenius.* "First after the second," *Campbell, Robinson, Greswell;* first after the Pentecost, *Norton.* *Secundo primo, Vulg.* Our Eng. Trans. is inexact, *Alexander.* First sabbath of the month of Nisan, *Epiphanius, Beza, Sir Isaac Newton;* first sabbath after the second day of the Passover, *De Wette*, *Brown*, *Olshausen*, *Lightfoot*, *Robinson*, *Greswell*; first sabbath before the new moon of Nisan, *Bengel*; sabbath immediately succeeding a festival, *Theophylact*. The fifteenth of Nisan, *Hitzig*. Jewish years reckoned by cycles of seven years; first sabbath of a year that stood second in a sabbatical cycle, *i. e.* April 9, *Wiesler*, *Ellicott*, *Tischendorf*, *Oosterzee*. Probably sabbath following first day of unleavened bread. *Ed.* διαπορευ. to attempt to pass through, to gain another point, *Stier*. σταχυασ the *spikes* of grain, or *heads*; that called Indian *Corn* was not discovered until 1492.

---

2. *And certain of the Pharisees said unto them, Why do ye that which is not lawful to do on the sabbath days?*

Pharisees. Luke v. 17. They made God's statutes to consist of *six hundred and thirteen precepts*.

Their contests of envy, bitter, and divisions numerous.

Scribes excelled in learning, but Pharisees in formal piety.

They began mechanical monastic penances, afflicting the body for the welfare of the soul.

Some wore caps, preventing them seeing any thing but their *feet*.

Others beat their heads against the walls, until the blood came.

Others walked as if so absorbed in meditation, they could not lift their feet from the ground.

They slept on planks, and put thorns in their garments, to *prick* themselves.

The day, divided into three parts, one of these, spent entirely in *prayer*.

If they forgot their devotions, they returned from the field to perform them.

They read the Decalogue twice—daily, without *moving* an eye, hand, or foot.

They would sell neither books, wax, nor incense, to *Samaritans*.

On meeting an idol, they went over the fields, to avoid passing it.

On the Sabbath, they would not place even an apple on the fire, nor put out a house in flames.

They went prowling after Christ, to catch at His deeds.

Listening behind—they watched for a single step taken beyond the prescribed limits.

There was no sabbath stillness in their souls, full of evil designs.

The disciples were listening to Christ's words, and offering praise in the Temple of Nature.

Their attendance on Christ, kept them from preparing a *regular* meal.

They exposed themselves to hunger, rather than lose the instructions of Jesus.

Their offence was the sin of *rubbing* the ears of corn, *plucking* allowed.

Pharisees under the mask of righteousness, were full of rapine.

They scruple at rubbing out a few grains of corn, but not at robbing widows and orphans.

They did not quarrel about taking *another's* grain, being indifferent to *justice*.

Why? Under what authority or right? implying a *censure*.

It was not the *act* itself, but the *time*, that gave offence.

When men become more righteous than Christ, their *hypocrisy* is *proved*.

Those who *commit* the greatest crimes, are most free to *censure trifles*.

It is no *new* thing for Christians, when harmless, to be *slandered*.

Lawful. One convicted of reaping and threshing, penalty was *death*.

Thirty-nine different acts were forbidden on the Sabbath.

Jesus upheld the Sabbath in spirit, while, in their view, He broke the Sabbath.

A mechanical keeping, and presumptuous contempt of it, alike sinful.

Behold! Mark ii. 24. As if they surprised them, at some great sin!

"Since the master is accountable, dost thou not rebuke thy followers?"

He would not descend, to discuss their miserable traditions.

Sacrificing the interests of *man* to preserve the *Sabbath*, they became *the* real Sabbath-breakers.

Sabbath, the harmonies of the day destroyed by the discord of sin.

οὐκ, gives intensity to the meaning. φαρισαίων Luke v. 17. They embraced the greater part of the nation. ἔξεστι, *it is possible*, referring to moral propriety. σάββασι *plural*.—Not their *habit*, but an assimilation to the *Greek names* of festivals—*singular* in meaning. ὁδὸν ποιεῖν Mark. *To make way, plucking* through the standing corn as though they pulled them up. The microscope of criticism, here finds a discrepancy between the Evangelists; because Mark omits the fact of their eating, cannot Luke add it? *Alexander*. αὐτοῖς, "*unto them*," and ποιεῖν, "*to do*," omitted, *Tisch.*, *Alford*.

---

8. *And Jesus answering them, said, Have ye not read so much as this, what David did, when himself was an hungred, and they which were with him;*

Christ defends His disciples by five distinct arguments.

Answered. When men unjustly assault, God shields His people.

He might have blasted them by a rebuke of divine *vengeance*.

In a Sabbath tone of mind, He stoops to overcome their folly.

The first, presupposes their acquaintance with the Old Testament.

David's acts were *examples*, unless disapproved by the Spirit.

Read. Our Lord felt Himself bound by the Mosaic law.
His first visit to the temple, and His last Passover, prove it.
David. Luke ii. 4. See Notes.
Hungred. Positive observance must gave way to self-preservation.
"Did your lauded David do that which Moses forbade?"
Even Doeg, Saul's spy, did not censure this act of imperative necessity.
David is rightly counted the great pattern of O.T. holiness.
"You admit it lawful, to do labor for Sabbath sacrifices."
"You admit circumcision is binding on that day." John vii. 22.

ἀνέγνωτε, *ανα* adds intensity, the *most careful perusal* of the sacred record, *ἐπείνασεν*, pressed with hunger, *famished:* necessity knows no law. "In the temple there is no Sabbath. Sacrificing drives away the Sabbath," Rabbis, *Lightfoot.*

---

4. *How he went into the house of God, and did take and eat the shewbread, and gave also to them that were with him: which it is not lawful to eat but for the priests alone.*

House of God, refers here to the *tabernacle*, sometimes to the temple.
Built near Sinai by Bezaleel and Aholiab, under Moses.
Length 55 feet, breadth 18 feet, and height 18 feet.
Built of shittim wood, supposed to be acacia; covered with plates of gold.
These were fixed upright in solid sockets of silver.
Bars, covered with gold plates, passed through a gold ring in each board.
On the east, were five pillars of acacia, overlaid with gold.
They stood in sockets of brass. All was covered with five curtains.
The *first* was colored dark blue, purple, and scarlet.
This hung inside, and covered the four sides with tapestry.
The *second* made of *fine wool*, the *third* of red morocco *leather*.
The *fourth* of thicker leather, perhaps the seal skin, taken from the Red Sea.
It was divided into two parts, by a curtain, or veil.
Looped at each end, rent at the time of our Lord's death, Matt. xxvii. 51, each side fell.
Four gold plated pillars in silver sockets sustained it.
Having no window, lamps were necessary. 1. Kings viii. 12.

Holy of Holies had the altar, shew-bread, golden candlesticks, &c.
The Ark of the Covenant, covered with wings of cherubim, was there.
Jews believe the ark still exists, and will be forthcoming, in due time.
While Israel wandered, the tabernacle was movable. Its *home* was the temple.

Shew bread. Heb. *bread of the presence.* Twelve loaves of *manifestation*, on a table of acacia covered with gold.
Sprinkled with salt and frankincense, represented the twelve tribes, even after the *separation.*
Implies, *true* Israelites are *ever* to be found among apostate churches.
They were a constant *testimony* against the wanderers.
There alone they were sure their sacrifices would be accepted.

Lawful. Our Lord takes for granted perpetual *obligations* of the 4th commandment.
He taught *how* *i.e.* in what spirit the Sabbath is to be observed.
He sanctions David's violation of an express ceremonial law.
The love of God consecrates the use of sacred things.
God's anointed is not to be left to die af starvation.
Christ does not teach, that any one *at will* may break a command.
But that the *end* of the Sabbath was—that it should be a blessing to mankind.
Pharisees had *no respect*, either for the *Sabbath*, or man's *welfare.*
They pronounced the hungry man supplying himself with food, a *sinner.*
But unrelenting *hostility* towards the Son of God, they thought *right.*

Alone. Shew-bread changed every Sabbath, and the incense burnt.
The bread might be eaten by the priests, *in* the Holy Place *alone.*
David, a type of evangelical liberty amid legal bondage.

οἶκον—not the Tabernacle, but the house of the High priest beside it, *Macknight*, *Mayor.* οἶκον, σκηνῆσ a *tent*, Heb. *tent of assembly*, *Kimchi.* Tent of testimony, *Sept.* The tabernacle, *Stier.* Jewish tradition of the Ark being found, derived Rev. xi. 19, xv. 5. L. H. V. D. προθέσεωσ, *bread of the presence*, set before the presence, or face of Jehovah. Also bread *arranged in order*, and *perpetual* bread. Ex. xxv. 30. 1. Chro. xxiii. 29, ἔξεστι, here, prolonged customary action, ἱερεῖσ Luke i. 8. The tabernacle and temple being God's palace, the weekly service of bread, wine, and salt, denoted His habitation among men, *Macknight.* A representation of the Table, as it existed in the Herodian Temple may be seen in the bas-reliefs within the Arch of Titus at Rome. Philo and Clement of Alexandria thought the Table a symbol of the world, its four sides typifying the four seasons. The table of the Second Temple was carried away by Antiochus Epiphanes, and a new one made under direction of Judas Maccabæus. Afterwards Ptolemy Philadelphus presented a magnificent table. The number of loaves (12) considered by Josephus and

Philo to represent the twelve months. No rite of Scripture so wholly unexplained as the *bread of the presence*, or literally, *bread of the face*, i. e. *face of Jehovah*. Probable meaning—*Bread of the face*, that bread through which God is seen, that is, with the participation of which the seeing of God is bound up, or through the participation of which man attains the sight of God. Whence it follows we have not to think of bread merely as such, as the means of nourishing the bodily life, but as spiritual bread or food, even Christ, the means of appropriating and retaining that life which consists in seeing the *face of God*. John vi. 51-58. See *Smith's* Dictionary of the Bible. *Ed.*

---

5. *And he said unto them, That the Son of man is Lord also of the sabbath.*

Son of Man. Luke v. 24. Refers to the abasement of His Divine nature in the human.

Dan. vii. 13-14. Doubtless alludes to the Messiah. *The Ancient of days* is Jehovah the Father.

Lord. They might answer, that the priests profane the Sabbath in the services of the Temple. Matt. xii. 5.

His reply implies—Here is One greater than the Temple.

The Sabbath gave place to the Temple, so Sabbath and Temple give place to *the* LORD of Temple and Sabbath.

Sabbath. Heb. *rest*, the institution enacted by Jehovah. Gen. ii. 2-3.

No mere man can be called,—LORD OF THE SABBATH.

It implies He is Lord of *human happiness*, as well as of the Sabbath.

His sovereign right to modify the rules for its observance implies the perpetuity of the *essence* of Sabbath obligations.

Christ kept the Sabbath in His life, and in His *resurrection* honored it.

Man was not created to do *homage* to any positive institution. Mark ii. 27.

That which injures man's highest interest, violates Sabbath sanctity.

What is compatible with the spiritual interests of all classes, is consistent with its sanctification.

Christ's refutation of the Pharisees, lessons not the obligation of the Sabbath.

The daily sacrifice continued, until the *Great Sacrifice* was made.

Hence the *Sabbath* is binding, until *that which is in part*, shall be done away, in the perfect *Sabbath* of heaven. 1. Cor. xiii. 10.

A God, to worship, implies there must be *time* to worship.

The reasons for founding the Sabbath exist through all time, for *fallen* beings.

While bread is earned by the sweat of the face, Sabbath is needed.

While souls are to be saved everlastingly, time for it is desirable.

God has also doubly blest the Sabbath, and added the mercy of *Redemption*, to the mercy of *Creation.*

His disciples, *priests* of the New Covenant in His *Sanctuary.*

As priests in the ancient temple were blameless, so are those in that "*not made with hands.*"

κύριόσ—(Adonai) *Dominus*, Lord, or Master. Gr. used with great latitude, always implied profound respect. *Augustus*, when declining the title of *Dominus*, answered: "*Imperator militum, Princeps reipublicæ: Dominus servorum.*" To assume the title would be calling the Roman citizens *slaves.* κύριόσ and δουλοσ, correlative terms among Orientals. Their ideas of paternal dignity being incomparably higher than ours, David's calling the Messiah *Lord*, confounded and *silenced* the Pharisees. To have the title of "*Lord of the Sabbath,*" was claiming for Himself authority over an institution founded by Jehovah, *Campbell.* It may refer to His signal authority, through the Apostles, in changing it from the *seventh* to the *first* day, *Doddridge.* As the Sabbath gave way to the Temple service, so must sabbath and temple service both give way to One still greater, (μείζων Matt.) even *the Son of man*, *Oosterzee.* ὑίοσ του ανθρ. Used to counteract Jewish error as to temporal glory, and to teach that His path to glory was through *humiliation*, *Beau-Dobre.* This verse seems unconnected, *De Wette.* Inserted after the 10, in Cod. Bezæ, one of the oldest Greek MS., from middle of sixth century. In its place we find these words, "*On the same day he saw one working on the Sabbath, and said unto him, Man, if thou knowest what thou art doing, blessed art thou; but if thou knowest it not, thou art accursed, and a transgressor of the law.*" Evidently spurious, *Author.* *Alford* inclined to think it an authentic narrative, *Ed.*

---

6. *And it came to pass also on another sabbath, that he entered into the synagogue, and taught: and there was a man whose right hand was withered.*

Sabbath. This was in Capernaum. Mark ii. 1.

Pharisees follow Him hither, malignant envy knows no respite.

This miracle was one of *seven*, performed on the Sabbath. John v. 9. Mark i. 21-29. John ix. 14. Luke xiii. 14; xiv. 1.

Synagogue. Luke iv. 15. See Notes.

The scene of our Lord's glory 1. His unprejudiced judgment.

2. His heavenly knowledge of the heart. 3. His merciful compassion.

4. His delivering power. 5. His long-suffering.

Man. The Redeemer's *presence*, an invitation to the diseased to be present.

Right hand. The means of working generally depend on its skill.

The organ of feeling—The Instrument of instruments.

Mechanism of the right *hand*, *foot*, *lung*, superior to the left.
The blood flows more forcibly through the right *arteries*.
The *vital energies* of the left side, limbs, and brain, inferior.
Paralysis and other diseases attack the left side generally.
The *tread* of the right foot, and *motion*, more equable.
The *nerves* of the hand more sensitive, than the naked heart.
Thus men are far more sensitive to outward wants than inward.
The right hand wonderfully executes the commands of the *mind*.
Emblem of *power*. Mark xiv. 62. Place of *pleasure*. Psa. xvi. 11. *Honor*. Col. iii. 1.
Moses laid *hands* on Joshua before Eleazar the priest. Num. xxvii. 18.

Withered. The work of nutrition had entirely ceased.
Blood no longer flowed—the pulse no longer beat.
The nerves and sinews were blasted and useless.
The Gr. implies, it was not congenital, but the result of *disease*.
Atrophy, like leprosy, was incurable by the skill of man.
No evidence that this man was *brought* to *entrap* the Saviour.
He was doubtless but *one* of many cured, on that occasion.
He may have come for the sake of his *soul*, Christ healed his *body* also.
Those expecting to be *cured*, must be willing to *learn* from Christ.

"*Another Sabbath.*" A feast sabbath, following that in verse 1, the seventh day of the first month, Ezek. xlv. 20, *Ellicott*, *Wieseler*. Two events on the same sabbath, *Meyer*. ἄνθρωπος—Tradition calls him a *builder*, who entreated a cure that he might not beg; Gospel of the Nazarenes, *Jerome*. Some detect a regular stratagem in the man being placed as a subject for questioning our Lord, *Ellicott*. χεὶρ δεξ—Cicero pronounces a eulogy on the right hand, De *Nat.*, *Deo.*, ii. 60 It has 21 bones, 19 muscles peculiar, *Sir C. Bell.* ξηρά, not mere luxation, but a kind of paralysis, *Alexander*.

---

7. ***And the scribes and Pharisees watched him, whether he would heal on the sabbath-day; that they might find an accusation against him.***

Scribes. Luke v. 21. Sacred and secular *teachers* of the nation.
Those who ought to *intercede* for the wretched, *cavil* at Jesus.
Pharisees prayed by the *hour*, but prayed not *for him*, who could not earn his bread.
Men defrauding innocent orphans, envy the poor, their crumbs.
Sin dries up all the streams of charity in the heart.

These men would rescue a *sheep*, but leave a *neighbour* to perish.
The race who regard *cattle*, more than *souls*, is not yet extinct.
Accuse. *i.e.*, bring Him before the council through a malignant envy.

παρετηρουν—to keep an eye with sinister intent. *κατηγορίαν* an *accusation, charge. κατα-αγορευω, to speak against, to accuse*, especially before judges, *Liddell and Scott.*

---

8. *But he knew their thoughts, and said to the man which had the withered hand, Rise up, and stand forth in the midst, And he arose and stood forth.*

Thoughts, not mere ideas, but *reasonings* and *plans* of action. Matt. xv. 19.
Their *secret* purpose, to encompass His death as an *offender*.
The heart is very small, but a *universe* of good or evil.
God was present searching their minds, but they knew it not.
A clear proof of Christ's Supreme Godhead.
He proves, that malignant stubbornness, will not yield to *compassion*.
His searching eye moves round their heart as in judgment.
Stand forth. The man's *rising*, *professed* his faith in Jesus, as Messiah.
Not ashamed to prove his loyalty to Christ.
Cold blooded Scribes, behold the sufferer's sad condition.
He would thus kindle their sympathies, and rouse their conscience.
Their bigotry had burnt out all their kind charities.
A challenge to detect any *trick* in the patient, or the healing.

"*Said.*" Doing all things openly, *Bengel.* *ἀναστάσ.* same term used (Acts ix. 18) to indicate Paul's posture when baptized by Ananias. Some have vindicated "*Anxious Seats*," *i. e. seats* to which persons are invited for special prayer, from this command. Under unwise hands, they have doubtless been sadly abused, *Sprague* on *Revivals.* The abuse of a thing no argument against its use; the best things are abused, even *the Gospel*, Rom. vi. 1, Jude, 4 verse, *Ed.*

---

9. *Then said Jesus unto them, I will ask you one thing: Is it lawful on the sabbath days to do good, or to do evil? to save life, or to destroy it?*

Ask. The question is not, the *sanctity*, but the *mode* of observing the Sabbath.

You, deeply emphatic. They *asked*, and had already *condemned* Him in their hearts.

Lawful. I leave it to yourselves. I will abide by your decision.

"Is it consistent with the law of Moses?" *Not*—Is it right in itself?

Divine gentleness! He *patiently* waits for an answer.

Their ignorance and malice effectually silenced.

A corrupt heart soon becomes *shameless* in its degradations.

Sabbath, on which the Lord, 1. Refreshes His friends. 2. Conquers His enemies. 3. Relieves the afflicted. 4. Advances His cause.

Do good. A Sabbath rest, 1. An active *rest*. 2. A holy *rest*. 3. A happy *rest*.

Evil. No truism, He points out the nature of an act, condemned beforehand by them.

Save. Rescuing, ransoming, blessing, legitimate labors on the sabbath.

Contrasts *His* benevolence, with their murderous designs.

He, who does not do good, does harm. James iv. 17.

They could not conceal their intentions from Him.

His words, His piercing look. Mark iii. 5. An illustration of Eph. iv. 26.

We are taught—1. The Christian solemnization of the Sabbath.

2. The grand objects for which Christ came into the world.

Not to save, in Oriental idiom, is equivalent *to kill*.

Not to love, equivalent to hate. Matt. xi. 25. Rom. ix. 13.

Life, including health, and all enabling one to enjoy life.

Destroy. This is now *your* desperate purpose. A withering question.

It was unanswerable. They held their peace. Mark iii. 4.

Here, for the Lord to refuse help was virtually to destroy.

With Jesus, works of *mercy* were ever works of necessity.

Mark says—*They held their peace.* They could not resist, but would not *yield.*

They persistently and inflexibly rejected the counsel of God. Luke vii. 30.

ψυχὴν—1, *breath.* 2, *animal life.* 3, *soul:* by meton., *a living being.* In the antistic declarations of Jesus, life beyond the grave. Departed spirits, Rev. vi. 9. The lower animal nature, as distinguished in Greek philosophy from the νόος, the higher nature, *Olshausen.* For "*I will ask you one thing,*" read "*I ask you whether,*" *Tisch., Alford.*

---

10. *And looking round about upon them all, he said unto the man, Stretch forth thy hand. And he did so: and his hand was restored whole as the other.*

Looking. Holy indignation, and compassionate love, blended.

A gaze of grief and anger, embracing all.

Round. They felt that omniscient glance, *searching* the depths of their souls.

In anger. Mark. Anger and sympathy contended in His mind.

Sin unrepented of, will bring another look of *vengeance*.

Grieved. Mark. Forty years, was he grieved with their fathers in the wilderness. Heb. iii. 17.

Christians like Jesus, mourn over the hardness of the obdurate.

Our anger ought only to burn, that sin might be destroyed.

Our danger is in hating the *sinner*, instead of the *sin*.

Said. Without drawing an inference, or answering His own question.

He left the arrow to burn its way into their consciences.

Stretch. The *command* to lift it, without imparting power, would have been *vain*.

The *attempt* to do it, without faith in God, *useless*.

Obedience might incur the vengeance of the Pharisees.

Opposition, dangers, death, do not deter earnest souls.

"Be it known to thee O king, we WILL NOT serve thy gods." Dan. iii. 18.

He *essayed* to obey, and God gave him strength. "As thy days, so shall thy strength be." Deut. xxxiii. 25.

Those looking to another source for help, will be put to shame. 1. Peter ii. 6.

The Scribes' malice could not deprive the poor man of Divine sympathy.

The world, flesh, or devil, cannot arrest the mercy of Christ.

Restored. The hand of the presumptuous Jeroboam was withered. 1. Kings, xiii. 4.

But our Lord spares the arm sacrilegiously raised against Him.

μετ', ὀργῆσ—Mark iii. 5. It is the uniform testimony of tradition among the Fathers, that Peter superintended the writing of Mark's Gospel. Hence that evangelist *alone*, records some vivid reminiscences of our Lord's *feelings*, *looks*, and *gestures* on several occasions, *Alexander*. υγιὴσ "*whole*," omitted, *Tischendorf*, *Alford*; also ὡσ ἡ ἀλλη, "*as the other*," *Alford*.

---

11. *And they were filled with madness: and communed one with another what they might do to Jesus.*

Madness. He had broken their traditions, and *silenced*, and put them to *shame* before the people.

He had healed a despised cripple on the Sabbath day.
But he had not raised His hand, or advanced a step to desecrate it.
Verily there was no law of Moses, against uttering a *kind word.*
Not the agitation, but the sediment, renders the stream turbid.
God's goodness to the wretched should kindle repentance. Rom. ii. 4.
When fire does not melt, it hardens. Fruit is ripened, or ruined by the sun.
Abel's innocence should have *disarmed* the *enraged* Cain.
Joseph's piety, instead of *conciliating*, *infuriated* his brethren.
No deed of piety is so lovely, but *envy* turneth it into reproach.
Many turned their eye to Jesus for *mercy*, the Scribes, with *revenge.*
Those who save a sheep, yet ruin a man, are verily monsters.
Men break the Sabbath without working, who find cause for persecution in deeds of benevolence.
The brighter the truth, the more the ungodly are irritated.
Even miracles cannot avail to convince despisers of truth.
Two days since, they said blasphemy was uttered.
Now, publicans were received, and the legal Sabbath profaned.
So his kindness to the wretched must be washed out by blood!
Thus the children of the Serpent ever persecute the children of God.
Communed. What a single arm cannot effect, the multitude unite to do.
Note.—It is professed religionists, and the officers of the Church, who conspire to murder the Anointed of the Lord.
The transient friendship of the wicked, is too often *cemented* by *blood.*
Blind madness, snatches at any weapon, that will destroy.

ἀνοίας from *α* and *νόος*—*without mind*, deprived of reason by either folly or madness. Were *wholly confounded*, *Wakefield.* A milder term than madness, *Meyer.* Ira est brevis insanitas.

---

12. *And it came to pass in those days, that he went out into a mountain to pray, and continued all night in prayer to God.*

Those days. Men from Tyre and Sidon flocked to Him after the above miracle.
Went out. He sought in solitude, that rest, which earth could not give.
All night. Many professors think half an hour very irksome.

"If any man have not the Spirit of Christ, he is none of His." Rom. viii. 9.

Sin is the only hindrance to our having the spirit of prayer. 1. Pet. iii. 7.

Closet prayer reveals our character to *us*, with singular exactness.

There, we ought to be *honest*, for the soul meets God, face to face.

There, we forget self-flatteries, God's hand is felt on the heart.

Vanity hiding our infirmities, has no place under the Eye of God.

There, many things appear sinful, which we thought innocent.

A conscience, dull in duty, proves a closet neglected.

There, *doubtful* schemes, dare not ask God's blessing.

Secret prayer loosens the hold of sin, and weakens the bondage of passion.

Dulls the glitter of earth, and clarifies our view of things unseen.

It fortifies the soul, while disarming temptations of their fascinations.

Secret prayer, the final test of the morality of our occupation.

Could Paul have asked God's blessing on slaying His Lambs? Acts xxvi. 9.

Prayer, an essential part of religion, and of all good works.

Prayer to God. Gr. *in prayer of God.* *Oratories* built for that purpose.

On the morrow, the Lord intended to *ordain* His Apostles.

Alone, deep affection, or affliction, dreads intrusion.

προσευχῇ τοῦ Θεοῦ—*An oratory.* Our translation violates the analogy of language, *Campbell, Mede, Wetstein, Doddridge.* Synagogue, *Grotius.* Different, *Calmet, Hammond, Prideaux.* Doubtful, *Meyer.* προσευχῇ and δέησισ commonly *prayer* in N. T., Acts xii. 5, Heb. v. 7, &c. The word was so common, that the Romans became familiar with it. Thus *Juvenal*, Sat. iii., v. 296, speaks to the mendicant Jew: Ede ubi consistas; in qua te quero proseucha?—*In what house of prayer may I find thee begging?* The *proseuchæ* or *oratories*, were enclosures of walls, without roofs, similar to the humble places of worship now common in the deserts around Egypt, *Campbell, Epiphanius.* A decree permitted the Jews of Caria to erect these proseuchas by the water banks, *Josephus.* "*Mountain,*" Tradition locates choice of apostles on the hill of *Hattin*, *Robinson, Stanley, Ellicott;* denied by *Thompson.* "*All night in prayer.*" On this account the apostles are said to have been *given* to Him, John xvii. 6, *Bengel.* Luke alone records the fact, that, before He ordained the twelve, He spent all the night in prayer to God, *Ed*

---

13 ¶ *And when it was day, he called* unto him *his disciples: and of them he chose twelve, whom also he named apostles.*

Day. The choice of apostles preceded by a whole night in prayer.

Disciples. After summoning many; out of them He chose twelve.
He was at first their visible, afterwards their invisible Head.
He devoted a large share of His time to their training.
Grace stoops low to select, but highly exalts its chosen ones.
Chose. Mark iii. 14. *ordained.* Thus the Church has ever solemnly *chosen* and *ordained* men.
To give judgment. Luke xxii. 30. Forgive sins. John xx. 23.
To bear the keys. Matt. xvi. 19. Sit on His throne. Matt. xix. 28.
The divine and chosen instruments in the foundation of His Church.
In sovereign wisdom and mercy, He chose Judas.
Twelve. Referring to the twelve patriarchs, and twelve tribes of Israel. Rev. xxi. 12-14.
Apostles. *Any one sent*, *commander*, *herald*, Christ is thus named. Heb. iii. 1.
Variously described, each *name* characteristic of progressively higher *relationship.*
Servants. Matt. x. 24. *Friends.* John xv. 15. *Brothers.* John xx. 17.
Their very name received the seal of their Master.
They seem to have been selected from John the Baptist's disciples. Acts. i. 21-22.
There are five characteristics which mark the twelve, chosen.
1. Personal acquaintance with the Lord.
2. Immediate designation to the office, by Christ Himself.
3. Effectual inspiration. 4. The power of working miracles.
5. Universality of mission. Compare 1. Cor. xix. 1-2, and 2. Cor. xii. 12.
They shared in the intercessions of the previous night.
Jesus Himself trained them, to organize the Church, and record her Faith.
He admonished the Jews, that the *Authority* of the Sanhedrim was at an end.
Also that the *Priesthood* was invested in Him alone. John x. 18.
The disciples are named the third time, and each time in a different order.
Precedency, claimed by prelates or popes, has no sanction from the Apostles.

ἀποστόλους, Attic Gr., a naval *armament.* N. T. an *ambassador*, one *sent*, a *messenger.* A counsellor of the high priest, who collected tribute. No authority for orders of ministry in the church, *W. & W.*

14. Simon, (whom he also named Peter,) and Andrew his brother, James and John, Philip and Bartholomew.

Simon. The change of name was not made, when first called.
Peter. Rock, not on account of firmness, but boldness and strength.
Not named first, because first called, Andrew called before him.
No superiority in office; as no *primacy* is ascribed to him.
He was betrayed into the gravest errors of judgment and practice.
Repeatedly rebuked with great severity, by Christ Himself.
Paul publicly rebuked him for dissembling at Antioch. Gal. ii. 11.
He alone was guilty of denying his Master.
His restoration was not completed till after our Lord's resurrection. John xxi. 15-16-17.
His historical position was *spokesman* for the college of the apostles.
It resembled the foreman of a jury, or chairman of a committee.
His qualifications, forwardness of speech, and energy of action.
Present at the transfiguration, and the agony in the garden.
With Jesus he paid tribute, may have supplied Him with a *home*. Mark i. 29. Luke iv. 38.
He alone of the twelve, is certainly known to have been *married*.
He was present at the judgment hall, at the grave, at the lake.
His threefold *denial* of Christ, remains for our eternal warning.
Union of courage and fear, strength and weakness, love and vanity, form the unstable Peter-like character.
After his visit to Antioch, nothing is certainly known of him.
Christ distinctly predicted his death, as a martyr. John xxi. 18.
Tradition claims him as a martyr at Rome by crucifixion.
Andrew, has the honor, of having first brought his brother Peter to Christ.
Native of Bethsaida, Galilee; at first, a disciple of John the Baptist.
After visiting Jesus, they *continued* their calling as fishermen.
He labored in Scythia, Thrace, Greece, crucified in Achaia, on St. Andrew's *cross* X
James and John. Sons of Zebedee; called *Boanerges*, "*sons of thunder.*"
This has been generally interpreted, *powerful preachers*.
Certain origin and intention of the surname are as yet *unknown*.
Their names in a remarkable manner, twice united. Luke ix. 54. Mark x. 35-37.
James, the only one of the twelve, (save "the son of perdition") whose death is recorded. Acts xii. 2.
John. *Whom Jesus loved*, leaned on Him at supper. John xxi. 20.

He remained faithful at the cross, when all the disciples had fled.

He received from Jesus' dying lips, the most precious legacy ever bequeathed by LOVE. The privilege of providing a *home for the Mother of our Lord.*

Banished to Patmos, for the testimony of Jesus, by Domitian.

He never mentions himself by name—but as, "that other disciple," &c. John xviii. 15; xx. 2.

He dwells much on our Lord's *Divinity*, hence called John *the Divine.*

Philip, of Bethsaida, the fourth apostle who attached himself to Christ.

He brought Nathaniel (Bartholomew) to Christ, was ordained with the twelve.

In feeding 5000, Christ singled out Philip to *prove* his *faith.*

His request—"Lord shew us the Father," implies him weak in faith.

His field was Phrygia, and it is said he suffered in Hierapolis.

Bartholomew or (Nathaniel) son of Talmai, occurs.—Josh. xv. 14.

A native of Cana—was hailed by our Lord—"*Behold an Israelite indeed, in whom is no guile!*" John i. 47.

Jesus appeared to him at Tiberias, he was present at our Lord's ascension.

He preached in Arabia Felix, and was crucified in Armenia.

Phillip was noted for *sincerity.* Nathaniel for his *candor.*

Σίμωνα Matt. has *πρῶτοσ* before the name. *Πέτρον.* Denying his pre-eminence, the fruit of ultra one-sided Protestantism, *Oosterzee.* No pre-eminence for, 1. None of the disciples so terribly rebuked by our Lord. 2. His prerogative conceded to all the Apostles. 3. The early church never admitted his primacy. 4. He never himself hints at it. 5. The most ancient fathers never attributed it to him, *Alexander.* He was born at Bethsaida, but lived at Capernaum. Named first because the oldest, *Lightfoot.* Luke xxii. 26. Never was at Rome, *Hug*, (a distinguished scholar of the Papal Sect) *Neander*, *Scaliger.* Peter's visit to Rome doubtful, *Baur*, *Spanheim.* Credited by *Casaubon*, *Usher*, *Pearson*, *Giesler*, *Olshausen*, *Hase*, *Tholuck.* John xxi. 19. *Ανδρέαν* a *strong man*, *Winer.* *Ιάκωβον*, *supplanter*, and John, sons of Zebedee and probably of *Salome.* The individual who accused James, saw him nobly confessing, and was so moved by his constancy, that he declared himself a *Christian too.* So they were both led away to death. On their way, the man entreated James to forgive him, on which James said, "*Peace be to thee,*" and embraced him. They were then beheaded together, *Clemens*, *Eusebius.* *Ιωάννην*, *mercyof the Lord*, given by Jehovah. *Φιλιππον*, *warlike.* *Βαρθολομαῖον*, *son of Talmai.* Some absurdly suppose his own name designedly repressed. *Talmai*, Heb., *cultivated field.* That Bartholomew and Nathaniel are the same person is most certain. John who twice mentions Nathaniel, never introduces the name of Bartholomew. Matthew, Mark, Luke, all speak of Bartholomew, but never allude to Nathaniel. Highly probable Nathaniel was his proper name, and Bartholomew his surname. Philip who brought Nathaniel to Jesus, is named by each of the first three Evangelists, in connexion with Bartholomew. By Luke, Bartholomew is coupled with Philip in the same way as Simon with his brother Andrew, and James with John, see *Smith's* Dict. *Ed.*

---

15. *Matthew and Thomas, James, the son of Alphæus, and Simon called Zelotes.*

Matthew. Life and character. Luke v. 29. See Notes.

Thomas, seems to have been of a melancholy temperament.

Surnamed *Didymus*. Aramaic and Greek synonymes for a *twin*.

Said to have been born at Antioch. Matt. xiii. 55. Noted for his slowness of faith.

His disposition to doubt, transcended the limits of cautious examination.

He exacted too rigorous evidence, for which our Lord gently censured him.

None willing to die a martyr by *mistake*, therefore we should investigate thoroughly.

Tradition located him in Judea and Parthia, and says his death was that of a martyr.

Son of Alphæus. Not identical with the *brother* of *Jesus*. Gal. i. 19.

Tradition is he perished, being cast from the temple.

Simon Zelotes. Surnamed the Canaanite. Mark iii. 18. The least known of the apostles.

Canaanite, Aramaic, synonymous with *Zealot*, a sect of that period.

Ferocious fanatics, whose zeal hastened the ruin of Jerusalem.

Tradition says he preached and died in Mauritania, Africa.

Μαθαῖον, *reward.* Θωμᾶν, a *twin*, out of this name has grown the tradition that he was a *twin* brother of our Lord. *Eusebius* says his real name was *Judas*. *Ed.* Αλφαιον, *learned.* Σιμωνα, *one who hears.* Ζηλωτήσ, *Zealot:* Canaanite, Matt. x. 4, formed from a *Hebrew* synonyme of Zealot, *Wakefield*. *James.*—Not the same with the brother of our Lord. John vii. 5, Luke ii. 7. 1. The James referred to, Acts xii. 17, cannot be the brother of our Lord. 2. Our Lord's brethren disbelieved until after His death. 3. Paul discriminates between apostles and brothers of our Lord. 4. James, Author of the Epistle, was the brother of our Lord, *Princeton Review*.

---

16. *And Judas* the brother *of James, and Judas Iscariot, which also was the traitor.*

Judas. Also called *Lebbæus* and *Thaddæus*, son of Alphæus.

His only record is, "*How is it, that Thou wilt manifest Thyself unto us,*" &c. John xiv. 22.

He labored in Arabia, and suffered martyrdom in Persia.

Iscariot. A man of *Kerioth*, a town in Judah, locality unknown.

Traitor. A synonyme for infamy in every language.

Covetous and unprincipled, but ambition was his ruling passion.

His feet were washed by the Redeemer, previous to the Last Supper.

He seemed solicitous that Jesus should assume the regal state.

He knew Christ's power, and thought no harm could be done Him.

Probably betrayed Him to hasten His kingdom, and in Jesus' day of triumph, hoped to be forgiven.

With other Jews, He believed that the Messiah could never die.

Finding Christ did not rescue Himself, but was surely condemned to die, he returned the money, and hung himself through remorse.

In life and death, Judas keeps his rank, as a *witness* of the Lord.

Christ forseeing his treason, in Divine wisdom, selected him.

As an *intimate*, but *faithless* companion his testimony to our Lord's holiness is valuable. Matt. xxvii. 4.

"*The foolishness of God is wiser than men.*" 1 Cor. i. 25.

If defection occurs in the militant Church, this case guards against despair.

Absolute purity is not to be found in the highest places of the Church.

In the Ark was Ham,—with Shem and Japheth.

In the spiritual Jerusalem, a Babel was in its bosom.

In the company of the twelve was a traitor apostle.

The privileges of those who *saw* and *heard* the Son of God were great.

"*Happy are thy men, and happy are these thy servants.*" Queen of Sheba to King Solomon.

Peter, James, and John, seem to have been the favorites of our Lord.

A kingdom founded by such frail instruments, must be the work of God.

The catalogue of apostles—a support for faith. It testifies—

1. To the truth of the gospel. 2. Its sublimity. 3. Its Divine origin. 4. Its imperishable nature.

Ιουδας—*the praise of the Lord.* Lebbæus, from *Libba*, near Carmel, *Gerlach*, *Liske*. προδοτης. Not evident that this word then signified the infamy, which is now attached to it. The verb from which it is taken (Matt. x. 4) simply means to *deliver* up by *judicial process*, or to commend one delivered to the favor of the judge *Stier*. Judas' life fulfilled the prophecy found in the 69th and 109th Psalms. *Docetae* taught, Christ foresaw the future traitor, and chose him *ad hoc*, *Cyril*, *Alexander*. He was mistaken in choosing a devil instead of an angel, *Ebionites Paulus*, (enemies of our Lord's divinity). A high venture of love, discerning many good qualities in him, doing the utmost to win him, but finding him evil, warning him, at length dismissing him as a son of perdition, *Oosterzee*. Four times we have mention of the twelve apostles, and four different arrangements of their names are given. *Bengel* thinks the order is important, and observes, that in each case Peter is styled the *first*, as expressive of *precedency*. The places where these arrangements of the twelve occur, are—Matt. x. 2. Mark iii. 16. Luke vi. 14. Acts i. 13-26. It is worthy of note, that while the places of the other apostles, vary, Peter is put first in each case, and Judas, the traitor, *last*. *Ed.*

---

17. ¶ *And he came down with them, and stood in the plain, and the company of his disciples, and a great multitude of people out of all Judea and Jerusalem, and from the sea coast of Tyre and Sidon, which came to hear him, and to be healed of their diseases;*

Came down. After a night of *watching*, He prepares for a day of toil.

Stood, Ruler of a kingdom amid His chosen ambassadors.

Plain. On a level flat below the mountain—while the multitude were on the plain beneath.

Judea. Luke i. 5. **Jerusalem.** History, &c. Luke ii. 25. See Notes.

Tyre. Heb. a *rock*—founded 240 years before Solomon's temple. Jeptha was judge.

1027 B.C. Hiram, its king, supplied the brass and timber for the temple. 1 Kings v. chap.

Their cunning and industry in the arts are celebrated by Homer.

Commerce of Syria, Persia, Greece, Egypt and Spain, enriched Tyre. Ezek. xxvii.

Famous for emeralds, purple, broidered work, fine linen, coral and agate.

Her merchants were princes, and their residences palaces.

Her fleets visited Britain, especially the Scilly Isles and Cornwall.

For *five* years, Shalmaneser besieged it, but could not take it.

Nebuchadnezzar took it, after 13 years, and destroyed it. Ezek. xxvi. 7. 584 B.C.

Lay desolate and forgotten 70 years, as foretold by Isa. xxiii. 15.

Besieged eight months by Alexander, was taken, but not destroyed, 332 B.C.

It had so grown, that Jerome, A.D. 390, stumbled at the prophecies.

"Thou shalt be rebuilt *no more*." Ezek. xxvi. 14.

Antigonus besieged it 13 months, and took it. B.C.

It was taken by the Saracens, A.D. 700. The Crusaders. A.D. 1200.

She rejoiced in the ruin of Jerusalem. Ezek. xxvi. 2.

Its site cannot now be determined with satisfaction.

Sidon. A city of Phœnicia, opulent and flourishing when Christ visited it. Luke iv. 26. See Notes.

It was called Tsidon Rabba, or Great Sidon. Josh xi. 8.

The best vessels of Xerxes fleet, built and manned by Zidonians. Its destruction was accomplished by Melek Adel, brother of Saladin, A.D. 1197.

Its present population Moslems, Jews, Maronites, and Greek Christians, about 7000.

Ancient Sidonians notorious for worship of Ashtoreth. "Queen of heaven," identified with Venus.

Medals are now found inscribed "*To the Zidonian Goddess.*" 1. Kings, xi. 5-33.

Sidonians followed Jesus. Mark iii. 8. Hence Paul found believers there. Acts xxvii. 3.

τόπου πεδινοῦ, Level place, *Stanley*, *Tholuck*, *Ebrard*, *Lichtenstein*. Matt. contradicts Luke, *Meyer*, *Alford*. "*In the plain.*" That is, not in the bottom of a valley, but on a plateau on the hill-side, a place more suitable than a dead-level for a large assembly to hear. Such a place as is referred to in Isaiah xiii. 2, *a high mountain*, i. e. *a mountain plateau* or *table-land*, *Bengel*. This explanation furnishes a reply to the unwarrantable statement of *Meyer* and *Alford*, that Matt. contradicts Luke! *Ed.* Table-land, *Thaber*, *Jerome*, *Wetstein*. This discourse is the same as Matt. v. &c., *Kuinoel*, *Rosenmuller*. A more modern *tradition*, *Meyer*. Descending to heal, He reascends to preach, *Andrews*, *Robinson*.

---

18. *And they that were vexed with unclean spirits: and they were healed.*

Vexed. The strange employment of lost spirits is to *torment men*.

Unclean. Luke iv. 33. Impure themselves, they defile every thing they touch.

The impure like the beasts, go with their eye down on the earth.

Sensual, "clothed in scarlet, yet embracing a dunghill. Lam. iv. 5.

All sin tends to debase the *body*, *soul*, and *spirit*.

Healed. Satan still "worketh in the hearts of the children of disobedience."

He blinds the minds of them that believe not, and who are taken captive.

But the Son of God was manifested to destroy the works of the devil.

ὀχλούμενοι from ὄχλοσ, *crowd*, *i. e.* they were tormented by a *crowd* of unclean demons, who, restless themselves, are determined none else shall have peace.

19. *And the whole multitude sought to touch him: for there went virtue out of him, and healed* them *all.*

Multitude. Tidings fly in the East with great rapidity.
Without a press, or telegraph, all society seem to be messengers.
The wonder-worker's fame, brought the deaf, blind, and lame.
A Touch, too slight it might be thought to heal a disease baffling all medical skill.
Virtue. Nothing magical, or beyond the power of His own will.
An exertion of the Divine prerogative by deliberate design.
He healed secretly, openly, quickly, gradually, always perfectly.

ἅπτεσθαι. Royal vanity never *presumed* to imitate more closely the acts of God, than in attempting to heal incurable diseases by a *touch.* It began with *Edward the Confessor.* Others trace it back to *Clovis*, 481. *Louis XIII* resigned all his power to the ambitious Cardinal *Richelieu*, but the curing sick with the *touch. Louis XIV* touched 1600 patients in April, 1686. The historians are *silent* as to their efficacy. *Wm. Cloyes*, physician to Queen *Elizabeth*, testifies, "Through her princely clemency, a *mighty number* of her majesty's subjects are daily cured."

"But at his touch,
"Such sanctity hath heaven given his hand,
"They presently amend." *Macbeth*, Act iv.

δύναμις. Fountain of miracles, *Theoph.* Efflux, *Euthymius.* Animal magnetism; mere emanations, *Le Clerc.* Intrinsic Divine power, *Grotius.* Cancels the passage, *Paulus. Inherent, underived power.* A beautiful expression, descriptive of the abundant "goings forth" of our Lord's Divine power and love in healing the bodies and souls of men. There is "*virtue*" going out of Him still, healing all who by faith "*touch Him.*" "*Wherefore he is able to save unto the uttermost,*" *&c., Ed.*

---

20. *And he lifted up his eyes on his disciples, and said, Blessed* be ye *poor; for your's is the kingdom of God.*

Lifted. Oriental heathen are silent, sad, and thoughtful.
This look was to attract attention. John xvii. 1.
At another time He stretched out His hand. Matt. xii. 49.
This look of *power* compelled the noisy crowd to attend.
Mount Sinai preached *condemnation*, and began with a *curse.*
This mountain brings *mercy*, and begins with "Blessed.
That law was given amid tempest, darkness, and earthquake.
The gospel proclaimed to those *quietly* sitting at the feet of the Messiah.
Benedictions, four in number, correspond to the four woes *unuttered.*
He addresses His disciples, *types* of all who should ever follow Him.
Eyes. The Lord's gracious look upon weak, but sincere disciples.
A different report of the Sermon on the Mount. Matt. v. 2.
This period of our Lord's life a culminating point.

Blessed. Never did a Teacher pronounce the word, with such authority.
No human discourse ever approached the gracious words of this Preacher,
Christ cries "Blessed" until sinners constrain Him to use another style.
His voice *pronounces*, and His grace *dispenses* blessedness.
We bless our friends, but *powerless* to make them happy.

"But feeble our compassion proves
And can but *weep*, where most it *loves*."

Blessed. A proclamation of the *Law*, with *Grace*, enabling men to fulfil it.
Originally applicable to *Divine* blessedness, and those sharing it.
Often referable to the felicity, enjoyed in this life.
Yet always connected with dependence on the *divine* favor.
This blessedness *begun* on earth, only completed in heaven.
The first beatitude on earth, the last, in heaven Rev. xxii. 14.
BEATITUDES. 1. Of *character*—Poor, hungry, weeping, hated of men. 2. The blessings of the citizens of Heaven, suited to those characters—Riches, full satisfaction, joy, children of the prophets.
THE RULER OF THE KINGDOM, 1. *Friend* of the poor. 2. *Bread* of the hungry. 3. *Joy* of the mourner. 4. *Judge* of the oppressed.
Poor. Jews believed the *higher classes* the Messiah's favorites.
Unrepining, not covetous, easily satisfied, content with little.
They are a *mirror* of the Kingdom, though broken into fragments.
It refers, say Papists, to voluntary poverty by way of penance.
Poverty of mind or body, a burlesque of the Redeemer's words.
Worldly prosperity is not unlawful, yet we believe, spiritual poverty *generally* coincides with external want.
It denotes, saints collectively, are *sufferers* on earth.
Believers, generally, destitute of what is essential to worldly happiness.
But pre-eminently they, who feel their *need* of *spiritual food*.
Realizing "an *aching void*," ere the fulness of grace enters.
Implies contentment in poverty, but grateful for all God spares.
Many *poor* in this world murmur, being *proud* in spirit.
Laodicea was *rich*, but spiritually *poor*; Paul, *poor*, but spiritually *rich*.
Poor in spirit, are willing to be esteemed *miserable*, to *do good*.
Blessed are the contentedly poor, as the righteous when *usefully* rich.
If the former cannot *spend* cheerfully, for Christ's sake, they can *want* cheerfully.
Kingdom. The Kingdom of *Grace*, prepares for the Kingdom of *God*. Daniel vii. 27.
The reign of the Messiah in its inception and consummation.
That part of the universe, where God gloriously manifests His presence.

Supposed to be the central point around which the Universe revolves. This laid in the dust the Pharisees' hopes of *monopolising* the kingdom.

ἔλεγε. Hitherto our Lord had *wrought*, now He *speaks*, *Ebrard*. This sermon the Magna Charta of the Kingdom of God, *Lange*. Different discourses, *Augustine*, *Osiander*, *Gratz*, *Neander*, *Kraft*, *Greswell*, *Andrews*. One before, the other after choice of Apostles, *Lange*. Identical with Matt. V., &c., *Calvin*, *Grotius*, *Elsley*, *Lightfoot*, *Robinson*, *Tischendorf*, *Stier*. Matt.'s Hebrew original changed by a Greek Editor, *Neander*. First addressed to disciples, then the multitude, *Augustine*, *Latin* and *Lutheran Churches*, A frivolous view, *Calvin*, *Ellicott*. Luke confounds the sermon on the mount with the advice to the Apostles after election, *Norton*. Luke only records those fragments of our Lord's discourse which suited the object of his narrative. Matt. gives it more fully, *Jacobus*. Matt.'s esoteric; Luke's exoteric, *Lange*. Luke's the more accurate, *Olshausen*, *Bauer*, *Calvin*. Luke's *MS.* only contained this extract, *Ebrard*. Oral tradition fuller form in Matt., *Meyer*, *Tholuck*. Luke's aim accuracy, rather than fullness, *Oosterzee*. Luke mistakes the *relation* of some parts, *Stier*. Neither authentic, *Strauss*. Lax moralists, taking a one-sided view of truth, have rejected all teachings, unless contained in this sermon. They reject the only aid necessary for their keeping these very precepts, *Gregory*, *Naz*. Writing for the Gentiles, Luke omits the glosses of the Scribes, concerning *oaths*, *divorces*, *fasts*, *alms*, *&c.*, *Lightfoot*. Delivered the longer sermon on the mountain, went lower and preached the shorter, *Augustine*, *Lange*.

μακαριοι. "*Blessed.*" Strictly applied to the gods, who are constantly μάκαρεσ θεοί in Homer and Hesiod, as opposed to *mortal men;* also applied to the dead, since the living world could never reach perfect bliss, the name μακαρεσ was specially given to *the dead*. μακάρων νῆσοι the islands *of the blest*, where heroes slain in battle and demigods enjoyed rest for ever, *Liddell* and *Scott*. μακάριοσ therefore means more than "happy;" it expresses supreme, heavenly bliss, freedom from all care and sorrow, such as can come from the abiding presence of God in the soul only, *Ed.*

πτωχοί *a* πτωσσω *to crouch*, the Oriental custom at this day, in the presence of the exalted. Literally *begging;* unrepining, easily satisfied, content with little, *Campbell*. Its synonyms are τăπεινὸσ πένησ. "*poor* and *needy;*" πτωχοι occurs 34 times, πένησ once, and τăπεινὸσ 8 times; the last is from πόνοσ *labor*, among the Greeks—compelled to toil for bread. πτωχὸσ *mendicus*, a beggar. Hence *Tertullian* changed the *Beati pauperes* of the Vulgate, and Old Italic, into the *Beati mendici*. *Socrates* called himself πενιă *i. e.*, if all he owned were sold, it would yield 5 Attic Minae about £20 sterling, The πτοχòι live on alms. Such mendicants, *Plato* would not admit into his ideal Republic: external poverty, *Neander*. Are *mendicants* as such, to be the inheritors of the kingdom of God? *Stier*.

---

21. *Blessed* are ye *that hunger now: for ye shall be filled. Blessed* are ye *that weep now: for ye shall laugh.*

Hunger, is influenced by habit, and intense mental emotion.
Debility, blindness, and delirium result from protracted fasting.
At other times the vision becomes supernaturally clear and strong.
Sensations are dreadfully painful, and the most tender affections are overcome. Deut. xxviii. 56.

Some have endeavoured in their delirium, to devour their own flesh.
The soul's desires unappeased, cause a hunger, but not for bread. Matt. v. 6. John vi. 35.
The promise is not to the *destitute*, merely as sufferers.
But it suggests the necessity of *spiritual* food.
There is a hunger which God did not create, the *aching void* of sin.
Its intensity is learned from the earthly pantings of the soul. Amos ii. 7.
Sleep of death broken, the soul first hungers after righteousness.
The feeblest desires after peace, are the earnest of felt deeper wants.
Our bodily and spiritual appetites, demand *daily* supplies.
Prosperity too often is a sweet poison, a Judas flower.
Affliction to the righteous, a bitter, but healing medicine.
Against a world of pleasure-seekers, Christ taught, *pleasure* not the chief good.
One who claims the kingdom, *because* poor, through pride, would no longer be among the hungry.
Filled. *Cranmer's* Bible, *satisfied. Rheimish* Vers., *have their fill.*
No soul satified, until awaking in the likeness of God. Psa. xvii. 15.
Weep. Tears belong to time, joy to eternity.
The reluctant cross-bearer—knows not its value.
The language of tears is understood among all the dialects of men.
Tears relieve. There is a sorrow, whose depth of grief cannot weep.
An angry sorrow, the soul indignantly dries its tears.
A *proud* sorrow, the soul disdains to shew its sympathy.
Sin is the cause of sorrow. Unfallen beings never weep.
Holy sorrow mourns not so much the loss of friends, health or wealth.
They alone truly weep, who feel they *deserve not* the comfort, the heart desires.
Some mourners are comforted, with but meagre scraps of good.
Penitential mourner's sorrow, has the eye fixed on Christ.
A godly sorrow weeps for the remains of heart corruption.
A sanctified sorrow weeps for the desolations of Zion. Zeph. iii. 18.
Jesus who is *never* said to have smiled, *often* wept.
Romantic writers speak of the "luxury of grief." This is only by contrast.*

---

* In the times of Louis XV., times of boundless profligacy in Paris, pleasure-seekers, through *ennui* committed suicide. A reverse illustration. The skeleton at an ancient Egptian feast. In the Palavicinni, near Genoa, an Epicurean luxuriance and splendour reveal a surprise of a *grave-yard*, with its broken tombs, and memorials of death.

We are commanded to weep for the fruits of the curse. Ezek. ix. 4.

God makes special enquiries for those who sigh for sin. Ezek. xxi. 7.

Laugh. The joys of the believer, though unseen, none the less real.

Lips filled with rejoicing, and mouth with laughing. Psa. lxiii. 8.

Weeping endureth for a night, joy cometh in the morning. Psa. xxx. 5.

"God will wipe away tears from off all faces." Isa. xxv. 8. Rev. vii. 17.

χορτασθήσεσθε—classically, to feeding animals, but by later Greeks, to human beings, feeding to satiety, *Alexander*.

"*Now*." This particle is added in speaking of matters which concern this world or the next, according to the different persons who are addressed, *Bengel*.

---

22. *Blessed are ye, when men shall hate you, and when they shall separate you from* their company, *and shall reproach* you, *and cast out your name as evil, for the Son of man's sake.*

When. The Greek implies contradiction,—*If* the world hate you.

Hate. The Primitive Christians as such, were almost universally hated.

Pliny, an amiable heathen, speaks of the NAME, being a *crime*.

Christianity demanded *sacrifice* of their *vanity*, and death to their *lusts*.

It required men to be *humble*, while they revered *ambition*.

It denounced their *reasonings*, as folly, and *self righteousness*, as *condemnation*.

Their *envy* kindled at the *degree of virtue*, they despaired of attaining.

Light is pleasant to the healthy eye, and virtue lovely to the pure mind.

Depraved philosophers hated the Gospel, since it destroyed their peace.

Christ's silent purity, loudly condemned the hypocritical Scribes.

If the martyrs were sure of glory, their enemies knew their own doom.

The Bible lifts an axe, against the foundations of their *only* home.

A persecuting world aims the blow at the Church, but meant for the Head.

Saul! Saul! why persecutest thou Me? Jesus to the Pharisee. Acts ix. 4.

"Christ also suffered for us, leaving us an example." 1. Peter ii. 21.

All who will follow Christ, must wear His livery.

No man is led *blindfold*, into a *hidden* snare, by the Gospel.

"These things, I have told you, that ye be not offended." John xvi. 1.

"Through much tribulation, we must enter into the Kingdom of God." Acts xiv. 22.

It is an unpleasant way, indeed, if we look no further. Deut. viii. 2.

But at the end of it is a KINGDOM. Jesus is a kind *Master*. Luke xxii. 29.

Separate. Implies excommunication among the Jews.

Three kinds of discipline. 1. Exclusion for 30 days from the synagogue.

2. Pronouncing a curse, and separating him from his family.

3. He was cut off from the congregation, and delivered over to Satan. 1. Cor. v. 5. Rom. ix. 3. 1. Cor. xvi. 22. The person was also spoiled of his goods. Ezra x. 8. Heb. x. 34. His sons were left uncircumcised, and dying thus, a stone was cast upon his grave.

Blessed are they whom the world forsakes, because Christ loves them.

Earth's anathemas, render the fellowship of Jesus, the more precious.

The hard task-master, made the Hebrews weary of Egypt.

Perils of land and sea made Paul long to be with Christ.

Reproach. The wicked first blacken, then persecute their victims.

Some reckon *that*, a slander, which is a rebuke *deserved*.

The *principle* of all slander, is, *rebellion* against the believer's God.

"Ye shall have tribulation in the world, but *peace* in ME." John xvi. 33.

Name. Primitive believers hated simply because of their NAME.

If our Saviour wore a crown of thorns, we need not look for one of gold.

They *misreckon*, who would *reconcile* the world with Christ.

He calls us to an inheritance, *and* the sufferings on the way to it.

Son of Man. Here the PERSONALITY of Jesus, first comes boldly forth. Luke v. 24.

Evidences a sublime consciousness of personal dignity.

At the end—"For *My* sake," He speaks in the person of JEHOVAH, as JUDGE.

ὅταν—*If at any time the world should, &c., Meyer.* μισήσωσιν—Virtue is loathesome to fiends, as light to the owl. The Tempter peering over the walls of Paradise exclaims—

"O hell! what do mine eyes with *grief* behold?" *Milton.*

ἐκβάλωσι, 1, disfranchise. 2, expunge from military rolls. 3, cashier, dethrone, hiss off the stage; hence reject with scorn, *Raphilius:* defame, *Le Clerc, Campbell;* civil banishment, *Kuinoel;* excommunicate, *Oosterzee, Meyer.*

ὄνομα. The name of Christian itself was hated, as it indicated character and faith. *Tacitus* in his Annals, Book xv, speaks of Christians as "*those who were hated.*"

He calls Christianity "*a pernicious superstition,*" and says that Christians "*were convicted of hating all mankind.*" On this account he justifies the cruel barbarities practised upon them. Pliny, in his celebrated letter to Trajan, asks "*Whether the bare name, without any crime, is to be punished?*" *Whiston* says that this was the just and heavy complaint of the ancient Christians, that they suffered commonly for the bare name, *Ed.* "*Separate you,*"—from the synagogues, and the common intercourse of life. *Meyer,* There was a gate through which mourners entered, *Grotius.*

---

23. *Rejoice ye in that day, and leap for joy: for, behold, your reward is great in heaven; for in the like manner did their fathers unto the prophets.*

Rejoice. Used as a salutation "*Joy to thee! I wish you joy!*"
Those not tolerated on earth, welcomed as *partners* of Christ's joy.
"If ye were of the world, the world would love its own. John xv. 19.
Romanists believe they do God service, in persecuting Protestants. John xvi. ii.
Man's craving nature, absolutely requires some support.
If the mind turn from God, it pursues EVIL with intense energy.
God, for wise reasons, permits His saints to pass through the fires.

The flame shall not hurt thee, I only design,
"Thy *dross* to *consume*, thy *gold* to *refine*."

He forewarns them of suffering and commands them to rejoice.
Reward. No legal *merit* enters into this indemnity.
By the Divine *decree*, they will be compensated in the presence of God.
Suffering was *inevitable*, but joy instead of grief should result.
Prophets. The Lord already ranks his newly called apostles with O.T. prophets.
Not that the apostles were impliedly their successors, in office.
He connects the apostles with the prophets as the *same church.*
Something is wrong, if the wicked treat us more kindly than the prophets.
No mean consolation, to be companions of prophets in sufferings.
If we suffer in the same cause, we shall be heirs of the same blessings.
Your righteousness shall be brought forth as light, &c. Ps. xxxvii. 6.

ἡμέρα, from one sunrise to another, Day of the Lord, *i. e.* Judgment, time in general, *Major.* σκιρτήσατε—Matt. ἀγαλλιᾶσθε. The former, the leaping of the animal creation, in their sportive hours. The latter, from Heb., implies the most intense gladness, *Meyer.* ταὐτὰ the *same things.* John xvi. 2. λατρειαν *oblation.* Rome, Pagan and Papal, in their fiery fanaticism, verily believed they offered an acceptable *sacrifice* to Heaven, in destroying the saints. Decrees of Trent contain 120 anathemas against Dissenters from Rome. "*Facit ac si sacrificium offerat,*" *Julkut;* cited by *De Wette.* The περικαθαρματα of Paul, 1. Cor. iv. 13, refers to the same idea. "Ye witnesses of the last time know ye the city in which the slayer of a heretic, hath an eternal indulgence?" *Heller.*

---

24. *But woe unto you that are rich! for ye have received your consolation.*

Woe. Five *benedictions* of Matt., omitted by Luke, and five *woes* are omitted by Matthew.

The four woes, Mount Ebal stood opposite Mount Gerizim.

Eight woes are opposed to eight blessings in Matthew.

This is not imprecatory, but declarative *i.e.* "Alas for you"!

Ye who make this world your chosen portion. 1. John ii. 15.

"*Deceitfulness* of *riches,*" proves the undoing of multitudes. Matt. xiii. 22.

Laodiceans, happy in their riches, but God pitied their poverty.

We are counselled to obtain of Christ, gold, tried in the fire, *true* riches have no woe!

Rich. The wealthy Chuza, and family at Bethany, did not incur this curse.

Rich Nicodemus came by night, and the young man went away sad.

Too many are gluttons, while some Lazarus is perishing at their gate. Luke xvi. 20.

They oft keep back by fraud the wages of their laborers. Jas. v. 4.

He is not rich enough, who possesses not heavenly riches.

Received. Have *already* received your gratification.

Consolation. The full comfort belonging to those, whose *trust* is not in *earth.* Luke xvi. 25.

Οὐαὶ.—These four woes, the modern creation of a later tradition, *Meyer.* A groundless opinion; bears every mark of inspiration, *Alford, Oosterzee.* Alas for you! *Campbell, Wakefield.* παράκλησιν.—1, a *calling near.* 2, a *petition.* 3, *exhortation.* 4, *consolation.* Temporal good, *De Wette.* In the N. T. includes *spiritual consolation,* illustrated by the *call* and *comfort,* Matt. xi. 28. Christianity has lifted various *terms of language,* as much *above* their original classical meaning as above the morals of the Greeks, *Author.*

25. *Woe unto you that are full! for ye shall hunger. Woe unto you that laugh now! for ye shall mourn and weep.*

Full. Those who pamper themselves with luxurious dainties.

Fulness of bread, and abundance of idleness, explain Sodom's doom. Ezek. xvi. 49.

Ye have lived in pleasure on earth, and have been wanton. Jas. v. 5.

Behold my servants shall eat, and ye shall be hungry. Isa. lxv. 13.

Hunger. The hunger of the full. 1. Painful. 2. Self-incurred. 3. An endless hunger.

Laugh. The mad earthly exuberance of the sons of pleasure.

Also, the *malevolent laughter* of those who hate the righteous.

As the crackling of thorns under the pot, so is the laughter of fools. Ecc. vii. 6.

I said of laughter, It is mad; and of mirth, What doeth it? Ecc. ii. 2.

Mourn. Dives laughed amid his luxuries, but in the end, he *mourned.*

I will also laugh at your calamity—Because ye have set at nought all my counsel. Prov. i. 25, 26.

Those abiding under the wrath of God, (John iii. 36.) have no right to be merry.

The righteous *alone* have good ground to rejoice. See 23 verse.

The laughter of the unrighteous will be turned into mourning. Jas. iv. 9.

γελῶντες—Laughter defined as pleasure, *Sir William Temple.* Ridicule of faults, *Aristotle.* Conscious superiority, *Hobbes.* Sudden contrast or surprise, *Hutcheson.* Incongruity of things, *Aikenside.* Malicious, "Death grinned a ghastly smile," *Milton.* This "woe" need not check natural cheerfulness, *Vers. Ger.* God has made man capable of *laughter*, therefore under *wise* restrictions it must be *right.* God himself is said to laugh, Psalm ii. 4, Prov. i. 26, *Ed.*

---

26. *Woe unto you when all men shall speak well of you! for so did their fathers to the false prophets.*

Unto you. Not spoken to the rich, but to the disciples.

Speak. World's entire approval, a stain upon Christ's disciples.

It makes them suspected—1, of unfaithfulness. 2, of want of principle. 3, subserviency.

Well. We are tempted by *flattery* to secure the friendship of men.

If faithful, men warned of their sins, become *enemies.*

To secure applause, *false* prophets prophesied smooth things. Isa. xxx. 10.

Our duty, to covet the approbation of the wise and good.

We should disregard the *reproaches*, or the *praises* of fools in Israel.

The *world* did not speak well of Jesus, or His disciples. Jas. ii. 7.

Paul was styled "The ring-leader of the sect of Nazarenes." Acts xxiv. 5.

A.D. 190, Celsus said that Christianity corrupts the human race.

A.D. 470, Hierocles ridiculed Christianity, and reviled the Lord's miracles.

Phocion, a heathen, wrote, "compliant temper secures friends, truth excites odium."

Elijah, Elisha, Isaiah, Jeremiah and the prophets generally, were reviled.

If teachers never displease the wicked, some truths are kept back.

To escape reproach on account of religion, indicates moral cowardice.

It is indeed a small thing to be judged of man's judgment. 1. Cor. iv. 3.

Persecution of our *creed*, proves not our doctrines from God.

Church history shows instances of men having suffered for erroneous theological opinions. Servetus was burnt to death for heresy, at Geneva, 1531.

The *shadow* oft mistaken for the *substance*: the *name* for the *thing*.

The prosperity of the wicked, being wrapped in a curse, not enviable.

False prophets. May depend upon public approbation. Jer. xxiii.

καλῶς. Hume and Gibbon speak of the unaccountable madness of men, in every thing relating to religion! The latter professes, in his history, to hold the balances with an even hand. His hero, the apostate *Julian*, receives some three hundred pages of eloquent praise from this *hater* of Christianity. While the immortal *Augustine* is *not lifted out of a foot note*. *Phocion*, when applauded, enquired what *wrong* thing had been said? *Plutarch, Wetstein.* A similar sentiment found in *Seneca.* What evil have I done? said Aristides, when one told him he had everyone's good word.

---

27. *But I say unto you which hear, Love your enemies, do good to them which hate you.*

The sin condemned is REVENGE in heart, word, or deed.

Hating an enemy, the undisguised heathenism of the carnal heart.

The Romans deemed that deity *unworthy*, who refused to aid in avenging an enemy.

Homer taught that revenge was *sweet*, and truly an *heroic* act.

They conceded forgiving an enemy was a noble thing.

In Attica, and Rome, temples were erected to *Nemesis*, goddess of *revenge.*

People stoned the gods, when their favourite young *Germanicus* perished.

Augustus defeated at sea, *dragged Neptune's* statue, and *flung* it into the waves.

The vanquished Egyptians, in revenge, threatened to disclose the mysteries of *Isis.*

The heathen never created a god, who was not of a *revengeful* nature.

The Romans flattered their gods, feared them, and then insulted them.

"They hate a God *condemning* revenge, with all their heart, mind and strength." *Burke.*

The *heroes* of this world, mostly men of *revengeful ambition.*

Declining a challenge to *revenge* an insult, *misnamed* cowardice.

Love. The *love of complacency approves* the *conduct*, as well as loves the individual.

The *love of benevolence, condemns* his conduct, but loves the guilty person.

Thou shalt not abhor an Edomite, or an Egyptian. Deut. xxiii. 7.

In our willing blindness, we *confound* the sinner with his deeds.

Loving our enemies can only come from having the love of God.

But the effort awakens the consciousness of our *inability* to do it.

No determination of the *will* avails, grace for it, must come from God.

Though *I* pronounce "woes" against them, yet I command *you* not to hate, but love them.

Loving our enemies—1. Its difficult struggle. 2. Happy victory. 3. Glorious reward.

The worldling seeks his own things, a Christian those of his Lord.

Enemies. Embracing all those hating, or persecuting us.

Jews taught that such ought to be treated in the spirit of revenge.

They limited *neighbours* to those, whom they chose *not* to esteem as *enemies.*

The love due to a Jew, did not imply a contempt for heathen.

But the pious Jew was not required to love the Gentiles, *as* Jews.

Nor can we love the *wicked*, as we love *holy* men.

Still, the love demanded, is a spirit directly *opposed* to revenge.

Our Lord did not *change* the Mosaic law, but *unfolded* its sense.

Christ announces no new law, but promises grace to fulfil the old.

Israel not separated for *aggrandisement*, but to *bless* the nations.

Their virtues among themselves, types of duties, they owed the Gentiles.

The law of Christ alone, leads to true *peace* of mind.

The emotions of hatred, and revenge, *torment* those indulging them.
Of *Cranmer* it was said, "If you would make him a friend, *injure* him."
Cleomenes said, "Favors for friends—Revenge for enemies."
It was *this* command extorted from an old believer—"*Either these are not Thy precepts, or we are not Christians.*"
Be silent ye scorners!—denying the Gospel teaches *friendship*.
If enemies are to be loved, how much more are friends!
The heart of sanctified love, is God's throne on earth.

ἀγαπατε—Heathen taught men to love their enemies, but [illegible]ver to requite deeds o. malice, by prayer for their injurers, *Oosterzee.* ἐχθρουσ—Like *hostis*, it originally signified a foreigner. Thus ξένοσ a *stranger*, then a *barbarian.*

"Highly they raged,
"Against the Highest, and fierce with grasped arms,
"Hurling defiance toward the vault of heaven." *Par. Lost.*

Cold blooded philosophy, dares oppose the spirit of the Gospel.—"Do not tell me, as a good man did to-day, of my *obligation* to put all your poor men in good situations.—Are they MY *poor?* I tell thee, thou foolish philanthropist, that I grudge the dollar, the dime, the cent, I give to *such men as do not* BELONG *to* ME, and *to whom I do not belong!* *Emerson.* This has the ring of the primeval fratricide: "*Am I my brother's keeper?*"

---

28. *Bless them that curse you, and pray for them which despitefully use you.*

Men need no incentive to injure a foe, or love the world.
Promise nor threat can scarcely urge us to bless them who curse us.
Publicans and ungodly were, doubtless, kind to their neighbours.
Bless. Oppose words of peace and love, to words of scorn and insult.
Curse. Canons of the Council of Trent *anathematize* Dissenters from Rome.
How Christ by degrees, narrows down the gate to the New Jerusalem!
An *answer* of kindness, may fail to melt the heart of an enemy.
We must then prove our *sincerity*, by deeds of love and self-denial.
Even the Pharisees by *displaying* kind deeds, put an enemy to the blush.
Pray. None but an *honest, holy heart*, can pray for enemies.
Praying for those persecuting us, highest test of a new heart.
Jesus Christ cried, "*Father, forgive them, they know not what they do.*"
Stephen's dying prayer, "*Lord, lay not this sin to their charge.*" Acts vii. 60.

Paul—"*I pray God that it may not be laid to their charge.*" 2 Tim. iv. 16.

Despitefully. The Church, ever *feeble*, needs all her friends.

Christ's "*little flock*" for 2000 years, has been persecuted.

Millions of Christians perished by the violence of pagan and papal Rome.

Vergerius boasts that in four years of Paul VI, 150,000 perished by the Inquisition.

Louis XIV, revoking the Edict of Nantes, exiled 2,000,000 of Protestants, 1685.

In 1641, 200,000 Protestants were massacred in Ireland.

Duke of Alva boasted that he destroyed 18,000 Protestants in Holland.

Under Paul III, 24 villages were destroyed, and thousands of Waldenses martyred.

"Thirty Years' War," 30,000 villages and hamlets of Protestants were destroyed.

καταρωμένους from *αρα*, a *curse*, more exactly, insulting or abusing you. A forensic term of *arraigning* one before a court, originally, *to threaten*, 1. Pet. iii. 16, too specifically rendered *falsely accuse*, *Alexander*.

---

29. *And unto him that smiteth thee on the one cheek offer also the other; and him that taketh away thy cloke forbid not to take thy coat also.*

Smiteth, Law of *retaliation* binding, actually carried out by *Rulers*.

The *error* was, transferring the rule for magistrates, to private life.

The *principle* of retaliation, like Earth's proverbs, is entirely *reversed*.

This revengeful spirit, would conquer *violence* by *violence*.

But our Lord would have us conquer in private *wrongs*, by *love*.

Does our Lord teach the non-*resistance* doctrine, as it is called?

It has never been literally and habitually carried out, by any class of believers.

Had our Saviour done this, when smitten, He would have tempted the wretch to *increase* his sin.

A precept never reduced to practice, must be *impracticable*.

It would deliberately sacrifice the injured, and encourage injustice.

Our Saviour Himself resisted violence by strong expostulation. John xviii. 22-3.

Paul, when injured, still more strongly resented the insult. Acts xxiii. 2, 3.

It was characteristic of our Lord's teaching, to use *strong paradoxes.*

Matt. v. 29, 30, prove *literal* construction is not intended.

No Christian literally *plucks out a right eye*, if it offend him.

Christ condemns the popular perversion, as a legal pretext for revenge.

The evident object is, to put down the indulgence of a *vindictive* spirit.

Refusing to avenge the widow, shews a judge fearing *neither God nor man.*

Rather than *revenge*, we should suffer any measure of wrong.

When society is dissolved, *individuals* may execute *law*, never *revenge.*

When government ceases to answer its end, it is to be *destroyed.*

Zulers may, when becoming curses, be tried and executed. Psalm cxlix. 8, 9.

)pposing capital punishment, a *morbid sensibility.*

'If I have done any thing worthy of death, I refuse not to die." Acts xxv. 11.

Jod, forbade taking any *ransom* for a murderer's life. Num. xxxv. 31.

Jloak. Roman *pallium*, the poor man's bed, the *upper* garment. Ex. xxii. 26. Job xxii. 6.

Ioat. The Roman *tunic*, folded closely to the body, the *inner* garment.

τύπτοντι—Revenge is honorable, *Aristotle.* Moderation to enemies, sign of valor, 'acitus. Mildness surest road to power, *Thucydides.* The precepts of Christ expounding ıe O. T. must themselves be tested in the Spirit of Christ, *Tholuck.* The Saviour's aim not to lay down definite rules, but indicate certain principles, *Oosterzee.* To the *reparation* of the heart, *Augustine.* Human ingenuity has accumulated too many xceptions to our Lord's rule, *Bengel.* Ever since our Lord suffered the Jews to take way His life, it is by *His patience* we must regulate our own, *Quesnel.* Do not retaliate, ıt be prepared rather to bear more injuries. *Wordsworth.*

χιτῶνα and *ἱμάτιον*—The former, the tunic, an under garment worn by the Jews and reeks. The *Dorian* worn by males, a short woollen shirt without sleeves. *Ionian*, a ng linen garment with sleeves. The latter used more anciently, and at length entirely ıperseded by the woollen. In female dress both continued to be used. *ἱμάτιον* resemed the Doric tunic, made of camel's hair coarser than wool, to the richest silk. It rresponded to the Roman pallium. It was clasped over the shoulders by a buckle, ıd the garment only reached to the knee. The other was flowing, and reached to the et. The sleeves generally only extended to the elbow. Both kinds of dress were stened by a *Ζώνη*, a *girdle*, worn by both sexes, especially when about to work, or walk. his was adorned at times with fine needlework, and fastened by a gold clasp, *Beckers tar.* We should be ready to sacrifice *private* comforts and advantages, for the sake of ıarity and peace, *Augustine.*

30. *Give to every man that asketh of thee: and of him that taketh away thy goods ask them not again.*

Give. A Pharisaic mind would say, I am not bound to give, until *asked.*
God, during a past eternity, infinitely blessed in giving.
Having His mind, we may be ever giving, and ever blessed.
Having nothing, we still can give *prayer* and *kind* words.
Every Man. Of any nation, Jew, Samaritan, or heathen.
To be regulated be the ability of the giver, and the worthiness of the object of charity.
Just claims at home are to be met, before *charity* to others.
Literally carried out, would beggar oneself, and form begging vagabonds.
The law of love must be regulated by *common sense,* not by fixed rules.
Some poor saints *refuse* from deeper love, than the opulent *give* from.
"I would rather some men *refuse* me, than others *grant* a favor."
Some *shun*, or *brow-beat* those worthily asking, to avoid their importunity.
Selfishness is Anti-Christ, and must be *consumed* by the fires of Love.
Be always ready to distribute, and willing to communicate. 1. Tim. vi. 18.
"It is more blessed to give, than receive,"—"Give a portion to seven and also to eight. Ecc. xi. 2. Acts xx. 35.
"A good man sheweth favor, and lendeth, he will guide," &c. Ps. cxii. 5.
Love requires us to act at times directly contrary to the *letter*, in order that we may obey the *spirit.*
Asketh. Some needy ones too timid, unworthy are often too clamorous.
"No beggar ever deceived me," is a miser's boast.
To refuse aid really needed, when *not* asked, is here condemned.
Goods, refers to the Oriental officials *grinding exactions* from subjects.
Rather than by law rouse bitter feelings, submit to impositions.
The Christian stand of Hampden, proves that submission has its limits.
Resistance is right, only, when government ceases to answer the ends of Heaven.
Ask them not. Rather suffer wrong, than indulge avarice.

"*Every man*" literally carried out would make a nation of thieves, *Markland.* αἰροντοσ—Taking by violence, *Pearce, Meyer.* Whether done under *process of law,* or by *violence,* our duty is to yield, so *long* as the Spirit of Christ's teaching can be attained. But if not, the literal compliance with it is a mere mockery. A Christian is bound to do many things, not by any external obligation of rights, but by the spirit and law of love, *Stier.*

31. *And as ye would that men should do to you, do ye also to them likewise.*

32. *For if ye love them which love you, what thank have ye? for sinners also love those that love them.*

As ye would. Our Saviour's rule is a two-edged sword.
The cold hearted world said, "First myself, then my neighbour, then myself."
It implied that the Jews esteemed *themselves*, their only *neighbours*.
A thousand limiting apologies silence natural conscience.
The Golden rule is ever limited, by "*similar circumstances*."
This rule shews what we *ought*, and what we ought *not* to do.
A poor man might desire a rich man to divide equally his fortune.
Such an extravagant wish, could furnish no rule of action.
The following questions, limit the Golden rule.
How do we expect our neighbours to treat us in their dealings?
Ought *they* to allow passion or interest to blind their judgment?
Ought *they*, by harbouring hatred or revenge, misrepresent us?
In seeking to be reconciled to *us*, ought they to insist on *degrading* terms?
Ought *they* to sympathize with *us*, if afflicted, and aid *us*, if in their power?
Our own *selfishness* will afford us the *true* key of interpreting the rule.
Neglecting it, embitters society, and causes alienations and strifes.
This maxim is rather a *test* of morals, than a *principle*.
Husbands, wives, brothers, children, servants find here a perfect system of conduct, in carying out the *two lines* of the Redeemer's Sermon.
The emperor *Severus* had it frescoed on his palace walls, though he failed to practice it.
The morals of Christianity the most elevated standard known to man.
"A Christian is the highest type of man." *Young's* Night Thoughts.
What do Christians more than others? asks an exacting world.
God expects more "*Unto whom much is given, of him shall much be required.*" Luke xii. 48.
Even the Heathen full of malice, treat their friends kindly.
No sinner is so essentially depraved, as not to have some friends,
"I love them *only because* they love me," is of the earth, earthy.

Benevolence to enemies, commended, *Xenophon*. καθὼσ. Do nothing to others which we ourselves would resent. *Thales*. A touchstone to compare acts with duty, *Oosterzee*. Not what others would have us to do, but what we would have them do to us, *Lange*. A rule not to be used by unrenewed hearts, *Tholuck*. This is an old precept

Higher in aim, purer in principle, holier in practice, happier in heart.
Communion with God, rendered Moses, *radiant* in holiness.
Highest. Alone said of Him, whose *Habitation* is *eternity*.
Unthankful. A fallen world's recompense for favors from God.

μηδὲν ἀπελπίζοντεσ—Without anxiety as to the return of principal or interest, *Alford*, *Campbell*. Do not cut one's hope, by rigidness to the borrower, *Junius*, *Pearce*, *Hammond*. *Nowise* despairing, *Chrysostom*, *Rosenmuller*, *Kuinoel*. Nothing from men, therefore all from God, *Beza*. μισθὸσ—Refers to the future life, *Meyer*. To the present also, *Oosterzee*. υἱοὶ 'Υψ. *Sons of the Highest.* Sharers in the Messiah's Kingdom, *Meyer*. The believer's adoption, *Alford*. Yearling lamb, son of a year: arrows, sons of a quiver; brave, *son of valor*: dweller, *son of Zion*; glory, *child of toil*; day, child of the sun; showers, children of a cloud, *Pindar*, *Meyer*. "*To the unthankful and evil.*" The vilest of men. Man may be *evil* before growing *unthankful*, *Bengel*. An unthankful man is a naughty man; nay, he is an ugly man, Psalm cxlvii. 1, *Trapp*.

---

36. *Be ye therefore merciful, as your Father also is merciful.*

Man being an imitative creature; a vestige of our original state.
Be ye. Not so much a command, as the *organic law* of His kingdom.
He gives the law a far more *comprehensive* scope, than the Pharisees *gave*.
Abraham's faith, Moses' humility, Joseph's integrity, Joshua's fidelity.
Elijah's fervor, John's love, Paul's zeal, not our models.
To be like Christ, is a fundamental principle in His kingdom.
Merciful. Our Lord perfectly observed all these precepts.
They contain the expression of His life and are His very image.
Christians, Godlike, do not let ingratitude hinder their kindness.
Mercy, the exercise of good will towards those not meriting it.
Reason, leads us to conclude God is merciful. He exercises forbearance towards sinful men.
Justice demands the punishment of rebels, against God.
But whether He will in mercy *forgive* sin, reason is silent.
Socrates doubted whether it was *possible*, for God to forgive sin.
Revelation declares—"The Lord God, *merciful and gracious*." Ex. xxxiv. 6
The Bible threatens *condemnation* to all who are unmerciful.
Rahab to spies, Boaz to Ruth, David towards Saul; instances of mercy.
He requires all homage paid Him, as One *merciful* in his nature.
His mercy is seen in the Incarnation, Life, and Death of the Redeemer.
Pangs, at man's entering and leaving the world, hint at no mercy.
Infidelity sends a man to judgment, with no hope of *acquittal* there.
If God is merciful, He must punish all who indulge in cruelty.

None but the merciful, need expect God's friendship hereafter.

Father. Divine mercy, 1, the pattern, 2, the reason. 3, the reward.

Merciful. 1, the source. 2, the fields on which it brings forth fruit. 3, the obstacles against which it strives.

οἰκτίρμονεσ—compassionate. Less strong than ἔλεοσ, *Tittmann,* *καθὼσ*—here in a casual sense, *even as*, or *since, inasmuch as*, John xvii. 2.

---

37. *Judge not, and ye shall not be judged: condemn not, and ye shall not be condemned: forgive, and ye shall be forgiven:*

Judge not. With the eye sharpened by distrust, but softened by lóve.

Believer, subject to a threefold judgment, 1, of his neighbour. 2, of his conscience, 3, of his Lord.

These words indicate the *presence of foes*, known by their looks.

We learn they *derided* Him. Luke xvi. 14. *Provoked* Him. Luke xi. 53.

The Greek in neither case implies, that they *spake* anything against Him.

These words have no reference to the *pronouncing* of judicial decisions.

They refer to the *disposition* of the heart, rather than *utterance* of the lips.

The religion of censorious moralists, consists, in blaming others.

The *desire* to *judge*, is the eternally valid principle, which God has implanted in those acting as judges in His name.

Be judged. Let us be *doers* of the law, the Lawgiver Himself is Judge.

It condemns judging our neighbours, apart from God's *forgiving* love.

Some act as if they were *assessors* with God, upon His Throne.

Condemn. Some appease their *own* conscience, by censuring *others*.

Condemned. By the judicial decision of God, not prudentially by our neighbour.

Prudential motives, Christ does not adopt in His teachings.

God's judgment, pronounced here, but executed hereafter.

The same high standard used in judging others, will be used towards us.

It may involve treatment from others, similar to ours, of them.

Those being daily forgiven, ought not to condemn others.

"Who art thou, that judgest another man's servants"? Rom. xiv. 4.

"Let not him that eateth, despise him that eateth not." Rom. xiv. 2.

Bigotry, anathematizing all who differ, condemned by these words.

"He shall have judgment without mercy, that shewed," &c. Jas. iv. 11.

Ishmael's hands were against every man, and every man's against him.

There is a strong inclination to treat men, according to *their* disposition.

A candid man, is generally spoken of by his neighbours with candor.
A censorious man's acts are all dissected, exposed, and condemned.

Forgive. Injuries must be known, before they can be forgiven.
"Lord, how often shall my brother sin against me?" &c. Matt. xviii. 21.
That God will forgive us, *because* we forgive others, a delusion.
Refusing to forgive others, God will refuse to forgive us.
However mildly we treat ourselves, we are ever more exacting towards others.
Infidels denying all moral *distinctions*, resent most severely an injury done themselves.
Applying rules to that *without*, rather than to that *within*, "the evil eye."
Believers *bemoan* their *neighbour's* sins, the more they think on their *own*.
The mind's eye gazing at others' faults, loses the power of seeing its own.
While losing charity towards a brother, we lose humility towards God.

μὴ κρίνετε.—The uncharitable "repels the word of God, which comes to his own heart, as the cold rock gives back the echo," *Braune*. ἀπολύετε—to *acquit by court*. To *release the captive*, or *debtor*. Those resolving to condemn, *implacable*, have no reason to believe they are forgiven. The fifth petition *binds* down ourselves under guilt, unless we have the spirit of forgiveness, *Augustine*. Matt. vii. 1-2, is greatly expanded and enriched here, *Alford*.

---

38. *Give, and it shall be given unto you; good measure, pressed down, and shaken together, and running over, shall men give into your bosom. For with the same measure that ye mete withal it shall be measured to you again.*

Give. Penurious economy, is not the way to become rich.

Measure. Murmur not when repaid in your own coin.

Pressed, dry goods. **Shaken,** grain. **Running over,** liquids.

Running over. Disciples even in this world, may at times expect overflowing compensation.

Bosom. The fold in the Oriental garment, falling over the girdle
"And render seven-fold into their bosom." Psa. lxxix. 12.
Such a *hard* measure was recompensed to Adonibezek. Judges i. 7.
Corn measured, and placed by Boaz, in veil of Ruth. Ruth iii. 15.
"He that soweth sparingly, shall reap also sparingly." 2. Cor. ix. 6.
"Thy floors shall be full of wheat, and thy vats overflow." Joel ii. 24.
"The liberal deviseth liberal things, and by liberal," &c. Isa. xxxii. 8.

"Blessed is he that considereth the poor, the Lord will &c." Psa. xli. 1.
"Charge them that are rich in this world, that they be rich &c." 1 Tim. vi. 17.
'There is witholdeth more than is meet, and it tendeth &c." Pro. xi. 24.
Infidelity denies, that the Bible motives to virtue are from God.
How the wisdom (folly) of men, differs from the wisdom of God!
Sin's penalty, and rewards of virtue, are Bible motives. Rom. ii. 7.
Mete. The law of retaliation belongs to God's kingdom, God, judge.

δοθήσεται alludes to the Divine reward of virtue. Our Lord here holds forth the assurance of *earthly* blessings, as a motive to liberality. The Bible motives to virtue, *mercenary*, *Shaftesbury's Enquiry*. Actions are virtuous though not prompted by the very purest and highest motives, *Webster* and *Wilkinson*. Verses 27 to 38 tend to solve the question of *disinterested benevolence*. (Amor pur, of *Fenelon*.) Some answer *negatively*, *Jer. Taylor*, *Erskine*, *Bossuet;* others affirmatively. *Molinos* expiated this belief in the Inquisition seven years. *Madame Guyon* in the Bastile. *Fenelon* was exiled from Paris, and the opinion condemned by *Innocent XII*, *Oosterzee*, *Macintosh*, *Hagenbach*. *μέτρον καλὸν*—measure *not falsified*. Aridis, mollibus, liquidis of *Bengel*, more ingenious than true, *Meyer*. *δώσουσιν* answering to the agents of *μετρεθήσεται* understood, or the *Angels*, who are in this matter, the ministers of the divine purposes. *Meyer*, *Alford*. *κόλπον* "*Bosom*." When *Crœsus* presented Alcmaeon with as much gold as he could carry about his person, he put on a very large robe, and filled the *bosom* with the precions metal. Almost all ancient nations wore long, wide, and loose garments; and when about to carry anything which their hands could not contain, they used a fold of their robe in nearly the same way as women here use their aprons, *Clarke*.

---

39. *And he spake a parable unto them; Can the blind lead the blind? shall they not both fall into the ditch?*

Parable. Luke iv. 23; v. 36. See Notes.
Blind. All following the maxims and customs of earth. 2. Cor. iv. 4.
Addressed primarily to His apostles, but to all ministers also.
Pharisees, awful examples of what religious teachers ought *not* to be.
The most terrible blindness, self chosen blindness—*to love darkness*.
The carnal have malicious pleasure, railing against Christ's ministers.
We are assured, there *are false* teachers in the world. 1. Peter, ii. 1.
"His watchmen are *blind*, dumb dogs, that cannot bark." Isa. lvi. 10.
"Evil men, and seducers, shall wax worse and worse." 2. Tim. iii. 13.
"Wandering stars, are reserved unto blackness of darkness. Jude xiii
He opposes to these blind guides, one True Master. 2. Peter, i. 19.
Pharisees, blind themselves, madly closed every avenue of light to others.

"*Blind*," labouring under his own *beam*, verse 42, destitute of compassion and love. "*Lead the blind*." A boon, if done by a seeing and experienced person, *Bengel*.

"*The ditch*." The blind guides fall undermost, and have the worst of it, *Trapp*. The falling into the ditch represents casting into Gehenna (hell,) *Meyer*. A warning against the sin of claiming absolute dominion over the faith of others on the one hand; and a warning also against the sin of submitting our conscience and reason to the dictates of any *human teacher* on the other, *Wordsworth*.

---

40. *The disciple is not above his master: but every one that is perfect shall be as his master.*

Disciple. Christ refers to the uncharitable, ignorant, *teachers*.
Beware, *ye* do not exercise *severer* judgment than I, your Master.
I, in my love, have shewn great *forbearance* toward you.
He warns the presumptuous, against entering the sacred office.
Nations have as often been ruined by *ignorance*, as by tyranny.
The *errors* of a Commander, are quite as dangerous as *treason*.
The Church's Head saith, "*No man taketh this honor unto himself*." Heb. v. 4.
Possessing *human learning*, many prove blind guides, lacking spiritual light.
"Woe to the idle shepherd, his right eye shall be *darkened*." Zec. xi. 17.
"Restore unto me the joys of thy salvation—then shall I teach transgressors thy ways." Psa. li. 12.
People are warned. "Understandest thou what thou readest?" Acts viii. 30.
"Thine eye shall see thy teachers—This is the way walk ye in it, when ye turn to the right hand or left." Isa. xxx. 20-21.
"Beloved, believe not every spirit, but *try* the spirits." 1. John. iv. 1.
"Cease, my son, to hear instruction causing to *err*." Pro. xix. 27.
"If any man teach otherwise—he is proud, &c." 1. Tim. vi. 4, 5.
As his Master. If the master judged none, neither must disciples.

κατηρτισμένος—adjust, put in order again, put into a complete state. The most accomplished scholar can only expect to be as his master. πᾶς is not *every*, but *totus quantus est*, *i. e.* when he has learnt all as a scholar, then he will be perfect as his master, *Meyer*, *Stier*. One modelled after his master, *Kuinoel*. ἔσται, a hortatory *promise*, like ἔσεσθε, verse 35. He who undertakes to teach others saving doctrines, should himself see the way of life clearly; should have no beam in his eye; should be a good tree; should lay up the good treasure in his heart, see verses 39, 42, 43, 45, *Vers. Gen.*

---

41. *And why beholdest thou the mote that is in thy brother's eye, but perceivest not the beam that is in thine own eye?*

Why? Direction how to escape the fate of the blind leaders.

Beholdest. A voluntary *officious* act, done in a censorious spirit.
An eye entirely *single*, or *whole*, has no mote or defect. Matt. vi. 22.
The sin is, in *not seeing* at all, what should *first* have been seen.
Mote. A *small dry body*, Gr. any thing *withered, a splinter.*
A keen, critical eye, for the slightest trifle in another, but *insensible* to all one's own faults; no self scrutiny or examination.
The gnat is strained out, and the camel swallowed. Matt. xxiii. 24.
One *sees* the mote, but *marks* not the beam, which he ought to have *felt.*
Thy Brother. Cold blooded; a heart, without charity for one so near.
Perceivest. Gr. *to understand thoroughly, observe attentively.*
Had he not been *morbidly sensitive*, he would not have seen the mote.
Beam. The hyperbole is not to be softened down, by any change in the original. Gr. *a beam*, sometimes *a shaft* or *spear.*
It is really most frequent in the dialect of common life.
Thine own. Not to do injury to others, one must know himself.

κάρφοσ, from κάρφοω, to wither, a *dry stalk, palea, splinter*, *W. & W.* The relative size, but the material is not expressed. Sticks or twigs used in bird's nests, *Herodotus*, *Aristophanes.* Small seed, *Doddridge.* Chip of wood, mote, *Bengel.* δοκον, thorn, *Campbell.* Illustration from Rabbis.—Foolish Jews are directed to the existing remains of their own wisdom, *Stier.* κατανοεῖσ—compound word from νοῦσ the mind, to *observe accurately, rightly to take account of*, *Stier.* *Apprehendest*, *Alford.* The eye of the mind, like other *media*, gives a coloring to our thoughts. "Were not thine eye sunny, how could it ever behold the sun?" *Goethe.* The *mote* is not a precious metal. It only is distinguished from the *beam* by its greatness. His *mote* becomes a *beam*, because he would silence his own conscience, by a censorious judgment of a brother, *Braune.* Some *desire* to find motes in themselves, and beams in others, *Alford.* The perception of a mote, is rendered the more acute, from the presence of a beam, *Cranmer.* Most men's minds are as ill set as their eyes; they can turn neither of them *inwards*, *Trapp.*

---

42. *Either how canst thou say to thy brother, Brother, let me pull out the mote that is in thine eye, when thou thyself beholdest not the beam that is in thine own eye? Thou hypocrite, cast out first the beam out of thine own eye, and then shalt thou see clearly to pull out the mote that is in thy brother's eye.*

How canst? Here are self *ignorance*, self *indulgence*, and unbounded *assurance* brought to light in this question.
Brother. In the deepest tone of *irony*, does Jesus adopt this term.
Proudly and dictatorially he says "*Stand!* Let me pull out the mote,"
"I can do it, I demand that thou submit obediently *to me.*"
The sin is in the *spirit* of beholding. A hasty uncharitable judgment.
An officious hand, and an unloving heart, often go together.

Pull. Tyndale, *suffer me to pluck.* Cranmer, *suffer me, I will pluck.*

Thou. Change from the plural to the singular, indicates a *personal* application.

Our Lord may have seen some *derisive* smile, or gesture.

Searching the secrets of the heart, He sends no doubtful arrow.

Hypocrite. One who pretends to be what he is not.

Hypocrisy easily creeps upon us, and grows quickly; it is difficult of cure, and when confirmed into a habit, irreparably ruins the soul.

Hypocrite! This is cast in the face of the Pharisees, very severely.

Art thou so well able to pull out the mote out of thy brother's eye? Then try thy skill on thy self, and remedy thy own faults.

Officious meddling involves inconsistency, and brings contempt.

Before condemning others, better to sit in judgment on thyself.

Self scrutiny qualifies one for examining others aright.

Cast out. One diligently examining himself, does not lightly condemn his neighbour.

First. It is easier to watch over others, than ourselves.

Some are cast away, while working for the salvation of others.

Beam. The *greater* and *graver* our sins, the more blind to them.

A Christian is severe to himself, and forbearing to others.

Clearly. Believers *can* see motes, but hypocrites *can't* see beams.

The Greek, implies, *seeing through* all obstructions and concealments.

Earthly wisdom begets presumption, but *heavenly* wisdom, humility.

No amount of skill, ever justifies an uncalled for censoriousness.

In order to reform, one must be sure, he is *himself* reformed.

"Wherein thou judgest another, thou condemnest thyself." Rome ii. 1.

It is generally true—The most censorious, are the most faulty.

Let us take another's place, and suppose our actions to be his.

It is as absurd for a *bad* man to reprove others, as for one *blind*, to turn *oculist*.

ἄφεσ ἐκβάλω—*Stand and let me pull, Stier.* *Suffer* (that) *I pull* (cast) *out, Alexander. Hold still, and I will take the mote out of thine eye, Doddridge.* βλέπων—*staring* at another's faults, attracts others to gaze also. διαβλέψεισ ἐκβαλεῖν—the most difficult and delicate office of Christian friendship, *Meyer.* ὑποκριτά. A mime, or one who made the *gestures* for the actor, while he was reciting his portion of the drama. 1st. one who answers, or responds, with particular allusion to *oracular* responses. 2nd. one who answers in a colloquy, with particular allusion to dramatic dialogue. 3rd. one who acts upon the stage. 4th. metaphorically, one who acts a borrowed part. And 5th. a dissembler or deceiver; not in Classics; modern usage gives a stronger sense than the original. (Luke xii. 56). Rather a self deceiver, than a deliberate deceiver of others, *Alexander.* The *hypocrite*, takes to himself the credit of virtue which he has not! but the *dissembler* conceals the vices that he has, *Stier.* δοκὸν—"*thorn*," *Campbell.*

It signifies a *spar* or *lance*.A grave error to call the "*beam*" a heinous crime. The figure is hyperbolical, but gives the exact proportions, *Stier*. Shrinking from *receiving* reproof, is hinted at, *Doddridge*. It was said of Antony, he hated a tyrant, not tyranny. It may also truly be said of the hypocrite, he hates sinners, not sins, *Dicke*.

---

43. *For a good tree bringeth not forth corrupt fruit; neither doth a corrupt tree bring forth good fruit.*

Good, in *kind*, fruitful in character, and pleasant to the sight.
The four parables are taken from every day incidents.
Blind leaders; and promising, but barren trees, ever at hand.
Bringeth forth. The motion of the sap, resembles that of blood in animals.
Corrupt. Gr. *rotten*, *putrid*, of a *bad quality*: depraved, vitiated.
Words and *acts*, are the infallible fruit of the *heart's nature*.
The *bloom* and *leaves* of profession, may often mislead.
Even the life deceives *men*, but at last, decides unerringly.
The well-ordered, resplendent conduct, makes false teachers *bold*.
The very *nature* of the tree, must be first changed.
It is vain to resolve *to do* good, till we *become* good.

δένδρον has sap, instead of *blood*, tubes, for *veins* and *arteries*, irritability, for *sensitiveness*, capillary attraction, for power of the *heart*, leaves, for respiring, instead of *lungs*, winter's rest, for *sleep*. All plants, like animals, love *light*. Sugar, mucilage, acid, oil or salt, form *sap*. καλον—1st. beautiful as to *form*. 2nd. good as to *quality*. 3rd. *influence*. 4th. *virtuous*. αγαθόσ, its synonyme, that which excels. The καλόν, *becoming*, and ἀγαθόσ, *absolute goodness*. ποιοῦν—Produces, *Aristotle*. καρπὸν καλόν.—It was the crafty *Wallenstein* who said, "Let me first search out the *nature* of the man, and I will tell his *will* and his *deed*." Such self-reliant minds, the sure victims of deceit, *Stier*. "For modes of faith, let senseless bigots fight," *Pope*.—A *delusion*. Contending for a right creed, is contending for a virtuous life. Men often contend for a *right* creed in a *wrong* spirit, and *vice versa*, *Ed*. No man is better than his creed. This has exceptions, but generallly true, *Grotius*. A person trying to extract a mote from the eye of another, while a beam is in his own, is like a *bad* tree endeavouring to bring forth *good* fruit, *Bengel*.

---

44. *For every tree is known by his own fruit. For of thorns men do not gather figs, nor of a bramble bush gather they grapes.*

Their spiritual guides just denounced, are thus detected.
Known. Honesty in nature, the result of the finger of God.
The *taste*, the *odor*, and *color* of the fruit, reveal a tree's nature.
Only half blind persons, mistake thorns, sloes, and thistles, for figs.

Vines of Sodom, from Gomorrah's fields, yield *grapes* and *wine*.
" Their wine is the poison of dragons, and the venom,"&c. Deut.xxxii. 33
Like, produces like, the immutable law of Nature.
Otherwise species would mingle, and *peculiarities* of fruit, be lost.
A pure doctrine, alone can produce pure thoughts and words.
A wild olive may by faith, be graffed into a good tree. Rom. xi. 24.
During the process, its *wild nature* must be changed.
A tree strung full of figs, may be a thorn tree still.
The occasional good deeds of evil men, seem *out of place*.

Own fruit. A tree may be of the fruit-bearing species, and yet barren.

Thorns. Supposed to be the *Spina Christi*, " the crown of thorns."

Thorns, symbolize the course, and *results*, of active sin, in the face of conscience. "*It is hard for thee to kick against the pricks.*"

Gather, the vintage done with a pruning hook in the East.

Figs. Luke xiii. 6. See Notes. **Bramble,** resembled the hawthorn.
A familiar instance of a fruitless bush, contrasted with the fig and vine.

ἄκανθα—*Spina Christi*; has leaves resembling the deep glossy green of the ivy. It is common in Palestine. *βάτου*—Seneh, hence Sinai is named, *Celsius*. It is the ordinary bramble *Rubus*, found at Sinai, Aleppo, Scandretta and Seide, *Shaw*, *Robinson*. τρυγῶσι, to harvest, to gather, from *τρυγή ripe fruit*.

---

45. *A good man out of the good treasure of his heart bringeth forth that which is good: and an evil man out of the evil treasure of his heart bringeth forth that which is evil: for of the abundance of the heart his mouth speaketh.*

Good Man. A renewed heart bears the image of the Redeemer.
Not in the Pelagian sense, but one made " good" by grace.

Treasure. Its early, wide sense, a *deposit*, without reference to *value*.

Heart. The heart, spacious, containing a vast amount of good or evil, and known by its utterances. " For out of the abundance of the heart," &c.

This innermost storehouse open only to the eye of God.
Forming fountains of influence, it determines character.
If the heart be false, one's good deeds are *hollow* and worthless.
Smooth words are so much the worse, from a venomous tongue.
Assumed virtues, resemble clusters of grapes *tied* to the vine.
An unrenewed, kind neighbour, the world calls a *good hearted* man.
Human laws, polish of civilization, amenities of society.
Regard to reputation, restraints of Providence,—produce *this fruit*.

Earthly parents value not *feigned* obedience in a hating child.
Those trusting alone to fancied virtues, are whited sepulchres.
An infidel may be benevolent, patriotic, but still *defraud* God.
Morality, integrity, purity, temperance, are implied in "good."
These external virtues, are the mere *leaves*; *holiness* is the *fruit*.
A man's heart is known by his words, as the contents of a vessel, from wine or water being drawn. Hence our word "tempt," from πειρω to *pierce*.
Benevolence to *bodily* wants, with indifference to *spiritual*, avails nothing.
An evil man. Cannot always disguise his corrupt mind.
In an unguarded moment, despite all care, the mask will fall.
Evil treasure. Impiety often desolates, long after death.
Abundance. The spontaneous expressions of an unrestrained heart.
A full heart, and a closed mouth, do not suit one another.
The very heart of the Redeemer, is here unfolded and laid bare.
Without *alluding* to His Divinity, He clearly *demonstrates* it here.

The second θησαυροῦ τῆς καρδίας αὐτοῦ,—"*treasure of his heart;*" omitted, *Tisch.*, *Alford*. The human heart has large capacities for good or evil; which break forth in words and deeds, *Bengel*.

---

46. ¶ *And why call ye me, Lord, Lord, and do not the things which I say?*

Lord, Lord. 1. Some neither say "Lord," nor do His will.
2. Others say "Lord," without doing His will.
3. Others, (sincere and timid) do His will, without saying "Lord."
4. Others say "Lord, Lord," and also do His will.
He who calls "Lord," disobeying Him, is a *mocker*. Mal. i. 6.
In *measured words*, He calls HIMSELF LORD, *i. e.*, JEHOVAH!
In His deepest humiliation, He never called any man, LORD.
He claims to be LORD in the present life, and LORD in Judgment!
To His disciples He said, "Ye call me Master and Lord, and so I am."
Jesus claimed, what no *created* being dare claim, without IMPIETY!
"If ye believe not that I am he, ye shall die in your sins." John viii. 24.
"I and my Father are one." John x. 30.
Some call him Messiah, and Lord, yet deny His *Divinity*.
Many wear the livery of Christ, but dwell in the house of bondage.
"What doth it profit, though a man *say* he hath faith?" James ii. 14.
Professing doctrines of grace, many are encouraged to continue in sin.
Previous warnings were given to *open enemies*, to rejectors of Jesus.

Some imagine themselves out of reach of trouble, when on the Rock.
But Christ is a *beacon*, against which, the waves rage the more.
The world will ever dash against the hope of the humble believer.
The wise neglect not the *superstructure*, building on the Rock.
A noble foundation, encourages the heart to go on more hopefully.
"Not as though I had already attained, or were already perfect." Phil. iii. 12.
"If any man's work abide, he shall receive a reward." 1. Cor. iii. 14.
Flood. A symbol of all possible trials of faith and hope.
1. The storm of unbelief. 2. The storm of affliction. 3. The storm of temptation. 4. The storm of death.
Floods and frosts test the stability of the *foundation* of a house.
Some build their houses as the moth; terrors take hold on him. A tempest stealeth him away in the night. Job xxvii. 20.
One class *will not build at all*, this is understood, although not named.
Flood. Severe afflictions. **Stream.** *Persecution*, or spirit of the age.
Shake. Perfect faith in God, renders the soul *secure and safe*.
A firm belief of final *perseverance* through Christ, not *presumption*.

εσκ. εβαθ. εθηκε θεμ. dug, deepened, laid foundation, describe graphically the *successive steps*, and diligent earnestness of the faithful, *W. & W.* In Egypt, an entire village founded on the earth, the writer saw *in ruins*, having been swept away by the flood from the mountains of *Abyssinia.* *θεμέλιον ἐπί τὴν πέτραν*—The parallel thought in Isa. xxviii. 16. The foundation of the temple *(Ewald)*, to the Law *(Umbreit)*, to Zion itself *(Hitzig)*, to Hezekiah *(Gesenius)*. Lapidem probationis, *Junius*, *Calvin*, *Vitringa.* Solely refers to Christ *(Alexander.)* "*Foundation.*"—Artificial.' "*Rock.*"—Natural. With the *foundation* is contrasted *without a foundation*, ver. 49, and with the *rock*, *upon the earth*, ver. 49. "*Could not shake*," much less destroy, *Bengel.*

For *τεθεμελίωτο γὰρ ἐπὶ τὴν πέτραν*, "*for it was founded upon a rock*," read *διὰ τὸ καλῶσ οἰκοδομεῖσθαι αὐτήν*, "*because it was well built*," *Tischendorf*, *Alford.* Christ built His church upon a Rock, *Petra* (Matt. xvi. 18), and Peter (Petrus) derived his name from this *Petra*. See Rom. ix. 33. 1. Pet. ii. 8. The foundation, which the apostle laid as a Master-Builder (1. Cor. iii. 10-16), is the one Lord Jesus CHRIST. On this solid and firm foundation, the church of Christ is built. But all doctrines of heresy are built on the sand, which is unstable, and cannot be consolidated; and they are built only to fall, *Jerome*, quoted in *Wordsworth.*

---

49. ***But he that heareth, and doeth not, is like a man that without a foundation built a house upon the earth; against which the stream did beat vehemently, and immediately it fell; and the ruin of that house was great.***

Heareth. Many have the *curiosity* to hear, but no *resolution* to do.
Their neglect, changes not their *relations* to eternal realities.

Without foundation A false faith, no better, than no faith at all.
It is *worse*, since it raises hopes, surely to be dashed.
The rain, flood, wind, will in no wise fail to come.
Earth. All creeds, dogmas, systems, fancies, apart from Christ.
Absorbed in cares, a *slight stay*, enough for the thoughtless.
Sand—Matt. *All* that was not *rock*, was earth or sand.
Vehemently. The *tearing up* the foundations of the false hope.
Immediately, indicates the sudden change at death.
Fell. The hour of storm, dwellers have the most need of refuge.
Too late to build on the *Rock*, or even another house on the *sand*.
The ruin. The simplest minds could understand His words.
Surely never man spake like this man. John vii. 46.
History of the creeds of all who have built, or ever will build, here condensed in three verses.
Fall of Judaism, of false religion, of false philosophy.
All not *in Christ*, will inevitably perish.
1. *Faith* makes the Christian. 2. *Works* show the Christian.
3. Storms try and prove the Christian. 4. Death crowns the Christian.
Great. Not the grandeur or value of the edifice.
But the complete, and everlasting shame and *loss* of the *ruin*.
His disgrace inconceivable, his loss irreparable.
"Some shall awake to shame, and everlasting contempt." Dan. xii. 2.
The higher they raised their hopes, the more terrible their fall.
As the *leaning* of the tree shews, which way, it will surely fall.
So the *chosen course* of the ungodly, *foreshadows* their doom.

χωρὶσ θεμ. in Luke only. Matt. has τὴν ἄμμον.

προσέῤῥηξεν, *broke upon*, *Campbell*. *Dash against*, *Gesenius*. Giving a specific sense to details, rock, sand, wind, &c., injures the force of this fine apologue, *Alexander* ποταμόσ, a rising storm might suggest the simile, and compel a speedy *conclusion* to our Lord's discourse. Without naming repentance, the idea pervades this discourse. The blind, the hypocrite, the tree, the foolish builder, all present the image of the natural man, *Stier*.

μεγάλη, "*great*." All the greater because such an one as is here supposed is a *professed disciple*; one *hearing the words* of Christ, *Alford*. Without a holy heart and a holy life, all is ruinous in the hour of temptation, and in the day of wrath, *Quesnel*.

We see from this example of our Lord's sermon that it is not necessary for every discourse to end with *consolation*, *Bengel*. Were a minister to deliver a discourse now-a-days upon the model of this sermon of Christ, there are many professors who would say "*He has not preached the* GOSPEL."

CHAPTER VII.

NOW when he had ended all his sayings in the audience of the people, he entered into Capernaum.

Ended. Gr. *fulfilled*, not that He had finished all He desired to say. He proportions showers to the wants of the field, so with His counsels. "I have yet many things to say unto you, but ye cannot bear them now." John xvi. 12.

People. Christianity, unlike Romanism, imparts her light to *all men.*

Capernaum. Luke iv. 31. The usual residence of the Saviour. Matt. iv. 13; Isa. ix. 1.

Its spiritual privileges, "exalted it to heaven." Matt. xi. 23.

The centurion's home a bright spot, amid its spiritual darkness.

"The Lord blesseth the habitation of the just." Prov. iii. 33.

"And the Lord blessed Obed-edom, and all his household." 2. Sam.vi.11.

Christ endorses His *authority* to teach, by showing His *power* to heal.

Unlike Rome, He let His light shine. "In secret, have I said nothing."

επλήρωσεν εισ—*He filled up all these words into the ears of the people.* Our ears are like vessels *into which* Christ's doctrine is poured. It is poured into our hearts through them, *Wordsworth.* καπερναούμ, Mark and Luke name a town, then record the miracles and discourses associated with it, without regard to time, *Greswell.*

---

2. *And a certain centurion's servant, who was dear unto him, was sick, and ready to die.*

Soldiers present, shewed the Jews *restless* under the yoke of Rome.

Centurion. Gr. *Ruler of a hundred.* The band varied from 30 to 100.

The first centurion bore the Eagle, the standard of Rome. Matt. xxiv.28.

Thoughtful heathen; deeply deplored the *emptiness* of polytheism.

Proselytes of the gate found in many cities of the Empire. Acts x. 2.

By profession they held to the Gentile *race*, and by *religion*, to the Jews.

By them, Providence broke down "the middle wall of partition."

They dare only worship, (under penalty of death) in the *outer court.*

But our Saviour honors and communes with a *soldier* of Rome.

Servant. Gr. a *slave*, not hired servant, *Doddridge & Alexander.*

From (*servi*) *preserved from being slain, when captured in war.*

Slave dealers followed the armies, and bought captives for 4 drachms.

Slaves, under the Patriarchs, were circumcised and educated.
Slaves did almost all the servile labor in our Lord's time.
Greek and Roman freemen esteem toil dishonorable.
Masters had power of life and death over their slaves and children.
In one night, Lacedemonian youths, slew 3000 Helots.
In Egypt to this day, masters have the same fearful prerogative.
Many were of fairer color than their masters, and some adopted as heirs.
Many educated as *amanuenses*, *actors*, physicians, and tutors.
Petronian law, forbade masters making them fight as gladiators.
Another, forbade putting them to death, without a sufficient reason.
Another, forbade separating by sale, husbands and wives.
Many poor parents *sold* their children to Roman masters.
Faithful slaves were buried in Rome, near their masters' sepulchres.
Those restless in their bondage, wrought in chains.
In 1806, British Parliament abolished slave trade. Due to Wilberforce and Clarkson.
In 1863, Abraham Lincoln, President, abolished Slavery in the United States, by proclamation.

Dear. The value of a faithful servant is only equaled by one's best friend, *Bacon.*
At Bethel, Jacob honored the fidelity of Rebecca's nurse. Gen. xxxv. 8.
"Servants be obedient to your masters, shewing all good fidelity." Tit. ii. 10.
Those rendering heart-felt services, are not recompensed by money.
"Thou shalt not rule over a servant with rigor." Lev. xxv. 43.

Sick. Matt. *palsy*, a relaxation of the nervous system, generally on the left side. Gr. *paralysis.*
A disease difficult of treatment to physicians.*

---

*The miracle same as Matt. viii. 5, *Lightfoot*, *Grotius*, *Tertullian*, *Origen*; different, *Calvin*, *Beza*, *Macknight*.

εκατονταρχοσ—Ruler of a 100; corresponding to a captain among us. A *proselyte of the gate;* one believing in God, without being circumcised, or conforming to the Jewish ritual. The same with Chuza, Herod's steward, *Sepp*. The centurion was figure and precursor of the Gentile world coming to Christ, *Augustine*. δουλοσ, for δεολοσ, from δεα to bind, signifying a slave or bond man, *Major*, 60,000 gladiator slaves, under Spartacus, were slain in battle A.D. 71. Matt. has παῖσ, both mean a slave; he was sick in the house af the centurion. Among the patriarchs, a slave was a servant, either bought with money from the heathen, (Lev. xxv. 46) or born in the house, (Gen. xiv. 14). Abraham's servants named, as the evidences of his *power*, (Gen. xiv. 14-15). The origin of slavery is lost in antiquity. The Hebrews (Lev. xxv. 46) were permitted to hold *heathen* as *possession*. But men-stealers were to be put to death (Ex. xxi. 16). The original Amer. Edition of the Confession of Faith condemned slavery as a violation of the eighth commandment. In *Homer's* time, *captives* were sold into slavery. *Philip* sold the *Thebans* into bondage. Attica had 21,000 free *citizens*, 10,000 *aliens*, and 400,000 *slaves*, *Beckers Char.* *Hecuba* laments that she was *chained* as a dog at the gate, *Euripides.* This was a common usage, as the iron ring at the gates of dwellings in Pompeii at this time shew. A slave was always present to open the gate. *Pollio* murdered slaves who offended him, and cast them as food to his fish. 30,000 of the *Tarrentians* were sold to the highest bidder. Timid masters shut them up every night. *Alfred the Great*, made the purchase of horses, oxen, and *slaves*, invalid, unless vouchers were given. In 651 A.D. slaves were sent by *African* princes to the king of Egypt, as *tribute.* Mohammed forbade his followers enslaving persons of their own faith. Slavery exists at present in the *Dutch* and *Spanish* colonies; in Turkey and in Egypt. It has existed for many ages in Africa. Notice the ruin of those nations who held slaves, *Babylon*, *Egypt*, *Greece*, *Rome*, *Etruria*, *Venice*, *Genoa*, *&c.*, and lately the Southern States of America. *εντιμοσ εντιμη*, *in honor*, *highly prized*, dear on account of obedience. Cicero *apologizes* in a letter to a friend, for mentioning the death of a slave in his family, *Ep. ad. Att.*

---

3. *And when he heard of Jesus, he sent unto him the elders of the Jews, beseeching him that he would come and heal his servant.*

Heard. Heathenism failed to supply the wants of such a spirit as his.

He longed to find One, who could hear, and answer his prayers.

As yet, he had not seen Him. "Blessed are they that have not seen," &c.

Sent. He supposed Christ's countrymen would succeed better than himself.

The centurion might have dreaded the presence of a superior being.

His deep *humility*, and profound *faith*, led him to send others.

Public men are said *to do*, that which is done by their orders.

Elders. Gr. *aged persons*, selected to rule on account of experience Num. xi. 16.

Probably, officers of the synagogue the centurion had built.

The elders of Egypt, among the highest officers of the nation. Gen. l. 7.

Seventy chosen to accompany Moses and Aaron to Sinai. Ex. xxiv. 1.

In the N.T. a title of dignity, not so much of age, as of office.

They *preached*. Tit. i. 9. *Visited* the sick. Jas. v. 14., and *ruled* in the church. 1. Pet. v. 1 and 5.

Jews. So called because the principle tribe was Judah's.

Our Lord's labours were as yet *confined* to this chosen people.

By his piety and prudence, the centurion had conciliated their prejudice.

While they were going, he may have earnestly prayed.

The elders, willing messengers, well-deserved their trust.

Beseeching. They imagined Christ's prejudices, as strong as their own.

They had faith, but not so strong as the centurion.

[T]hose having less grace, may nevertheless profit the more advanced.

[C]ome. They seemed to believe, He could not heal without being *present.*

[I]n this the faith of Israel, was far weaker than that of the Gentile.

[T]hey had forgotten their own oracles "*His mighty wonders.*" Dan. iv. 3.

ἀπέστειλε, *he sent.* Matt. says προσῆλθε, *resorted to Jesus, i. e.,* by his messengers, [a]nd by his *faith, Wordsworth.* He sent first and came afterwards, *Jacobus.* Such [v]ariations, the concise account making a man "facere per se" what the fuller one relates [h]im "fecisse per alteram" are common in all written and oral narrations, *Alford.*

πρεσβυτέρουσ. The apostles called themselves *elders* or *presbyters*, 1. Pet. v. 1, 2. [2]. John, 1 verse. It resembled the office of the ruler of the synagogue. The office of the [π]ρεσβυτερ identical with ἐπίσκοποσ—overseer or bishop. The Church of God has continued [t]o ordain a class similar in name and office. διασώσῃ, διά and σωζω, *to bring safely [t]hrough,* Luke v. 31.

---

4. *And when they came to Jesus, they besought him instantly, saying, That he was [w]orthy for whom he should do this.*

[B]esought. Matt. *Calling for aid.* "Yet for this will I be enquired of, by the house of Israel." Ezek. xxxvi. 37.

[I]nstantly. Gr. *earnestly, diligently, attentively.* Cornelius "prayed to God *always.*" Acts x. 2.

[J]ews interceding for a heathen, unusual, touching, and effectual.

Worthy. Centurion before a three-fold tribunal. 1. Judgment of men. "He is worthy." 2. Judgment of conscience. "I am not worthy." 3. Judgment of the Lord. "I have not found so great faith, No, not in Israel."

[P]recious testimony, from those who probably were strangers to the centurion's piety.

[T]hus scoffers dying, select Christians to be their *executors.*

[H]is humanity and humility had disarmed the prejudices of the Jews.

[T]he Roman idolater, and warrior, was humbled by divine grace.

[A]lthough he knew the confidence, and affection, his life had inspired, he counted it presumption, to ask the favor himself.

παρεκαλουν, "*besought.*" To call to one's assistance, to exhort, to comfort. [π]αρέξει, Attic for παρέξῃ. *Tisch., Lach. Extend this favor, Bengel.* Literally, *thou shalt [a]fford this favor, Wordsworth.*

---

5. *For he loveth our nation, and he hath built us a synagogue.*

Loveth. Romans in general treated the conquered with great severity.

Enslaving the wealthy, they made them *redeem* themselves from captivity.

Jews, specially despised for refusing to worship Roman gods.

For centuries they have been scattered, and peeled, and everywhere spoken against. Isa. xviii. 2.

A pestilence in 1348 A.D. was traced, by rumour, to springs poisoned.

The suspected Jews were massacred to the number of 1,000,000.

In 1492, 500,000 were banished from Spain, and 150,000 from Portugal.

Nation. To whom pertained the adoption, glory, covenants, &c. Rom. ix. 4.

No people once so highly *honored* of God, or so *despised* by men.

The religion of Jehovah, could not compromise with polytheism.

He hath. Gr. *it was he*, who built our synagogue.

Built. Romans wantonly destroyed them, to crush out the spirit of the captives.

Like Darius, he desired an interest in prayers offered to God. Ezra vi. 10.

Galerius and *Maxentius*, persecutors, dying, asked Christians' prayers.

Synagogue. Luke iv. 15. Very many had been either demolished, or *desecrated.*

Their sacredness rested not on the *founder*, but in the *worship*.

Augustus decreed, henceforth, they should be *spared*.

Their peculiar sanctity arose from their *dedication* to God.

ἀυτόσ, emphatic. τὴν—the only one in the place. A synagogue for us, *Campbell*. *The synagogue which we frequent*, There were many synagogues in so large a city as Capernaum. At Jerusalem there were upwards of 400. *St. Luke alone* records the words of these Jewish elders; and thus, while he repeats the substance of St. Matt.'s narrative, shows his own independent knowledge of the facts, *Wordsworth*. Romans wherever they encamped, generally built a theatre. "Where I have my tent, God shall have an altar," *John Howard*. *Philo* praised *Detronius*, governor of Syria, for the same act. Of his own accord, to build a synagogue for them, was something rarer still than to love their nation, *Bengel*.

---

6. *Then Jesus went with them. And when he was now not far from the house, the centurion sent friends to him, saying unto him, Lord, trouble not thyself; for I am not worthy that thou shouldest enter under my roof:*

Went. Our Lord refused many requests, but no call for mercy.

He refused to visit a nobleman at Capernaum. John iv. 48.

But now He goes, not for the synagogue he had built, but for the heroic faith the Gentile manifested.

We must come *earnestly*, if we would hope to succeed in prayer.

"The kingdom of heaven suffereth *violence*." Matt. xi. 12. Strive, (*agonize*) Luke xiii. 24.

Sent. This proves, his humility equaled his ever deepening faith.

Trouble not. True religion prevents us from unnecessarily troubling others.

Not worthy,—"of the least of thy mercies," said Jacob. Gen. xxxii. 10.

The Prodigal,—"No more worthy to be called thy son." Luke xv. 19.

How much clearer views of sin, had this Roman, than the Jewish elders!

He knew it might entail ceremonial uncleanness on Jesus until evening.

The prompt answer of our Lord, *increases* greatly, his faith.

He sent *elders* to intercede, *now*, friends to detain the Lord.

Enter. Jesus and he had already communed in spirit.

Roof. The honor was too great, though the *mansion* might have been noble.

He had received Him into his *heart*, although not into his house.

κύριε—Luke vi. 46, see Notes. *σκύλλου*, fatigue not thyself, *Meyer*. *μου*, emphatic; the roof of *me*, most unworthy as I am, *Wordsworth*. When aware of the Lord's readiness, humble faith increases in the centurion, *Bengel*.

---

7. *Wherefore neither thought I myself worthy to come unto thee: but say in a word, and my servant shall be healed.*

A word. His interest in his servant unusual and commendable.

The Romans regarded them as chattels, not human beings.

What an impression had our Lord's fame made upon him!

No *mythical* Christ, could have raised so bold a hope in him.

His faith was that of the most illustrious prophets.

"Am I a God at hand, and not a God afar off, saith the Lord?" Jer. xxiii. 23.

He knew unconditional obedience was exercised in the Roman army.

He believed that life and death hung on Christ's commands.

A Roman commander might order a guilty soldier to put himself to death, so perfect the discipline of the army.

To him, the Lord was the highest *Imperator* over the heavenly host.

His view of Christ's relations to the spirit-world, original and grand.

How far above that of Naaman, who said, "I thought he will surely come out and strike his hand," &c. 2. Kings v. 11.

Bodily diseases, as servants of God, executed His commission.

185,000 Assyrians, might have been destroyed *without* an Angel.

All this indicates child-like faith, with profound humility.

Servant. Anxious, not like Jairus, for an only *daughter*. Mark v. 22.

Nor for a *son*, like the nobleman. John iv. 47. But a slave.

Healed. Had not Christ been *Divine*, would He have sanctioned such views?

The centurion heard that the Lord was coming, and sent friends to Him with this second and still humbler message. He knew and felt himself to be out of the fold of God, a stranger to the commonwealth of Israel; and therefore unworthy to receive under his roof the Redeemer of Israel, *Alford.* His state of heart was that of all capable of embracing Christ; a consciousness of Christ's loftiness and our unworthiness, *Neander.* While owning himself unworthy the Lord should enter his house, he was accounted worthy the Lord should enter his heart. The more humility, the more room, and the more fulness: The proud hill tops let the rain run off; the lowly valleys are richly watered, *Augustine.*

εἰπὲ λόγῳ equivalent to "command," Speak by word of mouth, *Hammond.* παῖς, as *puer*, signifies a servant in general without reference to age. Master termed, *pater familias*, *Grotius.*

---

8. ***For I also am a man set under authority, having under me soldiers, and I say unto one, Go, and he goeth; and to another, Come, and he cometh; and to my servant, Do this, and he doeth it.***

Authority. An under officer, he paid prompt obedience to Tribunes.
Under me. My soldiers know no disobedience to my orders.
An officer, I know what it is to *command*, a soldier, to obey.
I say. Am accustomed to say, in the exercise of authority.
Go and Come, imply active, energetic service in general.
I sit still, yet my wishes are perfectly and promptly performed by others.
Servant. Not one hired, but a domestic slave.
The whole, a picture of brief command, and prompt obedience.
How much more Thou, Prince over the host of heaven! Luke ii. 13.
Only command, and winds, storms, seas, and demons obey.
This miracle no less a proof of the Lord's *willingness*, than his *ability* to save.

ἐξουσίαν—Authority of the *Principes*, Tribunes, and others high in command. He refers to Christ's supremacy over demons, *Fritsche.* Over angels, *Olshausen. Wetstein. Ewald.* Over ministering spirits, *Crusius.* Over diseases, *Meyer.* Some familiar servant of the Lord Jesus, he thinks, would suffice to restore his poor slave, *Lange.* Spiritual powers, healing angels, or disease and death, *De Wette.* The centurion could command his soldiers or his servant, but not disease. But the Lord is able to command disease; and that humanly speaking, with more ease than the oftimes rebellious will of man, *Bengel.* I know how to obey, being *myself* under authority; and in turn, know how others obey, having soldiers under me.—If then I, in my subordinate station, am obeyed, how much more Him, who acts over all, and whom diseases serve as their master, *Alford.* If I, who am *under authority* (i.e. of the "tribunus legionis" and of the "Imperator,") command and receive ready obedience from my soldiers, how much more Thou, who hast no superior? Thou canst command thy ministers (Diseases, the Elements, &c.) and they will obey Thee! *Wordsworth.*

---

9. ***When Jesus heard these things, he marvelled at him, and turned him about, and said unto the people that followed him, I say unto you, I have not found so great faith, no, not in Israel.***

Heard. He paused. *Complying* He conferred a greater honor on the centurion, than his *going* would.

Marvelled. *Admired*—It does not necessarily imply *surprise.*

Jesus marvelled at *faith*, and at another's *unbelief.* Mark vi. 6.

At faith, considering the general spiritual blindness.

At unbelief, considering the blaze of light around His hearers.

Christ marvelling, perhaps a part of "the great mystery of godliness." 1 Tim. iii. 16.

To the Divine *Logos*, there was nothing either new, or strange.

To His humanity, surprise and wonder were familiar.

Same wonder expressed by Jehovah, at "there being no Intercessor." Isa. lix. 16.

Our Lord approves great faith, even when mingled with error.

Belief, and unbelief, make up the history of our entire race.

I have. He claims the omniscience of God, to discern a *heart-faith.*

Found. A Divine finding, and solemn warning of His hearers' guilt.

I, who came to seek, and impart to all desiring it.

I came to seek it first of all, where it *should* be found.

Is not Israel, beyond all nations, the people of *faith?*

From Abraham, for long ages, have they not been trained to faith?

Great. First instance of faith healing at a distance, is a Gentile's.

Great, because 1. Candid in requesting. 2. Humble in approaching. 3. Joyful in receiving sovereign mercy.

Faith. A proof of its indispensible necessity, as a condition of gifts from God.

Great faith 1. Noticed. 2. Praised. 3. Rewarded. 4. Held up for imitation.

Self-interest prompts external works, but God looks on the heart.

It was the first mention of faith, as reposed in *Himself.*

The centurion's an earnest of Gentile faith, surpassing that of Israel.

Israel. Their rich inheritance was about to pass over to others.

The depth and strength of the Centurion's faith were wonderful.

Our Lord might have expected the highest type of faith in his chosen people.

Another Gentile, the poor woman of Cana, had a faith strong and deep.

Our Lord does not contemn *little* faith. "The bruised reed He will not break." Matt. xii. 20.

Lessons of love, 1. Love of a heathen to Jews.

2. Love of Jews to a heathen. 3. The Love of the Lord to both, exemplified in words and deeds of love.

"God is no respecter of persons." Acts x. 34-35; 1. Sam. xvi. 7.

God does not despise weak faith, but loves strong faith more.

ἐθαύμασεν—Twice only we read of this *nil mirari* of His divine perfection being suspended, namely, at the unbelief of the Nazarenes and at the faith of this Gentile. It was a proof of His humanity, *Oosterzee.* "A pleasing admiration," *Foote.* Admired, *Campbell.* That Jesus might have been *ignorant* of some things, seems to threaten a *Nestorian* severance of the Person of Christ. The *Manicheans* cancelled the passage, Matt. viii. 11., because it honored the chiefs of the Old Covenant, by seating them in the first places at the heavenly banquet, *Trench.* If surprise *was* felt, it is not our duty to reconcile it with omniscience, *Alexander.* If any wonder felt, it was only by His humanity. In the epistle to the Hebrews it is said, that our Lord *in all things was made like unto His brethren,* and if so, surely his knowledge as *man,* must have been limited. How else can we understand, Luke ii. 5-2. "*And Jesus increased in wisdom?*" Or how interpret His own words concerning the day of judgment. "*But of that day and that hour knoweth no man, no, not the angels which are in heaven, neither the Son, but the Father!*" That Jesus should have *wondered* at the faith of the centurion, seems as natural, and credible as that He should have been *tempted in all points like as we are, Ed.* We are not to imagine that our Lord's wonder was not *real.* Christ is *perfect* man, and the reality of His human affections, and His *regulation* of these affections, render Him a perfect example to us, *Wordsworth.*

---

10. *And they that were sent, returning to the house, found the servant whole that had been sick.*

Whole. The first miracle in Luke, wrought at a *distance.*
Thus Elisha cured Naaman at a distance. 2. Kings v.
Learn, 1. No man is too mean for His love. 2. No misery too great for His mercy. 3. No conditions of help so easy for all, as Christ's.
The sick slave at Capernaum, had the *best Physician.*
Jesus *now* as then, still "travels in the greatness of His strength" to save.
In this miracle, our Lord heals the slave on the *master's faith.*
How much more a child, on a believing parents faith!
It affords an analogy for baptizing children, *Alexander.*

ὑγιαίνοντα frequently used with reference to the health of the mind in faith and doctrine. In faith, Titus i. 13; in doctrine, 1. Tim. i. 10, Titus ii. 1. *Recovering, Paulus.* Not only sound, but using his health, *Bengel.* An invisible highway, for the conquering eagles of the Great *Imperator, Lange.*

Christ did not enter the centurion's house, but his servant was healed by Him, present in majesty, but absent in body, so to Israel and to them alone, He showed Himself in the Flesh; but to the Gentiles he was preached by others, *Wordsworth.* The Jews *saw* and crucified Him; the Gentiles *heard* and believed, *Augustine.*

---

11. ¶ *And it came to pass the day after, that he went into a city called Nain; and many of his disciples went with him, and much people.*

The following is one of the *three greatest* Miracles of Our Lord.
John alone describes that of raising Lazarus.
He raised one just dead, one on the road to burial, and one in the grave four days.

Day after. Gr. does not strictly imply more than, *a day following.*
Nain. A small village south of Tabor in Galilee, near Endor.
Heb. *fair*, the world a pleasant Nain but death spoils all its pleasure.
Christ was on His way to Jerusalem, to keep the *second* Passover.
He never could say with the Roman Emperor, "I have lost a day."
Went with Him. Christians follow Christ whether to *Cana* or *Nain, Tabor or Golgotha.*

The day after. The succession of events here set forth does not require very strict definition of time, *Bengel.* Nain.—From Heb. *fair* or *pleasant.* Three miles south west of Tabor, *Robinson.* In the tribe of Issachar, near Endor and Kison. A district two miles south of Tabor, *Eusebius.* But one of the four Evangelists naming this miracle, an unsolved mystery, *Alford.* No mystery at all, if we recollect that each Evangelist was inspired by the Holy Ghost, and that it is in their *fourfold* Biography we have a *complete* account of our Lord's life and miracles *only.* No one of the Evangelists intended to write as if he were ignorant of what had been written by any of his predecessors, nor did any of them omit through ignorance what a previous Evangelist had written, *Augustine.*

---

12. *Now when he came nigh to the gate of the city, behold, there was a dead man carried out, the only son of his mother, and she was a widow; and much people of the city was with her.*

Gate of the City. The sanctuary of the Lord's glory.
1. The Great Prophet proving His doctrine by a splendid miracle.
2. The merciful High Priest, drying the mourner's tears.
3. The Prince of Life spoiling death of his prey.

Generally towns in the East, of importance, are walled, and gates closed at night.
Behold, a marvellous coincidence, but only *seemingly* accidental.
The time of his death, of his burial, route of the procession, meeting the Lord at that moment, prove special Providence.
Dead Man. Biers sustained the bodies, wrapped in grave clothes, without a coffin.
Lazarus had no other covering, than clean linen for his shroud.
Egyptians embalmed their dead. Greeks and Romans burned theirs.
Ashes extinguished with wine, and funerals conducted by torch-light.
Ashes placed in urns of clay, marble, brass, silver, and gold.
They are found by the *way side* with "STOP TRAVELLER!"
Bildad said—"He shall have no name *in the street.*" Job. xviii. 17.
"Go by the *way*, and do ye not know their tokens (epitaphs)?" Job xxi. 29.
Carried out. Jews usually buried dead, the same day before sun-down.
All ancient nations buried outside the towns.
Pernicious custom of burying under the church began with *martyrs.*
Jews buried without the city. Kings were buried on Mount Zion.

Jehoiakim (burial that of an ass) was buried beyond the gates. Jer. xxii. 19.

Only Son. His mother's only remaining tie, binding her to earth.

Bereaved, childless, hopeless, her coal quenched in darkness. 2. Sam. xiv. 7.

David wept bitterly, over the death of Absalom, although profligate and traitor.

Rachel weeping for her children, refused to be comforted. Matt. ii. 18.

Much people. They showed their sympathy for the mourners.

Funeral rites are rather for the *mourners*, than the dead.

Why did not some bereaved hearts ask Christ to raise their dead?

Not even the sisters of Lazarus ventured making such a request.

Fear enchains us, paralyzing our hopes, and makes us slaves.

The funerals of large cities, harden the heart by familiarity.

As dead were unclean, and could not be buried within the city, sides of mountains, gardens, and unfrequented places selected.

Jewish funerals took place on the same day, as the death.

There was One nigh, pitying, and with whom to pity was to bless.

ἐξεκομίζετο—*was being carried out.* "*Much people,*" the miracle was done in the sight of numerous spectators. Luke's accuracy as an observer and an historian.—1. The city. 2. The gate. 3. The multitude. 4. The man's age and circumstances. 5. The mother's condition. 6. Our Lord's words. 7. The effects on the multitude; are all distinctly specified, *Wordsworth.*

---

13. *And when the Lord saw her, he had compassion on her, and said unto her, Weep not.*

Lord. Note this sublime appellation of Jesus—THE LORD.

Compassionating the sufferer, He everywhere relieved the wretched.

He could not begin with more of lowly sublimity, or simple majesty.

He did not reprove the mother's weeping, as He did noisy grief. Mark v. 39.

He hinted at his "wiping away all tears from all faces."' Rev. xxi. 4. Isa. xxv. 8.

Weep not. These words were not *prohibitory*, but *consolatory*.

1. How easy a word to use. 2. How difficult to obey.

3. How blessed the office to dry the mourner's tears!

Weep not, has carried consolation to thousands from age to age. Rev. v. 5.

Tears, a *speech*, understood by all Earth's tribes.

His *word* of comfort, as His *nature*, far above that of a mere man.

His voice *carried consolation* to the mourner, as *life* to the dead.

Mourners in the East, lament with *loud* and very bitter wailings.

"*The Lord.*" This mode of describing Christ almost peculiar to St. Luke among the the Synoptical Evangelists. To remind his readers that Jesus was co-equal with the Lord JEHOVAH of the Septuagint; proved by His mighty works. May also be a silent evidence that Luke's gospel is later than that of Matt. and Mark, and that it was written for those who had not seen Christ in the flesh, but who habitually thought of Him as the ascended and glorified *Lord*, *Wordsworth.*

ἐσπλαγχνίσθη—was moved with compassion. "*Weep not.*" In human creatures there is always something at first for God to remove, *Bengel.* He has come to make good one day the words in Rev. xxi. 4, *Trench.* These words express the only reason for the miracle—to comfort the living, *Stier.* Perhaps he willed also to awaken the young man's soul, *Olshausen.* The Redeemer's object was the relief of the mother, *Bib. Tub.* Imparting *spiritual* life to the dead, *Rieger.*

---

14. *And he came and touched the bier; and they that bare* him *stood still. And he said, Young man, I say unto thee, Arise.*

Touched. The oriental funeral trains moved rapidly.
That touch was full of power, as the bearers knew Him not.
Bier. Without a coffin to confine the corpse, as with us.
Egyptians and others were carried in marble coffins.
None but the higher classes of Jews had biers.
Jesus could touch the *leprous*, or *dead*, without defilement.
His *silent* approach, neither terrifies, nor dazzles.
God makes the sun to rise, seasons come, dews descend, *silently.*
Stood still. An *unseen might* ever the Lord's pleasure.
Young man. The sun of human hope, often *sets* in the morning.
"Man comes forth like a flower, and is cut down." Job. xiv. 2.
Young, should not put aside thoughts of death. Ps. xc. 12.
I say. Had not His Godhead been Supreme, this was blasphemy.
He performs the miracle with sublime repose.
He now opens the word "I am the Resurrection and the Life. Jo. xi. 25.
He pronounces the Almighty command with Divine majesty.
There is no calling upon a *foreign* power, as with the prophets.
No delay of preparation, as with Elijah, and Elisha.
Thee. Hereafter, the same voice will awake the countless myriads of the dead. John v. 25.
Arise. Our Lord awakes the dead, as easily as one asleep.

"*Stood.*" Bearers sympathizing with the mother, and knowing Jesus' fame, might have expected help, *Oosterzee.* "*He touched the bier,*" and so raised the dead; in order that we may know that His own Body is the Body of Life; and by communion with him we live, *Theophylact.*

According to the Levitical Law, uncleanness was communicated by touching a leper, or a dead body, but Christ touched both; and with His touch He cleansed the one and raised the other, and proved Himself to be above the Law, and to be the Giver of the Law, *Wordsworth.*

15. *And he that was dead sat up, and began to speak. And he delivered him to his mother.*

Dead. Such acts, unquestionable evidences of His Messiahship. Matt. xi. 5.

A writer of the Gospel period, *Quadratus*, preserved by *Eusebius*, tells us the young persons raised, were still alive, *Jerome* repeats it.

Sat up. Not only alive, but in health and strength.

Eternity dawning over the gate of Nain.

How the mighty word of the Lord changes all things!

1. A funeral procession, into witnesses of His miraculous power.
2. A bier, into a place of resurrection, a witness that He is Messiah.
3. A mourning widow, into a thankful mother.
4. A public way, into a sanctuary of God's glory.

Delivered him. Our Lord's *care* for the subjects of His power is here seen.

Jairus' daughter was fed, and Lazarus unbound.

What mingled majesty and grace shine here!

The Resurrection and the Life, meeting death and the grave, and with a touch achieving glorious victory!

Christ gave back the lost. He had ceased to belong to his mother.

What a meeting of mother and son.! Earth witnesses few such scenes

" This my son was dead, and is alive again, was lost, and is found."

A reference in this miracle to the *raised man himself*, is by no means excluded. Man as a conscious being, can never be a mere means to an end, and this would be the case, if we suppose the *consolation of the mother*, to have been its only object, *Olshausen, Alford.* νεκρὸς—When is the separation of the soul and body irrevocable? Only after complete dissolution, *Oosterzee.* There is a freshly trodden path between the recent dead and the spirit, *Lange.* Can he suppose it less an *Almighty act* to raise one dead an hour, than a mummy dead 3000 years?

---

16. *And there came a fear on all: and they glorified God, saying, That a great prophet is risen up among us: and, That God hath visited his people.*

Fear. God in the thunder, or in the earthquake, or in death, will *alone*, arouse some.

Glorified. Carnal and worldly souls reluctantly yield any tribute of praise to their Maker.

Supremely selfish, the unrenewed seek their own glory.

Prophet. It implies a Divine Messenger, greater than Elijah.

By flashes of Divine Power, darting hither and thither, the Messiah aroused the nation to a consciousness of His presence.

For 400 years, no prophet had appeared in Israel, since Malachi.

Visited. A visit of *mercy* to believing hearts; one of vengeance, to His rejectors.

How easily could the people of Nain have detected an impostor.

ἐγήγερται, hath been raised up, Meyer. *ἐπεσκέψατο—Visited. He had kindly considered, Wakefield.* Both Gr. and Eng. words convey the idea of *punishment*, as well as visits of *mercy*. The sense must be determined by the context, *Campbell.*

---

17 *And this rumour of him went forth throughout all Judea, and throughout all the region round about.*

Rumour. Some, doubtless, rejoiced, others feared it would be the *last visit.*

At sundry times, God has raised the dead, to teach the world, *immortality. Instances under both Dispensations.*

18. *And the disciples of John shewed him of all these things.*

John was imprisoned by Herod in Machaerus, a fortress in Moab.

But truth like the light of heaven, cannot be bound.

In his prison, tidings came to John, of wonders wrought by Christ.

Prisons have proved the joy and sorrow of many martyrs.

For ages, baronial castles had prisons *beneath* their halls.

The clank of chains contrasted with the music and revelry *above.*

Things. *The works of Christ,* those peculiar to the Messiah. Matt. xi. 2. *Evidences and manifestations of Messiahship.*

Heidelbergh Castle, and Lambeth Palace still shew the iron rings.

---

19. ¶ *And John calling* unto him *two of his disciples sent* them *to Jesus, saying, Art thou he that should come, or look we for another?*

Disciples. John's mission had been merged in that of Jesus.

They refused to acknowledge Christ, to be superior to their master.

Obstinate persisting, shews that they were not Christians.

He had already affirmed Jesus to be the Christ; but *they* believed him not.

He desired to silence their sceptical and envious misgivings.

Not the *words* of *Jesus*, but His *works* must convince them.

John had no doubts concerning the real Messiahship of Christ.

Repeatedly and passionately he affirmed his own *inferiority.*

But sixteen months before, he beheld the Spirit descend upon Him at baptism.

The Great Healer's deeds and fame pierced the dungeons of Machaerus.

Such *energetic prophetic* faith, not to be dimmed by a dungeon!

The Lord distinctly denies any *vascillation* of *mind* in John; verse 24.

Art thou? Variously answered, with the *No* of unbelief, with the *Yes* of faith, and with the *Hallelujahs* of gratitude.

Should come. A *proper name* for Christ, like "The Son of David." Ps. cxviii. 26. *The Desire of all Nations.*

He whose coming has for many ages been foretold and expected

A question of increasing impatience, rather than secret unbelief.

Or perhaps thus to offer his last public homage to the Lord from prison.

Do we look? Gr. *are we looking, i. e., Is it for another (not for thee) we are looking?*

Another. Gr. *one of a different sort, i. e.*, A Divine Messiah?

"*Calling.*" If Machaerus was in Perea, some days elapsed between the miracle at Nain, and this message, *Greswell.* δυο in Matt. xi. 2.—δια preferred, *Stier, Alford, Lachmann, Tischendorf, Tregelles, Meyer, De Wette.* ἔπεμψε—After long winter in castle of Machaerus. Herod living in sin with Herodias, at Jericho; Jesus accepting invitations to dine with publicans and sinners; no signs of the baptism of fire which he preached.—John sends this message, *Oosterzee.* His own doubts.—In this he incurred the same rebuke received by the mother of our Lord, John ii. 4. The purport of the answer was, that the hour had not yet come for such an open declaration. But sufficient proofs had been given, to render all inexcusable, who should be offended in Him. *Tertullian, Meyer, Olshausen, Neander.* To satisfy the doubts of his disciples, *Origen, Chrysostom, Calvin, Beza, Melancthon, Stier, Alexander.* Our Lord's course too spiritual for him, *Ebrard.* He desired liberation, *Lightfoot, Hase.* Dissatisfied with Christ's gentle course, *Paulus, Lange.* A message of *impatience* and *desperation* from John himself, *Brown.* He desired an open declaration to the world, of His Messiahship, *Alford, Wilkinson, Oosterzee.* Wondered at His slowness in assuming temporal dominion, *Kendrick.* The notion that John wavered in faith, and put this question in doubt is alien from the tenor of the narrative, and irreconcilable with the words of Christ, in verse 24, &c., and at variance with the exposition of the Ancient Church, *Chrys., Augustine, Jerome, Hilary, Gregory, Basil, Ambrose,* see *Wordsworth* in loco, ὁ ἐρχόμενος *the coming one, i.e.*, the Messiah, whose *coming* was expected from the beginning?

---

20. *When the men were come unto him, they said, John Baptist hath sent us unto thee, saying, Art thou he that should come? or look we for another?*

21. *And in that same hour he cured many of* their *infirmities and plagues, and of evil spirits; and unto many* that were *blind he gave sight.*

Another. His miracles, not those of judgment, but acts of mercy.

His expectations were that the Master of the Threshing-floor would use the Fan. Matt. iii. 12.

John's mind had its Gethsemanes, as well as Tabors.

Same hour, in which John's disciples were present.

Infirmities. Diseases which had been long standing, *chronic.*

Plagues, are by Luke, a *physician,* here studiously distinguished from *evil spirits.*

Blind. Human skill has never restored sight to those *naturally* blind. When Christ cometh, will He do *greater signs* than these? John vii. 31.
Gave. Gr. expresses the *grace*, *power*, and *dignity* of these miracles. It hints, that the gift of vision, is among the greatest blessings.

"*The men*," John's disciples, were men advanced in life; those of Jesus were chiefly youthful, *Bengel*. 'Ἐν αὐτῇ "*at that very hour*," He knew, as God, what John's design was in sending to Him, and He put it into his heart to send at that very time when He Himself was working many miracles, which were the true answer to the question, *Cyril*. *Basil* says—He replies by deeds. Believe your own eyes, they will tell you that I am doing the very works which it was prophesied that "He who should come," *i. e.*, the Messiah, should do (see Isa. xxxv. 5), and which are an answer to your question, *Wordsworth* in loco. An explanatory addition of Luke, *Ewald*, *Tischendorf*. μαστίγων—"*plagues*," a whip or scourge—met. for Divine punishment. πληγη—Lat. plaga, a *stroke*. ἐχαρίσατο—χάρισ *grace*, conferred with *dignity*, at the same time undeserved. χάρισ occurs about 150 times, generally translated *grace*, *charity*; derived from Lat. *caritas*. ἀγάπη, 1. Cor. 13, is most unfortunately translated *charity*, from the *Vulgate*. *Jerome* could not find a better Latin word by which to translate ἀγάπη, than *caritas*. *Amor* corresponds to φιλίᾱ, but not ἀγάπη. φιλία means *affection* or *friendship*: ἀγαπη means *brotherly love* and *love of* GOD, The word *grace* is a more exact synonyme of χάρισ, than any word in the Latin language, *Hodge*. 1. Cor 13.

---

22. *Then Jesus answering said unto them, Go your way, and tell John what things ye have seen and heard; how that the blind see, the lame walk, the lepers are cleansed, the deaf hear; the dead are raised, to the poor the gospel is preached.*

Go your way. He utterly declines declaring explicitly that he was the Messiah.
It is oft-times the glory of God to conceal a thing. Pro. xxv. 2. The hiding of His power. Hab. iii. 4.
Tell John. That he may tell *you* again, *the* signs of the Shiloh or Messiah.
Jesus withheld from John, what He told the Samaritan woman.
He might with a *word*, have declared Himself the Messiah.
Prophecy *foretold* these very *miracles*, ages before. Isa. xxxv. 5 and 7.
Light *centres* in, as well as *radiates* from Christ.
The *works* of Christ, go far beyond what prophecy foretold.
He gives John's disciples a *few* specimens of His power, as illustrations.
What things. Christians like Christ, known more by *deeds*, than *words*. *By their fruits ye shall knom them.*
Have seen. Doubt dies in the presence of Him who is Light and Love.
Blind. The eye, the greatest *wonder* of mechanism in the body.
Its derangement renders the person pitiably helpless.
Eyes of the blind, and ears of the deaf shall be opened. Isa. xxxv. 5.
Lepers. A plague midway between *disease* and *possession*. Luke iv. 27. See Notes.

Dead. John's disciples present, when the Lord raised the widow's son at Nain.

Poor. The *spiritual* poor generally found among the *literal* poor.

The climax of signs, the preaching of the gospel to the poor.

Christianity the only religion that can reach the wants of the poor.

To that age, this the most surprising of prophetic testimonies. Isa. lix. 1.

The chasm between rich and poor in the East deep and wide.

But Christ came to seek and save the *socially*, as well as *spiritually*, *lost*.

The prosperous not excluded. But the gospel is peculiarly suited to the miserable.

Preached. Gr. *evangelized*, *i.e.*, effectually enlightened.

ἃ εἴδετε—The Lord's Messiahship, discriminated by Messianic working. *Not about* the works of an individual known as *Jesus*, but whether the miracles, were those of *the* Messiah, *the promised Shiloh*, *Stier*. ἔργα,—Our Lord did not work miracles to be stumbling blocks, but aids to faith, *Oosterzee*. τυφλοὶ—The adjustment of the lenses of a telescope in an achromatic manner, was first suggested by those in the human eye. εὐαγγελίζονται—The glad tidings are preached to the poor *Tyndale*. The poor receive the Gospel *Geneva*. Poor receive the glad tidings of the Gospel *Cranmer*. To the poor the Gospel is preached *Rheims*. Poor men be taken to preach the Gospel *Wickliffe*, i. e. the poor preach the Gospel. But this is at variance with Isa. lxi. 1. *Stier* remarks the coupling of these miracles together and observes that with νεκ. ἐγ. is united πτχωοι εὐαγγ. as being a thing hitherto unheard of and strange.

---

23. *And blessed is* he, *whosoever shall not be offended in me.*

Blessed. Truly happy, with particular reference to Divine favor.

If we cannot find blessedness in Christ, we can get it nowhere.

Offended. Gr. *scandalized*, *i.e.*, through pride or passion.

"And He shall be a stone of stumbling and a rock of offence." Isa. viii. 14.

Some are offended at the *want* of *evidences* of Christianity. 2. Thess. ii. 10.

Some at Christ's Divinity, Mohammedans, Arians, Socinians and others.

Some at Biblical doctrines—Depravity, Regeneration, Trinity, Justification by faith, Helplessness of the sinner, Need of grace, &c.

Some at His precepts requiring *holiness* of heart. "Be ye perfect," &c. Matt. v. 48.

Some at the trials to which Christ's followers are exposed. Luke xiv. 27.

Some at the inconsistences of false-hearted professors, their covetousness, bigotry, &c.

Me. With Divine Majesty, He maintains a dignified silence concerning Himself.

Although these words are in the form of a beatitude, they contain a solemn warning against unbelief.

How delicately and skilfully does He treat the question of John's disciples! Without upbraiding, He shews the ruinous effects of scepticism.

σκανδαλισθῇ—*offended*, not *alienated in affection*. Not in the Lat. and old Eng. sense of *stumbling*. The theme in classic Greek, denotes *a trap*, or *snare*. In Hellenistic dialect—any hindrance in the path, over which one may *fall*. The derivative verb means to *make one fall*. A natural figure for both sin and error, and often representing both, as commonly connected in experience, *Alexander*. Not displeased but led into error, *Stier*. An actual mark of the Messiah that many should be offended in Him, Isa. lii. 14, *Bengel*. How corrupt must that man be who *is offended in* JESUS! *Quesnel*.

---

24. ¶ *And when the messengers of John were departed, he began to speak unto the people concerning John, What went ye out into the wilderness for to see? A reed shaken with the wind?*

Departed. He would not seem to flatter John in their presence.
But He leaves him not a moment, in a false position.
He would do away with the unfavorable impression produced by His question.
People. The promiscuous crowd who heard His answer to John.
Some would misconstrue, or invalidate John's testimony to Christ.
Went. Crowds had gone out to the wilderness, near the Dead Sea.
To see. Gr. Did you go out to witness a *spectacle* or *show?*
A Reed. Shewing that John had no doubts of His Messiahship.
One need not go to Jordan's banks, to see reeds shaken with the wind.
The Oriental form of the question indicates a *negative*. "Surely not a reed?"
Not wavering in opinions, like a reed bending before the breeze.
With divine art, He leaves them to apply the figure to John.
They knew John to be *firm*, unbending, and unsparing in his great work.
John would never retract testimony, solemnly repeated.
Had he like a courtier, bowed to Herod, he might have stood beside the throne.
But faithful, from first to last, he preached, "Repent ye, for the Kingdom of Heaven is at hand."
Wind. Luke xii. 55. See Notes.

θεάσασθαι—*to eagerly and curiously gaze;* Eng. *Theatre*. An idle gazing at a trifle, *Beza*, *Wetstein*, *Rosenmuller*. κάλαμον—*Kaneh:* Eng. *Cane;* Lat. *Calamus*. N. T. allusion to those plants, growing in dry barren situations, *Royle*. Reeds at this day wave along the banks of the Jordan, on the very spot where John baptized. Delicate *grasses* or *sedges* growing in wet situations, *Rosenmuller*. You looked to see a false prophet, a changeling, or a sensual teacher, *Stier*.

25. *But what went ye out for to see? A man clothed in soft raiment? Behold, they which are gorgeously apparelled, and live delicately, are in kings' courts.*

A man. Contradicts the idea that John had grown impatient in prison.

Soft. *Luxurious* or *sumptuous*. The reverse of the camel's hair and leathern girdle.

Raiment. A *secular* forerunner, to a *Spiritual* Messiah, were a contradiction.

A wilderness was no place for a courtier, attired for pleasure.

Behold! There are flatterers enough already in the palaces of Herod.

Ahasuerus allowed no one clad in *sackcloth*, to enter his presence.

Louis the Great, forbade an allusion to *death* at Versailles.

"Prophesy not *here*, for it is the king's court." Amos vii. 13.

Our Lord thus condemns wanton courtiers—royal parasites.

Such enter king's *houses*, but not often found in king's *prisons*.

John of the *wilderness*, now John of the *prison*, *consistent* to the end.

Gorgeously. Contrasting with his rough hairy garments and with the magnificent attire of his enemies.

The palace, and not the prison, the place for gorgeous apparel.

μαλακοῖσ—effeminate. ἐνδόξῳ—bright, splendid, or *purple*, *Wakefield*. τρυφῇ—sensuality, luxury, *Bloomfield*. Costly raiment, *Kuinoel*. Self-indulgent, courtly preacher, *Brown*. βασιλείοισ—Court-houses of the royal judges were called *Basilica*, Roman court-houses under the Empire. Equivalent to the royal dignitaries of the Empire. This was the sort of precursor, and even the sort of Messiah they desired, *Bengel*.

---

26. *But what went ye out for to see? A prophet? Yea, I say unto you, and much more than a prophet.*

Prophet. Luke iv. : Discarding all ironical questions He gives the anticipated answer.

"Ye went out to see a prophet," *i.e.*—Do *you* say he is a prophet?

Much more. Gr. *more abundant*, *more excessive* than a prophet.

Superior to most prophets, as to the circumstances of His *birth*.

Had clearer views of Christ's majesty, and office.

Not only *predicted*, but actually saw and *pointed* out the Messiah.

27. *This is he, of whom it is written, Behold, I send my messenger before thy face, which shall prepare thy way before thee.*

It is written. Gr. *has been written*, implying the passage exists.

The words are addressed to the Messiah, as a *promise*.

Here Jesus, gives an *authoritative exposition* of a prophecy.

Messenger. Gr. *an angel*, but here of wider import.

eference is made to messengers, Angel of the covenant, and John the Forerunner. Mal. iii. 1.

Before thy face. Added to the Heb. by the ORIGINAL AUTHOR, CHRIST.

Mal. iii. 1. Jehovah, speaking of Himself, says "*Before me!*"

In Luke, Jehovah speaks of Jesus Christ, before THEE.

Here the *unity* is clearly implied between the Father and the Son.

Isa. xl. 3. Alludes to John, "Prepare ye the way of the Lord," &c.

Prepare. Gr. implies making *fully ready, to equip, to furnish.*

γέγραπται—It varies both from the Heb. and Sep. But while retaining the essential meaning, our Lord, who first inspired Mal., has the right to change the wording as He pleases. Infidelity, with its lynx-eyed criticism, cannot detect a solitary contradiction in the Sacred Oracles, which remains inexplicable, *Alexander*, *Stier*. In the *Koran*, *two hundred and forty three* direct contradictions have been pointed out, *Princ. Rev.*, *Sale's* Translation of the *Koran*.

---

28. *For I say unto you, Among those that are born of women there is not a greater prophet than John the Baptist: but he that is least in the kingdom of God is greater than he.*

I say. He thus demands the solemn attention of those listening.

Born of Woman. An idiomatic phrase, meaning all mankind.

Greater. As forerunner of Christ. Being herald of the Sun of Righteousness elevated him to an eminence unsurpassed by the most distinguished of his predecessors.

No prophet gifted with clearer views, or called to so high a mission.

None more faithful in his ministry, or holier in his life: loyal to truth to death.

Baptist. Gr. *Baptizer.* His peculiar work as our Lord's forerunner.

Least. Gr. *less, i. e.* inferior to him in some respects, greater in others.

The humblest Christian enjoys a higher Dispensation than John.

One of more light, more liberty,— the special reign of the Holy Spirit.

"Blessed are your eyes, for they see," &c. "Many prophets desired," &c. Luke x. 23.

As our privileges are greater, so will be our responsibilities.

Some exalted to heaven through privileges, may be cast down to hell through unfaithfulness. Matt. xi. 23.

μικρότερος—*less.* *μείζων*—*i. e.* never entered the *state of Christianity*, *Bloomfield.* The translators have here made one of the few groundless innovations in King James's Vers. All the earlier versions from Wickliffe to the Rheimish have *less.* The most eminent Gr. and Lat. fathers, *Chrysostom*, *Augustine*, &c. understood this of Christ, who was John's *inferior* in the judgment of many, and really in age, to which the Gr. word is frequently applied. This would have been merely a repetition of what John had himself declared. Protestants generally apply it to any one belonging to the New Dispensation or Christian Church, *Alexander*. To our Lord, *Fritzsche, Oosterzee, Elsley*. Some MSS. and Editors omit προφητησ; but it appears to be emphatic. There is a contrast between the *prophets* and those ἐν τῇ βασιλεία τοῦ Θεοῦ, *in the Kingdom of God*,—*i. e.*, those who partake of the full privileges of the Gospel in the Christian Church. There is also a contrast between "*those who are born of women*" and those who are "*born of water and the Spirit*," *Wordsworth*. Major Propheta, quia finis Prophetarium, *Ambrose*. Although we may be inferior in holiness to some under the Law, whom John represents, yet now after the Passion, and Resurrection, and Ascension, and Day of Pentecost, we have greater blessings in Christ, being made, through Him, partakers of the Divine Nature, *Cyril*.

---

29. ***And all the people that heard*** **him,** ***and the publicans, justified God, being baptized with the baptism of John.***

People. The rank and file of humble poverty, despised by haughty Pharisees.

"These people, who know not the law, are cursed." John vii. 49.

The Talmud called the common people of the land, "*worms*."

Oppressed, but *open to the truth*. Christ uniformly sought to teach them.

The prosperous satisfied with earth, turned from the Gospel.

Publicans. Universally despised for their cruel exactions, contemned as miserable outcasts, from respectable society. Luke iii. 12.

This indicates the humble *class* of disciples of Jesus and John.

Rough honest people, more accessible to truth, than polished hypocrites.

Justified. *i. e.* acknowledged and commended the justice of God, that they deserved the punishment, John had pronounced.

Others were hardened, and deliberately closed their hearts.

Baptism. Luke iii. 3. Mode and objects. See Critical Notes.

John struck the first chords, but the sounds would soon have died out in silence, if a mightier Hand had not swept the yet vibrating strings, *Ellicott*.

The influence of this baptism was limited, Jesus revived it.

The 29th and 30th verses. Our Lord's words, *Campbell, W. & W. Meyer, Oosterzee, Wordsworth*. They would then read—"And now the great body of the people, who have heard Him, and even the publicans, have acknowledged and fulfilled the purpose of God, by being baptized by John." The words, those of Luke, *Schleiermacher, Bengel, Lachmann, Stier*. λαὸσ βαπτισθέντεσ should be βαπτιζόμενοι, if ἀκούσασ refers to hearing John, instead of Christ. The whole form of diction is historical, and not that of a discourse, *Alford*. ἐδικαίωσαν, thankfully received the kindness of God.—The word has a meaning similar to that in Psa. l. 6, *Wakefield*: reverently fulfilled God's commands, *Kuinoel*. *Vindicate*, opposed to rejection, *Beza, Hammond, Doddridge*. Declared God to be just, *Pearce, Le Clerc*. The use of the word δικαιόω, as employed in the New Test. for to regard as *just* and *holy*, to *pronounce* such, to *acquit*,—is derived from the Septuagint, and is very different from the sense in which it commonly stands in Classical Authors, where it signifies, when applied to a *person*, to pronounce sentence upon, *Wordsworth*. Complied with divine counsel, *Macknight*.

30. *But the Pharisees and lawyers rejected the counsel of God against themselves, being not baptised of him.*

Pharisees. Luke v. 17. vi. 2. Energetic enemies of our Lord.
Their schemes of political and ecclesiastical ambition, were in danger.
Their self-righteousness deadened their conscience to the truth.
Some minds are deeply *benumbed* by religious *delusions.*
Hearts preoccupied by error, are very rarely converted to God.
Lawyers. Skilled in the laws of the land, in Judea, those of Moses.
They taught the law to youth in synagogues and schools.
To the teaching, the *Scribes* added that of copying the law.
Learned in the Scriptures, yet they despised the doctrines taught.
Rejected. Gr. *frustrated within themselves*, or *with regard* to, &c.
They trusted, they needed not that repentance He required.
Offended at John's *severity* of manner, and Christ's *holy doctrines.*
Yet they crowded to hear His eloquence, and examine His miracles.
But our Lord was not the Messiah of their *carnal hopes.*
Practically He was *no* Messiah to them. The ark, was *no ark* to those, who refused to enter it.
Counsel, of the Lord, was, that the Jews should be prepared to believe.
Rejecting God's counsel, *for* us, we shall find it at last *against* us.

βουλὴν, always the decree of God, *Grotius, Elsley.* *ἠθέτησαν*—They set aside His counsel of mercy, and turned it against themselves, *Major.* Others *flouted, despised.* This is implied by their openly refusing baptism, *Grotius.* *Eleasar* said, though all perish, the Pharisees would not, *Josephus.* *εἰσ ἑαυτούς*—To their own ruin, *W. & W.* That God's will was right in John's baptizing them, *Meyer;* in themselves, *Erasmus;* against themselves, *Beza, Kuinoel:* towards themselves, *Wordsworth;* in regard to themselves, *Rosenmuller, Doddridge, Wetstein, Alexander.*

---

31. ¶ *And the Lord said, Whereunto then shall I liken the men of this generation? and to what are they like?*

Liken. Parables interest longer than naked truths.
They are like the money of *another* land, of great *value* by and bye.
The Spirit filled up these outlines, clothed the skeletons in flesh.
They grow with our spiritual growth, and open living fountains in the heart.

The clause *εἶπε δὲ ὁ κύριοσ, and the Lord said*, certainly spurious, *Tischendorf Alford, Meyer, De Wette, Oosterzee.* *γενεᾶσ* not the Jewish race in general, but those *living* then on earth. *ὁμοιοι*—"Write the vision and make it plain upon tables, that he may run that readeth it," Hab. ii. 2, *Trench.*

32. *They are like unto children sitting in the market-place, and calling one to another, and saying, We have piped unto you, and ye have not danced; we have mourned to you, and ye have not wept.*

Children. Jesus had noticed them playing in markets, and had observed them in their *little beds.* Luke xi. 7.
He saw them counterfeiting the *lively* music of the wedding.
He heard them imitating the *plaintive* notes of the funeral.
Sitting, does not refer to the posture, but their idly spending time.
Market. Orientals have places of concourse, but no market-place, crowds gather at the gates, open spaces, in the East.
Piped. Pipes had either one or two tubes, with four or eight holes.
Especially used, to enliven their periodical journeys to Jerusalem.
The humblest family must have two for a funeral.
Danced. Hired females with bell on ancles, and cymbals in hand, dance at wedding.
Mourned, is specially applied to lamenting for the dead.
Children foolishly play, without either earnestness or perseverance.
The Jews pleased with the miracles and eloquence of the Saviour.
But they dreaded the cross, and self-denial, to be encountered.
Preaching the rigors of the law reached its height under John.
Offering the kingdom, from the beginning, the joyful ground of all.
Jews' spiritual leaders, had all the caprice and petulance of children.
Children proverbial for instability, and thoughtless waywardness.
But sinners generally far more wayward towards the Gospel of Christ.
Wept. The *natural* man ever desires something different from the will of God. Luke viii. 53.
Either he wills another *mode*—another *time*, or another *measure.*
Ministers not to fashion their works to men's changeful humors.
Lamented. Would play neither at funerals, nor weddings, with them.

ὁμοιοί παιδίοις. A useless dispute, as to which set of children, our Lord likened the Pharisees, or Sadducees. A vicious practice of straining general illustrations into particular applications. Our Saviour simply teaches, that the wicked are always hard to please. The difficulty is not in that *without*, but the peevishness and petulance *within*, *Alexander*. A Hebrew adage, *Wordsworth*.

---

33. *For John the Baptist came neither eating bread nor drinking wine; and ye say, He hath a devil.*

Eating. Not the quantity, but quality, "locusts and wild honey."
An austere morality, abstaining from contact with sinners.
As a saint, he approached the highest type of Jewish holiness.
Bread. Made of millet, wheat or barley, mixed with beans.

Grinding. Luke xvii. 35. *Fuel*. Luke xii. 28. *Bread leavened*. Luke xiii. 21. See Notes.
Loaf, a span large, and thick as a finger. *Oven*. Luke xii. 28. See Notes.
Three loaves made an ordinary meal for a full grown man.
Baking done by the mistress (Gen. xviii. 6.) or daughters (2. Sam. xiii. 8.)
Ancient Egyptians kneaded dough with feet, Jews with *hands*.
Wine. Luke i. 15. The ordinary table-drink, *then*, and *now*, in the East.
Simply implies, he denies himself comforts everybody shared.
Devil, was under the unconscious influence of a demon.
An enthusiast, fanatic, or spirit-struck mind.
Not a charge of demoniacal assistance, in *pursuing* such a life.
But of demoniacal perverseness, in *adopting* it.
The Bible clearly discriminates between madness and possession. John x. 20.
Gospel *sobriety* ever condemned by the world, as delusion.
God's servants always slandered, need not expect to avoid it.
It is the world's old way to call evil, good, and good, evil. Isa. v. 20.
The teacher is yet to be born, who will please all men.

ἄρτον—Luke xi. 11. The *millet*, *barley*, *wheat*, sometimes eaten before ground into meal; sometimes *parched;* ordinarily but poorly crushed by hand mills, operated by women, Luke xvii. 35; raised by leaven, except that used for the Passover. Beans, lentils, and fitches eaten as bread. οἶνον—Luke i. 15. To render it *intoxicating* it was sometimes drugged, and then became *strong drink*, *Major*.

---

34. *The Son of man is come eating and drinking: and ye say, Behold a gluttonous man, and a winebibber, a friend of publicans and sinners!*

Son of Man. Used with reference to His *Divine* humiliation. Lk. v. 24.
Son of God, refers through his *humanity* to His Godhead. Rom. i. 4.
Is come, in His official character, the promised Messiah.
Eating, the same food as other men, without ascetic singularity.
Free from all the personal peculiarities condemned in John.
He did not despise the innocent pleasures of social life.
The self-righteousness of the age made them a stone of stumbling.
The Word and Spirit hallow a moderate use of blessings.
Behold, in scorn, as if they had surprised Him in some great sin.
Gluttonous. Gr. an *eating man*. **Wine bibber**, used it as everybody else did.
It was not the amount of His food, but His course of life.
He associated in an unrestrained manner with the masses.
Friend. Not merely a well-wisher, but a kind and genial *companion*.

This gave far *more* offence, than all else charged.

Christ a friend of sinners. 1. A base scandal. 2. A holy truth. 3. A high honor. 4. A joyful announcement. 5. A model for imitation.

Publicans. The Jewish tax-gatherers for Rome, universally scorned. Luke iii. 12. See Notes.

Sinners. They little dreamed that this would be His most honorable title.

It sets forth the captious, unreasonable spirit of those censors.

Hypocrites, they pretended to a godly strictness against Christ's *graciousness*.

Free grace, in their opinion, was too liberal a charter to all sinners.

Those having no heart to receive the truth, condemn those who do.

This is too violent, that too lax, this too severe, that too mild.

This too earnest, that too gentle, this too narrow, that too broad.

To such captious minds, the *true* Messiah never comes.

If a wise man contend with a foolish, rage, or laugh, there is no rest. Pro. xxix. 9.

οἰνοπότης—a felicitous translation (wine-bibber) of an Anacreontic term, *Alexander*: boon companion, *Alexander*. ἁμαρτωλῶν, ἁμαρτάνω—*erring from the way or mark*. 1, a sinful man. 2, obnoxious to the consequences.

---

35. *But wisdom is justified of all her children.*

Wisdom, calls fools to come, but few hear and become wise.

Wisdom, of God, in the apparent contradiction of the lives of John and Jesus.

Also in the two great systems which those persons symbolized.

Justified. Vindicated, approved, pronounced right, or praised.

Wisdom crossing the natural feelings of the unrenewed.

Ever finds a deep response in the sanctuary of their heart.

As long as there are children of wisdom, the foolishness of God has nothing to fear. 1. Cor. i. 25.

Diversities of gifts, but the same spirit. 1. Cor. xii. 4.

Pharisees, dare not openly affirm Jesus or John to be false teachers.

Thus now a searching ministry is harsh; if gentle, it is flattering.

If plain, it is weak; if polished, it is affected.

He is too simple; too flowery; too vehement; or too mild.

His dignity, is pride; his humility, meanness.

If retiring, he is indolent; if energetic, he is obtrusive.

Men of Gibeon deceived Joshua, Pharisees deceived *themselves*.

They wanted light, but of the *right color*—a Shiloh that suited them.

They loved darkness, rather than light, because their deeds were evil. John iii. 19.

Wrath could not drive: Love could not draw to Christ.

Such justice *Wisdom* meets at the hands of her *professed* defenders.

ἐδικαιώθη reproved by the Jews, *Elsner*. *Blamed—Luther*. Justified in fact by that foolish generation, *Ewald*. Wisdom had been dishonored by the Jews, but new children would be born to her, *Lange*. Encouragement to persecuted Christians, *Oosterzee*. And so was wisdom justified on the part of (απο) her favored and honored children, *Alexander*. Wisdom shall be absolved from the charges of her children, *Gerlach*, *Meyer*. Wisdom must justify herself against her children, *Nitzsch*. Those enlightened by wisdom, will justify both Jesus and John, *Chrysostom*, *Theophylact*. Wisdom manifested in Jesus, *De Wette*. The wisdom of both these masters, Jesus and John, is justified by all *their* children, *Sepp*. Men may condemn the wisdom of God, yet the children will acknowledge and discriminate the truth, and find that *consolation* in Christ, which is the key-note of that rest, which concludes the discourse, *Stier*. Reproved, *i.e.*, by the Jews who should have been its disciples, *Elsner*. The folly of the Jews really confirmed the choice of Christians, *Ewald*. The wisdom of *God*—in the baptism of John as well as the mission of Christ, *Wordsworth*.

τεκνων—*Publicans*, *Bengel*. *Prophets* and *witnesses*, *Chrysostom*. *Disciples*, *Campbell*. The undertone of *lamentation*, which και connects with the preceding words, confuses commentators, *Stier*.

---

36. ¶ *And one of the Pharisees desired him that he would eat with him. And he went into the Pharisee's house, and sat down to meat.*

Pharisees. Luke v. 17; Luke vi. 2. Character and history. See Notes.

Though there is a great resemblance between this narrative and that recorded in John xii. 3; Matt. xxvi. 6. and Mark xiv. 3., they are not identical.

Yet the name Simon is that of the giver of both feasts.

In both, misrepresentation was made, and an offence was taken.

In both, the Lord was honored by females, in an unusual manner.

Simon doubtless invited the Saviour through mere *curiosity*.

Christ's acceptance shews the social nature of Christianity.

He went. Jesus is always ready, when a *sinner* invites Him.

He went, though not invited in that capacity, *as* the Friend of publicans and sinners.

Sat. Luke v. 29. See Notes. All refined persons had adopted the custom of reclining at meals.

Our Lord readily accepted an invitation from an unfriendly person.

It illustrates our Saviour's self-denial and love.

Especially, He desires not wantonly to repel the Pharisees.

He would shew His disciples the *dark side* of Pharisaism.

He would silence the slanderous reports concerning Himself and His disciples.

Occurred at Nain, the last mentioned town, *Greswell*. At Capernaum, *Robinson*, *Meyer*. Magdala, *Friedlich*. A Romish tradition.

ἀνεκλίθη. κατεκλίθη. Alford. Gr. *lie down.* Our translators would reconcile ancient customs with modern. *Sat down to meat*—without washing or anointing, in order the sooner to receive the *repentant* sinner, *Bengel*.

---

37. *And, behold, a woman in the city, which was a sinner, when she knew that Jesus sat at meat in the Pharisee's house, brought an alabaster box of ointment.*

Behold. Surprise, not at the entrance of a spectator, but at the entrance of one of such a character.

The Author eating at Hebron, spectators crowded in to see.

When Christ appears, law loses its power, and grace bears the sceptre.

Woman. Nameless, neither Mary of Magdala, nor the sister of Lazarus.

She has been supposed to have been a *Gentile convert.*

Her narrative in the Gospel is perpetual history.

"When I consider it" said *Gregory the Great*, "I am more inclined to weep, than to preach on it."

City, unknown. Nain, and Capernaum, last two named.

Sinner. Known as such in the place, in a sinful occupation.

One under conviction, and desirous of amendment.

Penitents dread encountering the mockery of former associates.

Fear the proud contempt of their virtuous acquaintances.

She knew that no one dare thrust her from Christ's presence.

"Who can say, I have made my heart clean, I am free from sin?" Prov. xx. 9.

Knew. She seems to have enquired after her Lord. Song of Sol. iii. 3.

Sat. While guests *reclined*, (not sat) servants washed their feet.

Ancient bas-reliefs shew the *bare feet* of the guests at feasts.

Oriental houses have seats around the wall, of stone, or earth.

Couches, or divans, now very rare in the East, because of deep *poverty*.

Chairs are never seen in the East, among the *natives*.

Distinguished guests were sprinkled, with *perfumes*.

The more *costly* the odor, the greater the honor conferred.

Pharisee. Supposed to have been the landlord, or husband of Mary.

Brought. Oriental chasm between classes *wide*, social barriers *low*.

Love is fearless; *doubting* Nicodemus came by night.

She had reason to believe the Pharisee would not admit her.

However diffident, true faith will avoid denial of Christ.

Alabaster. From Alabastron, a town in Egypt; a compact variety of sulphate of lime, fine texture, usually white.

The alabaster of Damascus, and perfumes of Tarsus in Cilicia, celebrated.

Box. Sometimes made of marble, silver, gold, or onyx stone. Boxes of onyx stone among royal gifts to Cambyses.

Form of *box* or *vase*, like Florence flasks; broken if ointment hard.

Ointment. Gr. *myrrh*, oil scented with any kind of perfume, an aromatic oil distilled from various trees.

Myrrh; a white juice from a thorn tree, resembling the acacia, it is collected during July and August, valued by the ancients.

Obtained in Persia and India, but chiefly the produce of Arabia.

"All thy garments smell of myrrh. My hands dropped sweet smelling myrrh." Psalm xlv. 8. Song of Sol. v. 5.

γυνὴ. The same transaction related with different aspects, Matt. xxvi. 6-13. *Grotius*, *Schleiermacher*, *Weisse*, *Ewald*. Different in time, place, actor, and circumstances, *Meyer*, *Lange*, *Ellicott*, *Hammond*. *Elsley*. Different from that, John xii. 1, *Origen*, *Euthym.*, *Osiander*, *Lightfoot*, *Meyer*, *De Wette*. A narrative not found in any other Evangelist. *Augustine* has a sermon on the subject, and does not connect her with any other person. *Chrysostom* supposes that there were *two* different women that anointed Christ. *Origen*, *Theophylact*, and *Euthymius* that there were *three*. Certain there were *two* at least, this woman and Mary of Bethany. Luke conceals the name of this woman through delicacy and tenderness towards her, *Wordsworth*. The Greek fathers distinguished her from Mary Magdalene. The *Latins* identified them from the time of Gregory the Great, until the Reformation. In the 12 cent. the memorable *Dies Iræ* endorsed the error.

"Qui Mariam absolvisti
Mihi quoque spem dedisti."

The strongest argument in favour of their *identity* is, that Luke does not mention at all the anointing by Lazarus' sister, if he does not here. But John omits all mention of the institution of the Lord's Supper, and neither Matthew nor Mark alludes to the raising of Lazarus. *Magdalene*, a local name, has been thus made descriptive of repentant harlots, an assumption perfectly *gratuitous*, and possibly *calumnious* of this devoted Christian, *Alexander*, *Brown*. Same as Mary Magdalene, and Magdala same as Bethany, and twice anointed Him, *Lightfoot*, *Baronius*, *Oosterzee*: contrary, *Winer*, *Meyer*. ἥτισ ἦν. Her repentance and reform had taken place some time previous, *Grotius*. The turning moment of her life, the hour of a convert's first love, *Augustine*. ἁμαρτωλὸσ a Gentile—*Hammond*; a *fornicatress*, *Wetstein*. No classical authority, for rendering this word "*harlot*," *Bloomfield*. *A woman which was in the city, a sinner:* the proper order, *Alford:* the sentence bracketed by *Tisch*. *A sinner in the city*, *i.e.*, *publicly*, *Meyer*. Her *repentance* was as *public* as her *sin*, *Wordsworth*. Guilty of unchastity, the worst sin of woman, *Bengel*. A *Gentile*—a mere *political* term, used contemptuously by the Jews, of the *heathen* world at large. Matt. ix. 10; xviii. 17-20; xix. 26-45. Gal. ii. 15, *Wakefield*. A female abroad with uncovered head, or with arms bare, or seen spinning in the streets, with flowers on her eyes or cheeks; esteemed a sinner, *Lightfoot*. ἀλάβαστρον—Gypsum, forms our now well-known mantle ornaments, and perfume boxes. μύρου—myrrh. If it were mingled with the fluids of our system, man would be immortal, *Von Helmont*.

38. *And stood at his feet behind* him *weeping, and began to wash his feet with tears, and did wipe* them *with the hairs of her head, and kissed his feet, and anointed* them *with the ointment.*

Stood. Having pressed forward, she hesitates, adores, and weeps.
Behind. Her unostentatious modesty, in paying her debt of love.
Weeping. Tears are *words*, well understood by all nations. Lk. vi. 21.
Augustine calls them the "the flood of her heart." They fell on Jesus' feet.
The eye translates the feelings of the soul, joyful, or sad.
What more could her breaking heart give to her Redeemer?
Wash. Gr. *bedew* or *bathe*, *sandals* protect from bruises, but not from the dust.
Feet. Intending *ordinary* respect, she would have anointed His *head.*
By giving His foot to be kissed, He received *divine honors.*
He well knew, that in this way the Greeks and Roman honored deities.
Thus the Pope continually and *knowingly* receives *divine* homage.
Tears. Implied with Orientals, not grief, but earnest supplication.
Wipe. Girded with towels, servants dried the washed feet. John xiii. 5.
"Let thy handmaid be as a servant to wash thy feet." 1. Sam. xxv. 41.
Hairs. Gr. *unbound tresses.* "They are the glory of a woman." 1. Cor. xi. 15.
Had she expected the honor, a napkin would have been brought.
This natural veil, has ever been woman's chief ornament. Luke xii. 7. See Notes.
With Nazarenes, long hair the symbol of religious consecration to God.
At marriage, Greek females dedicated their cut hair to the gods.
Hair of an Oriental female flowing loosely, a sign of *mourning.*
At death, a lock cut by friends, implied *submission* to their doom.
A sign with Jews of a slave becoming his buyer's property.
Females, forbad disheveling their hair like heathen priestesses.
Priests officiating in the Temple shaved their hair.
Hair was the instrument of pride to females. Ezek. xvi. 39.
With gum, they imitated coronets, harps, wreaths, diadems.
Some wore many braids hung with gold and pearls, reaching to the floor.
Kissed. The Greek shews the accurate expression of minute distinction, kissed *tenderly*, and repeatedly; having touched them, she must kiss them.
Orientals a taciturn people, speak much by actions.
Kissing Christ's feet a token of subjection and obedience. Psa. ii. 12.
This touch of a sinner was an *abomination* to the Pharisees.
Unconstrained by holy love, it would have been *presumption.*

Much love springs from a sense of much forgiveness.
"Let *us* therefore come *boldly* unto the throne of grace!" Heb. iv. 16.
Absorbed in adoring gratitude, she thinks of no one around her.
In mercy, He does not interrupt these golden moments of the penitent.
Anointed. She owns Him as the *True Messiah*—the *Anointed One.*
Anointing, an Oriental custom believed conducive to health.
Priests and kings were consecrated to their offices by anointing.
Egyptians, Greeks, and Jews, thus welcomed guests to their houses.
Persons leaving home for a banquet, anointed themselves.

βρέχειν—*to water with a shower of tears, Meyer* and *Doddridge.* Her homage traced to a bodily cure, *Oosterzee.*

θριξι. Ital. *treccia.* Fr. *tresse.* Eng. *tress*, disheveled, as in mourning. Most exquisite reverence, *Bengel. Cæsar* ordered *Gauls* to cut their hair in token of submission. *Achilles* buried his hair in the tomb of *Patroclus* his friend. *Virgil* represents Iris as sent in pity by Juno to release the dying Queen Dido from her agony. Proserpine not having cropped her hair, she could not die. Iris having descended from heaven, says: "Hunc ego Diti sacrum jussa fero, teque isto corpore solvo." "I, commanded, bear away this (hair), sacred to Pluto, and loose thee from that body."

κατεφίλει. to kiss affectionately, or with *earnest gesture.* Kissing Rabbi's feet, special favour, *Wetstein.* Kissing the hand, adoration, Job xxxi. 27. Kissing princes, a token of homage. 1. Sam. x. 1. Kissing the dust, bitter humiliation. Psa. lxxii. 9. Kissing, among all nations, a symbol of peace and affection, Gen. xxvii., 26, xxix., 13. Luke xv., 20. Acts xx. 37.

---

39. *Now when the Pharisee which had bidden him saw* it, *he spake within himself, saying, This man, if he were a prophet, would have known who and what manner of woman* this is *that touched him; for she is a sinner.*

Pharisee. The true spirit of that self-righteous and heartless sect showed itself.
He was displeased that Jesus did not repel her homage, as she was a sinner.
His holiness consisted in external purifications. Religion, a thing of forms to him.
One, impenitent himself, cannot know how penitents feel and act.
Spake within. "Stand by thyself, come not nearer; I am holier than thou." Isa. lxv. 5.
He little knew how Christ was searching and reading his every thought.
This Man. Censorious persons believe that others must be like themselves.
It might have been supposed that all would have been pleased at her penitence.

If. All attempts to impose on the Divine searcher of hearts, vain. Psa. cxxxix. 1-2.

Prophet. The Jews held that "*discerning spirits*" was a sign of a *true* prophet. 1. Cor. xii. 10.

Nathanael broke forth in wonder, "Whence knowest thou me?" Jo. i. 48.

The woman of Samaria, "Come see a man who told me all things which ever I did." John iv. 29.

The Pharisee's thoughts put our Lord in one of two dilemmas.

Either He lacks the *discernment*, or the *holiness* of all *true* prophets.

Perhaps Simon repented his too hasty hospitality to Christ.

If he doubted before, he now seems to have denied that Christ was a true prophet.

Toucheth. He assumed a *false* axiom of the Pharisees, *i.e.* a *holy* man must not touch a sinner. The patient, of all persons, needs the touch of the physician.

How cold and hard his heart! "Touch" is all he has for her tears and kisses.

Many persons press to him by profession. How few *touch* him by faith!

Sinner. Spiritual pride cannot conceive the love, God shews to penitent sinners. *See this in the conduct of the elder brother.* Luke xv.

Simon did not see through his guest, but Christ saw through him.

He stigmatizes her a *sinner*. Alas! Simon himself was a *greater* sinner.

Jesus would not have been at *his* table, had *he* not been a sinner.

If not a *penitent*, she would not have sought her Redeemer.

Simon had yet to learn, what penitence and redemption meant.

Jesus knew Simon's *proud* heart, and her *believing* spirit.

It is to be hoped the parable flashed conviction on his mind.

If this man were a prophet He would have known that she is unclean; and knowing that He would not have suffered Himself to be polluted by her touch, *Augustine.* If thou hadst known that poor woman's heart, Simon, thou wouldst have judged differently, *Bengel.*

Christ refutes the supposition of Simon, and proves Himself more than a Prophet; and that He *did* know who and what manner of person the woman was, by reading Simon's heart, and by replying to his thoughts, and by forgiving the woman's sins, *Wordsworth.* ἐν ἑαυτῳ, gave vent to feelings by looks and gestures, &c., *Oosterzee.* Contrary to the letter of the text. ἅπτεται, some Rabbis highly extolled for keeping lepers at the legal distance by stoning them! *Lightfoot*

---

40. *And Jesus answering said unto him, Simon, I have somewhat to say unto thee. And he saith, Master, say on.*

Answering. Our Lord *answers* unuttered soul thoughts.

Simon, he must have felt that *Hand* pressing on his heart-strings.

He felt as *we* will, when under His eye, at judgment.
Mark the steps, from the heights of self-complacency, to conviction.
1. Christ sits at Simon's table. 2. He casts a look into his heart.
3. He proves his want of love. 4. He puts him to shame.

I have, &c. a courteous way of asking permission to speak.
He veils His rebuke under the well known form of a parable.

Somewhat. The Lord has somewhat to say to *every* Simon.
Christ's conversation at table tried by apostolic rules. Col. iv. 6.
The kindest entertainment, can never excuse neglect of duty.
"Thou shalt in no wise suffer *sin* upon thy brother." Lev. xix. 17.

Master say on. Simon had some modesty, if but little faith in Christ's high character.
He little suspected, his *proud self-righteous* heart was so soon to be revealed.

He *heard* the Pharisee's *thoughts, Augustine.* σοι, *to thee.* Emphatic—to *thee*, who hast harbored injurious thoughts of Me, I have something to say, *Wordsworth.* How tenderly our Lord brings home the truth! *Jacobus*

---

41. *There was a certain creditor which had two debtors: the one owed five hundred pence, and the other fifty.*

Debtors. Sinners differ in *degree*, but all *insolvent.*
All have sinned and come short of the glory of God. Rom. iii. 23.
Christ is the great *creditor*, who alone can absolve us.
Sinners are debtors to God, for a life of sinless obedience.
All having failed, we owe him a debt of punishment. Matt. v. 26.
"Thou shalt not go hence until thou hast paid the uttermost farthing."
Some are more heavily in debt to Heaven, than others.
"He that delivered me to you, hath the *greater* sin. John xix. 11.

Five hundred. An exact creditor, God knows precisely what each owes.

Simon and the woman both debtors and bankrupts. Our Lord puts the case in the gentlest terms, to convict Simon of being *without forgiveness*, because *without love*, *Jacobus.* δανειστῃ. Simon also had received a miraculous cure, *Paulus, Kuinoel.*

---

42. *And when they had nothing to pay, he frankly forgave them both. Tell me therefore, which of them will love him most?*

Nothing. Debtors brought to God. They never come of themselves.
How did the debtors discover their *inability* to pay? John xvi. 8.
This implies a *sense*, and a *confession* of helplessness.
Knowing this inability, sinners are *treasuring* up wrath, &c. Rom. ii. 5.

For peace of conscience many *sell* their hopes for eternity.
Instead of diminishing, men willingly increase the debt.
Impossibility of meeting this debt, urges us to our *surety*.

ἀποδοῦναι—1, to deliver up. 2, to render account. 3, to give in full, *i. e.* wages or debts. If men cannot pay 100 pence (representing our sins against man), how can we pay 10,000 talents (symbol of our sins against God)? ἐχαρίσατο from χάρισ *grace.* God forgives by *grace*, not *merit.* πλεῖον. Though the profligate's love may be intense of its kind; yet that kind is not so *high*, nor so *complete*, as the sacrifice of the whole life, the bud, the blossom, and fruit, *Alford.*

---

43. *Simon answered and said, I suppose that* he, *to whom he forgave most. And he said unto him, Thou hast rightly judged.*

Answered, properly, but he knew not that he condemned himself.
Our Lord shews the proud Pharisee his own deep necessities.
Simon invites through *curiosity*. Christ accepts for *salvation*.
He shields the poor penitent from censure poured upon her.
A Rabbi at a feast, had the right of uttering a parable.*
Rightly. Christ's wisdom, makes the accuser witness against himself.
He kindly treats him in not expressly blaming him.
He seriously intimates to Simon, that *his* sins are *unforgiven*.
Judged. He appeals directly to his *conscience*, as to the truth.
"Why even of yourselves, judge ye not what is right?" Luke xii. 57.
God has placed His representative in every bosom. John i. 9. Rom. ii. 15.

ὑπολαμβάνω—*I suppose, apprehend, take up an idea, Stier.* το πλεῖον, *the most; the* greater sum of the two. There is a contrast between the two *sums* as well as the two *debtors, Wordsworth.* ὀρθῶσ—holy irony, a weapon turned against him, *Oosterzee.* He had condemned himself as *the* one who loved little, or none, *Jacobus.*

---

44. *And he turned to the woman, and said unto Simon, Seest thou this woman? I entered into thine house, thou gavest me no water for my feet; but she hath washed my feet with tears, and wiped* them *with the hairs of her head.*

Turned, to the *woman*, but really was speaking to *Simon*.
A look of *mercy* to the penitent, and of *rebuke* to the Pharisee.
Seest thou? He would say, "Look on this woman, thou hast not seen her yet."
Jesus brings the despised penitent, in *contact* with our sympathies.
Contrasted with Simon's pride, she was no longer a great sinner.
A sight of a broken heart, should humble a proud professor.
She was a sinner, and yet a saint; a mourner, and yet happy; a despised one, and yet crowned with everlasting life.

Woman. Simon soon saw this great sinner, a great lover of Christ, therefore a great saint.

Himself, a proud and cold-hearted *egotist*, compared with her.

I entered. He speaks publicly of marks of respect, culpably withheld.

Thou gavest. Some read, Didst thou give ?—*i.e.*, What was my due?

No water. This time-honored usage, Simon had neglected.

If *accidental*, our Lord would not have reproached him.

Her tenderness, contrasts with his selfishness and coldness.

My feet. The custom still prevails in parts of the East.

Tears. Thou shouldst have *thanked* her for doing what thou hast neglected.

Simon avoided seeming *too intimate* a friend, therefore he did not kiss his guest. Worldly prudence waiting for Christ's success.

The *obtrusiveness* of her love, not censured by the Redeemer.

He was *humble* in His majesty, and *majestic* in His humility.

We see the poverty of an unloving, the riches of a loving heart.

In the presence of the compassienate Saviour, her broken heart poured forth its penitence and love in floods of tears.

Repentance never complete, till we feel the tenderness of that love that pardoneth and upbraideth not. James i. 5.

Hairs. Gr. *unbound tresses.* Members devoted to sin, become instruments of righteousness. Rom. vi. 19.

εἰσῆλθόν—*Tischendorf*, *Griesbach*. *ὕδωρ*—some extenuate the neglect, since the Lord had not come from a long journey, *Meyer*. *δάκρυσιν*—no water so costly as tears, *Bengel*. *τησ κεφαλησ*, *head;* omitted by *Tischendorf*, *Alford*. If not deficient in common courtesy, he had at least taken no pains for his guest. She so *loving*, and he so *cold*, founded in the difference of heart, *Jacobus*.

σου is emphatic. I came into thy house, and therefore might justly expect marks of hospitable courtesy from *thee;* and what *thou*, my *host*, didst not do for Me, *she*, a stranger, whom thou condemnest as a sinner, has more than supplied, *Wordsworth*.

---

45. *Thou gavest me no kiss: but this woman since the time I came in hath not ceased to kiss my feet.*

No kiss. Simon loving but little, failed to shew it in *little* things.

Life not made up of great trials, or illustrious triumphs.

Small favors ever repeated, "*Whatsoever things are lovely*," &c.

The despised one had far exceeded the Pharisee in *boasted* courtesy.

Pharisees and Rome put the rill before the spring. Faith the *fount*.

Faith without *works* of love, a fire without *heat*. James ii. 17.

A sun without beams. It is no *faith*, but reprobate *faithlessness*.

Kiss. Gr. *fondly kissing*. Males *salute* in the East.

Laban kissed Jacob, Ephesian elders kissed Paul. Acts xx. 37.
Cold worshippers give half reverence; "Having the form of godliness, but denying the power." 2. Tim. iii. 5.
They profess Christ, in public; but carefully avoid any *suspicion* of particular love for Him. Laodicean indifference.

καταφιλουσα. Kissing again and again, *Meyer*. An intensive form of the verb φιλέω to love, or show one's love by a kiss; hence to kiss, Matt. xxvi. 48.

---

46. *My head with oil thou didst not anoint: but this woman hath anointed my feet with ointment.*

Oil. Luke x. 34. Common *olive* oil, used by males, without perfume.
Myrrh formed part of the *holy oil*. Ex. xxx., rare and costly.
Guests at festivals were anointed with perfumed oils. Ps. cxli. 5.
"Thou anointest my head with oil, my cup runneth over." Ps. xxiii. 5.
Daughters washed their father's feet, and anointed them.
This custom omitted, implied one mourning a calamity.
The dwellers of Yemen believe it strengthens the body.
Gently He chides Simon, for condemning her great love.
Not a word of his *sin* in harshly judging the penitent.
Anoint. He gave no evidence of *gratitude*, forgiveness prompts.
Ointment. Oil perfumed with various aromatic spices.
The most precious, not too costly for the Lord.
Economy out of place, when God's honor is involved.

ἐλαίῳ—The simple oil, μύρῳ—that oil perfumed with aromatics. The former σμύρνα a *gum*. The latter from the olive tree. μύρω *unguent*. More costly than ἔλαιον *oil*. There is a contrast between the head and the feet; between oil and ointment; between Simon and the woman; between what was not done by the one, and what was done by the other, *Wordsworth*.

---

47. *Wherefore I say unto thee, Her sins, which are many, are forgiven: for she loved much: but to whom little is forgiven,* the same *loveth little.*

Wherefore. Sovereign grace the cause of her faith, faith led to forgiveness.
Her forgiveness the cause of her love, all traced to God.
The debt is not released, because the debtor loves the creditor.
The debtor loves, because his debt is forgiven him.
Many. Spoken in her presence, although not addressed *to her*.
Great sin, great repentance; great faith, great love.
Those forgiven the largest sum, have the most reason for gratitude.
Sinners of the deepest dye, *owe most* to Christ's cleansing blood.

Her sense of the *emptiness* of the creature, led her to Christ's *fulness*.
Life apart from God, is not life, but *death*. Rom. viii. 6.
Simon's faithless communion with Christ, awakened no reverence.
He who comes with most faith, bears away the greatest blessing.
It does not follow from this, we should continue in sin, that grace may abound. This is turning the grace of God into lasciviousness.
Those doing evil, that good may come; have a fearful doom. Rom. iii. 8.
From the gulf of *presumptuous* sin, but few ever escape. Psa. xix. 13.
Not her great *sin*, but her great *love*, our Lord approves.
Fifty pence would as certainly have sent the debtor to prison, as 1000 talents.
The escape of the one, as truly a cause of gratitude, as the other.
None of our fallen race can say, "I am forgiven little," "Whosoever offendeth in one point, is guilty of all." James ii. 10.
Not *great guilt*, but great *penitence*, makes us thankful. Psa. li. 15.
We cannot anoint *Jesus*, we can befriend His *saints*. Matt. xxv. 40.
We can shew our deep love to His gospel, kingdom, and people.
She intensely desired to know, that she was herself beloved of Him.

Forgiven. No longer *reproached* for sin, the weight is taken from her heart. Isa. xii. 1-6.

For. Gr. *inasmuch as;* the *forgiveness* of her sins unthought of by Simon, is proved by its *fruit*.

Loved much. Her love not the *cause*, but the *proof* of her forgiveness.
Her grateful love abundantly shewn, unjustly blamed, powerfully defended, blessed a thousand-fold.

Little. He who *thinks* he has but little sin *needing* forgiveness.
A sense of sin, not *measured* by the guilt others know of.
Our Lord's answer shews, He knew their thoughts and characters.

ὅτι *inasmuch as*, or *seeing that*. As a proof, not the procuring cause, *Neander*. *Since, for*, *Vulg*, *Beza*, *Grotius*, *De Wette*. Romanists explain it *therefore*, *Markland*, *Mede*, *Campbell*, *&c.* Like Simon, Romish faith is full of the leaven of *self-righteousness*. They who make her love, the procuring cause of the pardon, *reverse* the parable. Her sins are forgiven her (she knows this) and therefore she loves much. Gratitude brings her to Jesus, and she shews her strength of faith, by her love. She receives assurance of forgiveness not of *debt*, but of *grace*, *Oosterzee*. The object to show, not that any are forgiven *on account of their love*, as the meritorious ground; but that a sense of forgiveness is the foundation principle of love, *Jacobus*. Love, a *criterion* of forgiveness, *Bengel*. "*Little*." Simon having little or no faith, had little or no share in Christ's forgiveness, *Oosterzee*. *Receptive love*, as the *root* of her innermost life, in order to her being able to love, *Olshausen*. "The sun is risen, *because* it is broad day," *Braune*. Some writers disfigure the beautiful simplicity of the record, in the very spirit of Simon, *Stier*. "This is the great *paradox*, grace, out of the greatest guilt, can prepare for itself the greatest glory," *Roos.* ἠγάπησε Aorist.—Not, *she has loved*, and that her love is now *past*, but that she is *constantly living in love*. Rome infers the dependence of forgiveness, upon *merit*. For they understand "*loved*," of *active benevolence, Stier*. We are now beyond any polemical opposition to the Romish doctrine of justification by works, *De Wette*. It is still the natural resort of every impenitent heart. Our Saviour and this woman had met before, when her sins had been forgiven, *Lightfoot*. She owed *much;* but she *owns* that she owes much, and comes to Christ in faith, *Wordsworth*.

---

48. *And he said unto her, Thy sins are forgiven.*

Her. Jesus turns from Simon, and directly addresses the woman at His feet. The Divine Saviour speaks to the penitent sinner.
Having alone the power to pronounce *absolution*, He silences her fears.
All ought to strive after an *assurance*, but *few* attain it.
The clearer our evidence of assurance, the more deeply do we repent.
Ordinary boasted *assurance* affords but poor *evidence* of true faith.
How well paid for all her cost and tears, to hear those blessed words!
How *little* we love, considering how *much* we are forgiven!
None are hopeless. "Though your sins be as scarlet, they shall," &c. Isa. i. 18. The blood of Christ cleanseth from all sin. 1. John i. 7.
"Your sins and iniquities, will I remember no more." Heb. viii. 12.
Those who tempted you, will ever upbraid your efforts to believe.
So far from rejecting any, Jesus receives all returning penitents. Psa. lxviii. 13. Him that cometh unto me, &c. John vi. 37.
None need despair, while our Lord's record remains.
Forgiven. The happiness of the heart, reaching Jesus' feet.
Here at Jesus' *feet*, *there* on Jesus' *bosom*. John xiii. 23.
An absolved conscience, cares not for the judgments of earth.
She received an unsought assurance from God, of what she so deeply longed for. Divine Love anticipated her prayer.

The greatest sinners often become the greatest saints; even at the table our Lord exercised the power of the Keys, *Bengel*. Christ does not say "thy *many* sins," for His love can make the few or many clean, *Jacobus*. A *declaration* of pardon, already *anticipated* by faith, *Wordsworth*.

---

49. *And they that sat at meat with him began to say within themselves, Who is this that forgiveth sins also?*

Who is this? We need not wonder at this question.
Jesus sat on the same couch, shared the same hospitalities.
Now He assumed Jehovah's sole prerogative of forgiving sins.
Had He not been God, assuming this Divine act were blasphemy.
She did not come for an *assurance*, but God who is rich in mercy, gives beyond what we ask or hope for. He gives as GOD!

Insinuations against our Lord's character, did not move Him.
He firmly stood to what He said, and *reaffirmed her forgiveness.*
The question arises, How was one forgiven, and the other not?
The woman repented, but the Pharisee did not. This the answer.
We still ask, "Why did she repent and Simon remain in unbelief?"
"By *grace* are ye saved, through faith, and that *not* of yourselves, it is the gift of God." Eph. ii. 5.

"*Forgiveth.*" A youth, whose heart was black with sin, appeared before the cell of a dervish (a monk celebrated for his sanctity). He began to lament the depth of his sin, and imploring pardon. The proud monk indignantly demanded, how he presumed to appear in the presence of God's holy prophet? assuring him that it was in vain to seek forgiveness: adding, "My God grant that I may stand *far from this youth* on the *judgment* day." On this, Jesus spoke.—"It shall be so. The prayer of both is granted; this sinner, a penitent, shall then enter Paradise. But the monk's prayer is also granted; he shall be *far* from the youth in that day, even in torment." A *Persian* parable, *Tholuck* from *Saadi: Trench.* No *man* can forgive sins; but Christ, being GOD, forgives sins by those means He has instituted for that purpose, *Augustine* in *Wordsworth.* To forgive sins is a far greater thing than to heal the sick miraculously, *Bengel.*

---

50. *And he said to the woman, Thy faith hath saved thee; go in peace.*

Faith. Our Lord now first alludes to *faith*, the intermediate *link* of forgiveness. This is the key to her conduct—*Her Faith.*
Faith endorsed as the *instrument* by which the soul comes to Christ.
"By whom we have access by faith, into this grace, wherein we stand," *i. e.* Jesus Christ .Romans v. 2.
Love, the expression and proof to men, of the grace divinely given.
Allusion is made to the faith existing, before she saw Jesus.
The sealing assurance, differs from her first forgiveness.
Simon is taught that *he* must believe, to enjoy peace.
"Where sin abounded, grace did much more abound." Rom. v. 20.
Go in peace. A worthy climax to what preceded.
No going in peace without faith, no faith, without going in peace.
In peace. Gr. *into peace*, the abiding enjoyment of peace.
This points her to a new life of obedience. She must not remain at His feet.
She might have forgotten her home. He sends her forth to life's duties.
Observe the four steps in Christ's revealing Himself to this penitent believing sinner:—

1. Silently He accepted her coming. He knew her heart.
2. The light of His countenance He turned to her, and encouraged her.
3. He spoke to her, especially His assuring word of forgiveness.
4. He sent her away in the peace of faith and Divine love, *Jacobus.*

εἰς εἰρήνην—εἰς denotes a marked *transition* in the state of her feelings, a change from misery and wretchedness, to happiness and joy, *Stier.*

General Remarks.

John's message, and this repast took place in Galilee, just before the second passover, *Oosterzee.* The *woman* differs from that of Matt., Mark, and John. The host, in this case, an enemy, in the other, a friend; one anoints for love, other for burial; Jesus blamed by Pharisee in one, by disciples or disciple in the other; pride objects in one case, selfishness in the other; in one a sinner is pardoned, in the other a disciple honored. A vain tradition bestows the name of the earlier host on this, *Trench, Oosterzee, Lange, Kuinoel, Olshausen.* The Gentile world might see a beautiful picture of itself in this Woman that was a sinner, and despised by Simon the Pharisee, but blessed on her repentance by Christ; and might thus be taught to love much, and to present those members of the body, and faculties of the soul and estate, represented by her hair, her tears, and her ointment, which had before been abused to the service of sin and Satan, as living sacrifices to Christ, *Wordsworth* in loco.

CHAPTER VIII.

AND it came to pass afterward, that he went throughout every city and village, preaching and shewing the glad tidings of the kingdom of God: and the twelve were with him.

Village. We can see Him clad in a seamless garment: the gift of love, His feet bound with sandals.

His disciples about Him, without money, shoes, staff or scrip.

A bottle of oil, suspended from their shoulders. Mark vi. 13.

A band of females, veiled, caring tenderly for their wants.

With Jesus as their centre, moving from village to village.

Preaching. Gr. *heralding*, and *announcing glad tidings;* tidings that *all is well.* Luke viii. 1, ix. 2.

Neither Christ, nor His Apostles *preached*, as the word is now understood.

He doubtless conversed in familiar dialogue, and used familiar illustrations. Explained spiritual truth by analogies in nature.

"I must preach (announce the glad tidings) to other cities." Luke iv. 43. He came to seek and to save the lost.

Novelty of preaching has passed away; *value* of the inheritance remains.

Kingdom. The Christian Dispensation: spiritual reign of the Messiah.

Jews gave the prophecies a *temporal* meaning, thus they explained Dan. ii. 44; vii. 14-27; ix. 25.

They looked for the Messiah to restore the ancient religion.

Reform morals, make expiation, and free them from Roman yoke.

His actual kingdom in its *internal form*, is in the hearts of Christians.

Its *external* form embodied in the visible church of Christ. Matt. xxv. 1.

Twelve, as witnesses and teachers. Happy and honored servants of our Lord!

No one elected to succeed Judas, unless he had seen Christ. Acts i. 22.

"*Went.*" Circuit lasted a day or two, *Ellicott;* much longer period, *Andrews.* Each Evangelist records those journeys which suit his purpose in writing, *Bengel.* Second circuit in Galilee, *Jacobus.*

κηρύσσων—The *κηρύξ* a *herald, common crier*, answers to Lat. *caduceator.* He held in his hand a *caduceus*, a *white wand*, or *staff:* originally an olive branch. In times of war, it was the symbol of peace, and the bearer was held sacred. *Fabius* sent from Rome to the Carthaginians, a herald with a white *staff*, and a *spear*, offering them peace or war. From the heroic times their office was sacred, and their persons inviolable, as being under the immediate protection of Zeus, and they were Θεῖοι, Διΐ φίλοι, *Lidd. and Scott.*

κηρύσσων—not moral, or doctrinal instructions. εὐαγγελιζόμενος. Luke iv. 18, *Campbell.* βασιλείαν. In its typical form it existed under the O. T. Theocracy, *Lange.* Kingdom of Heaven, Dan. vii. 27, of Christ, and of God, all the same, *Major.*

---

2. *And certain women, which had been healed of evil spirits and infirmities, Mary called Magdalene, out of whom went seven devils.*

Women. Some of possessions, of diseases, and above all of *sin.*
Spirits. Malignant demons tormented them, but obeyed our Lord.
Infirmities. Luke, a physician, discriminates between possessions and diseases.
Mary. Tradition has unjustly identified her, with the nameless sinner. Luke vii. 37. See Notes.
This assumption is gratuitous, and possibly *calumnious* of her.
In social position, she was *above* the wife of Herod's steward.
Being generally named first by the Evangelists.
Magdalene. Magdala, of Galilee, beyond the Jordan.
This name, Rome falsely makes descriptive of repentant harlots, some Protestants perpetuate the error.
Seven. This number associated with the idea of *completeness.*
Seven abominations in his heart, *i. e.* complete depravity. Prov. xxvi. 25
Seven was a sacred number among *Greeks*, *Romans*, Persians.
An incidental proof of the inspiration of Moses. Gen. ii. 3.
Last at the Cross, Jesus chose Mary *first witness* of His Resurrection.
Thomas doubted, but *her* faith is held in everlasting remembrance.
From her case the most afflicted are encouraged, not to despair of relief.
The vilest are taught to believe, and hope for mercy.
Gratitude binds such to cling faithfully to their benefactors.
Those born again "follow the Lamb whithersoever He goeth." Rev. xiv. 4
"Were there not *ten* cleansed, but where are the *nine?*" Luke xvii. 17.

πονηρῶν—Luke xi. 4. Μαγδαληνή—From Magdala, an unfortunate notoriety. Others identify it with Bethany. Gomarists speak of Maria Magdila, daughter of a plaiter of women's hair, and an adulteress, *Lightfoot.* The Greek Church as steadily opposed the tradition, as the Romish Church fostered it. We have no right to exalt the compassion and Almighty grace of Christ by *assuming* a degree of degradation, which never existed. Being honored above Apostles at the tomb, we hesitate to receive this malicious tradition, endorsed, if not originated by Rome, *Alexander:* Luke vii. 37. δαιμόνια ἑπτα—The number *seven*, traceable to the Sabbath, *sacred* among many nations. Balaam built 7 altars, and offered 7 bullocks. Pharaoh's dream, 7 years, 7 ears, &c. Jericho surrounded 7 days. Job had 7 sons, and his friends sat 7 days. 7

years in the sabbatical year; 7 lamps, 7 viols, 7 trumpets, 7 spirits, before the Throne. Greek and Latin poets allude to it. Cicero calls it "The knot and cement of all things above and below." While Mary was under malignant demons, it no more follows that the person was unusually *dissolute*, than *insanity* proves an individual to be pre-eminently *depraved*, *Alexander*. Not the worst, but most unfortunate of our race, *Trench*. Jesus called vices, devils, *Lightfoot*.

---

3. *And Joanna the wife of Chuza Herod's steward, and Susanna, and many others. which ministered unto him of their substance.*

Joanna. Heb. *The gift of the Lord.* A witness of the Resurrection. Luke xxiv. 10.

The wife. Here, in the noblest sense, woman's emancipation is begun.

Women in Christ, no longer the slaves of men, but fellow-heirs of the grace of life. 1. Peter iii. 7.

Chuza. Probably an Edomite. See Haman's Genealogy.

Steward. Lieutenant, Treasurer, Procurator, or Guardian of Herod.

" Not many wise men after the flesh, not mighty, not noble." 1. Cor. i. 26.

But Joseph, David, Daniel, Naaman, Josiah, and saints of Cæsar's household, among the few noble *named*, or *noted* in the Scriptures.

Earth's honors or pleasures not promised to believers.

One is missed, and mourned for, by a circle of loved ones.

But even the tears, and eyes which shed them, are soon forgotten.

Their's a sad state, with no hope of immortality.

Portionless here, saints are had in everlasting remembrance. Psa. cxii. 6. The memory of the just is blessed.

Many others. The first Christian sisterhood in a work of love.

1. Their motive pure. 2. Operation powerful. 3. Fruit abundant. 4. Endurance steadfast.

Service to the poor, service to the Lord. Prov. xix. 17.

Among the women of Gospel History, not an enemy to our Lord is found.

Ministered. Gr. *supplied* Him with food, as angels gladly did. Mark i. 13.

In deep poverty, He *needed*, in deeper humility, *accepted* charity.

Females have ever been honored for their sympathies for the distressed.

Mungo Park, speaks the praises of Africa's degraded females.

Fainting from fever, he was refreshed with food and song—

" He hath no mother to make him bread, no wife to grind him corn."

In Redemption's history, we have Sarah's faith, Ruth's devotion, Abigail's humility.

Shunammite's hospitality, Esther's patriotism, penitence of her anointing Christ.

Canaanite's importunity, Mary of Bethany's love, Lydia's confidence.
Dorcas' benevolence, Phœbe's kindness, Priscilla's courage.
Tryphena, and Tryphosa's diligence, and Persis' affection—HONOURED OF GOD.
Some might turn from Mary, on account of the past.
At Christ's resurrection, she ranks *above* kings or apostles.
Many doubtless thought their charities bestowed in a silly manner.
He who was their spiritual Bread, disdained not their meat.
He fed others by miracle,—He lived on the love of His people.
Feeding thousands with a word, He lived on the bread of the poor.
Such a life must have been *lived*, to have been *recorded*.
Christ's indwelling Divinity, clothes itself in a human garb.
His glory strictly internal, only *seen*, when blessing others.
"He who was rich, yet for our sakes, became poor." 2. Cor. viii. 9.
Ministered, though He came *not* to be ministered unto. Matt. xx. 28.
Substance. The consecration of wealth to God's cause, our *duty*.

Chusa. This name occurs in the genealogy of Haman, Chusa and Herod were both Edomites, *Lightfoot.* He might have been a secret friend, like some of Nero's household, Phil. iv. 22, *Elsley.* ἐπιτρόπου—guardian, steward, Sax, *stew*, work *ward*, a guardian, *Bloomfield.* 'Ηρώδου Luke iii. 1. Σουσάννα—Shusan, susa, Heb. *Lily.* αυτω—Many MSS. and Editors have αὐτοῖσ, interpreted—*The ministering was to all the company, Oosterzee, Tischendorf, Alford.* αυτω *to Him, i.e.*, Jesus, preferred, *Wordsworth.* ὑπαρχόντων—of *their private* property. Our Lord left Capernaum, with the view of attending the Passover, to which these pious women were probably going, *Stier, Greswell.* It was a custom amongst the Jews, that women, especially widows, should aid Doctors and Rabbis out of their private resources, and should, for that purpose, accompany them on their journeys, *Simonius*, quoted in *Bengel.*

---

4. ¶ *And when much people were gathered together, and were come to him out of every city, he spake by a parable:*

Gathered. Gr. *flocked*, His power over demons drew crowds.
Parable. Luke iv. 23; v. 36. Gr. *compare*, a proverb in the O.T. Psa. xlix. 4.
A Divine painting, concealing truth from the foolish, but revealing it to the wise.
Always founded in analogy from nature, or daily life.
Like a cloud concealing the sun, and yet revealing its beams.
Parables unfold themselves, as spoken miracles.
Truth hidden in parables from certain minds shews—
1. Divine wisdom. 2. Divine holiness. 3. Divine grace.
"I will open my mouth in a parable, I will utter dark sayings of old." Psa. lxxviii. 2.

Nathan reproved David in parable. Job and Balaam spake in parables.
It secured the attention of the multitude, over abstract truths.
Not a *fable*, that relates to maxims of worldly prudence.
By the parable, the Lord hid in part, the sentiment from scoffers.
Wilful blindness alone, fails to understand a parable.
Docility, candor and piety, never fail to interpret aright.
He aids those willing to learn, but punishes the incorrigible.
They may expect the light taken from them, who shut their eyes.
Things hidden from *wise* and *prudent*, revealed to *babes*.

κατὰ πόλιν—rather city by city, in succession. ἐπιπορευομένων πρὸσ. people upon people, *Bengel*. Coming up one after another, *Alford*. παραβολῆσ—Heb. *meshalim*, from *mashal*, *to compare*, *make like*. From the frequent use of comparisons in short pithy sayings among the Orientals, the word *mashal* often signifies some sententious adage, apophthegm, or speech (αἶνοσ ἀπόλογοσ), and therefore Balaam's prophecy is called a *parable*, Num. xxiii. 18. The Sept. uses παραβολη in describing the Proverbs of Solomon, ἐλάλησε τρισχιλίασ παραβολάσ, 1. Kings iv. 32, *Wordsworth*. They contain the doctrine of the kingdom of heaven in all its parts, Theology, Anthropology, Soteriology, and Eschatology, *Neander*, *Lange*.

---

5. *A sower went out to sow his seed: and as he sowed, some fell by the way side; and it was trodden down, and the fowls of the air devoured it.*

A sower. The *article* defines the ideal individual, representing a *class*.
Went out Once upon a time, as you have often seen your neighbours do.
Sow. Since the curse, our bread must be obtained by labor.
Faith committing the seed to earth, trusts the ordinances of heaven.
When will men trust the revealed *promises* of the God of nature?
He sowed. That is *the field*, not merely on the way to it.
Way side. Not the highway, but the *trodden path*, through the field.
Trodden, *i.e.* The seed exposed upon the path, and then devoured.
Fowls, or *winged ones*, now confined to those *domesticated*.
The devil under the image of beautiful and harmless birds.
Air. Gr. of *heaven*. 1. The term embraced the special *residence* of God. The place where He manifests His glory.
2. The *starry heaven* composed of the sun, moon, and other bodies.
3. The *atmosphere* in which clouds, tempests, and birds move.
Flocks of small birds in the East, follow the sower, and enter houses.
A familiar fact, well understood by His humblest hearers.
Our Saviour exalted *familiar* doings, into chapter and sermon.
He gave dignity and significance to the toils of the husbandman.

The analogy between truth and the hearer, as seed to the soil, grounded deeply in nature.

ὁ σπείρων. *The* Sower, emphatically so, Christ, *Wordsworth.* παρὰ τὴν ὁδὸν—Some object that no sower ever wasted his seed on the trodden path. The opposite assertion can as easily be made, *Alexander.* οὐρανοῦ—This term also represents God Himself, in Matt. xxi. and Luke xv. 18. Paul alludes to the *spiritual paradise* in the presence of Jesus Christ, Angels, and Spirits blest, in 2. Cor. xii. 2.

---

6. *And some fell upon a rock; and as soon as it was sprung up, it withered away, because it lacked moisture.*

Rock. Not rocky grounds, for the soil between them, is generally good.

But the rocks which are covered with *thin*, warm, rich mould.

Soon. Gr. *springing it withered.* Matt. has "*immediately.*"

Withered. Either by heat, or spontaneous failure of moisture at the roots.

Little soil, little moisture; little moisture, little root, is Nature's law.

The processes of vegetation, *inscrutable*, as that of the resurrection. 1. Cor. xv. 36.

No richness of mould, nor prematurity of growth, compensates for depth of soil.

τὴν πέτραν. Matt. has τὰ πετρώδη (chap. xiii. 5). Mark has τὸ πετρῶδες (chap. iv. 5).

---

7. *And some fell among thorns; and the thorns sprang up with it, and choked it.*

Among. The strong faith of the sower, trusts his seed *everywhere.*

"In the morning sow thy seed, in the evening withhold not thy hand." Ecclesiastes, xi. 6.

Sprung up. Ministers sadly miscalculate, looking for native purity.

Choked. Gr. *stifled*, strictly applied to suffocating animals.

The ranker growth of weeds, have a fatal influence on the grain.

ἄκανθαι—Luke vi. 4. συμφυεῖσαι—The συν and φυω, *born together*: clearly indicating the *native* depravity of the soil and heart, *Stier.* ἀπέπνιξαν, root, *to choke, to throttle, to suffocate.*

---

8. *And other fell on good ground, and sprang up, and bare fruit an hundredfold. And when he had said these things, he cried, He that hath ears to hear, let him hear.*

Good ground. No true preaching ever entirely fruitless.

A ground of consolation to the humble ministers of Christ.

The curse fell on the unsinning earth, but not in vengeance.

Hundredfold. The fertility of our favoured land, is even greater than this.

Not that some hearts by nature are better than others.

Sovereign grace works in them to *will* and to *do*. Phil. ii. 13.

Cried. He would solemnly and tenderly rouse them by warnings

Hear. A formula often used, by no means pleonastic, or unmeaning.

A solemn, emphatic warning, of truths of momentous import.

They seem to have been *pauses* in our Saviour's discourses.

Why have we ears, if we fail to listen now? *Now is the accepted time.*

What can you listen to, if you turn a deaf ear to these words?

Now, if ever, he who can, must hear, or incur the penalty.

Close attention is necessary, or He imparts no knowledge, confers no benefits.

ἑκατον. Matt. and Mark add *sixty* and *thirty*. Luke giving but one genus, expresses the highest, in which the others are included, *Bengel.*

---

9. *And his disciples asked him, saying, What might this parable be?*

Disciples. Other followers beside the twelve apostles. Mark iv. 12.

Parable, excites the curiosity while veiling unwelcome truths.

It implies that His were but poorly understood at that time.

Enlightened hearers, through unbelief, found them obscure.

His answer is a key to unlock other parables. Luke iv. 23.

A parable, a pillar of *cloud* to those refusing to receive light.

A pillar of fire, ever turning a bright side to the teachable.

A shell keeping the precious kernel *for* the diligent, and *from* the indolent.

A diamond mirror, ever turning towards men, who must at some time look into it. Luke v. 36.

10. *And he said, Unto you it is given to know the mysteries of the kingdom of God: but to others in parables; that seeing they might not see, and hearing they might not understand.*

Unto you. He tells of a *sifting* process already begun.

It will continue dividing all men into two classes.

Given. No reward of intrinsic *merit*, or given as a *right.*

Discriminating sovereign grace, doing His pleasure. Eph. i. 5.

Why was it *not* given to others? Because "they desire not," &c. Job. xxi. 14. *The will to know, is wanting.*

Know. By the aid of infallible interpretation, without any veil of words. *The anointing of the Spirit.* 1. John ii. 27.

Mysteries. Truths *concealed*, until made known by revelation.

The personal duties of saints, and the establishment of the Church.

Kingdom of God. The spiritual empire of Christ, in the hearts of men.

Parables. Luke iv. 23; v. 36. See Notes.

Not see. The Pharisees that very morning, had reviled Him.

Blindness is sin, unchecked: *Sight* is sin counteracted by the Spirit.

Christ did not light the Lamp of Truth in vain.

To cause hardness through prophecy, only brings to light the hardness already existing.

Hearing. Many went away because they had heard enough.

To *chance* hearers, every sermon is a parable.

Words, from the fearful picture of judicial blindness in Is. vi. 10.

Parables plain to us, were enigmatical to the disciples.

Instruction by parables served as a test of character.

δέδοται. perfect passive, implying *authoritative predetermination.* τα μυστήρια, from μυστης, *one initiated: secret doctrines*, certain religious celebrations; first in *Herod.* of those of the Cabeiri in Samothrace. The most famous those of Demeter at Eleusis, first in *Aesch.* *Mysteries* were celebrated in every considerable city of Greece. They were always *secret;* but all Greeks, without distinction of rank or education, nay, perhaps even slaves, might be *initiated*, and, in later times, foreigners, *Lidd. & Scott.* The words *revelation* and *mystery* stand in the same relation to each other that the English words *discovery* and *secret* do. The revelation of the mystery is the secret discovered, *Campbell.* Something involved or concealed as the soul in the body, a *sacramentum, Wordsworth.* The common application of the word μυστήριον *mystery*, as denoting the *incomprehensible*, is not justified either from Classical or New. Test. usage: the word always means *a matter to the knowledge of which initiation is necessary.* ἵνα, strongly marks judicial blindness, *W. & W.* βλέποντες—*Demosthenes* and *Aeschylus* allude to this Greek proverb as *naturally* perceiving, without intellectual or *moral* conviction. Mark preserves the Heb., Luke the classic form. "*Ye will not perceive,*" simply announcing the certain fact. Remarkable words are those of a heathen, βλεποντας μη βλεπειν εκ των ειρημενων κ. τ. λ., *Polybius.*

---

11. *Now the parable is this: The seed is the word of God.*

The seed, needs a soil in which to grow, until the end of time.

It is of heavenly origin, and of inestimable value.

The ground, only at Creation, brought forth *without* sowing.

No science has ever comprehended this *forming* principle.

It transforms, under God, the soil and sap, into the fruitful plant.

The word of man, has wrought the heart and life into *barrenness.*

Word of God. A name given to the Saviour, Incarnate Truth. John i. 1.

The wisdom of God, and power of God, through the Spirit. Rom. i. 16.

Thus light, rain, air, electricity vitalize the dying seed.

By nature all hearts are closed, until God opens them.

"My doctrine shall drop as the rain, my speech distil," &c. Deut. xxxii. 2.
It makes the barren fruitful, and restores the lineaments of Christ.
It is vain to depend *alone* on eloquence and learning to sow the seed. 1. Cor. iii. 6.
A child's hand can *plant*, but an angel's might cannot *quicken*.
Its growth traced to the Lord of "the seed-time and harvest." Gen. viii. 22.
Pure seed, not made foul, by polluted hands of creature sowers.
All instruments as to their *inherent* efficacy, the same.
Note the Divine skill and originality of our Great Teacher.
Man would specify the *kind* of seed, *place*, and *plan* of sowing.
Our Saviour strikes at once at *essential* analogies, governing minor things.
Divine seed of the word transforms poor soil, into rich.
Even human words have a transforming power on the mind.
By a *seed*, Christ teaches us how to *live;* by it, Paul teaches us how to *die*.
Ministers will beware, that they sow no other seed than *His*.

σπόρος—*Luther's* famous saying "The word *understood* multiplies itself, and betters the man; misunderstood, wilfully, lessens the man's heart, and hurts the man." Words are germs of unfolded truths.

"His plausive words,
"He scattered not in ears, but grafted them,
"To *grow* there and *bear*." *Milton.*

Christ the Seminal Word, Physician and Medicine; Victim and redeeming Price; Door-keeper and Door; Sower and Seed, *Augustine*.

---

12. *Those by the way side are they that hear: then cometh the devil, and taketh away the word out of their hearts, lest they should believe and be saved.*

Way side. Implies Gospel of the Kingdom to be carried to all nations as a testimony. Mark xiii. 9.
God maintains his right to devils and men, with or without diligence.
The husbandman, year after year, tries to reclaim the footpath.
The unfeeling heart is like the trodden, barren pathway.
God on His part, sows diligently, always and everywhere.
Heathen confessed the fault not in the seed, but in the ground.
The margin of the field, wrongly turned into a trodden path.
Sensuality leads to the *boundaries* of Satan's empire.
The *indifferent* offer the seed no mould, in which it can grow
The secret beginnings of our hardening processes, are *sins*.
There may be no *susceptibility*, still, the sower sows the seed.
A false creed, overlaying the Bible, the most hopeless soil.
Hear, and Understand it not, *i.e.*, his relations to the Word.
Redemption, sin, and holiness, are unintelligible terms to him.

Hearts under evil influences, become like the *pavement*.
The word of God must pierce, and root itself in the wasted soil.
The ploughshare of the law, has not yet broken it up.
Devil. Gr. *accuser*. The unrelenting slanderer of the brethren.
With sleepless vigilance, he watches to take advantage.
He uses every weapon put in his hands, against men's salvation.
Birds of evil omen, wicked thoughts, worldly desires, lusts.
Taketh away. Satan can never coerce, but only persuade.
This counter-worker of the sower; overlooks no one, hearing.
Satan knows God's Word to be the instrument of salvation.
The seed lying in the memory might spring, if not devoured.
The arch-robber lets fly *little* birds, but very *many*.
Business, cares, carnal thoughts, make an atmosphere of *frivolity*.
The wind might scatter, but *living* agencies are abroad.
Hearts, of the majority of gospel hearers, in every age.
The Spirit can change the trodden paths, into a field of God.
Were there good and bad hearts from the first? Answer—
Where is the rich man, whom riches have not deceived?
Where is the poor man, whom wealth has not allured?
Where the rich man without disquietude, the poor man without cares?

ἔρχεται implies the coming of *another* person, apart from the deceitfulness of one's heart. We cannot prevent their lighting on our hearts, but we can their making nests, *Henry*. διάβολοσ—Luke; πονηρόσ—Matt; ο σατανᾶσ Mark. These varied names given, that we need not mistake the guilty party, ever ready to ruin the soul. Matt. has ἁρπάζει. One of his most wonderfully successful artifices, is the persuading so many wise men after the flesh, to *doubt*, or practically *deny* his *existence*. Our Lord's unambiguous allusions to Satan, proves it to be no pedagogic accommodation to an existing popular superstition, *Stier*.

The word *Satan* or the *Adversary* is used as a proper name only four times in the O. T., Job. i. 6-12; ii. 1; Zech. iii. 1; 1. Chron. xxi. 1. It is clear from this that the scriptural revelation concerning Satan is to be sought in the N. T., rather than in the O. T. In enquiring into the origin of Evil two tendencies have manifested themselves. 1st.—To regard evil, as a negative imperfection, unavoidable. 2nd.—To trace the existence of evil to a rival Creator. This is the old Persian and Manichæan notion. Holy Scripture meets the truth, and removes the error, inherent in both hypotheses. It asserts the supremacy of God, so that evil can only exist under His permission. It regards evil as an anomaly and corruption to be removed. It declares evil to proceed from the influence of an Evil Spirit, exercising the mysterious power of free will. The N. T. brings plainly forward the personality of the Tempter; he is a *spirit*, and all descriptions of his power imply spiritual nature and spiritual influences. We have hints which go to show that he is a *fallen angel*, for nothing *essentially evil* could have been created by God; his power over the soul is simply that of a powerful and evil nature on those in whom lurks the germ of the same evil: this power is both *negative* and *positive*, its *negative* exercise is referred to in the parable of the *sower*, its *positive* in the parable of the *tares*. The statement of *Beard* and others, that the "doctrine of devils" is the result of Persian and Chaldee modes of thought on the Jewish mind, is unwarrantable. See *Smith's* Dict. Satan.

ἀπὸ τῆσ καρδίασ, indicating the devil's power, *Bengel*.

---

13. *They on the rock* are they, *which, when they hear, receive the word with joy; and these have no root, which for a while believe, and in time of temptation fall away.*

Rock. *Rheimish—rocky places.* The *rock* comes very near the surface in *sensual* minds.

Roots, with mysterious instinct, seek the mould between the stones.
But here they cannot possibly *penetrate* the hard surface.
Slightly covered, this soil is soonest green, and soonest withered.
Shallow superficial hearing; false hearts are easily moved.
In the rocky bottom of the proud heart, this seed cannot root itself.

Receive the Word. 1. Christians with an external Christianity. 2. Christians with an easy Christianity. 3. Christians with a half Christianity. 4. Christians with a whole Christianity.

With joy. As the word of God: not cold assent, or forced submission.
Reason and *conscience*, compelled to honor revealed truth.
The affections are deeply interested. The heart is full of *wants*.
Not the joy of forgiven sin, or benefits of redemption.
Not that of the pearl-finder; "He went and sold all that he had."
Does not repel the truth, but sadly lacks deep earnestness.
He desires the blessings of discipleship, but fails to count the cost.
Promises are sweet, doctrines lovely, but no depth of nature.
Firmness and fruit depend on *unseen* roots—
"Whom not having seen ye love." 1. Pet. i. 8. "Seeing Him, who is invisible." Heb. xi. 27.
"Your life is *hid* with Christ, in God." Col. iii. 3.
Peter had this *root*, "To whom shall we go? *Thou* hast," &c. Jo. vi. 68.
They, who "took joyfully the spoiling of their goods." Heb. x. 34.
"Whose hope is anchored into that within the veil." Heb. vi. 19.

For a while. Gr. *convenient.* Policy is ever a broken staff.

Temptation. Gr. *trial*, Matt. *sun is risen.* Its heat is not intended to burn.
The winds are sent to strengthen, not overturn the trees.
Mark, has afflictions, and persecutions; or *pressure* and *pursuit.*
Providential chastisements, and evils inflicted by men.

Fall away. Gr. *apostatize*, without *vital* change, they return to the world, and to their old state and ways. Heb. iii. 12.

Falling away. 1. Fall speedily. 2. Fall inexplicably. 3. Fall miserably. Heb. x. 38-39.

A lamp without oil; so is a religion without *faith*. Heb. xi. 6.

ῥίζαν οὐκ—clearly shows that they fall not *from grace*. *πρὸσ καιρόν*, *for a while*, *unconstant*, *changeable*, Heb. xi. 25. *For a season*. In 2. Cor. iv. 18. *Temporal* as opposed to *eternal*. *πρὸσ καιρὸν* the *convenient* time, contrasted with *καίρῷ πειρασμοῦ* the *inconvenient* time, or dependent on time, *i.e.*, time serving, *Lange*. The difference between *fides temporalis*, and *fides salvifica* is deeply significant. A conversion in the understanding, sentiment or imagination, may be a flower, but will be fruitless, *Oosterzee*. *πειρασμοῦ*—Matt. *θλέψεωσ*—tribulation, Lat. from *tribulum*, the roller used in threshing grain, *Trench*.

---

14. *And that which fell among thorns are they, which, when they have heard, go forth, and are choked with cares and riches and pleasures of this life, and bring no fruit to perfection.*

Thorns. Symbols of sin. The curse extended from man to earth.

The earth had none other but a *thorn-crown* to yield its Lord.

Thorns need no planting, cares and lusts, no culture.

Grain planted, springs up into stalks, and puts forth ears. Gen. viii. 22.

Thorns and weeds *spring up* far more quickly than corn.

Go forth. After they have listened awhile, a picturesque addition.

Choked. Wickliffe—*strangled*. The soil poorly cleared of old roots.

Thorns overtopped the grain, and drank up the moisture.

Dwarfed in a good soil, shews lack of *careful husbandry*.

Profession remains, but fruit pines under *earth's shadows*.

Life of faith, power of godliness, by degrees eaten out of the soul.

The soul renewed, and bearing Christ's image, cannot lose it. John x. 29.

Cares. Poor man toils, to keep hunger from his door, not met by faith.

Greek, which *divides—cuts*. "They eat as doth a canker." 2. Tim. ii. 17.

Undue solicitudes,—anxieties, as to the interests of earth.

1. Earthly cares. 2. Earthly possessions. 3. Earthly enjoyments in their relation to the Gospel.

1. Inattention of childhood. 2. Ardent shallowness of youth. 3. Worldly seeking of age.

Riches. "*Deceitful*" in their *tenure*. "MAKE THEMSELVES WINGS," &c. Pro. xxiii. 5.

Deceitful in their *nature*, their hopes delusive, their joys fanciful.

As a source of pleasure, mocking their owners. Haman. Esther v. 11.

They fatally decoy those, *hastening* to become rich. 1. Tim. vi. 9.

Allowing these lusts to grow up with the seed, *half-hearted*.

To conquer, one must press on with *fire* and *sword* of self-denial.
Pleasures. Lusts springing from the *heart*, more dangerous than evil spirits.
Over these, the arch-fiend maintains his supremacy.
What creeps more stealthily on, more difficult to eradicate!
Our natural enmity *deepens*, as we attempt to *repress* it.
The guilt of the third, and smallest of the three, the greatest.
Insincerity and indecision, nullify all the earnestness of the will.
Satan sure of his prey, meddles not with this class.
How can the heart be freed from lusts, and *fitted* for seed?
This is a *miraculous seed*, which overpowers the thorns.
The three classes are solemnly warned, but irremediable.
The cares and pleasures of the world, though so opposite in their nature, agree in choking the word.

ἀκάνθας—Luke vi. 44. *πορευόμενοι*, *setting out*, *going their way*, not falling immediately, or very manifestly; nay, even with some degree of progress: this is the force of the verb, *Bengel*. *μεριμνῶν*—*μερισ*, *a part*. Care *cuts* both soul and body. *Care*, from the Welsh,—waste, pine. Cark, from *carcer*,—the wasting woes of prison. *πλούτου*, wealth, as estimated by the *desire* and *value* for it, *Alford*. A Threefold PROGRESS; The first receives a hindrance at the *very outset*. The second after it has *sprung up*. The third while coming to *maturity*, *Alford*, Matt., *ἀπάτη του πλούτου*—The *artifices* by which persons excuse themselves, while ardently pursuing wealth, or putting off the cares of religion to a convenient season. Cases not selected as *examples*, but as comprehensive *heads*, *Doddridge*. *βίου*, Life *extensive*—1, its *duration*. 2, *means*. 3, *manner*. *ζωή*, Life *intensive*, vitâ quia vivimus, *Trench*. *πορευόμενοι*, on their progress through life. *συμπνίγονται*, *choke*. The image of an evil growth, strangling a nobler, is *cockle;* Saxon, *ceocan*, to *choke*, *Trench*. *τελεσφοροῦσι*, used of trees, bringing fruits to maturity, *Stier*. Fruit perfected and ripened, *Bengel*.

---

15. *But that on the good ground are they, which in an honest and good heart, having heard the word, keep it, and bring forth fruit with patience.*

Good ground. Gr. *morally excellent*, sincerity, integrity of heart.
An humble and heart-felt trust in Divine mercy.
Before the plough and harrow mellow the soil.
Spirit's rain softens the mould, *His* plants, choke the thorns.
Heats of persecutions, scorch not, but mature *His* planting.
These hear, like the preceding, but *actively* accept the word.
Approving the truth, they resist temptations to unfruitfulness.
Honest. Gr. *Things which are lovely.* "Beauty of holiness." 2. Chron. xx. 21.
A heart firmly fixed for God and duty, receives and keeps the word.
Seeking *first* the kingdom, he cares for nothing *second*.

Fruit, of the Spirit, *Love, Joy, Peace, Long-suffering, Gentleness, Goodness, Faith, Meekness, Temperance.* Gal. v. 22.

Patience. Gr. *constancy of purpose*, and perseverance in practice.

Through the course of a life spent in duties, and amidst discouragements and trials.

It teaches, Divine Patience—does not give up bad land.

Whence comes the good honest heart? Where the good soil?

"He that is of God, heareth God's words." John viii. 47.

"Sons of God" understand the language of their Father's house.

"Every one that is of the truth, heareth my voice." John xviii. 37.

The "sons of peace" alone, receive the message of peace. Luke x. 6.

Loadstone thrust in this world's rubbish, attracts metal of celestial temper.

Divine goodness of the soil comes from God, as well as the seed.

Secret saving grace accompanies the preaching of the word.

The *rock* may be changed, by the power of God, into rich *soil.*

Shallow soil may become deep, thorns subdued, into mould.

Earthly seed uses the soil, as it finds it. Hence *morality* never makes *saints.*

καλῇ γῇ—A *receptivity* in man intimated, preparing for progressive development; and the *will* repelling heterogeneous influences, &c, *Olshausen.* These words mislead. There is no *tinder* in the human heart which ever kindles without the heavenly material being first deposited there. The good soil is prepared for the seed only by God's power and grace, *Jacobus.* καλῇ καὶ ἀγαθῇ—Adorned with the gifts of mind, body, and fortune; noble and good, *Thucydides.* Gr. expression for honesty, *Le Clerc:* one entirely good, *Aristotle.* Some naturally false-hearted; others by grace, earnest and simple minded, but not naturally, nor by irresistible grace, *Alford.* Not in an absolute and ethical sense, *Meyer.* *Gratia preveniens*, *Oosterzee.* A heart truly good, *Erasmus, Grotius, Wetstein, Rosenmuller, Beza.* Jewish Rabbis liken one class of hearers to the *sponge* which receives all, and then imparts it to others. Another to a *sieve* which lets all the fine flour through, and retains the bran, *Lightfoot.* ὑπομονῇ, Vul. *patientia* which modern versions wrongly follow; *persistentia*, *Beza; perseverate ad extremum et salvi eritis*, *Castalio.* ὑπομονῇ, Heb. xii. 3, *without intermission*, *Campbell.* Continue to bring forth with perseverance, *Bloomfield.* κατέχουσι, *retain, keep it fast*, not as on the wayside. καρποφοροῦσι, *bear fruit*, not as among the thorns. ἐν ὑπομονῇ, *with patience*, not as on the rocky ground. ὑπομονῇ is *strength of mind, sustained by good hope* This constitutes the sum of Christianity, *Bengel.*

---

16 ¶ *No man, when he hath lighted a candle, covereth it with a vessel, or putteth it under a bed: but setteth it on a candlestick, that they which enter in may see the light.*

Lighted. Philosophers taught a *secret* doctrine to pupils, and another to the public; *esoteric and exoteric.*

Apostles were not self-producing *lights*, but *light-bearers.*

overeth. God gives to none, mercies, merely for his own benefit.
Vessel. A candle cannot *permanently* be concealed, without absurdity.
A parable for a *moment* conceals, but eventually spreads light.
By nature, the mind has no more light than a candlestick.
By Divine agency, light springs, that men may diffuse it.
"Ye are the light of the world. Let your light so shine." Matt. v. 14, 16.
The unrenewed soul is *ignorant*, and *willing* to be dark.
False lights of reason and philosophy, render darkness *visible*.
Those walking in the steps of Jesus, walk not in darkness. John viii. 12
Better a small apartment well lighted, than a spacious hall with a sickly taper. **Bed.** Luke v. 18. See Notes.
Candlestick. Luke xi. 33. Antiquities. See Notes.
May see. Open and decided declaration of our principles.
With the mouth, confession is made unto salvation. Rom. x. 10.
Blameless in the midst of a crooked (depraved), and perverse generation, among whom, ye shine as lights, in the world. Phil. ii. 15.
The Christian, a candle lighted, and placed in darkness, to dispel the gloom.
Our light is to shine, not to glorify ourselves, but our Father. Matt. v. 16.
Fearful guilt therefore rests on the *inconsistent* professor.
Believers defeat the very end of being, by withholding benefits.
Rome, by suppressing *light* and *chaining* the Bible, proved Anti-Christ.

No man. Apostles hearing, bound to tell others, *Meyer, De Wette.* Fruits of preaching must be known, therefore receive it honestly, *Oosterzee.* λυκνον—Our Lord stood in full view of the golden candlesticks of the Temple, burning day and night, *Stier.* Christ is τὸ φῶς τὸ ἀληθινόν. His ministers are λύχνοι John v. 35, and φωστῆρες Phil. ii. 15, *receiving* their light, and only burning *for a time.* Johannes lumen illuminatum: Christus lumen illuminans, *Augustine.* *Demonax* a Greek sage, charged with neglecting the *Eleusinian Mysteries*, clothed in a white garment, pleaded his cause before the people. "If they were bad, he ought not to conceal them, if good, his love to mankind compelled him to reveal them." He was acquitted, *Athenaeus.* If they would spare my life, on condition that I should keep this truth to myself (the Unity of God) and not teach it to others, I would not accept it, *Socrates*, (Apology).

---

17. *For nothing is secret, that shall not be made manifest: neither any thing hid, that shall not be known and come abroad.*

Secret. Does not refer to bringing secret sins to light.
But to the partial obscuring of Christ's own teachings by *parables*.
He affected no *secret* instructions, characteristic of philosophers.
With great plainness, He declared the whole counsel of God. Acts xx. 27.
Philosophers taught the few, but left the multitude in the dark.
"What I tell in darkness, that speak ye in the light." Matt. x. 27.

"We have a sure word of prophecy, whereunto ye shall do well, that ye take heed." 2. Peter, i. 19.

Hid. Everything can, must, and will one day come to light.

κρυπτὸν. Eng. *crypt*, a secret chapel or cell in cathedrals. ἀπόκρυφον *hidden* Apocrypha, a book whose author is unknown, and whose inspiration is denied.

---

18. *Take heed therefore how ye hear: for whosoever hath, to him shall be given; and whosoever hath not, from him shall be taken even that which he seemeth to have.*

Take heed. Gr. *see to it*. Matthew has, *beware*. Hear with *prepared* mind.

1. You are bound to hear. 2. You may hear diversely.

3. It is no small thing how you hear. 4. Therefore take heed, &c.

"Everyone turned to his course, as the horse rusheth into battle." Jer. viii. 6.

Hear *reverently*, as creatures should regard God's oracles. Acts vii. 38.

Hear with an *unprejudiced* mind. We should be free from vain, captious spirit.

Hear with *humility*. A docility of mind characteristic of children. 1. Peter ii. 2. "Except ye become as little children," &c.

Hear with *self-application*. Receive the truth in *faith* and *love*.

Hear with *diligence*. "Gird up the loins of the mind," and remember it. "We should give the more earnest heed," &c.

Hearing aright, depends not on the *perfection* of preaching.

A *child* may point out the path, by which the captive may escape.

"They shall heap up to themselves teachers, having itching ears." 2. Tim. iv. 3. "The prophet that hath a dream," &c.

Many refuse the gospel-*milk*, unless it be sweetened.

Many refuse the gospel-*meat* unless it be *seasoned*.

Proclaiming salvation by Christ, many wonder if indeed they are *lost*.

The *earthen* vessel interests some, more than the *treasure* therein.

Some more highly *glazed*; ministers but earthen vessels still.

Gideon's vessels valueless, save for the lamp of truth they bear.

Whosoever hath, to him, &c. Giving and receiving, mutual as action and reaction. A universal law.

These words of Jesus are—1. A word of seeming contradiction. 2. A word of truth. 3. A word of wisdom.

If we receive instruction, we must in turn, give attention.

Hath not, kept and improved previous knowledge, *not faithful to light*.

A moral law. Our only choice is between *loss* and *gain*.

There is no standing still, we must either advance or recede.
We "treasure up wrath against the day of wrath" or the *reverse*. Rom. ii. 5.

πῶς. After spending twenty years among heathen, a missionary noted the *fastidiousness* of hearers in *Gospel* lands. δοκεῖ thinketh that he hath—*i.e.*, a reputation for godliness, *W. & W.* An expletive signifying a *reality*, not an *appearance*, *Pearce & Foote.* It is a just thing with the "FATHER of Lights," when he hath lighted any man a candle, by bestowing spiritual gifts upon him, and lent him a candlestick too, whereon to set it, by providing him a *stay* in the church, if that man shall then "hide his candlestick under a bushel," and envy the light and comfort of it to "them, that are in the house," either to remove his candlestick, or to put out his candle, *Sanderson.*

---

19 ¶ *Then came to him* his *mother and his brethren, and could not come at him for the press.*

Came to Him. Those loving Christ, cannot do long without Him.
His mother, desires Him to cease His labors to take food. Mk. iii. 20.
Jesus refuses with holy seriousness and tender forbearance.
Satan failing to baffle Christ by Pharisees, sends His *friends.*
By unseasonable visits, they would interrupt His work.
Mary had not learned (as Rome affirms) to *command* her Son.
She forgot, "He must be about His Father's business." Luke ii. 49.
Brethren. On the highest critical authorities, the *children* of Joseph and Mary. Luke ii. 7.
They were unquestionably *members* of His *mother's family.*
They are always named in connection with Mary.
"Neither did Christ's brethren believe in Him." John vii. 5.
Press. Without the circle, they would not *rudely* interrupt Him.
How has His relatives hitherto received His instructions?
His labors and fastings they regarded as dangerous excitement.

ἀδελφοὶ αὐτοῦ.—Superstition has involved the question; always called ἀδελφοι, and ...δελφαι; never called sons or daughters of Mary; always found in company with Mary. ...he had but four sons, *Hoffman.*

1. Theory, children of Joseph by a former marriage. Theory of the 2nd and 3rd ...nturies, *Thiersch.* This saves Mary's virginity during life, *Jerome, Augustine, Epiphanius, Hilary, Ambrose, Grotius, Stier, Vorstius, Bertholdt, Latin Church.*

2. "*Adopted children,*" *Hegesippus, Lichtenstein, Greek Church.*

3. "*Cousins,*" Children of Alphæus and Mary, *Chrysostom, Clement, Alexander, ...dner, Pearson, Sepp, Hug, Olshausen, Mill, Norton, Lange, Baumgarten, Eichorn, ...rike, Ellicott, Alexander, Tischendorf, Ebrard, Luthardt, Oosterzee, Ewald, Friedlieb, ...dsworth.*

4. Children of Joseph and Mary, *Eusebius, Tertullian, Luther, Hammond, Herder, ...ler, Fritzsche, Ruckert, De Wette, Meyer, Tholuck, Hase, Wieseler, Neander, Winer,*

Oosterzee, Riggenbach, Alford, Greswell, Ewald, Da Costa, Owen, Andrews, Stier, Lechler.

The following important fragment on the *four Maries* is from *Papias*, scholar of St. John (ap. Routh, Reliq. Sacr. i. p. 16, ex Cod. MS. Bibl. Bodl. 2397). "1. *Maria*, mater DOMINI. 2. *Maria*, Cleophæ sive Alphæi uxor, quæ fuit mater Jacobi Episcopi et Apostoli, et Simonis et Thadei et cujusdam Joseph. 3. *Maria* Salome, uxor Zebedei, mater Joannis Evangelistæ et Jacobi (confer Matt. xxvii. 56 et Marc. xv. 40 et xvi. 1). 4. *Maria* Magdalena," *Wordsworth.*

κρατῆσαι to *seize, arrest*, Mark iii. 21. An accumulation peculiar to Mark, *Schleiermacher.* The act implied, may have been recorded at Peter's suggestion, *Alexander.* Incident took place at Capernaum, *Greswell, Andrews.*

---

20. *And it was told him* by certain *which said, Thy mother and thy brethren stand without, desiring to see thee.*

Told. The message went from one to another, until it reached Him.
Desiring to see, Jesus, from wrong and from right motives.
A praiseworthy wish, may not always be truly a pious wish.
Mark uses terms implying *presumption* in His friends.
Mary was twice before rebuked, for the same spirit. Luke ii. 49; John ii. 4.

"*Thy Mother.*" That Mary after the admonition, John ii. 4, should have tried to influence her son's plans, proves the wide interval between the Mary of the Gospels, and the *Immaculate conception* of Rome, *Oosterzee.* His mother came according to prophecy (Luke ii. 35) to seek *consolation*, not to administer *reproof, Olshausen.* The Fathers more rightly infer, as he had twice before rebuked His relatives for their interference, it was unwarrantable now. Vain glory and unbelief prompted her to send the message or rather command. *ἑστῶτες ἀπέστειλαν*, &c., *Stier.*

---

21. *And he answered and said unto them, My mother and my brethren are these which hear the word of God, and do it.*

Answered. He neither *went out*, nor allowed them to *come in*
Looking round. All who *love* Me, are nearer than kindred.
My mother. An example of renunciation of earthly kindred.
Domestic ties, and endeared names, are real cords.
Feeble *in comparison*, with those of His spiritual household.
He did not ignore an affectionate regard for His relatives.
Those doing His will, alone claim the *sacred* relationship.
The poorest saints, are above all earthly household affinity.
Faith makes *natural* alliances the standard of *spiritual* ones.
Such professions in a *mere* man, would imply a want of natural affection.
A wide *diffusion* of human attachments, lessens their intensity.
He embraces myriads with equal warmth and tenderness.
There is a family *on earth*, of which, CHRIST is a member.

Believers on earth, *one* with Christ's family in heaven.
Hear. The implied reproof, was intended for His relatives.
We see the high value the Lord sets on *hearing* and *doing*
The Lord's spiritual family. 1. The family likeness.
2. The family ties. 3. The family blessing. 4. The family home.
Mary has no greater right to Christ, than other believers. Luke xi. 27-28.
Rome's worship of Mary—a compound of *idolatry and blasphemy.*
Absorbed in awful warnings, He felt the interruption unseasonable.
A Christian ever forgets his parents, in God's service. Matt. xix. 29.
Believers dearer to God, than children to parents. Is. xlix. 19-20-21.
If His friends were believers, His word embraced them also.
Do it, expresses the *limits* of the relationship of the Son of God, with man.
Even the Lord's brethren, without *faith in Him*, could not be saved.
Folly of *Mariolatry.* Mary was a sinner, saved by *grace* alone.
He turns a kind look to His disciples, as though some would take them from Him.—Behold my **mother and brethren**!
Away perverse generation! Away mother and brethren! I speak to those hearing and doing my Father's will.
All ties founded on nature, eventually *lost* in those of *grace.*
Those who hear *me*, are my mother, sister and brother.
These words, full of the profoundest humility and affection.
Timothy thus must treat aged saints as *mothers.* 1. Tim. v. 2.

τίσ ἐστιν—The words found Mark iii. 21, alone can explain this severe rebuke. *ὅτι ἐξέστη*—1, to put out of place. 2, to put out of one's self. 3, to be out of mind, deranged. The Pharisees having similarly charged Him, seem to have brought their blasphemous insinuations to His friends, and urged them to this folly, *Olshausen.* *μήτηρ μου*, not *ἡ μήτηρ*; *mother and brethren to me.* Those who hear the word of God and keep it, He calls thus, because, with reverence be it said, they daily bring Him forth in their hearts, *Wordsworth.* *αὐτόν* omitted, *Tischendorf*, *Alford*, *Bengel. Cod. Sin.*

I have read a story in Fox's Martyrs and monuments, of a woman who, when she ame to be tried for her religion, before the Bishop, he threatened her, he would take way her husband from her; saith she, "CHRIST is my husband." "I will take away y child;" "CHRIST," saith she, "is better to me than ten sons." "I will strip thee," ys he, "of all thy outward comforts." "Yea, but CHRIST is mine, and you cannot strip of Him," saith she. Rom. viii. 35-39, *Chr. Love.* *του θεου*, omit. *Cod. Sin.*

---

2 ¶ *Now it came to pass on a certain day, that he went into a ship with his disciples: he said unto them, Let us go over unto the other side of the lake. And they launched* h.

tain day. The same day that the parable of the sower was spoken.
ciples, familiar with real, feared no imaginary dangers.

Bound—1. To follow Him in every path. 2. To call upon Him in every danger. 3. To honor Him after every deliverance.

Let us. Dropping the majestic "I," He speaks humbly as one of them.

His motive in crossing appears to have been, that he might avoid the crowds curious only to see or hear Him.

Launched. He might have gone by *land*. He adopted the other course *designedly*.

Whither our Lord leads, believers may safely venture and follow.

Many willing to go to heaven by *land*, but dread *unknown* perils.

μιᾶ τῶν ἡμερῶν, one of these days, Wordsworth. Mark has ἐν ἐκείνῃ τῇ ἡμέρᾳ ὀψίας οὔσης, *in same day in which preceding parables were delivered:* this defines the chronology, see Mark iii. 31-35. Matt. xii. 46 has misplaced this occurrence, *Alford.* πλοῖον—Luke v. 2. ἀνήχθησαν—Lit. lead *up:* from the land, the sea appears to be higher than the shore. Loose the cable, *Wetstein.* It was probably near sundown when they left, *Andrews.*

---

23. *But as they sailed he fell asleep: and there came down a storm of wind on the lake; and they were filled* with water, *and were in jeopardy.*

Asleep. Exhausted by labours, the *man* Jesus slept.

Jesus asleep. 1. Manifests the greatness of the Lord. 2. Explains the perplexity of the disciples. 3. Fore-tells the peace of the Christian.

Redeemed humanity, shall at length rule over matter. Rom. viii. 21-3.

A sleep full of majesty after the labours of Capernaum.

A sign of a deep calm, amid a dreadful tempest.

If He *delay* His aid, we are prone to think the Lord asleep.

He sleeps not so much to be *refreshed*, as to be *awakened*.

A time to sleep even for the teacher in office. Ecc. iii. 1.

It is enough, "The God of Israel neither slumbers nor sleeps." Psa. cxxi. 4.

Why does the Lord so often sleep amid life's storms?

1. To unfold our impotence. 2. To rouse our faith in His power.
3. To lead us to pray for help. 4. To the praise of His name.

Storms, outward signs of weakness, not strength, in nature.

Against fever, germ of death, nature convulsively struggles.

A clear conscience, may *everywhere* sleep quietly. Psa. iv. 8.

Jonah's presence caused the *storm*, Christ's presence the deliverance.

Christ often invisible. His designs of mercy are wisely hidden.

Perhaps He intends to test His disciples, faith in His Divinity.

Surely they could not expect a *mere man* to quell the storm.

Storm. Gennesaret's towering sea cliffs caused these sudden gusts.

Work congenial to "the prince of the power of the air." Eph. ii. 2.

He raised the *storm* that destroyed the family of Job, see Job i. 19.
The Lord was about to invade his dominions in Galilee.
To Christians of every age he threatens danger, causing anxiety.
But the danger leads to manifestations of saving power, ending in praise.
Thus all Satan's machinations are overruled for good to the children of God.

Lake, under various names of *Gennesaret, Tiberias, Galilee.* Luke v. 1. See Notes.

Jeopardy. An humble fishing boat their only pleasure yacht.
Jesus teaches those embarking in His cause, to look for storms.
Storms, even when faithfully discharging our duties as Christians.
There is a world where no storms ever disturb the inhabitants.
No thunder ever shakes those serene skies, peace eternal reigns.
"And I saw a new heaven and a new earth, and there was no more sea." Rev. xxi. 1.

ἀφύπνωσε belongs to the later Greek, and even there more commonly signifies *to awaken.* *απο* gives it intensity: a sleep so deep, it was difficult to arouse one. An Antiochism, *Markland.* Rather a popular use of the term, *Major.* *λαῖλαψ—λάπτω, to pick up.* The tempest seems to lift up the billows. This sea is 600 feet lower than the Mediterranean, and the wind sweeps down from the deep wild mountain gorges on the north, which act like gigantic funnels, *Thompson.* *συνεπληροῦντο—were in the process of being filled, Vigerius.*

That small ship, *navicula illa,* is a figure of the Church, tossed in the sea, that is, in the world, by the waves, that is temptations and persecutions, while the Lord is as it were asleep, until being roused and raised up by the prayers of the saints, at the very last, *in ultimis suscitatus,* He appeases the world, and restores a calm to His people, *Tertullian.* As the kernel of the old humanity, Noah and his family, was once contained in the ark, which was tossed upon the waves of the deluge; so the kernel of the new humanity, of the new creation, Christ and His Apostles, in the little ship, *Trench.*

---

24. *And they came to him, and awoke him, saying, Master, Master, we perish. Then he arose, and rebuked the wind and the raging of the water: and they ceased, and there was a calm.*

Awoke. Three Evangelists allude to their awakening Him.
He was not roused, by all the wild uproar without.
They awoke Him by prayer. To whom else could they go? John vi. 68.

Master. Repeated as an evidence of their terror.

Carest thou not? Mark. Are almost words of *rebuke.* Mark iv. 38.

We perish. Includes the fear of the Lord perishing *with themselves.*
A cry of despair near the Lord, becomes a prayer.
All fearfulness in life springs from unbelief. Luke i. 12.
United prayer of faith, the hope anchor in the storm.
They inferred—Our Saviour, asleep, proved, He did not regard them.

"Can a woman forget her sucking child? yea," &c. Is. xlix. 15.

Arose. With the same *tranquillity*, with which He went to rest.
He never oversleeps the hour of deliverance, He appears at the right moment
His unapproachable *dignity* is seen, amid cries of distress.
Though asleep, His Divine EYE had seen all, His EAR had heard all.
The *man* Jesus was exhausted; for *others*, He was *Almighty*.

Rebuked. As though He addressed the arch-spirit of the storm.
Nature and demons in their wild uproar, yield Him obedience.
Commotions of nature, echoes of the soul's broken harmonies.
With one word, He rebukes His children, with another, the storm.
"Therefore we will not fear, though the waters roar." Ps. xlvi. 3.
He calmed a storm on Galilee, and raised one on Sodom.
He rebuked a *fever* (Luke iv. 38), and now rebukes the *winds*.
He reasserts man's dominion over evil powers in Nature.
His *word* sufficient, without Moses' *rod* over the deep.
He first rebukes the storm in their hearts, and then the elements. Matt. viii. 26.
Joshua conquered by the *ark*. Elisha by Elijah's *mantle*. Our Lord by His *word*.

Calm. Even the *ground-swell* after a storm, ceased.
Sign, the Son of man had entered on the government of the world.
"He sitteth upon the flood, and maketh the storm a calm." Psa. xxix. 10.
No storm too violent for the Lord to quell.—
1. In the world. 2. In the church. 3. In the house. 4. In the heart.

'Επιστάτα Luke, κύριε Matt., διδάσκαλε Mark. ἐπετίμησε 1, to *put honor upon*, N. T. sense. 2, *to judge* what is wrong. 3, *admonish, reprove*. *The* miracle was in calming the *minds* of the apostles, *Neander*. Uncertain whether He wrought a miracle, or predicted an event, *Hase*. Such anecdotes told of all celebrated persons, *Weisse*. A myth, *Strauss*. A natural subsidence, *Paulus*. Symbolical, *Ammon*. No connection between the storm within, and that without, *Meyer*. Sin in man causes an echo in nature's convulsions. Hidden spiritual effects are infinitely mightier, as they strike at the root of sin, *Olshausen*. Ultimate ground of the rebuke, the fact that demons caused the storm, *Lange*. κλύδωνι the *swell of the tempest*. ἐπαύσαντο—from which the Eng. *pause*. Contrast this with Cæsar's "Quid times? *Vehis Cæsarem*." The timid pilot showed more sense, and kept near shore. Simplicity heightens the grandeur. "Dicto citius tumidæ aequora placat," *Æneid*, i. 142, *Wakefield*. A stormy and tempestuous world is loved; what, if it were calm and tranquil? *Augustine*. Christ's sleep is the Divine acquiescence in our tribulations, and He is roused from it by the prayers of the righteous, *Origen*. Because the waves rise, the ship may be tossed, but because Christ is in it, it cannot sink, *Augustine*.

---

25. *And he said unto them, Where is your faith? And they being afraid wondered, saying one to another, What manner of man is this! for he commandeth even the winds and water, and they obey him.*

Where? *How have ye not faith?* Times of trial should bring it forth.
Faith, the key, that unlocks all blessings in Christ.
Their appeal to Christ—faith overpowered by *excess* of *fear*.
Could a ship bearing your Lord, possibly perish?
He chides not for disturbing His rest, but their disquieting fears.
Afraid. Timid believers dishonor their Lord. Faithful, honor Him.
But some should fear, "Let sinners in Zion be afraid." Isa. xxxiii. 14.
Storms within, and calamities without, hushed by faith.
Wondered. External signs overawed the senses, but were infinitely less mighty, than their *hidden* effects.
What manner? Words by some attributed to the crew, and not the disciples.
It seems they never yet had done justice to His greatness.
The deep impression of that scene never left the disciples' minds.
Obey Him. An echo of the O.T. notes of praise. Psa. cvii. 24-31.
"Hitherto thou shalt come, and no further," &c. Job xxxviii. 11.
"He maketh the storm a calm—waters still." Psa. cvii. 29.
"God alone stilleth the noise of the seas, and tumult,"&c. Psa. lxv. 7.
This miracle proves, He will redeem His people at last.
Though the vision tarry, at the end it will speak. Hab. ii. 3.
To obey Him is peace—to resist Him is ruin.
"Woe unto him that striveth with his Maker!" Isa. xlv. 9.

Ezek. xxvii. describes a worldly kingdom under the image of a stately galley, gorgeous with every circumstance that can heighten its glory and beauty. But that ship, with all its outward bravery and magnificence, perishes. "Thy rowers have brought thee into great waters. The east wind hath broken thee in the midst of the seas," *Trench.*

ποῦ ἡ πίστισ ὑμῶν, where is your faith? A child of God may be sorely tossed in a troublesome sea; but that ship shall never be shipwrecked, where CHRIST is the pilot, the Scripture the compass, the promises the tacklings, hope the anchor, faith the cable, the HOLY GHOST the wind, and holy affections the sails, which are filled thus with the gales of the Spirit, Isa. liv. 11, *Chr. Love.* *προσ αλληλουσ.* Omit. *Cod. Sin.*

---

26. ¶ *And they arrived at the country of the Gadarenes, which is over against Galilee.*

Gadarenes, of Gadara, on the Hieromax. 16 miles from Tiberias.
East of the Jordan. Strong fortress. Ruins two miles circumference.
Capital of Peræa. Captured by Antiochus 218 B.C.
Rebuilt by Pompey, to gratify Demetrius a *freedman.*
Captured by Vespasian, the people massacred, and the town reduced to ashes.
The pavements still shew the tracks of the chariot wheels.

Gadara added by Augustus to the territory of Herod the great.
Its most interesting remains, are the tombs in the cliffs around the city.
The warm springs flow on, and the tombs are still inhabited.

Γερασηνῶν, *Lachmann;* γεργεσηνων, *Cod. Sinai.* Γαδαρηνῶν, traced to *Origen.* Matt.'s reading preferred, *Alford, Andrews.* Mark and Luke's preferred, *Ellicott, Tischendorf.* Gadara, an hour from the sea, *Ebrard.* Wady Feik, *Stanley.* Luke names the more important city, *Meyer, Ewald.*

---

27. *And when he went forth to land, there met him out of the city a certain man, which had devils long time, and ware no clothes, neither abode in any house, but in the tombs.*

Met. Contest with demons, succeeds the storm on the lake.
Met, doubtless with purposes of violence, *overawed* by Christ.
The demoniac was coming out of the tombs, Mark, "*out of the city.*"
Matt. speaks of two. Mark & Luke of one, *i.e.* of the more desperate one.
Devils. Mark, *unclean,* a mysterious polluter of the soul.
Greatest victory of Satan, persuading men to *doubt* his *being.*
Our Lord had just shewn Himself the *Pacifier* of the outer world's tumults.
Lo! that, which is fiercer than floods or winds comes forth.
A spirit broken loose from the restraints of God appears.
A mightier deed, than hushing the tempest, is intended.
No clothes. This is characteristic of the insane in certain cases.
House. Driven from home by demons against his will.
Domestic comfort destroyed, by the powers of darkness.
A strange dread of the comforts, and habitations of home, haunt them.
Their fiery spirits repel all sympathies of kind hearts.
They haunt solitudes, lonely caves by day and night.
The insane dread their nearest and dearest friends.
The sinner made insane by sin, hates his best *Friend.*
Do the insane *realize* their misery and their bondage?
Medical men decide, that generally, they do *not.*
Tombs. At night, the mountains of Thebes, seem full of dwellings.
In the dark ages, thousands of hermits dwelt there.
Priest's Tomb, one and a half acres, is hewn out of solid rock.
Sarcophagi are now used for provisions, in a tomb at Gadara.
Sinners abandoning God, will hereafter have fellowship with fiends.

αυτω omitted, *Cod. Sinai.* ἀνήρ τισ—others insert the plural, *De Wette, Lange.* Matt. joined Mark's account with his, *Ebrard.* *One,* the principal sufferer, *Chrysostom, Augustine, Calvin, Alexander, Stier, Ellicott, Andrews.* His name, "*Legion,*" gave rise to the report of two, *Alford.* One became a disciple, the other did not, *Greswell.*

Madman and his keeper, *Strauss*. An unsolved difficulty, *Meyer*. The miracle in the synagogue at Capernaum, Luke iv, 33. Accounts confounded by Matt., *Olshausen*. The demoniac attacking a passer by, appear to be two, *Da Costa*. Plurality of spirits led to the use of the plural, *Neander, Hase*. Matt.'s Hebrew incorrectly rendered into Greek, *Oosterzee*. The Apostles being absent fishing, get different reports, *Ammon*. Mark's account, authentic, *Weisse*. One a Gergasene, other a Jew, *Lightfoot*. This account taken from Mark, *Ebrard*.

δαιμόνια—*demons*, from δαίω *distribute*: they *assigned destinies*. Heathen writers give this appellation to all orders of spiritual existences—1, to Providence. 2, to particular divinities. 3, to inferior divinities. 4, to a class between gods and men, some benevolent, others malignant. 5, it denotes fortune. Also beings *intercessory* between God and men, *Plato*. It included the souls of men, or heroes deified; malignant demons, *Plutarch*. By met. demons were the souls of lost men, *Jews, Josephus, Justin Martyr, Athenagoras*. Fallen spirits; first propounded by *Tertullian, Chrysostom*. ἱμάτιον οὐκ. Satan, when he can, brings a man down to such wretchedness, as to make him neglect natural decency. God loves order, decency, moderation, *Bengel*. Mark adds "*cut himself*." Peculiar disposition to self-destruction common, *Pritchard*. Apocryphal writers add, *they gnawed their own flesh*. "*Crying*," Mark; *sleeplessness* resulting from the unceasing stimulation of evil spirits, *Stier*.

---

28. *When he saw Jesus, he cried out, and fell down before him, and with a loud voice said, What have I to do with thee, Jesus,* thou *Son of God most high? I beseech thee, torment me not.*

Cried out, at the Lord, for intruding in their dread domain.
Or an instinctive feeling of the demoniac, that Jesus was the *Helper*.
The presence of a holy being, a torture to evil spirits.
Heaven would be no *heaven* to the rebellious.
Fell down. Uncertain whether the work of fiends, or adoration.
The demons usurped the man's lips, as well as his body.
Loud Voice. The unearthly shriek of an agonizing soul.
What? What have we in *common?* Why interfere with us?
Sinners wish the Spirit, Conscience, Providence to let them alone.
Why not let us alone? Confessing a doom unavoidable.
Son of God. This formula used, in dread of the great *Exorcist*.
They well knew Him. They had met Him before. Jude verse 6.
"Jesus I know, and Paul I know, but who are ye?" Acts xix. 15.
Demons, and sceptics, soon will own Him Divine. Mark i. 24.
Refusing to own Christ, our Lord, we are worse than devils.
Beseech. Mark *adjure*. Satan dissuades men from prayer, and *prays* himself.
The evil one feels his conqueror approaching. Rev. xxii. 1-3.
Fierce and terrible by nature, yet *suppliant* before Jesus.
Devils believe, but their faith causes terror, not love. Jas. ii. 19.
Torment. Evil spirits remonstrate, but do not quit their hold.
Devils knew him better far, and earlier, than men.

They recognized him as their Sovereign in a *pre-existent* state.
"Hasten not our doom, prolong our respite from hell!"
It was a torture to them, not to be permitted, to torment others.
Redeemer's triumph over His foes delayed, but certain. Rev. xx. 10.
"Reserved in everlasting chains, under darkness, till the great day." Jude 6 verse.
They dread hell, not as a place of *sin*, but of *punishment*.
To lose a victim, is a torment to their malignant dispositions.
But angels being God-like, *rejoice* over the sinner's deliverance.

προσέπεσεν—Luke v. 8. Mark has the stronger term, *προσεκύνησεν*—*δέομαι*, pray. Mark *ορκίζω*—from which *exorcise*, calling on God. Τί ἐμοὶ καὶ σοὶ, extorted by fear: *there is nothing in common between thee and us, Hilary.* *βασανίσῃς*—The *βάσανος*. The *Lapis Lydius*, the *touch-stone*, was anciently applied to gold, to test its purity. Term used of any kind of proof by *torture*. It was the opinion of the Fathers for the first three or four centuries, that the devils are not yet locally in hell (they are not *tormented before their time*); but have their mansions in the air, *Pearce*. *Personality* of Satan is here manifest, as *lunacy* could not possibly have ever suggested such a thought, *Olshausen*.

---

29. *(For he had commanded the unclean spirit to come out of the man. For oftentimes it had caught him: and he was kept bound with chains and in fetters; and he brake the bands, and was driven of the devil into the wilderness.)*

Commanded. Demons recognise One, with the *right* and power to command.
Unclean. Polluted himself, and polluting every thought he cherished.
Come out. A reason for the demon's request in this command.
On Christ's entering the heart, evil spirits retire.
Instead of shewing *rebellion*, they trembled in His presence.
Observe Christ's Divine composure, amid the fury of demons.
Caught him. The demon at such times, bore him away with him.
Human strength was powerless, in such paroxysms.
Bound. His keepers having succeeded in bringing him home.
Turks still bind the insane, as before *asylums* were founded.
Chains. Manacles for the *hands*, **fetters**, were for the *feet*.
Brake. His supernatural strength was due to the demon.
Sinners mad on their idols, fling off all restraints of virtue. Ps. ii. 3.
Medical observers, like *Pritchard*, have noted the *supernatural power* of the insane.
No one could bind his *limbs*, or subdue his *will*.
Driven. A province of humanity lying under the devil's ravages.

hose under Satan *say*—"Let us break their bands asunder." Psa. ii. 3.
atthew gives the result. "No man might pass that way." Matt. viii. 28.
/ilderness. Luke i. 80. See Notes.
in, selfish, destructive, tormenting, makes the earth a *desert*.

γὰρ—A remark of subsequent compiler, *Neander*. Like obstinate children, were erely making their proposals and subterfuges, having no inclination to obey, *Schleier-acher*. δεσμὰ may either refer to chains or cords. A marble pillar in a church, 7 nturies old, in old Cairo, still shows a staple, by which the insane were bound for ages, he pavement of marble is worn *several inches deep*, by the wretched victims, as their easeless rounds were year after year made in solitude. The prison of Chillon also mes to mind.

---

30. *And Jesus asked him, saying, What is thy name? And he said, Legion; because any devils were entered into him.*

.sked. Brought before this tribunal, a mysterious colloquy is held.
he Gr. examined as by a *judicial* investigation, not idle curiosity.
Tame. The object of the question was to *instruct* the bystanders.
mniscience needs no *information.* Inquiry put to Bartimæus for like reasons. Mark x. 51.
he answer magnifies the miracle and silences the Sadducees.
ur Lord suffered the demons *gradually* to relax their hold.
sudden change might have ruined the victim.
might help to bring the mad man to *self-consciousness*.
egion. A Roman brigade, from three to eight thousand.
iggests numbers, organized strength, and tried courage.
istinction of orders, unity of purpose, boastful of victory.
s serried ranks, long a fearful instrument of oppression to the Jews.
apudently, half-mockingly, though a prisoner, on self-defence.
ruth and error blended in his reply; his moral being almost ruined.
ae walls of his spirit broken down, open to the incursion of all evil.

'Ιησοῦσ and λέγων omitted, *Cod. Sinai.* τί ὄνομα—Who is interrogated? The moniac, or the devils tormenting him? We must modestly stand *aside*, when the Son God is speaking with an individual from hell, *Stier*. An attempt in psychological anner, to bring him to his senses, *Oosterzee*. Λεγεών—λεγιὼν, *Cod. Sinai.* Our viour now uses the singular, and then the plural, 1, a *collective*, signifying *personal* t not *individual* agency. 2, one fiend was in possession, but had many allies, whom could summon. 3, one as superior to the rest, as the commander of a Legion. Our rd showed a *kind* disposition, to enter into the disordered phantasies of a maniac, *eisse*. Better treatment of a sick man, *Lange, Braune*. First violent incursion of hell on Jesus calmly rebuked, *Stier*. Paraphrased—"I am myself an embattled host, orn to the cause, and serving under the same leader," *Stier*. These words will not bear any figurative rendering, but must be taken literally; viz., that in the sense in which other poor creatures were possessed by *one evil spirit*, this man was possessed by *many*. The fact of so many devils having entered him, shows the utter and awful break-up of his personal and rational being, *Alford*. Mark the omnipotent power of Jesus, who, by one word could cast out a *legion* (6000) of demons! *Ford*.

---

31. *And they besought him that he would not command them to go out into the deep.*

Besought. The *stronger* has come to bind the *strong* man. Luke xi. 22.

Prayers *answered*, often prove a judgment on the petitioner. Hos. xiii. 11.

Prayers of saints *refused* often proves the highest blessing. 2. Cor. xii. 7.

Command. Driven from Heaven, they felt the power of His resistless word.

Deep. Gr. *abyss*, *i.e. Hell.* Rev. xx. 1-3. *Deep* is applied to the *sea*. Mark has "*out of the country.*"

Our curiosity reproved by the severe silence of Holy Scripture.

ἄβυσσον—χώραν, *i.e.* Tartarus, 2. Pet. ii. 4. *Ταρταρώσασ*—These passages appear confirmed, as to the identity of the place, by *καὶ ἔβαλεν αὐτόν εἰσ τὴν ἄβυσσον*, Rev. xx. 3. Its N. T. synonymes are *Γεέννα*, Mark ix. 43; *Λίμνη τοῦ πυρόσ*, Rev. xx. 14; *Φυλακή*, 1. Pet. iii. 19; *Αιδησ*, Luke xvi. 23. All referring to the place of endless punishment, *Campbell*, *Grotius*, *Hammond*, *Olshausen*, *Oosterzee*. *τὴν ἄβυσσον.*—Not the Sea of Galilee as some have thought, nor yet *Gehenna*, or the *Lake of Fire*, which is the place of *future* torment, *prepared* for the devil and his angels (Matt. xxv. 41); and is distinguished from the *Abyss*, into which the devil is cast by Christ, *before* he is cast into the *Lake of Fire*, into which he will not be cast till the end of all earthly things, *Wordsworth*, *Alford*. *ἄβυσσοσ* is the word used in the Sept. for Heb. *tehom*, or *depth*, and it seems to describe the place of gloom into which the devils were plunged after their expulsion from heaven, and from which they are allowed to emerge from time to time. But it is not their final place of torment, *Mede*, *Fell*. The power of Jesus extends over *devils*, and the *abyss* itself; this the devils are compelled to *admit*, *Bengel*. *απελθεῖν*—Jews thought certain regions were assigned to individual good and evil spirits, Dan. v. 13 & 20. Thei proveden hym that he schulde not command hem that they schulden go into hell, *Tyndale*.

---

32. *And there was there a herd of many swine feeding on the mountain: and they besought him that he would suffer them to enter into them. And he suffered them.*

Many. Mark informs us, that there were about 2000.

Swine, flesh forbidden as *unclean*, by the Mosaic Law. Lev. xi. 7-8. Jews from that time to this, have eschewed its use.

Owners, probably Greeks, as they dwelt in the city of Gadara.

Besought. Jesus, by the mouth of the possessed man.

Inextinguishable desire, urges them to *harm* those, whom they *envy*.
They begged to be left undisturbed, but had been refused.
Their request a *disguise* for the malignant wish, to bring their conqueror into *reproach*.
It shews the fiends would have destroyed the man, if they could.
Suffered. Under a *permit*, He *forced* them out of their victim.
At His word, all Hell quits its grasp.
Jesus saw their malicious scheme,—gave the command, "Go!" Matt.
What mysterious power and depth, in that one word!
A concealed answer, to question (verse 28), "your time of judgment is not yet."
Their motive can't be concealed, *either of mockery*, *or of malice*.
Desperate malignity, unable to torment men, attacks brutes.
He makes the wrath of men (and devils) praise Him. Psa. lxx. 10.
Permission to do what they desire, ruins sinners. Hos. xiii. 11.

αυτοισ omitted, *Cod. Sinai.* εισελθεῖν—Ancient affinity between the serpent and the swine, *Lange.* The punishment of the fallen spirits, is, *divesting* them of bodies, *Gerlach.* (Reproduced in the "*Stars and Angels.*") Luke merely *inferred* that they entered the swine, *Neander.* A mythical addition, *Meyer.* Driven down by terror of the last paroxysm, preceding healing, *Ammon.* Dread of the Messiah, *Ewald.* The ruin of swine unexpected by Jesus, *Paulus*, *Hase.* They act entirely under the Lord's control, *Oosterzee.* Seized with madness, from some altogether undefined and unknown cause, *Schleiermacher*, *Henneberg.* If Gentile, they were guilty of insulting the national religion, *Neander.* A greater object was to test the Gadarenes, whether they would *accept or reject eternal life*, at the hands of One, who had rescued a neighbour from a legion of devils, *Major.* Mysterious fellowship of animals and devils, Isa. xiii. 21, Rev. xviii. 2, *Stier*; deemed necessary to convince the victim of his cure, *Chrysostom*; driven down by demoniacs, *Kuinoel*, *Milman.* *Swine* suited them because of their uncleanness, as serpents did because of their subtlety, *Ludolphus.* *He suffered them.*—The devil is not able, with all his might and malice, to hurt even *swine*, without God's *sufferance*, *Sanderson.* God's providence orders and directs sin and wickedness to such objects as He thinks fit, *March.* The Lord ordains for each class of sinners appropriate punishment. The *deep* is assigned to the devils, because of their *pride*, *Maximus.*

---

33. *Then went the devils out of the man, and entered into the swine: and the herd ran violently down a steep place into the lake, and were choked.*

Entered. Sadducees. Isa. xiii. 21. Rev. xviii. 2. Palpable evidence of *spiritual* being.
Jesus tested the Gadarenes how they would receive the destruction of their wealth.
He taught, the salvation of the soul is above earthly treasure.
That these fiends would destroy body and soul, if they could.
It might convince the man, of the fiends having left him.

The Hebrews must *see* their oppressors "dead on the shores." Ex. xiv. & xxx.

Gadarenes' sin, not so much keeping swine, as rejecting God.

God's taking away, is in a higher sense, *giving* greater gifts.

They saw the demons leave a neighbour, long tormented.

They saw them instantly shew their malice and presence, in about 2,000 swine.

They saw Christ's power, complete, over the spirit-world.

Their bold rejection of Christ, proves, *they deserved their loss.*

The deed is its own justification. He might have let them on the Gadarenes.

Why He permitted them to enter the swine, is answered by another question.

Why did Sovereign Mercy permit them to enter the *men?*

Instinct uncontrolled, would have saved the herd.

The essence of evil, in its true results, defeats itself.

It is stupid, blind, self-contradictory, suicidal.

Demons trying to ruin Jesus, among the Gadarenes, ruin *themselves.*

Choked. It was *no* unexpected event, or contrary to Christ's intention.

He gives no hint to the owners that He did not foresee their loss.

He simply grants the prayer of the demons, whether the herd endured the shock or not.

Unless chained, they would have plunged the Gadarenes, with their swine, in the lake.

Powers of darkness, always rushing to their own destruction.

Wilful violation of law, sooner or later punished.

A denial of the reality of demoniacal possession, in one believing the Gospels inspired, is plainly inconceivable.

Jesus' judgment on the *swine*, and not their *owners*, shews His *mercy.*

εἰσῆλθον—Through fear of the Messiah, they rush violently along, sweeping with their train, the vast herd of swine, *Ewald.* The fearful paroxysm preceding healing caused the terror and rushing of the swine, *Ammon, Lange.* The cause unknown, *Oosterzee.* A just retribution for their course, if corrupt Jews, *Neander.* The dwellers might still fish up the flesh for food, *Hug.*

εἰσ τοὺσ χοίρουσ—A poetical description of two mad men, chasing the swine into the deep, *Dr. Mede* and *Neologists.* Swineherds are watching the contest between the Saviour and the demoniac, the herds began to fight, and so tumbled headlong, *Paulus.* If the Gadarenes were guilty, Jesus would not have punished them so *circuitously, Stier.* Rights of property invaded, *Woolston.* "The cattle upon 1000 hills are the Lord's." It is no where said Christ *made* the demons enter the swine, and thus cause their ruin, *Doddridge.* It illustrates the great power of evil spirits over matter and mind. The courage or fear of the rider, is imparted to the horse, with electric celerity, *Trench.*

34. *When they that fed* them *saw what was done, they fled, and went and told* it *in the city and in the country.*

Fed. A district where swine had keepers, but souls were uncared for.
Fled. They knew not, what demons would next attempt.
Convulsions in the *spirit-world*, more terrific, than in the *natural.*
Satan makes the wicked, slaves of *fear*, as well as *guilt.*
Alarmed at the loss, they bear tidings to the owners.
Ungodly often care more for their swine, than for Christ.

ἀπελθόντες cancelled, *Tischendorf, Alford, Scholz, Lachmann;* omitted, *Cod. Sinai.*

---

35. *Then they went out to see what was done; and came to Jesus, and found the man, out of whom the devils were departed, sitting at the feet of Jesus, clothed, and in his right mind: and they were afraid.*

Found. A stranger thing than loss of property, a *demoniac cured!*
Sitting. Oriental pupils still sit at the feet of the teacher.
The sight of the famous demoniac, the terror of the whole region, converted.
Clothed. For years, broken fetters or rags, his only raiment.
Madness, like sin, makes men *shameless* in their degradation.
Glorying in their shame, a sign of deep depravity. Phil. iii. 19.
Jesus clothes his followers in the *garment* of salvation. Isa. lxi. 10.
Right mind. Not roaming like a madman, ruining all he met.
Symbol of the contest between light and darkness.
After heavy sacrifices, victory is sure to crown the truth.
God gives "a spirit of love, and of a *sound mind.*" 2. Tim. i. 7.
He *came to himself,*—"I will arise and go to my Father." Luke xv. 18.
"*Madness* in the heart of the sons of men, while they live." Ecc. ix. 3.
Afraid. Terror seizes the ungodly, at a superhuman sight. Lk. i. 12.
Clinging to sin, they dreaded His holy interference yet farther.
The righteous are bold as a lion, nothing in Heaven, Earth, or Hell, can harm them.
"The Lord is my salvation, of whom shall I be afraid?" Psa. xxvii. 1.

36. *They also which saw* it *told them by what means he that was possessed of the devils was healed.*

Means. Told, to *implicate* Jesus in the *prejudices* of the Gadarenes.
Insinuate, He could not heal a man, without destroying the swine.
Healed. A rectified understanding, a sanctified nature, a pacified conscience. *Christ healed both body and soul.*

δε add λεγοντες. και omitted, *Cod. Sinai.*

37 ¶ *Then the whole multitude of the country of the Gadarenes round about besought him to depart from them; for they were taken with great fear: and he went up into the ship, and returned back again.*

Whole multitude. Marks the *universal* resolve to reject Christ.
These high-handed rebels, deserved deeper punishment.
Often had Jesus used His power to bless, seldom to punish.
He smote the *swine*, the *figtree*, and *intruders* in Gethsemane. John xviii. 6.
Gadarenes dare not reproach Him for their loss.
Against their will, they shall have a *memorial* of His *mercy*, in the cured demoniac.
Heathen in solemn procession, besought their gods to avert calamities.
Thus Gadarenes went and besought Jesus to depart.

Besought. Their request proves *them*, as well as the demoniac, under Satan.
They forgot the blessing bestowed on the healed demoniac.
Unmindful of their region being delivered from this scourge.
They were indifferent to the PRESENCE of the Son of God Himself.
They could only think of their swine, which had been destroyed.
They were lost to all sense of gratitude for their Greatest Benefactor.
Chastisements, brought them very near to their *Redeemer*.
Their hour of *deliverance* had come, but they knew it not.

Depart. They would rather lose their *Saviour* than their *swine*.
A sad contrast to the Samaritans' prayer. John iv. 40.
The Lord granted both requests, the one in love, the other in vengeance.
He draws, but never *dragoons* men into His kingdom.
The most astonishing miracles, do not produce faith. Luke xvi. 31.
No judgment more dreadful, than when God grants sinners their requests.
Their *goods* in their estimation over-balanced their soul's *salvation*.
They put their loss down to *Christ*, instead of to the *fiends*.
Thus infidels charge Christianity, with fanaticism.
Their prayer, the final closing of the door of hope! 1. Thess. v. 19.
"Depart, we desire not the knowledge of thy ways." Job. xxi. 14.
He took them at their word, they were joined to their idols, HE LET THEM ALONE!
They cry "*Depart!*" Their Judge will say "*Depart!*" Matt. xxv. 41.
Christ forsaking the soul, seals its eternal doom.
The life-giving fluid failing, decrees the tree must die.
Sun, rain, dews, and winds, visit its withering branches, in vain.
Those refusing Christ as *Judge*, cannot have Him as *Redeemer*.

Men love not a religion that will cost them dear, *Taylor*. Hell has no project to keep out religion, like this,—to make religion thwart an *interest*. Rather no Christianity than lose an earthly satisfaction by it. Rather have the *swine* than CHRIST Himself, *Allestry*. It is as possible for devils to be saved, as the men, who take up their chief rest and happiness below GOD, *Baxter*. He who says "Depart" to Jesus, executes upon himself his own doom, *Gale*.

"*Depart.*" From motives of humility, *Jerome*. Fierce hatred, *Trench*. ἀπελθεῖν—Christ's mission to the Jews not appreciated by these Gentiles. The benefit was individual, the evils were general, *Alexander*. Presence of a holy being dreaded by all depraved beings.

---

38. *Now the man, out of whom the devils were departed besought him that he might be with him: but Jesus sent him away, saying.*

Besought. Fearing to be reduced again to the bondage of Satan.
He desires gratefully to be near his Benefactor.
His body cured, we infer his *soul* was renewed also.
He would disavow all sympathy with his rebellious countrymen.
Be with Him. The redeemed long to remain fast by their Lord.

ὁ Ἰησοῦς omitted, *Cod Sinai.* "*Sent.*" Melancholy by temper, he needs the healthy communion of friends, *Trench;* gratitude, *Alexander:* fear of demons, *Theophylact.* The man was by no means content with getting his cure. Nec mihi Tua sufficiunt, sine Te; nec Tibi placent mea, sine me, *Bernard.* He refused him, lest, if he was admitted to be an immediate follower, the works of CHRIST should be ascribed to the devil, and also, lest He should appear to seek his own glory in having such an attendant, *Ludolphus.* He refused him, to exercise his faith, and teach him that, though personally absent, He would be with him in His Divine power and love, *Wordsworth.*

---

39. *Return to thine own house, and show how great things God hath done unto thee. And he went his way, and published throughout the whole city how great things Jesus had done unto him.*

Return. A speaking memorial of the Lord's wonder-working power.
Own house, from which he had so long wandered, an exile.
To the circle of friends, from whom he had long been estranged.
Shew. Some healed are to be *silent*, others to publish their healing. Luke v. 14.
He may perhaps repair some of the ruin, he has wrought.
Great things. His deliverance from fiends, symbol of *higher* blessings.
Neither the fig tree, nor this, a miracle of *judgment.*
Judgment cannot be applied to irrational creatures.
Our Father daily destroys the less, to feed the greater.
He stops not the lightning, because some trees are shattered, and lives lost.
Nor the murrain that carries off thousands of cattle.
Power and Love, were still willing to save all who came.

God. Our Saviour attributes His own acts, to Jehovah.

Published. His neighbour must rejoice, and share Christ's blessings with him. Luke viii. 1; ix. 2.

"I will declare what God hath done for my soul." Ps. lxvi. 16.

Warm religious *feelings* are given as incitements to works of mercy and love.

Those feelings may die away in obeying them, as the seed changes into the herb, which bears the fruit.

Consistent obedience is more acceptable to God, than high transports, and passionate longings.

Goodness does not grudge that many should take part in it; rejoices in extending.

Andrew coming to Christ, calls Simon; Philip being called, calls Nathanael.

God will require of us no less account of the salvation of our neighbour, than of our own.

Negligence in usefulness, criminal, may cause our condemnation.

The slothful servant declared *wicked*, was cast out into outer darkness.

Infinite joy in having been instrumental in the salvation of one soul.

Healed demoniac not ashamed of the Gospel of Christ, knew it to be the power of God unto salvation.

κηρυσσων—Luke viii. 1, and ix. 2. See Notes.

---

40. *And it came to pass, that, when Jesus was returned, the people gladly received him: for they were all waiting for him.*

Received. Gr. *gave Him a reception*—received Him with a welcome.

The Gospel rejected at one place, is welcomed in another.

Gadarenes rejected, but Galileans *hailed* his approach.

An afflicted parent was longing and hoping for His Divine aid.

Waiting. They who desire to receive Christ, will never lack opportunity.

Order of time.—Paralytic healed. Matthew called. Matt.'s feast. Converses with the Pharisees. The *Twelve* chosen. Sermon on the Mount. Parables. Demoniac of Gergesa healed. Meets John's disciples. Discourse on fasting. Daughter of Jairus healed. *Andrews.*

---

41. *And, behold, there came a man named Jáirus, and he was a ruler of the synagogue; and he fell down at Jesus' feet, and besought him that he would come into his house.*

Behold. Our Lord was then in the house of Matthew. See Matt. ix. 10. Luke v. 29.

Jairus, ruler. Luke vii. 3. A national hereditary Jewish elder.
Duties, to conduct the worship and discipline of the synagogue.
Christian church, a copy of the patriarchal eldership.
Founded on the natural relationship of the family government.
Church, was not copied after the later Jewish bench of elders.
Church, the permanent arrangement of the old Theocracy.
These elders were ex-officio, rulers of the synagogue.
By birth, and office; highest in rank, and social position.

Synagogue. Houses dedicated to the worship of God, wherein it was lawful to pray, preach, and dispute, but not sacrifice. Luke iv. 15. See Notes.

Fell down. Our Lord never declined reverential salutations.
Gesture of *importunate entreaty*, not necessarily *adoration.*
Prostration common now in the East both towards God and man.

Come. Healing without being present, was incomprehensible.
His miraculous power through unbelief but dimly understood.
But the centurion's faith taught them a truer theology.
To whom shall *we* go, when borne down by our sorrows, if not to Jesus?

Our Lord was at a feast given by Matthew, *Alexander.* Ἰάειρος Heb. *My light.* By giving the name of this *certain ruler*, who, as the chief man in the synagogue at Capernaum, was well known to all the people of Galilee, Mark and Luke enabled any who might doubt the truth of the miracle, to ascertain the fact from the father himself, *Bost.* συναγωγῆς Luke iv. 15. Jairus formed part of the centurion's deputation to Christ. He who lately pleaded for another, is now touched by a nearer calamity, *Trench.*

προσεκύνει Matt. Their mode of expressing by *deed*, what we do by *word.* When this reverence was rendered by one Jew to another; they regarded it as *worship*, Luke iv. 7, *Herodotus*, *Campbell.* A recognition of the Divine power in Christ, for outwardly Jairus was of a rank superior to Christ, *Bengel.* Jairus had but imperfect views of our Lord's Divine power. Had he worshipped Him as Incarnate God, like the centurion, he would not have pressed Him to *come* to his house, and *lay His hand* on his sick child, *Chrysostom.*

An Armenian made 24 prostrations in succession before an image of Mary, in Jerusalem, in the presence of the Author.

---

42. *For he had one only daughter, about twelve years of age, and she lay a dying. But as he went the people thronged him.*

Daughter. The Greek a Hebrew form, *i.e., dearly beloved.* Psa. xxxv. 17.
At *Nain*, an only son: the *lunatic*, an only child: at Bethany, an only brother.

Twelve. Parental affections had clustered long and strongly around her.

hem of Christ's garment was not intended to *wound*, but to heal; and hence the woman laid hold of it, *Remigius*, in *Denton*. ἱματίου represents the Incarnation, which when received or touched by faith, heals and saves, *Athanasius*. ῥύσιο—Mark has *μάστιξ* a *scourge*, denoting the finger of God, *Major*.

---

45. *And Jesus said, Who touched me? When all denied, Peter and they that were with him said, Master, the multitude throng thee and press* thee, *and sayest thou, Who touched me?*

Who touched? He would not proclaim His own miracle.
Her testimony of the distinguished benefit would influence others.
He consciously and miraculously had imparted to her *health*.
Now He shews His miraculous *knowledge* of her experience.
No one had experienced a cure, from a similar disease.
Jesus was to her faith, the Fountain of all mercies.
Many healed by faith, are soon lost in the crowd.
Hidden faith must come to light—
1. For the glory of the Lord. 2. For its own confirmation.
3. For the encouragement of others.
Salvation a joy with which the stranger does not intermeddle. Prov. xiv. 10.
Our holiest devotions shrink from the gaze of men.
He asked, not because He needed *information*. John i. 48.
His conscious omnipotence healed her, having drawn her to His side by sovereign grace.
His own hand had sowed the seed of faith in her heart.
Carrying away her blessing in secret, would leave a false impression.
She must tell of her *disease*, *faith*, *cure*, *Deliverer*.
The Lord awakens *repentance* by "Adam where art thou?" Gen. iii. 9.
Elisha arouses *conscience*. "Whence comest thou Gehazi?" 2. Kings, v. 25.
A father humbles a guilty child. Who has done this wrong?
All denied. Possibly the healed female joined with them at first.
Throng. Others near, touched His body, without effect.
Faith, connecting link, between His *power* and their *need*, was absent.

It is not enough for any of us to believe that Christ's power can save—we must *touch* Him, *Coster*. Not a bare material touch—the crowd pressed around Him—*touch* of faith only, *Gand*. και λεγειο—μου omitted, *Cod. Sinai*. ἀψαμενὸσ—*Who touched?* He knew not the particular individual relieved, *Oosterzee*. Human nature is set forth in this woman. The useless efforts of physicians, showed the vain application of cultivated classic minds, to sages, for a balm to heal the diseased heart. But the moment humanity touched God in the *Incarnate One*, it was healed. Gentiles thronged to steal a blessing, taking the kingdom of heaven by violence, *Theophylact*, *Augustine*. *Credidit, dixit, tetigit. In his tribus speciebus sanitas omnis promeretur, id est in fide, verbo et opere, Maurus.*

46. *And Jesus said, Somebody hath touched me: for I perceive that virtue is gone out of me.*

Touched. Mark has, *looked around*, with a searching glance.
His energetic repetition, indicates the certainty of His Omniscience.
He rejoiced over her faith, well pleased to part with mercy.
Virtue. Gr. *power.* The only magic was His *Almighty will.*
He complains not, He was neither *weakened*, nor *wronged.*
He no more envied her aid, than the sun giving light.
Jesus' tranquillity contrasted, 1. With a pressing crowd.
2. The contradiction of the disciples. 3. The perplexity of the woman.
4. The anxiety of Jairus.
Religion, a work between the soul, and its God.
"With the mouth confession is made unto salvation." Rom. x. 10.
By this time, He may have fixed *His eye* upon her.
He would remove from her mind the fear that she had done wrong.
He would show her, that she could not be hidden from Him.
He would bless her with *peace* and *comfort* as a reward of faith.
He would set forth her faith, that all might imitate it.
He would shew, that He could not only cure disease, but that He knew all things.
He would confirm the faith of Jairus, shaken, at the tidings of his daughter's death, *Denton.*

Ἥψατό—The word signifies more than to *touch,*—to *fasten* oneself eagerly to a thing, to *cling* to it with a desire to derive something from it, *Wordsworth.* δύναμιν—The power of the Godhead, not His body or His garment, *Tostatus.* No miracle wrought by Jesus in which His humanity had not a part. He *called;* He *touched;* He *anointed;* but in each case it was the Divine power of the Eternal Word which went out from Him; His human nature but the instrument, *Cyril.*

His body healed not, but conveyed healing, united inseparably to Divinity, *Barradius.* As God He healed, as man He perceived that the Divine power had done the miracle, *Avendano.* Evident the healing power did not reside in His body, for on all sides it was pressed by the multitude, without giving forth any *virtue* to them; nor in His garments, for these the soldiers afterwards parted, without receiving any blessing, *Chrysostom.* Miraculous energy, similar to the shock of an electric battery, *Stier.* Consciously suffers healing power to flow, *Oosterzee, Lange.* Magical influence, *Strauss.* Jesus unconscious of the flow of virtue, *Meyer.* Every movement and result, Divine grace and power, *Doddridge.* τὴν τοῦτο ποιήσασαν Mark.—A wonderful precision of expression, indicating His *absolute knowledge, Olshausen.*

---

47. *And when the woman saw that she was not hid, she came trembling, and falling down before him, she declared unto him before all the people for what cause she had touched him, and how she was healed immediately.*

Not hid. Vain the hope to escape his power, or elude His presence.

This miracle, within a miracle, had no word spoken.

Trembling. Disheartening fears, consistent with saving faith.

Falling down. Oriental *prostration* shews by deed, what we express.

By a consummate stroke of justice and mercy, He *reproves* her fault, and rewards her faith.

Jesus seeks through bodily mercies, to heal her soul.

Her cure unacknowledged, would hardly have been a blessing.

This hour, a *crisis* in her spiritual life, she might have found confession too hard, *before healing*.

She publishes her deliverance from disease, if not also from *sin*.

The example of the crowd *warns* us, her touch, our plea.

Many press the body of Christ, who never touch Him in spirit.

Many utter words of prayer, who never lift their heart to God,—never pray.

Many thousands came out of Egypt—*only* two entered the Promised Land.

Many lepers in Israel in the days of Elisha the prophet, *only* Naaman, the Syrian, healed.

Many around the pool of Bethesda, *only one who first stepped* in, was healed.

Many thronged around Jesus on His way to the ruler's house, *only* this woman healed.

Ministers not to be discouraged, when they find, that so *few* are benefited by the word.

Though many are called, but few touch Jesus, to the saving of their souls.

If we find him in a crowd, we must *acknowledge* Him openly.

Jacob stealthily obtained, Isaac openly confirmed the blessing.

"*Woman.*" The *Veronica* of tradition, *Oosterzee*. *Trembling*. The Christian has too solid a view of Divine mercy in Christ not to rejoice; but he has too exalted a view of the Divine holiness not "to rejoice with trembling," Psa. ci. 1, *Arnaud*.

Declared. Our Lord always sought, through bodily cures, to reach the disease of the soul, *Olshausen*. She tries to secure blessings secretly, but the Lord requires honor openly, *Trench*, Rom. x. 9. ηλθε omitted, *Cod. Sinai*. δι ην—αυτου omitted, *Cod. Sinai*.

---

48. *And he said unto her, Daughter, be of good comfort: thy faith hath made thee whole; go in peace.*

Daughter. This indicates her *adoption*—her new relation to God.

Thy faith, saved her *mediately*, but Christ's virtue (Power) *energetically*.

The *garment* could do no more for her, than the physicians.

The woman's faith. 1. Secretly cherished. 2. Courageously shewn. 3. Immediately discovered. 4. Humbly confessed. 5. Happily rewarded.

1. *Praying faith heard by Jesus.* 2. Longing faith tried.
3. Fainting faith strengthened. 4. Steadfast faith rewarded.
5. Thankful faith perfected by words of assurance and consolation.

We see, Jesus ever delights rather to *give* than *receive*.

We know not how much ignorance is consistent with the new birth.

Go in peace. Be for ever healed of thy sad, long suffered, plague.

"My *peace* give I unto you, not as the world giveth," &c. John xiv. 27.

αυτῃ θάρσει cancelled, *Tischendorf:* omitted *Cod. Sinai.* *Courage, Daughter!* or *cheer up.* A fine Homeric word, always used to calm the apprehensions felt, *Trench. Alexander.* *Thy faith.* A lesson to the ruler, and to the nation, that it is not the Mosaic law saves, but faith in Christ, *Cyril.* Faith does not justify us *formaliter;* for so the righteousness of Christ justifies: but *effective: non tamen quod justitiam illam efficiat, vel effective nobis imputet:* for it is God who thus justifies, but only because *justitiam a Christo ablatam animæ peccatrici applicat, Barlow.* Faith is the beginning and source of all other virtues. *It is the root, and in its perfection comprehends all others, Nicole.*

---

49. ¶ *While he yet spake, there cometh one from the ruler of the synagogue's* house, *saying to him, Thy daughter is dead; trouble not the Master.*

Spake. The miracle and throng sorely tried Jairus' faith.

He evidently went with the approbation of his family.

They ceased to have any hope of aid from the Master.

Death was shaking the last few sands, in the hour glass of his daughter's life.

Mary and Martha saw death drawing near, yet Jesus *tarried.*

By faith, holding fast to God, Jairus shewed no impatience.

Saying. A strange pleasure among fallen beings, is bearing evil tidings.

They had faith, Christ might *heal* the sick, but not *raise* the dead.

Dead, *i.e.* all is over! Return to your house, and submit to your fate.

He delays both in Bethany, and here, until death ensued.

In both cases, He obscurely promises deliverance.

In both, He calls death a *sleep.* Acts vii. 60. 1. Cor. xv. 6.

Trouble. Do *not annoy* Him. There is no relief to *your* case.

Jairus' friends, surely do not share his faith.

Master. Gr. *Teacher.* It became the customary designation of our Lord.

Indicates the constant great work of His life.

ἐκόπτοντο—Mid. *To strike one's self*, *Meyer*: *plangebant*. Cp. *Aristoph. Lysist.* 397, κόπτεσθ' Ἄδωνιν, i.e., *beat yourselves in grief for Adonis*, *Wordsworth*. In Egypt, among a band of females on the Nile, one about 19, whose husband had been drowned, howled with frantic energy. She had her hair disheveled, dust upon her head falling on her garment. She was beating her bosom, laid bare to her strokes. Her words were, "Alas! my misery!" "Alas! the lord of my house!"

οὐκ ἀπέθανεν—She was in a syncope, *Origen*, *Olshausen*: *asleep*, *Hase*. Jesus denied she was dead, *Braune*. Luke writes as though he believed she was dead, *Von Gerlach*. So near death that she needed great quiet to be restored, *Ammon*. A trance *Neander*, *Paulus*, *Schleiermacher*. Actually dead, *Alford*, *Elsley*, and evangelical commentators. Jewish legends state, that the soul lingers awhile near the body, to which it has been bound by so many links. Even science itself conjectures, that the echoes of life ring in the body, much longer, than commonly supposed, *Trench*.

καθεύδει, is *sleeping* or *asleep*, the present tense, denoting actual condition; as the aorist before it, strictly understood, denotes a *previous* occurrence, *Major*. *She did not die, but sleeps.* Both terms are used figuratively. The first that she was really dead, but only for a time. The second, though her death was real, it was so transient, that it may be called a sleep, *Stier*. It was very common amongst the Jews to express the death of any one by the word which properly signifies *to sleep*. The phrase, *when he slept*, occurs hundreds of times in the Talmudists' expressive of the time of death, *Lightfoot*.

She is not dead to ME, to whom all things live: for to CHRIST, who is the essential *life*, there is nothing *dead*, *Jerome*.

---

53. *And they laughed him to scorn, knowing that she was dead.*

Scorn. Hired mourners dread, lest they might lose their fees. Familiar with death, they pass at a bound, from weeping to derision. They saw the contradiction between their *knowledge*, aud His *assertions*. Christ and His people ever laughed to scorn, by an unbelieving world. Unbelief laughs at the hope of immortality, though it trembles at death. **Was dead.** This statement rests on the *inspiration* of the *Scriptures*.

κατεγέλων—The particle in composition, equivalent to *laughing Him down*. They silenced Him by derision. A common method with the vulgar of silencing argument, *Hase*. Smiled with contemptuous pity, *Elsley*, *Stier*, *Alexander*. Their scorn, a testimony to the reality of the miracle, *Bengel*.

The light-hearted *minstrels* and pleasure-seekers of the world, are ready at every difficulty they meet with in Holy Scripture, to *scorn*—and are ever unable to see the mighty works of God, which He reveals only to the humble and reverent soul, *Denton*.

---

54. *And he put them all out, and took her by the hand, and called, saying, Maid, arise.*

Put, &c. Gr. *forcibly excluded*, or *peremptorily dismissed*.

Hired mourners fearing loss of pay, *persisted* in remaining.
The curious oft desecrate the solemnity of death chambers.
Hand, as though He would awaken a sleeping child.
Clasping the hand, *identified* Him as the performer of the miracle.
Elijah and Elisha *wrestled*, to *enforce* his prey from death.
Talitha cumi, (Mark v. 41) veils the loftiest dignity with the tenderest affection.
Arise. Gr. *Awake:* at Nain, *Young man arise:* at Bethany, *Come forth.*
Three resurrections—1. From death on the *bed*. 2. From death on the *bier*. 3. From death and corruption in the *grave*.
These three cases show Christ's power over death in *every form*.
Should teach us, that He is able to revive *dead* souls in every stage of spiritual mortality.

ἐκβαλὼν—καὶ, omitted, *Cod. Sinai.*, cancelled, *Tischendorf*, *Alford*. Ἡ παῖς—The nominative for the vocative. Luke has the fewest Hebraisms of all the Evangelists. Traced by tradition to Peter's supervision of Mark's Gospel, that he alone has preserved the very words in the Aramaic form, *Alexander*. *Talitha cumi*, must have long rung in Peter's ear, *Stier*.

Christ adapted His *manner* of working miracles to the occasion. He called the four days dead Lazarus from the grave with a *loud voice* (John xi. 43, φωνῇ μεγάλῃ ἐκραύγασε); but He *took this youthful maiden by the hand*, and woke her *gently* from the sleep of death, *Wordsworth*.

---

55. *And her spirit came again, and she arose straightway: and he commanded to give her meat.*

56. *And her parents were astonished, but he charged them that they should tell no man what was done.*

Came again. Gr. *recovery of one, from faintness.* 1. Sam. xxx. 12.
Here, actual return of the spirit, from the invisible world.
Meat. In their great joy, the parents may have forgotten food.
Miracles cease, when their necessity no longer exists.
Raising of the dead, the mightiest outgoing of our Saviour's power.
The boundary line between health and sickness, not clearly defined.
The fiercest tempests, by degrees, allay themselves into a calm.
The change of water into wine, may have remote analogies.
No imagination can bridge the GULF between LIFE and DEATH.
Hour cometh, when those who have slept thousands of years, shall awake. John v. 28.

Luke, the *physician*, alone of the Evangelists, notes that *her spirit came back to her again;* He thus corrected erroneous notions of popular belief and philosophical incredulity, and taught the Greeks, that the human soul, on its separation from the body, passes immediately into a place of joy or sorrow, *Wordsworth.*

He commanded to give her meat. The life which had been restored by supernatural means is to be maintained by natural means, *W. & W.* She *arose*, she *walked*, she *ate*, (Conf. Matt., Mark, Luke). These particulars furnish an answer to the objections of modern rationalism. Salvation consists in *new life, progress in holiness, and participation in Christ*, see John vi. 53-54.

καὶ ἀνέστη παραχρῆμα omitted, *Cod. Sinai.* *μηδενὶ εἰπεῖν*—He repressed their talkativeness, lest they should immediately *destroy again* the slight spark of life, which was but just enkindled, *Olshausen.* As though Almighty energy could be interrupted by the babblings of mortals. An unauthorized later tradition, *Meyer.* To show that He is the giver of good things, but not covetous of glory. In His humility there is "the hiding of His power," *Ford.*

Ancient Expositions.

Commentators, in olden times, loved to dwell on the picture presented in these two miracles, of the way in which Christ dealt with the two great divisions of the human race—the Gentile people and the Jewish Church. In the maiden lying *a dying* at twelve years of age, and the woman with her disease of twelve years standing, we have types of the Jewish Church and Gentile nations. Long time had priests, and prophets, and rulers longed for the coming of Christ, for the daughter of Zion was lying on a bed, sick with sin, and hopeless of cure, except from the hand of this Great Deliverer. For long time the Lord seemed to delay His coming; and when at length He was born into this world, the daughter of Zion lay at the point of death; so that whilst He was in the way she did die. When He came to her, sick and sore, wounded by long past sin, He did so, following in the footsteps of patriarchs, and prophets, and rulers; and He came with His disciples, that He might raise her from the sleep of death.

Whilst on His way thither, the Gentile world, perishing by inward corruptions, but strong in faith, weary of the many false physicians to whom it had recourse—the framers of the various systems of philosophy, which in vain had sought to cure the disease caused by sin, came to Him for healing. He stayed to cure, and to call these into His fold. To these His garment was no stumbling-block; an Incarnate God no offence. Of this they laid hold; they believed and were healed. When the fulness of the Gentile world shall have come in, then shall all Israel be raised from death, and be saved, *for she is not dead, but sleepeth.* See *Denton's* Commentary.

CHAPTER IX.

THEN he called his twelve disciples together, and gave them power and authority over all devils, and to cure diseases.

Called. This formal assembling, implies no ordinary business.
Twelve. History of the disciples. Luke vi. 14-16. See Notes.
Power. They were agents of the manifested purposes of God.
Authority. Delegates of the Messiah, they were commissioned.
They were endowed with *ability*, and *right*, to perform miracles.
Demons had power to perform "lying wonders." 2. Thess. ii. 9.
Hence our Saviour rebukes the eager desire for marvels. John iv. 48.
Disciples always wrought their miracles *in the name* of our Lord.
All. None expected. Hence their unbelief is rebuked. Luke ix. 41.
Cure. The Lord cares for the bodies, as well as the souls of men.
Devils and diseases. Discriminated by Luke, a *physician*.
Ability to *impart* miraculous gifts, the fulness of Deity.
"It pleased the Father, that in Him, should all fulness dwell." Col. i. 19.
Difference between Christ and all others who exercised miraculous gifts.
Christ is the Author, others are recipients; He the Source, they, only streams.
Miraculous power, the *seal* of fishermen's commission.

δώδεκα. The number twelve (3 X 4) in Scripture seems to indicate perfection and universality. "Hi sunt operarii," says *Augustine*, "qui mittendi erant et *quadrati* orbis partes ad finem *Trinitatis* vocaturi." It would appear that 3 is an arithmetical symbol of what is *Divine*, and 4 of what is *Created*. 3 + 4.=7 is the union of the two; hence signifying Rest, a Sabbath; 3 X 4.=12 is the blending and indwelling of what is Divine with what is created: e.g. as in Israel, the people of God, and in the Heavenly Jerusalem, Rev. xxi. 14. The *Twelve Apostles* were regarded by the ancient Church as typified by the *Twelve Sons* of Israel, the *Twelve wells* at Elim, and by the *Twelve stones* of the Urim and Thummim on the breastplate of the high priest, who was a type of Christ; the *Twelve loaves* of shewbread; the *Twelve spies* of the promised land, the type of Heaven; the *Twelve stones* taken from the Jordan. Joshua, or *Jesus*, the son of Nun, begins his office at the banks of Jordan, where Christ is baptized. He chooseth there *Twelve* men to carry *Twelve* stones over with them, as our Jesus thence began to choose His *Twelve Apostles*, those *foundation stones* in the church of God, whose names are *in the Twelve foundations of the walls of the holy city, the new Jerusalem*, Rev. xxi. 14. They seem also to be represented by the *Twelve stars* in the crown of the woman in the wilderness, who typifies the church on earth, Rev. xii. 1. *Baur*, *Arnoldi*, *Maldonatus*, *Jerome*, *Pearson*. &c., quoted by *Wordsworth*.

μαθητὰς αὐτοῦ—cancelled, *Tischendorf*, *Alford*, *Campbell*. Retained, *Lachmann*. *Cod. Sinai.* has *ἀποστόλους*. *δύναμιν*. Luke v. 17. *νόσους*—some *disingenuously* insert *ἄλλους*, as though the demoniacs had merely *natural diseases*. The article is wanting, implying that only such as *desired*, were to be healed, *Stier*.

---

2. *And he sent them to preach the kingdom of God, and to heal the sick.*

Sent. Those alone called of God, may look for His presence.

Preach. Proclaiming as a herald. Luke viii. 1. See Notes.

1. Heralds announced the *combat* at the Olympic games.
2. They summoned the contenders. 3. They declared the prize.
4. They exhorted those about to strive. 5. They explained the laws.
6. They proclaimed the victor. 7. They delivered the crown.
8. They convoked solemn assemblies, and oft slew sacrifices.
9. They entered between contending armies securely; free permission to enter besieged cities.
10. Commanded silence when kings were to speak, after handing them the sceptre.
11. They declared war and announced peace, Greeks styled them, "The messengers of gods, and of men."
12. Their rod given by Apollo was fabled to have power of life and death.

A herald cried before Joseph, "Bow the knee." Gen. xli. 43.

This offer of the kingdom from *such* a source, unexpected by the Jews.

Their appointment to preach, was not to afford *practice* for future employment.

Nor to prepare districts of Galilee for Christ's presence.

The Twelve were to follow, not to precede; to reap, not to sow.

They went not as strangers among enemies, but among friends.

Heal. Rude in speech, poorly clad, their warrant was "*Heal the sick.*"

Half of mankind, are thought to be under *disease*.

Christ's empire over the heart, one, not of *force*, but of *love*. Prov. xxiii. 26.

The Twelve had no promises of future conquest or glory.

They held out no hopes of earthly prosperity to followers.

Repentance and faith, of a *cross* to be borne, of a *crown* won.

Kingdom. Their hearts reluctantly yielded to a *spiritual* kingdom. Acts. i. 6.

Heaven forbids ministers mingling earthly with heavenly policy.

They preached a kingdom of righteousness, peace, and joy in the Holy Ghost. Rom. xiv. 17.

κηρύσσειν. The character of the herald was sacred, *Homer.* Achilles calls them Κήρυκες Διὸς ἄγγελοι ἠδὲ καὶ ἀνδρων. They carried a *rod*, given by Apollo to Mercury. Its fabled properties produced *sleep*, or raised the *dead.* It was entwined with serpents, emblems of wisdom; and with wings, emblems of haste. It was doubtless the *rod* of Moses, as handed down by tradition. *Potter's Gr. An.*

"*Preach.*" I do not remember that in any history or the framing of any state, there has ever been such a law, or practice, as that of *preaching*, which is only an ordinance of God Himself, for His own people, *Donne.*

τοὺς ἀσθενοῦντας—cancelled, *Tischendorf, Alford.* *Cod. Sinai.* has ἀσθενεῖς.

---

3. *And he said unto them, Take nothing for your journey, neither staves, nor scrip, neither bread, neither money; neither have two coats apiece.*

Nothing. They must go, just as they were, trusting in Providence.
Staves. Judea rocky, a staff so necessary, a spare one is taken.
Lean upon no other staff, than that, trusted by the Church.
Scrip. A leather bag used by shepherds, to carry food.
Swedish, skrappa—a wallet for carrying things.
Bread. Luke vii. 33. The ministers to be fed, serving at the altar. 1. Cor. ix. 14.
Money. "I have coveted no man's silver, or gold." Acts xx. 33. Nothing asked but *prayer.* 2. Thess. iii. 1.
Two coats. Luke vi. 29. Honors and pleasures of earth, not promised. Jews wore two coats. Simplicity of dress is enjoined.
Gehazi received Naaman's curse, with his changes of raiment.
These prohibitions intended to foster *faith*, not an *ascetic* spirit.
He will prove a "Jehovah Jireh," to all doing His work.
Desiring gold, miracles would not make them rich and great.
"No man that warreth, entangleth himself in the affairs," &c. 2. Tim. ii. 4.
In their own wisdom, they would have amply equipped themselves.
This *prohibition*, to the eye of faith, a truly glorious outfit.
Their first circuit finished, "They lacked nothing." Luke xxii. 35.
His Arm and Love engaged, none *He sends*, shall ever want.
An Arm, not of flesh, overshadows all who preach the cross.
Christ's Wisdom will guide, Christ's Power preserve, Christ's Love supply every want.

μηδὲν αἴρετε. The Apostles were under an extraordinary Providence, similar to that shown towards the Israelites in the wilderness, Deut. xxix. 5; that the Jews might believe in the Messiah, when they should observe Him so wondrously to protect His messengers, though surrounded with such inconveniences, *Lightfoot.*

For a needful use, Jesus Himself had money bags, and bread baskets too, *Luther, Stier.* ῥάβδους—ῥάβδον, *Cod. Sinai, Oosterzee, Tischendorf, Alford.* If they had a staff they might take it, Mark. If none, they must not buy, Matt. and Luke. χιτῶνας—Jews had 18 several garments, making up their dress. Season was winter—and He intended to show the *low estate* of that kingdom His disciples preached, *Lightfoot.* ἔχειν—Infinitive for Imperative, when *authority* is assumed, *Meyer.*

Our Lord gave this charge to His Apostles, to teach the church the duty of maintaining the ministers of the Gospel—for the labourer is worthy of his hire: therefore maintenance is a debt due to the teachers from the taught; not to discharge this debt is dishonest and unjust, and rebellion against Christ, *Chrysostom.*

---

4. *And whatsoever house ye enter into, there abide, and thence depart.*

Whatsoever. Not best inns, but hosts most *worthy* to be sought. Matt. x. 11.

True hearts seek not sumptuous fare, nor are hard to be suited.

House. Hospitality found most generous among the humble.

Choosing God for their God, they choose His people as companions.

Abide. Seek no special attention, give no unnecessary trouble.

Betraying restlessness, offends humble believers, and shows a heart ill at ease.

Follow not Jewish proselyte-makers, in their *fanaticism.*

Nor leave work half-finished. "A double-minded man is unstable in all his ways." Jas. i. 8.

ἐκεῖθεν—*Thence depart,* seems literal, but conveys no determined sense; rather, "*Until ye leave the place,*" *Campbell.* From that house leave the town.

---

5. *And whosoever will not receive you, when ye go out of that city, shake off the very dust from your feet for a testimony against them.*

Receive. On an errand of peace, they were to go in all the benevolence of the *sinner-greeting-mercy* of God.

"As ambassadors of Christ, we pray you in Christ's stead," &c. 2 Cor. v. 20.

Ministers responsible for *offering*, but not for the *rejection* of the Gospel.

Shake off. Symbolic action, of the *sternest testimony* against anyone.

Equal to denouncing them as pagans, and renouncing all intercourse.

Not of the true Israel, they voluntarily became as heathen.
"I shook my lap, and said, So God shake out every," &c. Neh. v. 13.
Paul and Barnabas shook off the dust of their feet at Antioch. Acts xiii. 51.
Jews returning home, shook their feet at the boundary, that the sacred soil might not be polluted.
Dust. Implied a renunciation of all fellowship with God's enemies.
They were thus absolved from all share in their *guilt*, or *doom*.
Dust may be a swift witness against some in judgment.
"We seek not *yours*, but you." 2. Cor. xii. 14.
Feet. There was *blood-guiltiness* attached to the shoes of the feet. 1 Kings, ii. 5.
In licentious Corinth, Paul shook his raiment, and said, "Your blood be upon your heads, I am clean." Acts xviii. 6.
Ministers not to remain in the company of those who will neither give, nor take good.

δέξωνται—undoubtedly the correct reading, *Lachmann*, *Tischendorf*, *Oosterzee*. *Cod. Sinai* has δέχωνται.

κονιορτὸν Naaman desired 2 mules burden of the sacred soil with which to build an altar to Elisha's God, in Damascus, on his return, 2. Kings v. 17. A similar superstition led *Ubaldi*, in 1188, when driven from Palestine, to bring 53 vessels laden with sacred soil. He thus formed the burial place of the Monks of *Campo Santo*, *Pisa*, surrounded with a splendid marble corridor, which is still a memorial of superstition.

---

6. *And they departed, and went through the towns, preaching the gospel, and healing every where.*

This third ministerial journey, the Saviour took alone.
Departed, from His presence, the *Arm* of the Lord was with them.
Preaching. "It pleased God, by the foolishness of preaching, to save," &c. 1. Cor. i. 21.
The apostles were uneducated men, but they were divinely qualified for their office by extraordinary *inspiration*.
For three years they were taught in Christ's *School*, Himself *Master*.
Ministers now need human as well as divine instruction. 1. Tim. v. 22.
Bishop or pastor "ought to be no novice—apt to teach." 1. Tim. iii. 2.
"Eldad and Medad prophesied," ordained by Moses. Num. xi. 27.
Unauthorized men have no right to minister. 2. Chron. xxvi. 18.

"Departed" from house of Jairus, *Andrews*, *Meyer* ; from Capernaum, *Alexander*.

κώμας villages, not cities. "*Preaching.*" Labors of the Twelve confined to Galilee, *Andrews.* Time occupied, one day, *Wieseler, Tischendorf;* two days, *Ellicott;* several months, *Kraft;* left February, returned in March, *Greswell, Andrews.*

---

7 ¶ *Now Herod the tetrarch heard of all that was done by him: and he was perplexed, because that it was said of some, that John was risen from the dead.*

Herod. Luke iii. 1. A frivolous worldling, and practical infidel.

Perplexed. The moral character of this tyrant, went from bad to worse.

His fear, proves the *splendor* of Christ's miracles, and the action of aroused conscience.

Even blunted sensibilities, and hardened hearts, wonder at Jesus.

They still tremble at the mere sound of His footsteps. Job xv. 20-21.

Conscience—its power and weakness exhibited in Herod.

Power. 1. It faithfully recalls past sin. 2. Justly condemns it. 3. Severely punishes it.

Weakness. 1. It cannot cancel the past. 2. Cannot tolerate the present. 3. Cannot make the future hopeful.

Without faith as an anchor, no one can have *rest.* Heb. vi. 19.

A Sadducee, conscience put his doubts of future existence, to flight.

Sensualists deny the reality of divine things, yet quake in *secret.*

Hidden remorse, ofttimes torments men amid palaces.

No man ever offended his own conscience, but one day it was revenged on him.

The days of affliction revive the memory of old sins, buried in the grave of forgetfulness.

"There is no peace saith God, to the wicked—they are like the troubled sea, whose waves cast up mire and dirt."

διηπόρει—διὰ intensive, *Wetstein.* A mixture of doubt and fear, *Doddridge.* A milder term than the original. *Harassed* is preferable, *Campbell.* *Was distracted, embarrassed,* knew not what to think, had no resource, *W. & W.* Paralleled by Nero the emperor taking refuge under his royal bed, in a thunder storm.

The scene in *Macbeth,* where the ghost of *Banquo* rises, gory and grim, and takes the vacant chair, reserved for the king, is a *powerful* illustration of the *force of conscience.*

Macbeth. Thou canst not say I did it.
Never shake thy gory locks at me.
The times have been
That, when the brains were out, the man would die,
And there an end! but now they rise again,
With twenty mortal murders on their crowns,
And push us from our stools.

For another powerful illustration in *Shakspeare*, of the force of conscience, see *Richard III.*, Act v., Scene iii. *Richard's dream, the night before his death.*

John. Not till John's death, does Herod seem to hear of Jesus. The king was absent from Galilee, *Greswell.* Matt. and Mark insert an account of *John's death*, the circumstances of which Luke, writing *after* them, assumes to be well known, and only *alludes* to them, *Wordsworth.* ὑπ' αὐτοῦ omitted, *Cod. Sinai.*

---

8. ***And of some, that Elias had appeared: and of others, that one of the old prophets was risen again.***

Elias. Gr. form of Elijah (God, Jehovah) Tishbite, Tishbeh, a village beyond Jordan.

Now men looked for his return, according to prophecy. Mal. iv. 5-6; Matt. xxvii. 49.

Old. All before Samuel were the *old;* after him, the *new.*

Prophets. The gift of prophecy, suspended four hundred years.

They believed a new Dispensation was approaching.

These errors concerning our Lord—*honorable* to His character.

Risen. Resurrection. Luke xviii. 33. See Notes.

Ἠλίας—by the Rabbis believed to be *Phineas*, the grandson of Aaron, or an *angel* sent to reform the abandoned Ahab, *Lightfoot.* ἐφάνη, not ἀνέστη, for Elijah had never died, *Major, Bengel.*

---

9. ***And Herod said, John have I beheaded; but who is this of whom I hear such things? And he desired to see him.***

Beheaded. Having got rid of him, he expects no more trouble from him.

Jesus knew His forerunner's death, prophetic of His own. Mark ix. 12.

Desired. Not through faith, but the curiosity of unbelief.

See Him. Too proud to go, He, by delay, *quenched* the Spirit. 1. Thess. v. 19.

At length they met, "But Herod set Him at nought." Luke xxiii. 11.

To the end of time, Herod found among the *murderers* of Jesus.

The KING of Israel here first *noticed* by the wretched Herod.

But his inner life was burnt out by the fires of passion.

He willingly heard the prophet, and unwillingly killed him.

He will be a Sadducee, yet must think of a resurrection.

With a superstitious dread, yet a curiosity to see Jesus.

Note the downward progress of crime, exemplified in Herod!
Sensible of the beauty of holiness, attracted by the stern preacher.
Conscious of the truth, he gladly listens, and partially obeys.
Under a criminal passion, he shuts up John in prison.
He kindly admits his disciples, and carefully guards his life.
A girl immodestly dances, and he orders John to be slain.
The Holy Heavenly Stranger never welcomed to *his* court.
Our Lord often among the lowly,—never visited a palace.
Wearing the Crown of the Universe, never honored by the great.
The high and lofty One who inhabits eternity, dwells with the humble and contrite.

The ἐγὼ being repeated, showed personal concern and alarm, at the growing fame of Jesus, *Stier*. "*Beheaded.*" The language of remorse, *Meyer;* of painful uncertainty, *Oosterzee*. The second ἐγὼ omitted, *Cod. Sinai.*

---

10. ¶ *And the apostles, when they were returned, told him all that they had done. And he took them, and went aside privately into a desert place belonging to the city, called Bethsaida.*

Apostles. Luke vi. 14-15-16. Characters of the Twelve. See Notes.
Told. Laborers must give an account to their Lord. Heb. xiii. 17.
Took. Neither sad, nor joyful news, disturbs His tranquillity.
Privately. He gradually withdraws Himself from crowds and public labors.
They needed repose and retirement after the day's toil.
Our Lord always avoided making a *sensation*. Matt. xii. 19.
Bethsaida. There was *one* city, divided by the Jordan, mistaken for two.
About three hours north of Capernaum, now *Tell-Hum*.
Our Lord bid them go to Bethsaida. Mark vi. 45.
This lay in their course to Capernaum. John vi. 17.
Philip rebuilt Bethsaida, calling it *Julias*, after *Augustus'* daughter.
There he was buried. The ruins are now called *Tell*.
In the evening, the disciples crossed the lake home. Mark vi. 45.
Our Lord had three places of retirement that we read of the Ship, the Mountain, and the Desert, *Remigius*.
His departure *after* he was told what had happened, manifests the reality of His Incarnation, *Chryostom*.

"*Returned.*" The time occupied and places visited are unknown. Some make it but a day, *Wieseler*. "*Desert place.*" A grassy level, not ploughed since the time of Christ, *Arculf*, (A. D. 700) near Butaiha, *Thompson*. βηθσαϊδά *House of fish*, on the western shore of Tiberias, *Winer*, *De Wette*. Two towns of the same name, *Reland*. *Fishing town*.—"Bethsaida" stood in Galilee and Gaulonitis, *both sides* of the Jordan, as Bethsaida Julias, *Thompson*, *Andrews*. No trace of it on the west coast, *Tregelles*. In the Syriac (Nitrian) version, name is omitted, *Ellicott*. It is wrong to say with *Alford* that Luke was not aware of Jesus' crossing the lake. All *proper* to be known or *recorded*, was *revealed*. Such *ignorance* is simply another term for the *Divine reticence*.

"*Went*" along the northern shore, *Robinson*. They hoped he would rejoin them there, *Wieseler*, *Newcomb*. *Not* the city of Peter and Andrew on the *western* coast of the Lake, but the other Bethsaida or *Julias*, and situated on the *northern* shore of the Sea of Galilee. Luke supposes his readers will compare the narratives of Matt. and Mark, where there is mention of their *crossing back* after the miracle to the *western* Bethsaida, *Wordsworth*.

τόπον ἔρημον omitted, *Tischendorf*, *Alford*, *Cod. Sinai.* εἰς πόλιν καλουμένην Βηθσαϊδά *Tischendorf*, *Alford*, *Cod. Sinai.*

---

11. *And the people, when they knew* it, *followed him: and he received them, and spake unto them of the kingdom of God, and healed them that had need of healing.*

People. On their way to the Passover, explains the presence of so many. John vi. 4.

Knew it. *It* is not in the Greek; *on recognizing Him.*

Followed, Him, round the lake on foot, to see the Wonder-worker.

Be thankful when ordinances are near, and follow them when distant.

"When ye see the ark of the Lord remove, ye shall go after it." Jos. iii. 3.

Received. Gr. *met them with a welcome*, He usually retired.

On disembarking, shores were crowded by Passover Pilgrims.

Their wants aroused the compassion of the Great Shepherd.

Fasting and wearied, He still began to preach and heal.

Cleave to Jesus, profess yourself His follower, this delights Him, you will be received.

Kingdom. The standing theme, SALVATION, His sole errand to earth.

Healed. Sickness oft a sermon of love, to believers. "Lord, he whom thou lovest is sick."

People willing to listen to One, whose *word*, demons and diseases *obey*.

He proved His claim as Messiah by His *works*, as well as *words*.

He feeds the soul, while He prepares to feed the body.

ὄχλοι—How could these crowds have been without food, if they had been on their way to Jerusalem? *Alexander*. In their intense curiosity, to behold the *Wonder* of the age, they left their provisions at their *encampment*. Our Saviour doubtless *selected* this very landing, with reference to the miracle. *Followed* on foot, Matt. and Mark. Jesus by ship, *Meyer*. As they could walk, but slightly diseased, *Ammon*. He forgets cripples may be carried, *Stier*.

δεξάμενος graciously entertaining their requests, W. & W. ἰάλλει——ἰᾶτο implies continued action, *Major : kept speaking, kept healing.*

---

12. *And when the day began to wear away, then came the twelve, and said unto him, Send the multitude away, that they may go into the towns and country round about, and lodge, and get victuals : for we are here in a desert place.*

The day. A glorious epoch in the lives of the 5000 fed.

Philip was asked, "Whence shall we buy bread, that these may eat?" John vi. 5.

His *weak* faith, the presumed cause why the Lord put this question. John xiv. 8.

By hasty calculation, 200 pence ($ 33 £7 3*s*. 0*d*.) would give each a little.

Multitude, in the East, generally at starvation point, extreme poverty.

Our Lord creates a *perplexity*, how could faith solve the problem?

We ought not to reckon too confidently where the power and grace of Christ are involved.—He can do more than we ask or think.

Great mercantile houses often neglect the column, *God's* BLESSING.

"How much bread?" Christ will multiply and divide, by another arithmetic.

Send. Our Lord was still discoursing at the time of the request.

Country round about. With no inns, they trusted entirely to their tents.

No one travels *now* in that land, without his tent.

Caravansaries *partially* supply shelter to pilgrims.

Deserts. Luke i. 80. Nature of Oriental wastes. See Notes.

κλίνειν—The proper time is now past, Mark. Much of the day is already past, *Campbell*. The time for healing and preaching being past, *Fritzsche*. Day-time, *De Wette, Meyer*. ἀπόλυσον—Applied to the dismissing of a congregation, Acts xix. 41. κύκλῳ—a *circle*, κειμένας—To farm houses, *Bloomfield, W. & W.* People did not dwell in farm houses in the East, but entirely in walled *villages*. καταλύσωσι, from καταλύματα—like our *stage*, from *stayage*, the unloosening the burdens of travel, *Trench*.

ἐπισιτισμόν—a commissariat word. Luke's phraseology here historically classical. ἐρήμῳ—not a barren waste, but thinly inhabited district, still common in the East. The three synoptical Evangelists agree in their account of this miracle. John differs, but *on every point of importance, the four are absolutely agreed, Alford.*

13. *But he said unto them, Give ye them to eat. And they said, We have no more but five loaves and two fishes; except we should go and buy meat for all this people.*

But he. His pity overcame His want of repose. His love an ever-flowing fountain.

Give ye. YE is emphatic. He would gently compel them to ask His Divine aid.

Owning our impotence, He shews His Omnipotence.

"Stretch forth thine hand." God's precept implies *His aid.*

God's commands often seem strange and impossible to man.

He knew that *they* had not the *food*, nor could they obtain it now.

The command implied, "I will take care we have *enough.*"

"Trust in the Lord and do good (right), and verily thou shalt be fed." Psa. xxxvii. 3.

Israel were bid "*Go forward,*" implying—"I will see a way is made." Ex. xiv. 15.

Divine command—a promise also. "*As thy days, so shall thy strength be.*" Deut. xxxiii. 25.

In working His miracles, Christ seems to take mankind into league with Him.

In condescension, He combines our will with His will, in the works of His goodness.

In the operations of His grace, he takes us into union with Himself, by faith.

If we do our best in our station, and commit in humble faith the issue to God, our exertions however small, will not be in vain.

Five loaves. Luke vii. 33. See Notes. **Barley.** Then, principally, food for beasts.

Roman soldiers thought it an *indignity*, to eat *barley.*

Barley no dainty, nor was there wine. God has promised, "Thy *bread* shall be given, and thy water *sure.*" Isa. xxxiii. 16.

Fishes. Jesus needed no *material* to work a miracle.

But even in miracle, the Divine law of *means to end*, is observed.

A slender bill of fare, compared with the number of guests.

But God can always provide a table in the wilderness. Psa. lxxviii. 19.

Except. We see human perplexity, contrasted with Divine wisdom.

Human compassion, contrasted with Divine mercy.

Human counsel, contrasted with Divine action.

Human poverty, contrasted with Divine riches.

Bring hither. Matthew. This teaches us to despise nothing we have, however humble.

Christian's faith should manifest itself in time of need—

In believing confidence in God—in due diligence in the use of lawful means.

In systematic order—in wise economy—in prayer and thanksgiving.

The loaves and fishes were with a lad (John vi. 9.) The young can serve the interests of the kingdom of God.

"What time the Saviour spread his feast,
For thousands on the mountain side,
One of the *last*, the *least*,
The abundant store supplied," *Lyra Innoc.*

Note, He first exhausts natural means before he performs a miracle.

Buy meat. Gr. *at a market;* too distant to reach that evening.

Meat, common name for all kinds of food: found in Eastern markets, only at stated periods.

The disciples utterly despair of getting adequate supplies.

"Shall the flocks and herds be slain, to suffice them?" Num. xi. 22.

παιδάριον, John vi. 9. A market boy, *Norton.* ἰχθύες—ὀψάρια, John, properly *flesh*, but used for *salt*, *olives*, or *butter*, as a *relish* for bread, *Major.* Our Saviour will not resort to a miracle, unless compelled. When there is a *door*, we do not break through the windows, *Stier.* ἐι μήτι *except*, *perchance*, an alternative highly improbable. ἀγοράσωμεν—Purchasing at a *market*, *Campbell.*

---

14. *(For they were about five thousand men.) And he said to his disciples, Make them sit down by fifties in a company.*

Five thousand. Matt., has—*Besides women and children* not included.

Many pilgrims take their entire family to Jerusalem.

Sit, *Reclined.* Mark, has, *green grass.* A memorial of His bounty in supplying the cattle.

He would reduce the world, to the simplicity and innocence of Eden.

Ahasuerus' guests sat on couches of gold and silver, a pavement of red, blue, white and black marble. Esth. i. 6.

Fifties. Proportionate to the five loaves, one *hundred* parties of *fifty* each. He is a God of order. 1. Cor. xiv. 33.

The women and weaker children, were thus not *overlooked.*

Company. Thus are they accurately *counted*, and carefully *waited on.*

The several Churches of Christ, form one Company.

Partakers of one heavenly Food, ministered to by the same Spirit.

Redeemed by the same Blood, united to the same Lord.

Pilgrims in the same unfriendly country, bound for the same *Home.*

κλισίας, Luke v. 29, *couches*—the Roman *triclinium*, N. T. *table companies*. συμπόσια, Mark, convivial parties: banqueting circles, *Xenophon*. Messes, *Alexander*. Companies, *Major*.

---

15. *And they did so, and made them all sit down.*

All sit. So that the Apostles might easily pass up and down to bear the wondrous bread.

Heaven's mercies arranged, that none need perish for *want*.

The Lord taking a repast with the *poor*, in the wilderness.

His presence meantime desired in vain, at Herod's court.

The time of this miracle, (*Passover*, John vi. 4.) the month of March.

The vast crowd was first seated, then openly fed.

16 *Then he took the five loaves and the two fishes, and looking up to heaven, he blessed them, and brake, and gave to the disciples to set before the multitude.*

Took. This *term* occurs in all the accounts of the *Lord's Supper*.

Ten thousand eyes were fixed upon the Son of God.

He avoids all secrecy or collusion, characteristic of false miracles.

God's works challenge the scrutiny of men and angels.

Five loaves. Luke vii. 33. Seed in the Great Husbandman's hands, yielded a thousand-fold.

Here the God of *peace* and *plenty*, in Jesus, supplies the wants of men.

" Thou givest them their meat, in due season." Psa. cxlv. 15.

Looking up. This gesture natural, and scriptural, in addressing God.

All men regard heaven, His special dwelling place.

Blessed. Gr. *speak well*. " When thou hast eaten and art full, thou shall bless the Lord," &c. Deut. viii. 10.

Paul gave thanks in the presence of all. Acts xxvii. 34.

Greeks and Romans sought a blessing on their daily food.

The quarries of Egypt still show the prayers addressed by the workmen to their gods.

The Twelve distributing, could tell of the *scantiness* of the provision.

Waiting on the multitude was quite ceremonious.

It aroused attention, and precluded all surmise of fraud.

Gave. He does not command the five, to become five thousand loaves.

To the first ranks, the disciples may have been *sparing*.

This foreshadows the disciples' future work, for their Lord.

They brake each loaf in faith that supplies would never fail.

It was impossible to make the mysterious process plainer.

The marvellous growth *eluded* observation, and defied the *understanding*.

Imagination cannot bridge the gulf, between *being*, and *not being*.

Bread is broken, but not diminished; half is given away, yet all remains.

Divided in parts, yet they sum up more than the whole.

"There is that scattereth, and yet increaseth." Prov. xi. 24.

There is analogy between the loaf multiplying in the Hands of Christ, and a grain of corn multiplying into many ears.

But these every day miracles of God are so common, that men fail to perceive them.

In turning *water* into *wine*, changes of *months* were compressed into *moments*.

A grain, by no natural process, can unfold itself into *bread*.

We can conceive of an acorn, by degrees, unfolding itself into an oak.

But an acorn cannot unfold itself into a *carved column* of oak.

By FAITH, we see the bread growing under His hands.

He imparted a seminal power of increase and multiplication, *Hackett*.

He who *created* the first grain, renews the miracle here.

A striking proof of our Lord's saying to Philip. John xiv. 9.

They saw Him *creating* bread. Is He not therefore the *Creator* of all things?

Ministers never fill the people's *hearts*, till God fills their hands.

They feed spiritually the faint, in the world's wilderness.

Temporal gifts *wane*, spiritual gifts *increase*, in the using.

λαβὼν—Our feeble minds comprehend somewhat more readily the *miraculous increase* of the 5 loaves,—than we would the *creation* of bread, out of *nothing*, *Trench*. He was the *Restorer*. He creates no *new* men, but *renews* the *old*. He creates no *new* limbs, but heals the *old*, *Olshausen*. ἀναβλέψας—It is a dictate of nature, to eye the *Source* of our mercies. Heathen generally *look up* when they pray, *Augustine*.

παρατιθέναι—*set before*. Mark has ἐμέρισε *divided*. He only fed those spiritually hungry, *Olshausen*. How fared unbelievers? *Strauss*. Doubtless both classes were fed—If he passed not *Judas* by at the Supper.

ἀυτοὺς—cancelled, *Wakefield*. Retained, *Lachmann*, *Tischendorf*, *Alford*; omitted, *Cod. Sinai*. εὐλόγησεν—κατέκλασε—ἐδίδου. Mark the change of tense, He blessed and brake *once for all*, but *continued* giving, *Wordsworth*.

---

17. *And they did eat, and were all filled: and there was taken up of fragments that remained to them twelve baskets.*

Did eat. *Jesus the Bread of Life and the Bestower of that Bread.*
He still meets the same need, and shews the same majesty.
Provides the same refreshment, and deserves the same homage.
On the same eve, while Paschal lambs were offered in Jerusalem.—
The Lamb of God fed his people in the wilderness.
The miracle in Cana, shews His creative power in *quality*, *this in quantity*.
Filled. Miraculous supply, only limited by the number of consumers.
God makes a little, go a great way. The cruse of oil failed not. 1. Kings, xvii. 16.
If he *blast*, even our abundance leaves us in eternal *want*.
By this miracle, Jesus proclaimed Himself the *Lord* of *Life*. John vi. 35.
Fragments. Wonderful union of Divine riches, and men's activity.
The power of God in nature, *lavish* and *economical.*
All faint-hearted anxiety about the future forbidden. Psa. xxxvii. 8.
In the miracle, Christ's *power* is seen; in this command, His *humility*, shines.
Divine grace, instead of exhausting itself, is richer still.
Annual harvests, are to *faith's* eye, far greater *miracles*.
Twelve baskets. One for each apostle.
A sure proof, that God's gifts are never *exhausted.* 1. Cor. x. 4.
This miracle was not a dream, but left *substantial* fruits.
It teaches wise *economy*, in the smallest affairs of life.
"He that is slothful, is brother to a great waster." Pro. xviii. 9.
There is no *waster* in the universe, like the sinner.
Bread failing, some walked no more with Christ. John vi. 66.
The moment miracles cease, the *laws* of *nature* bind us.
After this stupendous miracle, the people desired to make Him *King*.
They were far more dazzled by this miracle, than by His holy life and teaching.
Messiah who could miraculously feed their bodies, gained their hearts.
efusing the popular request, His followers diminished greatly, showing that their attachment was of the earth, earthy.
is miracle teaches 1. That all food comes of the blessing of God.
2. That Christ is able and willing to feed all *hungry souls*.
3. That none of God's blessings should be wasted.

χορτάσθησαν Luke vi. 21. κλασμάτων *fragments, broken food.* Luke omitted the miracle of feeding the 4000 since it occurred in the midst of a large section, which the accounts gathered by Luke did not contain, *Alford*. Luke depends no more on records, than Elijah ascending did on human chariots. Our Saviour uses κόφινοι twice (Matt. xvi. 9, Mark viii. 19), and σπυρίδας with the 4000. *Ostervald* translates the former *panier*, latter *corbeille*. σπυρὶς, in which Paul was let down from the window, the larger of the two; *Cophinus*, the usual baggage of a travelling Jew, *Juvenal*.

They took twelve baskets there, *Paulus*. This clumsy device of *Paulus* an exegetical *curiosity*, *De Wette*. The miracles of the 4 and 5000 are narratives of *one* event, *Schleiermacher*, *Strauss*. The miracle *symbolical*. Jesus broke the bread of Christian fellowship, *De Wette*. Originally a parable, *Weisse*. Natural process pursued, but quickened, *Luther*, *Olshausen*. Mystical increase of the *word* and *blessing*, *Origen*, *Meyer*. A narrative to illustrate Christ to be the Bread of Life, *Bauer*.

Germination, blade, ear, grinding, raising, cooking, could not have taken place in so brief a period. *Schleiermacher*. Selfishness put to shame, by the noble liberality of Jesus bringing forth its supplies, *Paulus*.

---

18. ¶ *And it came to pass, as he was alone praying, his disciples were with him; and he asked them, saying, Whom say the people that I am?*

Jesus now on the way to the Cross, His public labors in part closed.

He gathers the results of His teaching and life, in order to intimate His sufferings.

It came to pass. At Cæsarea Philippi near Jordan's source.

He leaves Bethsaida Julia near Laish, formerly Dan.

The beginning of our Lord's last departure to the northern regions of Palestine.

After the transfiguration, He visits Capernaum, Samaria, Galilee, Bethabara, Jericho, Bethany, on His way to Jerusalem.

Alone. Mark. *By the way.* The pious pilgrim can commune with the Lord *by the way*.

Praying. Every turning point of life, He hallowed by prayer.

He asks His disciples for a confession of their faith, *after prayer*.

He prays for that faith to be given them, whereof He demands account.

The revelation made to Peter, by the Divine Father, was the fruit of the prayer of the Son.

Whom say? Not, the slanderous Scribes and Pharisees, but the *people*.

Public opinion is despised only by the rash, and followed only by slaves.

I. Mark, "*Son of Man.*" (Luke v. 24.) He seeks not information.

The question intended to confirm their faith in His Messiahship.

All He did and said, was to *manifest* Who He was—THE INCARNATE LORD.

With stronger emphasis, this *vital* question is addressed to all men, *now*.

WHAT THINK YE OF CHRIST? *Eternity depends upon the answer!*

The gracious year in Galilee, was now ended.

συνῆσαν The interview took place about ten miles east of Laish or Banias, *Stier, Olshausen.*

---

19. *They answering said, John the Baptist; but some say, Elias; and others say, that one of the old prophets is risen again.*

Answering. They say all manner of things, but none, "The *Anointed One.*"

John the Baptist. Luke ix. 7. An echo of Herod's court.

Elias, the Gr. for Elijah. Forerunner of the Messiah. Mal. iv. 5, Luke iv. 25.

Jesus had said "John came in the spirit of Elijah." Mark ix. 13.

Old Prophets. In the Messiah's time, prophets were expected. Micah iv. 1-5.

All these *opinions* were highly honorable to our Lord.

His friends esteemed Him the *Forerunner* of the Messiah.

All mistakes of blind unbelief. His Works and Words proclaimed Him the *Sent of God*—the *true* and *proper* MESSIAH.

But His mean appearance satisfied neither their *curiosity*, nor their *pride*.

His Supreme Godhead, still rejected by many for the *same* reason.

"Blessed is he, who shall not be offended in me." Matt. xi. 6

"Elias." The Jews believed that at Messiah's coming, the prophets would rise, *Lightfoot.* Jews mistook Jesus for the forerunner of the Messiah, *Lange*, Matt., xvi. 14.

---

20. *He said unto them, But whom say ye that I am? Peter answering, said, The Christ of God.*

Say ye. It avails nothing what *others* think, if we are unconvinced.

The *confession* of our faith, will strengthen faith.

Speak out now in *private*, in due time you will be called to testify *publicly*.

The line soon drawn between those *for*, and those *against* the Lord.

Whom? 1. A question for conscience. 2. A disputed question. 3. A vital question. 4. A seasonable question.

Peter. Naturally forward and bold, the acknowledged spokesman of the Twelve.

Answering. There is a time to be *silent*, when it is wrong to *speak* concerning Divine mysteries: and a time to *speak*, when it is wrong to be *silent*.

Christ. Gr. *Anointed*, Heb. *Messiah*. His official Title.

The anointed Prophet, Priest, and King of humanity. Psa. ii. 2. Dan. ix. 25.

In Him, these offices for the first time, united and combined.

This claim a proof of His public mission, and personal veracity.

His miracles and public actions, implied this claim.

Previous incumbents only held these offices until He came.

They were set apart by *unction*, symbolical of spiritual gifts.

Jesus possessed these gifts "without measure." John iii. 34.

The Christ of God. In this one Name, His Divinity, Incarnation, and Passion are included. It comprehends everything, for it expresses both the Nature and the Name, wherein is all virtue, *Ambrose*.

To *receive* Christ as our *Prophet*, we must deny our proud carnal wisdom.

To *receive* Him as our *Priest*, we must deny our own merits and righteousness.

To *receive* Him as our *King*, we must renounce our own will and affections.

"And this is life eternal, to know Thee the only true God, and Jesus Christ whom Thou hast sent." John xvii. 3.

ὁ before Πετρος is cancelled, it being omitted in *Cod. Sinai.* and many MSS. Peter eagerly springs forward (προπηδᾷ) and becomes the mouth of the Apostolic body (στόμα τοῦ χοροῦ, *Chrysostom*); and utters these words full of love, and confesses Jesus to be *the* CHRIST, *the* Anointed One, above all Kings, Prophets, and Priests, and to be the Christ of *God*, or as St. Matthew says (xvi. 16), the Son of the Living God—the Only-Begotten Word of God, *Cyril*.

χριστόν—The Christ, same as John vi. 69, *Wieseler*.

This confession the turning point in the Apostle's history, *Andrews*. His confession brings out both the human and Divine nature of our Lord, *Alford*.

---

21. *And he straitly charged them, and commanded* them *to tell no man that thing.*

Tell no man. This was a time of preparation for the Kingdom.

Our Lord proves His Messiahship, by the benevolent nature of His words and works.

If men had known HIM, they would not have crucified Him. 1. Cor. ii. 8.

His apostles must have overwhelming evidence, to allege.

They must be filled with a larger measure of the Spirit. Eph. iv. 7. iv. 13.

Man is both unworthy and incapable of hearing Divine mysteries, til Christ has purchased by His death, grace requisite thereto.

ἐπιτιμήσας—1. honor. 2, rebuke. 3, adjudge. 4, admonish strongly, παρήγγειλε, they must not *tell*, in other places He uses δεικνύειν—*Tell no man.* Our Lord was almost shocked, *Fritzsche,*

---

22. *Saying, The Son of man must suffer many things, and be rejected of the elders, and chief priests, and scribes, and be slain, and be raised the third day.*

The Son of man. Luke v. 24. Indicating His humility.

Must. A necessity founded on prophecy, and the Covenant of Redemption.

Ought not Christ to have suffered these things, and to enter into His glory?" Luke xxiv. 26.

Suffer. Rejected, mocked, scourged, insulted, crucified. Psa. cxviii. 22.

What a thunder stroke upon all their lofty ideas of the Messiah!

Conceive the surprise of John and Nathanael, and the sadness of Thomas.

The questioning of Andrew, and the crafty testimony of Judas.

Peter's flesh and blood aroused, he gives the emphatic "No!"

Luke omits all notice of Peter's reply; Mark, Peter's friend and scholar records it.

The doctrine of a suffering Messiah, gradually lost to the nation, except to a few *divinely taught* souls, only.

The apostles shared the delusions of the Scribes and people.

Their Messiah must be a Temporal Conqueror, and Spiritual King.

Elders, Priests and Scribes. Those knowing the letter of Scripture best, most fit to persecute.

Rome's power crucified Jesus, but the *guilt* was on the *Jews.*

Slain. Moses and Elias, even *in Heaven*, knew Him as a suffering Messiah

His Transfiguration they "spake of His *death*, which He should accomplish," &c. Luke ix. 31.

Peter was offended at this declaration, what was it likely the common sort would feel, being first told He was the Son of God, and then seeing Him crucified and spat upon? *Chrysostom.*

ἀποδοκιμασθῆναι, to *assay metals*: δοκιμασία, *scrutiny* concerning magistrates' qualifications—hence ἀποδοκιμάζειν, to *reject* a candidate as disqualified. Our Lord did not realize their carnal views, hence His *rejection*, *Major*.

Slain. Some hint that the O. T. says nothing of a suffering Messiah, *Strauss*, *De Wette*. Their hermeneutics must have been above our Lord's, *Oosterzee*.

---

23. ¶ *And he said to* them *all*, *If any* man *will come after me*, *let him deny himself and take up his cross daily*, *and follow me*.

All. Multitude not far off, even when Christ was most retired.

His confidential conversations, held within *sight* of the crowd.

Any man. Universally binding, without reference to official duties.

Will. God's grace enables the will, paralyzed by the fall, to obey the truth. (Gr. θέλει wishes).

Resolution, resulting from convinced reason, and cheerful heart.

Nominal disciples, by education or interest; are many.

Deny. Abjure *Himself*, as the great object of regard.

Self denial crucifies our lusts; is submissive to *another*.

Surprise at their *Lord's* sufferings, increased by hearing of their *own*.

Our plans, pleasures, glory, must yield to God's Will.

No distinction of rank, privilege, or position, exempt.

We must say to *Self*, as Peter of Christ, "*I know not the man.*"

If a hard lesson, our Master willingly practised it.

Deny himself. 1. Ignore our own wisdom. Prov. xxvi. 12; Matt. xi. 25.

2. Renounce self righteousness. Our atonings as penance &c., mere barriers to Christ.

3. Crucify sinful desires. Rom. viii. 13. He saves *from*, not *in*, our sins, not minister of sin. Gal. ii. 17.

4. Sacrifice earthly joys interfering with duty, even reputation if necessary.

Moses refused to be called the Son of Pharaoh's daughter. Heb. xi. 24.

5. Sacrifice friends if they keep us from Christ. A man's foes often those of his own household. Matt. x. 36.

Take up his Cross. Criminals carried the transverse beam to the place of execution.

A *prophetic allusion* to the death He should die.

Means a patient endurance of any burden, God's *love* imposes.

The two embrace *inward* conflicts, and *outward* sufferings.

Penance only fosters the *pride* of the *carnal* heart.

An Indian Fakir suffers the keenest tortures, but they only *strengthen* his *pride*.

Daily. A disciple, is a willing, daily *cross-bearer*, after Jesus.

Demand of self denial, 1. Difficult. 2. Necessary. 3. Wholesome. 4. Practicable.

Follow Me. As though He had said, "Follow Me to Golgotha!"

His privations, humiliations, death and burial, voluntary.

Peter, with worldly thoughts and feelings in his heart, counsels a contrary course.

The love that urged Him on, constrains His people to self-sacrifice also.

Christ has many *servants*, but few *followers* of His cross and passion.

It costs *much* to *become* and still *more* to *remain* a Christian.

Paul's perfection is indicated, in, that he carried the cross in his body, and in his heart, *Gregory*.

No one has a *right* to shake off the yoke of the *cross*, but he who designs to have a *right* to nothing but *Hell! Quesnel.*

ἀπαρνησάσθω—*to resist resolutely*, and *absolutely*. καθ' ἡμέραν cancelled, *Wetstein' Bloomfield:* retained, *Campbell*, *Tischendorf*, *Alford*, *W. & W.*, *Wordsworth*. Its introduction attributable to the same *ascetic spirit* of the fathers, which prompted them to cancel εἰκῇ in Matt. v. 22, *Stier*.

---

24. *For whosoever will save his life shall lose it; but whosoever will lose his life for my sake, the same shall save it.*

Save. Attempting to save our present live, we risk that to come.

He who *loves* himself with respect to this *life*, *hates* himself with respect to *eternity*.

A blind carnality, seeks *life* in that which only yields *death*.

Life an ordinary Hebraism for *felicity*.

Lose. Gr. much stronger term, an antithesis to *save*.

ɪne cannot perpetuate his life on earth, by refusing to look higher.

'he life to be sacrificed, is the selfishness of the *old man*.

his command seems repugnant, it looks like self-destruction.

requires us to sacrifice a less good, for securing a greater.

)se his life for my sake, actuated by faith in Christ and in the eternal realities of His Kingdom.

ve. Transition to the promised victory, after life's struggles.

› *life* lost is that which pertains to *sense;* the *life* gained is that which pertains to *God*.

λῃ σῶσαι wishes to save; indulges his natural desire to preserve.

ολέσῃ—used of disregarding a thing, so that the owner is likely to lose it. ψυχὴν—

By antithesis, our Saviour lifts more than one word from an *earthly*, to a *spiritual* sense. ψύχω to *breathe*, *blow*, Lat. *Anima*.

---

25. *For what is a man advantaged, if he gain the whole world, and lose himself, or be cast away.*

Advantaged. Much in the world, we may innocently desire.

Gain. Esteem of men, protection of friends, society of those we love.

If one toils years to reach a throne, then loses his life, is he wise?

Saving a well-filled palace, and losing one's liberty, is hardly a gainer.

Jesus foreknew confessors must peril all, or lose heaven.

Their Faith needed strong support, when tempted to deny their Saviour.

Fires of martyrdom were *cold* to them, avoiding fire unquenchable.

They fear not *savage tormentors*, dreading *despair* hereafter.

Himself. Gaining the world, and losing one's soul, a spiritual bankrupt.

It is a good trial of a man's condition to know what he esteem to be *himself*.

He is not worthy of the name of man, who thinks his body to be *himself*.

Where the soul is, there is the man; *Lazarus* is said to be in Abraham's bosom, the *rich man* in hell.

Cast away. The *Soul's value.* Created in God's image—invested with great powers.

Contest of angels and demons over its possession. Redemption precious. Psa. xlix. 8.

Danger of its loss—loss of purity, of peace, of communion with angels, and with God.

No repentance in the grave—its loss complete. Matt. xxv. 46.

Nothing can compensate its loss. Those having most of earth, not satisfied. Pro. xii. 8. Psa. lv. 6.

Those who have not gained Christ have lost all, *Bernard*.

ἀπολέσας having destroyed himself, when he might have been saved. ζημιωθείς having *incurred loss*, (having become a cast away), when he might have gained himself, *Bengel*.

---

26. *For whosoever shall be ashamed of me and of my words, of him shall the Son of man be ashamed, when he shall come in his own glory, and* in his *Father's, and of the holy angels.*

Whosoever. Without distinction, as to class; Scribe, or Pharisee.

Ashamed. Through fear of man, refusing to own Him as his Lord.

The believer need not be ashamed of Christ.

He must not. He will not, if a Christian in deed.

Seeking *honor* from men, the way to get *shame* from the Lord.

My words. A hearty belief in his doctrines, as a rule of life.

Son of Man. Luke v. 24. See Notes, never used but by our Lord.

Because of His humiliation, bearing the form of a servant, rejected and disowned.

Ashamed. I will disown, and reject him in like manner.

Come, in Infinite Majesty, the reverse of what you see now.

Glory. Three-fold. 1. That of Messiah. 2. That of the Father. 3. That of the Angels.

The robes which belong to My Office, I have not yet put on.

Father's. Infinite, Eternal! Jehovah's glory added to His own!

Holy angels. Whose reflected glory, will enhance their Lord's.

They will testify how they ministered by the mission of God to man's salvation. Heb. i. 14.

Whosover is *ashamed* of the Truth, while it is humbled and oppressed in this world, shall be humbled and put to shame before the Truth in the day of its triumph and glory.

It requires holy boldness, not to be ashamed of the humiliation of Christ, His cause, or people; all of which are now debased before the world.

It is just, that he who in *Time* has preferred *himself*, should in *eternity* be abandoned to his *choice*.

In that *day*, positions will be reversed; the humblest believer will participate in the glory of His Lord, while the proudest unbeliever will be overwhelmed with everlasting contempt and ruin.

υἱὸς Luke v. 24. This remarkable formula, refers to the *depth of the humility*. "Glory."—*Shekinah*, *Elsley*. λόγους cancelled, *Tischendorf*; retained, *Alford*. If λόγους is cancelled the meaning is, *and of them that are mine.*

---

27. But I tell you of a truth, there be some standing here, which shall not taste of death, till they see the kingdom of God.

I, the Son of God, "*tell you,*" my disciples and followers.

Implies, His disciples would outlive Him.

That His cause would triumph over all His foes.

You. My confidential followers in the *regeneration.*

Truth. Autho:itatively propounded by a Teacher sent from God.

There be. Not a subjunctive, but an old indicative *i. e. There are.*

Some, referring to the Twelve, and some of the crowd present.

Which. Old English forms, applied to *persons and things.* Modern usage requires "*Who.*"

Taste. Death represented under the figure of a bitter cup. Psa. xi. 6.

Each guest had a cup or *portion.*

A cup of poison was given to those condemned to die.

Socrates the Greek philosopher and martyr, drank a cup of hemlock

Kingdom, of the Messiah, then actually set up.

Generally believed to refer to the Destruction of Jerusalem, the end of the Mosaic dispensation, and the erection of Christ's kingdom.

The gradual institution of a Spiritual Empire, in the heart.

The Kingdom of which Christ speaks here is His future Kingdom of Glory; of which He was about to shew them a glimpse in the Transfiguration, *Cyril.*

ἀληθῶς—Matt. ἀμήν, used by the Jews at the end of oaths, &c.—equivalent to γένοιτο or *fiat.* ἑστηκότων "*Hic stantes*"—Vul. οὐ μὴ γεύσονται—a strong negative, with the particle, μή. They neither *should, could*, or *would* taste, &c., *Alexander.*

βασιλείαν—*Until He comes*—Matt. *Transfiguration, Chrysostom.* End of the world, Primitive Christians. Destruction of Jerusalem, *Wetstein, Ebrard, Lightfoot, Alexander.* Conquests of the Gospel, *Dorner.* *Second Advent, Meyer.* His coming kingdom, *De Wette.* His resurrection, *Lange, Grotius.*

---

28. ¶ *And it came to pass about an eight days after these sayings, he took Peter and John and James, and went up into a mountain to pray.*

Eight days. Luke *includes*, Matt. and Mark, *exclude* the days of transfiguration and declaration.

The disciples had solemnly recognized His Divinity.

They might now look for clearer evidence of His Messiahship.

This would accord with the miracles during His *Infancy.*

This Transfiguration, a solemn *Installation into* the Messianic office.

Peter, John and James. Witnesses of the raising of Jairus' daughter.

Formerly partners in secular business, now a sacred *triumvirate.*

These three "Pillars" of the Church. Gal. ii. 9. "Eye witnesses of His majesty." 2. Pet. i. 17.

Some *Love* Christ, with Peter. Some are *beloved*, with John. Some *Suffer* for Him, with James.

Galilean fishermen were his first acquaintances, and the first *called*.

Abraham, Jacob, Moses, David, Hezekiah and Paul, also chosen with Sovereign independence, as His honored instruments.

Lifting the veil from their infirmities, He overruled their sins.

Yet left no stain on His holiness, or extenuation for their guilt.

Foreseeing Judas' guilt, did not prevent Him choosing him.

Mountain. Temptations, Transfiguration, Prayer, Suffering, Ascension on Mountains.

Here they beheld Him in *glory*, afterward in deepest humiliation.

Tabor, the inauguration of Golgotha, and foretaste of the Mount of Olives.

The Tabors of Christian life, like those of the disciples.

Pray. Luke alone assigns the *reason* for His ascending the Mount.

PRAYER, THE PATH TO GLORY.

By prayer the pilgrim's heart outstrips his footsteps.

Mountains of Judea, important in the Saviour's history.

Mount of Beatitudes, Mount of Tempta ion, Mount of Transfiguration.

Mount of Crucifixion, Mount of Ascension.

ὡσεὶ ἡμέραι ὀκτώ. Matt., and Mark have "*after six days.*" Luke's statement ὡσεὶ *about*, implies less accuracy of calculation. Probably he counts the days of the sayings with the event, *Bengel.* τὸ ὄρος, the two other Evangelists have here indefinitely ὄρος ὑψηλὸν, a proof that τὸ ὄρος is used by way of contrast with the plain, and not to specify any particular mountain, *Wordsworth.* ὄρος, Mount Tabor, a fortress there B. C. 219 years, *Robinson, Stanley.* In Galilee, *Neander.* Near Capernaum, *Alford.* Hermon highest in Gaulonitis, Mount Panias, near Cæsarea Philippi, *Lightfoot, Lange, Ellicott, Stanley.*

---

29. *And as he prayed, the fashion of his countenance was altered, and his raiment was white and glistering.*

And as. Time generally thought to have been midnight.

Prayed. To Luke we owe notices of Christ's devotional habits.

He was *praying* when owned at His *Baptism* and *Transfiguration*

We also gather glory, while communing with Source of *Light*.

Altered. Mark "*Transfigured*," His entire figure became refulgent.

At once the deepest *mystery*, and most glorious *revelation*.

Moses shone with *reflected*, Jesus with *inherent* splendor.

Light shone not *upon* Him from *without*, but from *within*.

His Godhead for a moment irradiated His human *vestments*.

In a servant's form, He assumes His CORONATION ROBES. Luke xii. 27; Phil. ii. 7.

Raiment. (The general term for clothing) lost in the divine effulgence.

White. Gr. *White as lightening*, or *flashing brightly forth.*

The Saviour thus glorious on the earthly mount,—what will He be on the heavenly?

No nations represent *divine* objects, under emblems of *darkness*.

An angel's *countenance* at the sepulchre, was as *lightning*. Matt. xxviii. 3.

Christ's was as the Sun, shining in its strength. Rev. i. 16.

"He covereth Himself with light, as with a garment." Ps. civ. 2.

Christ's shining raiment, the garb of believers.

It was "the Power and Coming (Gr. *becoming present*) of our Lord Jesus Christ." 2. Pet. i. 16.

Birth, Baptism, Temptation, Transfiguration, epochs in His Humanity.

Each signal points of glory, and flashings forth of Deity.

The Transfiguration tended to reconcile the apostles, to *any* future humiliation of Christ.

Satan's Kingdom and subject described as *under darkness*, Jude verse vi.

Christ's Kingdom and subjects described as being in *marvellous light.* 1. Pet. ii. 9.

τὸ εἶδος, literally, *the appearance*, ἕτερον, literally *was another*.

προσώπου—The oriental has no higher conception of human happiness and glory, than to look upon the "*golden face*," and dwell in the presence of his august sovereign.

ἕτερον—Partly a vision and partly an objective reality, *Meyer*, *Grotius*. A vision in a dream, *Kuinoel*, *Neander*, *Tertullian*, *Herder*. Accompanied by a thunder-storm, *Gabler*. A meeting with two unknown friends, *Paulus*, *Hase*. An atmospheric phenomenon, *Ammon*. A reality, with mythical embellishments, *Ewald*. A pure myth, *Shuls*, *Strauss*. An allegory, *Weisse*, *Bauer*. A waking vision, *Milman*. Historic reality, *D. Brown*, *Stier*, *Doddridge*, *Bengel*, *Wordsworth*, *Alford*, &c.

λευκὸς ἐξαστράπτων not glistering white, but whitely glistering, *Major*. Mark στίλβοντα—glitter of polished arms, *Homer*. Twinkling of stars, *Aristotle*. Flashing of lightning, *Euripides*. His life a continual process of glorification, *Olshausen*. This has a Docetic tendency, *Stier*. The unmeasured indwelling of the Holy Ghost, *Lange*. Moses' an external—this an internal illumination and external radiation, *Oosterzee*. Anticipation of His future glory, *Meyer*. Outward view of spiritual vision, *Lange*. Season of rest in half finished victory, *Gerlach*. A most exact pattern of our Resurrection, *Musculus*.

---

30. *And, behold, there talked with him two men, which were Moses and Elias.*

Behold. Implied, profound astonishment of the Apostles.

Talked. Were talking as long as they were within sight and hearing.
1. Spiritual communion of the church below, with that above.
2. Of the Lord and His disciples. 3. Of the Father and the blessed spirits.

Two men. The conflict waged on earth, known to dwellers in heaven.

We would have believed them *angels*, had we not been told.

Their presence proves, that death is not an *unconscious* state of existence.

We have here a delightful *earnest* of the kingdom of Christ above.

The church on earth and the church in heaven meet on the holy mount.

Saints on earth, and saints from heaven communed with *one* Saviour.

Moses. Luke ii. 22. Burial place unknown. The Lord supplied him with a body.

His Earthly sorrow compensated. He has entered the *Canaan*, which before death was sealed to him.

His presence on the mount a witness for *immortality*, under the New Testament Dispensation.

All the saints of former ages, will return in glory.

Elijah. Luke i. 17. As he was translated, he may have had his *glorified* body.

One, the *Founder* of the Ceremonial law, and the Theocracy.

The other, the *Restorer* of the 10 tribes from their apostacy.

Both fasted 40 days, and wrought stupendous miracles.

Through them, the *Law* and the *Prophets*, honored Christ.

Many types and shadows, fled before this bright vision.

The sacred narrative however is *severely* brief.

Μωϋσῆς καὶ Ἠλίας, Moses supposed to have been a type of souls before their blissful union of body and soul, and Elijah the representative of their ultimate state, of orification in the Resurrection, *Stier*. True to their nature, the Arabs pretend to ow the *burial* place of Moses, near Jericho.

"*Two men.*" They were known to Peter, &c., by *intuition*, *Wetstein*: intuitive and nediate, *Alford*. By subsequent information derived from the Lord, *Olshausen*. By lation, *Bengel*. By tradition, *Meyer*.

Moses and Elijah separated by 661 years, meet on the holy mount, and in heaven, r.

Who appeared in glory, and spake of his decease which he should accomplish at ulem.

In glory. These prophets came at *a crisis* in the history of Redemption.

One of the grandest historical scenes, a record of fishermen!

Is it a creation by transcendent genius, or a record of *facts?*

If *original*, by illiterate enthusiasts; it is unaccountable.

No where else do they give us the counter part of this conception.

Skill of its minute proprieties, only equalled by its grandeur.

Decease. Gr. *Exodus, i. e.* Passion, Cross, Death, Resurrection and Ascension.

The word, a tradition of the immortality of the soul.

It is seen engaging the *wonder* and *interest* of heaven.

Christ was the scope of the ancient economy, a DYING CHRIST.

In heaven, His death is the ground of their salvation.

They speak not of His *miracles*, or teachings, but of His *death.*

They read the O. T. amiss, who find no *suffering* Messiah there.

Our Saviour's *death*, the highway to the *Throne.* Heb. i. 8.

Typified ages before, by the *exodus* of these two prophets.

Elijah had stepped over the grave, and passed into heaven.

Michael seems to have had in *special keeping*, the body of Moses. Jude 9.

His death took place at the head of the thousands of Israel in the wilderness.

Law and promise demanded, Christ's death, and He was ready.

The transfiguration shows the Law and the Prophets, become part of the Gospel.

Apostles saw death *in keeping* with Christ, and their own future Glory.

His *Exodus* here figures as the accomplishment of the purpose of God.

Glorified saints come from heaven to speak of it.

The Mount of Transfiguration related to Mount Calvary.

1. The prophecy of His sufferings repeated. 2. The necessity of His sufferings confirmed. 3. The awful conflict alleviated. 4. The fruit of His sufferings foretold.

ἔξοδον Luke learned it from subsequent tradition, *Meyer*—a groundless assumption, *Bengel, Doddridge.*

θάνατον or τελευτὴν might have been selected. *Major.* Exodus of the Israelites from Egypt, *Beza, Lightfoot, Hammond.* A Euphemism for death, *Grotius, Rosenmuller, Tertullian, Irenaeus, Kuinoel, Wetstein.* *Decease* too literal,—*Departure* has the same latitude as the original, and refers to His ascension as well as death, *Campbell.* There may be an allusion to Israel's triumphant departure out of Egypt. Moses and Elijah both departed without pain. The term implied a *military victory*, and referred it to Christ's victory over the impenitent Jews, at the destruction of Jerusalem.

32. *But Peter and they that were with him, were heavy with sleep: and when they were awake, they saw his glory, and the two men that stood with him.*

Heavy. Note a similar drowsiness in Gethsemane. Luke xxii. 45.
Great agitations of mind, of joy or sorrow, fatigue.
The conscious presence of uncreated Glory oppressed them.
Agitations of joy or sorrow depress, but do not *obscure* the mind.
His glory. "The glory which thou gavest Me, I have given them." John xvii. 22.
It belongs to the *church*, in its *Waiting*, *Warfare*, and *Trial*.
Reflecting His spirit, "We are all changed from glory to glory." 2. Cor. iii. 18.
From the glory of Baptism, to that of *Salvation*, from the glory of *faith* to that of *sight*.
From the glory of regeneration, to that weight of glory, the Resurrection.
In the Transfiguration was seen the future glory of all the saints.

διαγρηγ.—they kept awake, though drowsy. Added to prove it a living reality, *Meyer*. At the great battle of *Shiloh*, some artillerists were actually seen by an officer present to fall asleep quietly beside their guns, amid the fury and uproar of 200 cannon. Here swoon from terror, *Olshausen*. Oppressed by the deep mountain solitude, *Stier*.

"*Awake.*" — When they were awakened, *De Wette*. Watching awake, *Lange*. Internal attention, *Neander*.

---

33. *And it came to pass, as they departed from him, Peter said unto Jesus, Master, it is good for us to be here: and let us make three tabernacles; one for thee, and one for Moses, and one for Elias; not knowing what he said.*

Departed. Gr. *While they were departing.* With the desire to hinder it.
This seems a *separation*, made by the surrounding *cloud*.
Peter feared it would be *permanent*, he pleads for their stay.
He is spokesman, and declares the *effect* of this august scene.
Bright manifestations here, and too often are *departing* visions.
To their half-darkened minds, a rapturous surprise.
Master. A synonym for *overseer* or *prefect*—the native Aramaic. **Rabbi.** Mark.
Good is it (for) **us here to be**—the *order* of *Peter's words* by all the Evangelists.
1. *For us* to be here. 2. For us to be *here*. 3. For us to be here with *heaven* and *Thee*.

Good, in every sense right, happy, useful, and agreeable.
Perfect satisfaction to remain, and reluctance to depart.

1. They there saw a vision—elevating in itself, important to their Master, instructive to themselves.
2. *Good* for a believer to be *there*—he finds a support for his faith, a lesson for his life, an emblem of his hope.

Three. Not selfish he desires one, for each majestic person.
Others think that Peter sought a refuge from the effulgent scene.
Tabernacles. *Tents*, *booths*, any temporary sheds. Luke xvi. 9.
Nothing resembling the sumptuous building The "*Tabernacle* of Moses."
"One thing have I desired to dwell in the house of the Lord." Ps. xxvii. 4.
No tent *needed*, "In my Father's house, many mansions." John xiv. 2.
Not knowing. Words divinely spoken, H. G. suffers them not to fall.
Peter, true to his nature, thought he *must* say something, even *here*.
Love will *stammer*, rather than remain silent.
He knew not what he *said*, but he knew what he *felt*.
Female Martyr "I cannot *argue*, but I can DIE for my Saviour!"
Peter was looking for heaven on earth, a crown without the cross.
Here is no rest, "We have no continuing city." Heb. xiii. 14.

"*Departed*,"—fearing the separation would be final, *W. & W.* ἐπιστάτα—Matt. has κύριε, Mark ῥαββί. Luke is more elegant and classic. καλὸν—good that we are to *provide*, &c., *Paulus*, *Crusius*, *Meyer*. Better here than in Jerusalem, *Chrysostom*. Preferred earth to heaven, in *such company*, *Lange*.

ποιήσωμεν—This form cannot include the *Lord* in this work. Peter would detain these august actors, in the belief, or hope, that the Redeemer would set up an earthly kingdom, *Meyer*.

"*Three*."—Greek church, Romish church, Christian church, *Bauer*. Enough for only half present, *De Wette*. The threefold ministry of the church, *Sepp*. "*Not knowing*," —evidence of drowsiness, *De Wette*.

---

34. *While he thus spake, there came a cloud, and overshadowed them: and they feared as they entered into the cloud.*

Cloud. Not a watery, but the Shekinah cloud, excellent glory. 2 Pet. i. 17.
The visible token of the presence of Jehovah, in the Pillar of cloud.
He thus came down on Sinai and thus entered the tabernacle. Ex. xix. 9; xl. 34.

He thus filled the Temple. 1. King viii. 10. Clouds His chariots. Ps. civ. 3.
The Shekinah, the symbol of the glory of the Lord.
This cloud again receives the three, in a sanctuary.
Overshadowed. The N. T. Dispensation one of *Light, Love and Liberty*. Heb. xii. 18.
Beneath this cloud, or "excellent Glory," (2. Peter i. 17.) Moses and Elias vanished.
This cloud broke, the otherwise intolerable effulgence, of uncreated glory.
The cloud to the disciples, was as the *parable* to the Jews.
It denotes the final abolition of the law.
Jesus seen above without *drowsiness, cloud or fear.*
Sun styled its "Maker's shadow," this cloud's shadow, was *glory*.
Feared. God's uncreated Majesty and Presence overpowered their minds.
Christ enters calmly, disciples under carnal fear.
God's voice inspires dread, since it was heard in the garden. Gen. iii. 9.
Our infirmities awake *alarm*, instead of kindling *courage*.
Christ's errand delivers saints from the *bondage* of *fear*. Luke i. 75.
"We followed no fable, but were eye-witnesses of His majesty." 2. Peter i. 16.

νεφέλη In opposition to the best MSS. Substitute φωτεινὴ of Matt. for φωτος, *Griesbach, Olshausen.* The difficulty is how a *bright cloud* could *overshadow?* Light so dazzling as to prevent the disciples from seeing those covered, *Olshausen.* A natural cloud conceals, *Meyer.* A mist lit up by the sun, *Paulus.* ἐκείνους refers to the celestial visitors, and not to the apostles, as our Eng. Tr. implies, *Stier, De Wette, Lange.* Jesus, Moses, and Elias, *Leclerc, Lightfoot.* Disciples, *Wolfius, Bengel.*

---

35. *And there came a voice out of the cloud, saying, This is my beloved Son: hear him.*

Voice. Came out of the cloud, in which the speaker is hid.
Formerly heard on the banks of Jordan. Mark i. 11.
Inaugurating Him King of the Kingdom of Heaven.
In the Temple consecrating Him High Priest. John xii. 28.
Here His Prophetic office, is adorned above Moses' and Elijah's.
Cloud. Our future blessedness is still hidden by a cloud.
Gr. **My Son, the beloved.** A sort of proper name, a distinctive title.
This epithet, in the same sense, not applied to any other being.
The same formula installed Him at *Baptism*. This for His *Passion*.

It is a species of second baptism, with *light*, and Glory uncreated.
In the presence of Moses, Elias, and Apostles as witnesses.
This foretaste of blessedness lightened His cross.
A pledge of support under trials, and of a resurrection.

Hear Him. The disciples doubtless desired to hear what Moses and Elijah said.
God speaks, "Nay not *those*, but My Son, the *Great Teacher.*"
Hear Him, "Except a man be born again," &c. John iii. 3.
Hear Him, "Come unto Me all ye that labor," &c. Matt. xi. 28.
Hear Him, "I am the way and the truth and the life." John xiv. 6.
Hear Him, "I am the Resurrection and the Life." John xi. 25.
"The Soul that will not hear Him, will be destroyed." Deut xiii. 3.
"We walk by faith, and faith comes not by sight, but by *hearing.*" Rom. x. 17.
Hear Him, 1. With deep reverence. 2. With unconditional obedience. 3. With joyful confidence.

ἀγαπητὸς—cancelled for *ἐκλελεγμένος*, *Alford*, *Cod. Sina.* Mark xii. 6, coincident, but not synonymous with *only-begotten.* Euripides uses *μονόπαις*, Homer ἀγαπητός. ἀκούετε an *endorsement*, on the part of the Father, of all that Jesus claimed to do, speak, or be, *Stier.* Father's testimony at the beginning (Luke iii. 22), and close of his Son's ministry, *Hoffman.*

---

36 *And when the voice was past, Jesus was found alone. And they kept it close, and told no man in those days any of those things which they had seen.*

Alone. Sadly the vision became *dim*, and all was dark again.
Law and prophets vanish, and Christ alone remains.
They had trusted, He was about to erect an earthly kingdom.
Expectations resting on *earth*, are vanishing *visions*. Matt. xvii. 9.
Jesus made no reply about *tents*, events decide the question.
Let who will depart, if but Jesus remains. Psa. lxxiii. 25.

Close. The Lord enjoined silence, until risen from the dead. Mark ix. 9.
Until *that* great event, *this* would appear *incredible.*
Matthew adds—*Jesus touched them, aud said, arise*, xvii. 7
"In a deep sleep, an angel touched Daniel." Dan. x. 10.
John, fell at the feet of the angel as dead," he laid his," &c. Rev. i. 17.

Things. The design of this visitation. O.T. Representatives would consecrate the Messiah to His death.

To the disciples, it counterpoised the shame of the cross.
A proof of Jesus' *sinlessness*, and the Father's complacency in Him.
Symbol of prophets retiring, and Jesus entering as Master.
The carnal views of the disciples corrected, and the supernatural character of His kingdom shewn.

οὐδενὶ Matt. himself did not receive information of this event until after the resurrection; and Luke not till after Paul's conversion, *Olshausen*. To know that one must be *inspired*. Israel, Psa. lxxviii. 41. "Those things."—ὅραμα—Matt.—The object of this scene, *Mayor*. To strengthen our Lord for the conflict, *Olshausen*. A fulfilment of the promise. v. 27, to Peter, James, and John. 1, the shekinah. 2, the Father speaking. 3, Christ in His coronation robes. 4, Moses a saint raised. 5, Elijah a saint changed. 6, three disciples still in the flesh.

---

37 ¶ *And it came to pass, that on the next day, when they were come down from the hill, much people met him.*

Met. When they met him, they were greatly *amazed*. Mark ix. 15.
Result of the lingering traces of *majesty* investing Him on the Mount.
These remaining vestiges, had not faded into the light of common day.
Moses brightness painful to the Hebrews, hence his veil. Ex. xxxiv. 30.

ἐξεθαμβήθησαν—Mark ix. 15. An undefined awe, *Euthymius*. The sudden appearance of one unexpected in a crowd, *Alexander, Meyer*. After lustre of transfiguration, *Bengel, Foote, Alford, W. & W., Trench, Ellicott*. An agreeable surprise, *Wakefield*. Struck with awe, *Campbell*. Struck with astonishment, *Doddridge*.

ὄχλος—Some affirm that the language of Matt. "when they came to the crowd," and of Luke "much people met him," form a *discrepancy*, which it is dishonest to attempt to reconcile. Sceptics of this school can do no harm, *Alexander*.

---

38. *And, behold, a man of the company cried out, saying, Master, I beseech thee, look upon my son; for he is mine only child.*

He questioned the Scribes, glorying in the defeat of the disciples. Mark ix. 16.
As a commander surveys the well-nigh lost battle, and helpless confusion of ranks,
And by his presence, turns the tide of threatened defeat, into victory—so now

Their own sinfulness—their own foolish ambition.
Some secret ban lay in their midst—anything but *unbelief!*
Perverse. Gr. *twisted.* Its moral sense—a perverted mind.
Those faithless, will be perverse; the worst aspect of sin. Psa. xxv. 9.
How long. A holy impatience to reach the goal, so near on the Mount.
Indignation of warm love and grief, bearing with perverseness.
Moses was *sinful*, presuming to rebuke, in his *own* might.
Not a longing to be gone from his work on earth.
But of a master complaining of the dulness of his scholars.
Very striking are these words, amid the discords of sin and unbelief resounding at the foot of the hill.
It expresses the longing of his soul for home, which for a moment had opened on Tabor.
How many cries in secret to His Father, may this indicate?
Suffer. He had laboured seemingly in vain, inculcating faith.
He suffered long the rebellious manners of Israel. Acts xiii. 18.
His life one of *suffering* the imputed weight of sin. Isa. liii. 6.
Complainings, known only to the father, He would not repress.
Must the child be ever carried? Will he never walk alone?
His deepest emotions, still move in the sphere of holy writ. Deut. xxxii. 5, 20.
Bring. *Indignant* with the faithless, but *merciful* to the son.
Every word is clothed with grief, that so brief an absence, had shorn them of strength.
When all other aids fail, Jesus is willing to receive us.

γενεά—Includes, 1, scribes. 2, apostles, *Stier.* Scribes alone, *Calvin.* People present, *Paulus, Olshausen, Neander.* Disciples, *Bengel, De Wette, Meyer, Chrysostom.* Disciples and multitude, *Trench, Ellicott.* Entire generation of the Jews, *Alford, Alexander.* "*How long.*"—Jesus blames their want of self dependence, *De Wette.* Directly the reverse. Had they *leaned entirely* on Him, they could not have failed.

---

42. *And as he was yet a coming, the devil threw him down, and tare him. And Jesus rebuked the unclean spirit, and healed the child, and delivered him again to his father.*

Yet a coming. Memories of the spirit world, not yet faded out.
This demon tested the *Almighty power* of the Incarnate Son.
Mark. **They brought.** Combined strength of several, overcame resistance.

Tare him. Satan's subjects nearing Christ, roused to fiercer energy.
The fiend seemed to set Christ Himself at defiance.
Like an out-going tenant, cares not what mischief he does.
Mark. Has "*How long?*" He wisely delays, that He may rouse faith, and tranquillize excitement.
Jesus seems to forget the malady, in His interest about faith.
Note the sublimity of this simple *element* of *power* in His Kingdom.
The father—"IF *thou* CANST *do anything?*" The *Saviour*—"If *thou canst believe?*"
Jesus *removes* want of faith, then *works*.
Saviour proves Himself the Author of the father's faith.
He endorsed the parent's faith, by healing his child.
He endorses the parent's act, by blessing the child baptized.
He endorsed the master's faith, by healing his servant. Matt. viii. 13.
He endorsed the mother's faith, by restoring her daughter. Mark vii. 30.
Rebuked. Mark has "*I charge thee.*" Implies the might of the fiend.
"I, *thy Creator and Judge charge*,"—military term of absolute authority.
Mark has "*Enter no more.*" This for ever bars the demon's return.
Healed. An *instantaneous cure* of the wounds, *another miracle!*
Greatness of the victory enhanced by the disciples' failure.
Mark has "*Many said he was dead.*" He arose in full health.
Delivered. "As though he said—"Remember the *source* of your mercies."

δαιμόνιον—Notes, Luke iv. 33.

---

43. ¶ *And they were all amazed at the mighty power of God. But while they wondered every one at all things which Jesus did, he said unto his disciples.*

Amazed. A mere man in appearance, controlling spirits of the invisible world.
Mighty power. The Greek is used of the divine power of Christ. 2. Pet. i. 16.
Wondered. He wrought as one Almighty, His name is "*Wonderful.*" Isa. ix. 6.

ἐξεπλήσσοντο—*struck with amazement;* Gr., *struck out*, *i.e.* of the normal condition of the mind, μεγαλειότητι—*majesty, greatness, Wickliffe.* The divine power of Diana, Acts xix. 27, *Alexander.*

---

44. *Let these sayings sink down into your ears: for the Son of man shall be delivered into the hands of men.*

Sink down. I have oft repeated them, but ye have never heard them before.
Points at a close connection between "Hosannas" and "Crucify, Crucify."
They were warned against trusting the fickle crowd.
When it is well with us, let us remember, it may soon be ill with us.
Your. Emphatic, to correct carnal views of the Transfiguration.
You have witnessed My glory, My power, the wonder of the crowd.
Know *ye* I must be delivered up, and suffer death.
Son of Man. Luke v. 24, referring to His Divinity.
Of men. This word is not used of just, but very wicked men.

Let them always sound in your ears, *Kuinoel.* ἀνθρώπων. Our Lord uses this term of the worst of men, Matt. x. 17, *Richter.*

---

45. *But they understood not this saying, and it was hid from them, that they perceived it not: and they feared to ask him of that saying.*

Preconceived ideas of a temporal reign had stopped their ears.
Understood not. Their ignorance is made prominent by the Spirit.
They asked not, the only One, able to remove the veil.
The Divine purpose, that they should not at present.
Hid. Not dark, but *veiled.* Doubts would in due time be dispelled.
The impression to be *deepened,* when the facts were comprehended.
God has been His own interpreter, with regard to things foretold.
Perceived. They cannot reconcile these words, with the scene on the Mount.
Their Messiah, according to their views, was to be *immortal.*
Others found in conflicting prophecies, TWO MESSIAHS.
Ben Joseph, the suffering; and *Ben David,* the triumphant Messiah.
Feared. The Transfiguration invested Him, with majesty.
There was no guilt in this reserve of the disciples.
Their vague forebodings, modified by the splendor of His deeds.

παρακεκαλυμμένον—The declaration was clear, but their minds obscured. Prophecy has been *veiled* until fulfilled. ἵνα is for ὥστε, *insomuch that* they might not. The stupidity of the apostles, unaccountable, *Schleiermacher*. αἴσθωνται—at first physically —afterward intellectually. Unable to reconcile the prophecies of a conquering, with a dying Messiah, the Jews made *two*, *Whitby*, *Elsley*.

---

46 ¶ *Then there arose a reasoning among them, which of them should be greatest.*

Reasoning. The idea is *calculation*, arising from human vanity.
Should be. May be translated "*was.*" John xiii. 24.
Greatest. The acting Master as a servant, they wrangling for the *mastery!*
While the Master was on His way to the cross, they are dividing crowns.
This envy might have been roused by the Lord's promise to Peter. Matt. xvi. 18.
Or the distinction of the three, on the night of the Transfiguration.
Or the miraculous payment of the tribute by Simon. Matt. xvii. 24.
Or the enthusiasm excited among the crowd, by the cured child.
If such grossness of views are held by the disciples of Christ,
How crude must the views of the unrenewed be!
While the Redeemer was absorbed in contemplating His death.
He by His inquiries shamed them into silence. Mark ix. 33.

47. *And Jesus, perceiving the thought of their heart, took a child, and set him by him.*

Perceived. He read their secret wishes, as at the Judgment.
Thoughts. Are heard by Jehovah on His Throne.
Took. "*Called,*" Matt., implying that He was then within a house.
The disciples instantly saw in the question the *sermon*, and felt the *rebuke*. Mark ix. 33.
Ashamed to ask Him on account of their *ignorance*. See verse 43.
Now they are ashamed to answer through *pride*.
A tender conscience, like a mirror, flashes its condemnation.
Our Redeemer was about to leave a sermon to coming ages, on *humility*.
In his arms.—Mark. He does not *speak*, but *shews* us the deep lesson.
The contentious apostles put to *shame*, by this child, before the bystanders.
He dignifies childhood, enriches poverty, ennobles meekness.
What a majesty of love and truth, in this act!
Every child preached *humility* before, but men understood it not.

Each child the symbol, and prophetic testimony of the doctrine.

Pride had fast bound the heart from comprehending the *reverence* due to a child.

Heathen sages knew nothing either of the *honor* or *dignity* of humility.

Christ speaks the great word, as unpretendingly, as though it had always been self-evident.

διαλογισμὸν, Gr., *reasoning*, it is the same word as in the last verse. Eng. *dialogue*. *ταπεινώσει*, Matt. xviii. 4. *Plutarch*, cited by *Tholuck*, stands in honorable signification. *Modestia* does not suffice for this. Humility, with classic nations, was meanness. Modern sceptics coincide with them,—pride is self valuation; humility, pusillanimity, *Hume*. In the parallels of Matt., &c., He teaches by the child, that to advance and become something, one must turn round, go backwards, and become a little child. *Puero debetur reverentia*, *Stier*.

---

48. *And said unto them, Whosoever shall receive this child in my name receiveth me; and whosoever shall receive me, receiveth him that sent me: for he that is least among you all, the same shall be great.*

Said. Every eye fastened on the child, *in the Saviour's arms*. Mark ix. 36.

This occurred at Capernaum, in the house of Simon and Andrew.

Receive. Gr. the form of expression is conditional, *should receive*.

In My Name. That is because he acknowledges My name.

With unwavering reliance on Me as entitled to send him.

Humility is pointed out, as the true road to greatness.

True greatness is spiritual greatness. Attainable by all conditions of life.

A child, though depraved, is comparatively humble.

A *truthful*, *guileless* child, a model for believers.

Feeling its ignorance, weakness, helplessness.

It is teachable—obedient in its simplicity, *with perfect confidence*, until deceived.

Faithful, with fearlessness it follows mid great perils.

Free from *ambition*, it covets no honors.

A wigwam or palace—princes or peasants alike.

"I was not haughty, nor lofty; but behaved as a child." Psa. cxxxi. 1.

Free from *malice*, its quarrels are soon forgotten in love. 1. Cor. xiv. 20.

Receive Me. The same objection made by proud Jews, to an humble Christ.

It required humility to renounce their *lofty expectations*.

And if they would not, from pride, receive a humble Messiah.
They could not, by reason of pride, receive The *Father* who sent Him.

Least. God trains His children to be small or lowly.
We train ours to be great, *i.e.*, vain and proud.
A child need not humble itself, for *it is* humble.
"He resists the proud, but giveth grace to the humble." Jas. iv, 6; 1. Pet. v. 5.
God humbles the exalted, exalts the humble. Ezek. xxi. 26. Isa. lvii. 15.

In humility, we behold—

A childlike understanding, free from vain imaginations.
A childlike heart, free from ignoble jealousies.
A childlike will, free from insubordination.
A childlike life, free from dominion of sin.

Without the temper of a child.
It is impossible to acknowledge the King of this Kingdom.
To obey the fundamental law of this Kingdom.
To enjoy the happiness of this Kingdom.
The world makes its servants great, Jesus makes His *little*.
He taught them humility by *actions*, by *emblems*, and by *words*.

Among animals, He chose not the lion but the lamb.
Among birds, He chose not the eagle but the dove.
Among trees, He chose not the cedar but the vine.
Among the elements, He chose not the thunder but the gentle voice.

Humility the first and chief lesson taught by the Son of God.
Taught, not by words only, but by actions, and by His whole life.
Man, innocent, had God for his image—guilty, had a child set before him as his example.
Humility, the gentle nurse that fosters all infant virtues.
The soil in which all Christian graces flourish and bear fruit.
True humility discovers itself only to the spiritual searcher.
It brings the soul to the feet of Jesus, and leads to practical holiness.
It is the pathway to glory, honor, immortality, and eternal life.
He who lives on earth the life of an humble Christian, shall reign victorious in heaven.

"*Receive this child,*" literally, *Bengel*, *Neander*, *De Wette*. Spiritually, *Beza*, *Calvin*. An orphan, *Paulus*. *Young disciple*, *Bolten*. The point is its innocency, *De Wette*; humility, *Oosterzee*. Not moral purity, *Olshausen*. Tradition makes this child Ignatius, *Eusebius*.

μικρότερος—Gr., comparative form. The Pope styles himself *servus servorum Dei*—*servant of the servants of God*. The dispute had been, who, among the Twelve should be greatest,—*i. e.* greatest *in the kingdom of heaven*, about to appear: and our Lord reminds them, that no such precedence is to be thought of among those sent in His name; for that even a little child, if thus sent, is clothed with His dignity; and if there be any distinction it is this, that he who is like that child, humblest and least,—*i. e.* nearest to the Spirit of his Lord, *he is the greatest*, *Alford.*

---

49 ¶ *And John answered and said, Master, we saw one casting out devils in thy name; and we forbade him, because he followeth not with us.*

In sending out His Apostles, absolute *equality* was implied.
If any difference, a deeper humility alone caused it.
Zebedee's son thought of the exclusive dignity of the apostolic company.
John appreciated the *peculiar* honors of office.
He felt rebuked, and Christ intended he should.
He accounted him a *stranger*, who wrought in Jesus' name.
Answered. It awoke their conscience, instead of wounding self-love.
One, not emphatic, some one, whose name they had forgotten.
Devils. He was *successful*, wherein the apostles had *failed*.
Thy name. Proof of the importance strangers attached to Jesus' name.
Forbade. Through ill concealed jealousy and ambition.
Followeth. Belongs not to our authorized body of disciples.
Among the disciples, but not crowned with apostolic honors.
Bigotry springs out of the selfish depths of our nature.
"Our religion" (Acts xxvi. 5.) with many, the spirit of Pharisaism so strongly condemned by the Lord.
Us. A self-convicting, self-condemning pride, in this word.
It confounds following the Messiah, with following disciples liable to err.
God may *vary* any of His appointments at His will.
Moses rebuked Joshua, for forbidding Eldad's prophecy. Num. xi. 29.
Confessing Christ's Messiahship, not partisanship, but discipleship.
Wherever demons are expelled, *there* is the Spirit of God. Matt. xii. 28.
"By their fruits ye shall know them." Matt. vii. 20.

ἐπὶ τῷ ὀνόματι—John strangely misconceived these words, *Neander.* δαιμόνια—notes, Luke iv, 33. ἐκωλύσαμεν—literally, *hindered him;* a noble soul is at first intolerant, *Neimeger.* μεθ' ἡμῶν—*i. e.* followeth not *Thee*, with us. He may have invoked the Saviour's name, but he was not of John's party, *Stier.*

---

50 *And Jesus said unto him,* Forbid him *not; for he that is not against us is for us.*

Forbid. God's *ordinances* are only *bound* by His sovereign pleasure.

Our Lord regards casting out devils in *His name*, as homage, involuntarily paid Himself.

That homage proved good-will, and was a pledge of friendship.

A glorious example of His holy divine gentleness.

Christ's garment was "without seam," yet the Church's garment was of divers colors, *L. Bacon.*

Paul rejoiced at Christ being preached, though through envy. Phil. i. 18.

A standard to judge of deeds, when ignorant of men's faith.

Jesus taught that men might cast out devils, and be lost. Matt. vii. 23.

Therefore, ordinary grace more to be desired than extraordinary.

Against. Absence of hostility, to be regarded in a certain sense, a sign of friendship.

Nicodemus *not* acting with the Sanhedrim, proved his secret attachment to Jesus.

On the arrival of the crisis, the same course would prove his emnity to them.

For us. Generally we say those against Satan, are for Christ.

No neutrality for the heart in the kingdom of God.

Christ teaches that no person should be discouraged from the good he has attained in part.

Rather, he should be stimulated by the pursuit of the good that remains to be attained.

"Not the man, but the grace of God in the man," *Cyril.*

"Dost thou forbid one who conquers Satan by Christ?" *Cyril.*

Mark the bright side of the act, and carry it back to the source whence derived.

True love approves good, whensoever, and by whomsoever, done.

"*Forbid him not,*" literally, *hinder him not.* ἡμῶν often confounded with ὑμῶν. *Bengel, Lachmann, Alford, Campbell, Olshausen, Stier*, and *Tischendorf.* ἡμῶν, *Bloomfield, W. & W., Oosterzee.* There is no choice, *Alexander.*

---

51. ¶ *And it came to pass, when the time was come that he should be received up, he steadfastly set his face to go to Jerusalem.*

Came to pass. This was our Lord's *last* journey from Galilee to Jerusalem.

It was neither *direct* in time, nor in the *road*, chosen.

He was in Jerusalem at the Feast of Dedication, at the close of December.

Three months before the Passover He spent in the following tour.
After the attempt to stone Him, He returned to Galilee. John xi. 8.
From thence, He retired to Bethany, beyond Jordan. Matt. xxi. 17.
Thence called by Mary to Bethany, where Lazarus was raised.
Returned to Bethany 6 days before the Passion, and was anointed.
Luke again takes up the narrative of Matt. and Mark, in chap xviii. 15.
From chap. ix. 51, to chap. xviii. 14, the contents almost wholly peculiar to Luke.

The time, &c. Too *definite.* "*As the days of his receiving up were being accomplished.*"

Received up. Took place on the Mount of Olives, 500 brethren present. Acts i. 9; 1. Cor. xv. 6.

One travelling to a city, omits rugged ways, and speaks of the *arrival.*

Set. "I have set my face as a flint, I shall not be confounded." Isa. l. 7.

A firm resolve is of much help in difficulty, *Bengel.*

The hierarchs at Jerusalem, had long planned His death.

Jerusalem. Luke ii. 25. See Notes.

If travelling towards the heavenly Jerusalem, the fear of Death should not depress us.

συμπληροῦσθαι—*the days were being fulfilled*, or approaching their fulfilment, *D. Brown.* "*The Time*"—Identical with John, *Hug.*, *Lucke*, *Weiseler*, *Oosterzee.* Others place John vii. 1, after Matt. xvi. 13; and suppose our Lord stayed three months at Jerusalem, *Stier.* His reception in Galilee, *Lange.* Luke mixes two journies *Schleiermacher.*

ἀναλήψεως—*assumption*, ascension—can have but one meaning (as it is found no where else), and must be determined by the cognate verb, *Alford.* The word ἀνελήφθη had been already prepared for this sense of *ascension* by the LXX. applying it to Elijah (2 Kings, ii. 9-11). Our Lord's Agony, Cross, and Passion were at hand. But He looked through them all to His glorious ascension, *Wordsworth.* Reference to His ascension natural, if ἔξοδον includes it, *Lightfoot*, *Bengel*, *De Wette*, *Olshausen*, *Alford*, *Oosterzee.* Elevation to the Cross, *Heyne*, *Hammond.* Going up to Jerusalem, *Beza*, *Michaelis.* Removal, *Campbell.* A renewed entertainment, *Isaac Newton.* Death, *Calvin.*

πρόσωπον—Entire ministry a journey to death, *Bengel;* firmness of mind, *Grotius.* He never lost sight of his destination, *Baur.* *Set His face*—a Hebrew way of speaking, implying determinate, fixed purpose; see Isaiah l. 7, the sense of which, as prophetic of the Messiah going to His sufferings, seems referred to in this expression, *Alford.*

This portion of Luke unchronological, *De Wette.* Others make two journeys, *Olshausen*, *Neander*, *Bengel.* No chronology; but historical importance, *Meyer*, *Alford.* Three journeys—1. At the Feast of Tabernacles. 2. Some three months after. 3. Shortly before last Passover, *Ellicott*, *Ebrard*, *Weiseler.* "*To go.*" He left Capernaum, *Andrews*, *Ephraim*, *Greswell.*

52 ***And sent messengers before his face: and they went, and entered into a village of the Samaritans, to make ready for him.***

Messengers. The two sons of Zebedee were among them, it is believed.

Face. Heb., they knew He was going to Jerusalem. 2. Sam. xvii. 11; Luke xii. 50.

At feast time, rivalry between Jerusalem and Gerizim, was bitter.

Samaritans. The country, geography, &c. Luke xvii. 11. Character of people. Luke x. 33; xvii. 11.

Pilgrims to Jerusalem tried to avoid this route.

Samaria, their capital, about 40 miles north of Jerusalem.

Jeroboam with 10 tribes, renounced Rehoboam son of Solomon.

Idols at Dan and Bethel, drew from the worship at Jerusalem.

Samaria 724 B.C. captured by Shalmaneser with Assyrians.

Land vacated, settled by heathen, Levite sent to teach them.

The Samaritans were *entirely*, not *half* Gentiles, as some write.

Their race and religion *mixed*, until Ezra rebuilt the temple.

Their offers to *unite*, being repulsed, made them bitter enemies.

Baal's temple built by Ahab, was destroyed by Jehu.

Herod rebuilt Samaria, or *Sebaste* (Gr.) for *Augustus* his friend.

A splendid temple here, failed to draw them from *Gerizim*.

They believed Messiah would sanction Gerizim and not Jerusalem.

Our Lord condemned this heresy. "Into any city of the Samaritans enter ye not." Matt. x. 5.

Ruins of Helena's church, and Herod's palace still seen.

Pelagius was the Heresiarch bishop of this place A.D. 526.

Samaritans treated Jews more kindly than *they* were treated.

Make ready. The Lord will not give offence. A Christian is "*courteous*." 1. Peter, iii. 8.

The solemnity of the sentence, forbids the idea of simply providing board and lodging.

Their aim, to announce the coming of Jesus as expected Messiah.

He had not done this before; but now, instead of avoiding, He courts publicity.

Events were rapidly hastening to maturity. His hour had almost come.

"*Messengers.*" Sons of Zebedee, *Euthymius, Zigal.* No reason for the assumption, *Alford.* Denied, *Meyer.* κώμην—As their land, waters, dwellings, roads were clean, the Jews did not hesitate to pass through Samaria, *Lightfoot.* The Galileans in going to the festivals at Jerusalem, usually took the Samaritan route, *Josephus* Antiq. xx. 6. 1.

53 *And they did not receive him, because his face was as though he would go to Jerusalem.*

Receive. In the widest sense, the services of hospitality. Matt. x. 14

Hospitality could hardly be shewn a Messiah, preferring Jerusalem to Gerizim.

A type of the Christian's reception, by an unbelieving world.

But the world gives a welcome to the *time-serving* professor.

"Behold I stand at the door and knock," saith Christ. *The heart is closed.* Rev. iii. 20.

Prejudice against Him, as a Jew, closed their hearts.

They refused the greatest BLESSING that could be tendered.

The sad effect of religious bigotry springing from religious error.

Our Lord's publicity, contrasts with His former retiring habits.

His going up to Jerusalem to the feast, a reproach to those who did not go up.

Christians should solemnly observe the public and stated ordinances of the Church of God.

54 *And when his disciples James and John saw* this, *they said, Lord, wilt thou that we command fire to come down from heaven, and consume them, even as Elias did?*

James and John. Not Peter as might have been expected, but those "*sons of thunder.*"

Saw. Some insult of manner, or refusal to allow the Lord to enter their village.

Persecuted by the Sanhedrim, He might side with them.

Invoking fire in their presence hints at some open insult.

This fiery zeal, reveals their conviction of the Lord's Majesty.

Christ wrought miracles in all the elements but *fire*, that is reserved for *the End.*

Human vengeance stretches its hand, to grasp at the weapons of God.

We. How many never wait for Christ's consent to persecute.

Malice skilfully finds here the purest act.

Fire. Their indignation was kindled by remembering Tabor.

Moses and Elijah had there paid homage to their Master.

A spark of the latter's fiery zeal. inflamed their hearts.

They forgot that Sodom's doom, prefigured the *future* judgment.

Elias. They endeavored to imitate the saints, where they ought not.

The prophet sat on one of those hills, and it *reminds* them of it. 2. Kings i, 9.

Those slain in Elijah's time the involuntary agents of a tyrant.

Elijah's act was to reprove an idolatrous king, court, and nation.

Some trace their name, "*sons of thunder*," to this event.

If so, then their sin is *immortalized* as a warning, that Christ would not sanction persecution.

The revenge He took on Samaria was one of *love*. Acts viii. 14-17.

Disciples did not allow for prejudice, education, and accustomed train of thought.

Forgiveness, not destruction, is the characteristic of the Gospel of Christ.

Their conduct was self-seeking, not God pleasing.

Offended pride, the anger of the natural heart.

God must not be honored by unlawful means.

The wrath of man worketh not the righteousness of God.

Pride, anger, and prejudice retard the progress of the Gospel.

In mercy, the lightning of the skies is not under the control of man.

πῦρ—fire, not lightning, 1. Kings, xviii. 38. *καταβῆναι*—Descent of the thunderbolt. Jupiter called *καταιβάτης*. *ἀναλῶσαι*—*use up*, *spend*, destroy, kill. This feeling of revenge had its origin in the Samaritans offering the temple to Antiochus for an idolatrous use for Jupiter.

ὡς καὶ Ἠλίας, doubted. *Mill*, *Griesbach*. Cancelled, *Tischendorf*, *Tregelles*; because an indirect censure of the example in the Lord's answer, *De Wette*. Omitted by some ancient authorities, *Alford*. Genuine, *Oosterzee*, *Chrysostom*, *Theophylact*.

---

55. *But he turned, and rebuked them, and said, Ye know not what manner of spirit ye are of.*

Turned. Gr. *suddenly turning*, as if greatly surprised.

He condemned their fanaticism, more than that of the villagers.

Know. Some regard this as interrogative, the affirmative sense preferable.

Spirit. They overlooked the difference between the Old and New Covenants.

As if saying, "Let not your grace despise those who are without grace."

"The thing you demand, though in keeping with the *legal*, is unsuited to the genius of the *evangelical* dispensation.

They mistook Satan's promptings, for the zeal of the Holy Spirit.

Theirs a mixture of daring faith, and simple presumption.

In reality their *own* rejection. They have rejected us, was the sting.

Their supposed zeal for Christ, concealed a wounded pride.

They flattered themselves as having Elijah's holy zeal and spirit.

They felt assured his precedent, would be their warrant.

Elijah's examples, not precepts to Christ's followers.

True zeal never calls for fire from heaven to destroy those who differ.

We see, the best of men, are but men at the best, "I have seen an end of all perfection." Psa. cxix. 96.

Their fiery zeal was inflamed, rebuked, purified.

They had seen the Lord insulted by Nazarenes, Gadarenes and Pharisees.

Christ had forbidden them to enter Samaritans' villages. Matt. x. 5.

Must the entire town be destroyed, for the sin of a few?

Spirit of Christ, was love to all. He was the Prince of Peace.

We should never do anything for religion that is contrary to religion.

This reproof contains the true doctrine of Christian charity.

Erring friends to be reproved by the faithful, but in the spirit of meekness.

Unpalatable medicines are wholesome and restore to health.

---

55 and 56 verses cancelled, *Lachmann*. Omitted, *Cod. Sinai.* Retained, though considered doubtful, *Alford*. οὐκ οἴδατε, &c., doubtful, *Tischendorf*. Because a direct censure on Elijah, *Oosterzee*. Omitted by most of our oldest MSS., but contained in the most ancient versions, and quoted by some very ancient writers, *Alford*.

πνεῦμα, general meaning of the word,—1, Holy Ghost. 2, gift of the Spirit, Eph vi. 18. 3, an angel, Rev. i. 4. 4, an apparition, Luke xxiv. 39. 5, spirit of a man, Gal. v. 17. 6, a dispensation, Rom. viii. 15. 7, an affection, Luke i. 17, *Hammond*. Here, disposition of mind, *Wall*. What a *bad* spirit! *Bornemann*. Samaritans, ignorant and superstitious, objects of pity, *Grotius*. The Spirit meant is the Holy Spirit. The Spirit in Elias, was fiery and judicial, as befitted the times, and the character of God's dealings then; but the Spirit in Christ and His disciples, a Spirit of love and forgiveness, *Alford*.

---

56. *For the Son of man is not come to destroy men's lives, but to save them. And they went to another village.*

Son of man. His *humiliation*, as the *Eternal Word of God*. Luke v. 24. See Notes.

Destroy. Persecution, ever the badge of Satan's kingdom.

Fanaticism is *selfishness*; malignant, unrestrained, energetic.

The fire of zeal is to be sustained by the oil of mercy, *Aquinas*.

The Israelites, though conquerors, found that the Canaanites were still in the land.

The self-denying love of the cross consumes selfishnes.

Men's lives. Life of body, soul, and spirit.

Save. Implies both the suffering and the glorified Messiah.

His entire mission: He came to seek and save the lost. Luke xix. 10.

Christ compelled no one to receive Him, and when received, it is "by a people made willing."

Went. His turning from that village, a terrible judgment.

Another. Ministers not bound to preach to resisting people.

"*Come.*" The interrogative form does violence to the Greek, by making ἐστε mean, Ye ought to be.

ὁ υἱὸς, &c., cancelled, *Griesbach*, *Olshausen*, *Tischendorf*, *Oosterzee*. Genuine, *Stier*, *Bengel*. Apostles excused, trained under the O.T. dispensation, *De Wette*.

It is interesting to remember that this same John came down to Samaria with Peter, to confer the gift of the Holy Spirit on the Samaritan believers, see Acts viii. 14-17, *Alford*.

"*Village.*" In Galilee, *Meyer*, *Andrews*.

---

57 ¶ *And it came to pass, that, as they went in the way, a certain* man *said unto him, Lord, I will follow thee whithersoever thou goest.*

Came to pass. This incident occurred during a visit to Capernaum.

A certain man. Mark, "*Scribe*"—a professional expounder of the Law.

Follow, in personal attendance and adherence as a disciple.

It implies a partial conviction of our Lord's Messiahship.

Renouncing home attractions, something still wanting at heart.

Whithersover. A tacit condition of submitting to trials and dangers.

Our Lord's reply hints at a wish to share the *honors* of the kingdom.

Still it implies a *consciousness* of difficulties involved.

Our Lord's answers to the persons who came to Him are keys to their motives.

The *natural man* weighs not the greatness of the self-denial.

It is not purposes, but performances, that mark the Christian.

Man oft resolves and re-resolves, yet dies the same. Hell is paved with good intentions, *Luther*.

We have here an instance of undue precipitation in discipleship.

This candidate for Christian honors and glories had not counted the cost.

A *Scribe*, in our Lord's train, a "Saul" among ths prophets.

"*It came to pass that*," omitted, *Alford*, *Cod. Sinai.*

ἀκολουθήσω—These callings refer to apostleship, and the scribe offers to follow as one, *Lange*.

58. *And Jesus said unto him, Foxes have holes, and birds of the air have nests; but the Son of man hath not where to lay his head.*

The resolution, made without urging, seemed sincere.
But the Searcher of hearts saw that his motives were *low* and *carnal.*
Jesus said. "My kingdom is not of this world." I am a homeless pilgrim.
Foxes. Luke xiii. 32. The humblest animals have a settled home.
He hints he had taken his resolution too suddenly.
That he had not maturely considered its consequences.
Not the poverty and meanness, but wandering and unrest.
Nests. Some seek high places (nests) in prosperity.
Others seek places of concealment (caves) in adversity.
Many like to be pious, if they can retain their riches and honors.
A man is soon enlisted, but is not soon made a soldier.
He is easily put into the ranks to make a show, but not so easily broug to do the duty of a soldier, *Cecil.*
Our Lord's reply a strong contrast to honors anticipated by the Scribe.
Not a complaint, for friends were able to support him.
Extreme destitution was not one of the *griefs* of the "man of sorrows."
He would have the people clearly see His humanity.
Not of want absolutely, but voluntary poverty.
Son of Man. Luke v. 24. See Notes.
Lay. Gr. a place to *sleep.* The Apostles had no certain dwelling-place. 1. Cor. iv. 11.
Head. A renunciation of everything a man calls his own.
Even in *death,* He had no home of His own for His mother. John xix. 27.
A man without a home on earth, and yet Creator of heaven's palaces.
Most wonderful contrasts all through His life, deepest humiliation and highest glory.
Our Lord, owner of all things, became poorer than the beasts which perish.
His resting places were a manger, the side of a well, a ship, a garden, the cross!
Hard fare for Himself, and contempt from others.
Our Lord sanctified poverty, and sweetened life's trials.
He disjoined worldliness from piety. Let us not unite them.
Yet piety blesses for both worlds. "Godliness is profitable for all things."
The Redeemer became *poor,* but makes many rich. 2 Cor. viii. 9.
The Scribe to his surprise, was *repelled* from following Christ.
No worldly policy may mingle with the elements of His church.

A mere *man* would have concealed all that is forbidding.
Mohammed flattered the ambition, and pampered the lusts of his followers.
Jesus desires no disciples, but from pure principle.
Fearless faith and integrity are beyond the reach of a bribe.
He went back to the *world*, he had never actually *renounced.*

ἀλώπεκες—*The foxes*, a familiar animal, remarkable for its cunning, Luke xiii. 32. They oft damage the vines in the south of France, Song of Sol. ii. 15. φωλεοὺς—lurking places. πετεινὰ—*The birds of the air* to the boastfulness, *Augustine*, foxes to the cunning of scribes, *Lange*. κατασκηνώσεις—shelters, not nests, *De Wette*.

"*Lay.*" Where He should sleep that night, *Herder*. Divine Spirit felt oppressed within the four walls of a chamber, *Weisse*. He would follow the Lord either road He took to Jerusalem, *Schleiermacher*. Ittai's words to David illustrate it, 2. Sam. xv. 21, *Oosterzee*.

---

59. *And he said unto another, Follow me, But he said, Lord, suffer me first to go and bury my father.*

Follow. Our Lord saw one *procrastinating* at a critical moment.
The Scribe deterred by *difficulties*, others held back by *duties*.
This more honest man is *urged forward*, the Scribe is *discouraged*.
The Scribe was too *hasty*, this person too *slow*.
The dark image of *death* haunts him in the presence of the Prince of *Life*.
He must choose promptly, or he will never choose.
Christ treats him with loving severity, yet with loving wisdom.
Suffer me. Spurious scruples, and spiritual hesitation.
A collision of duties impossible, as a contest among angels.
Good works, when a pretext for not following Christ, are dead works.
Bury. (Luke vii. 12.) Saviour knew the effect of funeral ceremonies and patrimonial inheritance.
Those spiritually dead busy themselves much with ceremonials of life.
Man ever opposes the will of God, under some pretence.
He either lags behind, or runs before he is sent. Jer. i. 7.
The Bible sanctions no neglect of friendship's sacred duties.
Family duties never really stand in the way of *earnest* souls.
An earthly father should be honor'd, but the heavenly Father must be obeyed.
A want of *leisure* is rather often a want of *inclination*.
Obligations due to the world, must yield to those *due* to God.

"Whoso loveth father or mother more than *Me*, is not worthy of *Me*." Matt. x. 37.

As Ruth to Naomi, he doubtless clung to Jesus. Ruth i. 16.

Father. A *dead* father, and a *living* Gospel.

To follow Christ is a weightier matter than to go to the burial of a father.

Spiritual ties are more sacred than earthly ones, when they are opposed, the former are paramount, the latter must yield.

ἕτερον—Philip, *Clement of Alexander*. ἐπίτρεψον—Luke vii. 12, Gr., *turn over*, entrust, permit. θάψαι—He must wait till his aged father dies, *Hase*. His father was then dead, and he ceremonially unclean, *Oosterzee, Lange*. In Egypt and Palestine they frequently embalmed. 100 pounds weight of spices prepared for Jesus. In Greece and Rome bodies were burned, and ashes collected in urns. They are still found in their gorgeous tombs. Greeks could utter no deeper malediction than, "*May you never be buried*," *Freidleib*.

---

60. *Jesus said unto him, Let the dead bury their dead: but go thou and preach the kingdom of God.*

Let the dead. Gr. *leave the dead.* Those about to die, or mortals bound to the laws of death.

Let those dead (in spirit), bury those who are dead (in body).

If the dead cannot be buried without drawing away from Christ, let them be unburied. There are interests *above* those of dust.

Such persons more fit for burying the dead than preaching the gospel.

The tenderest obligations of earth must yield to Christ.

His self-denial will be a thousand fold requited in preaching Christ.

Nazarites *not* to mourn even for parents. Num. vi. 6-8.

Bury. Earthly pleasures, earthly love, earthly sorrow are three great forces drawing men back from Christ.

Our Lord intended to teach us that whatever withdraws us from Him, or impedes us, is *death*, *Calvin*.

He no more discourages respect to a deceased father than He recently disclaimed His own duty to a living mother. Luke viii. 21.

To respect the memory of a deceased father good; but to follow Christ, far better.

Those "dead in sins," could bury the lifeless corpse, but none but a regenerate soul could preach the kingdom of God, *Hall*.

ὁ Ἰησοῦς omitted *Cod. Sinai.* ἄφες—*Leave, Alexander.* νεκροὺς, first, spiritually dead:—its double meaning adds beauty to the passage, *Oosterzee.* Gentiles, the blind, the leprous, the poor, and the children, accounted *dead, Lightfoot.* νεκροὺς—That grave-diggers, or buriers of the dead, are here implied, is monstrous. The dead differed in nothing, essential from the living, *Alexander.* Sceptics insinuate Christ's demand to be disrespectful to parents, *Baur.*

---

61. *And another also said, Lord, I will follow thee: but let me first go bid them farewell, which are at home at my house.*

I will. As if determined to renounce all others, and follow Christ.

Bid farewell. Notwithstanding his apparent determination "I will," he was *irresolute.*

Elisha asked a similar privilege, but the request unreasonable here.

The dangers of Christ's service might make their parting final.

He might do more *for them*, with Jesus, than with them.

Some out of a funeral used to make a festive entertainment.

Heathen usually *rejoiced* with the world, before leaving it.

He is willing unnecessarily to expose himself to temptation.

"Demas forsook me, having loved this present world." 2. Tim. iv. 10.

Christ rejects none coming in sincerity. John vi. 37.

ἀποτάξασθαι—renuntiare rebus domesticis, *Vul.:* arranging them, *Heyne, Doddridge.* ἀποτάξασθε τῷ Σατανᾳ; and συντάξασθε τῷ Χριστῷ; Form of renouncing the world. Ancient *Liturgies, Stier.*

---

62. *And Jesus said unto him, No man, having put his hand to the plough, and looking back, is fit for the kingdom of God.*

Plough. Every *sowing time* preceded by a *ploughing time.*

Strong arms and stout hearts persevere in exhausting toil.

Irresolution or procrastination in reference to the service of Christ, sinful weakness and device of Satan.

It often happens that when a man goes home, and is engaged in bidding farewell to his friends, some of them will draw him from God to the world, *Theophylact.*

In this vital matter, decision for Christ, a man's foes are often those o his own household.

Think nothing done while aught remains to be done.

Looking back. Confuses our plans, and arrests our progress.

It is more than we can sustain without *going back*, *Cecil.*

"Whoever looks back" the proverb says "makes no straight furrow."

So will they come short of salvation who prosecute the work of God with distracted attention or divided heart.

Christ demands a deliberate, a courageous, and an unconditional surrender.

He who thinks of following Christ mnst follow wholly, or not at all. Luke xvii. 32.

Lot's wife's sin was giving her heart to the perishing world; looking and longing for that which was condemned.

She *looked back;* and God never gave her leave to *look forward* again.

"Blessed is the man that endureth temptation." Jas. i. 12.

"He that endureth to the end shall be saved." Matt. x. 22.

"But we are not of them who *draw back* unto perdition." Heb. x. 39.

Who ever *required* more, or *requited* more than Jesus?

These three cases designed by the Holy Spirit to teach these lessons—

1st. In following Christ we must follow Him for His own sake, and if need be, by sacrifice of all earthly advantage.

2nd. No earthly tie, however dear, may draw us from prompt obedience to His call.

3rd. Christ must have the chief place in our affections, He must have the whole heart.

A Christian must not be like Hezekiah's sun that *went backward.*

Nor yet like Joshua's sun that *stood still.*

But like David's sun, that, *like a bridegroom cometh out of his chamber, and rejoiceth as a champion to run a race*—*Boys.*

ἄροτρον—*Delirare*, acting foolishly, from *de* and *lira*, a *furrow*, to make a crooked furrow; spiritualized, *misses the gospel track.* A faithful ploughman is one who, attending to his business, draws the furrows straight, by no means looking round. 4 characters drawn:—51-56, the choleric. 57-58, the sanguine. 59-60, melancholic. 61-62, phlegmatic, *Winkler.* The three followers supposed to have been Judas Iscariot, Thomas, Matthew, *Lange.*

The man seems to have had in his mind the case of Elisha, to whom Elijah gave leave; for Jesus in reply employs the figure of a *plough*, (1. Kings xix 19.) The Kingdom of God requires more zeal of us, than the discipline of the law, *Bengel.*

CHAPTER X.

AFTER these things the Lord appointed other seventy also, and sent them two and wo be 'ore his face into every city and place, whither he himself would come.

,uke alone records this mission, probably he was one of them.

After these things. The Seventy were sent out before the Feast of Tabernacles.

The Lord. This expression fitly designates the ordination of the Seventy by the Divine Head of the Church.

Appointed. Designated. There is the idea of choice, as ambassadors.

ppointment of the Twelve differs from that of the Seventy in nature and duration.

The former, an office permanently founded: the establishment of a regular ministry.

The latter, to present duties, and preparation for the Lord's last journey.

The services of the Seventy limited to places the Lord designed to visit.

The Twelve to accompany their Master, as special witnesses of His life, death, and resurrection.

The Apostolic office involved a work and consequences wide as humanity.

Other Seventy also. *Others also, seventy in number.* There were not seventy *before.*

The number *seventy* points from afar to an *Anti-Sanhedrim* of the new kingdom.

uke fitly records the appointment of the Seventy. He is the Evangelist of the Gentile world, and the Historian of the universal church.

Two and two. Thirty-five pairs as pioneers, calling those he had healed.

Christ seizes the social principle, and sanctifies it to the highest use—to proclaim words of peace, to exhibit deeds of love.

Two and two: mutual aid, friendly counsel, brotherly affection, conjoint prayer, helpful sympathy, testimony to miracles.

That two should be joined in service, seems from Scripture an ancient custom.

God led Israel out of Egypt by the hand of Moses and Aaron.

'oshua and Caleb united together, appeased the people provoked by the spies.

A brother assisted by a brother is as a fortified city.

Two by two: to justify the Gospel they were to preach "*The testimony of two is true.*"

Also to signify say some, that they were to preach unto *two*—Jew and Gentile.

Also that they were to preach out of *two*—the Law and the Gospel.

Also that they were to preach the love of *two*—God and our neighbour.

These *two* precepts, the substance of religion, contained in the *two* tables.

Also that they were to preach by two works—Doctrine and good life.

That the end of their preaching was to save *two*—Soul and Body.

And to join the great *two*—Heaven and Earth: God and Man, *Austin.*

The kingdom of Christ aggressive, progressive, expansive.

First, 12 Apostles; then 70 preachers; then 500 brethren; then thousands!

Before his face. In advance: to publish this, His last journey.

The Lord *follows* His preachers—they go *before His face.*

Preaching comes first—then the Lord enters the tabernacle of the heart.

Through the word going before, Christ is received into the soul.

μετὰ—besides, Olshausen; after, Alford. ἀνέδειξεν—to proclaim any one to an office, *Wetstein.* "*Appointed.*"—Their names not given by *Eusebius.* "*Seventy,*"—a round number, answering to that of the Sanhedrim, *Oosterzee.* Foreshadowing the number of Cardinals, *Sepp.* Why the Vulgate has 72, the translators themselves could not tell, *Lightfoot.* Such as the 70 elders selected by Moses. The 70 Palm trees in the desert, Ex. xv. 27. 70 members of the Jewish Sanhedrim. 70 Translators of the Sept., *Wetstein.* The 70 *Gentile Nations, Neander, Lange.*

δύο—Vul., *duos.* Seventy others, *Campbell.* Others, also 70, *Markland. Tischendorf* cancels it. *Fabricius* has made a catalogue of their names, as *Agabus, Amplias, Ananias,* who baptized Paul, &c., *Epiphanius.* Luke was one, *Origen.*

"*Sent them.*" To strengthen their own faith, *Hase, Krabbe.* The journey made a final offer of the Messiah, *Meyer, Andrews.* Some of the disciples were dismissed and made teachers in synagogues, *Ammon.* Rather a net of love which the Lord cast over Israel, *Riggenbach.* Seventy sent to Samaria, *Wieseler, Lange;* to Perea, *Lichtenstein, Robinson, Andrews.* When? Before leaving Galilee, *Robinson;* after, *Wieseler.* Before the Feast of Dedication, *Tischendorf, Alford, Oosterzee.*

---

2 *Therefore said he unto them, The harvest truly is great, but the labourers are few: pray ye therefore the Lord of the harvest, that he would send forth labourers into his harvest.*

Said He. A band of Israelites ever roused the compassion of Jesus.

The O. T. dispensation a *seed time*. All felt the need of an atonement.
A nobler harvest, expected at the coming of the Messiah, is ready.
A scattered, hungry, fainting, shepherdless flock.
In answer to prayer, the Seventy were now commissioned to go.
The Seventy as pioneers prepared the way of the Lord.
The Twelve followed His track and *reaped* His sowing.
Harvest, summer, and winter, only seasons named in the Bible.
Barley harvest in the plain of Jordan about the middle of April.
In Sharon and Esdraelon plains, the 1st of May, wheat 2 weeks after.
The Gospel sickle garners for heaven and for future vengeance.
Laborers. Worthy the name. There were *many*, but not for God.
Ministers as Husbandmen must labor.
Ministers as Watchmen must guard.
Ministers as Shepherds *must* feed their flocks.
Ministers as Soldiers of the Cross must war a good warfare.
Pray ye. The solemn key-note of this commission.
Prayer directs men's thoughts to the magnitude of the work.
Prayer teaches men their insufficiency for so vast an undertaking.
Prayer shows the need of the perpetual presence of God.
He challenges His disciples to pray unto HIMSELF.
Power of prayer, a thousand-fold attested, but an inscrutable mystery.
He who prays for laborers, must be disposed to labor.
The sending forth of laborers, still suspended on human prayer.
Lord, &c. 1. He determines the time of the harvest. 2. He appoints the laborers. 3. He watches over the growth. 4. He alone deserves the praise.
Send forth. With the vehement impulse of his burning love.
Importance, urgency. The eternal welfare of multitudes.
Rigorous strivings with God are the bitter pangs, by which Ministers are born unto the Church, *Allestry*.

ἐκβάλῃ—Tischendorf, Stier, Cod. Sinai. ἐκβάλλῃ—W. & W. and Alford; to *expel. Would speedily send forth, Bloomfield.* Thrust forth, *Doddridge.*

---

3. *Go your ways: behold, I send you forth as lambs among wolves.*

Go. The origin and authority of the gospel ministry, *Divine*.
The enemies of the ministry, ever the enemies of God's Truth.
Behold. Mark's transition, calls attention, impresses the mind.

For a mere man, such a *formula* were impiety.

I send. I, expressed in the Greek denotes ***high authority.***

Reorganizing His Church, and completing Revelation.

Angels never honored with such a commission.

Christ's "*safe conduct*" secures from wrath of men and demons.

"Ministers immortal as angels, until their work is done."

"*I send you:*" as if He said, "This will suffice for your consolation, this will be enough to make you hope."

Lambs. Implies simplicity, helplessness, and needing a guide.

Suggests the idea of *value.* Wolves useless and therefore valueless.

Also an endearing and intimate relation to the Shepherd.

They were unarmed and helpless against cruel and powerful foes.

To go with unwavering faith in the Supreme Shepherd.

To abide faithful to the only work, to which they were called.

Wolves. A well known beast, specially dangerous in the evening. Jer. v. 6. Crafty, ravenous. Gen. xlix. 27. Of exquisite power of scent.

First fact, note, the world will be your enemy.

Contrast value and helplessness of sheep with worthlessness and cruelty of wolves.

The Gospel a proclamation of *peace*, and a declaration of *war.*

As howlings of wolves, so revilings of persecutors, terrify.

Serpents. Mark. Avoiding danger, not malignant; cunning is noted.

Doves. Luke ii. 24. Matt. Emblems of gentleness, innocence, and purity.

Their bearing offers of *peace*, prove them "sons of peace."

"The wolf shall dwell with the lamb." Symbol of the Millennium. Isa. lxv. 25.

ἀποστέλλω is equivalent to *I ordain* (or constitute) you apostles, *Alexander.* ἄρνας—*lambs:*—The Twelve were sent forth as *sheep.* A verbal difference, *Meyer.* Seventy held a lower rank, *Euthymius.*

---

4. *Carry neither purse, nor scrip, nor shoes: and salute no man by the way.*

Purse. Luke ix. 3. Omit all that prevents dispatch. See Notes.

Luggage forbidden proves disinterestedness, and dependence on the Lord.

He promises no riches, honors, or pleasures, but rather persecutions and sufferings.

A perpetual warning to the Ministry against *covetousness.*

Christ puts the trust and confidence of His ministers to the test.

He who sends them forth will *guide* and *guard*.

Salute. A remarkable injunction given to no other followers.
Oriental forms of civility very tedious and heartless.
Serious and silent orientals grow talkative in travelling.
Our Lord discountenances no ordinary tokens of civility.
Attention *demanded* by the world, cripples Christian energy.
The trifles of fashion *impede*. Christ's affairs need *haste*.
Christians trained in the court of *the King:* true courtiers urge with vehemence, but not obtrusiveness their claims.

Shoes. Sandals, pieces of leather bound with *latchet*.
Servants always loosed them when guests entered the house.
Some interlaced and beautified with needle work. Sol. Song vii. 1.
Warriors protected their limbs by greaves. Eph. vi. 15.
Sandal delivered to one buying real estate. Ruth iv. 7.
Sandal-bearer, the office of the humblest servant. Matt. iii. 11.
Those mourning refused salutations, as waste of time. 2. Sam xiv. 2.
Pharisees loved salutations to feed their vanity. Mark xii. 38.
"If thou meet any man, salute him not," Elisha. 2. Kings iv. 29.

Way. Orientals live in the street, so one never wants cause of loitering.
Inferiors remain standing, while superiors pass.

ἀσπάσησθε refers to seeking *favor* of men, *Olshausen*. The command means—*Haste: delay not in salutation, Meyer, De Wette, Alford*. Luke xi. 43, ἀσπασμοὺς He was a man of sorrows,—and would have all conform to His pattern, and testify their sympathy with the afflicted, *Lightfoot*.

τὴν ὁδὸν—The population are lounging or smoking in the shade of their hovels, as the Athenians, Acts xvii. 21. ὑποδήματα—*under-bound*.

---

5. ***And into whatsoever house ye enter, first say, Peace** be **to this house.***

Whatsoever. Implying, what thou doest, do quickly. John xiii. 27.
An errand of mercy, and the souls of high and low are precious.

Peace. Messengers of the King of peace; proclaim a *truce* to men.
Guides to eternal peace, ministers of reconciliation to those at war with God.
Peace, the mother of all good things, without it all other things are vain.
Peace, a divine authorization of benediction by the ministers of the Gospel.

Peace to be offered alike to the evil and to the good. *Peace to all.*

The peace of the Gospel is as health and sunshine within the dwelling.

He forbids official severity, as contradicting humility.

"Go to Nabal at Carmel, and greet him in my name." 1. Sam. xxv. 5.

"Pray for the peace of Jerusalem: they shall prosper that love thee." Psa. cxxii. 6.

The messengers of God should pray for men's salvation before beginning to reprove them, *Bengel.*

6. *And if the son of peace be there, your peace shall rest upon it: if not, it shall turn to you again.*

Son of peace. Worthy to receive the blessings of the Gospel of peace.

With disposition suitable for the reception of the proffered blessing.

We are not to suspect or suppose evil in any, till by their works it is manifest.

Sons of *Belial*, depraved persons following after Satan.

Shall rest. In a manner perceptible to yourselves.

No unmeaning form. It *conveyed* the intended blessing.

Blessings of salvation, not *fitful*, but *abide* for ever. Psa. xci. 1.

"This day is salvation come to this house." Luke xix. 9.

Peace having gone forth, does not cease seeking till it finds a place to rest.

Upon it—or *upon him.* Upon *the house*, in the first instance; upon its inhabitants, in the second, *Bengel.*

Return. Peace, like the dove from the ark, finds a resting place or returns.

No prayers of faith lost—"vials filled—the prayers of the saints." Rev. v. 8.

His prayers (for his enemies) returned to his own bosom. Psa. xxxv. 13.

Woe to the houses whence the proffered blessing returns.

"Though Israel be not gathered, I shall be glorious." Isa. xlix. 5.

If no one be willing to accept *peace*, the preacher shall not be without his fruit.

Peace returns to him, while the Lord gives him the recompense of reward for his labor and work.

ἐφ' ὑμᾶς—cancelled, *Griesbach*, *Tischendorf.*

ἀνακάμψει—The turning back of travellers, the omens unfavourable for a prosperous journey. The heathen accustomed to commence their journeys with prayer, *Plutarch.*

7 *And in the same house remain, eating and drinking such things as they give: for the labourer is worthy of his hire. Go not from house to house.*

In the same house. Read, *in the house itself: in that house.*

Remain. Poverty of entertainment no reason for a speedy departure.

Not to change lodgings, as if hard to be pleased.

Such things. Not desirous of dainties, with Christ as an example.

Sparingly or freely, as the case may be; satisfied with such things as were offered, if the message of peace was accepted.

Give. *Fasts* of Pharisees, and *feasts* of Epicureans condemned.

The laborer, &c. The hire is worthy of a *laborer*, not of a *laggard*, *Bengel.*

It was permitted them to take food, but not to ask for money; though not expressly forbidden to receive even that.

Go not. Content inculcated: the appearance of evil to be avoided.

Preserve consistency in your love towards your hosts, nor lightly loose any bond of friendship.

8. *And into whatsoever city ye enter, and they receive you, eat such things as are set before you:*

Set before you. Reference to the multiform usages of Pharisees, about food.

The traditional rules very irksome and perplexing.

From these restraints, Christ absolved all His disciples.

The Gospel leads to liberty, never licentiousness.

Dishes set before pampered palates, raise scruples. 1. Cor. x. 25.

The Pastor's motto: "I seek not *yours*, but *you*." 2. Cor. xii. 14.

9 *And heal the sick that are therein, and say unto them, The kingdom of God is come nigh unto you.*

Heal the sick. First heal and then teach; evidence of miracles necessary.

Miracles—the ringing of the great bell of the universe, to call attention to the doctrine, *Foster.*

When men were healed in body by special Divine power, they would believe the kingdom of God had come to them.

10 *But into whatsoever city ye enter, and they receive you not, go your ways out into the streets of the same, and say,*

11 *Even the very dust of your city, which cleaveth on us, we do wipe off against you: notwithstanding be ye sure of this, that the kingdom of God is come nigh unto you.*

Wipe. A visible reproof—a symbolical act full of meaning.

Their severest words must bear no resentment.

Righteous indignation ever to be combined with patient love.

Very dust—lest they carried it back with them: they must shake it off to show that so far from seeking anything earthly from them, they suffer not even the dust of their land to cleave to them, *Bede.*

Those who despise Christian teaching turn the labors and dangers of the teachers into a testimony of their condemnation.

Conquerors take away kingdoms—the heralds of Christ offer a kingdom.

The connexion which the Holy Spirit has adopted in the four Gospels is that of *substance*, rather than of *time*, or *place.*

Be sure. Proclamation made on entering, repeated on leaving the city.

Refusing allegiance to God, we leave you to your doom.

We free ourselves from all share in your condemnation.

The peace rejected on earth will become your accuser at the bar of God. Pro. i. 24.

Though "*The kingdom of God is come nigh unto you*" the separation may be eternal.

They who pass from the love of themselves to the love of God inherit the kingdom.

The *kingdom of God* may come *nigh*, and yet we may be *far* from the *kingdom of God.*

Where *the kingdom of God* comes not as a *blessing*, it comes as a *curse.*

The Gospel is a savour of life unto life, or of death unto death.

ἀπομασσόμεθα—*We wipe off unto you, i.e.*—We return the dust back to you, *i.e.*—We renounce all intercourse. A Mussulman saluting a Christian by mistake, insists on revoking it, *Lord, Hennike.*

---

12 *But I say unto you, that it shall be more tolerable in that day for Sodom, than for that city.*

Tolerable. Breaking many express laws *aggravates guilt.*

No *reparation* possible against clear convictions.

Laws violated *deliberately*, frequently, obstinately.

Sins against *mercies*, *judgments*, *admonitions* and *vows*.
Terrible judgments, prove the high rank He assigns them.
Note the consciousness of His own unapproachable dignity.
Mercies *withheld*, even when they should have been *improved*.
Evidence of the *sovereignty* that dispenses them.
Increased by the *station*. Against the soul, rather than the body.
" To whom much is given, of them much required." Luke xii. 48.
"Why," the caviler asks, "did he not bestow them?" Answer: Rom. ix. 20.
" I will have mercy on whom I will have mercy." Ex. xxxiii. 19. Rom. ix. 15.
Here is Christ's farewell offer of Himself, and Salvation.
The people mocking Lot, would have believed in Christ.
Sodom. In the vale of Siddim, well watered, as the garden of God.
" Lot pitched his tent towards Sodom." Gen. xiii. 12.
Abraham, warned of Sodom's doom, intercedes for it.
He began with fifty, and ended with *ten*—ten *righteous* not found.
Transcendent power of prayer.—*God gives, whilst Abraham pleads.*
Abraham left off asking before God left off granting.
Angels urge Lot to leave. His wife made a pillar of salt.
Sodom's ruin introduced with unusual solemnity. Gen. xviii. 23-33.
In the morning " lo the smoke went up as a furnace." Gen. xix. 28.
Dead Sea distinctly *seen* from Mount of Olives, where Christ stood; supposed to cover the cities of the plain.
Mountains in height 1500 feet, appear burnt, and *entirely* desolate.
A standing type of great guilt, and fearful retribution!

δὲ is not the beginning of the verse, nor the usual connective; omitted, *Alford*. ἀνεκτότερον—more *endurable*; implies different degrees of punishment. Involves those like the Tyrians, &c., *in mitissima damnatione*, *Augustine*. If more warnings would have saved the lost Sidonians, it is not for the infidel to ask, Why were they not given? Every act of Jehovah, towards saving sinners, is one of *pure* MERCY! The proportion is ruled by a holy, just, Sovereign, who willeth not the death of the sinner, but whose ways are past finding out. It is enough for us to know, that all are *inexcusable*, Rom. 1 and 2 chaps. Our feelings should be profound gratitude for Gospel light, and redeeming grace, *Alford*.

---

13 *Woe unto thee, Chorazin! woe unto thee, Bethsaida! for if the mighty works had been done in Tyre and Sidon which have been done in you, they had a great whi ago repented, sitting in sackcloth and ashes.*

Woe! Woe *is* unto you; not woe *be* unto you.

An interjection of grief and concern, not an imprecation denouncing vengeance.
As regards the Saviour, implying knowledge past and future.
As regards these rejecters of the Gospel, implying—
Obduracy, guilt, folly, wretchedness, responsibility, final impenitence and eternal ruin.
To reject the Gospel of Christ is the highest crime.
It is an offence against the Trinity in the Godhead.
It is to despise the wisdom of God the Father, in devising Redemption.
It is to reject the atonement of God the Son, making Reconciliation.
It is to sin against God the Holy Ghost, the Teacher and Sanctifier.
Upbraid. Matt. xi. 20. He had long been preaching, now *sternly rebukes.*
Unbelief under privileges, provoked His long suffering.
Contrast His sighings over the cities, and joy over babes. Verse 21.
Woe. His inmost thoughts, deepest emotions disclosed.
His message rejected, where He had labored most. Isa. xlix. 4.
The sins of men made Him "acquainted with grief." Isa. liii. 3.
His blessing carried life, His curse death.
Chorazin, or land of Zin, west of Galilee lake.
In the time of Jerome, 382 A.D. no vestige could be found.
Chorazin named twice, its situation unknown, probably on the shore of the lake.
Bethsaida. Luke ix. 10. Town of Galilee, west of Jordan, near Sea of Tiberias.
Birth place of Peter, Andrew and John.
Once rich and populous, now a miserable village.
Mighty works. He admits things might have been otherwise.
The Bible has no allusion to them in particular.
It proves the N. T. records of miracles rather scanty than profuse.
Our Lord esteemed miracles, as means of grace.
Satan's wonders were wrought in behalf of error.
Heathen deceived by Satan's miracles, discredited Christ's.
Tyre. (Luke vi. 17. See Notes.) They had been warned. Ezek. xxvi. xxviii.
They despised the Jews, their God, and His warnings.
Then is mercy exhausted, "The wrath of the Lamb." Rev. vi. 16.
The ruined cities of antiquity are preaching to unbelievers now.
Great while ago. Refers to actual warning, which they heard.
Tyre and Sidon to *us* forgotten, wiped out from the earth.
To God, a *living reality*, a breathing crowd awaiting their summons.
The sinner dead, *reserved* for punishment; the righteous for glory.

Repented. Godly sorrow precedes seeking rest in Christ.
Repentance hates *sin*, remorse dreads its *punishment.*
Christ's omniscience knew what *would* have taken place, had their privileges been greater.
God is under no obligation to enlighten any sinner.
Note the absolute sublime assurance of Jesus!
None but the SEARCHER of HEARTS, could thus speak.
A sacred mystery. The Gospel preached to those who reject it.
Not preached to those, who would have repented. Rom. ix. 33.
Sitting. Universal posture of mourners, in the East. Job. ii. 13.
As descriptive of a spiritual state it implies the lowliness of conscience.
Sackcloth. *Haircloth* of camels' and goats' hair, used for mourning, black.
Intended to signify a sharp and painful remembrance of former sins.
Nineveh repented clothed in sackcloth. Jonah iii. 8.
Chinese use yellow, Turks white, and Europeans black mourning.
Jacob put sackcloth upon his loins, and mourned, &c. Gen xxxvii. 34.
Lord bids Isaiah put off sackcloth from his body. Isa. xx. 2.
Rejoicing, it was flung off. Psa. xxx. 11. And white put on. Ecc. ix. 8.
Ashes. Symbol of grief. Job. ii. 8. Hints at death by which we are returned to dust.
Females deeply mourning, still cover themselves with earth.
Ash-Wednesday, the first day in Lent, so called from the custom of putting ashes on the head, still observed in the church of Rome.
Our Lord thus mourns over the cities which after so great miracles repented not.
Their guilt greater than that of those who violate the law of nature only.
Having despised the written law, they dared also to despise the Son of God and His glory.
Similar guilt rests on all who neglect or despise the *great salvation.*

"*Chorazin.*"—*Tell Hum*, *Robinson.* Near the second milestone from Capernaum, *Eusebius.* *Khorazy*, *Thompson.* But one Bethsaida, both banks of the Jordan, *Ewald.*

δύνάμεις—Luke v. 17. σάκκῳ—Heb., Gr., Lat., and Eng. express the unchanging name of this article. Authenticity of these four verses questioned, *De Wette.* μετενόησαν—Never in the N. T., *temporary grief;* always *permanent* reformation, *Olshausen.*

---

14 *But it shall be more tolerable for Tyre and Sidon at the judgment, than for you.*

But it shall be, &c. The doom of otherwise correct persons who, amidst a blaze of light, reject the Saviour, shall be *less endurable* than that of any of these, *Brown.*

Wilful impenitence is treason against God, *the* condemning sin.

Tolerable. Not as sharing Tyre's guilt, but surpassing it.

Increase of light, increases responsibility.

Light enlarges the capacities of the soul, for joy or woe.

Angels visited Sodom, *Prophets* warned Tyre and Sidon.

But *Jesus Christ* preached in Bethsaida, and Chorazin.

These words teach there will be different *degrees* of punishment as of glory.

Degrees in wickedness have answerable degrees in endless punishments, *Hooker.*

ἀνεκτότερον—The coming sorrows of the Galilean cities, *twice* wrung this cry from the Saviour's heart, *Meyer.* The Lord does not refer to external judgments as seen in the use of the future, ἔσται, instead of the past. *It was more;* not, *It will, &c., Stier.*

---

15. *And thou, Capernaum, which art exalted to heaven, shalt be thrust down to hell.*

Capernaum. "*Town of pleasure.*" Earth's names specious. Luke iv. 31.

Preferred to Nazareth, as His chosen residence, *second* birth place.

Chorazin and Bethsaida guilty cities, but not the *guiltiest.*

Capernaum was the centre of the Lord's missionary labors.

Miracles of love were their daily *bread,* now they hear of the *wine* of His wrath.

Exalted. The sense has been variously interpreted—

1. Some suppose it to allude to the *distinguished honor conferred* by our Lord's residence there.
2. Others suppose it to allude to the *rich fisheries carried* on, by which the town became proud and prosperous.
3. Others refer the expression to the *lofty situation* Capernaum.

The first interpretation the most probable. It was called "*his own city.*" Matt. ix. 1.

Thus it was honored above Jerusalem, in the sovereignty of God.

Mercies despised, far from saving, increase responsibility and guilt.

Believers in Gospel lands the greatest debtors to *mercy,*

Gospel rejecters the greatest debtors to Divine *justice.*

Hell. As antithesis to heaven, extremest moral degradation.

Includes loss of external greatness, and oblivion of the foundations.
Capernaum's location nowhere certainly to be found.
We see darkness resting on Capernaum, Divine light rising, enmity prevailing, the light withdrawn, the sentence pronounced.
"None sink so far into hell, as those that come nearest heaven, because they fall from the greatest height," *Gurnall.*
"Then I saw, that there was a way to hell even from the gates of heaven, as well as from the City of Destruction," *Bunyan.*

ὑψωθεῖσα—The best MSS. read—*Shalt thou be exalted unto heaven? thou shalt be, Alford.* Exalted situation, *Stier.* *Pride, W. & W.* *Rich fisheries, Grotius.* Lord's residence, *Alford.* Interrogatively—*Shalt thou be exalted to heaven? Campbell.* μὴ ὑψωθήσῃ, *Alford, Cod. Sin.* ἕως ᾅδου according to classic usage, does not refer to future torment, but the *place*, or *state* of *the dead.* Unseen world, *Alexander* Neither *Sheol* nor ᾅδης are ever used in a good sense, *Augustine.* Holle or hole, *Luther, Ewald.* Too *human* a conception, *De Wette,* Like Phlegethon, *Tertullian.* An intermediate state, *Josephus, Jerome, Justin, Alford, Trench.* Hell, originally an old English word, used in this sense, though now confined to *Gehenna.* Hence some have retained the word *Hades* here, *Campbell, Alexander.*

---

16. *He that heareth you heareth me; and he that despiseth you despiseth me: and he that despiseth me despiseth him that sent me.*

Our Saviour hinting at Judas, warns his disciples. John xiii. 18-20.
The Saviour's trials, would be *their* trials, and His triumphs, theirs.
Heareth. This encourages them to resist all persecutions.
Despiseth. Mankind *generally*, will reject mercy's message. Matt. vii. 13.
Yet, a remnant would never bow the knee to Baal. 1. Kings, xix. 18.
Their labours not in vain, "My word shall not return unto me void." Isa. lv. 11.
Sent me. The disgrace through you, reaches Me, and Him that sent Me.
For the Master is heard in His disciple, the Father honored in His Son.
God is a most severe avenger of the Ministry of the Gospel, *Queen Eliz. Bible.*
Honors and insults to ambassadors, reflected on the king sending.
"Thy cause shall be my cause,"—saith Christ to all his servants.
Ministers' honorable duties, overlooked by the world.
Receiving them, is entertaining the *Lord*, and angels. Heb. xiii. 2.
"Thou shalt love as the apple of thine eye, every one, that speaketh to thee the Word of God," *Barnabas.*

Such kindnesses valued not by their *cost*, but by *love* bestowing them.
Widow's *mite* stamped high above many talents of gold.

17 ¶ *And the seventy returned again with joy, saying, Lord, even the devils are subject unto us through thy name.*

A considerable interval elapsed between the 16th and 17th verses.
Returned. The tour must have been short, about eight days.
They met Him at Jerusalem before the Feast ended.
Joy. No higher rapture felt by saints, than Christ's triumph. Psa. iv. 7.
Saying. Nothing whatever, of the reception of their *great commission*.
Devils. Strange they speak of no other cures than this.
The nine apostles had lately failed in their attempts to cast out a devil, Luke, ix. 40.
He had not authorized the Seventy to cast out devils.
So they had actually attempted greater things than Jesus had expressed.
Subject. If demons are *subject*, saints need fear no other foe.
Through thy name. Render, *in thy name.* Not sufficiently emphasized—hence the rebuke.
Or they manifested a *boastful* spirit in success.
Or having been formerly defeated, they now triumphed over demons. Luke ix. 40.
That this was a ground of joy not to be *prominently brought forward* is the purport of our Lord's answer.
They seemed to rejoice more that they had power over devils than that they were Ministers of the Gospel of Salvation.
Christ's universal presence implied, miracles in His Name.
Christ's miracles by an original power, disciples' by a derived power.
Christ's Divinity implied in the success of His servants.
Satan a defeated foe. 1. By Christ. 2. By disciples of Christ.
Satan contended for victory: weapons, wonder, elation, pride, he failed.

18 *And he said unto them, I beheld Satan as lightning fall from heaven.*

Their Lord confirms, elevates, and hallows their just joy.
Satan a real and personal being. The prince of evil spirits.
Satan called the prince of this world to denote his dominion.
Satan called the prince of the power of the air, to denote his abode.
Satan is said to rule in the hearts of the disobedient, to denote his subjects.

Satan is called the prince of darkness to denote the nature of his deeds.

Satan has fallen from his glory. He that captured is led captive.

The fall of Satan, 1. Purposed by Jesus. 2. Affected by Jesus. 3. Celebrated by Jesus.

The fall of Satan compared to that of lightning. 1. In the duration of both. 2. In the rapidity of both. 3. In the depth of both.

The preached Gospel aims at the destruction of Satan's kingdom.

Beheld. He speaks, as though all things were present to His eye.

Satan. Luke iv. 2 and 3. Character and history of demons. See Notes.

Heb. *to lie in wait, to oppose.* **Devil,** *to thrust through—to accuse.*

Lightning. Reference to the suddenness, brightness, and fall of Satan's character. Zech. ix. 14.

Fall. Implies its rapid, decisive, and terrible nature.

Refers to the *original* apostacy, or *present* victories of the disciples.

He beheld, as present, the annihilation of Satan's dominion.

Or to the entire period, *past, present,* and *future* conquest of Christ.

In His disciples' success, He beheld the pledge of His complete triumph.

From heaven, implies loss of pre-eminence and power. Rev. xx. 2.

By nature Satan shone as lightning, but by sin became darkness, *Bost.*

Lucifer, a *light bearer* no longer, but a bringer in of darkness, *Bernard.*

Now cast down, he transforms himself into an angel of light, *Bede.*

Satan's fall—from the highest power to the lowest impotence.

Before the coming of the Lord, he had subdued the world; men worshipped him.

But by the coming of the Lord, he is cast down, and trodden under foot by those who worship Christ, *Cyril.*

At Christ's resurrection all the gods of the heathen expired, *Hammond.*

Ἐθεώρουν, like *contemplari. I was contemplating, i. e.*—Be not surprised, when I sent you forth, I was contemplating, &c., *Grotius, Lightfoot.* He accompanied them in spirit, and witnessed Satan's overthrow. No isolated vision :—the spiritual intuition of the God-man, to whom the secrets of the spirit-world are naked, *Oosterzee.*

The words refer to Satan's original fall, which has been proceeding ever since, step by step, and shall do so till all things are put under the feet of Jesus. He is to be the Great Victor over the Adversary, and the victory began when Satan fell from heaven, *Alford.* To the motion, not the fall, *W. & W.* To the victories before the Crucifixion; a period of *six* months, *Lightfoot.* The Crucifixion, *Stella.*

ἀστραπὴν—The *violence* of the fall is indicated, *Gerlach*. By the glance of the Spirit, our Lord anticipates the development of the future, *Neander*. *Cicero*, speaking of *Pompey's* ruin, says *cecidisse ex astris*, Ep. Att. Allusion to "How art thou fallen from heaven," Isa. xiv. 12, *Wakefield*. Psa. lxxviii. 48.—Hot thunder-bolts.

"When we fled amain, pursued and struck
"*With Heaven's linked thunder-bolts*, and besought
"The deep to shelter us, this Hell then seemed
"A refuge." *Par. Lost*, B. 2.

πεσόντα—*falling headlong*. Satan retains something of the rapidity of lightning, and *deceptive* outward splendor, *Elsley*.

---

19 *Behold, I give unto you power to tread on serpents and scorpions, and over all the power of the enemy; and nothing shall by any means hurt you.*

Behold. Gr., and Heb., introduces something unexpected and surprising.

I give. Read, *have given*. Note the majesty and sublimity of the Saviour's Godhead.

He who bruised the *Old Serpent*, can crush all serpents.

Power. All power given to Christ, in heaven and earth. Matt. xxviii. 18.

To those improving divine gifts, He imparts greater skill.

To tread. Nothing can hurt them, which does not hurt Himself.

Serpents. Symbolizes crafty, dangerous adversaries.

Some traditions make the serpent hide in the sand. Gen. xlix. 17.

Another that he can stop his ears at pleasure. Psa. lviii. 4.

His poison is concealed under his perforated fangs. Pro. xxiii. 32.

The *curse* fell on the animal and on the vegetable worlds.

Disorders in the *spirit* world, express themselves in the natural world.

He who was *lightning* in heaven, becomes a *serpent* on earth.

Scorpions. The more *minute*, but more active manifestations of evil. Ezek. ii. 6.

The noxious influences which *sting* and embitter life. Num. xxi. 6.

"Thou shalt tread upon the lion and adder," &c. Psa. xci. 13.

God promised Eve, her *seed* (Christ) *should bruise the head of the serpent*. Gen. iii. 15.

Paul's deliverance from a viper at Melita (Malta) a literal fulfillment of the promise in the text. Acts xxviii. 3-5.

Tradition says that John drank poison and was not harmed by it, *Isidore*.

Serpents who bite with the teeth, and scorpions who sting by the tail, signify two classes of enemies, those who rage openly, and those who plot secretly, *Bede*.

Serpents are those which visibly hurt; scorpions those which invisibly injure, *sins of the spirit*, *Theophylact*.

Power of the enemy: the singular number, meaning the *arch-enemy*, the *devil.*

Hurt. Refers to final, and complete *spiritual* victories. Luke xxi. 18.

Those giving up earthly things walk with a free step in heaven, dreading not the prince of the air, *Athanasius.*

Christians connot be *hurt* but by doing that which is wrong, *J. Martyr.*

God will never leave it in the power of any creature to hurt us, but by our own treason against ourselves, *Sibbes.*

Uprightness, as a rock, breaks the waves into foam, that roar upon it *Leighton.*

δίδωμι—δέδωκα—*Tischendorf, Oosterzee, Alford, Cod. Sinai. Serpents* and *lightnings* in their serpentine courses, images of fallen spirits, *Oosterzee.* ἐξουσίαν—*delegated* power. ὄφεων—The Jews had a legend, that all the venomous beasts of the wilderness, must lie under the feet of God's people. Traditions ascribing superhuman and mysterious knowledge and power to serpents, traceable to the history of the *Fall.* Hence the types occurring in *fable, history,* and *astronomy.* The dragon guarding the gardens of Alcinous, Golden Fleece, and Lernean Hydra, distorted facts of Revelation. The story of the Brazen Serpent is interwoven with the history of Egypt. ἐπὶ πᾶσαν—ἐπὶ implies *aggressive authority;* to proceed against.

σκορπίων—Luke xi. 12. ἐχθροῦ—The *singular* after the plural, ὄφεων, &c., indicates the *leader* of the fallen angels. These words following the mention of the fall of Satan, who is the δράκων (Rev. xx. 2); the ἀρχαῖος ὄφις (Rev. xii. 9) suggests that there is some connexion between his power, and the operation of venomous reptiles, *Wordsworth.* οὐδὲν ὑμᾶς—Three negatives strengthen the negation, *Markland.*

---

20. *Notwithstanding in this rejoice not, that the spirits are subject unto you; but rather rejoice, because your names are written in heaven.*

Rejoice not. An impure element lurks in rejoicing, even over demons.

In *vain* triumphing, there lurks pernicious *self-praise.*

He forbids not rejoicing, but directs it in the proper channel.

Such joy must be transient and give place to disappointment.

It was possible for the children of darkness to cast out devils. Matt. vii. 22.

The gift of miracles implied not a new heart. Matt. vii. 22.

The disciples rejoiced in the manifestation of power.

The Saviour rejoiced in the bestowment of salvation.

The life of God in the soul more to be prized than miraculous gifts.

Gifts and graces, by Satan's craft, may become snares.

In working miracles, man has not necessarily communion with God.

Spirits. This was a confirmation of their mission.

The disciples said *devils*. Jesus enlarges it to *spirits*. Eph. vi. 12.

Not the mere subjection of evil to you, at all.

But positive, and infinite display of God's mercy to *you*.

Names. Anciently, citizens were recorded in public rolls.

Unworthy, lost citizenship, and their names were erased. Ex. xxxii. 32.

"The Lord shall count, when He writeth up the people." Psa. lxxxvii. 6; lxix. 28.

"Whose names were not written in the book of life," &c. Rev. xvii. 8.

"Laborers whose names are in the book of life." Phil. iv. 3. Dan. xii. 1.

"Departing from God, *their names written in the earth*." Jer. xvii. 13.

The Almighty has his book of servants. Ex. xxxii. 32-33. Mal. iii. 16.

Written. Equivalent to acquiring heavenly citizenship.

The true cause of joy is not the power shewn forth by you in *my name*, but that *your names* are in the book of life.

The words "*your names*" seem a reference to "*in thy name*," which, perhaps, was to them a *medium of self-praise*, as so often with Christians, *Alford*.

Those whose self-love make their joy excessive, may come to resemble Satan, *Bengel*.

The names of the saints are written in the *book of life*, not in ink, but in the memory and grace of God, *Theophylact*.

Can a name once written there, be blotted out? Ex. xxxii. 32-33. Rev. iii. 5. Rev. xxii. 19.

Your name in the world's book, cannot aid, may ruin you.

Written in the earth, implies one is to perish. Jer. xvii. 13.

A higher source of joy, union with heaven, imparts felicity.

Happiness the most sublime; pure, substantial, abiding, supporting, consoling, and enriching.

In Heaven. In that heaven whence Satan hath fallen.

The devil fell from *above*, but ye being *below*, have your names inscribed *above* in heaven.

The way to hell is by pride, the way to the mountains of glory by humility.

Returned.—Not a trace has been preserved of the abiding results of their labors, *Oosterzee*. χαίρετε—These *confessions* and *rejoicings* in Matt. and Luke, repeated on two separate occasions, *Alford.* μᾶλλον—cancelled, *Tischendorf, Alford;* retained, *W. & W.* ἐγράφη—Some see no immutable predestination, others are of opinion that it is taught elsewhere, as Eph. i. 5 and 6; Rom. viii. 30; 2. Tim. i. 9, *Olshausen:* but the contrary, Ex. xxxii. 32-33, *Grotius, Whitby, Alford.* Citizens of heaven, *Le Clerc.* The Heroes, κοσμοκρατόρες, worshipped by millions for their genius, will find such rare gifts availing nothing to secure their names being written in heaven, *Stier.* The dying *Haller,* when congratulated on account of the visit of the Emperor Joseph II, repeated this text, *Oosterzee.*

---

21 ¶ *In that hour Jesus rejoiced in spirit, and said, I thank thee, O Father, Lord of heaven and earth, that thou hast hid these things from the wise and prudent, and hast revealed them unto babes: even so, Father; for so it seemed good in thy sight.*

Hour. At that *juncture,* the Spirit guided the *arrangement.*

This is one of those rare cases in which the veil is lifted from the Redeemer's soul.

Rejoiced. Extraordinary emotion, at a moment of critical solemnity.

They exulted over the external splendor of the work.

He drew his delight from the hidden glory.

He felt Himself the *organ* and *object* of these revealings of God.

No victory like that of grace, no hire so precious as immortal souls.

They rejoiced in the *greatness.* He in the *good* effected.

1. Proof of the joy tasted by our Lord on earth. 2. An image of the joy He has now in heaven. 3. A foretaste of the happiness He will hereafter enjoy.

The assurance of salvation is a privilege to be enjoyed only by those who live in holy communion with God. 2. Tim. iv. 8.

O Father! God never called HIS LORD, but LORD of HEAVEN and EARTH.

First recorded invocation of the Father before the people.

Jews believed He made himself equal with God. John x. 33.

He never corrected the error, if it was one. Phil. ii. 6.

Lord. Spoken under a veil of prophecy, in His deep humiliation.

He claims the most *intimate* personal relation with Jehovah.

Hid. God is said *to do,* what he certainly foresees *will* be done. Rom. ix. 18.

Not that the mysteries of the Gospel, were hid from any.

But what was hid from the wise, was *revealed* to the humble.

A fulfilling of a righteous judgment against sin.

A withholding grace, without which, *these things* are invisible.

It may be hid from many now, *theoretically* wise.

"The light of the knowledge of the glory of God, shines in the face of Christ Jesus." 2. Cor. iv. 6.

"The brightness of His glory, and the express image of His Person." Heb. i. 3.

God's essence, and Triune relations, *mysteries*, reserved for eternity.

The Son. In His eternal generation, and incarnation, "The mystery of *Godliness*." 1. Tim. iii. 16.

The Son Himself can only be known by omniscience.

The Father reveals the Son; The Son reveals the Father.

Thus, the Son glorifies the Father, and the Father glorifies the Son. John xii. 28.

Reveal. This is that eternal "covenant of peace," alluded to by Zec. vi. 13.

No comfortable intercourse between man and God, except by the *Mediator*.

Worship, not through *Christ*, is to an *unknown* God. John v. 23.

How can man understand God, since he does not yet understand his own mind, with which he endeavours to understand Him, *St. Augustine*.

The essential nature of Christ, as the Son of God, is just as profound a mystery as the being of the Father; whilst the relationship between the two is a depth which we can never fathom.

The highest exercise of reason is to cease to reason about those things which are above our reason.

Many things are *above* our reasoning powers that are not contrary to them.

καὶ στραφεὶς πρὸς τοὺς μαθητὰς εἶπεν, and He turned to His disciples and said, *Tischendorf*, *Alford*, *&c.* So most editions of *Rec. Text.*, but not *Mill*; omitted, *Cod. Sinai.* *πάντα.*—Limited to the teaching of Jesus, *Grotius*. The essence of shallowness and assumption, *Oosterzee*. Addressed to his disciples, *Stier*. *μοὶ* emphatic,—"to Me, *to none other*, *Wordsworth*. *οὐδεὶς*—The adding of "*man*" to this, in our E. V. almost stultifies the sentence, to the modern reader, by appearing to call *God*, *Man*, *Alexander*. These words are found three times in *Justin*, *Clement*, *Marcion*, *and Tertullian*, in *reversed* order.

γινώσκει τίς ἐστιν—This assertion of mutual knowledge between the Father and the Son, which *no other* being possesses, is a *clear declaration* of the *Son's supreme Godhead*. This can never be an obstacle to research, nor a covering for wilful ignorance, *Gerlach*. The 21st verse can never be made a charter for stupidity, or a reproof to true Christian science, *Oosterzee*. This is in the style of John, showing that his conception of the character of Jesus, did not differ from that of the other Evangelists, *Stier*. Because all wrote under *one Spirit*.

23 ¶ *And he turned him unto his disciples, and said privately, Blessed are the eyes which see the things that ye see.*

Turned. Luke particular in noting pauses and transitions in our Lord's discourses.

Jesus had been praying to the Father; then had spoken of the Father; and now addressed the disciples privately.

Blessed, *i. e.* human felicity begun here, and continued after death.

Always dependent on the Divine favor. Not the same as *happy*.

"*Blessed* are they that know the joyful sound." Psa. lxxxix. 15.

Eyes. Many then had good vision who never saw Jesus by faith's eye.

An indirect admonition to continue to regard Him with the eye of faith.

That kings and prophets would have deemed Him worthy of reverence.

Which see. The Apostles saw the Lord of life and glory, the desire of all nations.

They saw the holiness of His life, and the lesson afforded by His conversation.

They saw the tokens of His power, the miracles which he wrought.

They saw the exceeding glory which shone around Him at His transfiguration.

They saw Him die upon the cross, by which sin was abolished, God in the highest sense became our Father, and Jesus our Elder Brother.

But beyond all others, blessed are they who shall see Him eternally, and dwell for ever in His glory.

The hearing ear and the seeing eye, are God's gifts. Prov. xx. 12.

"Now we see through a glass darkly, then face to face." 1. Cor. xiii. 12.

O. T. saints looked through types and shadows toward the *substance*.

Glimmerings of light, made them long for the *Sun* of righteousness.

"Abraham saw my day, and was glad," John viii. 56.

God has scattered the clouds, and we behold as in a *mirror* the GLORY of the LORD.

The fathers of the Old Covenant had only a dim candle, we have the bright sunbeams.

They had only the green blade of corn, we the increase, as in time of harvest.

They had only a drop, we have the river of water of life, clear as crystal.

Blessed are our eyes, for we see by faith the Word made man for us, and shedding upon us the glory of His Godhead, that He may make us like Himself, *Cyril*.

και στραφεις, &c., cancelled, *Beza*, *Ebrard*, *Tregelles*. Retained, *Tischendorf*, *Alford*, *W. & W.*

24. *For I tell you, that many prophets and kings have desired to see those things which ye see, and have not seen* them; *and to hear those things which ye hear, and have not heard* them.

Many. A sight of the Messiah, the object of hope with O. T. saints.

Prophets. Who testified beforehand of His sufferings, and the glory that should follow. 1. Pet. i. 11.

An indirect admonition to them, to hear Himself.

Kings. Reference probably to David who united both offices, and perhaps to Solomon.

David's last words a prophecy of the Redeemer. "This is all my salvation." 2. Sam. xxiii. 1-5.

The bunch of grapes, carried from the promised land, was borne by two strong men upon a pole.

He who went before could not see the grapes, but he behind could both see and eat.

So the fathers of the O. T. did not in like manner see the bunch of grapes, the Son of God made man.

But those that went behind in the N. T. saw and tasted, *Boys*.

This is comparing humble fishermen with kings.

Desired. Christ was the "DESIRE OF ALL NATIONS." Hag. ii. 7.

Socrates uttered the longing of all thoughtful heathen.

"We must wait," said he "till One shall come and teach us our duty to God."

The Cumaean Sibyl taught that a Great Ruler should be born, of heavenly extraction, whose reign would be *universal*.

"To give a *universal peace*, and exercise His Father's virtues."

"To abolish all violence, and restore *original simplicity*."

"To kill the serpent, and purge all vegetables of poisons."

"The blessings would extend to the brute creation."

Thus unconsciously did the heathen world prophesy of, and long for, the Redeemer.

Augustine desired to see *Christ* in the flesh, *Solomon* in his glory, and *Paul* in the pulpit.

ἠθέλησαν. See *Trench's* Unconscious Prophecies of Heathendom; The *Hulsean* Lectures; and *Horsley's* Dissertation on the Prophecies among the heathen, vol. ii. 27.

---

25 ¶ *And, behold, a certain lawyer stood up, and tempted him, saying, Master, what shall I do to inherit eternal life?*

Lawyer. Versed in the (casuistical) interpretations of Mosaic law.

One skilled in the law, and obeying the letter, while ignorant of its spirit, *Ambrose.*

Hearing the blessing, verse 23. "Let *me* hear what *great thing* He has to say about salvation."

Stood up. *Fearless* of defeat, and *defiant* of the gathered crowd.

Tempted. The act of *trying* the motive, may be good or bad.

He had no design to make Christ *politically* suspected.

That about *tribute money*, maliciously endangered His life.

Not hostile, but vain, and self-righteous in his curiosity.

He doubtless expected some *great deed* to be named.

He may have had trouble in his inmost heart.

Trammelled by tradition, he seeks some outward rule.

He would bring out, whatever was *peculiar* in the Lord's views.

Prove the famous Galilean Teacher, and measure His depth.

Master. With respect real, or feigned. Jesus was a "*Teacher*" in truth.

Appeals to Him as an *acknowledged* Teacher.

Shall I do? Doubtless expecting to hear of *some great deed*, or *sacrifice*.

Or with the Philippian gaoler perhaps to ask for knowledge. Acts xvi. 30.

Wishing to establish a *meritorious* claim to eternal life.

Our Lord shews him a kind of doing, which would not *earn*, but prove a *mark*, of the inheritor of life.

Inherit. The promised land, a type of *eternal rest.* Deut. xxv. 15.

An inheritance a *filial* right; the *portion* of *sons.*

Eternal life. The *way* to it the supreme concern of this life.

Jesus the Way, the Truth, and the Life: *i.e.*, 1. The Author of the Way. 2. The Teacher of the Truth. 3. The Giver of spiritual Life.

Jesus the best *guide* on the road to eternal life.

A right *question* from a *wrong* motive, a thing of frequent occurrence.

No life but *spiritual*, no inheritance but heaven, worth the name.

Incorruptible—moth, rust, fire, foes, spending, affects it not.

Undefiled. Not stained in the *gathering:* it *clogs* not in the using.

Fadeth not. Gr. it never becomes *less*, never *dim*, never *lost.*

Earth's pleasures, within the scope of the *scythe* of the curse.

The question of questions, but it lost its goodness, if the design was bad.

The doctrine of the lawyer was that salvation is obtained by the law. Rom. iii.

The doctrine of the Gospel is, that salvation is obtained by faith. Eph. ii. 8.

Unwise men seek righteousness and life, *i.e.*, salvation, by a law which no man fulfils.

νομικός—used by the classical Luke; γραμματεὺς—generally by the Hebraizing Matt. "*Lawyer.*"—No Sadducee, asking ironically the way to *Utopia*, but prompted by curiosity. *Olshausen.* Wanted a *talk*, as many go to hear a sermon. *Stier.*

φαρισαῖοι—a particular class of the νομικόι. A different version of Matt. xxii. 37. *Strauss.* Entirely different. *Lange, Oosterzee.* ἀνέστη—Standing posture, assumed by the *pupil* anciently, desiring information. ἐκπειράζων—*Putting Him to the full proof,* Luke iv. 2. Expecting to ensnare Christ into giving some command contrary to the law. *Euthymius* in *Meyer.*

Διδάσκαλε—*Instructor, Disciple,* (μαθητής) *learner.* κληρονομήσω—Matt. v. 5. τὴν γὴν—This hope, resting primarily on the promised land, the *foundation* of all the *future prospects* of the Jews. They identified their national existence with that of the Temple. Hence, when it was ruined, multitudes committed suicide. *Milman.*

---

26. *He said unto him, What is written in the law? how readest thou?*

Written in the law? An appropriate question to a *lawyer*, and putting him in turn to the *test.*

Our Lord ascribes absolute authority to the "law" in these things.

The law of God has reference to secret motives and to internal character.

Not speculative, but practical knowledge profitable to men.

The great problems of life are to be settled by the Scriptures.

Christ refers him to the law which he professed to expound.

Thou art a lawyer versed in the record.

What thou askest, has lain from old, in the revealed word.

Not to the 613 *commands* of Moses, collected by the Scribes.

What? Demanding, intense desire, to learn God's will.

How? Christ may have pointed to the text (Deut. xi. 13) on his phylactery.

The Scriptures were read privately as well as publicly.

Readest. Gr. implies *that but* FEW READERS *were then found.* Dost thou read for *thy* benefit, or that of *others?*

Not what thinkest thou? but how *readest* thou?

Gr. read, and know accurately by reading.

Not as a *special pleader*, looking for evasions, and excuses.

He readeth rightly that discovereth the Gospel in the law, and the law in the Gospel.

He readeth rightly that discovereth the Gospel to be the law fulfilled.

He readeth rightly: 1, who is daily less proud. 2, less wrathful. 3, less covetous. 4, less worldly minded. 5, less eager for the present: more mindful of the future.

We read amiss unless we discover that not the letter, but the Spirit enricheth.

The Saviour's answer differed from what he expected.

His receiving nothing new, was his first repulse.

Dost thou read as an heir, the record of an inheritance?

He accepted the reading, with limitations and explanations.

We read *amiss*, unless with docility, faith, and humility.

"*How readest thou?*" A common Rabbinical formula for eliciting a text of Scripture. *How? i.e.* to what purport? *Alford.* ἀναγινώσκεις—to *know accurately* by reading. *Alexander.* Acts viii. 30, and Cor. iii. 2, evidence that Luke follows Paul's lusus verborum, and Paul superintended Luke's writings. *Stier.*

---

27 *And he answering said, Thou shalt love the Lord thy God with all thy heart, and with all thy soul, and with all thy strength, and with all thy mind; and thy neighbour as thyself.*

Answering. The Jews used daily to repeat the text here quoted.

Scripture should be read not only frequently but attentively.

To ascertain the *scope* of Scripture a most important object.

The Lord. In this word is asserted His power as a Ruler—rightful authority.

God. The Maker and Preserver of all men—the eternal wisdom that directs all.

Thy God. Dwelling in our hearts, and sanctifying us by His presence.

It is not one person, but the Holy Trinity who is our Lord and God.

All sufficient, and infinitely blessed, He *needs* no creature's love.

Our Supreme Source of happiness, and *deserves* our love.

He gives us our fellow men to share our love, instead of Himself.

To love God supremely, embraces our neighbor. 1. John, iv. 21.

To love our neighbor as ourselves, is to love God *aright.*

"Heart, soul, and strength," acumulated synonymes.

With all thy soul, *i.e.*, with thy warmest affections.

With all thy strength, *i.e.*, with the most vigorous resolution of thy will.

With all thy mind, *i.e.*, with thy understanding guiding thy affections and thy will.

Mark, uses understanding for mind, to guard against the undue influence of imagination in religion.

This teaches the utter impossibility of being justified by the law. Gal. iii. 11.

But theoretical correctness will not atone for practical disobedience.

Love to God implies—

It must be *heart* work—the fulfilling of the law. Rom. xiii. 10.

It must be *ardent* with *all* thy strength. Matt. xxii. 37. Deut. vi. 5.

It must be supreme, with all thy *soul*. Deut. xxx. 6. Psa. lxxiii. 25.

It must be purely for Himself, His inherent excellencies. Cant. i. 3.

It must be intelligent. The more we know of God the more we will love God. Mark xii. 33. Psa. ix. 10.

It must be active, eating or drinking, or whatever we do, all must be done for His glory. 1. John iii. 18. 1. Cor. x. 31.

Performing our duties to our neighbor, *evidence* of love to God. John xiii. 35.

Christ doth not command the love of our neighbor, until he hath commanded and explained the love of God.

Love to our neighbor assumes divers forms—

In a family it is tenderness and care.

In a neighbourhood it is courtesy.

In friendship it is sympathy

In business it is integrity.

In distress it is mercy.

To our country it is patriotism..

To the world it is benevolence.

To the Church it is brotherly kindness.

True *self*-love, and true *brotherly* love, are at one, in God.

Hence the *second* and all commands, are like the *first*. Matt. xxii. 39.

We are bound to love all with the love of benevolence. To do them all the good we can. Gal. vi. 10; 1. John iii. 18.

To esteem the virtues of an enemy, because "every good gift is from above." Jas. i. 17.

To love our enemies, by blessing those who curse, and praying for those who persecute us. Matt. v. 44.

Our love must be the same in *degree*, *truth*, and *sincerity*. Matt. vii. 12.

This principle not *natural*, but *divinely* implanted.

Love desires constant *communion* with God and saints.
Love to God and man should regulate every opinion we adopt.
Every connexion we form and arrangement we make.
Every course we pursue and hope we cherish.
The Bible deals with great principles.
If love to God prevail, there would be—

1. No idolatry. 2. No superstition. 3. No profanation. 4. No opposition to truth. 5. No corruption of truth. 6. No perjury. 7. No despising the good. 8. No ingratitude. 9. No pride. 10. No discontent. 11. No suicide. 12. No violent deaths. 13. No duels. 14. No wars. 15. No rivalry. 16. No breach of contracts, national or individual. 17. No envy. 18. No wrongs. 19. No slanders. 20. No intrigues. 21. No deceit. 22. No fraud. 23. No false statements. 24. No oppression. 25. No injury to person, to property, or to character. 26. No cruelty. 27. No ingratitude. 28. No disobedience. 29. No unkindness. 30. No resentments. 31. No haunts of wickedness. 32. No social evils. 33. No complaining in our streets.

Then the precept would be obeyed, "Do good unto all men."
Then the prayer would be realized—
"Thy will be done on earth, as it is in heaven."
Thus love to God is the motive power to action.

Deut. vi. 5, and Lev. ix. 18, were repeated every morning and evening in the synagogue, as a summary of the whole law. Part was written on the phylacteries. *Meyer* thinks the man answered thus, because he had before heard our Lord cite these in connexion. *Alford.*

In the creation of the world God gave the water unto the fish, earth unto the beasts, air unto the fowls, heaven unto the glorious angels and then after all these glorious seats were bestowed, Almighty God made man, according to his own likeness and image, that He might say with the Psalmist,—*Whom have I in heaven but Thee? and there is none upon earth I desire beside Thee. Boys.*

Sep. translates the *Heb.* διάνοια, ψυχή, δύναμις.

---

28 *And he said unto him, Thou hast answered right: this do, and thou shalt live.*

Right. True words, but he was *ignorant* of their import.
This Do. In the effort to obey he would discover his own inability and his need—
1, of God's grace to enable him to keep the commandments.

2, of Christ's sacrifice to atone for sin.
3, of Christ's obedience for his justification before God. Rom. v. 19.
The law is our schoolmaster to bring us unto Christ. Gal. iii. 24.
Do this in me, and I shall do it, cause me to live, and I shall live.
Give Lord what Thou hast commanded, and then command what Thou hast given.
Godliness is knowledge put into practice. Love to God and man pervading, directing, and ruling man.
Earnest *tones* of Christ, might imply, "Do this, if thou art able."
Our Lord lays emphasis on the words "*This do*," showing where the real difficulty to a sinner lies.
Let this law pass from *dead* knowledge into living practice.
Speaking, is not enough,—the whole heart must be in it.
Our Lord intended to draw a *confession* of his utter failure.
Depravity and perverseness prevent him confessing his weakness.
He seeks by the *cunning* of his lips to evade this home-thrust.
Most, that perish, it is not their disease kills them, but their physician.
They think to cure themselves, and this leaves them incurable, *Gurnall.*
Note three things in our Lord's answer to this lawyer—
1. His approbation of the answer.—*Thou hast answered right.*
2. His bidding him put in practice that which the law taught him, and which he knew to be right.—*Do this.*
3. His promise of the life sought.—*Do this, and thou shalt live.*
So that he who truly loves God and man shall live beloved of God to all eternity, *Kenn.*

ζήσῃ—Our Lord endorses the interpretation, put upon this term by the scribes, Lev. xviii. 5; Ezek. xx. 11. He places the lawyer on the same platform, and he must abide by the same law, given to our first parents,—"*Do, and live*," *Stier.*

---

29 *But he, willing to justify himself, said unto Jesus, And who is my neighbour?*

Willing. To get himself out of the difficulty by throwing on Jesus the definition of neighbor.
Justify. Christ's omniscience perceives conscience first touched.
On this *earnestness*, our Lord seizes, and leads him on.
Jesus tries this *tempter*, but out of fervent *love* to his soul.
He had been led to an answer, which condemned him.

It implied on his own theory, he had not lived up to it.
The question indicates wounded sensibility, and a desire to resist.
As to loving God, he was willing to say nothing about that.
"But if I have not loved all men, it is because all have not a *claim*."
"I, interpreting *neighbor* as I do, wherein have I failed?"

Who? He starts *another question*, as an excuse for dropping the former.

Or, dost *Thou* profess to give a *new* meaning to the word?
Must I love those who hate me, and whom I hate in return?
Whom shall I love? An excuse for stopping short of his *whole* duty.

Neighbor. Rabbis taught *strangers* (Gentiles) were not *neighbors*.

Who is? &c. 1. Its high importance. 2. Its single answer. 3. Its manifold application.

A Jew killing a Gentile (being no neighbor) was esteemed no murderer.

Jews refused to direct a traveller unless he was going to worship at their Temple.

God transfers *Covenant* favors, to those denied *Common* favors.
How often shall I forgive? was a question wrong in the *design*.
This of the lawyer, was a mere *excuse* for his humbled vanity.
How blind to the meaning of the great words he had uttered!
He hints, his question was by no means easily solved.
The very heathen rebuked his narrow minded selfishness.
A Roman amphitheatre trembled with thunders of applause at the words *I am a man*, and I regard no human interest as estranged from me.
This feeling *sanctified*, renders every man a *brother*.
Love has no limits, but its own inability to go further.
Love forgets all antipathies at the sight of another's woe.

δικαιοῦν, *δικαιῶσαι*. *Tischendorf*. To excuse himself, *Kuinoel*—to vindicate himself from the implied charge of disobeying law, which he professed to teach. *πλησίον*. HOMO SUM, nihil humani a me, alienum puto, *Terence*. If a Gentile was drowning, not being a neighbor, a Jew need not attempt to save him, *Lightfoot*.

---

30. *And Jesus answering, said, A certain* man *went down from Jerusalem to Jericho, and fell among thieves, which stripped him of his raiment, and wounded* him, *and departed, leaving* him *half dead.*

Answering. Literally *taking him up*, implying the question was made the occasion of saying more than the mere answer.

With delicate and divine skill, He takes his eye from the *object*, and turns it back upon the *subject*, him, who is to shew the love.

Abstract morals, do not open the eye of the blind self-righteous.

He wishes to know what neighbors are *to be loved.*

The answer tells him, what neighbors are *to love.*

If *one's own heart is right*, there will be no difficulty about the *object.*

Certain. No mention of nation, or character, for wise reasons.

But evidently a Jew, for this is the point of the application.

He was a *fellow-man*, therefore had a neighbor's claim.

No Samaritan was permitted alone to visit Jews.

Went down. *To go up* is the common expression for journeying towards a metropolis.

Jerusalem. Stands 2400 feet above the Mediterranean Sea, and 1500 above Jericho.

Religion and commerce caused very much intercourse.

Jericho. "City of Palms." Deut. xxxiv. 3. Heb., *His Moon.*

About 18 miles 6 furlongs east of Jerusalem, in the valley of Jordan, 9 miles north of the Dead Sea.

A blooming oasis in the midst of a sandy plain.

Fruitful in palms, balsam and roses.

The Serpent not wanting, the *Canaanite* was there.

Rahab here entertained the twelve spies.

Surrounded by Joshua and the Israelitish army 7 days, the walls fell and the city was destroyed.

520 years after, under Ahab, *Hiel* the Bethelite rebuilt Jericho. 1. Kings xvi. 34.

A school of the prophets was there. 2. Kings ii. 5.

Herod rebuilt and adorned it, with palaces and theatres; dwelt there in winter, and died there.

Zaccheus was converted, and Bartimæus healed there.

Destroyed by Vespasian, the city pillaged and burnt.

700 A. D. it was a ruin. Rebuilt by Saracens, now in ruins.

The fountain sweetened by Elisha, flows near the ruins.

Thieves. Gr. *robbers*, a wonder of Divine forbearance.

Travellers still pay *armed guards*, to protect life and property.

The Author in 1855 was obliged to procure a guard in going down to Jericho.

Jericho; the Scriptural type of the city of the world.

Jerusalem; the Scriptural type of the city of God. Josh. vi. 26. 1. Kings xvi. 34.

About 12,000 priests and Levites who used to attend the Temple, in courses, resided at Jericho.

In the time of Jerome it required a fort garrisoned by Roman soldiers to protect travellers.
Said to be the most dangerous road in all Palestine.
Wild Arabs still lie in ambush at the fords of Jordan.
The road (a mere camel's track) lies through *desolate* gorges.
Towering cliffs, dark recesses and narrow defiles. Then as now the resort of robbers.
Wilderness of Adumminn or "bloody way," lies along the road.
Did the lawyer *thank* himself, *his hands* were not *stained?*
40,000 workmen were dismissed from work on the Temple of Herod at this time.
Stripped. Having no gold to *redeem* himself, he is thus left.
Wounded. Implies he tried to *defend* himself.
Half dead. Refusing even robbers' mercy, in shortening his agony.
Some Commentators, with good reason, regard this as true history.
An incident related by Jesus in order to convey a deeper and spiritual truth.

ὑπολαβὼν—*taking him up, i.e.*, answering—usus loquendi still among certain classes, *Stier.*

ἀπὸ Ἱερυ—*a man of Jerusalem.* Such transpositions are not unusual. Matt. xv. 1., Matt. xxvii. 57, John xi. 1, *Campbell, Wakefield.* Not a *heathen* but a *Jew*, in contrast with the Samaritan, *Meyer, Olshausen.* λησταῖς—robbers. κλεπτὴς—a thief. Fancy prompts Commentators to locate this robbery at Adumminn, from its signification—"*place of redness,*" *Stier.* *Leaving him*—Heedless whether he lived or died. "*Half-dead.*" *In the state of being half-dead, Alford,* or *just as he was*, or *happened to be*, namely, *half-dead, Meyer, Bengel.*

---

31. *And by chance there came down a certain priest that way; and when he saw him, he passed by on the other side.*

Chance. Gr. *coincidence.* In God's empire, there is no chance.
It is our ignorance of the cause which makes an event fortuitous.
Chance is only another name, for man's want of knowledge.
That which occurs without previous design of the doers we term chance.
The *falling in* of one event, with another; all of Divine ordination.
Opportunities beneficial to us or to others lie hid under those things which to us seem matters of chance.
The fine weaving of life's threads in one woof by Providence.
Summonses to acts of mercy, are these *side-calls.*

Many opportunities of doing good lie under seeming *chances*.
The word, an appropriate addition to the force of the parable.
Contrasted with anything that *must* have taken place.
God, directs these chances, and will require it at our hands, if we neglect these opportunities, however casual they may seem to be.
Without a sensitive heart, we fail to see the finger of God.
This meeting undesigned of *man*, but overruled by *Jehovah*.

A Priest. Luke i. 8. Probably returning home to Jericho.
The appearance of this character may perhaps shake his high opinion of himself.
There would be a fine *irony*, if the priest was returning from *official* service.
Sympathy and compassion might have been expected from one exposed to the same dangers.
Holy occupations do not of necessity, make the *heart* holy.
Familiarity with sacred things diminishes reverence in men prone to be irreverent.

That way. The only road must have been the camel's track.
No "great road" has ever existed along these steep gorges.

Came down. Gr. implies no haste. If we might say, "He was going *along down*."

He saw him, *lying on the road*, crying loudly to every human heart.
He does not look, whether it be an enemy or friend.
His only idea: "This is a dangerous place, and I must escape."
If some compassion stirs his heart, "He is too far gone, what can I do?"
Or his robes, might be soiled with blood.
He may tell others, "I saw a poor creature dying, and I prayed for his soul."
Yet this Jewish priest would have aided a *brute* in danger. Luke xiv. 5.
"If thou meet an enemy's ass lying under a burden, thou shalt surely help him." Ex. xxiii. 5.
God prefers *mercy* to sacrifice. Even the heathen condemn such cruelty.
He omitted the weightier matters of the law, *judgment*, *mercy*, and faith.
Not an ox or an ass, but a *brother*, was left in his blood Deut. xxii. 4.
Those passed by on earth, will *lie in our way*, before the *Throne*.

Passed by. Selfishness stronger than the voice of humanity, than nationality, than the voice of religion.

συγκυρίαν—by a coincidence, Trench. ἱερεύς—Luke i. 8, see Notes. κατέβαινεν—

This compound does not denote *haste*, *Stier*. ὁδῷ ἐκείνῃ—The impression that there are great highways in Palestine, because Solomon and others had *chariots*, is a mistake. ἀντιπαρῆλθεν—He passed *right over against* him, *Grotius*. He passed on *the contrary* side of the way, *W. & W.*; *near to him*.

---

32. *And likewise a Levite, when he was at the place, came and looked* on him, *and passed by on the other side.*

Levite. Set apart at Sinai, instead of the *firstborn*.
The firstborn of the 12 tribes were 22,273. Tribe of Levi, 22,000.
They carried the ark, tabernacle utensils, offered no sacrifice.
Musicians, and porters by day, by night guards of the temple.
Entered full service at 25 years of age, had 48 cities, 6 for "*refuge*."
Hebron both a *priestly* city and city of *refuge*. 350 Levites returned from Babylon.
Having no land, they received tithes of *corn*, *fruit*, and *cattle*.
Students of the law, and under the priests, *judges* of the land.
Came. It was not inadvertently he acted. He gave no passing glance.
Curious to know more, he approached cautiously.
Looked. Men often *see* that, which they do not *care* to *examine*.
If a priest passed, not bound to stop; therefore, "*I* am excused."
As the example of the superior, so will be the conduct of the inferior.
One sinner follows another, in neglecting urgent duty.
He may have pitied, but selfish, he also *passed by*.
Here a *neighbor* dying, had *no good claims* on their aid.
What a withering of the heart-strings, doth sin produce!
Neither knowledge, dignity, nor worship, can do the work of love.
A dread of the sight of misery, possibly the *priest's* excuse.
The dread of labor, and of self-denial, the *Levite's* apology.
Priest *instinctively* selfish, he would not stop to look.
Levite exhibited selfishness through *calculation*.
There was pride, they were superior in station, of the sacred tribe, and despised the poor wounded man.
There was selfish fear probably—they might be attacked by the same robbers.
There was over-sensibility probably—they shrank from the sight of an object so deplorable.
He who unfeelingly keeps to himself his property, and he who steals it from another are influenced by the same motive.

Viewed in this light, the priest and the Levite had some share in the guilt of the thieves. James iv. 17.

Our Lord referred to presumptuous and prejudicial enquirers.

The highest in religious *position* demanding the sternest censure.

The kind-hearted pagans will rise up and condemn such cruelty.

The conduct of the priest and Levite—a warning to those who have the care of souls in God's church.

Many, like these two, disregard the wounds of sin, and the anguish of the sinner.

Passing by the terror-stricken sinner, who, it may be, is waiting but for a word to turn to his Saviour.

At the last day God will require the blood of souls at the watchman's hands.

Among the *Assyrians*, it was unlawful to pass by in *silence*, any one in distress, without first inquiring the cause, *Herodotus*, Lib. 1.

---

33. *But a certain Samaritan, as he journeyed, came where he was: and when he saw him, he had compassion* on him.

Samaritan. Luke ix. 52. Their name a bye-word of contempt with the Jews.

A type of our Lord—He still encounters the same misery. Luke ix. 51.

He feels the same compassion. He furnishes the same aid.

He requires the same disposition, "Blessed are the merciful, *for they shall obtain mercy.*"

The followers of false systems of faith, oft by their deeds, censure those professing *true* religion.

A despised heretic shows Scribes and Pharisees what is true *love.*

Of an *alien* race, Christ calls him a *stranger.* Luke xvii. 18.

Children of Jews and Samaritans taught to despise and curse one another.

They repaid hate, insult, and wrong, with insult, hate, and wrong.

Samaritans anathematized as Cuthites, and worshippers of the dove.

Jews prayed Samaritans might have no part in the resurrection of life.

Entertaining a Samaritan laid up judgments for one's children.

Eating meat in his house was as though he ate *swine's flesh.*

A Samaritan had secretly defiled the temple with *human bones.*

This deep hatred of the Samaritan gave a *sting* to the application.

Journeyed. The priest comes from the sanctuary, without the spirit of the sanctuary.

The Samaritan full of business, but with a soul *glowing* with love.

Saw him. Christian's double eye; 1, of *Faith*, verse 23. 2, of *Love*. verse 33.

He might have had ten excuses, where the priest and Levite had one.

Compassion, for *past* misfortunes, help for *present* need, care for *future* wants.

Discriminate between this love, and that of John xiii. 34.

John has *believers* for the *object*, Christ's love its *measure*, and faith its *foundation*.

Luke's conception of love founded on the relation of man to man.

Universal philanthrophy asks not, "Who is my neighbour?"

Its reward, an approving conscience and approving Lord.

A whole chapter of Christian ethics, in this *one* word.

Christ took the features from His own divine *Original*.

He knew not the *nation*, only a man in his blood was there.

Service of love willingly undertaken, indefatigably continued, never ended.

A stranger near by, would have said, "They are brothers."

The Jew rejoiced to see, a hated Samaritan, aiding him.

Our Lord respects the feelings of Jews, by selecting a *heathen*.

He intends to reprove their foolish and wicked *prejudices*.

Though of the regal tribe, He was an *alien* in His family. Psa. lxix. 8.

The deepest indignity to Christ was, "*Thou art a Samaritan and hast a devil.*"

Note, though He replied to this last accusation, *I have not a devil*, He does not reject the hated name *Samaritan* with which they reproached Him.

Σαμαρείτης—The chosen example proves the wounded man a *Jew*, *Olshausen*. A type of Jesus Christ, *Luther*, *Melancthon*, *Stier*. ἐσπλαγχνίσθη—Hellenistic, not classical, *Major*. The *heart* in all languages, marks the seat of the affections. But the Greeks extended this figure to the *liver*, *lungs*, and *bowels*. Hence we read of *bowels* of *compassion*, *Olshausen*. αὐτὸν, *him*, after ἰδών, *seeing* omitted, *Tischendorf*, *Alford*, *Cod. Sinai*.

---

34. *And went to* him, *and bound up his wounds, pouring in oil and wine, and set him on his own beast, and brought him to an inn, and took care of him.*

Went. He forgot business and danger in anxiety about the dying man.

"Where in this wilderness, can I get aid to save the sufferer?"

Bound. He may have torn his own garments into bandages.

How love restores, what sin has ruined!

Real love does not ask *how little*, but *how much* it can do.

Their intense enmity forbade a Jew to *touch* a Samaritan.

An earnest *will*, finds things necessary for works of love.

Oil. In the East used instead of butter for food. Ezek. xvi. 13.

All travellers in the East still carry their own food.

Used in offerings. Lev. v. 11. And mixed with oblations. Num. vi. 15.

A perfume for anointing the person. Luke vii. 46. As luxury. Deut. xxviii. 40.

Fuel for lamps in the Temple and dwellings. Zech. iv. 11. to the 14.

Oil of Samaria was noted for its medicinal qualities.

Principal article of traffic anciently with the Syrians. 1. Kings v. 11.

Beaten, or fresh, pressed from the berries, when green. Ex. xxvii. 20.

Presses in which the *feet* crushed the berries. **Gethsemane.** "*Oil Press.*"

Wine. Luke i. 15; vii. 33. See Notes. *Oil and wine*, the remedies used in such cases all over the East.

The *wine* to cleanse the wounds; the *oil* to assuage their smarting.

Own beast. He sacrifices his comfort to save the man.

Inn. No building among the ancients answered to this term.

Kahns or *caravanseras* are square, with open court and well.

Moslems now build them, as acts of *meritorious* faith.

Open stone sheds, accommodating 50 to 100 families.

Used by pilgrims having tents for *protection*, not *shelter*.

Beasts, as well as owners, housed together. Luke ii. 7.

There is not now a single dwelling between Bethany and Jericho.

Took care. Out of love, his only reward an approving conscience.

Who can tell, whether of the two, had the greater satisfaction?

Trajan rent his clothes to bind up his soldier's wounds, *Gurnall.*

The way to be sensible of another's misery is first to feel it ourselves.

If it be not ours, we must make it ours before our hearts will melt.

I must take my brother into myself, before I help him.

I must be that Lazarus, that begs of me, and then I give.

I must be that wounded man by the wayside, and then I pour my wine and oil into his wounds, and take care of him.

I must feel the hell of sin in myself, before I can snatch my brother out of the fire.

They require more than one remedy. At one time, *wine;* at another, *oil.*

The ministers of God will remember that the wounds of sin are not cured in a moment.

The pastor must unite patience with charity.

Human charity often for a moment only, Christ's charity unending.

The Samaritan *going* to the wounded man, a type of Christ.

Unless Christ approaches the sinner, the sinner will not come to Christ.

κατέδησε—a surgical term, binding *down* the swollen wounds. *Bloomfield.* ἐπιβιβάσας with labor, placing, and with difficulty, retaining, the poor man on the beast. πανδοχεῖον literally, *hold-all,* Luke ii. 7. κατάλυμα—*guest*-chamber, Mark xiv. 14. It had no partition, dividing men from cattle. A difference between πανδοχεῖον and κατάλυμα. Uncertain. *Pearce, Campbell.* The former a Roman stabulum for the reception of travellers; the latter a tavern. *Macknight, Elsley.* κτῆνος—beast, horse. *Wetstein;* ass, *Syriac. Kuinoel.* Robbing himself. *Wetstein.*

---

35. *And on the morrow when he departed, he took out two pence, and gave* them *to the host, and said unto him, Take care of him: and whatsoever thou spendest more, when I come again, I will repay thee.*

Morrow. The picture shews the boundary lines of different duties.

Required to shew mercy, but not to sacrifice his business.

Took out, of his girdle,—ample wages for two days. Matt. xx. 2.

He spares from his slender supply. The amount indicates poverty.

Host. Benevolent himself, he treats the host as guided by *self-interest* alone.

Love when weak, engages others to carry out her designs.

He is introduced as receiving pay for a work of mercy.

The picture contrasts heartlessness, with disinterestedness.

Lest any comfort be withheld, he *anticipates* every scruple.

In the khan, ordinarily, *no* provisions are found.

I come. After such self-denials, the host trusts the stranger's honesty.

He helps the needy, and yet pursues the journey.

Note 1, the compassionate heart. 2, the helping hand. 3, the willing foot. 4, the future provision.

He who gives his money to the wretched, gives that which is *external.*

He who gives his toil, and sacrifices comfort, gives *himself.*

Men are prone to pervert truths and to forget injunctions.

The tone of supererogation has been derived from this narrative.

It is argued that the Samaritan did more than his duty.

The Scriptures declare that when we have done all, the all that was done was our bounden duty, and we are still unprofitable servants.

Take care of him,—In giving this command to the host, Christ leaves a charge to all His ministers.

Mark how He says not, *cure him;* but *take care of him.*

The sinner may resist the means for healing, but cannot hinder that *care* which God requires from His ministers.

In the deeds of mercy of this Samaritan, we have set before us—

1. The mission of Christ to man; He came on earth, and *journeyed* on the same road as His brethren, *yet without sin.*
2. The incarnation of Christ; He took upon Him the weaknesses of our nature, and so *came where man was, even close to him.*
3. The mercifulness of Christ; when He *saw* man's wretched state, *He had compassion on him.*
4. The cure of man's sins; Christ *bound up his wounds* by forgiveness, and instituted *two* sacraments for cleansing and strengthening the enfeebled nature of man, *pouring in oil and wine.*
5. The sufferings of Christ for man's sake; *He bore our sins and carried our sorrows.*
6. The establishment of His Church for the safe keeping of those called out of the world, *He brought him to an inn.*
7. An image of Christ's constant love and solicitude, *He took care of him.* *Denton's Commentary.*

ἐξελθών, *when he departed*, omitted by many of the oldest authorities. *Alford;* omitted, *Cod. Sinai.* ἐπιμελήθητι.—The nursing of the sick, distinct from medical care. ἐκβαλὼν—Casting down, evidently by loosening his girdle. *Meyer.*

---

36. *Which now of these three, thinkest thou, was neighbour unto him that fell among the thieves?*

Three. Embraces the *magnates* of Israel, and the *despised* Samaritan.

God is no respecter of persons; so these three men of different classes are mentioned together.

Thinkest thou? Appeal from the prejudiced Jew, to an *honest conscience.*

Neighbor. Not, who *thought*, but *who* WAS neighbor to him?

Not whom your narrow-minded creeds, call *your neighbor.*

But who acted the *part of a neighbor* to the victim of robbery?

Judicious teaching. Jewish prejudice not offended.
Our Lord did not say the Samaritan is thy neighbor. But constrained the enquirer to say it.
God oft makes men their own judges that they may be self-condemned.
Neighbor implies not nearness in place, but in kindness and in care.
Our common nature makes us all neighbors, "*one touch of nature makes the whole world kin.*"
Whosoever is another is our brother and our neighbor.
Common proverb, "*I am my nearest neighbor,*" is the sum of selfishness.
To do our duties, is to change places with the unfortunate.
Thieves. Our Lord leaves them to their career, and coming doom.

Omit οὖν, *now. Tischendorf, Alford, Cod. Sinai.*

---

37. *And he said, He that shewed mercy on him. Then said Jesus unto him, Go, and do thou likewise.*

Shewed mercy. Ashamed to name the Samaritan, a crowd listening.
All *encountering* the Lord, sooner or later, put to confusion.
We do not lack *knowledge*, but the *will*, to do our duty.
True love's glory: 1. It asks no question. 2. It does not hesitate. 3. It fears no harm. 4. It does not delay. 5. It makes willing sacrifices. 6. It leaves nothing unfinished.
A despised Samaritan *knew* his duty, and tried to perform it faithfully.
The truth avails nothing without *love*, and without love, works have no truth.
Dives feeding Lazarus through *vanity*, had still been condemned.
Had robbers seized him before he began this work of mercy.
His act of kindness would have been *complete*, before God.
Lazarus's heart to feed the starving, had been accounted done. 1. Kings, viii. 18.
Men judge our creed from life. God from our heart.
Christ disarms prejudice. " The Samaritan is thy neighbour—love him."
Some have *opportunity*, but no *heart*, to do good.
Go and do. Not as the priest or Levite, but as the good Samaritan.
Christ's command the rule of action: His life the example.
We live not in the world for ourselves.

Man is to be blessed through the instrumentality of man.

If God so loved us, we ought also to love one another.

Nothing is good unto us, unless we communicate that good.

A Christian man would not willingly pass one day of his life without some act of mercy.

We do not want precepts so much as examples. *Pliny.*

Example is the softest and least invidious way of commanding.

The Master not only rules the scholar's book for him, but writes him a copy with His own hand.

Christ's command is our *rule*. His life our *copy*. *Gurnall.*

Keep close to the text, and apply the substance of it to thyself. *Bengel.*

The *practice* of Bible doctrine, the best help to its understanding.

Our Lord leads from *calculating* the number of the objects of our charity, to the *exercise* of love.

The Bible proposes to school the *heart*, as well as enlighten the mind.

Happy world, if it was as full of compassion, as of misery.

The lawyer felt his *question* and *state* of *mind* were *false*.

Gospel love, loves, and asks no questions—*whom? how? where?*

It ignores the whole world of *prudential calculating* rules.

The humble sublime faith, that *God will honor all its drafts.*

"He that pitieth the poor, lendeth to the Lord." Pro. xix. 17.

Into this world of *glowing love*, the lawyer's heart, hardened by legal subtleties, is brought.

Our Lord shewed him that *very love*, and *blest* the man, *tempting* Him.

His answer *designating* the kind heart, settles the question, he himself asked.

It is only by laying aside sectarian or national prejudice that men can find ready access to free and full grace. *Bengel.*

Another lesson—we should love *all* who are imitators and followers of Christ.

The early fathers of the Church saw a deep spiritual meaning veiled under the letter of this parable.

Human nature forsaking the seat of innocence. (Jerusalem the dwelling of peace.)

Is going down to the city under the curse—our earth.

The enemy of our souls stripped us of our robe of righteousness.

We were grievously wounded, and our spiritual life fast flowing away.

Our state one of spiritual death, when the law passed by.
But no law had been given, "which could give life." Gal. iii. 21.
The Redeemer (the Good Samaritan) drew near by the Incarnation.
He came with the "balm of Gilead" to heal our perishing souls.
The oil and wine, represent the *word*, and *sacraments*.
Others think the *two sacraments—others still, the blood* and *Spirit*.
The victim riding, the traveller walking, Christ's deep *humiliation*.
The *inn* represents the *Church* for the reception of "pilgrims" going to a better country.
The host typifies the ministry of the Gospel—*two pence* the *O. and N. Testaments*.
The Samaritan's *departure*, the Lord's *ascension* to heaven: the *promise* of *further reward—the honors and glories He will confer on His ministers at His second coming in the last day. Wordsworth.*

A true history. *Grotius.* Loving our enemies *one*, but not *the* aim of the parable. *Stier.* τὸ ἔλεος.—Circumlocution avoids naming the Samaritan. Luke xvii. 18, ἀλλογενὴς one of a *different stock*. The popular impression that Samaritans were mixed with Jewish blood is *groundless*. Christian antiquity knew nothing of this view of their origin, but saw in them a people of an *unmingled heathen blood*. No mingling of Cuthite or Assyrian blood, 2. Kings, xvii. Not named in plea to Zerubbabel, Ezra. iv. 2. Our Lord sanctioned no popular prejudice, Matt. x 5. Called ἀλλο-εθνής, *Hammond, Trench.* Their features were not Jewish. *Robinson.* The spiritual application of this narrative has frequently diverted the attention from the great practical lesson "Go and do likewise."

---

38. *Now it came to pass, as they went, that he entered into a certain village; and a certain woman named Martha received him into her house.*

It came to pass. Probably on his arrival at Bethany. Luke xix. 29.
Village. Towards the close of life, He seldom entered a village.
Bethany. Luke xix. 29. Heb. *House of Dates.* Now called *El Aziriel, i.e.*, Lazarus.
Certain woman. Mary and Martha, sisters of Lazarus.
Martha. Generally named last, probably the elder and a widow.
Received. Gr. *receiving* and *entertaining*. Luke xix. 6.
Her house. She the owner felt honored in having such a guest.
Though King of Zion, our Lord had *no house*, He called His home.
In humiliation, He borrowed His *cradle, home, raiment*, and *grave*.
He visited some friends, more than others. John xi. 55. *Spiritual attractions.*

His visits to friends tokens of *mercy;* to enemies—of *warning.*
Those entertaining Christ's servants never *lose* by their hospitality.
Martha welcomes for His sake, all His disciples also.
It had become dangerous to befriend Him, but *love* knows no *fear.*
Thousands rejected Him, *one* welcomed Him.
While the world stands, a *remnant* will be steadfast. Rom. ix. 27.

ἐγίνετο, omitted, *Cod. Sinai.* κώμην—of the village of Galilee. *Meyer.* No allusion to Lazarus. *Strauss.* Not proved that he lived in the same house with them. *Oosterzee,* They show the same characters respectively as in John ii. *Stier, Alford.* Sisters had residences both in Galilee and Bethany. *Greswell.* γυνὴ does not necessarily imply a widow. *Campbell.* Formerly married to *Simon,* the leper. *Grotius.* ὑπεδέξατο implies the idea of *entertaining.* "Caesarem recipere oppidis," *Major.* Hospitably entertained. *Wetstein.*

---

39. *And she had a sister called Mary, which also sat at Jesus' feet, and heard his word.*

Mary. 5 Marys:—1. Mother of Jesus. 2. Magdalene. 3. Wife of Cleopas. 4. Sister of Lazarus. 5. Mary the mother of Mark.
Which also. Who for her part, as opposed to Martha.
Sat, literally, *sat close* by; the word is constrasted with, *was cumbered.*
This Jewish custom, not unknown to Greeks and Romans.
It implies *readiness* to hear, submission and obedience.
They who sit now to *learn,* will shortly share his throne. Rev. iii. 21.
All must sit at His feet, or be made His footstool. Psa. cx. 1.
Jesus' feet. For instruction, as the repast was not yet ready.
Paul sat and learned at Gamaliel's feet. Acts xxii. 3.
The restored Gadarene sat at the feet of Jesus, clothed, and in his right mind.
Heard, rather, *kept listening;* indicating her spiritual attitude towards the Great Teacher.
His Word. As soon as the Lord enters, He begins the great work.
Family circle preaching, sanctioned by our Lord.
When Christ instructs, we should "be swift to hear." Jas. i. 19.
Mary improves present mercies, as she may not have others.
The good Samaritan practised love *actively,* Mary, *passively.*

παρακαθίσασα. Thus Luke sketches the whole situation at once. καὶ—refers to the *disciples,* who sat with Mary at his feet. *Major.*

Jesus' feet,—many ancient authorities have *the Lord's. Alford.* παρὰ τοὺς πόδας. These were not expressive of *attitude*, but refer to being educated near anyone. *Vitringa, Ernesti. Mutual relation* rather than training. *Trench, Alexander, Buxtorf.* ἤκουε—kept listening, implies continued action. *Campbell.*

---

40. *But Martha was cumbered about much serving, and came to him, and said, Lord, dost thou not care that my sister hath left me to serve alone? bid her therefore that she help me.*

Cumbered. Gr. *distracted by thought-scattering anxieties.*
Pride and indolence, render many homes miserable.
Things belonging to the outward service of God may distract the minds of loving Christians.
There is a time for everything, if only we seek to do everything for Christ.
Worldly affairs are a snare to us when they hinder us from gaining good for the soul.
Trifles disturb, and rightly regarded—what are not trifles?
Ills that have never happened have made half the world sad.
If troubles come, let them meet us in the path of duty.
Let them be divinely appointed and not our own creation.
When diligent in business, it behoves us to be also fervent in spirit.
Observe the smallness of the household, and humble nature of events
She entertains the Lord of Heaven, and *alone* prepares the meal.
Let the proud forget their pride. Poverty inherits the blessing.
Serving. Preparing the meal, her heart evidently was in having a fine entertainment.
Martha perhaps envied her sister enjoying more than herself.
But her envy is mingled with vanity.
Martha should have commended, not reproached her sister.
Those resolute in Christ's service, often censured by relatives.
Daniel's fasting before God, is turned to his reproach.
Worldly business a *snare*, hindering our way to Christ.
Cumbering *anxieties*, not *cares*, hostile to spirituality.
Millions *pining* in want, and Christians seeking after dainties.
Came. Gr. *a sudden earnest coming into His presence.*
Lord. A reverent beginning, but she becomes uncourteous.
Those in the *wrong*, sometimes the first to appeal to God.
Dost thou? She would thus draw Jesus into her restlessness.
It implies, He was as desirous of a fine feast, as herself.
Care. She chides His want of "care," and dictates to her Lord.

He never kept Mary from her proper domestic labors.
Martha's *intention* was good, but her *manner* wrong.
Happy is the house where there is a Mary for a Martha to complain of. *Bernard.*
We may have Mary's privileges wherever we are, *Jesus ever nigh.*
Ejaculatory prayer would harmonize Martha's employment with Mary's devotion.
Passion gained the mastery, else she had not troubled Jesus.
Thriftless believers are too oft said to neglect their families.
My sister. She had no quiet, Mary must have none either.
She cannot call Mary away, therefore interrupts the Lord.
She boldly speaks, as if it were a *waste* of *time*, to listen to Him.
Left me alone. Here is *vain boasting* of superior industry.
She desires to give the repast a *festive* appearance.
Martha desires to *bestow* much. Mary to *receive* much.
Martha is the Peter, and Mary the John, of female disciples.
Martha a type of those, who work untiringly for Christ,
But neglect close communion with the Redeemer.
Martha's type, may degenerate into self-righteousness.
Christians should be mutual helpers, not complainers.
Must the Lord be "left alone," as if He had only come for *food?*
Jealous of Mary, she wished her to be as herself.
She testifies that Mary really loved Jesus more than herself.

περιεσπᾶτο—*was in a state of distraction.* Literally *to draw from around. Bez.* Distrahebatur; it exactly answers to torqueor. "Omni solicitudine districtum," Hor., lib. ii., sat. 8. It answers to the provincialism of Eng.; *to be put about, i.e.,* distracted with officious care. *Alford.* American provincialism is *fussy, i.e.* much ado, when less work would answer. Cumbered, from *kummer*, Danish, *trouble.* ἐπιστᾶσα—*suddenly coming into presence, Alford.* It denotes a solemn, deliberate, emphatic action. *W. & W.*

μέλει—A term tinged with indignation. *Stier.* Gr., *Does it not concern you? How!* She is restlessly hurrying hither and thither, and cannot enjoy calm thoughtfulness. *Wakefield.* διακονεῖν—preparation of the meal, hence Eng. *deacon.* συναντιλάβηται—to lend a hand. *Hammond.*

---

41. *And Jesus answered and said unto her, Martha, Martha, thou art careful and troubled about many things.*

Answered. She looked for justification, solicitous for Christ's comfort.
Self-righteousness insinuates itself in our busy zeal.

Some willing to receive and serve Christ in their *own way.*
We must not always be *seeking*, but must *find* Him.
While *busy* about Him, we cannot *rest* in Him.
Running about impetuously, many wonder how the meek find Him.
Martha, Martha. Repetition alarms her in her busy confusion.
Those entangled in the world, with difficulty, rescued. 2. Tim. ii. 4.
"Oh earth! earth! earth! hear thou the word of the Lord." Jer. xxii. 29. Mic. i. 2.
Nathan said unto David "Thou art the man." 2. Sam. xii. 7.
The mild but *Divine solemnity* of our Lord, arrested her.
When Providence calls us, be sure, He has something to say.
Careful. Gr. refers to the *cutting nature of* painful *cares.*
Troubled. Gr. *fretting anxiety. Iron* of *care* entereth the soul.
In ministering to her Lord, Martha chose a blessed portion.
She knew, weary, "He oft had not where to lay his head."
If hospitality was ever honorable, it was then and there.
But seeking to withdraw Mary from Christ, she is *rebuked.*
"As many as Christ loves, He rebukes." Rev. iii. 19. Heb. xii. 6.
"Nevertheless I have somewhat against thee." Rev. ii. 4. Job. xxxiv. 31.
Our Lord rebukes Martha not for *serving* but for *much serving.*
To hearken is better than the fat of rams. 1. Sam. xv. 22.
Christ says to the troubled, submit thyself to God, and desire nothing but His will.
Anxiety is the parent of much sin, and much misery.
Many things. Refers to the manifold cares of the household.
Our Lord by no means condemns household activities.
Prompt, untiring energies in the daily affairs of life, often solemnly enjoined. Pro. vi. 6, x. 5. 1. Tim. v. 8.
He did condemn the *state* of *mind,* she had in her work.

For ὁ Ἰησοῦς, *Jesus*, read ὁ κύριος, *the Lord. Tischendorf.*

μεριμνᾷς—the inner anxieties, Luke viii. 14. τυρβάζῃ—the outer bustle. *Cod. Sinai.* has θορυβάζῃ. "*Martha,*" repeated, not in a tone of serious admonition, but with the half sportive manner of friendly intimacy. *Oosterzee.*

---

42. *But one thing is needful: and Mary hath chosen that good part, which shall not be taken away from her.*

One thing, in opposition to the "many" in the previous verse.
Martha had with self-gratification given herself up to cares.
External activities were in reality, more *agreeable* to her.
Her heart was a little *too much* involved in earth's cares.
Our Lord thus entwines minute daily incidents, with the loftiest eternal verities.
With Divine skill, He makes everything *chapter and lesson.*
The desire of Martha was to satisfy and please the various appetites.
He makes this a text for a sermon, on the chief food for the soul.
She, exalts enjoyments of *time*, Christ, those of *eternity*.
Needful. Changing from the needs of the body, to those of the soul.
Man's wants are strictly, *all for the soul.*
Our Lord says, but one thing is needful, the world says everything is needful but that one.
The favor of God is needful to our happiness.
The salvation of Christ is needful to our safety.
United they constitute the "one thing needful."
Nothing is *needful*, but what is *eternal*, or leads to *eternity*.
Honor is but air, and is lost in the grasping.
Riches are but earth, and sink from us in the digging.
Pleasures are but shadows, and slip from our embraces.
Who hath God, hath all, who hath him not, hath less than nothing.
Nothing is needful that stifles the spirit of prayer, or draws us from the presence of God.
The things of life will be taken from us, or we shall be taken from them.
He came to bless her house with His presence.
I came not to *feast* with you, but to *teach* you.
Kind *warnings* among the highest gifts to the soul.
Many things useful, but one *indispensable*, viz., HOLINESS.
Food, raiment, health, wealth, honor, are *desirable*.
Health lost, has proved a blessing through eternity.
Jesus the best family friend. 1. He enhances the pleasures. 2. He lightens the cares. 3. He hallows the duties. 4. He strengthens the union. 5. He promotes the highest end of domestic life.
One thing needful 1, in order rightly to use our time.
2, rightly to taste life's joys. 3, rightly to bear its burdens.
4, rightly to expect the end of life.
"The words of His mouth more than necessary food." Job xxiii. 12.
Life itself, not necessary to our peace, "*To die, is gain.*" Phil. i. 21.

Chosen. Each soul obtains that which it chooses.
Mary leaves her defence entirely with her Lord.
Martha expected Christ to blame her *sister*, but He blamed *herself*.
Good part. A portion assigned to each one at a feast.
Not in the sense of *good* in opposition to *bad*.
Of two *good* ways of serving and pleasing the Lord, choosing the *better*.
Let our choice be sanctioned at the day of judgment.
Martha resembles the church of earth, in the *service* of Christ.
Mary the church in heaven, in devout *adoration* of God.
Martha still at sea, Mary in port. *Augustine*.
Not taken away. Martha's services, of the earth, would die with her.
Mary's being spiritual, were eternal in their nature.
A church of Marthas, is activity, without contemplation.
A church of Marys, is contemplation, without activity.
Believers partake of an enduring inheritance. 1. Pet. i. 4.
God said to Aaron, "Thou shalt have no inheritance in the land."
"I am thy portion, and thine inheritance." Num. xviii. 20.
No wearied strangers to *need* hospitality in heaven.
Our Lord kindly accepted her hospitality.
But he condemns her thinking *her way*, the only right way.
LOVE is seen speaking, ruling, deciding a domestic conflict at Bethany.
Love condemns Martha's *spirit*, but rejects not *Martha*.
Both true hearted disciples, one was absorbed in the higher, the other in the lower of two ways of honoring their common Lord.
Yet neither despised, or would willingly neglect, the other's occupation.
A church full of Maries, perhaps as great an evil as a church full of Marthas.
Both needed, each to be the complement of the other.
The judgment of our Saviour is according to truth. Rom. ii. 2.

πολλά embrace the culinary preparations of Martha. Not a general care for eternal things. *Oosterzee.* μερίδα.—The disposition Mary was at that moment exhibiting, while at the feet of Jesus. *Oosterzee.* ἑνὸς—Although taken from a feast, points to an *election of grace. Olshausen, Stier.* An allusion to sending the best dish to the guest to be honored. *Wetstein.* Land of Levites unalienable. *Wolfius.* Business or occupation. *Grotius, Elsner, Kuinoel.* For ἑνὸς δέ ἐστι χρεία, the *Cod. Sinai* has ὀλίγων δέ ἐστιν ἢ ἑνὸς: also for γὰρ—δὲ, and omits ἀπό.

ἐξελέξατο—*hath chosen out;* the choice of a distracted taste among many viands. *Major.* Man's moral responsibility. ἀφαιρεθήσεται—"No man can deprive us of a virtuous habit." *Hierocles.*

CHAPTER XI.

1. *AND it came to pass, that, as he was praying in a certain place, when he ceased, one of his disciples said unto him, Lord, teach us to pray, as John also taught his disciples.*

It came, &c. The time and place of this incident indefinite.

Praying. Luke, more than the other evangelists, notes our Lord's devotions.

Luke alone records His prayer for His murderers, and the dismission of His spirit into His Father's hands when expiring.

Luke alone records the two parables which show the success of frequent importunate prayer.

Jesus, fresh from communion with God.—Heaven seems to linger in His words.

Earth, and its sins and miseries have vanished for a moment from His eyes.

In Him, the words of the King of Israel were fulfilled,—"But I give myself unto prayer." Ps. cix. 4.

His whole life, one continuous act of communion with His Father.

Certain place. Perhaps Bethany, or the Mount of Olives.

Our Lord's example teaches that ministers must take time to pray as well as preach.

Public life has a tendency to dissipate the mind; spiritual energies are spent.

Prayer the divinely appointed means for procuring new supplies of grace.

The children of Israel required to gather their manna daily—our heavenly food obtained in a similar manner.

Ceased. His divine fervor did not allow the liberty of interruption.

One. He is thought to have been some new convert.

Struck with either the matter or the manner of our Lord's prayer.

God often affixes a great blessing to a good example.

Christ's prayer urged His disciples to pray, and led them to seek divine instruction.

Teach us. A prayer in itself.—We all need to be divinely taught.

None can teach to pray but those who have first learned to pray.

Believers must *pray*, must *learn* to pray, must learn from *Jesus*.

It is ever pleasing to God that we desire to pray,—the desire is of His Spirit.

Prayer brings the impotence of man into connexion with the omnipotence of God.

The prayer "*Lord teach us to pray*" increases the blessing sought for.

It is a confession of our ignorance, and of God's knowledge.

It is a confession of our dependence, and of God's power.

It is a confession of our sin and misery, and of God's grace

It is looking to the wise for wisdom, to the strong for strength, to the merciful One for mercy.

Christ teaches us to pray, 1. By His Word. 2. By His Spirit. 3. By His example. 4. By His providential dealings and deeds.

Encouragements to prayer.—1. The influence of the Spirit. 2. The advocacy of Christ. 3. The exceeding great and precious promises of God. 4. The testimony of men of prayer, to its reality and blessedness.

"If I omit prayer in the morning,—nothing goes well with me all day." *Hale.*

As John also, &c. From this reference to John, it is probable the disciple had not heard the Sermon on the Mount.

The prayer of the Jews contained adoration, praise, doxology.

The prayer of John doubtless contained confession, petition, thanksgiving.

Tertullian says John brought in a new order and method of prayer.

Nothing of John's *inner* teaching to his own disciples preserved to us.

His prayer, however good, is lost. Christ's is heard in every land under heaven.

We may be sure John never taught his disciples to address Jehovah as "OUR FATHER."

There are *degrees* in prayer. "They go from *strength* to *strength* in Zion."

Prayer in some form is the natural cry of the human soul after God.

Greeks and Romans, heathen, were often at their temples before day, praying.

Heathen mariners urged Jonah, in the storm.—"Arise; call upon thy God!"

Can Christians neglect a duty that even heathens perform?

Can Christians neglect a privilege that Christ has consecrated and honored?

Backsliding begins in the neglect of prayer.—"Thou restrainest prayer before God." Job xv. 4.

"Tarry ye in Jerusalem, until ye be endued with power from on high." Luke xxiv. 49.

Private prayer, family prayer, social prayer, public prayer,—steps in the spiritual ladder by which the soul ascends to God.

2. *And he said unto them, When ye pray, say, Our Father which art in heaven, Hallowed be thy name. Thy kingdom come. Thy will be done, as in heaven, so in earth.*

When. *As often as.* It refers to oft repeated action, "*Pray without ceasing.*" 1. Thess. v. 17.

Ye. Those having the Gospel, preeminently under obligation to pray.

Children should, and may be taught to pray, as soon as they can say, "father."

Earthly relationship and love, means of ascending to heavenly things.

"Father," said a child, "I have said my prayers, have you said yours? or are you too big to pray?"

When ye pray—Remember the nature of prayer.

As a *man*, it is the language of *worship*.

As a *creature*, it is the language of *dependence*.

As a *subject*, it is the language of *submission*.

As a *sinner*, it is the language of *repentance*.

As a *pardoned believer*, it is the language of *adoration* and *praise*.

As a *needy man*, it is the language of *supplication*.

As a *receiver of mercies*, it is the language of *thankfulness*.

As a *grateful man*, it is the language of *obedience*, desiring to *do* what the word of God *enjoins*, to *believe* what it *declares*, to *rely* on its *promises*.

Say. Forms of prayer are found in the O. T. Num. vi. 23. Deut. xxi. 8 xxvi. 13. Joel ii. 17.

This prayer, except "as we forgive our debtors," said to be contained in the Jewish Liturgy.

Thus it appears our Lord condescended to adopt a form already in use.

The Lord of the Christian Church did not seek unnecessary novelty.

It may have been to show the union existing between the Old and New Covenants.

A simple, brief, comprehensive *model* for our petitions.

Adapted to His disciples on the threshold of a new dispensation.

Intended as a *framework* for the perpetual use of believers.

It contains no allusion to the Redeemer personally, and no distinct recognition of His peculiar work.

Yet it embodies the substance of Prophets, Evangelists, and Apostles.

The honoring of God in the *Father*, the testimony of faith in the *Name*, the offering of obedience in the *will*, the remembrance of hope in the *kingdom*, the petition for *life* in a twofold sense in the *bread*, the confession of *debts* in the prayer for *forgiveness*, the anxious care about *temptations* in the call for *defence*. *Tertullian.*

God alone could teach, how He would have Himself prayed to. *Tertullian.*

Twice God wrote the Ten Commands, twice Christ said this prayer.

The Decalogue is divided into two tables, this prayer divided into two parts.

Those parts contain *seven* clauses, *three* to God, and *four* for men.

Three and *seven* with the Jews, sacred numbers: *three* represents the Trinity: *seven* the Sabbath.

Four, say the curious, is a secular number denoting the world, *seven* denoting perfection.

Therefore if *three*, *i. e.* the Trinity, is brought into union with *four*, *i. e.* the world, perfection is attained.

Augustine traces a connexion between *seven* of the Beatitudes, and *seven* requests in the Lord's prayer.

Our Father, 1. A *Father*. 2. A *heavenly* Father. 3. *Our* heavenly Father.

Our *selfishness* would prompt " MY Father, forgive *my* sins, &c."

Fellowship of supplication, turns petitions, into *intercession*.

Thy closet must be large enough, for all the Church to enter with thee.

It is only through Christ, this spiritual *sonship* exists.

Jesus Christ alone, could have a right to say " *My Father*."

Our Father, reminds us of our *brotherhood* in Christ.

By faith, we are His *adopted* children in Christ. Gal. iii. 26.

This adoption our *warrant* for approaching " Our Father."

Father. God is never thus addressed in prayer, in the Old Testament.

At Sinai, He said, " Thy God," now graciously " *Our Father*."

Intractable Israel were governed by motives of *fear*.

The relation of Master and servant prevails in the O.T.

Father, by *creation*, *preservation*, *adoption*, and *grace*.

He is the *wisest* Father. 1. Tim. i. 17. *Most loving* Father. 1. John, iv. 16.

He is the *richest* Father. Eph. iii. 8. *Owner of all things*. " My Father made them all."

None but adopted ones have a right to family privileges. John i. 12. Eph. ii. 18-19.

Every good and perfect gift, cometh from our *Father*. Jas. i. 17.

The Creator is here shown to be an *objective*, *personal* Being.

This cuts up by the roots—Pantheism, Atheism, Polytheism, and mere Deism.

Every child lisping " Our Father," shames such vain thinkers.

" Our Father " cheers us amid our orphaned desolation. Isa. lxiii. 16.

It reminds us, against " Our Father," we are in rebellion. Isa. i. 2.

Christ lays the foundation for praying through His name. John xvi. 23.

In heaven. He is all-seeing, all-ruling, invisible, infinitely holy.

"Father" here inspires *confidence*, "in heaven," *awe*.

The Bible speaks of heaven, as His proper dwelling-place. Isa. lxvi. 1.

It is heaven where He is. "He inhabiteth eternity."' Isa. lvii. 15.

No heaven for the soul, *out* of communion with God.

Each believer's soul reflects God, as the rain-drop, the sun.

προσεύχησθε—*Ye*, is emphatic. The extreme brevity of this form contrasts with the vain *repetitions* of heathen: *long* prayers of Pharisees. For *hours* priests cried, "*O Baal hear us,*" 1. Kings xviii. 26. For *two* hours, "*Great is Diana,*" &c., Acts xix. 28.

Πάτερ—Peculiar to the N. T., *Chrysostom, Augustine, Bengel.* Even childhood is not without its distinctive feeling of brotherhood. *Lange.* ἡμῶν and ὁ ἐν τοῖς οὐρανοῖς—These words not found in the most ancient MSS., omitted, *Cod. Vat., Cod. Sinai.* Doubtless inserted by copyists from Matt. *Alford, Tischendorf, Tregelles, Meyer, Mill, Wetstein.* Retained by *Lachmann, Brown.*

The discrepancies in the two authoritative forms of Matt. and Luke occasion much embarrassment to scrupulous *liturgists. Alexander.* Words first merely spoken in Matt., here prescribed as a prayer. *Tholuck, Stier.* Only used by Him *once. Oosterzee.* A form given twice. *Olshausen, De Wette, Neander, Alexander, Schleiermacher, Mede, Lightfoot.* Matt. records this incomparable form as given on one occasion to the people, at greater length: Luke has delivered more briefly, on a different occasion, at the request of the disciples. The sum of the prayer is always the same; on one occasion all the topics are employed; on the other, some out of all, with a free choice of words and subjects. *Bengel.*

οὕτως. Matt. Thus briefly. *Maldonatus, Tholuck, Meyer.* A formula. *De Wette.* A specimen of things to be prayed for. *Mede, Lightfoot, Doddridge.* Petitions taken from Hebrew forms. *Wetstein.* Others find but two allusions to Hebrew forms. *Schottgen, Vitringa.* Omitting allusion to *redemption* authenticates the Lord's Prayer. *De Wette.* Heb., forms as *suggestions. Olshausen.* Great verities of the Scriptures found in this prayer—*Theology, Anthropology, Pneumatology, Soteriology.* But the *Christian* element is not announced. *Oosterzee. Father*—our Lord confines our hope of acceptance to the paternal feeling even among sinful men. *Oosterzee.* Its *arrangement* refers to the *Trinity. Lange.*

Hallowed be thy Name.

It begins with *God's glory, the end* of all things.

Embraces—1. Means for its *promotion.* 2. For man's good.

Shews the comparative value of things Divine and human.

Hallowed. Revered, as sacred, therefore to be glorified. Lev. xxii. 32.

But God's glory, infinite, is incapable of increase or loss.

Yet if all the world were *blind*, the *sun would shine on.*

Sanctified. "If I be a Father, where is mine honor?" Mal. i. 6.
God's *name* only hallowed, by *owning* Christ as the Saviour.
God in *Covenant*, God of Revelation, God of Grace.

Thy name. His various *names*, titles, attributes, Father, Son, &c.
Primarily a particular allusion to JEHOVAH.
"Not unto us, not unto us, but unto Thy name," &c. Psa. cxv. 1.
Psa. xxii. 22. Psa. ix. 2. Psa. lii. 9 Psa. cxl. 13.
Self in man, asking for its *own*, is cut up by the roots.
It goes over the world, as far as "Our Father," rules.
The Pharisaical "*Mine be the glory*," rises in God's children.

Thy, distinguished from all *false* gods, self-existent, eternal.
Reveal thy *Character*, that we may *love* it, and thy *laws obey*.
The highest of all good things is to glorify God's *name* in our lives.
Who is there so debased, as when he sees the pure life of the believer, does not glorify the *name* invoked in such a life. *Grey Nyss.*
When a man gazes on the beauty of the heavens, he cries out *Glory be to Thee, O God;* so the holy lives of believers glorify the Divine *name* far more than the heavens. *Chrysostom.*
Let *thy* holiness be known to all the world, and let it worthily praise *Thee. Augustine.*
Since among those to whom the faith has not yet come, the name of God is still despised, let the ways of truth shine on them, and they will confess the *Holy of Holies. Cyril.*
Christ teaches us to pray that the *name* of God may be appropriated to the *only true God. Origen.*
Because the *name* of Jesus is the glory of God the Father, the *name* of the Father will be hallowed wherever Christ shall be *known. Bost.*

ἁγιασθήτω—Imperative, *entreats* as well as commands. *Treat as holy. Tholuck. Make holy. Olshausen.* The 3rd and 7th petitions omitted in the Latin copies of that age. *Augustine, Origen, Mills.* ὄνομα—Not *name*, but *idea* we have of the *Being* of Jehovah. *De Wette.* Into the depths of His Being, no created soul can penetrate. *Tholuck.* The manifestation of God in his true character.

Thy Kingdom Come.

Kingdom Come. 1. In the heart. 2. In the home. 3. In the Church. 4. In the World.
Not God's *essential* Kingdom, *i.e.* all things *created.*

Kingdom of grace and glory, with Messiah as *Head.* Eph. i. 22.

"*Thy Kingdom of thy Messiah come*" formed part of the Jewish prayers.

Christ leaves out the words "Thy Messiah" to teach them the Messiah had come.

This prayer embraces the *Kingdom* in its hidden beginnings, and triumphant consummation.

Also all the ulterior results of the Messiah's Advent.

That Kingdom will extinguish sin, and establish holiness.

The kingdoms of the world shall become the Kingdom of our God and His Christ.

Christ's first preaching announced, this Kingdom at hand.

Faith looks for a time, when there shall be no more *reason* for this prayer.

"The Kingdom is the Lord's, and He is the governor," &c. Psa. xxii. 28.

"He shall set up a Kingdom, that shall never be destroyed." Dan. ii. 44.

That Kingdom also in the *heart*, we trace the *desire* to pray for it.

The *spirit* of supplication, evidence of its *fruit* and *seed.*

It will continue, until the Kingdom of grace becomes the Kingdom of glory.

Until *then*, this petition has the force of a *promise.*

The want of a *missionary impulse*, which is a fruit of this prayer,

A mournful evidence of *blindness* and *unbelief* in the church.

Children's Hosannas tended to destroy the Adversary.

This prayer, offered in faith, *the seed* of a future harvest.

A prayer for *growth in grace*, in ourselves and others.

"This Kingdom of God is come nigh unto us." Luke xxi. 31.

The stone, seen by the prophet, is cut out of the mountain. Dan. ii. 34.

The prayer anticipates great voices heard in Heaven. Rev. xi. 15.

It includes the hastening of the Kingdom "Surely I come," &c. Rev. xxii. 20.

Come. From without, as descending from above.

As Luke wrote his Gospel for the Gentiles, he never uses the phrase "the Kingdom of Heaven," but always "the Kingdom of God," lest he should countenance the heathen idea of a local deity. *Wordsworth.*

βασιλεία—Spread of Christianity. *Kuinoel.* Christian fellowship. *Tholuck.* Psa. lxviii. 1. The ruin of *Antichrist*, and of *Islamism* and *Romanism*, the great organized enemies of the cross. It secures the conversion of the Jews, Rom. xi. 25. *ἐλθέτω*—The Lutheran catechism adds, *even to us.* This limits that which Jesus made universal. *Stier.*

Thy Will be done, as in heaven, so in earth.

Thy will. Universal terms, not referring to temporary changes.
The height of Christian attainment to be able to say,—Not *my will*, but *Thine* be done.
Will. That which God *wills*, embodied in Revelation.
At present, the earth is full of *contradiction* to that will.
The *coming* of the Kingdom, and *doing* His will, coincident.
Of ourselves, we cannot know His will. "It is spiritually discerned." 1. Cor. ii. 14.
God alone can make us submit. "He worketh in us to will and to do of His good pleasure." Phil. ii. 13.
"He doeth according to His will in the armies of heaven, and amongst the inhabitants of earth." Dan. iv. 35.
We pray, that the heathen may know and do His will also. Ps. lxvii. 2.
That we should submit to His will, as the angels, &c. Ps. ciii. 20.
To will, what God wills, is heaven begun below. Heb. x. 7.
To do the will of God, is meat, the world knows not of. John iv. 34.
Done. As *cheerfully* and as *fully*, as in the upper world.
Many pray "*Thy Will*" while secretly wishing for *their own*.
It is a *promise*, rising above the *tumult* of humanity.
The godless, in uttering this petition, condemn themselves.
Persecuted ones are assured, all will be for their *good*.
The slothful, are *invigorated*. The self-willed, *rebuked*.
As in heaven. No *suspension*, or opposing influence found there.
The only place it is done—1. *Constantly*. 2. *Perfectly*. 3. *Cheerfully*. 4. *Immediately*.
Sons of God, in *festal service*, active in rest, shout for joy. Job xxxviii. 7. Ps. xl. 8, and ciii. 20.
The Church, uniting, will give thanks for ever and ever. Ps. lxxix. 13.
Enable us, O Lord, to follow the heavenly life, that whatever Thou willest, we may will also. *Chrysostom*.

θέλημα—This petition cancelled. *Tischendorf, Meyer, Alford, Tregelles, Lachmann.* Introduced from Matt. *Grotius, Mill, Bengel, Wetstein.* If this clause was interpolated from Matt., why was not the whole prayer here made identical with its form in that gospel? *Wordsworth.*

I prayed it, but secretly, with an unrenewed heart, wished God would not hear my prayer. *Augustine's Confessions.* Our *Forerunner*, in the weakness of our flesh, prayed this prayer, before us, yet without sin. *Stier.* The great *conflict* of sceptical minds, has ever been with the *manner* in which Providence executes His sovereign *will*. *Foster.*

---

8. *Give us day by day our daily bread.*

Give us day by day our daily bread.

This portion refers to man's wants, subordinate to God's glory.

Give. Believers receive as *gifts*, what the impenitent only seem to *stumble on.*

"Pensioners on God's bounty," we have lost all title to bread.

Blessings, *double* gifts; fruit of God's *love* in Christ.

Give us, &c. 1. *Give*, a lesson of dependence. 2. *Bread*, a lesson of contentment. 3. *Our bread*, a lesson of industry, 4. *To-day*, a lesson against care. 5. *Daily*, a lesson of trust. 6. Give *us*, a lesson of love.

Day by Day. Literally, *for that day's bread*, or *for that day.*

What we need is *daily* bread for *body* and *soul.*

To be ever anxious about the future, is sinful. Matt. vi. 34.

Daily. In allusion probably to the manna which was given day by day.

Our daily bread, includes all that soul and body need in this life. *Augustine.*

Grant us food for the day, and faith for the morrow.

Bread. Luke vii. 33. Bodily subsistence among old civilized nations.

Note His goodness.—Bread might have been *tasteless* like *chalk.*

Or if like *sugar*, would soon have *cloyed* on the appetite.

Had it been *bitter*, sustaining life, were painful.

Adapts itself alike to the wants of the infant, and to the man of three-score and ten.

The simplest fare, and no promise is held out, of *more.*

"Having food and raiment, we ought to be content." 1. Tim. vi. 8.

Temporal goods proper objects of prayer—"If God give me bread." Gen. xxviii. 20.

God's providence is felt in the gifts, and acknowledged in the prayer.

His blessing makes mercies, *mercies indeed.*

The blessing of the Lord maketh rich, and addeth no sorrow. Pro. x. 22.

Prayer for temporal gifts *limited*, but not for spiritual.

Sinners hold mercies by *common* favor, believers by covenant title.

Daily bread, without *spiritual* blessings will prove a curse.

The only true BREAD which imparteth *life* is, JESUS. John vi. 35.

"I AM THE BREAD of LIFE *that came down from heaven.*" John vi. 48-51.
The Lord mindful of us in *this* life, as well as hereafter.
We need *daily bread*, we need seek it by *daily prayer*.
God will *supply* all that his children *want* here.
He who has *bread* has much more than he *deserves*.
He will *starve* in *eternity*, who secures not the *Bread of life* in *time*.

The word translated "*daily*" is not to be found in any Greek author, except in this passage of Luke's, and in a similar passage in Matthew.

ἐπιούσιον—Among the most disputed terms in the N. T. Matt., supersubstantialem. *Vulg*. The bread of the Sacrament. *Rheimish Notes*, Matt. vi. 11. Luke, quotidianum. *Vulgate*, from ἐπί and ὀυσιά substance. *Rheimish*. Necessary for our *subsistence*. *Chrysostom*, *Theophylact*, *Origen*, *Parkhurst*, *Luther*, *Campbell*, *Tholuck*, *Lange*, *Alford*, *Kendrick*, *Ebrard*, *Major*. Necessary for our existence, *Oostersee*. Others from εἰναι; others ἰεναι. see *Tholuck*. Spiritual nourishment. *Jerome*, *Olshausen*, *Stier*. A word coined by the evangelist himself. *Origen*. *To-morrow's* bread; the word is compounded of ἐπὶ and ἰοῦσα coming *to-morrow*. *Arabic*, *Ethiopic* Versions. *Bengel*, *Scaliger*, *Lightfoot*, *Meyer*. *Of our necessity*. *Syriac*. Give to us by *the* each day:—*i.e.* as it succeeds—that bread which is needful for us. *Wordsworth*. Necessary for *subsistence*, more than *existence*. The physical must be kept in the foreground. But the spiritual is there by *implication*. Either derivation may answer. *Alexander*, *Meyer*. *Our daily bread* includes all that soul and body need in this life. *Augustine*, *Tholuck*, *Alford*.

---

4. *And forgive us our sins; for we also forgive every one that is indebted to us. And lead us not into temptation; but deliver us from evil.*

And forgive us our sins, for we also, &c.

Forgive, *i.e.*, *send away*, not to *impute* them.
In this we confess we are fallen creatures.
God forgives *completely*, *absolutely*; man only *partially*.
Reveals the entire fullness of His love, through His Son.
First gift of grace, to earth's returning prodigals.
His act of forgiveness is *free*, we have no *claims*.
Our sins. No heathen had either the *idea*, or *word* for *sin*.
It embraces all *words*, thoughts, deeds, against God's law.
Its entrance into the universe, involved in deep mystery.
Its *entrance* into the world, *infection* and *fruits*, revealed.
Contrary to God, called *ungodliness*; against law, *trespass*.
Proceeding beyond prescribed bounds, *transgression*.

Actions contrary to appointed rules, *misdoings*.

Against rectitude, *iniquity;* transmitted, *original* sin.

The penalty, *death*, Rom. vi. 23, and unrepented, destroys for ever.

***One* sin, as a single broken link in an ocean cable, ruins all.**

Its *guilt* measured—1. By the holiness and goodness of God. 2. By the *eternity* of misery caused. 3. By the greatness of the *atonement* necessary. 4. By the wisdom despised, and the mercy rejected by the unbeliever.

All true disciples of Christ struggle after holiness, yet each one is bound to utter this petition *daily*, until he enters heaven.

A debt *no man can ever pay*. A burden ever increasing.

A debt the sinner is *ever trying to diminish*.

Not by paying it, but by persuading himself it is not *so much*.

A debt *continually growing*, despite all efforts to *cancel* it.

"Treasuring up wrath against the day of wrath." Rom. ii. 5.

A debt *constantly exciting* his *hatred towards God*.

He cannot consent to be *compelled* to render an *account*.

A debt, *fairly stated in the book of God*, which will be *exacted to the last farthing*.

A debt, for which *God will soon prosecute the sinner*.

For we also. ***For it is our own practice also to forgive*.**

"How terrible may this prayer become to us, if we be unforgiving." *Augustine*.

We are not forgiven because we forgive. But if we forgive not we are not forgiven.

1. This is not the ground of our hope. 2. Not the motive of our prayer. 3. Indicates not the measure of our hope to be forgiven.

A sign—1, of *humility*, conscious of our guilt. 2, of *love, Forgive us*. 3, of *sincerity*, before God.

As we. **Bringing our sins to the *Mercy Seat*, we are already reconciled.**

First petition puts away *idolatry;* so this puts away *revenge*.

We cannot forgive our enemy's *sin*, only his debt to *us*.

David forgave Shimei's sin against *himself*. 2. Sam. xix. 23.

At his death, he judges his sin against God, to be punished.

This is a petition that cannot be offered in our *own* strength.

All are naturally unforgiving. "Revenge is sweet," said *Homer*.

The most difficult lesson of practical Christianity is to forgive enemies.

Wounded pride will ever recoil at the injunction.

Being able to forgive others a token of regeneration.

Indebted. **We must forgive cheerfully, and continually.**

It demands *grief* at calamities befalling enemies. Matt. xxiii. 37.
Those *living* and *moving* by mercy showed them—must *shew* mercy.
We have the example of Christ,—Luke xxiii. 34, and of the saints, Gen. l. 15-21.
A revengeful spirit, closes the gate of mercy.
We owe many and great debts to the Lord—if the least should be exacted, we must perish everlastingly. *Chrysostom.*
Who dare say—"Forgive my sins, but not those of my enemies?"
God hath bound together our *forgiving*, and being *forgiven.*
Cherishing revenge in prayer, reveals the spirit of *Satan.*
Forgiving others, no *motive* to prevail with God, to forgive us.
It removes a great obstacle in our way of asking forgiveness, but not a meritorious cause.
It is one *evidence* of our having been *forgiven* of God.
A proof, how much God is forgiving Love.
To us. Sins toward man alone, are here embraced.
He that sins against God or man, is in Syriac termed a debtor, and so a sin is a debt. "This people have sinned a sin." Ex. xxxii. 31. The Targum reads *hath owed a debt.*

ἄφες—1, *let go, send away.* 2, *let alone.* 3, *leave, go away.* 4, *leave out*, omit. 5, *leave unpunished, forgive, absolve. Hammond, Elsley.* ἄφες is used about 140 times in N. T.; *leave*, and *forgive*, the principal meanings. Matt. iii. 15, *permit, pardon*, or *suffer.* καὶ γὰρ—This does not determine the measure of our forgiveness. ὡς—Matt. The measure. *Crosius.* Ground of forgiveness. *Fritzsche, Meyer.* Indicates our feelings. *Lange.* Implies those seeking pardon, willing to forgive. *Alexander.* Psa. ciii. 3; 1. John i. 7. A proof that a *sinless* state is not attainable in this life, as held by Pelagius. *Augustine.*

And lead us not into temptation.

Lead. Suffer us not to be led by others, nor by our hearts. Jer. xvii. 9.
Providentially led, we may be tempted, but never *compelled* to sin. Matt. iv. 3.
Humbly shrinking from trials of our loyalty to heaven.
It confesses, our *strength*, as well as our *innocence*, is lost.
It suppresses all presumption and flattery of the heart. Prov. xxviii. 26.
Prayer for bread, raises us above *present* care.
This furnishes us with a weapon for *future* trials.
The key note of each strain, ascends from earth to heaven.

Temptation. Luke iv. 1 to the 7. Gr. *trial, test of character.*
God cannot directly solicit any one to sin. Jas. i. 13.
He tests the *existence* and *endurance* of faith. Gen. xxii. 1.
"The Lord can deliver the godly out of temptation." 2. Pet. ii. 9.
"Being tried (tempted) I shall come forth as gold." Job. xxiii. 10.
God's way is often dark, temptations great.
Our hearts weak, the ruins of our fall sad.
Therefore "pray that ye enter not into temptation." Matt. xxvi. 41.
Self-confidence our greatest danger, "When I am *weak*, then am I *strong*."
To be tempted, and supported, like Christ, will crown us.
"God will not suffer you to be tempted, above what you are able to bear." 1. Cor. x. 13.
"Resist the devil," &c. Jas. iv. 7. There are perils in his assaults.
He is *maliciously* aiming at the ruin of our race. Rev. ix. 11.
He is *unwearied*, "he goeth about as a *roaring lion*. 1. Pet. v. 8.
He is *powerful*, "*the strong man armed*," "*god of this world*."
He is *cunning* in selecting the seasons of his onsets. Gen. iii. 1.
He chooses the *most fitting instruments*, Job's wife, Peter, Judas.
He selects the fittest objects—idleness, 2. Sam. xi. 2. Pride, Esth. vii. 10. Luxury, Ezek. xvi. 49. Ambition, 2. Sam. xviii. 18. Covetousness, 2. Kings v. 26.
He turns lawful things into baits. Gideon's ephod became a snare unto him, and to his house. Judges viii. 27.
The Brazen Serpent becomes a *Nehushtan*, a vain thing. 2. Kings xviii. 4.
He leaves his victims for a while, by way of a *feint*. Luke xi. 24.
He is the author of all false doctrines, and persecutions. Jude, 4 verse.
He assumes the form of an angel of light, that he may deceive. 2. Cor. xi. 14.
He tempts us to delay repentance to our own time and way. Acts xxiv. 25.
He endeavors to weaken and destroy our *faith*.
His acts are called *wiles, devices, depths, fiery darts.*
Discriminate between *his* acts, and those of the *heart*.
Wealth, honor, pleasure, office, become sources of temptation.
Troubles, sickness, poverty, reproach, persecution, sensuality.

εἰσενέγκῃς—inducas. Vul. *εἰσφέρειν*—Sept. Suffer us not. *Augustine, Bengel.* Lead us not into conflict with evil. *Alford.* Subject us not to too hard a test. *Stier.* Introduce us not into trial. *W. & W.* Experience of strong temptations, fruits of our sin. *Lange.* Abandon us not, 2. Thess. ii. 11; Gen. xxiv. 54, 56, 59. Not only let us not be led by others, but *providentially*, let us not be involved in *circumstances*, which afford us *opportunities* and *motives* to sin. *Alexander*. Believers ought not to pray for deliverance from trials for their good. *Ebrard*, Rom. v. 8; Isa. i. 25; 1. Pet. i. 6. πειρασμὸν—Luke iv. 2. The opportunity of sinning, and the peril of it. *Alexander*.

But deliver us from evil.

Evil. Should we be led into temptation, then, *Deliver us from evil.*

Evil of *sin*, the greatest, because the *cause* of all others.

From the evil of *temptation*, and power of Satan.

Yet "all things *work together* for good to them that love God." Rom. viii. 28.

Implies the *desire* of deliverance from all evil in this life.

That believers leave themselves in God's hands, to do His pleasure.

The end of this prayer, the perfect sanctification of the believer.

The closing doxology wanting here, is wanting also in all the best and most ancient copies of Matthew's gospel. Perhaps our Lord purposely left that part *open;* and as the grand Jewish doxologies passed immediately into the Christian Church, probably this prayer was never used in the Christian assemblies, but in its present form, as we find it in Matthew, while in Luke it has been allowed to stand as originally uttered. *D. Brown.*

"*Deliver.*" The *desire*, but not the *deliverance*. *Stier.*

τοῦ πονηροῦ—cancelled. *Tischendorf, Meyer, Alford, Tregelles;* retained. *Lachmann, Lange.* ὁ πονηρός—*Meyer, Alexander, Olshausen, Bengel.* τὸ πονηρὸν—*Augustine, Tholuck, Lange, Brown, Alford, Stier.* From moral evil. *Luther, W. & W.* The whole sphere of the πειρασμοὶ. *Tholuck*, Luke iv. 2.

The prayer recorded by Luke was delivered by our Lord, at a time, and under circumstances, differing from those to which Matthew refers. The one was spoken in Galilee, the other in Judea. The one unasked for, the other at the request of a disciple. The one as He was preaching, the other after He had been praying.

---

5. *And he said unto them, Which of you shall have a friend, and shall go unto him at midnight, and say unto him, Friend, lend me three loaves:*

And he said. He follows the lesson *how to pray*, with an assurance of *an answer.*

Friend. A word oft misused among the languages of earth.

"He that hath friends, must show himself friendly." Prov. xviii. 24.

Midnight. Orientals often *travel* during the cool of night.

Having no *inns*, they tax their friends' hospitality.

His *own*, or *father's* friend, gave him this right.
But in every land, midnight a most unseasonable hour.
Yet *midnight* beggars are God's delight. Isa. xxvi. 9. Cant. iii. 1. *Augustine.*
Night devotions have been early in the world. God often appeared to men at night.
Before day, Abraham rose to sacrifice his son.
In the night, Jacob wrestled with God, and obtained the blessing.
In the night, God led the Israelites out of Egypt.
Samuel cried unto the Lord all night.
David "washed his couch with tears in the night."
In the night, the Son of God was born, and angels announced it to the shepherds.

Lend. Often one is asked for aid, and the answer is, *nothing.*
But *he* has a friend who will aid him in extremity.
Without apology, he loudly knocks. *Friends* have *rights.*
"If thou dost not help me in difficulty, thou art *not* my friend."

Three. One for the guest, one for the host, third for hospitality,
He will continue knocking, until his friend opens.
His friend must rise and grant it, to get rid of him.
Believers have a *Friend* ever accessible in distress.
They are their own enemies, to make so little use of such a Friend.
Some are *willing*, others *able*, but *few* find a HEART to pray.
We must go to the Lord with confident boldness. Heb. x. 9.
For that, as *needful* for the soul, as *bread* for the body.
We must plead for *others*, as for ourselves. 1. Tim. ii. 1. Job xlii. 10.
Midnight or midday the mercy seat is accessible. Rev. xxi. 25.

Loaves. Luke vii. 33. At present about the size of a small plate one-half inch thick.
In weight less than half a pound; thus Abigail could prepare 200 loaves for David and his men.

χρῆσον—to furnish what is needful. Hence the needful answer, the *oracular response.* τρεῖς. Represents the Trinity, or faith, hope, and charity. *Augustine.* *The guest*—The heathen world. *Vitringa.* ἄρτους. The oriental loaf of *millet*, ground coarsely by hand, is about the size of a breakfast plate, and proportionally thick.

---

6. *For a friend of mine in his journey is come to me, and I have nothing to set before him?*

A friend. I am not pleading for myself, but for another.
Mine, and therefore of *thine.* Orientals bound for *mutual* friends.
Nothing. In the East they bake every day, and keep none over.
Borrowing bread was common with the Jews, they had certain rules on the subject.
He would not have *wanted,* but his friend came unexpectedly.
Believers can go to God, if their necessities are *Providential.*
The cares Providence casts upon them, they can *roll* back on Him. Ps. lv. 22.
We are not to pray as though it were to overcome a reluctance with God, but rather to lay hold of His willingness.
With God delays are not denials.
He is more willing to give than we are to pray.
And is wont to give more than we desire or deserve.
His ears are ever open to the supplications of His people.
"Limit not the Holy One of Israel." Ps. lxxviii. 41.
"Open thy mouth wide, and I will fill it." Ps. lxxxi. 10.
God's ears are open to our prayers, and His eyes are open to our wants.

φίλος typifies the spirit of man wearied by the cares and sorrows of life's journey, returns seeking rest, thirsting after better fare. *Origen.* A heathen coming to a Christian for light. *Augustine.*

---

7. *And he from within shall answer and say, Trouble me not: the door is now shut, and my children are with me in bed; I cannot rise and give thee.*

Within. Comfortably retired, he dislikes to be aroused.
Trouble. He does not respond to the friend. He may forget many favors.
The selfish world actuated by interest, not by *principle.*
Doors, were of wood, brass, and stone.
Locks were of wood or iron—sometimes *sealed.*
Inscriptions, warnings, or *charms* written above them.
A slave frequently chained to the post opened the door to Romans.
Curtains in summer caused less noise by the servants entering.
Humble houses in Egypt are generally without doors.
Shut. Gr. *locked.* "Disturb me not, thou midnight intruder!"

Doors without locks *unbarred* with difficulty.
A *prophetic* meaning, to those delaying repentance.
Children, by timely application have entered, and are safe.
Lost opportunities, by-and-bye, never recovered.
Our Father (though to unbelief, asleep,) never slumbers.
The golden gates, which prayer enters, never closed. Rev. xxi. 25.
He has no *favorite* children to divert His regard.
No trouble to Him to hear and grant fervent cryings.
Men are *willing*, but alas! unable. Not thus with God.

Children. Our Lord glances kindly at the details of *domestic life.*

The *mother* unnoticed, the *dignity* of the parable is preserved.

In bed. Bedsteads unknown among the common people in the East.

A raised floor, of clay or stone, next the wall, is their cot.
Orientals generally sleep in their garments, covered by a rug.
Divans are the ornamented beds of wealth.
Skins or dry herbs spread on the floor for the poor.
Bedsteads of iron, ivory, tortoise-shell, silver and gold. Deut. iii. 11.
Anciently boxwood and maple. Beds filled with wool and rushes.
"I am glad my children are asleep. I wish no more trouble."
"I ought not disturb them to help night-disturbing friends."
Most houses in Egypt have but one room.

κόπους from *κόπτω* to *beat, i.e.*, beaten by *weariness. κέκλεισται.* The first watch called by the Romans—torch-lighting—by Greeks *κλεισίθυρον*—door-shutting. The door being shut expresses the lateness of the hour. *Elsley.* It is usual in the East in humble life for a whole family to sleep in the same room, laying each a bed or mattress on the ground.

"*I cannot rise and give thee,*"—the speaker had risen when he addressed his friend; an Eastern traveller is of opinion that the request was not only that the loaves might be lent—but that it implied "Bake them for me. I have no meal in the house, and am unable to bake bread for my guest."

Locks seldom used, and were of primitive make. Judges iii. 23. The keys of Cairo gate, are huge wooden affairs. *παιδία—domestics. Elsley. εις* for *ἐν*, *have gone to bed, and are in bed. κοίτην—bed*, not *chamber, as Newcombe. Middleton.*

---

8. *I say unto you, Though he will not rise and give him, because he is his friend, yet because of his importunity he will rise and give him as many as he needeth.*

I say unto you. He knowing God's mind from eternity, thus encourages us.

He welcomes in *prosperity*, at noonday; in *adversity*, at midnight.

Bartimaeus' importunity *offended* the crowd, but *pleased* Jesus. Mark x. 47.

This importunity distinguished from "*praying*" as urged by Paul. 1. Thes. v. 17.

Latter, like the pulse, never rests, but beats on even during sleep.

The former perseveres for a given object, until it is obtained.

If our prayers were answered immediately, how could men exercise the graces of *faith*, *love*, and *hope*?

Although God may be *silent* let man persevere.

Will not. Even evil men yield to troublesome importunity.

The midnight applicant consents not to be refused.

Persisting, and refusing to take a denial.

Importunity. Gr. *shamelessness*. He asks until his friend is *ashamed*.

The oriental rites being *sacred*, he dreads to violate them.

Importunity, regardless of time or place, urgently troublesome.

He asked for "*three*," but receives as *many* as he wants.

Reluctance once overcome, friendship triumphs.

Rises. He might send a servant, but rises *himself* to befriend.

Faith needs *resistance*, to call it forth in its strength.

The ANGEL, contending, allows Himself to be overcome by Jacob.

Jacob, by perseverance, obtains a new name and a blessing.

All God's children, as spiritual Israelites like Jacob, have power with God and prevail.

All like Jacob are ready to exclaim "I will not let Thee go, except Thou bless me."

The Syrophenician and Patriarch, blest by their trials.

God for a time withholds the answer to prayer.

But the blessing is sweeter, when obtained.

It is the Christian's duty to ask in faith, and to wait in hope.

Perseverance in prayer effects no change in God, but effects a change in the petitioner.

Miracles have ceased: wonders have not: perseverance in faith and prayer will accomplish wonders.

Diligence, perseverance, and importunity are honorable terms applied to prayer.

They offend not God, but are enjoined by command, and taught by example.

God is urgent with us, to make us urgent with Him.

1. Our petitions never unseasonable. 2. No time unsuitable. 3. No spiritual mercy too great to ask. 4. No needed blessing exceeds God's power. 5. God never disinclined to hear. 6. Never unwilling to bless. 7. He is ready to answer. 8. Able to grant. 9. Willing to bestow. 10. Waiting to be gracious.

Therefore:—In pleading be urgent, in expectation be confident, the answer cometh, success is at hand for Christ hath thrice said, "*ye shall*," "*ye shall*," "*ye shall*."

This divine hesitation proves who are earnest and who are not.

God much kinder to his friends, than men to theirs.

If the self-indulgent, by entreaty, be overcome—

How much more shall perseverance in prayer, prevail?

God will not only give *what* we desire, He will give *more* than we desire.

ἀναίδειαν—shamelessness. Alford. Improbitatem—Vulg.—unweariedness. Like *improbus*, it may be exercised in a good or a bad cause—"Imprudentia est regnum sine corona." *Jew's* proverb. Abraham's importunity in behalf of Sodom approaches *ἀναίδειαν. Indefatigableness. Oosterzee.* Persevering importunity. *Major.* The arrangement of the words, premeditated: *δοῦναι ἀναστάς, ἐγερθεὶς δώσει*—though he will not *give rising up*, yet *when he is aroused*, he will give. Friendship might have urged him *to give:* continued importunity in knocking obliges him to the effort of *rising. Bengel.*

---

9. *And I say unto you, Ask, and it shall be given you: seek, and ye shall find; knock, and it shall be opened unto you.*

Ask. Christian prayer renders the mind offering it, tranquil.

It obtains from God, what otherwise He would not grant.

Trust and prayer are not at variance, but co-incident.

Ask of whom? Not of the *inexorable* deities of pagans.

Not of our neighbor. "Who can ransom *a soul?*" Ps. xlix. 7.

But of our heavenly Father, who is more willing to give than we to ask.

The more we trust in God, the less we trust in man.

Seek. Implying earnest zeal and deep anxiety.

As we would search for lost gold, so let us anxiously *seek* after God.

Implies also that we must not only ask (pray), but wait upon God.

There is a gradation in the words—*Ask*, but stay not there.

Seek, but rest not satisfied there—*Knock*, strive to enter.

Seek, all things necessary to salvation, and to sanctification.
All spiritual assistance for final perseverance.
All that the sinner needs: all that the believer requires:
1. Pardon of sin. 2. Strength to resist temptation.
3. Increase of faith. 4. Power to overcome evil habits.
5. Deeper humility. 6. Prompter obedience.
7. Greater devotion to Christ. 8. More of the Spirit's influence.
9. A daily victory over besetting sins and infirmities.
10. Grace to ascribe all to the undeserved love of God in and through Christ Jesus.

Knock. At that door, from which we are *shut out*.
Our sins have *barred* the door to heaven, we should *knock*.
By nature men torment themselves with forbidden cares.
The remedy is, faith in God's paternal care.
All true prayer is prompted by Divine grace, agreeing with His will.
Within God's heart, lie all the blessings we can desire.
It implies pressing urgently our suit at the *same* door.
God would not *bid* us knock, if unwilling to *open*.
The door is kept closed, that we might *knock*.
Many prayers are *said*—Happy is he that *prayeth* in sincerity and faith.
"Ye shall find Me, if ye seek Me with *all your heart*." Deut. iv. 29.
Christian men should never hold their peace, nor give him rest, &c. Isa. lxii. 6.

Ask. To prevail with God in prayer—
Ask with the humility of a beggar.
Seek with the carefulness of a good servant, and
Knock with the confidence of a friend.

The believer *asking*, reverses the begging man's usual plea.
1. The beggar pleads his former condition—He has seen better days.
2. He pleads his goodness—I am reduced, not by my fault.
3. He pleads the unusualness of his request—It is my first, I shall not again beg.
4. He pleads the smallness of the boon—I ask only a trifle.
5. He promises not to tell others so that others may not apply.

Seek. For Divine things—for they are hid from the natural heart.
To know the secret of the Lord, it is revealed to them that fear Him.
To know God in Christ and be blessed for both worlds.
For a new heart, and a right spirit.
For the teaching, sanctifying, and comforting influence of God the Holy Spirit.

That needed blessings may be granted.

That dreaded evils may be averted.

Knock, make applications to Christ to be admitted into His service.

To be received into His family.

To be fed by His bounty, comforted by His presence.

Knowing that none shall seek His face in vain.

It shall be opened to you. It shall be given.

What shall be opened? Heaven, its joys, its inmates, its King.

What shall be given? MERCY, and GRACE, *i. e.*:—

1. Srength to contend. 2. Guidance to direct. 3. Comfort to console. 4. Support to animate. 5. Help to aid. 6. Deliverance to rescue. 7. The friend to assist. 8. The food to nourish. 9. The pardon needed. 10. The peace desired. 11. The purity sought for. 12. The wisdom required. 13. *The* "*anything*" asked. 1. John v. 14. 14. *The* "*Whatsoever.*" Matt. xxi. 22. 15. *The* "*blessing desired.*" Mark xi. 24. 16. "*What ye will.*" John xv. 7. "*Whatsoever ye ask.*" John xvi. 23.

How? Liberally, without rebuke. Jas. i. 5-6.

Who shall receive? "Ye." "We." "All." "Everyone."

When? "In time of need." Heb. iv. 16.

Therefore: "Come boldly unto the throne of grace." Heb. iv. 16.

Ask. Seek. Knock. Persevering prayer implies:—

1. Consciousness of need. 2. Sense of weakness. 3. Earnestness of soul. 4. Intensity of desire. 5. Faith in the Son of God. 6. Reliance on Jehovah's power. 7. The sovereignty of God. 8. Belief in the promises. 9. An acknowledgment of Divine goodness. 10. Of the universal presence of the Deity. 11. Of the Almighty's knowledge of the heart of man.

It is the application of want to Him who alone can relieve it.

The voice of sin to Him who only can pardon it.

1. The urgency of poverty. 2. The prostration of humility. 3. The fervency of penitence. 4. The confidence of truth.

It is not eloquence, but earnestness.

It is the cry of faith to the ear of mercy.

It is the contrite sinner's voice.

It is the Christian's vital breath.

It is the believer's sincere desire, uttered or unexpressed.

It is the voice of God speaking in the soul of man.

It is a voice that heaven has given—crying to heaven for aid.

The first true prayer—is life from the dead.

Αἰτεῖτε. Greeks and Romans sought mercies, but half in *despair*. They prostrated themselves on the earth, and clasped the god's cold marble knees, fondly believing, mercy had her dwelling there. But the gods themselves were subject to an iron *Fate*. "I see no reason to *trust* the gods, since our enemies triumph." *Cato*. "Tears cannot restore the dead, lamentations are vain. Nothing remains, but to forget the blessings of the past, and submit to the future." *Hecuba in Euripides*. "The world is a gloomy theatre. Everywhere, are the altar and the victim." *Cicero, Tusc.* "The best thing, the gods can give, is *eternal sleep*." *Plutarch*. The world by wisdom knew not God. In the Gospel immortality is made known to man.

---

10. *For every one that asketh receiveth; and he that seeketh findeth; and to him that knocketh it shall be opened.*

Every one. Repeats in stronger terms the assurance above.
Here is a *great law* of our Father's spiritual kingdom.
A clause out of the eternal covenant, not to be changed.
A parent is not bound to grant a *rebel* child a favor.
Asketh. We must ask aright, that is in *faith*.
Some ask *amiss*, asking for merely selfish purposes. Jas. i. 5-7. Hence their prayers are not answered.
"We know not *what* we should pray for as we *ought*,"—ignorance limits our petitions. Hence we should ask, "Father thy will be done."
We are wanting in the proper spirit of prayer,—hence we should trust to the Holy Spirit, who is promised, *to help our infirmities*.
Receiveth. Not only shall, but actually *now* receives the blessing.
This records the actual experience of all who pray in faith.
Believing prayer is never unsuccessful, never.
It will be answered in some *way*, but *how*, may not be known until Judgment. Matt. xxi. 22. Mark xi. 23. John xiv. 13.
Findeth. Hid treasure, "a pearl of great price," riches for *eternity*.
Opened. Mercy seat accessible, in all *places*, at all times. Rev. xxi. 25.
Prayer *refused*, the highest act of infinite love. 2. Cor. xii. 8-9.
Granted *afterward*. 1. Sam. viii. 6-9. In *wrath*. Psa. lxxviii. 18-31.
A king given in anger. Hos. xiii. 11. Gadarenes lost the Saviour. Matt. viii. 34.
Refused, but afterward granted. Deut. iii. 23. Luke ix. 28-33.
Promptly granted. Gen. xxiv. 12. Hezekiah's prayer. 2. Kings xx. 3.
Daniel's prayer. Dan. ix. 3-20. *Gabriel* assures him. Dan. x. 12.
While *Saul* prayed, Ananias was sent. Acts ix. 11.
Our blessed Redeemer refused, and yet granted. Luke xxii. 42. 3.

The cup could not pass from Him, but an angel appeared *strengthening Him.*

Paul obtained grace sufficient for the day of need.

THE RESULTS OF PRAYER.

1. Abraham's servant prays—Rebekah appears. Gen. xxiv. 12.
2. Jacob prays—Esau's mind is wonderfully turned from the revengeful purpose he had cherished for 20 years. Gen. xxxii. 24.
3. Moses cries to God—the sea divides. Ex. xiv. 15.
4. Moses prays—Amalek is defeated. Ex. xvii. 11.
5. Joshua prays—Achan is discovered. Joshua vii. 7.
6. Hannah prays—Samuel is born. 1. Sam. i. 10.
7. David prays—Ahithophel hangs himself. 2. Sam. xv. 31.
8. Asa prays—a victory is gained. 2. Chron. xiv. 11.
9. Isaiah prays—185,000 Assyrians are dead in 12 hours. Isa. xxxvii. 36.
10. Hezekiah prays—his life is lengthened. Isa. xxxviii. 2.
11. Daniel prays—the dream is revealed. Dan. ii. 17.
12. Daniel prays—the lions are muzzled. Dan. vi. 10.
13. Daniel prays—the 70 weeks are revealed. Dan. ix. 21.
14. Ezra prays—God answers. Ezra viii. 21-23.
15. Nehemiah darts a prayer—the king's heart is softened in a minute. Neh. ii. 6.
16. Elijah prays—a drought of 3 years succeeds. 1. Kings xvii. 1.
17. Elijah prays—rain descends in torrents. 1. Kings xviii. 42.
18. Elisha prays—Jordan is divided. 2. Kings ii. 14.
19. Elisha prays—a child's soul comes back. Prayer reaches eternity. 1. Kings xvii. 21. Elijah. 2. Kings iv. 33. Elisha.
20. The apostles pray—the Holy Ghost descends upon them. Acts ii. 1.
21. The disciples pray—Peter is delivered by an angel. Acts xii. 12. *Campbell.*

11. *If a son shall ask bread of any of you that is a father, will he give him a stone? or if* he *ask a fish, will he for a fish give him a serpent?*

Son. The parental relation, among the tenderest on earth. Hungering in the soul, none can satisfy, but God.

Ask. A parent grants not *wisely* to a child refusing to ask.

Bread. The loaf in its color and roughness like a flat stone.

Father. Bad as our nature is, the *father* is not extinguished.

Will he give? Strongly oriental in form. "*He will not, will he?*"

Stone. God never trifles with *honest* hearts, coming to Him.

1. No *useless* gifts from God. 2. No *dangerous* gifts from God. 3. No *deceitful* gifts from God. 4. *Love* prompts the gift. 5. *Adaptation* gives value to the blessing.

Persevering prayer and *pleading* prayer honor God, and will by Him be honored.

The importunate widow though repulsed prevailed.

The host, unrepulsed by refusal, obtained the food, and the traveller was fed.

God gives not to our wants, nor to our wishes, but to our requests.

Though the promises be free, yet for these things will He be enquired of.

Ask and *ye shall* have, seek and *ye shall* find, knock and it *shall be* opened.

Prayer obtains all things, for it moves the hand that moves the world.

Short sighted, we too oft ask for stones, instead of bread.

Fish. Serpent, a fish, with concealed fins.

Should anyone in his folly ask for a serpent or a scorpion,

He would be no *father*, if he should grant the request.

A child might mistake a serpent for a fish. *Bengel.*

12. *Or if he shall ask an egg, will he offer him a scorpion?*

Egg—Scorpion.—Both could be grasped in the hand.

Scorpions vary from one inch and a half, to six inches in length.

They resemble a small slender lobster, and their sting is fatal.

"Their torment was as the torment of a scorpion." Rev. ix. 5.

Their sting brought over their head strikes in front.

If in danger, they destroy their parents, or sting themselves to death.

Curled—resemble an egg. They attacked the Hebrews. Deut. viii. 15.

"*Of any of you that is a father.*" Gr., τίνα δὲ ἐξ ὑμῶν τὸν πατέρα, *but, of what one of you who is a father.* There is a gradation from a friend to a parent. *Bengel.* "*Or if,*" Gr. ἢ καὶ ἐὰν, *or even if.* His confidence in asking is increased. ὁ υἱὸς omitted. *Cod. Sinai.*

ἄρτον λίθον. Luke vii. 33. The loaf of *millet* coarse, ground by hand, resembles a flat granite stone, in color and roughness. *Wheat* pays their rent and tax. πατέρα—*Jehovah* true *Pater familias* of the household of faith. *Alford.* αἰτήσει—a suppliant act of an inferior. *Lat. peto.* ἐρωτάω—an equal asking another a question. *Lat. rogo.* Thus Christ never uses the former to His Father as a *petition*, but the latter as a request. *Trench.* "*An egg*"—The children's request advances from necessaries to luxuries. *Bengel.* *Fides in pisce; spes in ovo: charitas in pane.* Faith intimated by the *fish*, hope by the *egg*, charity by the *bread*. *Augustine.* σκορπίον. *Aristotle* calls it the manslayer. Pliny makes nine species. Scorpions are of various colors. One species is white. It is said that in Judea scorpions are about the size of an egg. Mr. Fox, in his travels in Palestine, gives an account of two children who lost their lives through the stings of scorpions. In the Zodiac, the scorpion represents *Typhon*, one of the symbols of the evil spirit among Egyptians. *Stier.*

---

13. *If ye then, being evil, know how to give good gifts unto your children: how much more shall* your *heavenly Father give the Holy Spirit to them that ask him?*

If ye then. A formal inference from truths, felt by all, to be *truths.*

Evil. Points to the corruption of man's nature (original sin).

Good things. Matt. The Holy Spirit's influences, repentance faith, &c.

Our importunity to be limited. "Speak no more." Deut. iii. 26.

It may become unauthorized *obstinacy* to pray. Isa. i. 15. 1 Sam. viii. 19.

Depth of earnestness to a child, our rule toward God.

Heavenly Father. In contrast with the *earthly father*, best of whom is sinful and imperfect.

The argument *à fortiori.* If an earthly parent, so far less careful, wise, and loving, will give his child, &c., How much more our heavenly Father give the gift which includes all others!

Holy Spirit. The *best* gift of all, the gift of gifts, and with it all things. Chap. xxiv. 49.

The Holy Spirit, the Spirit of goodness and of joy. Ps. cxliii. 10.

He is more needful to the soul than food to the body.

Our Lord illustrates *God's* love, by that of a *creature.*

Ask Him. The indispensable condition of obtaining favors.

The *reasonableness* of importunity in prayer.

What can He refuse to the prayers of His children, who has already given them the grace of adoption to be His children? *Augustine.*

But although He gave us His Son without asking, He will not give us His Spirit unless we ask. *Ford.*

Mark the Saviour's change in the terms of comparison.

It removes doubt, and imparts confidence.

It is not—your heavenly Father shall give His Holy Spirit to *His children.*

But, He shall give His Holy Spirit *to them that* **ask Him.**

"*Being evil*,"—comparison of frail, sinful man with God. *Meyer.* The ὑμεῖς instead of ἡμεῖς. Direct testimony of His own *sinlessness.* No human teacher without presumption, could have thus spoken. *Oosterzee.*

"*Heavenly Father*."—Gr. ὁ πατὴρ ὁ ἐξ οὐρανοῦ, *the Father who is of heaven*, "*your*" is not expressed at all. *Alford.*

"*Holy Spirit*."—This discriminates between conditional and unconditional prayers. Prayers for spiritual gifts always heard, (doubtful?) Desires for temporal blessings only, when we ask for *bread*, and not for a *stone*. *Oosterzee.* A general promise graciously held out to all. *Bengel.* Confined to God's children. *Stier.*

οἴδατε—idiomatic for δύναμαι *know how to do, have the power.* Thus "*king*" means *able one*, and the *knowing one.* Saxon *can* and *ken* (know) are the same. *Trench.*

---

14. ¶ *And he was casting out a devil, and it was dumb. And it came to pass, when the devil was gone out, the dumb spake; and the people wondered.*

Casting out. Gr. *was actually at that time casting one out.*
Devil. Luke iv. 2. Gr. *demon*, a superhuman being, good or bad.
There were many *demons*, but *one devil.* Luke iv. 2.
Demons embraced all kinds of gods among the *Greeks.*
Dumb. One having no intercourse with men, was cured.
A *double* miracle, made the "people wonder."
They inferred Christ to be superior to spiritual powers.
Matt. speaks of a demoniac *deaf*, *dumb*, and *blind.*
Three miracles were performed on him at the same moment.
The like miracle is daily accomplished in the conversion of sinners.
Christ still unstops the ears of the *deaf*, unloosens the tongue of the *dumb*, and opens the eyes of the *blind.* *Bede.*
Dumb, metonymically, *i.e.*, made the person possessed to be dumb.
The ungodly are dumb upon subjects relating to God, to the soul, and to eternity.
The devil makes his servants *dumb*, and hinders them from—
1. Praying to God. 2. Praising God. 3. Confessing demerit. 4. Instructing the ignorant. 5. Admonishing vice. 6. Bearing witness to the truth. 7. Comforting the godly.
The whole race of mankind rank under one or the other of two antagonistic powers.
The Spirit of Good, or the Spirit of Evil.
Christ Jesus is the federal head of one division. The company of the faithful.
Satan is the head of all who reject Christ as their Redeemer and their King.

Multitudes pass daily from the camp of Satan to the army of the living God.

καὶ αὐτὸ ἦν—omitted. *Cod. Sinai.*

κωφόν—Blind, as well as dumb. Luke i. 20; Matt. xii. 22. The demon had closed these avenues by means of a delusion. Christ restores the right balance. *Olshausen.* Devil was dumb but the man spake. *Ryle.* The miracle identical with Matt. xii. 22. *Neander, Tischendorf.* "I leave the difficulty where I find it. The authority of the record remains, however it may be settled." *Alford.* Located out of its historical connection. *Robinson, Andrews.* This portion of St. Luke's narrative (v. 14-26) affords a striking instance of the manner employed in his gospel by the Holy Spirit, of grouping incidents and sayings together according to their *spiritual connexion.* Incidentally also this mode of writing supplies a silent proof, not only of Luke's *posteriority* to Matt. and Mark, but also of the divine origin of the Gospels. Time and place are needful for *man.* And the Holy Spirit, by Matt., and Mark had fixed the time and place of those incidents. (See Matt. xii. 23-37. Mark iii. 22-30.) He now deals with them by Luke according to their *inner* relation to each other. *Wordsworth.*

---

15. *But some of them said, He casteth out devils through Beelzebub the chief of the devils.*

Some. These Pharisees had been challenged. Matt. xii. 23.
They saw Christ would annihilate their influence.
Hence the blasphemy they breathed into the people.
Casteth out. A humane act, foolishly imputed to Satan.
Their charge is yet involuntary testimony to the truth of His miracles.
They knew the primeval promise, of a *long conflict.* Gen. iii. 15.
By this master stroke, they intended to blight the Saviour's fame.
As though the cast out demons, had fully *possessed* their own souls.
No *miracle* is great enough to conquer unbelief.
Miracles may make men wonder, but it is only the Spirit of God that can make men believe.
Wicked men often mistake God's works for the devil's.
Beelzebub. Gr. *Beelzebub.* "*Lord of the flies,*" an idol deity of the Ekronites.
His favor sought as a protection from the torment of gnats and flies.
Supreme male divinity of tho Canaanitish nations.
Moabites and Midianites worshipped him. Num. xxii. 41.
Ahab and Jezebel introduced the worship of this god into Israel.

Temples mentioned. 1. Kings, xvi. 32. Altars. Jer. xi. 13. Hills and houses. Jer xxxii. 29.

In their robes priests offered incense. Jer. vii. 9. Human victims. Jer. xix. 5.

Chief. "The prince of the power of the air." Eph. ii. 2. Prince of demons. Eph. vi. 11-12.

They ascribed to an *obscene devil*, the Divine power of Jesus.

It was in the highest degree INSULTING to Jehovah, to identify Him with evil spirits.

Thus they madly flung themselves *against* the eternal God, reckless of the denunciation, "Woe unto him who striveth with his Maker."

Ascribing God's work to wicked conspiracy with Satan—the highest blasphemy.

In the refutation, we discern the Divinity of Christ.

The Jews accused Christ of two opposite offences.

1. Making Himself "the Son of God."

2. Casting out devils by the aid of the devil.

The Saviour repudiates the one charge, but not the other.

Thereby claiming His right to the Sonship of God: therefore Divine.

Observe: The Jews said Christ was the Son of the devil.

The devils said Christ was the Son of God. Mark iii. 11.

Christ would not suffer the evil spirit to bear testimony to Him.

He would not receive even the word of truth from so polluted a source.

The Divinity of our Lord proved by His own deeds and not by the words of demons.

The evil spirits, as celestial beings, had seen Christ as God.

As fallen angels they beheld Christ as man.

The disciples by faith beheld Jesus as both God and man, in one Christ.

To accuse Jesus of casting out devils by the aid of the devil was an act of wickedness prompted by the devil.

And proves that the devil had no fellowship with Christ.

And he that thus accuses hath fellowship with the devil.

Jesus opposed all tradition. Jews made it the sum of religion.

Devils. Because demons confessed Him, He was said to be in compact with them.

Ἐν *in*, not *by*, as E. V. *Beelzebub*—βεελζεβοὺλ—*god of the dunghill.*—Hebrew. Preferred. *Tischendorf, Alford. Lightfoot.* Four Baals—1. Phenician. 2. Baal-Berith. 3. Peor. 4. Zebul. Dominus Stercoris. Achor a tutelar god of the Cyrenians was lord of flies. *Lightfoot.* The prince of devils was called *Asmodeus.* ἄρχοντι—leading Athenian magistrate. Elder of Sanhedrim. Here prince of the abyss of Hades. *Stier.* Of all the heathen deities, the Jews, in the time of the Redeemer, regarded Beelzebub with the most intense abhorrence and contempt. By the term, chief of the devils, they meant to give expression to their hatred, and to imply that our Lord was so much under the influence of evil that he cast out demons by the aid of the most contemptible of all demons.

---

16. *And others, tempting* him, *sought of him a sign from heaven.*

Tempting. Envious of Christ's glory increasing, and their influence decreasing.

Sign. One *from heaven*, distinct from our Lord's *miracles.*

Unbelief strangely flutters, when at a loss for an excuse.

They challenged Him to equal the wonders of the Pentateuch.

The Lord righteously refused, knowing their caviling spirit.

Those resolved to neglect *present* duty, seek any excuse.

A craving for miracles, as evidences of truth, sign of an unregenerate spirit.

He *had* wrought miracles, but they now demand something *from heaven*, in which *God* will be *visible. Calvin.*

σημεῖον. Supernatural token, by which the power of God is manifested.

---

17. *But he, knowing their thoughts, said unto them, Every kingdom divided against itself is brought to desolation; and a house* divided *against a house falleth.*

Knowing. Christ answered not to the words uttered, but to the thoughts cherished.

Proving that "to Him all hearts are open, and from Him no secrets are hid."

His hearers, conscious of His omniscience, are *ashamed* to speak.

Kingdom. Idea of a self-inclosed, firmly compacted *unity.*

Satan's power fearfully well arranged, but conquerable.

Styled "king," but a deposed *usurper*, still *in arms.*

Strife, discord, and anarchy, the elements of his empire.

A *falling, divided* Babel. Sinner wars with sinner.

In the back ground, Satan maintains an *inexplicable harmony*, when he moves *against* Christ.

All wicked beings, become *instruments* in his hands.

Throughout, is seen the plan of one *will*, one *central power*.

There is power in ruins. His throne is *fiercely upheld*. Rev. ii. 13. Eph. vi. 12.

Divided. Can such folly be imputed to one, so crafty?

It implies three *contradictions*, whick he is *too wise* to adopt.

1. That he will at once *extend*, and *crush* his own power.

2. That the means he employs will *build up*, and *pull down*.

3. That he desires to *do good*, and to *do evil* at the same time.

A suicidal policy, never pursued by one, so cunning and selfish.

No "house" destroys itself, until *infatuated*.

Satan resists not himself, nor hurts his servants, but rather strengthens his kingdom. *Chrysostom*.

Errors in conduct lead to errors in creed.

So also, an erring creed tends to produce a persecuting spirit.

Satan stupefies the sinner by the love of sin, or lulls him into a false security.

Thus men unaided are unwilling, and unable to contend against their spiritual foe.

Nevertheless, it is a *moral* and not a *physical* inability.

The inability being *moral* increases the demerit of the transgressor.

By the consent of the transgressor's own will, the gifts of God are subjugated to Satan.

1. The understanding. 2. The will. 3. The affections.

4. The memory. 5. The conscience, under the influence of the "strong man armed."

All men by temptation come under the dominion of this hostile power.

But by Christ, the taker of captives is now led captive, and Satan is a conquered foe.

"*House*,"—that is, *family*. "*Against a house*,"—that is, *a house divided against itself falleth. Bengel, Alford. And house falleth against house. Meyer's* rendering.

---

18. *If Satan also be divided against himself, how shall his kingdom stand? because ye say that I cast out devils through Beelzebub.*

19. *And if I by Beelzebub cast out devils, by whom do your sons cast* them *out? therefore shall they be your judges.*

20. *But if I with the finger of God cast out devils, no doubt the kingdom of God is come upon you.*

If Satan. Our Lord takes their own stand point.

Herod and Pilate combined to crush the Redeemer.

" Though *hand join in hand*, the wicked shall not go unpunished." Prov. xi. 21. Ps. ii. 2.

Your sons. Some understand these words of the Lord's apostles, Jews according to the flesh.

Pharisees *believed* their sons actually cast out demons.

Your own sons' attempts convict you of malignity, and of inconsistency.

If they cast out devils by the power of God, Why not in my case attribute the work to the same cause ?

Sin debases the judgment as well as hardens the conscience.

Children, often their parents' judges in this world. 1. Sam. xix. 5.

Finger. Divine power manifested, but hardly perceived.

Matt. has *Spirit, i.e.*, Spirit of God, indicating the meaning of the phrase *finger of God.*

Only the finger of God can expel Satan from the heart.

Kingdom. They knew the Messiah would work these wonders.

For centuries their King had been expected by them. Matt. ii. 6.

Herein He shows His own Kingdom to be *undivided* and *everlasting.*

Come upon you. If I as a man cast out devils by the Spirit of God, human nature is enriched by me, and the Kingdom of God is come. *Cyril.*

Or He means: The Kingdom of God is *against you*, not *for you*, for dreadful is the *coming of His Kingdom* to unbelievers. *Bost.*

The Devil—a real existence—a Person.

1. He speaks. 2. He reigns. 3. He tempts. 4. He lies. 5. He murders.

In Greek—a calumniator. In Hebrew—an adversary.

The Scriptures reveal him as the enemy of man.

The enemy of God—of holiness, and of happiness.

They make known—1. His nature. 2. His character. 3. His work. 4. His agencies. 5. His plans. 6. His treachery. 7. His malice. 8. His devices. 9. His success. 10. His destiny.

He is the god of the world. The prince of darkness. The ruler of the disobedient. The federal head of fallen spirits, and the moving power of men revelling in sin.

This enemy has studied the human mind in all its varieties.

His assaults have continued for nearly 6000 years.

He has prostrated the entire race of man under his despotic sway.

Deceiving others, but not deceived; yet often defeated.

He facilitates declension, and impedes amendment.

1. His attacks on worldly men are by deception and seduction.
2. His attacks on godly men are by counteraction.
3. His attacks on the church of God are by imitation and substitution.

The voice though it be the voice of Jacob, yet the hands are the hands of Esau.

Only in destroying can he find ease. *Milton.*

He it is that maketh it to his followers—an awful thing to die.

For after death cometh the judgment.

In his dominion, truth is wisdom learned too late.

In Satan's kingdom there are no infidels, and in his gloomy abode "the perpetuity of woe increases woe."

All men have fellowship with the Father and the Son, or with Satan and apostate spirits.

To deny the existence of the Devil, is a thought suggested by the Devil.

He may tempt, but he cannot constrain. He cannot force the will.

Serve God with an undivided heart, and Satan is compelled to flee from you.

ὁ σατανᾶς—The objective reality of the N. T. Satanology receives the strongest proof from this discourse. *Oosterzee.* The reality of ἐκβάλλουσι seems to be as unquestioned as Christ's ἐκβαλλ. *Alford, Stier, Oosterzee, D. Brown.* A concession built on a supposition. *Neander.* Demons were exorcised after the Apostles' time. *Irenaeus, Tertullian, Origen.* *Damascius* relates that *Theosebius*, a pagan philosopher, exorcised a demon. *Jortin, Beausobre.* Charms used, which came down from Solomon. *Josephus.* Jews only *attempted* exorcism. *Alexander.* υἱοὶ—Disciples of Pharisees. *Lange, Bengel, Schleiermacher.* Christ's disciples. *Gerlach, Chrysostom, Jewel.*

δακτύλῳ—*Arm*, *Hand*, and *Finger* of God express varied *degrees* of strength. Psa. viii. 3; Isa. lix. 1-2. ἔφθασεν—stronger than ἤγγικεν—*has broken unexpectedly upon you.* There might have been *solemn irony*—"That in spite of their murmuring, the Old Promised Conqueror might have come, after all their unwillingness." *Stier.*

---

21. *When a strong man armed keepeth his palace, his goods are in peace:*

Strong man. Gr. *strong one*, "*man*" is not in the original.

Satan, Abaddon, the Dragon, the old Serpent, the Devil. Rev. ix. 11.

He was one of "the angels who excel in strength." Psa. ciii. 20.

Armed, with "power," "wiles," "fiery darts," "depths."

He arms men with unbelief, impenitence, prejudice, pride, &c.

Keepeth. The palace scarcely needs a guard in times of *declension.*
Drowned in lust, pleasure, secular or scientific pursuits.
Cravings of the soul for peace, systematically quenched. 2. Thes. ii. 11.
Palace. This present world; up to our Lord's coming he enjoyed supreme power.
Or the individual soul fortified against the truth of God.
Goods. Powers of the soul, affections of the heart, the *entire* man.
Peace. They flatter themselves "Soul, take thine ease." Luke xii. 19.
They say "*Peace*, peace, when there is no peace." Jer. vi. 14.
"I will have peace, though I add drunkenness to thirst." Deut. xxix. 19.
His peace is *bondage.* He bound a daughter of Abraham. Luke xiii. 16.
Christ's service is perfect freedom.
It is better to be God's servant, than to be our own master.
For *four thousand years*, Satan kept the palace of the world.
"He shall divide the spoil with the strong." Isa. liii. 12. Evident allusion to Satan.
The *person*, *equipment*, *guardianship*, *goods*, are in peace.

ὅταν—whenever. αὐλήν—*hall*, Lat. *aula*, palace. *Olshausen.* Court. *Meyer, Brown.* *Courtyard*,—word used eight times in the history of the crucifixion, when our Lord encountered Satan in the αὐλὴ of the High Priest, *Wordsworth.*

---

22. *But when a stronger than he shall come upon him, and overcome him, he taketh from him all his armour wherein he trusted, and divideth his spoils.*

When. Whenever the devil is driven out, then the Kingdom begins.
Stronger. *The* stronger, stronger than all, glorious name of *Jesus.*
Now its *real*, always the *rightful* owner of the soul.
Speak of *strength*, Jesus is *Almighty.* Isa. liii. 12.
John calls our Lord "THE MIGHTIER ONE." The Gr. is the same. Mark i. 7.
Shall come. Unexpectedly, sublime expression of the approach and deadly encounter.
Clearly expressing the Redeemers's approach to save.
The world, especially the unrenewed heart, Satan's palace.
Overcome. Matt. bind: Satan's energies were crippled.
He is partially disarmed of his aids and allies.

One individual rescued, predicts the Church's universal triumph.

Taketh. Breaks chains, opens eyes, and humbles the heart.

Affections exalted, desires purified, veil removed.

Robbed of his captives, Magdalene, Zaccheus, and others.

Christ, by His death and ascension, "led captivity captive." Psa. lxviii. 18.

He still rescues myriads of victims, and will, until he binds him. Rev. xx. 1.

The Holy Spirit dispossesses the usurper and restores the heart to God.

Satan is constrained to surrender the palace he can no longer keep.

Christ appropriates to His service, the armour in which Satan trusted.

The time, the talents, the knowledge, the wealth, and the influence devoted to selfishness, to pleasure, and to pride are now consecrated to the Deliverer.

There is a change of service, as well as a change of masters.

Man's heart once the abode of Satan becomes the habitation of God.

Men cannot be sure that God reigns in the heart until it is seen that "the lust of the flesh, the lust of the eyes, and the pride of life" are cast out.

Then the usurper is rejected and the man becomes the faithful soldier of the true King.

Armor. Gr. *panoply.* Ignorance, superstition, the law, sin, death and hell. 2. Cor. x. 4.

Trusted. How deep the *mysterious dismay* here revealed!

The victory of Christ all the more glorious from Satan having advanced so confidently for many ages.

Woe! unto them who trust in Egypt and stay on horses, &c. Isa. xxxi. 1.

Divideth. Our Lord re-enters the soul, and it becomes a purified palace.

A palace freed from the usurped dominion of Satan.

"If the Son make you free, ye shall be free indeed." John viii. 36.

In vain will the house be swept and garnished, if it be not occupied by a Divine Master.

The strong man armed.—His palace, spoils, false peace.

The stronger than he.—His courageous attack, His complete victory, His dazzling crown.

Spoils. Endowments of mind and body, *stolen* at the *Fall.*

Discriminate between Satan's *retiring*, and being *expelled.*

At times, his forces *retreat*, by way of a *feint.*

Christ gives him a total and final rout.

Energy of terms, paints the rapid conquest of the Victor.

πανοπλίαν αὐτοῦ—contrasts with πανοπλία τοῦ Θεοῦ—Eph. vi. 11. σκῦλα—Luke vii. 6. Spoils; with these, *i.e.* their *capacities*, he is *clothed*, *armed*, which he *brightens* for use. *Trench.* Homeric goods made of spoils. Satan's arts are turned against himself, as captured weapons against the enemy. *Reynolds.* The gold of Egypt was formed into vessels for the use of the Sanctuary. The spoils of the Egyptians enriched the Tabernacle. διαδίδωσιν—*distribution of spoils* which regularly followed conquest. *Wetstein.*

---

23. *He that is not with me is against me; and he that gathereth not with me scattereth.*

With me. Fellowship of the heart, *spiritual life.* John xv. 5.
Indifference to sin is sin. Neutrality is hostility.
He that said "Cease to do evil," said also "Learn to do well."
He who has commanded us to love the Lord our God, has also told us to love Him—
1. With all our heart. 2. With all our mind. 3. With all our soul. 4. With all our strength.
To serve God with an undivided heart, is to serve Him acceptably.
Neutrality here, no neutrality; but a siding with the enemy.
It embraces indifferent spectators, careless listeners.
By nature, every man is at heart, against God. Rom. viii. 7.
Man's heart was God's by creation and right of ownership.
It became Satan's by craft and usurpation.
Gamaliel would be neutral, and not fight—Jehovah, Acts v. 39.
In the great contest, neutrals are the worst enemies.
To dissent from the blasphemy of the Pharisees, was not enough.
The happy medium between friendship and enmity, impracticable.
The *urgency* of the Lord's demands, proves *intense* opposition.
Indirect testimony to the matchless dignity of His person and work.
Indifference was but a mere *mask* for enmity.
The Lord prefers *open* enemies, to *pretended* friends.
He who tries to begin neutral, often ends by open opposition.
Enmity to Christ shows—1. Ingratitude. 2. Betrays folly. 3. Prepares for perdition.
Against me. A *judicial sentence* reaching into eternity.
Denying our enmity to religion, no proof of neutrality.
The *feeblest promptings* towards Christ, may not be scattering.
Having no *relish* for His service, betrays an enemy.
All in religion, apart from Christ, will come to nothing.
Having no love for Jesus, involves actual hostility.

Gathereth. A figure derived from the *harvest* field.
He who is *with* Christ, must also *gather* with him.
To add names to this, or to that *sect*, is no gathering.
Satan through *nominal churches*, is *gathering* his spoils.
Once the furniture of the house of sin, now vessels of honor.
Fruit gathered, and sheep brought by the Great Shepherd into one *fold*, one *fellowship* of conflict and victory.
"He gathers the children of God scattered abroad." John xi. 52.
The watering, tending, serving, for the great harvest.
True hearts cannot but gather: light will shine.
His anointing will give forth a savor of life. 2. Cor. ii. 16.
Roman emperors' titles were—"ALWAYS EXTENDER OF THE KINGDOM."
Christ will have no drones, none but laborers.
Scattereth. Refusing to take arms for Christ, is to be *on Satan's roll.*
1. He who does not believe in Me, speaks against Me.
2. He who does not walk with Me, resists Me.
3. He who does not work with Me, works against Me.
4. He who does not fight with Me, betrays Me.
Gleaners labor in vain, unless they follow in the wake of the reaper.
Separation begins, wherever the Gospel comes.
The unfruitful tree, an *offence*, a cumberer of the ground.
A warning, "They shall be as the *chaff* of the threshing floor."
The suppression of Christ's praise, a virtual *denial.* Luke xix. 40.
A Pastor, not gathering for Christ, is *scattering.*
Standing at the door, refusing to enter, as a *workman.*
Proud laborers, with *selfish* friendship and activity.
Jehu builds up the Church, to build up his throne.
Selfishness brings Babel's confusion into Zion. 2. Peter ii. 3.
Christ knows of no man, who is neither to be rewarded as a friend, nor punished as an enemy.
From the throne of God, to deepest hell, there is not a moral being who is not either a friend or an enemy of Christ.
In one or other of these lights, every man will stand at the day of judgment.
Mere indifference to Christ, is positive evil, and will be punished as such.
No neutrality in Christ's service.
The human race is divided into two classes.
Governed and guided by antagonistical powers.
Both representative Beings.
The one the Source of all Goodness.

The other the Source of all Evil.

Jesus Christ, the Great Captain of Salvation, rules over one class.

Satan, the prince of the power of the air, controls the other.

The name of the one Leader, or Federal Head, is indicative of 1. Freedom. 2. Forgiveness. 3. Knowledge. 4. Holiness. 5. Happiness. 6. Light. 7. Life.

The name of the other Leader indicates.—1. Evil. 2. Bondage. 3. Guilt. 4. Condemnation. 5. Ignorance. 6. Impurity. 7. Misery. 8. Darkness. 9. Despair. 10. Endless woe.

The one elevates the thoughts to glory in the highest.

The other debases the thoughts to the bottomless abyss.

There is a way that seemeth right, but the end thereof is death.

The path that Christ has trod, leads to life.

Ὁ μὴ—Satan. *Chrysostom.* συνάγων—an allusion to amassing money. *Kuinoel.* The *forking of hay or corn* together. *Bloomfield.* μετ' ἐμοῦ—No man could have *assisted* our Lord. *Bengel.* This text cannot apply to any *particular Church.* "He who is not *with you*, is against *Me*" our Saviour will not affirm, of any visible organisation on earth. This is "*Extra ecclesiam, nulla salus,*" a doctrine of bigots. *Stier.* The moment the Gospel is published, the *separation* begins. *Scattereth*, Jewish exorcists. *Schleiermacher, Neander.*

---

24. *When the unclean spirit is gone out of a man, he walketh through dry places, seeking rest: and finding none, he saith, I will return unto my house whence I came out.*

He patiently refutes, kindly warns, sharply rebukes, now *retorts.*

Mankind Satan's house, now it is *Israel* collectively.

Israel under blind leaders, was the great demoniac.

Idolatry, an unclean spirit, left them at Babylon.

Pharisaism, a sevenfold worse spirit, took its place.

Unclean. Luke iv. 33. Polluted and polluting all they touched.

First parable shews the enemy's *strength*, the second his *uncleanness.*

Gone out. In no case can a soul thus vacated be thought *regenerate.*

A convert's heart is *lost* to Satan, but the avenues, he knows still.

This seldom occurs in periods of religious indifference.

Gone out at leisure and voluntarily, not cast out. Satan feels *sure* of his prey.

The heart of the unconverted man is the devil's palace.

In this palace he dwells, and in this palace he rules.

The deliverance of the palace, is Christ's victory over the devil.
This victory is the rescue of the heart from Satan, and the conversion of the soul to God,
As only the power of God is superior to Satan's strength.
In vain he contends against his spiritual enemy who contends in his own strength.
By Christ's Divine strength, Satan was conquered.
This strength is the strength imparted to all who contend aright.
And the language of assurance precedes the Christian's triumph.
" Greater is He that is for us, than He that is against us.
" Our weakness is made perfect by His strength."
" And we are more than conquerors through Him that loved us."
There is no real exchange of masters or service.

A man. That is, an unbelieving generation of blaspheming Pharisees.

Dry places. Gr. *places without water*. Isa. xiii. 21.
Some mysterious fact lies at the foundation of the assertion.
Veil of the invisible world here trembles, as about to part.
He is *restless*. Believers have rest, and quietness. Isa. xxx. 15.
" The wicked like the troubled sea, cannot rest." Isa. lvii. 20, xlviii. 22.
Evil beings " go to and fro in the earth, walking," &c. Job. ii. 2.
Dwellers at Babylon's ruins, believe demons now reign there. Isa. xiii. 21.
"Babylon, habitation of demons and foul spirits." Rev. xviii. 2.

Rest. Not another victim, or the pleasure of a new possession.
Where can devils find *rest*—which alone is found in God?

Seeking. Where can the wicked soul find lasting repose?
A terrible word. The unwearied craving of the wicked to do mischief.
Causing misery, the only element of sad repose.

Will return. A soul away from Divine protection, *open* to demons.

My house. How impudently he speaks of it, as always *his own*.
He knows the *secret avenues* to the soul's strongholds.
He had left the heart. but *owned* it still—" MY HOUSE."

ἐξέλθῃ—The victim seems to have been actually *reformed*, and the demon to have been *expelled*. *Stier*. Mere *appearance*. *Neander*. ἀνύδρων—without water, *uncultivated*. It was not the desire of doing mischief, but to avoid mankind reminding him of lost blessings, and thus renew his anguish. *Foote*. Spiritual desolation of Heathenism. *Whitby*. οἶκόν μου—the demoniac temporarily abandoned. *Alexander*. *Desert*.—Demons chose such resorts. *Tobit* viii. 3. The ruins of Babylon. Rev. xviii. 2. Neither superstition, nor poetic embellishment. *Alexander*.

25. *And when he cometh, he findeth it swept and garnished;*

Comĕth. Pictures the energy of a fallen spirit, ruining our race.
He reconnoitres—Demons limited in their knowledge.
Swept. Matt. *empty*, hypocritical *conceit*, void of truth.
Unwashed. "If I wash thee not, thou hast, &c." John xiii. 8.
Attrition not contrition. Reformation but not renovation.
The besetting sin is untouched. The heart never given to Christ.
The mind of the man uninfluenced by indwelling of the Holy Spirit.
Therefore; The form of godliness without the power—
1, a forced confession like Pharaoh's. 2, a feigned repentance like Ahab's.
3, a partial reformation like Herod's.
Garnished. Assumed devotions are garnishings of the evil heart.
The good works of which hypocrites boast.
Balaam, Saul, Simon Magus, awhile *respectful.*
The enemy loves high, and privileged persons.

26. *Then goeth he, and taketh* to him *seven other spirits more wicked than himself; and they enter in, and dwell there: and the last state of that man is worse than the first.*

Then. Having reconnoitred, and found the avenues all open.
Seven. No indefinite plurality. A complete occupation. Luke viii. 2. See Notes.
Enter in. Re-entrance upon the scarcely forsaken path of sin.
"Better not to have known the way of righteousness." 2. Pet. ii. 21.
Expelled, he lies in wait still to *deceive*, if not *ruin.*
Believers safe only because the Almighty guards them. John xix. 29.
Enter. No resistance now, no rival to dispute the ground.
The devil was out, but Christ was not in.
Although the house of our conscience be made clear Satan can again enter, and again assume authority as the ruling power.
If we cease to watch Satan, Satan never ceases to watch us.
He who prays for power to contend, must *watch*, as well as *pray.*
To *watch* without *praying* is presumption.
To *pray* without *watching* is neglect of duty and leads to danger.
Strikingly parallel runs the history of the Christian Church.
What the effect of the captivity to the Jews, the Reformation was to Christendom.
The first evil spirit had been cast out, but by worldliness and rationalism, the house has become emptv, swept and garnished.

Swept and garnished by the decencies of civilization, and discoveries of secular knowledge.
But empty of living and earnest faith.
These improvements are preparing for the final development of the man of sin.
Another important fulfilment of this parable may be found in the history of individuals.
By religious education or impression, the evil spirit has been cast out of a man.
But often the *religious* lives of men expend themselves in sweeping and garnishing with hypocrisy, or mere formality.
Till utter emptiness of real spirituality and faith prepares for final ruin. *Alford.*
Dwell. Never more to go forth or be put out.
God gives such over to a reprobate mind. Rom. i. 28.
Habits, once abandoned, then resumed, are *inveterate.*
Last state. Backslider with his grace, loses his amiability.
The mask falling, the last features of his natural face are struck out.
Worse. Not more wicked, for one demon is as bad as another.
But more *numerous* and *energetic* in the work of ruining.
A relapse is often worse than the original malady.
Heathenish *idolatry*, the *first* possession of the Jews.
Their national *rejection* of the Messiah, was their *last.*
Their insane fanaticism, and ferocity, defied God and Rome.
The malignant spirit of rebellion is styled *unclean.*
Hypocrisy, cupidity, blindness, in rejecting all counsel.
Gives terrible *exactness* to the parable, in their downward progress.
Savage beasts, apparently tamed, fall back to their native ferocity.
So from the Ascension to Jerusalem's ruin, all self-control was laid aside.
In their final catastrophe, their fathers' sins and their own, filled their cup of vengeance.
Their blindness and ruin foreshadow the world's destruction.
In *our* superior *privileges* and *guilt* the handwriting on the wall may be seen.

For εἰσελθόντα, *enter in*, read ἐλθόντα, *come. Tischendorf, Alford.*

This parable applies with terrible exactness to the downward progress of the Jews, with partial interruptions, until the final catastrophe. Then their fanatical insanity, resembled demoniacal possession. *Alexander.*

27. *And it came to pass, as he spake these things, a certain woman of the company lifted up her voice, and said unto him, Blessed is the womb that bare thee, and the paps which thou hast sucked.*

Woman. Nameless, tradition makes her Mary's servant.

Company. Gr. *from among the multitude.*

Blessed. With true womanly feeling she envies the mother of such a teacher.

A *new heart*, a greater honor, than the *motherhood* of Christ.
The near relation of a mother, would have been of no service to Mary.
Had not Christ been formed in her heart, the hope of glory.
Contrast the Pharisee's scowl with Mary's emotions. Mark iii. 20.
Orientals invoke blessings on the parents of those they esteem.
Mary's happiness modified. At His *birth*, exposed in a *stable*.
She periled her Son's life and her *own*, by flying to Egypt.
At 12 years old she sought Him *sorrowing*.
A sword pierced her soul when *He* was crucified. Luke ii. 34.
Being risen, He ascended, and left her bereaved and mourning.
"A wise son maketh a glad father." &c. Joseph to Jacob. Prov. xv. 20.
Parents have a right to mourn, "Daughters of Jerusalem," &c. Luke xxiii. 28.
This touching incident is related by Luke alone.

Woman.—Tradition names her *Marcella*, servant of Mary and Martha. *Oosterzee.* Μακαρία—Epaminondas, the *Theban*, on conquering, said, "My chief pleasure is that my *parents* will hear of my victory." *Blessed*, &c.—We are prone to judge of persons by external privileges. We judge by outward acts, but God judges by the state of the heart.

---

28. *But he said, Yea rather, blessed are they that hear the word of God, and keep it.*

It is necessary for all the members of Christ's holy family.
1. To hear. 2. To believe. 3. To obey His hallowed word.

But. *Not so*, but *otherwise*. Her mistake is corrected.

He reproves her for not taking His words in their *true spirit*.
Her admiration for His humanity, was untimely.
He denies, the cause given, the true one of His mother's blessedness.
Her *faith and obedience alone*, rendered her blessed.
Her blessedness rested, as any other sinner's, on God's mercy.
It was not Christ in the womb, but Christ in the heart.
Spiritual relationship more to be prized than earthly ties.

Yea rather. Peculiar honour belonged to the Virgin as Christ's mother.

Far higher honour belonged to her as one of Christ's followers.

Blessed are they that hear. The woman had heard *wrongly*.

She forgot the *sermon* in word, in admiration of the *mother*.

He repudiates all praise; He calls it "*God's word*," not "*my* word."

He did not deny Mary's title, accorded her by the angel.

The mother of such a Teacher is pronounced blessed; but *blessed rather* are they who follow the Teacher.

She, whose paps He sucked, must not glory that she fed Him; but that He fed her, and gave her living waters to drink.

Keep. They who bear Christ in their heart, as His mother had borne Him in her womb. *Augustine.*

Obedience, *the test* and the *fruit* of rightly hearing the truth.

The law of God observed, not so much by *hearing* as by *doing*.

My mother *is so far* blessed, as she has heard and kept the *word*.

True believers more blessed than Christ's mother, *as such*.

The believer has a closer union with Christ than the mother of Jesus (as mother).

Christ was bone of her bone, and flesh of her flesh.

To His people, Christ is more; the union is closer.

For 1, Christ is found in their *souls*.

2, He dwells in their hearts by *faith*.

3, He is *in them*, the hope of glory.

The one is like the union of the parent and the child.

The other is like the union between Christ and His heavenly Father.

As such, Christ gives to His people a throne, a crown, and a kingdom.

Word. "My sheep hear my voice;" it worketh effectually in believers.

In *prophetic* view, he cuts the roots of all future Mariolatry.

Intruders, creeping into the Church, deified *Mary* instead of *Jesus*.

At the Reformation, the Church of God came out from idolaters.

Council of Trent anathematizes all, refusing Mary divine honor.

Repelling *truth*, they are a *Maranatha* unto themselves.

How utterly alien the spirit of Rome from this glorious saying of our Lord!

This **Blessedness** is, 1, of a higher character; 2, firmer foundation; 3, more enduring than any other.

Μενοῦνγε—*imo, vero, yes indeed, but*, or *yea rather*, Rom. ix. 20. The speaker was assured her blessedness might equal, or surpass Mary's, if she *excelled* Mary's *obedience*. *Stier.*

Father *Newman's* exposition, that our Lord, but still further exalts the honor of Mary, in that besides being His mother, she heard His word and kept it, shows the follies to which able men are abandoned, who once desert truth and simplicity. *Alford.*

---

29. ¶ *And when the people were gathered thick together, he began to say, This is an evil generation: they seek a sign; and there shall no sign be given it, but the sign of Jonas the prophet.*

Gathered. Gr. *crowding towards*; not desirous of instruction, but to see a *miracle.*

Evil. Men were intensely wicked, and under demons' power.

Adulterous. Matt. They professed themselves the true Church and spouse of God.

They had broken covenant, and treacherously departed.

He *sighed deeply*. Mark. At their *infidelity* and *doom.*

Idolatry was spiritual adultery. Jer. ix. 2. Mal. iii. 5.

Generation. The race of Jews then living. Ordinarily embraces 30 years.

Pharisees sought a sign to crown their own ambitious views.

Jesus in sovereign wisdom, refused the insolent demand.

Their obduracy of heart, had no right to more evidence.

"If any man will do (is *willing* to do) His Will, he shall know of the doctrine." John vii. 17.

Christianity as it is now *without*, far more inexplicable, than *with*, miracles.

Infidels are by far the most *credulous* of all mankind.

Seek. Gr. *demand*, they would *dictate* what their Maker should do.

Sign. To satisfy fastidious unbelief, captious scepticism.

The demand was *insolence*, the aspersion, *blasphemy*.

Craving after miracles rebuked by Christ, John iv. 48; and by Paul, 1. Cor. i. 22.

The origin of the desire is Satanic. Luke iv. 9-10.

Our Lord refers to signs in proof of His divinity.

"The works I do in My Father's name, bear witness." John x. 25.

"If I do not the works of My Father believe me not." John x. 37.

From Heaven. Mark. Similar to the manna, or deliverance from Roman power.

An indirect proof of the reality of miracles He had already wrought.

No sign. He had miracles for the *sick*, the *hungry*, and the *blind.*

But none for proud Pharisees or envious Scribes.

Jonas. Given in solemn prophetic warning, condemning while refusing.

Our Lord testifies to the truth of Jonah's history.

He could never compare Himself to a fabulous hero.

From Abraham down to Christ, they had had signs enough.

He continued to work wonders, until the last words were uttered on Calvary's mount.

Suspicious minds, generally demand *unreasonable* evidence.

There is an economy of power in all God's dealings.

Miracles are not employed when ordinary means are adequate.

Miraculous deeds are performed to create faith, but not to gratify idle curiosity.

Christ will work miracles to relieve the afflicted; to give the impress of Divine authority to His teaching; to confirm faith, but not to satisfy the unjust requirements of prejudice and unbelief.

The lessons addressed to the ear the Jews regarded not, but required lessons addressed to the eye; whereas they had both heard and seen.

Divine power had accompanied Divine teaching, and still unbelief prevailed.

Let us not desire more evidence than the Gospel affords, but grace to profit by the evidence afforded.

γενεὰ—Third person, implying contempt. *πονηρὰ*—Matt. xii. 39.—*Adultress, Alexander.* A spurious race degenerated from their fathers, Isa. lvii. 3, 4; John viii. 39. The multitude of youthful wives *divorced*, noted by the *present* Jerusalem Mission. *Nicolayson.* Demons took the place of idols, in the age of our Lord. *Theophylact.* *σημεῖον*—The preaching of Jesus. *Schleiermacher, Neander.* Attributing our Lord's miracles to *magic*, they desired a sign from *heaven. De Wette.*

Ἰωνᾶ τοῦ προφήτου, *the prophet*, omitted, *Tischendorf, Alford, Cod. Sinai.* The sign refers to the *resurrection. Lange, Meyer, Ellicott. Preaching. Neander.* Jonah's history a foreshadowing in the O. T. of the resurrection. 1. Jonah was cast in the sea, to save many lives.—Christ crucified for the salvation of believers. 2. Jonah received in the body of a great fish, he calls "the belly of hell."—Christ lay in the dark sepulchre. 3. Jonah comforted himself with the hope of deliverance.—Christ, "Thou wilt not leave my soul in hell," Psa. xvi. 10. 4. In due time Jonah was set free.—Christ was loosed from the pains of death. 5. Jonah was confined until the *third* day—so was our Lord. 6. After Jonah's resurrection, he preached to the Ninevites. For 40 days Christ "spake of the things pertaining to the Kingdom." Christ came without observation, "in the form of a servant." Solemn *irony*, viz.—Unless they will accept the case, &c. *Alexander.*

ἐπιζητεῖ—*ἐπὶ* not expressed in our version, simply *intensive. Gesenius.* Like *θέλομεν* of Matt., it combines the idea of *demanding.* The inquiring *authoritatively.* *αἰτέω*—ask with a *suppliant* spirit. *ἐρωτάω*—to *plead, pray*, or *ask* by supplication, 1. John v. 16. *Alexander, Trench.*

30. *For as Jonas was a sign unto the Ninevites, so shall also the Son of man be to this generation.*

31. *The queen of the south shall rise up in the judgment with the men of this generation, and condemn them: for she came from the utmost parts of the earth to hear the wisdom of Solomon; and, behold, a greater than Solomon is here.*

A sign. A thing brought openly to view, containing in itself the manifestation of something hidden.

The fact that Jonas was a sign here *first* revealed to the Church.

Jonah announced that after forty days Nineveh, if unreformed, would be destroyed.

So Jerusalem, after forty prophetical days (i.e. years), would be overthrown.

Thus Jonah was an emblem or sign to the Jewish nation.

Ninevites. Heathen, inferior in advantages, rank above Gospel despisers.

So. This word has the force of a promise, contemplating a distant period.

Son of Man. Luke v. 24. See Notes.

Queen of the South. Sheba. 1 Kings x. 1. Arabia, south: of the race of Shem, Gen. x. 28. Yemen or Arabia Felix.

She surpassed the Jews in *faith*, coming from far to learn.

This heathen queen came *uninvited*, sinners are *pressed*.

Solomon was wise, Christ had the treasures of God's wisdom.

Her journey long and *perilous; Jesus knocks at our door.*

She came on *uncertainties;* fame hath a flattering tongue.

Who was ever disappointed, asking *wisdom of God?* Jas. i. 5.

She came through *curiosity;* Christ's wisdom involves SALVATION.

She could only *hear* the words of Solomon; "Christ Jesus is of God made unto us WISDOM." 1 Cor. i. 30.

Rise up. Anciently, witnesses and criminals stood at the bar.

The guilt of impenitence is to be seen, 1, By contrast; 2, By the vastness of the mercy rejected.

Our Saviour's *endorsement* of the truth of the O. T. record.

Men travel years to gather the wisdom of earth.

Many despise the heavenly wisdom of Christ, which is at their door.

A year before, He announced this great sign. John ii. 19.

Now He meets His enemies with the same answer.

Greater. Gr. *There is more than Solomon here.* An evidence of our Lord's humanity and Divinity.

His wisdom higher in its origin, wider in extent, more beneficial in purpose than Solomon's.

Solomon. Heb. Peaceful. Son of David and Bathsheba, born 1033 B.C.
Crowned at 18 years of age, prayer for wisdom answered. 1. Kings iii. 9.
Wisest, richest, most honored, and, while faithful, the most fortunate of men.
His learning a proverb now in the East; his kingdom embraced Judæa, Syria to Euphrates, Nile, Palmyra, and Ezion-geber.
His temple, built by Hiram of Tyre, one of the seven wonders of the world.
Commerce with Babylon, Egypt, Tyre, Arabia, India.
He had 70,000 bearers of burdens, 80,000 hewers in the mountains.
3,300 overseers; he spake 3,000 proverbs, his songs 1,005.
Author of *Proverbs*, *Ecclesiastes*, and *Solomon's Song*. 1 Kings iv. 32-3.
Became proud, luxurious, and an open idolater.
Example corrupt, taxes oppressive; reigned 40 years.
Life a sermon—grandeur blended with weakness.

καθὼς γάρ.—When our Saviour formally institutes a comparison, we may know the type was *prepared*. The resemblance is not *arbitrary*. *Stier*. *Queen, &c.* of Sheba, district in Arabia Felix. Traditions make her name *Maqueda*. *Lange*. The king of Egypt, called the king of the South, Dan. xi. 5. πλεῖον—something more. The very act of refuting a Satanic accusation, causes Him to utter this most sublime expression of self-consciousness. *Oosterzee*.

---

32. *The men of Nineveh shall rise up in the judgment with this generation, and shall condemn it: for they repented at the preaching of Jonas; and, behold, a greater than Jonas is here.*

Condemn. Each renewed person condemns his unconverted neighbor.
Repented. Ninevites repented under warnings; Jews were hardened.
Jonah, a man of like passions with us; Jesus the eternal Son of God.
Jonah preached *one* short sermon; our Lord for *three years and a half.*
Jonah preached *wrath* and *ruin;* Jesus proclaimed *salvation.*
Jonah wrought no miracle; our Lord wrought many.
Those saved by twilight, shame those groping at noon-day.
Heathen, blindly striving after virtue, condemn us.
Sins are heightened, and guilt increased, in proportion to the means afforded to bring men to obedience.
Even the works of creation proclaim the wisdom, the power, and the goodness of an ever present God.

When He who sent Jonah to the Ninevites condescends to teach,
And He who is wiser than Solomon instructs mankind,
What must be the ultimate condition of the men who reject the Instructor and despise His teachings?
It is said of Cyprian, one of the Latin fathers of the third century, that he was led to embrace Christianity by reading the history of Jonah.
The mercy of God to a sinful people, and the forbearance of God to a sinful servant, were the means employed by the Holy Spirit to bring him to the mercy seat of God.
Greater. Gr. *more than Jonas;* a greater sign by far this generation shall reject.
A *sign*, greater in its *actuality*, its *significance*, and its *consequences.*

εἰς—The action implied in *μετενόησαν* was performed so as to *come up with, fully to answer*, or in accordance with.

---

33. *No man, when he hath lighted a candle, putteth it in a secret place, neither under a bushel, but on a candlestick, that they which come in may see the light.*

No man. To exhibit an object, to a man who will not regard it, is as profitless as to light a lamp and then conceal the light.
Christ did not light the candle of the Gospel in the world to be hidden, but that all who are willing to see it may see it.
So also a Christian's usefulness is designed for God's glory and for man's good, and therefore must not be hid.
Candle. Gr. *a lamp* fed by oil, Jews used no candles.
Greeks and Romans used lamps oft fed by *perfumed* oil.
Unbelief and blasphemy, put out spiritual light.
Jesus the true light was never *kindled*, and never shall be *put out.*
"I am the light of the world, he who followeth me," &c. John viii. 12.
Author of the light of *revelation, conscience, reason, grace.*
Church of God, owes all her light to Christ. Isa. lx. 1. Hab. ii. 14.
A holy *life* burns brightly and loftily, in this dark world.
The Church no secret institution, like heathen mysteries.
No policy, no ordinance, no false shame may obscure it.
God kindles and places light in the heavens, when He pleases.
What He has kindled on earth, let no man *dare* obscure.
Our indolence, fanaticism, ignorance, often darken it.
He had pronounced (Matt.) a solemn warning on the *saltless salt.*

Now He warns us against bearing a *dark lantern.*
Suspect one's religion, if he is content to go to heaven *alone.*

Secret place. Gr. *a crypt, a vault or cellar, a covered place.*

Bushel. Matt. v. 15. Then found in every house, a little larger than our peck.

Would ye have ME work miracles, and ye believe ME not?

Candlestick. Gr. *lamp stand*, wood, bronze, marble, silver.
Some had branches of delicate workmanship, of the richest design, hung by chains and elaborately ornamented.
They vary from twelve *inches*, to five *feet* in height.
Primitive stands were *reeds*, placed on the floor, to raise the light.
Small lamps were placed in sepulchres, supposed to cheer the departed.
Churches "*golden candlesticks*," graces purified. Rev. ii. 5.
They only hold forth the light, having none *inherent.*
Christian examples lighted for His use, who kindles them.
Ungodly men hate the light, and those holding it. John iii. 19.

οὐδεὶς—third person, like, *on dit.* Lighted for their *Author's use. Trench.* "Johannes lumen illuminatum, Christus lumen illuminans." *Augustine.* *Hypocrisy*, like a phosphoric light, *cold* and *dead.* The Pacific ocean on a stormy night, is seemingly on fire with this phosphoric flame. It seems as though—

"The lightnings there,
"Had spent their shafts, and left their fragments
"Glittering on the field."

λύχνος—φῶς classically, the light of the *sun*, Rev. xxii. 5. φέγγος—the light of the *moon*, Matt. xxiv. 29. φωστῆρες (luminaria) *heavenly lights*, Phil. ii. 15. λαμπάς—a *torch*, in the Par. Ten Virgins, *Stier.* At this time, in Judea, torches are fed with oil from a bottle. *Elphinstone's His.* λύχνος—*not* a candle (*candela* from *candels*, the white wax light, a taper,) but a hand *lamp.* The humble Romans used as candles, wicks of *rushes.* "*The smoking flax*" refers to a wick made of flax, *i.e.* He will not extinguish a flickering lamp, *i.e.* will cherish the feeblest beginnings of repentance. But lamps were used in towns.

---

34. *The light of the body is the eye: therefore when thine eye is single, thy whole body also is full of light; but when* thine eye *is evil, thy body also* is *full of darkness.*

Light. Gr. *candle* or *lamp;* it is the same word as used in the preceding verse.
A comparison between the *eye* and conscience.
Philosophy and theology have detected no *error* in our Lord's teaching.
The *lenses* of the eye, first and finest of optical instruments.

Light was made for the eye, and the eye for light. Eccl. xi. 7.

The eye. The out-shining, or manifestation of the soul of man.

The eye is to the body, what the lamp is to the chamber.

The thoughts, the words, and the actions of the man should be viewed by a divine light to judge correctly of the man.

A dial may be seen by artificial light, but it is only by light from heaven that it is seen practically and profitably.

If our leading principles be wrong—our actions will also, of necessity, be wrong.

It is a principle in philosophy that water cannot rise above its own level.

If the source from which the light flows be dim—no object can be more than dimly seen.

We sometimes read in the eye that which is not spoken, or indicated by action.

"The *spirit* of a man is the *candle* of the Lord, searching," &c. Prov. xx. 27.

Single. Gr. *simple*, not double; two sound eyes see but *one* object.

The *confusion* of double *seeing*, typifies a *dishonest* mind.

It were well some were *blind*, when sin enters the eye.

Eve's eye begat *lust* in her heart, but *darkness* in her soul.

Achan and Gehazi's eyes made them *traitors* to their God.

A *single* eye implies *simple* faith in God alone.

A *double* heart, or *divided soul*, a source of sorrow.

Full of light, Gr. simply *light*.

Eye evil. In the East diseases of the eye are painfully common.

In Egypt the proportion of *blind* exceeds any other nation.

All sin begins in the *heart*; thought, word, and deed, fruits of sin.

Lot's wife *travelled* rightly, but her heart *lingered*.

Hypocrites, boatman-like, look one way and row another.

Full of darkness. Translation too expressive. Gr. simply *dark*.

Inner light obscured, renders one's state hopeless.

It is dark within him, dark around him, dark before him.

ὀφθαλμος—The Creator had always been forming the lenses of the eye, on acromatic principles of the highest science. ἁπλοῦς—Lat. *simplex*, presenting a clearly defined image on the brain. *Stier*. διπλοῦς would be the antithesis of ἁπλοῦς sound. *Chrysostom*, *Campbell*. Without film, *Doddridge*. Clear, *Parkhurst*. Being the opposite of *single* must mean *double*, confused. *Alexander*. σκοτεινόν—*full of darkness*, means *total darkness*, which is the opposite effect of ἁπλοῦς. As φωτεινόν—lightful. *Tyndale*; lightsome. *Rheimish*; in the sunshine, so σκοτεινόν, *in the dark*. *Major*. Add σου after θαλμός *thine eye*; omit οὖν. *Tischendorf*, *Alford*, *Cod. Sinai*.

35. *Take heed therefore that the light which is in thee be not darkness.*

Take heed. Conscience, like the eye, needs careful protection.
Its nature is to reflect, not originate truth. John i. 9.
The Spirit's influences, by open or secret *sin*, are *obscured.* 1 Thess. v. 19.
Heaven's fire goeth out from want of *fuel*, or by *exposure.* 1 Thess. v. 19.
Conscience *seared*, passions darkened, leave the victim *blind.*
The light. Thought, reasoning, conscience, making us responsible.
One's own guide, dishonestly treated, becomes a traitor.
Be darkness. Gr. *is* darkness, more forcible than *be.* Much, held as sound religious truth, is pernicious error.
Human mind too *willingly* deceived as to its highest interests.
Eternity contracts to a span—life's span spreads into eternity.

φῶς—The better part of man's spiritual nature. *Alford.* μὴ followed by the indicative implies their light was darkness. *W. & W.*

---

36. *If thy whole body therefore* be *full of light, having no part dark, the whole shall be full of light, as when the bright shining of a candle doth give thee light.*

No part dark. The processes of the mind darkening, various.—
1. Plans, embracing *time*, and excluding *eternity.*
2. Persisting in *ignorance*, or infatuated by *conceit.* Prov. iii. 5.
3. "Spoiled through philosophy, after the tradition of men." Col. ii. 8.
4. Self-righteousness. The Laodiceans thought they were rich, and in need of nothing. Rev. iii. 17.
5. "Covetousness, which is idolatry." Col. iii. 5. A *parent* sin.
6. Loving darkness rather than light, because their deeds are evil. John iii. 19.

Envy, malice, uncharitableness, "Is thine eye evil?" &c. Matt. xx. 15.
The god of this world hath *blinded* their *minds.* 2. Cor. iv. 4.
"They who knew God, but glorified him not as God," &c. Rom. i. 21.
Give the Lord glory, lest you stumble on the *dark mountains.* Jer. xiii. 16.
Result, wandering *endlessly*, and perishing *eternally.*
Bright shining. Gr. *as a candle lighteneth thee with its brightness.*
The *celestial origin* of the light Christ gives the soul.
To do deeds of light, one's soul must be illumined.
Night, dawn, day—illustrate the soul being converted.
Soul illuminated amid bigotry, fanaticism, and ignorance.

Nicodemus among Pharisees, *Pascal* among Romanists.

Our Lord is speaking of His teaching, as apprehended by the simple, single-seeing soul.

If the soul have no part darkened by prejudice or selfish lusts, it shall be wholly illuminated by the doctrine of Christ.

The Pharisees sought a *sign from heaven*, but they sought with *evil intention*.

No sign therefore would the Lord give to *them*.

But signs enough in His miracles and doctrines were afforded those who *desired to see*.

Christ lighted the candle of His Gospel in the world, that all might *see it*.

But no one can see it, if he has an *evil eye*, as the Pharisees had.

If the intention is *holy*, the whole man is full of *light*.

If the intention is *evil*, the whole man is full of *darkness*.

Our mind is our *candle*, which shines only, when it has the *light of God*.

Take heed therefore, that what God intended for thy *light*, be not *darkness*.

Let no cloud of passion or prejudice darken the light of the spiritual eye.

If thy *inner man* be *light*, everything will be *full of light*, for all will be *illumined by the light of Christ*.

ὅλον φωτεινὸν—bracketed. *Doddridge*. λύχνος—Rheimish, *lamp*; often *lucerna fulgoris* of the Vul. ἀστραπῇ—*sprightly lustre*. It signifies a strong vivid flame, commonly applied to the lightning's flash. *Doddridge*; gleaming flash. *Olshausen*; by its flame. *Campbell*; *bright flame*. *Bloomfield*; its blaze. *Wakefield*.

---

87. ¶ *And as he spake, a certain Pharisee besought him to dine with him: and he went in, and sat down to meat.*

As He. Gr. *while speaking*, *interrupted* by the crafty Pharisee.

Probably spoken in the temple, the last week of His ministry.

It formed the solemn closing of His public teaching.

At the end, He departed to return no more.

Pharisee. (Luke v. 17; vi. 2.) Here is the key-note of this passage to the end of the chapter.

As usual, neither name nor place is given.

The Lord uses the occasion as one of exhortation and warning to the *Pharisees* generally.

This incident, like the former, peculiar to Luke's gospel,
The host seems to have been no friend of the Lord.
Besought. Invited through curiosity, or with a bad heart.
Maliciously, they watched, how He would act among His *enemies.*
Dine. Not the principal meal, but a noon day refreshment.
Jews, Greeks, and Romans, had but two meals a day.
In heroic ages the first at *sunrise*, the second at noon.
Their supper, their principal meal, about sun down, or later.
The first meal of the Jews may be called their breakfast, or their dinner because it was both; it was but a light meal.
Different classes dined at various hours, as among us.
Patriarchs at noon. Gen. xliii. 16. Had but one dish.
Milk, cheese, bread, fruit, rarely meat.
Knives, forks, spoons,—tables, were unknown.
Orientals gather food with fingers, or on a piece of bread.
Sat. Reclined, Jews borrowed Greek custom. Luke v. 29.
Our Lord converts meals for the body into banquets for the soul.

For ἠρώτα, *asked*, read ἐρωτᾶ, *asketh:* omit τις, *certain. Tischendorf, Alford, Cod. Sinai.*

ἀριστήσῃ—Lat. *prandium*, *take breakfast*, the morning meal, not *dine. Meyer, Alford.* Morning meal, taken between breakfast and dinner time. The legal hour on the Sabbath was *noon. Josephus.* With the Greeks it was a *lunch.* Breakfast at sunrise, (as it was in Homer's time) dinner at 11, and supper (their principal meal) at 5. The Romans ordinarily bathed at 2, and dined at 3. Peter's hour, in Palestine, was about 12 (the 6th hour, Acts x. 9). *Plutarch's* at noon. *Aristophanes* places the ἄριστον after attending court. *Lightfoot.* ἀνέπεσεν—Luke vii. 36; see Notes.

---

38. *And when the Pharisee saw* it, *he marvelled that he had not first washed before dinner.*

Saw it. That he had reclined without washing.
Marvelled. He had broken a superstitious tradition, observed by all.
The Saviour, in humility, complied with *harmless* customs. Phil. iv. 8.
Washed. There is no evidence He *usually* omitted the washing.
Outward purification, without inward purity, is vain.
Sympathy for the wicked, not social intercourse, defiles.
God's favour depends not on washing of hands.
Rabbis said, Moses received their traditions from God at Sinai.
Babylonian *Talmud*, composed A.D. 190; Comment. *Gemara*, A.D. 370.

Jerusalem Talmud, A.D. 220; Gemara, A.D. 500.

Our Lord knew the result, and *intentionally* refused.

Men ask.—What harm in merely washing one's hands?

Our Lord saw that *outward washing* was substituted for *inward holiness*, and chose the occasion to reprove the Pharisees.

Therefore He did *not* wash before dinner, that the Pharisee might wonder, and that He might teach the necessity of an *inward washing* of the soul.

Sanctioning their custom, as if of divine authority, would have *endorsed* other superstitions.

The Lord's repast embittered by the wickedness of men. Prov. xvii. 1.

The word here used is "baptised;" this use of the word shows that it did not, necessarily, mean immersion of the whole body, for it was the washing of the hands only which was here meant.

ἐθαύμασεν.—Because a Teacher, famous for his holiness, should presume to refuse, what all others did. Talmud declares "eating with unwashed hands, was, as the committing of adultery. A Jew, dwelling in *the land*, eating in clean vessels, reciting his phylacteries, cannot be finally lost." "The words of the *Scribes* are lovely, above those of the *Law!*" *Lightfoot.* ἐβαπτίσθη—Gr. *baptized*, immersion of *the body*, not involved as necessary, when one was ἐβαπτίσθη, for only the hands were washed before meat, *Alford.*

---

39. *And the Lord said unto him, Now do ye Pharisees make clean the outside of the cup and the platter; but your inward part is full of ravening and wickedness.*

He said. He never suspended His work out of compliment.

This discourse probably mainly spoken at table.

Now. Marking perhaps their degeneracy from the ancient law and better times.

Ye Pharisees. Who deal with *yourselves* as with your cups and platters.

As if He said, You who regard yourselves as better than your fathers, are worse than they.

Fearlessly He speaks now with cutting *severity*, again with *benignity*.

He *had* only expressed in *act* what their secret guiltiness had hinted.

Without a "Woe unto you" He rebukes their hypocrisy.

Petty externalities had pushed aside *essentials*.

He passes by the *drink* they *strained*, to the cleansing of the *dishes*.

Remarkable example of our Lord's way of illustrating the greatest truths by the commonest incidents.

He points to *conscious inward* uncleanness by sin.

Outside. Figurative of legal, external purifications.

A compromise between conscientious scruples and love of sin.

Some unscrupulous, both in little things and in great duties.

Hypocrisy, united with covetousness, is quite incorrigible.

They had elevated mere *decency* into *soul* religion.

Satisfied to eat the *fruit* of *fraud* out of *clean platters.*

Scandalous sins would spoil their reputation for sanctity.

Cup and platter. Under the metaphor of vessels human beings are represented.

The body answering to that which is without, and the soul to that which is within.

Meat and drink—daily tables furnished by oppression.

Heart-sins, though intensely hateful to God, they *regarded not.*

Inward. Corrupt *heart*, contrasted with the *outside* of cleansed cups.

In this He eyes the *persons* not the *vessels.*

Common place *decorum* yields to an infinitely higher duty.

The Pharisee must somehow have *expressed* his surprise.

Reigning *rapacity*, characterized their secret plans.

Wickedness. Reigning *malice* prompted their concealed desires.

Under forms of *humanity*, they concealed a *proud lust* of honor.

Sinful *getting*, and sinful *engaging* involved in the Greek words,

"Behold, Thou desireth truth in the *inward* parts." Psa. li. 6.

Therefore, the cleansing to be good must extend to the whole.

It is folly to attend only to the external observances of religion.

The soul of piety lies in the piety of the soul.

εἶπε—Spoken mainly in the temple. *Stier;* first in Galilee, afterwards at Jerusalem. *Bengel.* τὸ ἔξωθεν—being taken to denote the *body;* and τὸ ἔσωθεν the *mind*, bears, in its simplicity, the stamp of truth. *Bloomfield.* *Outside* and *inside* of the vessels. *Elsner.* Body and mind. *Rosenmuller, Euthymius.* The Evangelists group our Lord's sayings of earlier discourses into later ones. *Lange, Oosterzee, Olshausen.* νῦν can hardly intimate that this is a fragment of a long discourse. It has the force of *atqui*. *Bengel.* νῦν contrasts with an understood πάλαι. *Meyer.* Well, *i.e.* this must be expected; vero. *Beza;* indignation. *Raphel:* now. *Wetstein, Kuinoel.*

ὑμῖν instead of ὑμῶν would correspond to the Attic elegance of Luke. *Wakefield.* ἁρπαγῆς—evidently the root of *rapax* and rapacious. "*Ravening,*" from *raven*, Sax. *reafian*, to plunder. πονηρίας—Luke vi. 22. This divine roughness was entirely in its place. *Ebrard, Oosterzee.*

40. *Ye fools, did not he that made that which is without, make that which is within also?*

Ye fools. A term of reproof, not of reproach. Ye foolish men.
Supposing that God was as easily *deceived*, as their neighbors.
Or of separating that which, by nature, is inseparable.
They dreamed the *leprosy* of *their heart* was nothing, if the *body* was clean.
Christianity friendly to *bodily* cleanliness; heathen were filthy.
When God's works are soiled, *partial* cleansing avails not.
Maker of soul and body being *pure* demands *purity* in both.
Ye fools, did not He who made the outward man, i.e., the body, also make the inward man, i.e., the soul?
He that planted the ear, shall he not hear? Psa. xciv. 9.
"Man looketh on the outward appearance, but the Lord," &c. 1. Sam. xvi. 7.
He seeth *secret abominations* under the fairest robes. Ezek. viii. 9.
Since to Him belongs the outer life, is the inner man less His?

'Αφρονες—*Ye thoughtless creatures. Doddridge.* ποιήσας—translated by *purgare. Has he not cleansed?* &c., while ποιεῖν has this sense sometimes. *Stier.* Our Lord, denying that the Creator made the *unclean inner man*, is not found in the text. *Alford.* Adorning. *Kuinoel.* What is within the cup. *Wetstein.*

---

41. *But rather give alms of such things as ye have; and, behold, all things are clean unto you.*

Give alms. In place of coveting that which belongs to others, give liberally of that which is your own.
Thus evince a change of heart by a change of conduct.
Often, by a figure put for repentance, only the *fruit*.
Charity was selected as a generally neglected virtue.
The Jews erroneously thought to *purify* fraud and robbery by alms.
Restore to their owners that obtained by deceit.
Such amends will tend to show your repentance sincere.
Communicate to others, that God may bless what remains.
Job ate not his morsel alone, but shared with the fatherless. Job xxxi. 17.
Mosaic law enjoined gifts to Levites and strangers. Deut. xxvi. 12, &c.
Clean, among the Jews signified that which may be lawfully used.
Unto you. Live holily, and nothing *external* can stain your soul.
Our Lord never taught, that alms-giving was meritorious.

As they were, they polluted everything they touched. Only "to the *pure*," &c. Tit. i. 15.

"*Give alms*," &c. Some Commentators understand our Lord's words as ironical, as if He said, "*but ye give alms of their contents* (vessels), *and, behold, all things are clean* (in your estimation) *to you*." But our Lord never cast a slur on alms-giving. *Alford.*

τὰ ἐνόντα in proportion to your substance; corresponds to ὑπάρχοντα—Luke xii. 33, and θησαυροὺς οὐρανῷ. *Lightfoot, Erasmus, Kuinoel, Neander, Brown.* *What is within*, articles of food and drink *within* the vessels. *Bengel.* Rabbis taught that alms had a value which served for an *atonement*. *Lightfoot.* Rome teaches that rapine and injustice may be *purified* by alms. *Decrees of Trent.* Give according to your ability. *Euthymius, Coccejus, Hammond.* Give as freely as you have acted rapaciously. *Brown.* Give your *heart* first. *Ryle.* Rom. xii. 1; Psa. li. 17. *Owen.* Our Lord does not mean to say, that by giving alms purity is bestowed on food and drink. *Bengel.* Give what is *within* in alms: deal *that* out in acts of love to God and man, *Wordsworth.* To give alms is to shew mercy. If thou art wise begin with *thyself;* in judgment and love give alms to *thy soul*. *Augustine.*

ὑμῖν ἐστιν, *i.e.* vestro (perverso) judicio. This addition would have been superfluous, had he spoken of real purity. *Oosterzee.*

---

42. *But woe unto you, Pharisees! for ye tithe mint and rue and all manner of herbs, and pass over judgment and the love of God: these ought ye to have done, and not to leave the other undone.*

Woe! Not an outburst of *passion*, but of *deliberate condemnation.*
His righteous indignation shews His exalted greatness.
Ever gentle towards the penitent, but inexorably severe, to hypocrites.
Tithe. Moses commanded a *tenth* to be given. Num. xviii. 21.
The *usual tax* paid in Babylon and among Romans and Greeks.
Mint, rue, &c. Our Lord purposely names the most trifling products of the earth, as examples of what they punctiliously exacted the tenth.
Human additions, to the Divine statutes.
By perjury, encompassing the death of the Lamb of God.
Yet they greatly dreaded *defilement* in Pilate's hall. John xviii. 28.
All manner. Boundless charity without faith, is worthless. 1. Cor. xiii. 3.
Judgment. Of themselves, and of justice to their neighbors.
Love, and obedience were better than sacrifice. Isa. i. 11.
Reference to Micah vi. 6-8, whose third element of acceptable piety, "*walking humbly with God*," comprehends both *love and faith.*
Ought ye. He sacredly enjoins obedience to those in Moses' seat.
God's commands cannot be esteemed as trifles.

There is no duty so little as to be neglected, no command so small as not to be obeyed.
Hypocrites buy reputation with that which costs little.
Those loving a *cheap* gospel, *come short* of even the Pharisees.
Instead of abrogating, He enjoined little duties.
Proves His heavenly tranquillity, and impartiality.

ἀποδεκ.—tithes voluntary, not compulsory among Jews, *Lewes*, *Brown*.

It was a rule among the Jewish Doctors, that a man should single out one of the Commandments, and pay especial regard to it, that thereby he might make God his friend and atone for a defective obedience of the rest.

πᾶν λάχανον every (other) trifling herb, *Doddridge*. *Literally everything planted.* κρίσιν, ἀγάπην, ἐλεὸς and πίστις—Matt.

---

43. *Woe unto you, Pharisees! for ye love the uppermost seats in the synagogues, and greetings in the markets.*

Pharisees. Luke v. 17 and vi. 2. Their hypocrisy and *malignancy* deserved these woes.
Pharisaism, *outgrowth* of depravity, not an *accident* of Judaism.
His rebuke does not proscribe all distinctions of honor.
He forbade calling *one's self* Rabbi, yet made some Apostles. Eph. iv. 11.
Love. Where the *heart* is there will he seek his treasures. Matt. vi. 21.
Uppermost. Jesus *marked* how they chose out the chief places. Luke xiv. 7.
How *sad* such petty distinctions will appear in death.
Synagogue. Luke iv. 15. Professedly to worship God as *sinners*.
The house of prayer should witness our deep humility.
A strange place wherein to *contest* for earth's hollow honours.
To *idolize* one's self, and go to the house of God to *worship* it.
David would gladly at the threshold act as doorkeeper. Psa. lxxxiv. 10.
A religion that must *shine* in the Church is a deception.
Greetings. Luke x. 4. Orientals ever delight in compliments.
A profession of *flattery* ever speaks a *false* heart.
A parade of salutations ever avoided by truly humble souls.
The *vain* covet to be pointed out in the *crowd*.
In *solitude* these compliments would be but little valued.
Proud lust of honour a *mockery* of their *pretensions*.

ἀσπασμοὺς—salutations of the Oriental sometimes *profane*. "*Hail, thou incarnation of righteousness!*" Another—"The sun hath shone more brightly upon me, since I have looked upon thy nobility." Lodiana Pundit to *Dr. Newton*.

---

44. *Woe unto you, scribes and Pharisees, hypocrites! for ye are as graves which appear not, and the men that walk over* them *are not aware* of them.

Hypocrites, only deceive *men*, never their Maker. Luke vi. 42.
Graves. Matt. sepulchres, whitened, that men may avoid the polluting touch.
Orientals now whiten them through affection.
Here, concealed by long grass, men are defiled unknowingly.
Yearly, Moslems and French decorate the graves of friends.
Men are defiled by the concealed profligacy of hypocrites.
Graves! a new and terrible figure from Levitical uncleanness.
A *human heart* can be a *temple of God*, and a human heart can be a GRAVE!
Their *cold forms* of service covered the vilest treason to God!
Let men beware; he that toucheth *you*, toucheth *death*.
The contagion, like leprosy, defiled all who approached.
There is a degree of depravity, from which escape seems hopeless.

Scribes and Pharisees, hypocrites! These words are supposed to have been inserted by copyists from Matt. Omitted by *Tischendorf*, *Alford*, *&c.*, and by *Cod. Sinai.*

---

45. ¶ *Then answered one of the lawyers, and said unto him, Master, thus saying thou reproachest us also.*

Lawyer. Our modern idea differs entirely from that in the N. T.
Lawyers explained *traditions*, scribes *text* of the law.
The woe against Pharisees and Scribes, but a lawyer answers.
Reproachest. Gr. *insultest*, different from *justly reproving*.
Himself the repository of truth he thought his dignity trifled with.
They furnished the Pharisees with their theological ideas.
Daring acknowledgment of a smitten conscience.
Our Saviour convinces them that He penetrated their *hearts*.
A sad state of the mind! Jesus' words felt a *reproach*.
The *kindest reproof* felt as *reproaches* by unhumbled hearts.
The word of the Lord is a *reproach* to them. Jer. vi. 10.

This teacher, defending hypocrites, a *partaker* of their *sins*.
There is a sympathy between *formalists* and *hypocrites*.
Beware of men of *religious* pretensions *ridiculing* holy persons.
"I hate him, for he doth not prophesy good, but evil." 1 Kings xxii. 8.
The world hateth *Me*, because I testify that it is *evil*. John vii. 7.

Νομικῶν—traditionary doctors of the law. If a difference, the νομικοὶ had a school, but the γραμματεῖς none. *Lightfoot*. γραμματεῖς—public. νομικοί—private teachers. *Camerarius*. Those skilled in the law. *Kuinoel*. ὑβρίζεις—Thou dost *insult*. ὀνειδίζειν—to *reproach*. ὑβρίζειν—meanest treat with *insolence*? *Meyer*.

---

46. *And he said, Woe unto you also, ye lawyers! for ye lade men with burdens grievous to be borne, and ye yourselves touch not the burdens with one of your fingers.*

Woe! Flattering themselves they stood high with *God*.
Omniscience reveals *dross*, where men dream of *gold*.
Lade. Their sin was, thundering out "*Thou shalt, and thou shalt not.*"
Heartless proclamation of laws, they broke constantly in spirit.
They loved to show their power over slaves.
Burdens. They bound commandments thickly, without mercy.
They prescribed *trifles* to themselves, but *burdens* to others.
Rome's penances, fastings, flagellations, contritions, attritions, confessions, and pilgrimages, are similar burdens now.
Grievous. Jesus condemned the *rigor* of these interpreters.
Our Saviour bore the heaviest burden, to make it easy for His people.
Fingers. They would neither lighten, nor repeal them.
Dispensing rigors with both hands, they spared themselves.
There are now also many severe judges of sinners, yet weak combatants.
Burdensome imposers of laws, yet weak bearers of burdens.
Men who neither approach nor wish to approach strictness of life, although sternly requiring it from others. *Gregory*.
He rebuked their *remissness* of God's commands.
He condemns their *tenacity* concerning their own.
Christ's "Thou shalt hate father and mother," &c., was a *harder* law.
What He commands, in *mercy*, He enables to perform.
Namely, to love Him and His service even more than we love the best and kindest of our earthly kindred. "*To hate*" is a Hebraism often used to denote an inferior degree of affection.

"Give what Thou commandest, and command what Thou givest." *Augustine's* prayer. There is a shade in the original, not in the E. V. *καὶ ὑμῖν τοῖς νομικοῖς οὐαί—and to you, ye lawyers, woe!* The fearless boldness of the Saviour overawed the *hypocrites. Stier.* "*Fingers.*"—Note the gradation, touch, with a *finger;* raise, with a *hand;* place on the *shoulder. Bengel.* You absolve them from the *moral* law, but not a finger's weight of your own *traditions. Lightfoot.*

---

47. Woe unto you! for ye build the sepulchres of the prophets, and your fathers killed them.

Ye build. Ye profess profound regard for martyrs' memories.
They persuaded the people, they condemned their fathers' crimes.
Christ put another construction on these pretended honors.
Sepulchres. Oriental sepulchres are found hewn in the rocks. Isa. xxii. 16.
Ancients prepared their tomb among their first public acts. 2. Chr. xvi. 14. Job. iii. 14. Isa. xiv. 18. Matt. xxvii. 60.
Pyramids are tombs, among the 7 wonders of the world.
Tombs at Thebes cover acres in the mountain rock.
Hadrian's and the Appian way, are the glories of old Rome.
Catacombs of Rome of vast extent contain remains of early Christians.
Our Lord condemns no proper respect for the departed.
A rage for monuments over departed virtue, without imitating, a bad sign.
"What inscription is this?" asked Josiah, "The man of God," &c.
"Let him alone, let no man move his bones." 2. Kings xxiii. 18.
Epitaphs undeserved, mockeries of the *real* state of the dead.
Herod the Pharisee built a splendid sepulchre to David.
These sepulchre-builders could not deceive our Lord.
The mask of veneration for the *dead*, concealed hatred of the *living* prophet.
Some feel glad they have *only* to honour the memory of the dead.
These lawyers doubtless rejoiced they were not *alive* to rebuke them.
Arisen from the dead, those prophets would find these persecutors, fiercest.
They *crucified* the MAN who came in the *same spirit.*
Killed, their ancestors, slew God's heralds, and descendants build their tombs.
Men judge the heart by the deed, God the deed by the heart.
Your fathers killed them, and ye *hide* the murder in a grave.
They persecuted a living Prophet infinitely superior to those slain.
Rome *canonizes* dead saints and sends the living to the *Inquisition.*

Splendid churches cover the dead while she *anathematizes* the living.
We oft praise the pious dead yet follow not their godly teachings.

48. *Truly ye bear witness that ye allow the deeds of your fathers: for they indeed killed them, and ye build their sepulchres.*

Truly. Gr. *therefore* or *consequently*. Our Lord *translates* their deeds.
Bear witness. In fact, honor the *murderers* rather than their *victims*.
Their treatment of John and the Redeemer proves it.
When the vile praise the virtuous it is the kiss of the traitor.
Blessing a friend with a loud voice counted a *curse*. Prov. xxvii. 14.
Sepulchres. Solon made laws against Greek extravagance to the dead.
Athenians once a year required the tombs repaired.

Omit *αὐτῶν τὰ μνημεῖα, their sepulchres. Tischendorf, Alford, Cod. Sinai.*

---

49. *Therefore also said the wisdom of God, I will send them prophets and apostles, and some of them they shall slay and persecute:*

Therefore. Their reception of the Apostles proves their final *test*.
His long-suffering, a closing offer of repentance.
The measure of *grace*, as well as of *guilt*, may be filled.
Wisdom of God. CHRIST HIMSELF, the Divine Logos, is the sender of the prophets, and spake by them. Matt. xxiii. 34.
He sent prophets to them to bring them back to the Lord. Matt. xxiii. 34.
They conspired against Zechariah and stoned him. 2 Chron. xxiv. 21.
Jesus is here majestic; He looks beyond present humiliation.
He speaks of Himself as the Jehovah of the O. T. who sent the prophets.
Surely, He can be none other, than the Lord God of Israel in the flesh!
I send. He names not His blood, which they would shed.
Apostles. Treated by *them*, as *prophets* by their fathers.
Slay. Their fathers' spirit, fathers' crimes, they would continue.
Here we learn the fact, nowhere else stated, that some of His Apostles were *slain* before the destruction of Jerusalem.
Synagogues. God's messages of *mercy* would be answered by blood.
Persecute. No wonder faithful preachers are reviled.

σοφία τοῦ θεοῦ—Paul calls our Lord the *Wisdom of God*, Col. ii. 3. And in the O.T.

Prov. viii. 22. The whole *saying* a reference to 2. Chron. xxiv. 18-22. In Matt. the *Lord Jesus Himself* stands forth as the sender of the Prophets and Apostles. *Alford.* The WISDOM of God in Christ. *Ambrose*, and all the Fathers. This quotation has not precisely been found in the O.T. A wise as powerful God. 1. Cor. i. 30. *Kuinoel.* He speaks of Himself, *Oosterzee.* An expression of 2. Chron. xxiv. 19. *Olshausen.* The same as Λόγος of John. *De Wette.*

Remarkable our Lord calls them γραμματεῖς (see Matt. xxiii. 24) contrasting with Pharisaic Scribes; *i.e.* I will send you men *truly* versed in Scriptures. *Olshausen.*

---

50. *That the blood of all the prophets, which was shed from the foundation of the world, may be required of this generation;*

Matt., "*Fill ye up.*" There is *unity* in the plans of Providence
"Until their cup is full," Amorite, nor Israelite perishes not. Gen. xv. 16.
A terrible censure, on all the towering schemes of the Pharisees.
Without *Divine permission*, even the wicked cannot go on.
The blood. Guilt; colour of sin—*scarlet* and *crimson.* Isa. i. 18.
Because *sin* demands *blood* as atonement. Isa. lxiii. 1.
In the settlement of nations, as individuals, a *balance sheet* is struck.
Blood-guiltiness of Israel—1, an old debt; 2, an accumulated debt; 3, a justly visited debt.
Proof—"The Lord is slow to anger, and great in power." Nahum i. 3.
Required. A terrible property of Divine judgment.
A generation sanctioning the sins of the past.
Pays the *accumulated debt* in its own punishment.
The iniquity of Israel was allowed to accumulate from age to age till in *that* generation the vengeance of heaven burst upon a guilty people.
In the first French Revolution this awful principle was fearfully exemplified, nor is the end yet come.
He will visit the sins of the fathers upon the children. Ex. xx. 5.
The father's treason beggars and taints his children.
Piety transmits its *blessings* to our offspring. Acts ii. 39.
The fellowship of guilt, secures a fellowship of doom.
Above all, the blood of *Jesus*, was required of this generation.
Why does He not *definitely* allude to it?
Although His crucifixion did call it down upon their heads.
Yet to the last judgment, "it speaks better things than that of Abel."
It speaks grace, not vengeance. Its burden is "*reconciliation.*"

51. *From the blood of Abel unto the blood of Zacharias, which perished between th altar and the temple: verily I say unto you, It shall be required of this generation.*

Abel. Heb. *transitoriness;* second son of Adam, His name *prophetic* o the shortness of his life.

There were prophets in all ages: Abel a shepherd was one.

His trustful obedience honored God's righteous law.

Cain proudly rejected, Abel thankfully accepted means of grace.

Cain by envy *murdered* one whom God had *honored.*

With Abel's death the warfare between righteousness and unrighteousness commenced.

Evil men strike at God's *image,* in the life of man. Gen. ix. 6.

Zacharias. See verse 49. This martyr's death is found 2. Chron. xxiv. 21. His last words were "the Lord *require it,*" so they are warned that of that generation it should be *required.*

In their malignity, they were fully up to their fathers.

Yet they pretend a *holy horror* at their fathers' crimes.

This wicked generation repeats, and sums up, all previous guilt.

These words are from the lips of our Merciful Saviour, who was too wise to err, and too just to be untrue.

How tremendous an evil is sin! It destroys nations as well as individuals.

"The evil that men do lives after them."

Communities as well as individuals have a character, and we are helping to mould the character, and through it the destiny of the community, the family, the church, and the nation, to which we belong.

Ζαχαρίου—Son of Barachias, another name for Jehoiada, who had three names. A frequent custom among the Jews. *Lightfoot, Beza, Olshausen.* Zacharias, father of John Baptist. *Origen* and many of the Fathers. Grandson of Jehoiada. *Lange.* A prophecy of the death of Zacharias, son of Baruch. *Sepp. Hugg.* A grandson of Jehoiada. *Ebrard, Oosterzee.* The Jews themselves regarded it as an act of proverbial cruelty. Legend runs, this blood *bubbled up,* and could *not be stayed* for 252 years, until the Temple was burned, and until Nebuzaradan had carried off 745 captives. Some apply it to Barachias' son; descendant of Iddo, or son of Baruch, as slain in the Temple, previous to its ruin.

Our Lord cites from the Book of Chronicles, regarded as the conclusion of the Historical Canon of the O.T.; and in going back to the martyrdom of Abel, as recorded in Genesis, comprises all Jewish History as given in the O.T. *Wordsworth.*

ἐκζητηθήσεται—same as *the* Heb. word used in 2. Chron. xxiv. 19-22. αἵματος used *three* times in Matt.

52. *Woe unto you, lawyers! for ye have taken away the key of knowledge: ye entered not in yourselves, and them that were entering in ye hindered.*

They arrogated all wisdom and the control of others' consciences.

Key. A key is to open a door *closed.*

Key taken, is shutting the door in the face of those desiring to enter.

Right knowledge of God's word is life eternal, but this they took away, substituting vain traditions.

Their hierarchal influence had blocked the way to the *people.*

Their enmity to the Lord had closed their *own.*

They had *misused* the key, shutting and *locking* the Kingdom.

Falsifying doctrines of faith and repentance: they had *stolen* the key.

They had prevented the people acknowledging Jesus to be the Messiah.

Their daring, *silenced* the man cured—"We *know* this man," &c. John ix. 24.

Rome, by her Latin prayers and suppressed Bible, hides the key.

To let it *lie rusted* will bring a *woe* upon the neglecters.

κλεῖδα—Luke xi. 7. A key was handed a steward on assuming office. One was given a Rabbi, when authorized to expound the law. On the death of Rabbi Samuel, a key was hung on his tomb. The early fastenings were made of chains, but later, keys were made of iron, wood, bronze and gold. When the bride was introduced into her husband's house, a key was handed her; and when one was divorced, the keys were taken from her. Keys of a large house usually trusted to a janitor.

---

53. *And as he said these things unto them, the scribes and the Pharisees began to urge* him *vehemently, and to provoke him to speak of many things.*

54. *Laying wait for him, and seeking to catch something out of his mouth, that they might accuse him.*

Scribes and Pharisees. No men hate each other too much to prevent their *uniting* against Christian truth.

Provoke. They could not bear cutting reproofs, unmasking their hypocrisy.

Wait. They laid a snare (in vain) to throw Him off His guard.

"Every day they wrest my words." *David,* Psa. lvi. 5, 2 Pet. iii. 16.

Evil men dig up mischief—create what they cannot *find.*

In the "multitude of words there wanteth not sin." Prov. x. 19.

They would anger Him, and cause Him to *betray* Himself.

Convicted, not converted, they filled up the measure of their iniquity, endeavoring to entrap the Teacher of Truth.

Awful evidence that the charges He brought against them were true.

His speech and His silence were alike a reproof to the Scribes and the Pharisees.

λέγοντος—κἀκεῖθεν ἐξελθόντος αὐτοῦ—*and when he was gone out, Alford, Cod. Sinai. Tisch.* This plot doubtlessly concocted after His departure. Conscience or indignation, for the moment, deprived the lawyer of the power of replying. *Oosterzee.* "*Urge*," grieviously agenstonde. *Wickliffe:* urge sore. *Coverdale;* wax buisy about Him. *Tyndale;* press Him hard. *Luther:* fasten upon Him. *Dieu.*

ἀποστοματίζειν—*harass Him with questions. W. & W.; or stop His mouth with many* questions. *os ejus opprimere. Vul.;* classically to *speak anything memoriter.* To give *vent to random words. Bengel.* To force words from the mouth. *Parkhurst.* As an angry schoolmaster vexes a pupil. *Hesychius. To mouth, or bear down with the violence of their words. Theophylact. To examine in a magisterial way. Grotius.*

δεινῶς ἐνέχειν—began *fiercely to fasten on Him. Doddridge.* θηρεῦσαι—The eagerness with which sportsmen beat about to start their game from its covert. To *start some unguarded word. Doddridge.* Omit καὶ ζητοῦντες, *and seeking. Tischendorf, Alford, Cod. Sinai.;* the latter omits αὐτὸν, also ἵνα κατηγορήσωσιν, *that they might accuse Him.*

These things Matt. records to have been said after our Lord had come into Jerusalem, Luke relates them here, when our Lord was on His journey to Jerusalem; from which they appear to be similar discourses, of which Matt. has given one, Luke the other, *Augustine.*

CHAPTER XII.

1. *IN the mean time, when there were gathered together an innumerable multitude of people, insomuch that they trode one upon another, he began to say unto his disciples first of all, Beware ye of the leaven of the Pharisees, which is hypocrisy.*

Meantime. Gr. *during which occurrences*, in close connexion with the foregoing scene.

Gathered. Curiosity to see, rather than a desire to *protect* Him.

Multitude. Gr. *the myriads being collected.* Oriental curiosity is great, and the words of the Prophet have an *inchoate* fulfilment.—

"Unto Him shall the gathering of the people be." Gen. xlix. 10.

"Who are these that fly like clouds, and as doves to their windows?' Isa. lx. 8.

It denotes the mighty success of the Seventy in preaching.

Began to say. Our Lord spoke more plainly as events were drawing to a close.

Our Saviour acted more *publicly* as He approached the cross.

Trode upon. Gr. *were likely to trample on one another.*

Disciples. They were about to meet trials, demanding strong faith.

First of all. First in importance. He well knew the weak points.

Beware. In the presence of a vast crowd, the Lord denounces the sins of the most powerful Jewish sect.

Leaven. Sour dough kept over, with which, to raise the new mixture.

A very small quantity, affects a very large mass.

Leaven and honey, easily fermenting. Forbidden in sacrifice. Lev. ii. 11.

Priests of Jupiter were prohibited from touching leaven.

Salt a symbol of *incorruption*, leaven, of *corruption.*

All leaven was carefully removed during the Passover.

It *secretly*, silently and powerfully transforms.

Its peculiarities—souring, swelling, spreading, and corrupting.

Their doctrines led to bigotry, pride, fiery zeal, and depravity.

Hypocrisy. Luke vi. 42. This vice was singled out by the Saviour.

Hypocrisy, i.e., wickedness concealed under a show of goodness.

Like leaven, hypocrisy infects the *whole* man, and many by means of one.

Nothing so changes the characters of men as hypocrisy.

As a little leaven leaveneth the lump, so hypocrisy robs the mind of all its virtues. *Bede.*

Hypocrites have existed in all ages of the world. Cain in the first age; Canaan in the second; Ishmael in the third; Esau in the fourth; Saul among the prophets; Judas among the Apostles; Nicholas among the deacons; and Ananias among the early Christians.

Hypocrisy is professing to be what in reality we are not. It is the negation of sincerity.

Its essence is imitation, and its success is deceit.

Hypocrites have been classed under four kinds:—

1. The worldly hypocrite, who professes godliness from worldly motives.
2. The legal hypocrite, who resigns his vicious practices to win heaven, but has no love to God.
3. The evangelical hypocrite, whose religion is an acknowledgment of sin, but with no desire to lead a holy life.
4. The enthusiastic hypocrite, who has an imaginary notion of the Saviour, and relies on impulses and feelings, and yet clings to vicious deeds.

Grace is the Christian's new nature, and hypocrisy is the art that counterfeits it.

The hypocrite affects the innocence of the dove to hide the cunning of the serpent.

By the hypocrite good men are oft deceived for—

"Goodness thinks no ill
Where no ill seems." *Milton.*

The hypocrite like Judas may salute Christ, but it is to betray Him.

"Satan was the first
That practised falsehood under saintly show." *Milton.*

The hypocrite's life is a falsehood to heaven and to earth.

The hypocrite gives his tongue to virtue, but his heart to vice.

If there be "the head of gold" there are also "the feet of miry clay."

Hypocrisy is the homage which vice pays to virtue.

The more plausible hypocrisy is before men, the more detestable it is to God

The hypocrite serves Satan and from Satan receives his reward.

The religious hypocrite is at best a man of dark deeds, though clad in garments of light.

He may approach the portals of heaven but he does not enter.

A hypocrite was discovered at a royal supper but the king rejected him from the banquet.

Man esteems him hateful because he seems not what he is, and God hates him because he is not what he seems.

The Christian's heart oft speaks without the tongue, but the hypocrite's tongue always speaks without the heart.

The hypocrite, like a bird of prey, although his course be towards heaven, yet is always looking and longing for something upon earth.

The Christian gives to God the fruit of his labors, the hypocrite gives to God the fruit of his lips.

The hypocrite is led by ostentation and not by a sanctified conscience.

Jehu's zeal was for the Lord, but his project was for his kingdom.

Hypocrites may be "Christians in the skin, but they are demons in the core." "their rhetoric may be pretty, their logic witty, but their practice is naughty."

Hypocrisy is insulting to the virtuous, and cruel to the poor and afflicted.

For he who hides his vices by hypocrisy, suspects the virtues of others to be hypocrisy.

And the poor and afflicted remain poor and afflicted because the sin of the hypocrite closed the hand of charity, and in consequence thereof genuine sorrow is oft suspected in place of being relieved.

An impostor who asks for alms is a hypocrite in the lower grade.

Hypocrisy may prevail in morals as well as in creed. Some men are hypocritical in both.

Hypocrisy shall be detected, as in the case of Saul. 1. Sam. xv. 14.

Hypocrisy shall be detected, as in the case of Gehazi. 2. Kings v. 26.

Hypocrisy shall be detected, as in the case of Judas. Matt. xxvi. 50.

Hypocrisy shall be detected, as in the case of Ananias. Acts v. 3.

Hypocrisy shall be detected, as in the case of Simon Magus. Acts viii. 20-21.

Hypocrisy may be seen in the history of Jacob; Gen. xxvii. 20. Pharaoh; Ex. viii. 28-29. Balaam; Num. xxiii. 10. Absalom; 2. Sam. xv. 7. Hazael; 2. Kings viii. 12-13. Samaritans; Ezra iv. 2. Herod; Matt. ii. 8. High Priest; Matt. xxvi. 65. Pilate; Matt. xxvii. 24.

Let the Hypocrite tremble, lest he perish by his own hypocrisy, for God is the God of Truth; Christ is the Word of Truth; and the Holy Ghost is the Spirit of Truth.

Sadducees, in their pretended search of the truth, were more candid.

Pharisees wished to *appear*, rather than *be* pious.

They paid the accustomed tribute to virtue, by assuming its guise.

An honest man *seems* to be what he *is*, and *is* what he *seems*.

"The hope of the hypocrite shall be as the spider's web." Job viii. 13-14.

Strange he should have any hope.—"Can the flag?" &c. Job viii. 11.

He is unwise who decries religion because some professing to be religious are hypocrites.

None would take the pains to counterfeit pearls if true ones were not of value.

Men would not personate piety were it not of itself a noble quality.

We best show our abhorrence of hypocrisy by holding the truth free from hypocrisy.

The characteristic mark of Christ's disciples is sincerity.

They are "Israelites indeed, and without guile." 2. Their *repentance* is not partial. 3. Their *faith* is not partial. 4. Their *zeal* is not partial.

ἐπι—intensive, indicating the extent of the gathering. μυριάδων—*many thousands. Doddridge. The ten thousands of the multitude. Alford.* An indefinitely large number. *W. & W.* We might suppose the number to have been over 20,000. *Lightfoot.* At this period of our Lord's history, feelings of love and hatred had reached their utmost intensity. *Oosterzee.* ὥστε, followed by the infinitive describes an act contemplated but not realized; an event capable of occurring or likely to occur. So Matt. xxvii. 1. ὥστε, followed by the indicative denotes a fact which actually takes place, Matt. xxiii. 31; Gal. ii. 13; iii. 24; iv. 7. *Webster's Syntax.*

πρῶτον—*First of all in importance. Meyer, Olshausen, Oosterzee.* Refers to the disciples. *Bengel, Alford, Tischendorf.* ζύμης—The putrefaction af any substance, destitute of nitrogen. The carbonic acid gas escaping is arrested by the dough, and forms numerous *cells*, and renders bread *light* or spongy. ζύμης—doctrines of which hypocrisy was their *essence. Meyer, Oosterzee.* ἄζυμοι—the principle of incorruption, 1. Cor. v. 7. *Unleavened.*

---

2. *For there is nothing covered, that shall not be revealed; neither hid, that shall not be known.*

The darkness of the night and the light of day to God are both alike.

He who will be our Judge is every moment our Witness: be it for evil or for good—He is at our side, seeing us but Himself unseen.

Covered. *Concealed from view;* refers to conflicts and snares of believers.

Revealed. All secrets made known, no human mind can grasp its full meaning.

A warning against hypocrisy, and fear of man.
Hypocrisy not only wicked, but *useless*.
By this warning all deception assaulted in its foundations.
Their Almighty Friend *foresaw* all their secret snares.
Faint-heartedness, unfaithfulness, would be disclosed.
A *promise*—the faithful may refer every trial to the Judgment.
They would commend themselves to the *consciences* of men.
"We have renounced the hidden things of dishonesty." 2 Cor. iv. 2.
Those dreading the least *sin* fear not the greatest *perils*.
Hid, *from knowledge*. Heathen connected *mysteries* with their religions.
The ignorant were warned to retire from their sacred rites.
Their abominations were such that heathen Rome endeavoured to suppress them by *law*, as Livy testifies.
Christianity always and everywhere lets its light *shine*. Matt. v. 16.
Gives free and fearless utterance to all the truth.
It is in vain to conceal that which will one day be revealed.

3. *Therefore whatsoever ye have spoken in darkness shall be heard in the light; and that which ye have spoken in the ear in closets shall be proclaimed upon the housetops.*

In darkness. Probable allusion to the oppression and gloom under which the Apostles commenced their ministry.
Philosophers kept their instructions as *secrets* for the few.
All error, like Pagan fables, dreads the light of truth.
Persecutions, Pagan and Papal, aimed to stifle the truth.
Light. Every secret thing shall be brought to the light of God's judgment.
Where God kindles lights they *are* the lights of the world.
Secret societies, social, civil, or religious stand *opposed* to the genius of Christianity.
Secresy should be the exception, candour the rule among believers.
That which. Truth must be proclaimed and nothing else.
In the ear: somewhat fearfully. **Closets;** Gr. in *the closets*.
Our Lord had no *esoteric* and *exoteric* doctrines.
Amongst the heathen the favoured few kept the light, and shut out the many.
Some refer this to the custom of the elder of the synagogue whispering the text to the interpreter.
Inspiration addressed to an open ear. Isa. l. 5.
Proclaimed. Gr. *heralded*. Office and duties anciently. Luke viii. 1. ix. 2. See Notes.

Housetops. The roofs are generally of stone, because wood is scarce.
Their *pulpit*, when temple and synagogue were closed.
Roofs sometimes made of layers of branches and covered with clay.
After rains the owners level their earthen roofs by rollers.
They erect booths and sit there for *air*, *prospect*, and *slumber*.
Moslems often are seen praying on the housetop. Acts x. 9.
Our Lord's words may be paraphrased; Beware of hypocrisy, for all shall be made evident in the end, and ye are witnesses and sharers in this unfolding of the truth. *Alford.*
Whatever ye have hitherto preached privately henceforth preach publicly. *Kuinoel.*
Whatever you may have said privately in your ministry shall be known publicly, and your Father who heareth in secret will reward you openly in the Great Day. *Origen.*

Ἀνθ' ὧν—*Because, wherefore*, used for ἀντὶ τούτων ὅτι "in requital for this that." So Luke i. 20; xix. 44; Acts xii. 23; 2. Thess. ii. 10. *Webster's Syntax.*

ταμιείοις—mysteries, *esoteric*, *i.e.* were for the private instruction of the few; *exoteric*, *i.e.* for the public instruction of the many. Their vulgar prejudices were flattered. *Enfield.* εἴπατε—*with some degree of fear.* Spoken secretly, through fear of persecution, &c. *Meyer.* Not confined to the Gospel or Apostles. *Oosterzee.* ἀνθ' ὧν—hence, *Dean.* Oriental houses built entirely of stone, have roofs all *domes*, no chimney is seen.

---

4. *And I say unto you my friends, Be not afraid of them that kill the body, and after that have no more that they can do.*

I say. As fearless speaking of truth might endanger their lives, our Lord comforts them.
My friends. He speaks as a general—"Brothers in arms, Fear not."
The Redeemer is *able* and willing to shield even the least friendly.
Be not afraid. Gr. elsewhere: *Fear not.*
Racks, tortures, dungeons and fire, cannot harm you.
"The fear of man bringeth a snare." God controls our foes. Prov. xxix. 25.
A life-guard of angels protects the saints of the Lord. Psa. xxxiv. 7.
Kill the body. They may go that far, but there, their power ends.
"Slay me, they may: hurt me, they cannot," *Socrates.*
In view of heaven, He taught them to *despise* death.
They die, but death touches not the proper *life* of saints.

Immortality the ground tone of all these promises.

No more. The *malice* and *kindness* of man, end at the grave.

They can do. Implies *another* can destroy the soul.

Only destroyed, when driven from God "a vessel of wrath."

Created power can crush the *cabinet*, but not destroy the *jewel*.

Our Lord implies the soul can perish, but will not be annihilated.

Through *fear* of man religious duties are often neglected.

Through *fear* of man we are sometimes tempted to guilty pleasures.

"Who art thou that thou shouldest be afraid of *man?*" Isa. li. 12.

"Let HIM be our fear, let HIM be our dread." Isa. viii. 13.

This precept of our Lord, a protest against the notion of a *sleep* of the *soul* after death.

He clearly distinguishes between the state of the *body* after death, and the state of the *soul*.

But the state of the soul would *not* be different, *if* the *soul sleeps* after death.

Therefore the *soul* does *not sleep*, but retains its consciousness.

It passes immediately from the body to the abode of departed spirits—the Hades or covered place.

A portion thereof being a place of joy, a portion thereof being the region of sorrow.

There to dwell separated from the body, until the Resurrection morn.

When the body and the soul are again to be united and for ever to be inseparable.

In the perfection of felicity prepared for the believer in Christ—

Or in the extremity of wretchedness, the predicted doom of the finally impenitent.

In these new states of existence the one class rises higher than the angels, the other sinks lower than demons.

φίλοις—*loved ones*, objects of the Divine complacency, (John xv. 15.) a distinguished honor. Our Lord calls them "*friends*," from the feeling, perhaps, He then had, that in this "*killing of the body*" He and they were going to be affectingly one with each other. *D. Brown.* ἀποκτεινόντων—only the body. When soul and body are involved, ἀπολέσαι, Matt. x. 28, is used, or ἐμβαλεῖν, &c.

τὸ σῶμα—*Immortality* of the soul, is not philosophically taught by our Lord, any more than the existence of God. He assumes, however, these truths, and the *resurrection* of the body. *Stier.*

5. *But I will forewarn you whom ye shall fear: Fear him, which after he hath killed hath power to cast into hell; yea, I say unto you, Fear him.*

Forewarn. However heathen fare hereafter the hearers of the Gospel are faithfully warned.

Pagans' consciences *accuse* or else *excuse* one another. Rom. ii. 15.

Pre-eminent privileges, bring heavy responsibilities.

Fear. Used three times with great power, in this verse.

Fear neither the revilings of their tongues nor wrath of man. Isa. lvii. 11.

Those who censure ministers for appealing to any other *motive*, than *love*;—profess to be wiser than our Lord.

Only the fear of the *greater*, will expel fear of the *less*.

He concentrates the mind at once on the final issues.

After he hath killed. Gr. *after the killing;* the verb is used as it were impersonally.

Power, of God, eternally to punish, is *the one* reason given.

Cast. Matt. *soul and body.* Weighty, and stern language, even to *friends.*

Our Lord guards against the *error* of the soul's annihilation.

Also against the notion that the body will escape the ruin of the soul.

Perdition, not destruction of the *being* of either, but of the *well being* of both.

Knowing the terrors of the Lord we persuade men. 2. Cor. v. 11.

Hell. Gr. *Gehenna,* used to signify the place of everlasting punishment.

No mawkish refinement prevents Him using plain terms.

Meekness and gentleness, consistent with awful fidelity.

Learn—To play false to convictions to save life will fail of its end.

God can inflict a violent death in some other and more awful way.

a. There is a *hell* for the *body* as well as the *soul;* consequently sufferings adapted to the one as well as the other.

b. Fear of hell is a divinely authorised and needed motive of action even to Christ's "*friends.*"

c. As Christ's meekness and tenderness were not compromised by this language, those ministers want their Master's spirit who soften it to please "ears polite." *D. Brown.*

Bitter-wholesome is a safe receipt for Christians. *Augustine.*

φοβήθητε. *Olshausen* and *Stier* suppose these words to refer to Satan, rather than to God, but this is wholly inconsistent with the scope of our Lord's teaching. God alone

throughout the Bible, is the Almighty Dispenser of life and death, temporal and eternal. Satan is ever represented as the condemned of God. Besides, if this chief enemy, and his subordinates, whom Christ has just commanded us not to *fear*, are introduced in the midst of this great subject, it would indeed be an ἅπαξ λεγόμενον, horrendum. Our Heavenly Father is intended as the right object of our fear. *Alford*. Contrary to the connection and universal scripture tone. *Alexander*. Matt. parallel, καὶ σῶμα prove immortality, since the body is not killed, even in hell.

γέενναν—the "valley of Hinnom;" a deep narrow glen, south of Jerusalem, where, after the introduction of the worship of the fire-gods, by Ahaz, the idolatrous Jews offered their children to Moloch (2. Chron. xxv. 3). It became, in later times, the image of the place of everlasting punishment. *Smith's* Dict.

---

6. ***Are not five sparrows sold for two farthings, and not one of them is forgotten before God?***

Five. In Matthew, two for one farthing; for two farthings an additional one is thrown in.

A charming variation from the saying in Matthew x. 29.

Sparrows. Small brown birds still found in Palestine.

The birds used in the Temple by cleansed lepers. Lev. xiv. 4.

In Judæa they annoy at meals as flies in America and England.

They feed on seeds and insects; even in *winter* God feedeth them.

Yet do they fall and die, but it is by Divine order and permission.

God's government extends to trifles—a truth, 1, too certain to be doubted; 2, too glorious to be slightly valued; 3, too instructive to be forgotten.

Two farthings. One tenth of a penny (Roman).

Roman coins and power extended over the world.

Not one. Not even an odd or stray one. How incomprehensibly *minute* is His providence!

With God they have value; permitted to rest under altars. Psa. lxxxiv. 3.

He satisfies the desires of *every living thing*. Psa. cxlv. 16.

Forgotten. He remembers the young lions when they suffer hunger. Psa. xxxiv. 10.

And stilleth the raven's clamorous nest. Psa. cxlvii. 9.

Surely then He will watch over, protect, and supply the wants of His people.

But an angel is not always sent to release them. Acts v. 19.

The mouths of lions are not always stopped. Daniel vi. 22.

The violence of fire is not always quenched. Dan. iii. 21.

Earthquakes do not always open prison doors. Acts xvi. 26.

Jesus remembered us on His throne, in the garden, and on the cross. Realised, it redeems life from its drudgery and dreary emptiness.

στρουθία—Sax. spears. Hence Eng. *spare*, from the smallness of the sparrow. *ἀσσαρίων* Lat. *as*, *assis*, fourth part of an *uncia*, *one-tenth* of a denarius. A Roman penny equal to one-and-a-half cent. *Elsley*, *Major*. Homer noticed the particular providence of the gods, which so many baptized unbelievers deny. A stag escapes the snare, because it was not *ordained* he should be taken, Il. xv. 274. Yet the Epicureans, Academics, and Aristotelians denied the *particular* providence of their gods. *Major*.

---

7. *But even the very hairs of your head are all numbered. Fear not therefore: ye are of more value than many sparrows.*

Hairs. *Ornament* of man, *protection* of beasts. Luke vii. 38.
Colour and flexibility due to the oil filling them.
Its horny covering never changes; nutrition failing, it turns grey.
Numbered. He counts the stars, and calleth them all by name.
To God there is nothing small or great—the least is great, and the greatest little.
Numbering of our hair, implies His accurate knowledge; it manifests the minuteness of His care. *Cyril.*
Has reference not so much to the act of reckoning, as capability of knowing.
Yet said to be numbered, because those things we wish to preserve we number. *Ambrose.*
If the mere excrescences of the body are thus preserved, how great the security of the soul! *Augustine.*
We are taught thus not for curiosity but for *encouragement.*
Neither His infinite *glory* nor the *repose* of His mind disparaged.
Implies *He* takes better care of *us* than we of ourselves.
If He numbers our *hairs*, He guards our *lives.*
Men number their treasures, seldom their *mercies.*
Fear not. The timid heart oft needs *reassurance.*
Flesh and blood meet life's conflict with dread.
Persecutions heighten our vigor and brighten our graces and virtues.
"Thou tellest my wanderings: put Thou my tears," &c. Psa. lvi. 8.
More value. The market value of the sparrow is given.
The computation how far *they* excel sparrows in value, is left to the disciples.

Christians' value, 1, as reasonable beings. 2, as immortal. 3, as redeemed by Christ's blood. 4, as being like God.

The mention of the sparrow one of the few allusions to those *mysterious beings*, irrational creatures.

The charm and power of our Lord's teaching, heightened by its wonderful simplicity.

ἀλλὰ augments and strengthens the idea conveyed in ἐπιλελησμένον, "on the contrary," "more than this." *Webster's Syntax.* τρίχες—Luke vii. 38.—light hair grows on light skins, &c.; witness the leopard. Mental anguish has been known to turn hair grey in one night. This received a painful illustration in the case of the unhappy Maria Antoinette, Queen of France. The hair thus changed was formed into a brooch, with the expressive motto, "Bleached by sorrow."

ἠρίθμηνται—*have been numbered*, consequently are known. *Numbered*,—this teaches a Special Providence towards Christ's friends. *Oosterzee.* The doctrine of Special Providence perfectly consistent with government by General Laws. The Bible gives no uncertain sound upon this subject; it is full of illustrations and instances. The experience of the Christian gratefully attests it in many an Ebenezer,—"Hitherto the Lord hath helped me." οὖν, omitted by some ancient authorities. *Alford.*

---

8. *Also I say unto you, Whosoever shall confess me before men, him shall the Son of man also confess before the angels of God:*

9. *But he that denieth me before men shall be denied before the angels of God.*

Son of man. Luke v. 24. Points to His Godhead in humility.

Confess. *Christ as Master*, and His *doctrines* the rule.

Christ mainly rejected by man's bitter pride. Matt. xi. 6.

Confession in those days was a test involving *life* itself.

Exile, prison, loss of goods, loss of office and good name.

Martyrs by way of eminence, divine heroes, *confessors*.

He is confessed more by *suffering*, than by *serving*.

Some *profess* Christ, but in works *deny* Him. Tit. i. 16

Me. Gr. IN ME, showing the spirit in which the confession must be made, and the ground on which it rests.

It is not in our own strength we confess, but by grace from above.

Denieth Me. Observe, He does not say "*in me*," as in confessing Him. The fault lies at the sinner's door.

We deny Him by remaining *silent*, when we ought to speak.

If we now acknowledge Christ to be our Master, He will hereafter acknowledge us to be His disciples.

We must confess Him in our hearts, with our tongues, and by our lives.

We deny Him by sitting still, when we ought to go to the Lord's table.

By conforming to *customs*, *fashions*, and *spirit*, of earth.

Apostacy and *blasphemy* are denounced in verses 8-9.

"I will speak of thy testimonies also before kings." Psa. cxix. 46.

He would have us fearless, as Nathan, 2. Sam. xii. 7., or Gad, 2. Sam. xxiv. 13.

John before Herod, Matt. xiv. 4. Jehu before Jehoshaphat, 2. Chro. xix. 2.

Or Micaiah before Ahab, 1. Kings xxii. 8-15. Or the three Hebrews before Nebuchadnezzar, Dan. iii. 13.

Or the Apostles before the Sanhedrim. Acts xxi. 19.

Denial of our relation *to*, or expectation *from* Christ.

We have infinitely more need of Him, than He of us.

Angels. In their presence at the day of Judgment.

"Encompassed by a great cloud of witnesses." Heb. xii. 1.

A worthless worm acknowledged by Christ, "MY FRIEND," verse 4.

The point lies in confessing Him "before men," because one has to *despise the shame*.

But when done, the Lord holds Himself bound to repay it *in kind* by confessing such "before the angels of God."

If we must give an account of every "idle word," take care, lest you have to answer for an idle silence. *Ambrose.*

The Lord is not content with an inward faith, but requires an outward confession. *Chrysostom.*

ὁμολογήσει—same opinion, *acknowledge. Doddridge.* ἀπαρνηθήσεται—renounce. *Doddridge.* "Life is sweet, and death is bitter," said Hooper, at the stake:—"But *eternal* life is more sweet, *eternal* death more bitter." ἐνώπιον—Here our Lord sublimely assumes to Himself, the *judicial decision*, and that highest *personality*, on the confession or denial of which, all is suspended. *Stier.*

---

10. *And whosoever shall speak a word against the Son of man, it shall be forgiven him: but unto him that blasphemeth against the Holy Ghost it shall not be forgiven.*

Whosoever. Ye calumniators, and gain sayers!

Word. Decided evidence of the principles of the heart.

From denial, the advance to blasphemy is easy.

Son of Man. Offended by His *outward appearance*, supposed to be the carpenter's son.

Blasphemeth. In classic Greek any evil against man, as slander. In Hellenistic usage denotes evil speaking against *God*.

Holy Ghost. The third person in the adorable Trinity. Luke i. 15.

Wilfully rejecting and reviling what the blasphemer *knows* in his own conscience to be the testimony of the Holy Ghost and God's truth and grace.

To those who thus sin our Lord's prayer not applicable—"Father forgive them, they know not what they do." Luke xxiii. 34.

Shall not be forgiven. Because in a state of deadly impenitence.

There is a conscience seared as with a hot iron. Tim. iv. 2.

A heart, gospel hardened "Twice dead." Jude verse 12.

Unsanctified familiarity with sacred things. Lev. x. 1.

The fire which melts the wax hardens the clay.

Malignantly and defiantly they had *reviled* the Spirit.

The essence of the unpardonable sin is *presumptuousness.*

"The soul that doeth aught presumptuously is cut off." Num. xv. 30.

No *sacrifice* under the Levitical dispensation for blasphemy.

No forgiveness under the Christian, for blasphemy against the Holy Ghost.

This does not arise from inability in God to forgive, or from insufficiency in the atonement of Christ, but from the utterly hopeless state of the blasphemer himself.

"Because they said, He hath an unclean spirit." Mark iii. 30.

The impossibility of pardon turns on the impossibility of repentance.

Luke *καὶ*, Matt. δὶα, Mark ἀμὴν begin this momentous declaration. ὅς ἐρεῖ. Matt. has εἴπῃ. Mark βλασφημήσῃ. Confined to the age of our Lord. *Meneken, Horsley.* It may be committed in any age. *Baxter, Hammond, Doddridge, McKnight.* "For all other sins, forgiveness is *possible*. The sin against the *Spirit*, being more heinous than the sin against the *Son*, results from the nature of the Holy Spirit's work in the Divine plan of salvation. Saul spake against Christ, yet was forgiven. The murderers of Christ were *pardoned*, Luke xxiii. 34. The mockers on the day of Pentecost were *forgiven*. The person who thus offends must be entirely convinced, and sin with complete knowledge and *will*. The sin against God the Holy Ghost has been committed in all ages, but is peculiarly the sin of the *last times*. The guilty soul is not merely *under* the influence of Satan, but has become a freely acting and conscious *Satan*. It is the eternally unpardonable rejection of the perfectly known, immediate testimony of the Spirit. No Satanic *deceit* is practised upon the understanding (Gen. iii. 13), nor compulsion of any kind. Pure evil is willed, spoken, and done, instead of known and rejected good. It is unpardonable, not on *God's account*, but the creature, who has put himself under such a *ban*. He remains incorrigible, and incapable of repentance." *Stier.*

The blasphemy of those who, acknowledging God, and seeing His present power working by His Holy Spirit, *openly oppose* themselves to it. *Alford.* Ascription of miracles He wrought, by the Holy Ghost, to powers of darkness. *Athanasius, Jerome, Chrysostom. Ambrose*, and nearly all the Fathers, *Vers. Ger., Hales, Bengel, Wordsworth.* The blasphemy against the Holy Ghost is a sin of the tongue. *Ford.*

Whoever *grieves*, thinking he has committed this sin, may rest assured he has not. The really guilty will not grieve, but will defend himself against the charge. This passage, with its parallels, has been always and unanimously received as one of the most alarming in the word of God. But it acquires increased solemnity and terror, when considered in its true connection. It is no insulated and detached expression of a fearful and mysterious truth. Instead of formally reproving the scribe for insinuating that He had an unclean spirit, He describes the nature of a sin which they had perhaps committed. "I, the Son of God," (verse 8) "yet the Son of Man, declare to you, my enemies and false accusers, on account of your groundless and malignant charges. All sin of every kind shall be forgiven. There is but one exception, and to the last degree insulting to God."

ἀφεθήσεται repeated gives it the impressive tone of a judicial sentence. *Neither in this world*, &c., convey the idea that the sin described shall NEVER be forgiven. *αἰών* properly denotes *duration*, sometimes definite, as dispensation or age. But when limited by nothing in the context, indefinite and even infinite duration. If some sins are forgiven they are forgiven *to eternity*, and if unforgiven they will *eternally remain so. Alexander.*

No man can blaspheme unconsciously. *Lange.* Contemptuous indifference. *Gurlitt, Nitzsche.* Rejection of the Gospel. *Irenaeus. Mortal sins after baptism. Origen.* Hardness of heart to the end of life. *Augustine.* Hatred of that which is holy. *Grashof, Tholuck.* An outward *expression* of inward *hatred. Waterland.* The lost ability of fulfilling the conditions required for forgiveness. *Muller. Henry* and *Whitby* suppose that this sin could not have been committed till after Pentecost.

Sin and blasphemy against the Holy Ghost are very different things. *Bengel.* The terrible act of one who, in defiance of light and knowledge, rejects of set purpose, opposes after due deliberation, the work of the Spirit. The deliberate quenching and cursing of the Spirit. It involves the obstinate, persevering, and malicious rejection of the Gospel. *Foote.* Although not named in the former dispensation, yet Cain and Saul were probably guilty of it. It is no special act, but made so by the circumstances. In one case it is *blasphemy*, another *persecution*, another *perverting the truth.* It must be against the specially imparted light of the Spirit. It is unpardonable, because it wilfully tramples under foot the blood of the covenant, the only possible way of escape from eternal wrath. He despises the Spirit, the only agent who can bring the soul to God. The deliberate renouncing all lot or part in the offers of Redemption. All the sins which men commit are capable of being classed under three heads, as being either in thought, in word, or in deed; but blasphemy against the Holy Ghost can only be referred to the second of these, and must not be confounded with sinful thoughts, or with erroneous actions. Sin against the Holy Ghost, but not blasphemy, is committed by every reader of the Bible, or hearer of the Gospel who dies finally impenitent.

Practically this unbelief pronounces Jesus an imposter, His blood useless, the Spirit worthless, Bible a fable, death a sleep, judgment a dream, and its eternal realities, mere illusions. *Fuller.* Possibly the veil is left on the precise nature of the sin, that men might avoid *all* known sin, lest *the one* committed, peradventure might be to himself, the unpardonable sin. It was a maxim of ancient law—"*No sanctuary for sacrilege.*" So here—"No sanctuary for blasphemy." *Henry.*

From this passage it is rightly inferred, that the Holy Ghost is a Person, and that He is God. *Pearson.*

11. *And when they bring you unto the synagogues, and unto magistrates, and powers, take ye no thought how or what thing ye shall answer, or what ye shall say:*

Synagogues. Their nature, use, and history. Luke iv. 15. See Notes.

This was for purposes of excommunication.

Magistrates. First in office, wisdom and power. Eph. i. 21. Col. ii. 10.

Powers. Herod, Agrippa, Felix, Festus and Nero.

Great ones of earth, at that time, great *enemies* of the Gospel.

No thought. Old English word for *solicitude* or anxious care.

Martyrs were bound to prepare themselves for duty.

"Yet *suspect* thy heart, fearing thou wilt utter it wrong."

They who speak in faith, will be furnished in that hour.

As those who in faith took no money, were divinely supplied.

Without *diligence*, prayer for wisdom, is *presumption*.

Neglecting study, and expecting the Spirit's aid, is *fanaticism*.

As an excuse for study, the plea is a refuge of indolence.

In what could unlearned apostles trust? Acts iv. 13.

The gold of gospel truth, needs no human gilding.

The three champions not careful to answer the king. Dan. iii. 16.

True ministers labor rather to *do well*, than to *speak* well.

Anxious to *keep*, rather than *vindicate* their integrity.

Special trials, bring special grace, "As thy days, so shall thy strength be." Deut. xxxiii. 25.

Jacob wrestled all night, *preparing* to meet Esau.

David *prepared* with all his might, for the temple. 1. Chron. xxix. 2.

"Oh! Lord I am not eloquent" said Moses; "I will be with thy mouth," saith God. Ex. iv. 10-12.

"I am a man of unclean lips," said Isaiah, when lo! A seraph touched them. Isa. vi. 6.

"I cannot speak for I am a child," said Jeremiah; "Behold: I have put my words in thy mouth," saith God. Jer. i. 6-9.

συναγωγὰς—Luke iv. 15. *ἐξουσίας*—authorities, human magistrates, *δι ἐν τέλει*, Titus iii. 1. Angelic powers, both good and evil, Eph. iii. 10; vi. 12; Col. i. 16; ii. 5; 1. Peter iii. 22. *Webster's Syntax.*

μεριμνᾶτε—*μερις*—division, distracting of the mind, Matt. vi. 34; 1. Cor. vii. 34; Phil. iv. 6; Luke x. 41, not *solicitous*. *Rheimish.* *Anxiously solicitous. Bloomfield.* Phil. iv. 6; not "*careful for nothing*," but *anxious* for nothing. *Ne solicititi sitis.* Vulg. *Solicite cogitando. Beza.* *πῶς ἤ τί* does not imply *verbal* inspiration. *προσφέρωσιν*—Mark xiii. 11. *ἄγωσιν*—a forensic term *rapere in jus.* *ἀπολογήσῆσθε*—English *Apology.*

Hence, *what apology you shall make. Doddridge.* This term has changed, anciently synonymous with *defence.* Hence Watson's "Defence of the Bible," an "Apology," evidently in its *classical* sense.

---

12. *For the Holy Ghost shall teach you in the same hour what ye ought to say.*

Holy Ghost. Matthew—*Father.* In Christians' conflicts individual *personality* vanishes.
Among the enemies of believers there is *one adversary.*
The Spirit the *one Friend* and *Ally* in danger.
Teach you. He who teaches wrong cannot live aright.
He who does not live aright cannot teach aright.
Outward and inward teaching of the Spirit united.
He imparts instruction and the capacity to receive it.
He would spare them the necessity of self-defence—"*I am thy shield.*"
Nor must they interfere with the mysterious advocate.
They would be the vehicles of conveying the Divine answer.
Without such a Friend they had good cause to be dismayed.
In the same hour. Gr. *at the time itself.* "A *present* help in time of trouble."

"*Holy Ghost.*" Our Lord's promise of the Holy Spirit is the highest authority for the inspiration of the Apostolic writings. *Oosterzee.*

---

13. ¶ *And one of the company said unto Him, Master, speak to my brother, that he divide the inheritance with me.*

One of the company. A foolish listener, who forgot the *heavenly* for earthly inheritance.
Even the preaching of the Son of God had worldly-minded listeners.
Master. Gr. *Teacher.* Great preacher of righteousness, Help.
This rude interruption deserved a severe rebuke.
The appeal, earthly in spirit, sought the *dead* among the *living.*
The love of earth was fast hardening him against all truth.
Brother. Some kindred are without natural affection. Rom. i. 31.
It implies he *designed* defrauding his relative.
No one unjust to *God* can be just to his *neighbor.*
Earthly riches cause strife between brothers as "bars of a castle." Prov. xviii. 19.

Divide. Law's delays and costs suggest a motive for appeal.
Confidence in Christ and love of earth here unite in one heart.
Anxieties about earthly riches contrasted with the holy tranquillity of the children of God. Phil. iv. 11.
Wealth is a blessing if God send it—a temptation if men ask for it.
Men misplace their discontent—they are satisfied with what they *are*, dissatisfied with what they *have*.
The reverse ought to be the case.
Men generally care first for their property, secondly for their health, lastly for their soul.
The only desire to which no bounds should be set is desire for holiness.
The wisdom and piety of the Great Prophet will divide justly.
Inheritance. The *title* of all the earth, at first, with the Creator.
Man *tenant*, not proprietor, held his portion in *trust*.
These rights fearfully violated before the deluge. Gen. vi. 13.
Creator, by the deluge, revoked the grant and took back the gift.
Canaan, divided by lot; each received title *directly* from God.
The eldest son received a double share, daughters received nothing.
The parable is against *covetousness* and not *unrighteousness*.
Too much *eagerness* in gaining his own was his sin.
Many who admire their spiritual teacher are apt to fall into the error of wishing him to settle their domestic and civil quarrels. *Bengel.*

εἶπε—The speaker a stranger. *Kuinoel.* κληρονομίαν—the *usage of lot*, evidently pointing to the original manner of receiving one's inheritance. Each *deed* of land was a sermon, as with us, each mortgage—*mort, gage; death, pledge*—reminds us of our *brief* control of earth.

---

14. *And he said unto him, Man, who made me a judge or a divider over you?*

Man. A mild, but indignant *reproof*, contrast with "My Friends," verse 4.
Made me. *Instituted.* A distinct *endorsement* of human laws.
This *question* is equivalent to a strong *negation*.
Judge. Gr. a *public* officer; "*Divider*," a *private* arbitrator.
He acknowledges the just prerogative of those appointed.
"I have not my commission from men." "My kingdom is not of this world." John xviii. 36.

I am a Redeemer from sin, not a judge of civil matters.

Over you. It was not control among His *disciples*.

The Saviour, no usurper of judicial functions. Heb. v. 5.

He might have acted as judge, or as physician. Matt. ix. 12.

A warning to His ministers, not to meddle with earth.

The world ever envious of such interference. Ex. ii. 14.

Leaving the altar, to attend to earthly affairs, often soils the garments of ministers. 2. Tim. ii. 4.

Ministers' influence *immense*, when *indirectly* exercised.

Christianity leaves civil rights, where it finds them.

It will change the social selfish *framework*, of the world.

Its power is *moral*, It works from *within*, outwardly.

He would have gained a suit, asking a *heavenly* portion.

If brethren battle among themselves, Christ is not *with* them.

The man asked the division of the inheritance. The Lord gave a prohibition against covetousness.

He did not dismiss His petitioner empty. He sent him away filled with precious truth. *Augustine*.

15. *And he said unto them, Take heed, and beware of covetousness: for a man's life consisteth not in the abundance of the things which he possesseth.*

Unto them. Not only the intruder, but all carnal ones.

Both seemed desirous of securing the larger portion.

Take heed. We have here a striking illustration of our Lord's manner of teaching.

He seizes the occasion to deliver a discourse on the sin and folly of covetousness.

Its secret approaches deceive many.

Beware. Gr. *keep watch by night*, unslumbering vigilance.

Under the guise of *economy*, the tempter instills poison.

Warning does not prove that his request was unjust.

He does him better service than if He had made him rich.

Covetousness. Luke xvi. 14. Read "*all*" before "*covetousness*," that is, *every* kind of covetousness.

Too greedily keeping one's own, as well as desiring the goods of another.

"A foolish and hurtful lust," of having *much*, and of desiring *more*.

Man's life. Rest, confidence, satisfaction of its every need.

Life, or happiness; our being's end, and aim.

How *poor*, a rich man may be! how *rich*, a poor man!

Consisteth. Earth suits not the *nature*, nor satisfies the soul.

Its fruits are not *contentment*, but envyings and frauds.
One half of the sins of mankind, may spring from this source.
Ahab's throne left him *fretting* about Naboth's *garden*.
This sin visited on Balaam, Achan, Gehazi, Ananias, Simon.
More are made covetous by riches, than rich, by covetousness.
Abundance. Not on wealth, but on the will of God.
"The little that a righteous man hath is better than the riches," &c. Psa. xxxvii. 16.
We do not live a day longer by having bread for another day.
The rust of riches forewarns by witnessing against them. Jas. v. 3.
The Kingdom of Christ cannot grow from an *earthly root*.
So abundance is not *the soil* for man's blessedness.
Lacking *permanence* it may slip any moment from us. Prov. xxiii. 5.
"He that loveth silver, is not satisfied with silver." Ecc. v. 10.
What is Alexander now the greater for his power?
What is Cæsar the higher for his honour?
What is Aristotle the wiser for his knowledge?
What delight hath Jezebel in her paint?
What happiness hath Ahab in his vineyard?
What is a delicious banquet to Dives in hell? *Farindon.*
The only foundation of *true life* must be God Himself.
Life is well lived on little; Man's *life* is of *God*, not of his goods.
He who hoards wherewith to live, ought to gather wherewith to die.
The love of Christ in the heart, can *alone* master covetousness.

αὐτοὺς, to those about Him. *Norton.* ὁρᾶτε—*mind and carefully guard against. Bloomfield.* πλεονεξίας and φιλαργυρία—πλεον. or covetousness, seeks to *grasp* what it has not; φιλ. or avarice, to *hoard*. πλεον. *is* bold and aggressive, often free in squandering, as unscrupulous in getting "*rapti largitor.*" The Pharisees were φιλ., and this was in keeping with an outward show of holiness. *Cowly* defines covetousness as "a rapacious appetite for gain, not for itself, but for the pleasure of refunding it, through all the channels of *pride* and *luxury*. Avarice, an insatiable desire of riches, for no other end than hoarding them. The covetous man resembles the greedy ostrich devouring any metal, with the intent to feed upon it. The avaricious, like the foolish *chough*, which loves to steal money, only to hide it.' *Bengel* calls covetousness "the highest kind of revolt against the Creator." It is frequently joined with *impurity*.

πλεον., is the *root*, out of which they alike grow, viz., the fierce and ever fiercer longing of the creature, turning from God, to fill itself with objects of sense. *Plato* likens πλεον., to the *sieve* of the *Danaids*, which they were ever filling, but might never fill. By a just retribution, it would stay its hunger with the swine's husks, instead of the children's bread. *Trench's Synonymes.*

ὑπαρχόντων—*superfluous possessions. Richter.* "A man must live on what he has—

more would be of no avail." *Michaelis.* He misses the meaning of ζωή. Our Saviour never uttered such flat morality. "*For not, because a man hath abundance, doth his life consist in the things which he possesseth.*" The word *life* includes time and eternity. *Alford.* Happiness consists not in wealth. *Kuinoel.* For not even if one has plenty, is his life, his goods. *De Wette.* Ζωή, not happiness, but equivalent to ψυχή. *Schott.* Add πάσης (instead of τῆς) before πλεον. πάσης—*Tischendorf, Lachmann, Alford, Brown, Wordsworth, Cod. Sinai.*

---

16. *And he spake a parable unto them, saying, The ground of a certain rich man brought forth plentifully;*

17. *And he thought within himself, saying, What shall I do, because I have no room where to bestow my fruits?*

Parable. More *parables* against taking no thought of heavenly things, and taking too much about earthly things.

Ground. Gr. *region.* His plantation had been growing into a *region.*
"Woe unto them who add field to field, until they are *alone.*" Isa. v. 8.
Agriculture, the *least exceptionable* manner of getting wealth.

Rich. Not by unfair or unjust means, but by God's blessing.
"If riches increase, set not thine heart upon them." Psa. lxii. 10.
"The prosperity of fools shall destroy them." Prov. i. 32.

Plentifully. In O. T. times, a sign of God's favor. Deut. xxx. 9.
"The Lord thy God will make thee plenteous in the fruit of thy land."
"The goodness of God leadeth thee to repentance." Rom. ii. 4.
God's richest earthly blessings oft crown the *fields* of the ungodly.

Thought. Gr. *questioned.* God ever holds us accountable for secret *thoughts.*
His secret resolutions and God's secret counsels in strange contrast.
God knows our secret desires better than we ourselves.

What shall I do? The first want of this prosperous man was contentment.
Care and anxiety without faith beget discontent.
He has no thankful song, bringing his harvest home.
No proper responsibility of being entrusted with heaven's gifts.
He does not ask, "What shall I do for others' happiness?"
There is no mention of anything for God or the poor. *Augustine.*
The hungriest beggar could not ask a more *anxious* question.
"The abundance of the rich will not suffer him to *sleep.*" Ecc. v. 12.
The character of a mind at *rest* yet void of real *repose.*
The very bounty of Providence perplexed him.

His sin was not his *possession* but his *abuse* of wealth.

No room. Alas! bosoms and sad homes of widows and orphans were "*rooms*."

My fruits. Note "*my* fruits," "*my* barns," "MY" used five times.

Just as Nabal talked of "*my* water," "*my* bread," "*my* flesh." 1 Sam. xxv. 11.

His *brief tenure* a mockery of all his proud boasting.

He may, by religious *forms*, have quieted his conscience.

Goods. He exalts his *earthly* fruits into his highest *goods*.

Mark the *misery* of the *selfish enjoyment* of the rich.

Covetous people seem unhappy in this world and in that to come.

How faith and unbelief keep their *harvest feasts*.

1. They differ in their view of blessings received. 2. In their use of them. 3. In their dependence upon them.

The more acres the more cares.

παραβολὴν—Luke iv. 23. It is hardly a parable, so clearly referring to God. *Riggenbach.* χώρα instead of χωρίον, a strictly classical distinction. τί ποιήσω may not imply a *painful* anxiety through wealth, as others through poverty. "Suppose a friend come to thee and finds thy goods stored near the *ground*, and ready to *spoil*; and kindly bids thee remove them *higher*; thou wouldst listen. But Christ bids thee raise them to *heaven*, and they will be safe there for ever." *Augustine.* διελογίζετο—He leisurely *deliberates*, that his sentence might be seen to be more just.

---

18. *And he said, This will I do: I will pull down my barns, and build greater; and there will I bestow all my fruits and my goods.*

This will I do. What boldness to plan without consulting God!

He only, who could bring about success, left out of the reckoning.

"If the Lord will, we shall live, and do this, or that." Jas. iv. 15.

I will pull down. The cares of abundance disturb his eating and drinking.

But his plans begin, continue, and end in *self*.

He entirely forgets he cannot use all these goods *himself*.

Build greater. "Their thought is, their houses shall continue forever." Psa. xlix. 11. **Barns.** Luke iii. 17. See Notes.

Bestow all. His all was embarked on a single sinking plank.

Nothing laid up, where "there will be *no more sea*," i.e., wrecks. Rev. xxi. 1.

Fruits. His thoughts are on his fields, not, of Him who made them fertile.

Not a word about his *soul*—his dying body fills his vision.

Goods. He uses this term not as his *possessions* but *treasures.*

He willingly forgets the *true good* which God pronounces *good.*

My goods —was he not God's steward, and these things merely *lent?*

Nothing is good to us, unless we communicate the same good to others.

"*It is my corn*, saith the Lord, *and my wine.*" Hosea ii. 8-9.

If asked about his mercies God would coldly have been thanked.

Within, his plans and thoughts effectually shut out his Maker.

A man is happy indeed who is not undone by his happiness. *Augustine.*

Contented opulence retiring, as usual, from the cares of life.

In all this the world finds nothing to *blame*, but much to *covet.*

His riches gathered without a stain, "Why can't he enjoy them?"

ἀποθήκας—Luke iii. 17. *γεννήματα—γεννάω*, to *produce*, *progeny*, *produce;* only used thus by later writers. ἀγαθά, neuter—*something useful;* plural, *blessings;* really, *stables*, not *chattels*. *Xenophon, W. & W.*

---

19. *And I will say to my soul, Soul, thou hast much goods laid up for many years; take thine ease, eat, drink,* and *be merry.*

I will say. On the credit of such frail security, without God's endorsement.

> "The spider's most attenuated thread is cord, is cable
> To man's slender tie on human bliss."

Was he sure the moth, the thief, the lightning would spare his barns?

May not sickness rob him of the power of taking his ease?

What interest had his *soul* in barns pressing out with corn?

Could his treasures soothe his remorseful spirit?

Soul. The self-deceit of false hope now added to discontent.

He involuntarily owns his long-desired ease is not his.

Repetition of *soul* equivalent to "Mark what I say!"

Profound *irony* in addressing his *soul*, when his goods could not sustain his *body* one day more.

For the eternal wants of his soul he had made no provision.

What folly to put off what comfort he might enjoy!

Thou hast. He understood *not* the only good *title*—through the covenant.

Much of earth's splendor and treasures are only held by the *eye.*
Men have no real *grasp* of their houses or lands.
What Christ brings is *all* the soul truly *owns.*

Much goods. Epicurean-like, his *chief good* is in the earth.
These words a mockery of his almost departing spirit!
Goods worth the name he had never desired or sought.

Laid up. What! secured against fire and foe, robbery and death?
No promise secure without the Redeemer's consent.
Treasures trusted with God the only riches really safe.
All that a dying man *possesses* is that which, as God's almoner, he has *given away.*

Many years. Hast thou a store of *years* laid up too in thy barns?
"I will multiply my days as the sand"—Job xxix. 18; a vain boast!
He felt secure of wealth remaining with him until death.
Reverses blasting others would not injure his comfort.
The dew would lie all night on his branch. Job. xxix. 19.

Take, &c. Gr. *rest, eat, drink, feast.*
God never said "Enjoy thyself," but "*Deny thyself.*" Matt. xvi. 24.
Not eat, drink, feast, but "*watch, pray, agonize.*" Matt. xxvi. 41. Luke xiii. 24.

Be Merry. Gr. generally *sensual* delight.
That night's summons spoiled his rest, meat, drink, feasting.
He forgets the Giver and greedily reserves all for *himself.*
Love of pleasure, the only sin laid to his charge.

ἀγαθὰ—He does not say χρήματα or ὑπάρχοντα, but epicurean like, ἀγαθὰ, *summum bonum.* ἀναπαύου—To an Oriental, perfect freedom from all exertion, *the* idea of happiness, similar to the *far niente* of the Italians. φάγε πίε—*Ede, bibe, lude; post mortem nulla voluptas:*—an inscription found to this hour, on the tombstone of a Roman Epicurean, in the Vatican. Our Saviour well knew how universally the unrenewed were slaves of sense.

εὐφραίνου—*Indulge, genio, make merry. W. & W.; regale. Wakefield.* It generally refers to sensual delight. εὔφραινε σεαυτόν. *Euripides, Foote.*—"Cras serum est vivere, vive hodie." Epicurean motto.

---

20. *But God said unto him,* Thou *fool, this night thy soul shall be required of thee: then whose shall those things be, which thou hast provided?*

God said. How diverse from the "Take thine ease."
By decree, while the worldling was cheering his heart, God was deciding his dreadful surprise, and eternal doom.

Or perhaps some awful judgment is meant.

"Men will praise thee, when thou doest well to thyself." Psa. xlix. 18.

"The wicked *blesseth* the covetous, whom the Lord *abhorreth.*" Psa. x. 3.

Thou fool. Pronounced by *Him*, the infallible and holy judge.

Nabal and Belshazzar trembled at their feasts.

It opposes the estimate he made of his own prudence.

1. His painful discontent. 2. Increasing care. 3. His deceitful hope. 4. His irreparable loss.

His folly was *fourfold*—

1. He forgets the Giver, God: he says "*My fruits, my goods.*"
2. He greedily reserves all for *himself.*
3. He imagines such things to be food for his immortal *soul.*
4. He forgets *death*, which was each day possible.

He devised what he should leave behind, not what he should send before him.

Eternity writes "folly" on many boasted schemes of men.

This night. Divine communications to men mostly occur at night.

There is a correspondence between *night* and the *darkness* of his soul. *Gregory.*

This decree cuts off all his long years of promised enjoyment

Epicures soon enter on their eternal award.

Thy soul. Which thou didst shut up in thy barns, and thoughtest happy.

Gr. *this soul of thine*, thou hast so gaily addressed.

Soul, which thou didst neglect, corrupt, and ruin.

Shall be. Despite thy forming plans, "My counsels are fixed."

Required. Gr. *they require*, the ministers of the Divine purpose, angels.

Not a *gracious* summons, but by force of an *arrest.*

Painfully rendered up, to My inexorable demands.

Terrible angels, like pitiless exactors of tribute, shall seize thee.

Not as a vessel when the signal is given, joyfully lifts anchor and departs.

But torn by winds, and dragged from its moorings.

Death to the righteous, comes as the dawning of the morning. Amos v. 8.

Sinking to rest. Stephen "fell asleep," Acts vii. 60. "They sleep in Jesus." 1. Thess. iv. 14.

To the wicked, death is the approach of a *tempestuous night.* Job xxvii. 20.

The rich fool appears before God's judgment, 1, with a lost name. 2, a lost soul. 3, a lost world. 4, a lost heaven.

Then whose? Not his surely, for dying, he taketh nothing. Psa. xlix. 17.

Some would rather *burn*, than adorn their houses, if they knew their future owners.

Those things. "He heapeth up riches, and knoweth not who shall gather them." Psa. xxxix. 6.

Provided. Not for himself; Where are the *I* and *my* of this boaster?

What shall *we* carry with *us* through the gates of death?

"This their way is their folly: yet their posterity approve their sayings." Psa. xlix. 13.

The curtain falls sadly over one living and dying a *fool*.

Grace is the only lasting possession. 1. Pet. i. 4.

εἶπε—By alarm of conscience or mortal sickness. No direct communication imparted. *Stier.* A silent decree of God. *Grotius, Kuinoel, Trench.* The King actually speaks. *Oosterzee.* By some judgment. *Alford.* 'Αφρον Tex. Rec. The word used by the LXX for *Nabal*, and with a reference to his history, 1. Sam. xxv. 25, 36, 38, to whom the fool in this parable bears a striking resemblance, in his words, acts, and end. *Vitringa* in *Trench*

ἀπαιτοῦσιν—without an involuntary requisition. *Theophylact;* personal for impersonal. *Grotius, Kuinoel.* ἀπαιτοῦσι.—We may supply ἄγγελοι as the nominative; angels, God's ministers and messengers demand. The impersonal form is perhaps used to soften the announcement. So in Ezekiel xxiv. 14, "shall they judge thee," *i.e., thou shalt be judged.* The subject of a verb is often omitted when some customary or familiar action is expressed; when it is some unknown or imaginary agent and the action alone is regarded. Thus we supply ἄνθρωποι, Luke xii. 48; John xv. 6. ὁ Θεός 2. Cor. vi. 3; Heb. viii. 5. ἡ γραφή, Gal. iii. 16. *Webster's Syntax.* Evil angels. *Trench.* God Himself. *Bengel, Meyer.* Angel of death requires back the debt of life. *Gerlach, Wetstein.* Robbers and murderers. *Bornemann, Oosterzee,* Luke vi. 38. Jewish doctors taught that angels kissed away the souls of the righteous. Among the catacombs of Rome, we read the epitaph—*In osculo Domini obdormivit.*

---

21. *So is he that layeth up treasure for himself, and is not rich toward God.*

So is he. The ground note of verse 20 a *sad eternity.*

These words emphatically refer to the *doom* of his soul.

Layeth up. His folly was toiling for treasures he could not *use.*

He gathered treasures but lost *them*, his *soul*, and *God.*

Enriching himself *outwardly*, impoverished himself *inwardly.*

Linking his being with perishable things he perishes with them.

Thus he became poor, blind, naked, in one hour. Rev. iii. 17.

Treasure. Restless and fruitless contrasted with the quiet abiding "rich unto God."

Not rich. *True* treasures; the world has changed its meaning.

Rich in faith—righteousness. Rev. ii. 9. Jas. ii. 5. 1. Tim. vi. 18.

His crowning error; God alone could make him rich.

To become rich one must possess God—the SOURCE of all.

A true Christian prays, believes, loses, loves, lives himself *into God.*

Rich. 1, the only true; 2, the inalienable; 3, the only all-sufficing riches.

Riches did not harm *Abraham, David, Solomon,* or *Josiah.*

Yet riches destroy more souls than poverty.

Laying up unto *himself* one gains nothing; creditor takes all.

A wise man desires no more than what he may get justly, use soberly, distribute cheerfully, and leave contentedly. *Bacon.*

Love and *faith* of the *heart* "the unsearchable riches." Eph. iii. 8.

A believing *beggar* dying, *quits* his poverty, and *goes* to his riches.

Millionaires oft in time are *beggars* in eternity. Luke xvi. 23.

Without faith, 2. Pet. i. 1. God's favour, Psa. xxx. 5. Good works, 1. Tim. vi. 18.

Toward God. Not *for God, for* HIMSELF. Nothing can be added to, or taken from *God.*

God is the believer's depository of all treasures.

HE holds Himself accountable in the world to come.

οὕτως—Thus, in utter confusion, and sudden destitution of all provision for eternity, he is dragged away. *Trench.* *θησαυρίζων—treasuring up.* A bag of gold, stolen from a *Western* steamer, was found bound to the neck of the robber, his treasure having sunk him. A striking similarity to this parable is found in Ecclesiasticus xi. 18-19. πλουτῶν—works of charity and virtue. *Beza, W. & W.*

---

22. ¶ *And he said unto his disciples, Therefore I say unto you, Take no thought for your life, what ye shall eat; neither for the body, what ye shall put on.*

23. *The life is more than meat, and the body* is more *than raiment.*

Therefore. Since your conditions are such as I have said.

I say. Your Creator, Preserver, Law-giver, and Redeemer.

The parable had condemned selfish sensual complacency.

His poor disciples were in danger of dreading *want.*

Over anxiety, another form of covetousness, the sin here spoken of.

Take no thought. Gr. *no cutting thought*, no *carking* care.
Cares *lacerate* the heart, and *furrow* the brow.
Neglecting lawful means for daily bread, we *tempt God.*
Holy freedom from care, differs widely from light-minded carelessness.
Care from *love*, is commanded; aside from *faith*, forbidden.
Difference between a blind heathen's care, and a believer's.
Christ forbids not labor of the *hands*, but mistrust of *heart.*
Earthly care—1, unworthy of us. 2, highly dangerous. 3, extremely foolish. 4, utterly useless.
Pride says, "To beg I am ashamed." Faith says, "*Give us this day*" &c.
Thoughtlessness as certainly condemned, as *over* anxiety.
Distrusting God, when over anxious, *jealousy* of His wisdom.
If willing to starve us, *would* "He give His angels charge?" &c. Psa. xci. 11.
He who gives life, withholds not food to preserve it.
His promises and covenant relations, forbid these cares.
Anxiety cannot *lengthen* our lives, or supply our wants.
A gracious *carelessness*, rolls all care on the Lord. Psa. lv. 22.
"Bread and water" promised, but no *dainties.* Isa. xxxiii. 16.
"The righteous not forsaken, or his seed begging bread." Psa. xxxvii. 25.
Your life. Care not how *long*, but *how* thou livest.
Meat. Ought to be the servant of life, but it is the master.
God bestowing the greater, pledges Himself to give the less.
The body. Food and clothing absorb nine tenths of man's cares.
Yet the *body* is but the husk or shell, the *soul* is the kernel.
The *body* is but the cask, the *soul* is the precious liquor.
The *body* is but the cabinet, the *soul* is the precious jewel.
The *body* is but the vessel or ship, the *soul* is the pilot.
The *body* is but the tabernacle, the *soul* the tenant.
The *body* is the machine only, the *soul* the animating principle.
The *body* is the dark lantern, the *soul* the candle of the Lord that burns in it. *Ray.*
If anxiety be condemned, how offensive is *ambition!*
Anxiety is so much belief, that *wealth* is safer than *God*, as a trust.
Unbelief asks not *How?* but shall I get food *at all?*
We are not so much troubled by the events of life, as by our own reflections upon them.
Venture the holy *investment*, God is able and willing to repay.

μεριμνᾶτε—Luke viii. 14; the best exposition is *μετεωρίζεσθε*—Luke xii. 29. *Do not distress yourselves by excessive solicitude.* "Take no thought for," used by *Bacon* and *Shakespeare*, as synonymous with *being over anxious. Alexander.* ψυχῄ—The soul considered as the vital principle, and rendered *life* and *soul*, in different connections. Here it should be *soul.*

φάγητε—aorist sub., suggesting doubt or contingency, translated by an Eng. *future. What ye are to eat* would be more exact. *Alexander.* The argument is from the ordinary course of Providence. Neither honors, pleasures, nor *outward* blessing, mark out the favorites of heaven, *Stier.* ὑμῶν after ψυχῄ, in the 22nd verse, omitted, *Tischendorf, Lachmann, Alford, Cod. Sinai.*

---

24. *Consider the ravens: for they neither sow nor reap: which neither have storehouse nor barn; and God feedeth them: how much more are ye better than the fowls?*

Consider. Gr. *examine accurately*, not carelessly, *investigate.*
The mysteries of Eleusis were not learned in one visit.
God's works demand long continued study.
Their loftier lessons will only be learned in heaven.
Ravens. Intensely black, with gleams of purple, passing into green.
A bird, heavier, of greater sagacity, than the crow.
Its scent, acute; voice, loud; inhabits solitary cliffs.
Its courage great, flight very high; associated with superstition.
Egyptian priests clothed in black, uttering *oracles*, called *Ravens.*
With Scandinavians emblem of *slaughter*, with Danes a *banner.*
Noah sent forth a raven from the ark. Gen. viii. 7. They fed Elijah. 1. Kings xvii. 4.
God sends proud men to school to learn faith from the ravens.
The preaching of the ravens as follows—
Excessive care is, 1, unnecessary; 2, in vain; 3, hurtful to our higher interests.
To rise above petty cares, look at greater gifts bestowed.
God seems literally to feed their young, so early forsaken of them.
Neither sow. These stages of agriculture are *binding* on men.
"The king himself is served by the field." Ecc. v. 9.
Birds a sermon on *care*, *ants* against *sloth.* Prov. vi. 6.
Storehouse, sunk some three or four feet in the dry soil.
They are covered with straw, and rise about four or six feet.
Barns. Not found in the East, were *rare* anciently.
God. Matt. *Heavenly Father*—that tender relation secures food.
Will His kindness to birds surpass that to His children?
Feedeth. Birds the least serviceable to man—the *ornaments* of earth.
"He remembereth and knoweth all the wild fowl of the mountain." Psa. l. 11.

They are fed we know not how, often the best in the severest weather.

The patriarchs wondered how their young were fed. Job xxxviii. 41. Psa. cxlvii. 9.

Very rarely birds ever perish for want of food.

Free from care, full of faith, they sing among the branches. Psa. civ. 12.

They are the *merriest* and most *musical* of God's creatures.

Their pure life and song seem an affinity with heaven.

Poets say they are half-way between flowers and angels.

Saints are nearer and dearer than birds, being *heirs*.

He that remembers His birds cannot forget His babes.

By faith saints are wiser than the fowls of heaven. Job. xxxv. 11.

Earthly anxieties *dampen* our zeal and *silence* our songs.

Unbelievers without the wisdom even of the storks. Jer. viii. 7.

Better. Of more value in the estimation of the Creator.

Hints about the irrational creatures in the Bible, very few.

Here He indicates that they have *some value*, hence cruelty to them is an insult to the Creator.

Fowls. Gr. *birds;* now restricted to domestic species. In old English, birds in general.

κατανοήσατε—*κατα* intensive. *ἐμβλέψατε*—Matt. scrutinize. Comparing by the microscope, the finest velvet of human skill, with the texture of flowers, the *contrast* is seen to be literally *infinite. Bridgewater Treatise.* *κόρακας*—The raven's association with the ark, doubtless the origin of the superstition with respect to it. The priests of *Ammon* were similar to a class in *Greece*. Those seen in the catacombs, playing on the harp, are clothed in *black*. As a symbol it occurs among the *Normans. Smith, Kitto.*

θερίζουσιν from *θέρος* summer. *ταμεῖον*—*ἀποθήκη*, former for *fruit*, the latter for grain. *Lightfoot.* *μᾶλλον διαφ.*—are ye *not much more valuable? Doddridge. Have ye not greatly the advantage? W. & W.* *τρέφει*—No chance, no blind iron handed fate, governs the world. *Stier.*

---

25. *And which of you with taking thought can add to his stature one cubit?*

26. *If ye then be not able to do that thing which is least, why take ye thought for the rest?*

Which of you? As opposed to God, who feeds all His creatures.

Taking thought. Gr. *cutting* or corroding cares.

Fretting brings no relief but doubles our cares.

Our *stature* as our *features* entirely depend on Providence.

Our strength and stature relate to the magnitude of our earth.

As the density of the air relates to the strength of our lungs,
So the light, and whole economy of nature, to our body.
Our growth *mysterious* in its process, and without our will.

Stature. Gr. also for *age*. In God's measure a hand-breadth, a span. Psa. xxxix. 5.

" Teach me to know the measure of my days." Psa. xxxix. 4.

Cubit. Generally reckoned about eighteen inches.

The length from the point of the elbow to the end of the middle finger.

If *our own* stature is not in our power, much less all the creatures from which we derive our meat and drink.

To God leave the care of the body, by whom, the body and its particular stature, are determined. *Bede.*

That which is least. The argument proceeds from the greater to the less in verse 23.

Now by the contrary process it is shown that our cares are useless.

To add a cubit to our stature, a small thing with Almighty God.

On the contrary, it is a great thing, that He has given us the stature necessary to us.

Nay, more, has given us daily and yearly produce for our wants.

These things are the rest, and they are less in our power than the height of our stature.

Yet they are much more needful to our support.

μεριμνῶν and ἕνα omitted by *Tischendorf*, *Alford;* retained, *Lachmann*, *Wordsworth*. ἡλικίαν—primarily *age*, *Rosenmuller*, *Stier*. *Olshausen*, *Tholuck*, *Alford*, *Alexander*. Its secondary sense, stature; staturam. *Vulg.* We speak of an *inch* of *time*. "If our earth were the size of Jupiter, gravity would be eleven times greater. The *stature* and strength remaining the same, the lightness of the fawn, the speed of the deer, the power of the horse, the energy of man, would be gone. For man to lift himself erect, or crawl from place to place, would be a labor more painful and tedious than the motions of the sloth." *Whewell.* πῆχυν—*cubitus*, a measure from the elbow to the end of the finger. Orientals question the *vain:*—"Has your money made you a cubit higher?" Life here compared to a race-course or stadium. *Wetstein. Campbell.* Life a continuous thread. *Alberti.*

---

27. *Consider the lilies how they grow: they toil not, they spin not; and yet I say unto you, that Solomon in all his glory was not arrayed like one of these.*

Consider. Our Lord would accustom us to habits of reflection.

Lilies. The royal color, except in Persia, was white.

The robes of kings defeated left, on the field. Psa. lxviii. 14.
The battle field was "white as snow in Salmon."
Solomon's robes were white. Ecc. ix. 8; Josephus Lib. 8, c. 7.
Mordecai's royal robe of blue and white; Esther viii. 15. Alexander in white entered Jerusalem.
Our Lord on Tabor in coronation robe of *white;* Luke ix. 29. Herod's robe white. Acts xii. 21.
It seems to have been silver tissue, it glistened exceedingly. *Josephus.*
Angels sent to Cornelius and at the sepulchre were in *white.*
The *coronation* robes of kings are *white.* Rev. i. 6. Rev. iii. 4-5.
He might have named the gorgeous plumage of the *birds.*
He descends to flowers, the lowest scale of creation.
Grow, to a tall and slender height, *how* is a mystery.
Their beauty, unlike fine dress, unfolds from *within.*
As nothing from *without* can *defile,* so nothing, unless from *within,* can *adorn.*
All true ornaments proceed from the Spirit working *within.* 1. Pet. iii. 4.
Toil not, as men in the field; labour ever honoured of God. Gen. ii. 15.
Spin not. He glances at, and *elevates* work into sermons.
Art known in Egypt; Joseph's *vestures of fine linen.* Gen. xli. 42.
Hebrews wrought with *spindles.* Isa. xix. 9; Prov. xxxi. 19.
The priest's robe seamless. Ex. xxxix. 27.
I say. Not to the *importance* but improbability of the remark.
Solomon in all his glory. Solomon on state days, or days of glory was accustomed to sit upon an ivory throne arrayed in a white robe, and bearing in his hand an ivory sceptre; yet though invested in dazzling brightness, resembling the magnificent lily in its color—"I say unto you, that Solomon in all his glory was not arrayed like one of these."
1. Solomon with glory. 2. Lilies with more glory. 3. Christ's people with more than both.
All his glory, not moral excellence, but external splendor.
The O. T. *glory* refers to the Shechinah primeval *theophanies.*
Here, to regal costumes, worn publicly, present to Christ's eye.
Queen of Sheba wondered at the attire of Solomon's servants. 1. Kings x. 4-7.
Arrayed. Gr. *flung around.* Ease and luxuriance seen in all the works of God.
Solomon surpasses our *wisdom,* the lily, his *glory.*
God neglects and forgets nothing, as to man, beast, flower, birds.
He lavishes the treasures of beauty and glory on a *fading* flower.

He thus rebukes our vanity, in vain efforts to *shine.*
Garments at the beginning, a mere modest covering of nakedness.
Of that monument of our *guilt* and *shame*, we became *vain.*
"The fine linen is the righteousness of saints." Rev. xix. 8.
"They washed their robes, and made them white in the blood of the Lamb." Rev. vii. 14.

λέγω referred to Solomon's known, proverbial illustrations, drawn from nature. *κατανοήσατε*—Matt. has *καταμάθετε*, an intensive compound, to *discern.* *πῶς αὐξάνει*, an interrogation. *Bengel:* Luke xii. 27. *Campbell;* omitted by *Tischendorf, Alford;* probably inserted from Matt. *τὰ κρίνα*—Persian term signifies "*white.*" *Gesenius.* It is not necessary to suppose pomp of gorgeous colors, but delicacy and beauty of texture. *Alford*, The Byzantian lily. *Royle, Smith, Kitto;* white lily. *Bengel.* The Roman princes and Jewish monarchs wore *white. Friedlieb;* some few, purple. *Henry, Potter, Elsley, Meyer, Jennings, Ho'den.* Hirleh, lily of Tabor. *Thompson.* The Siriaca lilia of brilliant red, growing wild around Galilee. *Bowring.* Some gaudy, gay looking, flower. *W. & W.*

ἐν τούτων—Pattern makers forsaking the divine, and following the ever changing fashions, have been compelled to return and use the *same blending of colors found in nature. Hutchinson.* God, with rare kindness, adapts each bird and beast in its *covering*, to the climate it inhabits. Among icy regions we find *furry skins* and thick *down;* wool in temperate climes; and in tropical, silk and cotton. *Kirby.*

---

28. *If then God so clothe the grass, which is today in the field, and tomorrow is cast into the oven; how much more* will he clothe *you, O ye of little faith?*

If God. He has robes for flowers, and raiment for His children.
So clothe. Thus he attires frail ornaments in gorgeous colors.
He lavishes matchless splendors upon footstool carpetings.
Grass. Flowers are grass—glory of the grass, but *fairer* and *frailer.*
Somewhat gayer, comelier, and better apparelled. 1. Pet. i. 24.
Like men of honour fading and shorter lived. Psa. xc. 6.
Disease quickly blasts our vigor and wastes our beauty.
The *grave* the *oven*, into which great and humble are cast.
Knowledge and piety the only apparel outlasting the tomb.
To-morrow. "So also shall the rich man fade away in his ways." Jas. i. 11.
Cast into. No trees but fruit-bearing in Judæa. Isa. x. 19. Num. xiii. 20.
Grass, grape, vine, roots, and ordure the common fuel.
Ovens, of *copper, earthen,* or *stone* ware, all portable.

Fire kindled on the top, and loaves are placed inside.
Small cavities with stones are heated and dough laid on them.
How much? Painful anxieties cherished, reproach Providence.
Early rising and bread of sorrow show distrust in God. Psa. cxxvii. 2.
Children perplex not themselves with their parents' affairs.
Our Father has the POWER and WILL to provide for His own.
Trust the curious builder of these bodies for their support.
Clothing His humblest works in matchless splendor.
He will not forget His heirs, bearing the image of His Son.
Little faith. No amount of anxiety betters our estate.
"Be careful for nothing, but in everything by prayer, let your requests be made known unto God." Phil. iv. 6.
In a sad hour of prayer, at the Cape of Good Hope, *Henry Martyn* found a lonely flame colored flower, recalling this text, girded his mind and praised God.
Want of faith, causes more heart-aches, than want of raiment.

χόρτον—enclosure, pasture, grass. Little girls, in oriental towns, seen mixing millet straw with camel ordure, thus forming cakes, and drying them, sell them for *fuel*. *κλίβανον*, Attic *κρίβανος*—a covered copper vessel, larger at the bottom. Orientals, in domestic utensils, only one remove beyond Western Indians. ὀλιγόπιστοι—but one word for five English words. *ἀμφιέννυσι*—*invests*, referring to *sumptuous* apparel.

---

29. *And seek not ye what ye shall eat, or what ye shall drink, neither be ye of doubtful mind.*

Seek not. Gr. has the idea of *earnestness* and *anxiety*.
To the poor the gospel is preached, words of *warning* and *promise*.
While pledging food and raiment, it notes the evil of *solicitude*.
It warns against striving after *luxuries* and dainties.
Poverty has wondrous privileges, and splendid promises.
It has peculiar dangers, and needs peculiar warnings.
Doubtful, easily tossed to and fro, by contending hopes and fears.
Do not rise and shine like a *meteor*, and meet its fate.
Flights of fancy create imaginary wants and discontent.
Serenity of mind alone found building on the ROCK OF AGES!

μετεωρίζεσθε—originally to the driving about of the clouds. *Major.* Eng. *meteor.* *Nolite in sublime tolli. Vulg., Meyer,* and *Luther.* Be not in suspense. *Alford,* Be not like ships tossed aloft on the billows of worldly anxiety. *Wordsworth.* *Be not unsettled in your mind.* Be not anxiously fluctuating between hope and fear. *Theophylact. Grotius, Wetstein, Kuinoel.* "Ne fluitem dubiæ spe pendulus horæ." *Hor.,* Epis, I. "Float on the balance of the wavering hour." Originally *pride* or *loftiness* ;—clouds floating high. *Hammond.* Exposes the troubles of men's minds in war. *Thucydides.*

---

30. *For all these things do the nations of the world seek after: and your Father knoweth that ye have need of these things.*

These things. Grovelling pleasures of earth, were all they knew.
Life becoming intolerable, they sought refuge in suicide.
Ignorant whether the gods heard their prayers, or could help, if they did.
Ye cherish *heathenish* doubts about God's omniscience.
Ye are no strangers to a better inheritance.
Nations. All not Israelites, were counted *heathen.* Psa. ii. 8.
Will ye return to heathenism in your *hearts?*
Leave care to Gentiles, who, so far as they know have *no Father.*
Heathen in prayer, only knew or sought *temporal* blessings.
Father. Our Lord's way of speaking is extremely to be observed.
He does not say "God knoweth," or "the Lord knoweth."
But, *your Heavenly* Father, knows your wants, and regards them with a Father's feelings.
Precious name, the ground of assurance and victory
1. There is One who knows what we want. 2. This One is our Father. 3. Jesus leads us to this Father.
Children of kings, need not torment themselves with petty cares.
If He purposes to bestow *heaven,* He will not withhold *bread.*
Knoweth. Pagan gods were deemed disgraced by regarding trifles.
Sages, heroes, crowns and realms, claimed their notice.
Earth's down trodden millions, they disregarded.

ἔθνη—plural: refers to the heathen who were restless in their deep ignorance of the powers above. *Doddridge.* Πατὴρ οἶδεν—Tully thus sadly writes: *De Nat Deo.* "*Magna Dii curant, parva negligunt.*" Stoicism was but the bright side of heroic despair. *Ireland's Ann. Mor.*

31. ¶ *But rather seek ye the kingdom of God; and all these things shall be added unto you.*

Seek ye. *Ye*, emphatic, in contrast with heathen.
Greeks and Romans *persistently, passionately sought* life's pleasures.
As if the gods were *ignorant* of or *unable* to supply their wants.
First, Matt. Not with the intention of seeking the world *afterwards*.
Some with prayer *begin* days of avarice and anxiety.
First, as to the morning of the day, and morning of life.
First in *value*, earth's joys are of little worth.
Religion so fills the heart there is no room for vanities.
He does not say *above;* experience brings out the rigorous strictness.
No one begins *well* whose plan does not embrace *the Kingdom*.
No one who seeks in *earnest* will find his labor in vain.
Solomon sought *wisdom*, riches and honour were flung into the scale.
He who buys a treasure of jewels hath the cabinet into the bargain. *Reynolds*.
He who buys goods has paper and twine flung in. *Henry*.
Kingdom. The Jews desired an *external* kingdom without the *internal*.
This kingdom, existing of old, typified by the Mosaic theocracy.
Bestowed in Christ, essentially complete in its form.
Secretly advancing in the world, destined to a final conquest.
Kings and statesmen toiling for thrones resemble children making palaces in sand.
His righteousness, Matt. Conformity to God's will only rule of right,
Seeking a kingdom above excludes anxiety about earthly comforts.
Cares of earth not expelled by a mere act of the *will*.
The heart must be filled with other interests.
Religion is nothing unless *heaven* be involved in it.
Yet, "Godliness has the promise of the life that *now is*." 1. Tim. iv. 8.
These things. The outer mercies, perishable gifts of time.
Our Lord condemns not earthly comforts nor proper diligence.
He rigorously demands that they shall not be our *treasure*.
He would fix our gaze on the *crown*, not the trappings of royalty.
Added. Matt. Gr. *shall*, as we say, "BE GIVEN" into the bargain, to believers.

βασιλείαν, ἐπουράνιος, τοῦ Χριστοῦ, τοῦ Δαυίδ, Mark xi. 10, are all the same terms, as the everlasting kingdom. Dan. ii. 44. *προστεθή*.—shall be given unto you in the bargain. *Oosterzee*. Omit "*rather*," not in the Greek. For *βασιλείαν τοῦ Θεου* read *βασιλειαν αὐτοῦ*, and omit *πάντα*. *Tischendorf, Lachmann, Alford, Cod. Sinai.*

32. *Fear not, little flock; for it is your Father's good pleasure to give you the kingdom.*

Notice, 1, the command—Fear not; 2, the title—Little flock; 3, the reward—God has promised a kingdom.

The comparison sheep, i.e., creatures useful, harmless, defenceless, clean, sociable, with many foes, prone to wander, never returning of themselves; of them it is said that, they know their Shepherd and are all known by Him. The Christian's rule in life, and the departed Christian's epitaph—"The sheep of the flock following their Shepherd. The disciples of Christ gone to take possession of the Kingdom. Gone to abide with the Great Shepherd."

Fear not. Forethought distinguishes man from brutes.

It often renders him unhappy by over anxiety.

While the *Chief Shepherd* rules, no cause for dreading want.

"He that cometh to me shall never hunger." John vi. 35.

A word of consolation; 1, to those dreading inward foes; 2, to those dreading the wrath of men; 3, to those dreading invisible foes.

Little flock. A diminutive, very sweet and very full of love. A chosen term, as *Shepherd* is with Christ.

Contrasted with the vast multitude crowding round. Verse 1.

Free from cities' sorrows and crimes the shepherd tends his fleecy store.

"I will give you pastors, who shall feed you with knowledge." Jer. iii. 15.

Cyrus, His shepherd, sent back His flock to Canaan. Isa. xliv. 28.

"I will set up one SHEPHERD over them, He shall feed," &c. Ezek. xxxiv. 23.

The good shepherd giveth his life for the sheep. Acts xx. 28; Isa. liii. 6; John x. 15.

"Awake, O sword, against my shepherd." Zec. xiii. 7.

By His *death*, He opens the door. By His *Spirit*, brings them in.

"My sheep hear my voice, I know them, and they follow Me." John x. 27.

Little. Gr. *the little;* especially in its beginnings, and despised as such by the world.

A term 1, of endearment. 2, helplessness. 3, insignificance.

Christ's converts few, but He always had a flock.

"He came to His own, and His own received Him not." John i. 11.

How few converts at the Flood, few at the calling of Abraham.

A gleaning of grapes, two or three on the uppermost boughs. Isa. xvii. 6.

Five hundred brethren, and one hundred and twenty gathered. 1. Cor. xv .6. Acts i. 15.

"Narrow is the way;" Matt. vii. 14. "But few are chosen;" Matt. xx. 16.
His church a *garden* spot, in the wilderness. Isa. lviii. 11.
This little flock is sent forth as sheep among wolves.
No danger of being overpowered: "*Fear not,*" cheers them.
All who belong not to Christ's flock, belong to the *world's herd.*

Good pleasure. Free, but sovereign grace.
"As many as were ordained unto eternal life, believed." Acts xiii. 48.

To give. Salvation not of *merit*, but of *grace*. Eph. ii. 5-8.
"The gift of God is eternal life, through Jesus Christ our Lord." Rom. vi. 23.
I told you to *seek* the kingdom. I now say "*He will give* it."
Be it your chief care, and earnest prayer, to prepare for it.

The kingdom. God has *kingdoms*, *crowns*, *thrones*. 1. Pet. v. 4. Rev. iii. 21.
The encircling love, and high inheritance are in reserve.
Doubting believers sometimes ask—if bread be promised?
A king's son has no cause for anxiety about meat or raiment.
1. Fear not *calamities*. "The Lord is my helper, and I will not fear what man can do unto me." Heb. xiii. 6.
2. Fear not *spiritual foes*. Erring man seeks strange pastures.
Sheep of themselves prone to wander, but seldom or never return.
Peter had *one look*. He felt the gathering arm of His grace.
3. Fear not *death*, "Though I walk through the valley." Psa. xxiii. 4.
This kingdom is in *reversion*. Grace given, is glory begun.
It is not called *a* kingdom, but *the* kingdom, worth all those Satan showed our Lord. *Donne.*
Of all the gracious words, that ever preceded from the lips of incarnate love, this may be accounted the most gracious. *Ford.*
"O taste and see how gracious the Lord is." "Blessed is the man, that trusteth in Him." 2. Pet. i. 4.

ποίμνιον—a *diminutive*, μικρὸν makes it a *double diminutive*; equal to a *very little flock*,—giving great emphasis to ὀλίγοι εὑρίσκοντες of Matt. vii. 14. *Olshausen*, *Major.* Double diminutives, after the manner of the *Italian*, indicate *affection* or *tenderness of appellation*. *Bloomfield.* τὸ—equivalent to *My little* flock. *Campbell.* εὐδόκησεν—*God takes pleasure in the thought.* He enjoys his prescience.—*Silently rests in His love.* Zep. iii. 17. The tenderness and energy of many texts relating to *election*, heretofore *dry rods of controversy*, when thus viewed, bud out into a thousand fair leaves and fragrant blossoms of hope and joy. *Doddridge.* βασιλείαν. Luke xi. 2. Note.

33. *Sell that ye have, and give alms; provide yourselves bags which wax not old, a treasure in the heavens that faileth not, where no thief approacheth, neither moth corrupteth.*

Sell all. Do not hoard it for yourself; do not like the rich fool, call them *your fruits.*
Do not consider yourselves *proprietors* of your goods.
Regard them not as *your's* but as *God's.*
Sell them to God, and dispose of them in *mercy* for the wants of others.
This is not a command that no money be kept for own use, but that righteousness should not be neglected through fear of poverty. *Bede.*
They make the best of bargains, who secure eternal life.
They obtain the best of treasures, who carry them through the grave.
Self-righteous, lazy, mendicant friars, a *burlesque* on the text.
Men may part with all, only to be more covetous than before.
The command was given in good earnest, to the young man.
It demands the soul to be *unfettered* of earth-born weights.
It requires a consecration of all our means to God.
Mariners save the vessel, by throwing the cargo into the sea.
Possessions cease to be *harmless*, the moment they acquire the *mastery.*
Esteem it no *loss*, if your *all* is destroyed for Christ's sake.
No sacrifice of treasure, *meritorious* in purchasing heaven.
Some give their *all* to the poor and still lose heaven. 1. Cor. xiii. 3.
That ye have. Gr. *possessions*, property, substance.
Believers must be benevolent at their *own* expense.
No investment on earth can ever approach acts of love in *security.*
Alms. The art of giving, so as to become not poorer, but richer.
Believers rich in good works. 1. Tim. vi. 18. Pity lends to the Lord. Prov. xix. 17.
Provide. Christians *seek* for, not *wait* for, objects of charity.
Bags. Luke x. 4. Treasure of unbelievers, in "*bags with holes.*" Hag. i. 6.
Bags, purses, refers to small sums; *treasure* to larger amounts.
Wax not old. The securities of earth uncertain, and fail at death, entirely.
Treasure. Goods lent for a season—stewards misnamed owners.
Earth's title to *personal* and *real* estate will mock the *soul.*
Thoughts, *plans*, *pleasures*, point to one's real treasure.
Heavens. Earthly homes are doomed to the flames.
Wise invest in a city that hath *foundations.* Heb. xi. 10.
Ask thyself, O soul! where are thy treasures and thine heart?

Faileth. Sin essentially curses earth's good things.
Heavenly treasures spoil not by keeping, nor waste by spending.
Spiritual in origin and heavenly in nature, therefore imperishable.
Eternity uses, never *exhausts* or *lessens them.*
Thief. In that golden city marauders cannot *enter.*
Darkness cannot conceal—no night there. Rev. xxi. 25.
Moth. Treasures in garments were formerly immense.
Crassus, a wealthy Roman, had 30,000 changes of raiment.
Moths, like thieves, go by night and *secretly* destroy. Hosea v. 12.
They prefer the foul to the clean, *destroying* what they do not *consume.*
Corrupteth. Gr. *thoroughly destroys.* At death, the last vestige disappears.
He is no fool who parts with that he cannot keep, when he is sure to receive that he cannot lose. *Henry.*
We visit the sick, and the Spirit of comfort visits us.
We help our brethren, and holy angels minister unto us.
We cover the naked with garments, and God covers us with joy.
We are instruments in the conversion of a sinner, and shine as stars.
We part with a few pieces of gold or silver, and the hand of mercy turns them into a glorious crown.
We sow temporal transitory things, and reap eternal joys.
The best *gains* are those we purchase with our *loss.*
The best way to "find bread is to cast it upon the waters." *Farindon.*

πωλήσατε figuratively, *Rosenmuller;* literally, *Kuinoel.* ὑπάρχοντα, *that ye have,* denotes possessions. This Divine portrait of Christian Communism has been caricatured by Fourierism, and other offshoots of infidelity. *Stier.* βαλλάντια, Luke x. 4, *purses;* βάλλω, to lay up. ἀνέκλειπτον, only used here, *inexhaustible.* ἐγγίζει—implying they cannot *enter,* much less *rob.* Rev. xxi. 27. σὴς—Land moths never enter wool or fur goods carefully attended; water moths deposit themselves in straws that they may float, if too *heavy,* they add a piece of *straw* or *wood,* if too light, a bit of gravel. *Kirby.* διαφθείρει *thoroughly destroys.* Matt. ἀφανίζει, *disfigures.*

---

34. *For where your treasure is, there will your heart be also.*

Treasure. Plans, words, pleasures, define this term.
Objects supremely loved, infallibly determine character.
What men value they will love—the two not divorced.
Depraved hearts practically deny this truism.

Our hearts follow our treasures to heaven while we are here.
We keep our eye upon them—they cheer our hopes, enliven zeal.
Heart. This gives us a deeper insight into the soul.
Men *profess* to love, "while in works they deny God." Tit. i. 16.
Many admit the truth in *theory* yet deny it in *practice*.
The Divine paradox, "Heart and treasure must go together." Luke xiv. 26.
The friendship of the world enmity with God. Jas. iv. 4.
Men believe they can serve God and mammon. Luke xvi. 13.
The heart *identifies* itself with the object sought—
1. Loving gold intensely, the heart becomes *hard* and *cold* as metal.
2. Loving flesh, one becomes supremely *sensual*.
3. Loving God, it becomes *spiritual*—pure and heavenly.
Supreme love of the world idolatry, *treason* against God.

Καρδία. This sentiment is key to that noble thought, "Domine quia nos fecisti ad te, cor nostrum inquietum nobis, donec requiescat in te." *Augustine.* Nam ego sum hic, animus domi est. *Plautus.* I am here, my heart is at home (with my treasure).

---

35. *Let your loins be girded about, and your lights burning;*

Loins girded. Loose, flowing, oriental dress needs a *girdle*.
Made of leather, highly ornamented with needlework.
Also *cotton*, *linen*, and rarely *silk*, like a military sash.
Ancient boatmen, shipbuilders, hunters, all were girded.
Type of courage—it promotes the power of *endurance*.
A loosened girdle, symbol of an *unprepared* mind.
"Relax not the girdle of your *diligence*."—*Greek Proverb*.
With soldiers it meant to *arm* one's-self—Eph. vi. 14—a warrior's postr
Money, ink-horn, carpenter's rules, carried in it.
Desiring *haste*, Elijah girded his loins to run. 1. Kings xviii. 46.
With citizens it meant to *prepare* for work. Luke xvii. 8.
Robes often torn or defiled when flowing loosely. 1. Pet. i. 13.
Truth binds our souls from being entangled. 2. Tim. ii. 4.
As we walk around briars and thorns, so avoid snares.
The highest part of the unrenewed soul, *glued* to earth.
Partakers of the Serpent's curse, they mind earthly things. Phil.
Fair weather tempts to ungird; Satan's blasts nerve the soul.

Girding depicts *diligence;* lamps, *watchfulness.*
Lights. Gr. *lamps*, made of earth or brass, silver or gold.
Burned throughout the night, hence "*outer darkness.*" Matt. xxii. 13.
In temples, imply unceasing devotion; in sepulchres, unceasing affection.
Lights of morality and virtue all go out.
Olive trees supplied temple lamps perpetually. Zech. iv. 2.
Lamps burned all night, confusion of lighting them avoided.
Being ready to open cheerfully at their Lord's first knock.
Working by a wrong rule, to *slumber* with earth's treasures only.
To be girded, signifies activity; to have the light burning, knowledge and love. *Cyril.*

Ἔστωσαν ὑμῶν—οἱ λύχνοι καιόμενοι—*Let your lamps stand burning. Gesenius*, Luke xi. 33. A reminiscence of these words is found in 1. Peter i. 13. *Oosterzee.* λύχνοι, plural—various energies. *Braune.* Remove all obstacles. *Lisco.* A very meagre idea. *Stier.* εὔζωνος—well girded, or *active. Alte præcinctus. Hor.* The English word *expedition*, gathering the garment, *expede*, from the feet, by the girdle. Glass lamps were used in Egypt, at the time of our Saviour *(Wilkinson)*, they may have been in Palestine. Animal oils never used, always *olive* oil. These counsels allude to the parable of the Ten Virgins. *De Wette.* ζώνη—The entire armor. *Homer.* ἐν ταις χερσὶν ὑμῶν added. *Tischendorf;* omitted. *Alford, Lachmann.*

---

36. *And ye yourselves like unto men that wait for their lord, when he will return from the wedding; that when he cometh and knocketh, they may open unto him immediately.*

Ye yourselves, i.e., that your whole conduct and demeanor.
Wait. Gr. waiting with a longing *desire* for His arrival.
Connexion between death and judgment *near* as to *result.*
Remote in point of *time;* some thought His advent near.
"Watch and pray"—shew the constant *expectation* of believers.
Probation ended when men on trial fell.
We are now "prisoners of hope"—Zec. ix. 12, but not of despair.
We are all under condemnation but respited. John. iii. 18.
An unfolding of character ever going on. Matt. xiii. 30.
Believers should look on death with chastened joy.
As servants, earnestly and impatiently long for their master.
Return. Hour of death closes for ever our mercies and works.
Servants made great preparations for the bridegroom's return.
Wedding. Luke xiv. 16. Oriental marriage customs.

Knocketh, by loss of property, health, character and friends.
When *God* knocketh, our hearts should open. Rev. iii. 20.
Open. A *ready, waiting posture,* becoming faithful servants.
Immediately. Few will thus *open immediately* when He knocks.
They will have something to do first, they will have to get ready.
They will need time to collect themselves, and summon their better thoughts and affections.
Life is short, death is certain, the world to come is eternal.
"That ye be not ashamed before Him at His coming." 1. John, ii. 28.
The absolute necessity of being constantly *prepared.*
No pause long enough to *light* a *lamp,* or gird the loins.
Coming not so early as *impatience,* nor so late as *indifference,* desires.
Parable of virgins a type of the *wedding; here,* the *return* from it.
The blessed ones are those who watch *longingly,* patiently.
Patience makes longing mighty; longing makes patience watchful. *Braune.*

ἀναλύσει—σῃ. *Tischendorf.* Latin, *solvere;* to weight anchor, *intrans.,* to *depart* or *return.* About the fourth century, it was thought the Second Advent would be literal—1, Jerusalem rebuilt, and become the centre of His kingdom. 2, the just would rise first. 3, Christ would appear in person. 4, the terrestial paradise would be restored. These views held, with variations, by many distinguished and excellent men, charmed by their novelty; yet it is questionable, whether ultimately, they prove as vigorous aids to piety, as the common faith. *Foote.*

τῶν γάμων. Messiah seems to celebrate His nuptials in heaven, and returning to His dwelling, to crown His faithful servants—The festivities are furnished. *Oosterzee.* doubted by *Bengel, Stier.*

---

37. *Blessed* are *those servants, whom the lord when he cometh shall find watching: verily I say unto you, that he shall gird himself, and make them to sit down to meat, and will come forth and serve them.*

Blessed. Servants no longer, but wedding *guests,* of the king.
Even a faithful servant may not have *such order* as he ought.
If he can open immediately, his blessedness is enviable.
It will then be a time of reward, to the persecuted.
Servants. Believers of every name, "following the Lamb." Rev. xiv. 4.
The Lord. Gr. *their* Lord.
Cometh. The hour uncertain, to some, an awful *surprise.*

Watching. A time of prevailing *security* among many.
Verily. With a solemn "*Amen*, I say unto you," a wonder of mercy.
Indicates not so much assurance, as *improbability*.
Gird. Bridegroom in England formerly waited on the guests.
Transcendent honors are in reserve, for the faithful.
Our Redeemer thus girded, washed His disciples' feet. John xiii. 5.
It implies an exaltation, beyond our highest expectations.
Sit. Thus favorite slaves, freed, were treated, by *Roman* masters.
To meat. Lord's supper, a prelude and *prophecy* of that immortal banquet. Rev. xix. 9.
"Eat, O friends, drink abundantly, O beloved." Sol. Song v. 1.
Come forth. Gr. act of *coming* forward, presenting one's self to speak.
To serve. Stephen saw Him *standing up from His throne*, to welcome Him.
Figure expanded to *sharing His throne*. Rev. iii. 20-21.
He served the church, assuming the "form of a servant." Phil. ii. 7.
Bridegrooms rarely assumed the office, or duties of a servant.
The Lord Himself, in the great day of His glory, will invert the order of human arrangements.
In the fulness of His grace and love He will serve His brethren.
The Redeemer will serve the redeemed.
The Master wlll serve the servants.
The King will serve the subjects. *Alford.*

περιζώσεται—shall take the place of the servant himself. *παρελθὼν*—*coming in turn to each.* *διακονήσει*—*Romans* had their *Saturnalia*, *Cretans* their *Hermaea*, and Babylonians their Succa. The agricultural labors of the year at an end, public business courts, schools, were suspended; no malefactor was punished; slaves, both good and bad, wore the cap of freedom *(pileus)*, had freedom of speech, and sat down to banquets, in the attire of their masters, who waited upon them. *Elsley*, *Bekker's Gallus.* To displace this festivity, Christmas was located during this season, by *Julius I*, and the *carnival* proves the merry *making* of the *Saturnalia*.

---

38. *And if he shall come in the second watch, or come in the third watch, and find* them *so, blessed are those servants.*

Second watch. The first watch is not mentioned, since that was the hour of the nuptial feast.
The Jews and Greeks had but *three* watches.

Jews conquered, adopted the *four* watches of the Romans.
The second and third watches the time of *deepest sleep*.
Blessed. Servants' fidelity *tested* become wedding guests.
Men generally seek those things causing eternal misery.

τριτῃ φυλ.—Our Lord follows the *Roman* division of four watches. *Oosterzee*, *Alford*. The Greek division of three. *Lisco*, *Olshausen*. The marriage occurs on the first, and *decorum* would hasten the return. The first and fourth are not named. *Alford*. οἱ δοῦλοι—omitted. *Tischendorf*, *Alford*, *Cod. Sinai*. Read—*Blessed are they*.

---

39. *And this know, that if the goodman of the house had known what hour the thief would come, he would have watched, and not have suffered his house to be broken through.*

This know. *Forewarned* is to be *forearmed* for believers.
Goodman. Gr. *the master of the house*. Represents the impenitent, unprepared to meet Christ.
Even believers may be more or less *surprised* at death.
Things might have been in a little better *order*.
Conscious of general fidelity he opens, trusting to mercy Divine.
To him always ready "an entrance abundantly," &c. 2. Pet. i. 11.
What hour. He gives no other warning save the word of His Gospel.
Thief. Represents *sudden*, *violent* loss of wealth, health, or life.
The possession of false and unwarrantable goods.
Unfaithful servants will lose all their privileges.
Moth represents *silent* waste or *gradual* exhaustion.
The Judgment day will be unexpected. Rev. xvi. 15, 2. Pet. iii. 10.
The day of *death* is as secret as the day of Judgment.
That which follows clothes it with deepest solemnity.
Watched. The uncertainty as to the hour makes watchfulness constantly necessary.
Men guard their treasures with vigilance.
The soul, the only thing worth the pains, unguarded.
A believer has, 1, an eye open to the light; 2, a hand active for work; 3, a foot ever ready to open unto Him.
Broken through. Mud walls still exist in Palestine. Ezek. viii. 8-12.

οἰκοδεσπότης—Representative of all unbelievers. *Olshausen.* Believers. *Stier.* κλέπτης—the house ruler. *Olshausen.* The Lord Himself. *Oosterzee, Stier.* The ἄρχων.—Our Lord does not enforce truth by motives drawn from the certainty of death, itself a mere transition, being a slender motive. *Olshausen, Oosterzee, Lange.* διορυγῆναι—*to dig* or *break through.*

---

40. *Be ye therefore ready also: for the Son of man cometh at an hour when ye think not.*

41. ¶ *Then Peter said unto him, Lord, speakest thou this parable unto us, or even to all?*

Son of Man. Luke v. 24. See Notes.
Ready. Equipped for eternity—"That I may be found *in Christ.*"
Threatenings of instant judgment were not for believers.
Parable. Luke v. 36; iv. 23. See Notes.
Unto us. It indicates Peter's characteristic—over confidence.
First to them as stewards, then to all servants of His house.
No state or condition exempt from the Judgment. Heb. ix. 27.

42. *And the Lord said, Who then is that faithful and wise steward, whom his lord shall make ruler over his household, to give* them their *portion of meat in due season?*

Our Lord makes no direct answer to Peter's curious question.
He proceeds with His discourse, and thereby furnishes an answer.
Who then? As frequently—the Lord gives back the question.
This is *the* supremely important question.
He appeals to each one's conscience with the emphatic, *Who?*
A salutary fear in this warning, that *possibly*, we may not be that servant.
As if He said, not everyone, even of you, My disciples.
The more exalted, the more rigorous the responsibility.
Faithfulness. The fruit of heavenly prudence or wisdom.
An unfaithful steward, a rebel, playing the master himself.
Faithful ones "declare all the counsel of God." Acts xx. 27.
Wise, steward, a servant realizing his full responsibility.
Honesty suffices for a servant, a steward needs *wisdom.*
Steward. Gr. *House-steward* between the master and the slaves.
Eliezer in Abraham's and Joseph in Potiphar's house.
By this, He draws the cord with a more rigorous application.
Under-shepherds have a twofold relation to Christ and the flock.
Not to prescribe new ways, but to lead in "old paths." Jer. vi. 16.

Steward expresses 1, a minister's high rank. 2, his holy calling. 3, his heavy responsibility. 4, the strict account he must render.

Shall make. Future faithfulness yet to be proved.

Ruler. Distinction only makes responsibility more rigorous.

Many high in influence, may hereafter wish *it had been less.*

Our *weakness* needs the allurements of reward.

Our *stupidity* requires the threatenings of judgment.

He demands not the *proud self-deception of disinterested love.*

Household. Christ's church is His *family* here, and in heaven.

Promotions in heaven, unlike those of earth.

Pre-eminence of one, excludes not that of another.

Diffusion as love, the more each has, the more there is for all.

Give. He is to give, not to take, give his *life*, not authority.

Portion. Each one's share undiminished and unadulterated.

Meat. The faithful shepherd is to give *meat*, not *law.*

Anciently servants received six pecks of corn per month.

Food has for many ages been exceedingly scanty in the East.

Due season. Paul demands high qualifications.—"Who is sufficient for these things?" 2. Cor. ii. 16.

"*Said.*" Concerning all. *Friedlieb:* the Apostles. *Ewald, Bengel;* Peter only. *Oosterzee.* ἐπὶ τῆς—Here some find a clear allusion to Episcopacy. Others are of opinion that so large a claim cannot be fairly deduced from these words. θεραπείας—familiam. *Vulg.;* familitium. *Doddridge.* His whole estate. *Thompson.* A numerous servitude. *Milton.* σιτομέτριον—measured allowance of corn. *Campbell.* Determinate measure of wheat. *Doddridge.* A minister is not to shake out of his school-bag whatever may be in it. *Roos.*

---

43. *Blessed is that servant, whom his lord when he cometh shall find so doing.*

Blessed. 1, in the deed; Jas. i. 25. 2, to be so found. 3, with high promotion.

Our Lord's "Blessed," *carries* a benediction through eternity.

Honors of earth become dim at the grave.

Of the faithful He said, "Him will My Father honor." John xii. 26.

Dying on the field of *service*, next to martyrs at the stake.

Servant, no longer; a priest and king. Rev. i. 6; v. 10.

1. Honorable distinction. 2. Perfect satisfaction. 3. Corresponding elevation.

Cometh. To one writing to *Calvin* to spare his exhausted frame, he said—"What! would you have my Master find me idle?"
Find. Sincerity, humility, diligence and constancy.
Even a believer may be taken more or less by surprise.
His house might have been in better order.
So doing. The question is not, what shall one do to be *saved?*
But what shall the sinner saved, be *doing?*
Without a purpose of life established, then too late to begin.
Doing nothing, or that not required, shows the unfaithful shepherd.

44. *Of a truth I say unto you, that he will make him ruler over all that he hath.*

Of a truth. Promise confirmed with an oath. Heb. vi. 17.
Ruler. The labor is great, the reward without measure.
Over all. Servants in the East at times become prime ministers.
Joseph was prime minister in the court of Pharaoh for 80 years.
"Only in the throne, will I be greater than thou." Gen. xli. 40.

45. *But and if that servant say in his heart, My lord delayeth his coming; and shall begin to beat the menservants and maidens, and to eat and drink, and to be drunken;*

But and if. Sadly implies—solemn vows broken.
Servant. Still in the sacred office.
Worthless pastors "feed themselves, not the flocks." Ezek. xxxiv. 2.
A single person named, significantly points at *Rome.*
In his heart. He throws off the servant, and plays the master.
My lord. He continues to use the language of Canaan.
He is not among the mockers, sitting in the seat of the scornful. Ps. i. 1.
He does not even deny the return of the Lord.
Treason at heart, often cries "Lord, Lord." Isa. xxvi. 13.
Delayeth. The unfaithful servant says, It will yet be a long time.
"Since the fathers fell asleep, all things continue," &c. 2 Pet. iii. 4.
Begin. He played the lord mannerly at first.
A quarrel or some controversy made his spirit rough.
He assumes the lordship, and becomes a *pope* as far as he *dare.*
Privileges abused lead men into deeper sin.
The barriers gone, pride and selfishness run riot.
Malignant jealousy of others' piety poisons their peace. Esther iii. 5.
Idolatry and infidelity are by nature intolerant.
Beat. Civil power has often aided priestly ambition.
Persecution frequently results from *envy* of superior *virtue.*

Religion oft the *cloak* of Satan's rage against the church.
Men servants. *Peers* of the steward, in office and privilege.
Angels are "fellow servants" with believers. Rev. xix. 10.
Eat, drink. Secure from fear he riots with earth's devotees.
Drunken. Luxury, corruption, depravity.
Depravity in the sanctuary exceeds ordinary guilt. Jer. xxiii. 14.
Ruling with severity, followed by idle indulgence, constitutes a double sin.

ὁ δοῦλος—1. Peter v. 8. *Leighton's* fervid eloquence is *silent* upon this subject. μεθύσκεσθαι—giving way denotes the *habit* formed. Soldiers indulging in drink had beer found in the trenches, bayoneted during their perilous slumbers. *Beak.*

---

46. *The lord of that servant will come in a day when he looketh not for* him, *and at an hour when he is not aware, and will cut him in sunder, and will appoint him his portion with the unbelievers.*

Will come. Putting off thoughts of Christ's coming delays it not.
In a day. unknown to us, and those unprepared then will be so for ever.
Looketh not, 1, unexpected death; 2, everlasting banishment; 3, torment without end.
The gods have feet like noiseless wool. *Taylor.*
We have no security but a perpetual preparation.
So live, knowing the Judge is at the door. Jas. v. 9.
In sunder. Quartering, or sawing asunder. Dan. ii. 5.
Refers to severing the animal for sacrifice. Ex. xxix. 17.
Xerxes laid the fragments of Pytheas on either side of the road.
The background of the picture uncovers the evil intents of the heart.
He whose heart is divided will be himself *cut in sunder.*
Divine wrath will fall heavily on the unfaithful servant.
There is a heaven for the faithful, a hell for the unfaithful.
Unbelievers. Matt. *hypocrites.* Ezek. xviii. 24; Luke vi. 42.—See Notes.

διχοτομ.—Excommunication. *Grotius, Pearce, Major.* Sent to mines or prison. *Chrysostom.* Exclusion from office. *Beza.* Discarded. *Thompson.* Theocratical punishment. *Lange.* Estate confiscated. *Rosenmuller, Kuinoel.* Turn him out of his family. *Valckner.* Qui cor divisum habet, dividetur. *Bengel.* An everlasting dying, and yet not dying. *Stier.* The E. T. endorsed by *Wakefield.* Figurative. *Doddridge, Heuman.* Scourge to the utmost. *Parkhurst.* ἀπίστων—Infidels. *Doddridge.* Faithless. *Campbell.*

47. *And that servant, which knew his lord's will, and prepared not* **himself,** *neither did according to his will, shall be beaten with many* stripes.

That servant. Ye are not your own—"bought with a price." 1. Cor. vi. 20.
Knew. Head knowledge useless unless the heart is sanctified.
How dreadful is knowledge without corresponding fidelity!
Lord's will. If done from fear, not love, unavailing.
Christians labor because Christ's love constrains. 2. Cor. v. 14.
Prepared not. Great responsibilities go with great privileges.
Many stripes. The number was limited to forty among the Jews.
Slaves were frequently beaten to death by their masters.
The number of stripes for slaves was unlimited.
The crime being repeated the number was doubled. 2. Cor. xi. 24.
The stripes proportioned to the offence by Moses. Deut. xxv. 2.
Terrible sins demand terrible punishments.
Envy not these having many gifts, as few improve them.
Many at Judgment will wish that they had had *fewer*.
As our talents increase so does our responsibility. Amos iii. 2.
The greater the *light* of the impenitent, greater their *guilt*.
Future punishment will vary according to each one's guilt.

"*Prepared not himself.*" Gr. μὴ ἑτοιμάσας, made no preparation. These two verses resemble Hebrew poetry. *Herder.* πρὸς denotes the relation between different objects, here conformity to a rule. *Webster's Syntax.* πολλὰς—An intimation that there will be different degrees of glory and misery hereafter. *Chrysostom, Ambrose.*

---

48. *But he that knew not, and did commit things worthy of stripes, shall be beaten with few* stripes. *For unto whomsoever much is given, of him shall be much required: and to whom men have committed much, of him they will ask the more.*

Knew not. *Ignorance* of the law part of the *guilt* of those violating it.
Though he knew it not, yet is he guilty. Lev. v. 17.
All ignorance of that, which a man is bound to know, and may know, is wilful and will be punished.
Conscience in the heathen leaves them without *excuse*. Rom. i. 19-20.
The Gentiles not having the law are a law to themselves. Rom. ii. 14.

"Our ears have heard the voice Divine—
We cannot be as they." *Keble.*

Ignorance, if self-willed, ceases to be a plea in extenuation of punishment; it is wilful blindness, and as such a sin to be chastised with many stripes.

Worthy of stripes. Shall be punished, such is the sentence. Lev. v. 19.

Few stripes. Difference in degree but not in duration.

All the principles and circumstances will go in the account.

Much is given. Gr. given as *treasures* anciently on *deposit.*

How the *covetous* and *ambitious* recklessly widen and deepen responsibilities!

The thoughtless often plume themselves on their privileges.

Worldlings wisely *unburden* the ship in a storm.

Faithful teachers tremble under their responsibility.

Much required. More than was committed.

"I might have required mine own with *usury.*" Luke xix. 23.

A solemn truth of *general* application, and discloses a momentous principle in the awards of eternity.

πληγῶν. Degrees of future punishment in proportion to the knowledge sinned against. *D. Brown.* ἐδόθη—great knowledge and confidence. *Kuinoel.* Official activity required. *Meyer.* Sins of omission and great light greater than of commission and less light. *Jebb.*

---

49. ¶ *I am come to send fire on the earth; and what will I, if it be already kindled?*

Send. Gr. *cast*, implying *coercion.*

By a figure of speech the effect produced is put for the cause producing.

Fire, 1, warms that which is cold; 2, purifies what is unclean; 3, consumes what is evil. Luke iii. 16. See Notes.

There never can be a compromise between sin and holiness.

In Christ it burns up all opposing elements.

To resist God is to seal one's own ruin inevitably.

What will I? *And what will I? would that it were already kindled!*

This abrupt ejaculation seems unlike our Lord's discourses.

A similar expression in John xii. 27, and under similar circumstances.

Our Lord seems to say, Such is the corruption of man and Satan's malice that MY COMING, which is an embassy of love, will be the signal of a conflagration of strife.

I Myself, who am Love itself, shall be the first object of its fury.

The fire is *now* kindled which shall consume Me as its victim.
But what do I will?—to do My Father's will, to suffer.
He guards against the notion that He is the Author of the fire.
It is kindled by Satan and of man—and Christ is its victim.
But far from shrinking from the fire, He is ready to be offered. *Wordsworth.*

πῦρ—Holy Spirit. *The Fathers, Coccejus, Stier, Alford, Brown, Alexander.* Gospel preached. *Theophylact, Cyril, Bucer.* Word of God. *Bullinger, Watson.* Love. *Jansenius, Bengel, Stellar.* Persecution, *Beza, Poole, Hammond, Lightfoot.* A purer faith, *Wakefield.* Contest between Lutheran and United Churches, *Tholuck.* Interest holy or unholy. *Starcke, Oosterzee.* Higher spiritual elements of life, *Olshausen.* All-quickening fire. *Novalis.* Divine love. *Quesnel.* τί θέλω—*This I will. Lightfoot.* Nihil jam restat amplius. *Raphelius.* Quid volo nisi ut accendatur? *Vulgate, Campbell, Le Clerc.* Would it were already kindled. *Meyer, Stier, Alford.* What do I wish? &c. *Neander, Doddridge.* What wish I more? since it is already kindled. *Major, Schleiermacher.* Sceptics misquoting this text as referring to persecutions, have pronounced Christianity a failure. Ans.—The salvation of one soul *outweighs* all the temporal misery that ever existed. εἰ—oh that! *Doddridge.* How wish I that it were already? &c. *Rosenmuller, De Wette, Olshausen.* What will ye? *E. V., Euthymius, Beza.* What should I have to desire, if it were but once kindled? *Brown.*

---

50. *But I have a baptism to be baptized with; and how am I straitened till it be accomplished!*

Baptism. The mode and design. Luke iii. 16. See Notes.
The first trace of Christ's conflict in the near approach of death.
Baptized. A threefold baptism—1, external baptism of water; 2, spiritual baptism of renewal; 3, fiery baptism of trial.
Our Lord could only share in the third.
Straitened. Gr. *pressed*, Acts xviii. 5; *constrains*, 2. Cor. v. 14.
The nearer His passion the greater His emotion.
Straitened—His holy will struggling through obstacles.
The first utterance of the Saviour's mysterious anguish.
Christ's sufferings—1, their *origin*—the eternal counsel of God. 1. Pet. i. 20. 2, their *nature*—a person devoted to God. John i. 29; Isa. xlii. 1. 3, their *severity*, number, variety, complication, continuance.
Christ had His passion ever before Him.
His love for the cross condemns our timidity.
He desired to purify the church by His own blood.
I have a baptism of suffering—the baptism of My own Blood.

I am straitened till it is fulfilled; for so, and so only, can the world be saved.

By the fire which Satan and evil men have kindled, and by that baptism of blood which they will shed, I shall overcome Satan and deliver man from his power. *Wordsworth.*

The salvation of the world was our Lord's ruling passion.

συνέχομαι—from longing desire. *De Wette;* anxiety. *Meyer.* The technical term for constriction of breathing. *Stier.*

---

51. *Suppose ye that I am come to give peace on earth? I tell you, Nay; but rather division:*

Suppose. Question, with orientals, a strong *denial.*

A terrible saying in the lips of the Prince of *Peace.*

Peace. Genius of Christianity "peace on earth." Luke ii, 14.

It would bind all nations into one loving brotherhood.

"There shall be abundance of peace as long as the moon," &c. Psa. lxxii. 7.

Men shall beat their swords into ploughshares. Isa. ii. 4.

True peace first of all, disturbs all *false* peace. Not the peace that unites heterogeneous good and bad.

The fire separates heterogeneous, and unites homogeneous principles.

"The wisdom that cometh from above is first pure, then peaceable."

The Messiah is the predicted peace, His kingdom one of Peace.

The peace which our "gentle household ethics bring," is no peace.

Salvation brings the only enduring peace. Luke xix. 9.

Apostles trusted the Gospel would receive universal welcome.

This text prevents all hope of building up peace *this side* Jordan.

Through the perversity of a corrupt nation the Sun of righteousness kindles the torch of discord.

Resistance of unholy hearts, to a pure God, is inevitable.

Division. Not the object, but necessary *consequence* of Christ's coming.

Result of corrupt hearts, not the fruit of the Gospel.

Water quenches fire, but on *cold lime* brings out the flame.

"Because ye are not of the world, therefore the world," &c. John xv. 19

The tendency of the Gospel to the Jews was peace, but rejected, was ruin.

The Spirit of Christ cuts off evil, and him clinging to it.

The heavenly kingdom does not *give up* the earth.
On it, the heirs of Christ, in hot conflict, must win their inheritance.
This circle of ideas, never *before* came from *mortal* lips.
Divisions prove the unparalleled importance of His coming.
Such deadly strifes shew men's highest interests, involved.
The announcement proves—1, our Lord's infallible *omniscience;* 2, holy severity; 3, infinite love.
Many unwisely demand *unity*, even to the sacrifice of *truth.*
But even gold may be bought too dear.
How are we to "pursue peace?"—
Christ is set forth in Scripture as Captain, Leader, Man of War, Lion of the Tribe of Judah—the victorious tribe.
So is He also as Prince of Peace; honoured at His birth with the style of Emmanuel—a name of peace.
Crowned in His baptism with a dove—emblem of peace.
Holding in his hand a sceptre—the Gospel of peace.
In the temple a "corner stone"—the place of peace.
Coming into the world with a song of peace.
Going out of the world leaving a legacy of peace.
A perfect Moses, the meekest man; yet the mightiest warrior.
A true David, versed in battle, yet all love.
Sending a sword in one place, sheathing it in another.
Careless of offending in case of piety, tender in case of liberty.
Thus He, and thus His church—Jerusalem, a vision of peace.
Yet therein a fort, and an armoury for shields and bucklers. *Reynolds.*

δοῦναι—Matt. βαλ. to force men, &c. *Alexander.* Micah iv. 8; iv. 10 hints that war and the sorrows of Zion will usher in the kingdom of peace. *Stier, Lange.* ἀλλ' ἤ—not so much so as. *W. & W.* διαμερισμόν—Matt., a sword. The legitimate effect is peace; the *abnormal*, contention; not the purpose, but inevitable results. *De Wette.* With God, results are all purposes. *Alford.*

---

52. *For from henceforth there shall be five in one house divided, three against two, and two against three.*

Five. It was literally fulfilled in Abraham's household.
Christian sympathies prevent family hostilities.
No union too close for evil passions to rend asunder.

House. A scheme framed by God, to promote universal peace.
Results in sowing discord in family circles.
Shows the human heart terribly depraved.
We are not to shrink from human opposition.

Two against three—five; number of imprecation in the East. *Sept.* The five confessions in the household. *Lange.* Merely proverbial. *Stier.*

---

53. *The father shall be divided against the son, and the son against the father; the mother against the daughter, and the daughter against the mother; the mother in law against her daughter in law, and the daughter in law against her mother in law.*

Divided. Unnatural consequences of alienation—resistance.
Our Lord teaches uncompromising decision.
The more *resolute* believers are, sooner opposition ceases.
Consistent perseverance often wins the bitterest foes.
Small temporal interests oft jar families.
But a miracle of grace necessary to unite them. Prov. xviii. 19.
Daughter in law. Gr. *bride.*
The very binding powers of the Gospel become so many *chains of fire* to unsanctified tempted minds.
Many strive to make religion an aid to pleasure.
Whosoever puts on Christ takes upon him His sufferings.
It is a religion of self-denial and taking up the cross.
The Christian is bound to renounce all those things that would rob him of his Saviour, or make him false to the Covenant, into which he has entered. *Patrick.*

For διαμερισθήσεται, read διαμερισθήσονται, and connect with verse 52. *Lachmann, Tischendorf, Alford, Cod. Sinai.*

---

54. ¶ *And he said also to the people, When ye see a cloud rise out of the west, straightway ye say, There cometh a shower; and so it is.*

People. Not the disciples are here addressed.
A special warning to the careless crowd about to leave.
See. Curiosity and interest stimulate these studies.

Cloud. Luke xxi. 27. Oriental skies generally cloudless.
One appearing, excites universal expectation of rain.
A man false to his promise, a cloud without water. Jude, verse 12.
Cloud, a chosen symbol of Divine Presence. Deut. iv. 11.
On Sinai. Ex. xix. 18. Shechinah. Ex. xxix. 42. Ezek. xliii. 4.
West. Clouds generally rise from the west, *i.e.* the Mediterranean.
Shower. "Go up now and look towards the sea," Elijah to his servant. 1. Kings xviii. 43.
They only have the early rains, November, December; and latter, in March.
No rain ever falls during harvest. Prov. xxvi. 1.
The great rain in harvest under Ahab, a miracle. 1. Kings xviii. 45.
So it is. All pretensions to foretelling human destinies, are *impious.*
"The astrologers and star-gazers of Babylon shall burn." Isa. xlvii. 13-14.
We understand not the balancings of the clouds. Job xxxvii. 16.

ὄχλοις—the mixed multitude. ὄμβρος—a heavy shower. *Homer* notices similar signs, and *Bruce* in Abyssinia. A similar saying of our Lord in Matt., but differing in its occasion and substance. *Alford.*

---

55. *And when* ye see *the south wind blow, ye say, There will be heat; and it cometh to pass.*

South wind. Called by Arabs *Simoom*, by Turks *Samiel*, by Egyptians *Camsin*, *i.e. poison.* This wind in Palestine is modified by the sea.
The air in motion, but the causes little understood.
Ascribed to God's agency. Psa. cxxxv. 7; cxlvii. 18. Amos iv. 13.
Medium of Divine agency. Job i. 19. Isa. xi. 15. Jonah i. 4.
Metaphor, "Inherit the wind," denotes disappointment. Prov. xi. 29.
To "hide the wind," an *impossibility*, Prov. xxvii. 16: to labor for it, *vanity*, Ecc. v. 16.
To sow to the wind—extreme *folly*. Hos. viii. 7.
A symbol of calamities. Isa. xli. 16. Of conquest. Zec. v. 9. Of chastisements. Isa. xxvii. 8.
At its coming the heavens assume a yellowish haze.
The skin becomes dry and full of stinging sensations.
Eyes and ears become inflamed, tongue parched.
A fever seems kindled through all the system.
It causes in summer much ruin to the vines.

It destroyed a small army of Cambyses west of Thebes.

Heat. "He quieteth the earth by the south wind." Job xxxvii. 17.

Cometh to pass. Daily concerns are wisely judged of by men.

Contrast with this their blindness in spiritual things.

Despite the mockings of sages the weather ever will continue a source of much *comfort* or *misery* to mankind.

The writer faced this Simoom at the Petrified Forest in the Arabian Desert, during six hours. The flesh seemed all inflamed, as with a fever; the voice hoarse; eyes inflamed; and the entire system prostrated. Three days elapsed before the painful effects passed away. *πνέοντα—ἄνεμος*—the usual term. *νότον*—a wind blowing any point between east and south and east and north is thus named. *Shaw.*

---

56. Ye *hypocrites, ye can discern the face of the sky and of the earth; but how is it that ye do not discern this time?*

Hypocrites. Luke vi. 42. Origin and history of the word.

A hypocrite affects the character or appearance of a good man, but disregards the greater good itself.

All the people willingly deceived by the arch Pharisees.

How is it, that you rise not from natural to spiritual judgment?

It implies if they *wished* they could easily do it.

Spiritual *proof* should be much easier to man than physical.

Voluntary blindness prevents the infatuated from seeing duty or danger.

Ignorance wilful and persisted in, *great guilt.* Luke xix. 44.

Discern. Unable to see what a critical period that was for the Jewish church.

Events in the spiritual world reveal themselves to the eye of faith.

Rightly interpreted, changes in the heavens and the earth contrast with profound insincerity of heart.

Wilful misapprehension blinded their minds.

As those in love with sin—do not wish for light.

Such ignorance either wilful—the result of sin; or judicial—the punishment of sin.

Both will meet a terrible punishment hereafter.

Nothing incomprehensible necessary for us to know.

The mysteries of religion an excuse assigned by those who have no heart to believe.

Face of the sky. The countenance varies, the face is the same.

Men judge wisely of things that are dear to their hearts.

This time. This time of God's gracious visitation. Luke xix. 44.

"Yea, the stork knoweth her appointed times," Jer. viii. 7.

Children of Issachar had understanding of the times. 1. Chron. xii. 32.

Signs, Matt. Daniel's seventy weeks expiring: Christ born of a virgin.

Star in the East: our Lord's baptism: Holy Ghost's descent.

Sceptre departing from Judah: dead raised.

The Jews in mad impiety fast drifting to ruin.

Jews in a blaze of miracles perished, demanding *more.* 1. Cor. i. 22.

Sceptics, under noonday evidence perish, asking for light.

ὑποκριταὶ—Diviners or foretellers. *Raphelius.* Verb, to utter oracles. *Homer, Herodotus.* The word sometimes means an *interpreter of dreams*, but here a *malicious hypocrite. Bengel.* The πρῶτον ψεῦδος in the way of the man's acknowledging the truth. *Stier.* δοκιμάζειν—*cerno*, to separate, *i.e.* decide or judge after separating the particulars, and assigning a value to each. *Olshausen.*

---

57. *Yea, and why even of yourselves judge ye not what is right?*

Of yourselves. You might learn these things from the word of God.

But why not use your common sense?

Apply the rule of conscience, as in other matters.

Judge. The exercise of *conscience* in view of truth and duty.

The moral power of deciding what is and is not right.

It was secured by Christ's death for all men. John i. 9.

Insanity distorts this power, hence they are *irresponsible.*

Depravity dims, and long indulged, *obliterates* it.

Conscience, like *seared* flesh, may cease its office.

Right. Human science cannot secure saving knowledge.

Those wise in temporals far less inexcusable for their fatal ignorance of spirituals.

The *highest right*, righteousness incarnate, Jesus Christ.

Him, they *could* not recognize, because they *would not.*

It is a great mistake to suppose that the obligation of moral duties depends wholly on the Bible. *Tillotson.*

Moral lessons derived from the dictates of nature, no less divine than those of the Bible. ***Melancthon.***

" This is the condemnation, that light is come into the world, and men love darkness better than light, because their deeds are evil." John iii. 19.

κρίνετε—proves the right of private judgment in religious matters. *Tertullian. Horsley.* δὲ, what precedes refers to *faith*, what follows, to *love*. *Bengel.* δίκαιον—reasonable. *Grotius.*

---

58 ¶ *When thou goest with thine adversary to the magistrate*, as thou art *in the way, give diligence that thou mayest be delivered from him ; lest he hale thee to the judge, and the judge deliver thee to the officer, and the officer cast thee into prison.*

Agree, Matt. Instead of an adversary He will prove a Father.

Make peace, even at the sacrifice of your just *rights*.

Our brief privileges preserved, may cost an eternity of woe !

Adversary. Apply your prudence in law, to religion.

God, by our rebellion, has become our adversary.

We owe him a debt, which we can never pay.

A debt of obedience, and of punishment.

Magistrate. Christians as sons of peace, make law, a *last resort*.

There is a suit against us, which cannot be avoided. Rom. xii. 10.

Diligence. Men *improve* moments of earthly interest.

Years are *squandered*, involving everlasting life.

Judge. Whom none can escape, none can bribe.

" If the righteous scarcely be saved, where shall ? " &c. 1. Pet. iv. 18.

Officer. Instead of vengeance, angels will bear thee, &c., Luke xvi. 22.—If thou hast found an advocate in Christ. 1. John ii. 1.

Prison. Will God spare thee, if He did not sinning angels ?

Agree with thine adversary, and instead of a judge—thou shalt find a merciful Father.

Instead of a cruel officer—angels shall carry thee to glory.

Instead of a prison—a paradise of God.

All things are changed *in the way*, because thou hast " agreed with thine adversary." *Augustine.*

Did we only see how needful Christ is to us, we should esteem and love Him more. *Leighton.*

Without a mediator there can be no communion with God. *Pascal.*

ἀντιδίκου—The reference to a *human* enemy, makes the Lord close a solemn discourse with a foreign subject, and in an abrupt manner. *Stier.* Refers to God. *Meyer;* to Satan. *Euthymius;* the poor. *Michaelis;* the law. *Olshausen, Braune;* impersonation of the law. *W. & W.* A mere illustration from common life, without specific meanings to the terms. *Alexander.* Remorseful conscience. *Quesnel.*

πράκτωρ—Exactor, executor, a Roman official. ὑπηρέτης—Matt., term used by Luke known to Theophilus. *Oosterzee.* Collector of taxes at Athens. δὸς ἐργασίαν—pay interest as well as principal. *Theophylact, Le Clerc,* ὡς γὰρ—"*For instance, when,*" connection with preceding lost. *Kuinoel, De Wette.* Discern your true state:—You are going with your adversary (the law), before the magistrate (God Himself); therefore, take pains by the way to be delivered (through faith, &c). *Alford.* Do all thou canst. *Wakefield.* κατασύρῃ—detraho, cum in judicium *detrahi* non posset. *Cicero.* ἀπήλλαχθαι—forensic term equivalent to dismissing the suit—hurry thee off by force. μήποτε—Lest the Messianic crisis be so near that, &c. *Meyer.*

---

59. *I tell thee, thou shalt not depart thence, till thou hast paid the very last mite.*

I tell thee. This seems only to complete the ideal case.

The solemn formula alludes to a more awful case.

Life-long imprisonment for debt on earth reminds us of perpetual imprisonment in hell for sin.

Paid. Implies the possibility of the debtor's payment.

But suggests the debtor's *hopeless incapacity* to do it.

No payment in hell—hence, unending woe.

Our Lord is a chosen Ransom for all debtors.

Happy they who secure a discharge in proper time.

Rome, in forlorn hope, builds the dogma of *Purgatory* on this text.

Mite. Rather more than one-third of a farthing (i.e., 0,375).

It was the smallest coin made or milled.

None bearing a *heathen inscription* received in the Temple.

Last. Such as God finds us at death, such will He judge us at the last day. *Cyprian.*

It is absolutely impossible for needy man ever to pay his debt, seeing he has not even the *first* mite. *Stier.*

An earthly debt can be paid in most cases, but the spiritual debt, never. *Alford.*

"And these shall go away into everlasting punishment." "Their worm dieth not, their fire is not quenched." "The smoke of their torment ascendeth up for ever and ever." These and many other texts which might be quoted show, that the loss of the soul is unalterable and eternal. The Scriptures know nothing of a Purgatory or of Universalism. "How shall we escape, if we neglect so great salvation?" The question is left unanswered, because answer is impossible.

Objections to eternal punishment are alike unphilosophical as well as unscriptural. Let it be conceded that the terms are figurative; but they are images emblematical of a terrible reality, which is, that no one can fly from himself; no one, at his own will, can lose self-consciousness, and forget his crimes. Blood-thirsty persecutors, vile seducers, all who have taken pleasure in fraud and falsehood, in malice and revenge, must lose the remembrance of their conduct and of its consequences, before their remorse and anguish can cease. The sufferings of the lost may proceed from internal rather than external influence. If this be so, the question as to eternity of punishment comes to this.—Is a God of love bound to interpose, and provide means for checking the penal action of the mind on itself? We may go further, and ask:—On what principle is the Judge over all bound to render the disembodied spirit, dull, callous, insensate, unfeeling, so as to suspend the operation of the immutable law—What a man sows, that shall he also reap?

μὴ ἐξέλθῃς—Implies the debt can never be paid. *Bede*, *Euthymius*. λεπτὸν—24 made a quadrans, 4 quadrantes made one *as*, equal to 2¼ farthings. The mite was one-eighth of this sum. Two coined in the reign of Hadrian, found in the Baths of Titus, are in the writer's collection. "*Depart*." The Messiah will appear against them as *complainant*. *Neander*

END OF VOL I.

Milton Keynes UK
Ingram Content Group UK Ltd.
UKHW041118161223
434388UK00008B/97

9 783752 520378